The Devil's Memoirs
(Vol. 1)

OTHER TITLES TRANSLATED
BY STUART GELZER

Paul Féval - *The Hunchback*
Paul d'Ivoi - *Miss Musketeer*
Paul d'Ivoi - *Queen of Illusions*
Anonymous - *Harry Dickson vs. Mysteras*
Anonymous - *Harry Dickson vs. Krik-Krok, The Walking Dead*

The Devil's Memoirs
(Volume 1)

by
Frédéric Soulié

Translated from the French by
Stuart Gelzer

A Black Coat Press Book

ISBN 978-1-64932-346-0. First Printing. January 2025. Published by Black Coat Press, an imprint of Hollywood Comics.com, LLC, 18321 Ventura Blvd. Suite 915, Tarzana, CA 91356.

TABLE OF CONTENTS

Introduction

Les Mémoires du Diable (here translated as *The Devil's Memoirs*) was first published in *Le Journal des Débats,* a daily newspaper which ran from 1799 to 1944. The novel appeared from February 10, 1837, till March 8, 1838, in a hundred installments. It was then republished in book form by Ambroise Dupont in 1838. This monumental work is a combination of Gothic romance, novel of manners, and Satanic fiction.

Melchior-Frédéric Soulié was born in Foix on December 23, 1800. His birth crippled his mother, Jeanne-Marie Baille. His father, François-Melchior Soulié, after having taught philosophy at the University of Toulouse, had enlisted in the army in 1792 and reached the rank of adjutant-general, but was forced to leave the military because of illness. He then joined the public finance administration as an employee in the tax revenue service. Frédéric lived with his mother in Mirepoix, not far from Foix, till the age of four, when his father took him to live with him. Young Frédéric followed his father when he was transferred to Nantes in 1808, then to Poitiers in 1815, where Frédéric completed his secondary education. His sister, Antoinette-Françoise, remained with their mother at Mirepoix. The family had not been reunited by the time of Soulié's death in 1847.

After the fall of Napoleon, Melchior-Frédéric Soulié was fired from the tax service for being a supporter of the exiled Emperor. He went to Paris; Frédéric accompanied him there and attended law school. Expelled for having signed a Republican petition and for taking an active part in a student revolt against the law school dean, he was banished with several of his fellow students to the University of Rennes, where he completed his law studies under the watchful supervision of the police.

Upon getting his degree, Frédéric rejoined Melchior-Frédéric in Laval, where he had been reinstated in his job. He first worked with his father, and then joined the civil service himself. In 1824 Melchior-Frédéric was fired again for supporting the "wrong" candidates in the elections, and Frédéric resigned from the civil service. Father and son resolved to settle once more in Paris.

Frédéric, using the name "F. Soulié de Lavelanet," published some poetry he had written earlier, followed by three elegiac songs, all under the title *Amours françaises* ("French Loves"). That small volume went unnoticed, but it allowed him to make some contacts in the literary world: Casimir Delavigne lavished his encouragement on Soulié, and he became a friend of Alexandre Dumas. To ensure his subsistence, he took a job as the manager of a mechanical sawmill. Driven by his literary vocation, he translated and adapted Shakespeare's *Romeo and Juliet*, which was performed at the Odéon on June 10, 1828. At the same time, Soulié wrote an original play, *Christine à Fontainebleau* ("Christine in Fontainebleau"), which was performed at the Odéon on October 13, 1829, but failed to attract much attention.

Discouraged, Soulié became a journalist and began writing short stories. However, on June 17, 1830, he returned to the theater with a two-act play entitled *Une Nuit du Duc de Montfort* ("A Night with the Duke of Montfort"), which was more successful and generated some income. A little over a month later the 1830 July Revolution broke out, and Soulié fought among the insurgents, rifle in hand, in the streets of Paris. He was decorated with the July Cross.

When order was restored he took up his pen again, contributing stories to many smaller newspapers, including *La Mode* and *Le Voleur*. In the theater, however, he had yet another failure with *Nobles et bourgeois* ("Noblemen and Bourgeois"), a five-act play. But he was not discouraged. His three-act play, *La Famille de Lusigny* ("The Lusigny Family"), performed at the Théâtre-Français on October 15, 1831, was a success.

Encouraged by that, Soulié next simultaneously staged a play, *Clotilde*, first performed at the Théâtre-Français on September 11, 1832, and published a Gothic novel, *Les Deux Cadavres* ("The Two Corpses"). The play received enthusiastic applause from a large audience; the novel, a tale full of horrors, murders, and bloody scenes, was also a great success. From that moment on, Soulié's reputation as a great playwright and novelist was established.

In 1833 he published a collection of short stories, *Le Port de Créteil* ("Créteil Harbor"), which was also successful. At that time he founded a newspaper, *Le Napoléon*, which he soon sold to Émile Marco de Saint-Hilaire. In the theater, two plays he staged on the Grands Boulevards, *L'Homme à la blouse* ("The Man in the Smock") and *Le Roi de Sicile* ("The King of Sicily"), were his last two failures.

During the two years that followed, Soulié was very prolific. Another play, *Une Aventure sous Charles IX* ("An Adventure under Charles IX"), performed at the Théâtre-Français on May 21, 1834, was highly acclaimed. He also published many novels, including *Le Vicomte de Béziers* ("The Viscount of Beziers"), *Le Magnétiseur* ("The Hypnotist"), and *Le Comte de Toulouse* ("The Count of Toulouse") all in 1834; *Le Conseil d'Etat* ("The High Council") in 1835; and a short story collection, *Un Eté à Meudon* ("A Summer in Meudon") in 1836. On August 6, 1835, his play *Les Deux Reines* ("The Two Queens") was performed at the Opéra-Comique, also to great acclaim. But despite all those successes, Soulié remained in a rather precarious financial position.

His uncle, Marshal Clauzel, on becoming governor-general of Algeria for a second time, made him an offer he had already proposed in 1831: that of a lucrative job in the administration of the colony; but Soulié refused again, preferring to devote himself to his literary career. Nor did he accept the proposal made to him by Count Molé, then President of the Council, to join the High Council of the Republic, on condition that he give up his literary career.

It was around that time that Soulié conceived the idea of *The Devil's Memoirs*, a gigantic, powerful work, probably inspired by Alain-René Lesage's *Le Diable Boîteux* ("The Lame Devil") from 1707. *The Devil's Memoirs* offered a picture of society at its most hideous: crime, incest, adultery, lies, all the evils human souls were capable of, were depicted in characters seemingly good, innocent, and pure. A well-regarded man, enjoying a reputation for probity, was secretly infamous; a woman, lauded for her virtue, was an example of hypocrisy and debauchery. The immense fame that *The Devil's Memoirs* garnered for Soulié placed him at the pinnacle of literary glory.

At the same time, his translation of *Romeo and Juliet*, relaunched at the Odéon, was greeted with unanimous applause. During 1839 three more of his plays were performed at the Théâtre de la Renaissance: *Diane de Chivri*, *Le Fils de la Folle* ("The Madwoman's Son"), adapted from his own 1839 novel *Le Maître d'école* ("The Schoolmaster"), and *Le Proscrit* ("The Banished Man"); all were successful. And that did not stop Soulié from also contributing articles and reviews to *L'Europe littéraire*, *La Mode*, *La Revue de Paris*, and *La Chronique de Paris*, and serialized novels to *Le Journal général de France*, *Le Journal des Débats*, *La Presse*, *La Quotidienne*, *Le Messager*, and *Le Siècle*. He also cooperated with the elite of French literature to publish several collective works.

Between 1840 and 1847 Soulié published more novels, and had several plays performed at the Théâtre de l'Ambigu, all of which were successful, including, on October 14, 1846, the now classic *La Closerie des genêts* ("The House with the Broom Hedge"), which was a triumph. Soon after that, however, Soulié came down with heart disease; after three months of suffering he died in his country house in Bièvres, on September 23, 1847.

A large crowd attended his funeral on September 27 at the Church of Sainte-Élisabeth du Temple and his burial at the Père-Lachaise cemetery, where Victor Hugo gave a speech and where Alexandre Dumas, pressed by the crowd to say something, collapsed in sobs.

Dumas later wrote:

"Soulié was twenty-six when I first met him. He was a lusty young man of medium height; he had a prominent forehead, dark hair, eyebrows, and beard, a well-shaped nose and dark eyes, thick lips, and white teeth. He laughed readily, although it was never a fresh, young laugh. It sounded ironical and strident, which gave it the quality of age. Being naturally of a bantering disposition, irony was a weapon he wielded admirably.

"He tried his hand at most things, and retained some slight knowledge of everything. After receiving an excellent education in the provinces, he studied law, I believe, at Rennes, to which we owe the admirable description of a student's life in his book entitled Confessions Générales. *He got his degree and was called to the bar, but did not take kindly to the legal profession.*

9

"He lived at the rue de Provence, on the second floor, in a bewitching apartment that seemed like a palace to us. There was, above all else, a most unusual luxury in that room: a piano, on which Soulié could play two or three tunes. He was both radical and very aristocratic, two qualities which then often went together."[1]

Le Musée des Familles, a publication which had often disagreed with Soulié's darker works, praised him:

"A courageous pen, a strong imagination, and an undisputed talent. His name remains attached to more than a hundred volumes: novels, plays, short stories, opera, even criticism; he tried everything... Without having the microscopic view of Balzac, the compassionate touch of George Sand, the splendid verve of Alexandre Dumas, he gloriously conquered a place at their side. He had wit, grace, fantasy, love, passion; he had strength, which often took the place of everything else."[2]

By 1875 Soulié's tomb had fallen into disrepair, and a subscription was taken up to restore it and to place a monument beside it. The formal speech at the unveiling ceremony was given by the great Paul Féval, who said:

"On September 25th, 1847, the cemetery where we stand now could scarcely contain the crowd who followed Frédéric Soulié's coffin. A vaster gathering had never glorified a man's funeral more. He was a man, in fact, who was loved even more than he was admired, a gentleman in the truest sense of the word. And when the voice of Victor Hugo, as loud as his genius, pronounced these words, which still resonate after so many years, 'He lived by his heart; he died by his heart,' the same sob rose in thousands of breasts. A less sad ceremony brings us together today. Two fraternal societies that Frédéric Soulié honored are now visiting his restored tomb. Auguste Maquet brought him the eloquent remembrance of dramatic authors; I myself come to tell my illustrious friend, my well-beloved master, that French writers are still proud of him and that they will never forget him.

"Some owe Soulié a tomb, and think that their debt is paid. What we, the writers of France, owe him is immortality! I know that he was a master and that you who allocate fame have too long forgotten him. It isn't a favor we ask for him; it's his due that should be his."[3]

The speeches given at that time became the introduction to a new 1876 edition of The Devil's Mémoirs. The editor quoted Féval's speech, adding, *"It is in response to the wish so eloquently expressed by M. Paul Féval that we republish this edition of* Les Mémoires du Diable, *that masterpiece where sparkling strength vies with a prodigious imagination."*

---

[1] Alexandre Dumas, *Mes Memoires,* Vol. II, Chapter IV. New York: The Macmillan Company, 1907, pp.349-359.

[2] Notice Nécrologique de Frédéric Soulié, *Musée des Familles,* 1848, p. 3.

[3] Paul Féval, *Introduction, Les Mémoires du Diable,* Paris : J. Le Clerc, 1876.

Of all the *feuilletonistes* of that time, Soulié seems to us the most modern in style. He is casual, chatty, and ironic. He couches his satire in innuendo, allusions, and circumlocutions in order to criticize the falsity of social hierarchy, affectation, marriage, and, most of all, women. Since he was both a dramatist and a novelist, his novels retain some of the theater's techniques. He uses dialogue extensively to delineate character and to move the plot forward when narration would be boring. The poet in him sprinkles verse throughout even the darkest passages. He died dictating a poem he had composed about those gathered at his bedside. His novels and articles became parts of plays, and his plays were turned into novels and short stories, making him one of the best-paid *feuilletonistes*. His allusions, though almost always apt, are sometimes too locked in nineteenth-century life to be completely meaningful to a twenty-first century audience. Many of Soulié's stories never definitively conclude: their open endings resemble modern television series, which always have the next season in mind when one season wraps up. Soulié left his endings vague enough to be followed with a sequence or a spin-off in another *feuilleton*, if it seemed likely to sell. If there was no sequel, readers could continue the story in their imaginations and end it to their own satisfaction.

In most of his output Soulié is a critic of human and society's failings, showing little or no pity or charity. In *Le Lion amoureux ("*The Lion in Love")* from 1840, he portrays the rich, vain, useless young men of Parisian society, but does not spare the bourgeois who are awed by them and envy them. In *Physiologie du Bas bleu* ["The Physiology of a Bluestocking"] from 1841, he is a misogynist who mocks women writers, including George Sand, sparing only the woman who "scratches" with her pen on paper in order to feed her family. In all his work he castigates pride, vanity, self-interest, self-delusion, the hypocrisy and corruption of government and government officials, and the artificial stratification of society.

In the Prologue to *The Devil's Memoirs,* Soulié sets up his version of the Faust legend. Barons of an ancient aristocratic family from the Toulouse area have for generations sold their souls to the Devil for knowledge, worldly status, and wealth. Each new Baron de Luizzi must renew the contract with Satan on January 1st of the year following that in which he inherits the title, by returning to the ancestral chateau to meet with the Devil in person. He will remain there for only twenty-four hours. When his contract with Lucifer has been agreed on and signed, he leaves, never to return during his lifetime, even though the residence is always kept ready for his imminent arrival. The new baron is aware of the terms of his ancestors' contractual agreement with the Devil and how to initiate the required interview. On his arrival at the ancestral chateau, he summons Satan with the small bell used for that purpose. When the Devil appears, Luizzi finds him to be an impudent rascal. As his attitude toward Satan changes, so does Satan's appearance, going from a dandy to a conniving servant, before finally assuming his real persona, the fallen Principality and Power, Lucifer, Son of Light.

Soulié changes the Faust legend to allow a *proviso*: if Satan's gifts make any recipient consistently happy for a ten-year period, the contract will be null and void and the baron does not have to render his immortal soul to the Devil for eternity. However, no recipient has yet avoided repayment to Satan. Since Armand de Luizzi has not yet decided what to ask for, the Devil allows him to sign the contract but delay his choice. During that time he will allow the baron access to his memoirs to use as he likes, to reveal them, to publish them, even to sign them with his own name. These become *The Devil's Memoirs*.

Before beginning his history, Soulié explains and justifies the tone of the narratives to follow, the same tone as in most of Soulié's preceding novels. Speaking for authors unappreciated by a cruel, coarse, and debauched public, Satan declares that he will reveal the true corrupt soul of the generation that at present he finds himself condemned to serve.

In the second chapter of the novel, Soulié tells the reader:

[W]hen you've asked the public to pay attention to someone who speaks well and honorably, you'll find that public hanging on the vulgar words of some petty scribbler, on the manic nonsense of some ink-spiller, on the frightening tales in some crime gossip sheet. You'll see the public—that old libertine—smile at the virginity of your muse and defile her with an indecent kiss before calling out to her, "All right, hussy, get out, or entertain me: I need astringents and burning Chinese remedies to wake my dormant senses. Have you got wild incest, monstrous adultery, horrifying criminal debauchery, or impossible desires to tell me about? If so, speak, and I'll listen to you for an hour—for as long as I can feel your acrid, venomous pen moving across my calloused and gangrenous feelings. If not, shut up, and go die in misery and obscurity!"

You hear, young friends? Misery and obscurity! Misery, that vice punished by contempt! Obscurity, that aptly named torture! Obscurity means exile from sunlight—when you're someone who needs the rays of the sun to keep your heart from freezing to death! Misery and obscurity—you don't want that! So then what'll you do, young friends? You'll take a pen and a sheet of paper, and at the top you'll write The Devil's Memoirs, *and you'll say to your century, "Oh, you want to take pleasure in cruel things? So be it, my lord, here's a slice of your own story."*

In some ways the Devil, as Soulié presents him, resembles Satanic figures from earlier literature. French critics frequently mention Le Sage's 1707 novel, *Le Diable Boiteux*[4]. However, since Soulié's English was strong, he was not limited to French. He created, edited, and published a revue called *Keepsakes*, which ran from 1830 to 1848, the year following Soulié's death. *Keepsakes* featured previously unpublished French and English short stories by contemporary

---

[4] Q.v.

authors, with previously unpublished illustrations by contemporary English and French artists. His first dramatic work was a French adaptation of Shakespeare's *Romeo and Juliet.*

Soulié could therefore have been familiar not only with John Milton's Satan as portrayed in *Paradise Lost*, and the Devil's personas, Mephistopheles and Lucifer, as depicted by Christopher Marlowe in *Dr. Faustus,* but also with the Devil's character as conceived by Blake, Hazlitt, and Shelley. Hazlitt said the Devil was one of the most heroic figures ever chosen for a poem, and Shelley claimed Satan was morally superior to Milton's God. In the first few pages of *The Devil's Memoirs,* at the Devil's last manifestation and change of persona into his real form as the Fallen Angel Lucifer, Soulié exclaims: "*It was indeed the fallen angel evoked in poetry,*" alluding to Milton's Satan in *Paradise Lost.*

Though translated into Danish, German, Hungarian, Spanish, and Turkish, *The Devil's Memoirs* was not translated into English.[5] An early and rare review in a British publication, *The Monthly Review* of May 1840, praised Soulié's novel and translated several pages into English, writing:

"*Of all the remarkable works that have emanated the last few years from the French Press,* Les Mémoires du Diable *by Frédéric Soulié, is one of the most conspicuous.* Les Mémoires du Diable *extend to eight volumes, and comprise, in one continuous tale, varied by numerous episodic constructions, a series of lessons of human life... The idea of introducing into the tale a personage whose universal knowledge shall work out the scheme of the author and make the hero acquainted with all the mundane vicissitudes, mysteries, and hypocrisies is as ingenious as it is well executed....We cannot do otherwise than bestow our decided approval upon the style and moral of the volumes now before us, and earnestly recommend all our friends, who are acquainted with the French language, to peruse it.*"

Several well-known nineteenth century English authors commented on Soulié's masterwork in their correspondence, quoting from the work in French. Edward Bulwer-Lytton, writing to Mary Elizabeth Braddon, told her in detail about the horrors elaborated on in the novel: "*blood, corpses, ghastly murders, ghoulishness, revolting tales of disease or torture or decomposition,*" and "*unusual crimes such as rapes, incest, and sequestration, treacheries.*"

Elizabeth Barrett Browning mentions Soulié more than a dozen times in her correspondence with Mary Russell Mitford. Although she frequently deplores the raw, sometimes ghastly descriptions, she also writes: "*Frédéric Soulié*

---

[5] A publisher of penny dreadfuls, Benjamin D. Cousins, did publish another of Soulié's works in English, *Crime and Vengeance: A Tragedy of Real Life,* in London in 1845. He, or another penny-dreadful publisher, may also have published *The Devil's Memoirs*, perhaps adapted. Many penny dreadfuls have yet to be found and catalogued.

was one of the new French schools I ventured to approach, and he made me open my eyes very wide indeed." (24 December 1844). In another letter (4 February 1845), she writes: *"Do you think you could take courage & attempt the eight volumes of Frédéric Soulié's* Mémoires du Diable? *Eight rather thick volumes? I am in the midst and heat of them, and though they stink in one's nostrils not infrequently & are full of the most gorgeous extravagances, the variety and power, the invention (flash upon flash), and the vividness of life all through, render them to my mind, a most remarkable work (...) Much of it is most disgusting, but you must be struck by the variety of power in it; & I can't keep back any new sight from you. Yes, indeed! How nearer and nearer we are drawn in this 'palpitating literature' as you call it so truly! Palpitating is just the word & and it sets me palpitating too, whatever it may do by yourself."*

A modern analysis by a German critic, Jörg Türschmann, of the University of Göttingen, *Le héro en guise de genèse de texte: Les Mémoires du Diable* (2003), is an extended and erudite examination of the background of the work and of the history of the Devil in world literature. In addition, Türschmann questions the point of view of the narrator of the text. He finds the hero to be Luizzi, and he maintains that the novel is not pessimistic, as some critics claim. He points out *"the comic, the irony in the novel and Luizzi's attitude, which is from time to time completely moral and shows something else, if the end of the novel and Luizzi's weakness do bring out an image which is not unequivocal."*

Türschmann also examines the shifting point of view of the narration. Is the speaker Soulié, as he sometimes appears to be, as when he rails against *"the public, that debauched old man,"* and criticizes his contemporaries, writers whom readers prefer to better, more honest, and more polished authors? He condemns public taste, saying it prefers: *"the stories of a trivial writer, the hysterical madness of a scribbler on paper, the gross stories of a crime gazette."* At other points in the narrative, it is Satan who speaks to the reader and directs his satire to the reading public. When Luizzi, the hero, is in control of the narrative, his point of view, when reporting the events, evolves as his choices are more and more out of his control.

More than a hundred and fifty years later, Alex Lascar, in the preface to the latest French edition of *Les Mémoires du Diable*, published in 2003, wrote: *"A satiric tableau of French society worthy of Balzac. Bankers and society women, journalists and prostitutes, restaurateurs and men of the theater: all parade through in a hellish sarabande—which will leave Luizzi famished. But his good fortune and his bad fortune are valuable to us as an astonishing story half-way between a novel of manners and the fantastic."*

Nina Cooper & Jean-Marc Lofficier

A Guide To Navigating the Plot

The Devil's Memoirs takes the form of several dozen not quite self-contained episodic tales, some involving the hero directly but many consisting of nested stories he is told, by the Devil or by someone else—a form that might be called "parlor picaresque." Many of those nested stories are long enough that they could stand on their own as novellas. It would be easy to assume that, as in a true picaresque like *Gil Blas*, when Soulié ends a story and moves on it means he (and the reader) are done with it.

In Soulié's use of the form, though, there is in fact some spillover; and the further into the novel you get, the more you'll find the narrative referring back to much earlier episodes, and—even more taxing to the reader's powers of re-call—drawing to the foreground of the plot a character who might've been mentioned once briefly in passing, forty or fifty or more chapters earlier. Soulié's first readers experienced the story either in its hundred-installment periodical form or in the eight-volume original book edition. That Soulié clearly expected them, over and over, to remember characters and incidents from many months earlier in the newspaper version, or several volumes earlier in the book edition, speaks highly of the powers of recall of ordinary readers in the 1830s.

We, however, live in lesser times. Since there are almost a hundred and fifty recurring characters, I have provided an index at the start of volume one (which also includes those characters who first appear in volume two) listing the chapter in which each of those characters first appears, so that the reader has the option of flipping back to that chapter for a quick refresher. In addition, in the course of doing the translation, whenever I myself was confronted—especially in the last third of the novel, as Soulié accelerates his pulling together of earlier strands of the story—by some half-familiar name and found myself thinking, "Wait, *who*?!" I have footnoted an explanatory chapter reference, generally to the most recent or most relevant appearance of that character; again, that might be hundreds of pages earlier. If you find those footnotes unnecessary, having the characters or incidents Soulié refers to firmly and clearly in your mind, you can simply enjoy a feeling of superiority over your more forgetful translator.

Stuart Gelzer

A Note on Currencies

In the post-Napoleonic era in which the novel is set, so many political regimes had come and gone in the previous decades that various overlapping units of currency were still in circulation. In addition, two parallel hierarchies of coinage coexisted, one based on gold, the other on silver; their exchange rate, so to speak, was periodically reset by government fiat as the values of gold and silver fluctuated.

However, broadly speaking, the units of currency commonly referred to in *The Devil's Memoirs* had the following relative values:

• One **centime** was a hundredth of a franc.

• The **liard** was an obsolete unit, originally worth a quarter of a sou, that, by the time in which the novel is set, was mostly used metaphorically to mean any insignificant amount, like the British farthing.

• One **sou** was 5 centimes, so there were 20 sous in one franc.

• One **franc** was roughly equivalent to one **livre**—silver coinage versus gold—and the words are used interchangeably in the novel, sometimes in the same conversation.

• One **écu** was worth 5 francs, which is to say 100 sous. At least that's what modern references quote as the official value at that time. At several points in the novel, however, a character converts from one of those units to the other in conversation, and it's clear that to Soulié one écu was worth only 3 francs—and therefore represented a much less convenient number of sous.

• One **louis d'or** or gold **Napoleon** was worth 20 francs or 4 écus (at the official, non-Soulié rate) or 400 sous. Louis d'or and Napoleons were equivalent in value, though the latter were minted under the Empire and the former under the Restoration and the July Monarchy.

Stuart Gelzer

BIBLIOTHÈQUE
MARABOUT

FRÉDÉRIC SOULIÉ

LES MÉMOIRES DU DIABLE

Seul le Diable lui-même
pouvait évoquer,
en maître du Mal,
les plus bas instincts
d'un monde condamné

1

TEXTE INTÉGRAL

Index of Recurring Characters

X – (First appears in chapter…)

Faynal, Eugène (XI)
Félix, Monsieur (LXXX)
Fernand (XI)
Finon, Mademoiselle / later Madame
  Béru (XXVII)
Firet, Madame (XXXVII)
Firion, Nathalie / later Madame du
  Bergh (XVII)
Firion, Monsieur (XVII)
Follard, Citizen (LXVIII)
Furnichon, Désiré Anténor (XXX)
Ganguernet, Aimé Zéphirin (XI)
Ganguernet, Gustave / later Gustave de
  Bridely (XXVI)
Gargablou, Marianne / née Marianne
  Libert (XXVI)
Gelis, Madame (XLVII)
Gelis, Juliette (XLVII)
Gilet, Madame(XXXVI)
Humann (XC)
Humbert, Madame (XXIV)
Jacob (LXXXIX)
Jean-Pierre (VII)
Jeannette (XI)
La Chesnaie, Marquis de (XXXV)
Labitte, Ernest de (V)
Lannois, Léon (VI)
Lannois, Monsieur (VII)
Legalet, Madame (XXXVII)
Legalet, Monsieur (XXXVII)
Legalet, Sylvie (XXXVII)
Lémée, Count Alfred Henri (XXX)
Lémée, Countess (the count's mother)
  (XXX)
Lémée, Countess Ernestine (the
  count's wife) / née Ernestine
  Turniquel (XXX)
Libert, Marianne / later Marianne
  Gargablou (XXVIII)
Libert, Antoine / later Monsieur de
  Marignon (XXVIII)
Lili (LXXXIX)
Little Pierre (XXX)

Louis (XXIV)
Loré, Monsieur de (LXXXII)
Lozeraie, Count Lucien de (LXXXII)
Lozeraie, Viscount Arthur de
  (LXXXII)
Ludney, Arthur (XXXVI)
Ludney, Lady (XXXVI)
Ludney, Lord (XXXVII)
Luizzi, Baron Armand de (I)
Luizzi, Baron Hugues de (I)
Malize, lords of (LXXV)
Marcoine, Louis Jérôme (XXX)
Mareuilles, Cosmo de (XV)
Mareuilles, Lydie de / née Lydie de
  Marignon (LIV)
Marianne (VII)
Mariette / see also Mariette Bricoin (II)
Marignon, Antoine de / see also
  Antoine Libert (XXIX)
Marignon, Lydie de / later Madame de
  Mareuilles (XVI)
Marignon, Olivia de / née Olivia Béru1
  (VI)
Mère, Victor de (XXIX)
Mérin, Monsieur de (X)
Molinet, Father (LVI)
Niquet, Monsieur XL)
Paradèze, Madame de (LXIV)
Paradèze, Monsieur de (LXIV)
Périne, Madame / Mother Périne
  (LXXXIX)
Petithomme (XLIX)
Peyrol, Eugénie / née Eugénie Turni-
  quel (XXX)
Peyrol, Alfred (XXXVIII)
Pierre (XXIV)
Ridaire, Captain Félix (IV)
Rigot, Jeanne / later Jeanne Turniquel
  (XXXV)
Rigot, Monsieur (XXVI)
Roquemure, Alix de (LXXV)
Roquemure, Ermessinde de (LXXV)
Roquemure, Gérard de (LXXV)

Roquemure, Hugues de (LXXV)
Roquemure, Lionel de (LXXV)
Séjan, Monsieur (LXXIX)
Sérac, Adrien Anatole Jules de / later
    Father Sérac (XII)
Souvray, Monsieur de (XXXVI)
Stive, Lord (XXXVII)
Thérèse (XXXV)
Turniquel, Ernestine / later Countess
    Ernestine Lémée (XXX)
Turniquel, Jeanne / née Jeanne Rigot
    (XXX)
Turniquel, Jérôme (XXXV)
Val, Marquis du (II)
Val, Marquise Lucy du / née Lucy de
    Crancé (II)
Vaucloix, Marquis de (XLII)
Vaucloix, Louise de / later Louise de
    Carin (XLII)
Virelei, Blanche de (LXXV)
Zizuli (LXXVI)

MUSÉE CONTEMPORAIN, A 20 CENTIMES LA LIVRAISON

FRÉDÉRIC SOULIÉ

LES

MÉMOIRES DU DIABLE

Prix : 2 francs

PARIS

MICHEL LÉVY FRÈRES, LIBRAIRES-ÉDITEURS

RUE VIVIENNE, 2 BIS

1858

PROLOGUE

Chapter I: Ronquerolles Castle

On the first of January, 182*, Baron François Armand de Luizzi was seated by the fire in his castle at Ronquerolles.

Though I haven't seen that castle in twenty years, I remember it perfectly. Unlike typical feudal castles, it lay at the bottom of a valley. In those days it consisted of four towers joined by four wings; both the towers and the connecting buildings were capped by steep slate roofs, a rarity in the Pyrenees. As a result, from the hills that surrounded it the castle looked more like a dwelling from the sixteenth or seventeenth century than a fortress from 1327, which is when it was built.

I was often inside the castle as a child, and I remember I especially admired the large flagstones that formed the flooring in the attics where we played. Those flagstones—which put to shame the puny floor tiles at my house—had protected the ramparts of Ronquerolles when it was a stronghold; later they'd been covered over with peaked roofs, like those you can still see on the Vincennes Gate, but without altering the original structure.

Nowadays we know that of all durable materials, iron is the least durable. So I'll be careful not to say Ronquerolles seemed to have been built of iron, so respectful had the centuries been to it; but I can say the great building was in a remarkable state of preservation. It looked like the whim of some wealthy connoisseur of the Gothic style, who just yesterday had built those walls, not one stone of which had deteriorated, and carved those floral arabesques, not one line of which had been broken nor a single detail marred. And yet in living memory no one had ever been seen working on the upkeep or repair of that castle.

Still, it had undergone several changes since its original construction, the most striking of which was visible on the southern approach to Ronquerolles. Of the six windows in the façade on that side, no two were alike. The first window on the left, as you faced the castle, was ogival in shape; a stone cross with sharply defined edges divided it into four panes filled with ordinary glass. The next window was like the first, except each pane, held in a hinged iron frame, contained clear glass divided into a lead-outlined diamond pattern. The third window had lost its ogive and its stone cross; the ogive had been bricked in, and the glass in the iron frames had been replaced by a heavy wood-framed sash win-

23

dow, opening vertically like a guillotine. The fourth window had two casements, one on the inside and one on the outside, both latched, and both divided into small panes, and besides that it was protected by a shutter painted red. The fifth window had only one casement, with large panes of glass, plus a louvered shutter painted green. Finally the sixth window held mirrored glass, behind which could be seen a brightly colored shade; that window too was protected by thick shutters.

The wall continued unbroken after those six windows, the sixth of which the people of Ronquerolles had noticed for the first time on the first of January, 182*, which was also the day after the death of Baron Hugues François de Luizzi, Baron François Armand de Luizzi's father, without anyone being able to say who'd added that window and placed it where it was. The strangest thing was that, according to local tradition, all the other windows had appeared the same way, in similar circumstances: that is to say, without anyone seeing any work performed, and always the day after the death of each successive proprietor of the castle in turn. And it was certainly a fact that each of those windows belonged to a bedroom that had been closed, never to be reopened, at the death of whoever had occupied it all his life.

If its owners had lived at Ronquerolles full time, that peculiar mystery would probably have upset the locals more; but for over two centuries each new heir of the Luizzis had spent only twenty-four hours at the castle before leaving it, never to return. That had been the case with Baron Hugues François de Luizzi; and when his son François Armand de Luizzi arrived on the first of January, 182*, he announced he'd be leaving the next day.

The caretaker had only learned his master was coming when he saw him enter the castle; and the good man's astonishment turned to terror when, meaning to prepare a room for the newcomer, he saw him head toward the corridor which led to the mysterious rooms we've spoken of—and then, with a key he drew from his pocket, the baron opened a door the caretaker had never seen before, and which had appeared in the corridor just the way the new window had appeared in the façade.

The doors were as varied as the windows, each designed in a different style; the latest one was made of rosewood with copper inlay. Beyond the doors, the wall continued unbroken along the corridor, just as outside the façade continued unbroken beyond the windows. Between those blank interior and exterior walls there were presumably other rooms, but—since no doubt they were intended for the heirs of the Luizzis yet to come—they, like the future to which they belonged, remained sealed and inaccessible. Those we might call the bedrooms of the past were locked and unknown as well, but the doors and windows opening onto them remained. The new room—the bedroom of the present, if you will—was the only one open; and throughout that day, the first of January, anyone who wished could enter it freely.

That corridor, which strikes us as somewhat fantastical, just felt damp and cold to Luizzi, and he ordered a roaring fire built in the white marble hearth of his new room. He spent the whole day there, going over the accounts of the Ronquerolles property. Those concerning the castle itself didn't take long: Ronquerolles brought in nothing and cost nothing. But Luizzi now owned several nearby farms whose leases had expired and whose contracts he wanted to renew.

Anyone besides those farmers entering the baron's room would've been struck by its fashionable elegance. The room was entirely done in Louis the Fifteenth style, which is to say the furniture was both grotesque and uncomfortable. Since a few of the old houses in the area had kept original specimens from that period as souvenirs, what passed for modern elegance among the Luizzis looked merely old-fashioned to the good country neighbors, who rated the fussy rococo furnishings of the new room well below the mahogany desk and chest of drawers of the lawyer's wife.

Anyway, the whole day was spent in negotiating and settling on the rates for the new leases, and it was only when night fell that Luizzi found himself alone. As we've said, he was seated by the fire, with a table next to him on which a candle burned. While he sat there, lost in thought, the pendulum clock rang midnight, then twelve thirty, then one, then one thirty. At the chime announcing that last time, he rose and began to pace with agitation. He was a tall man, with a figure that conveyed forcefulness; the natural look on his face expressed resolve. Yet now he trembled, and his agitation grew the closer the hands of the clock came to two. Several times he stopped, as if he'd heard some noise from outside, but nothing broke the solemn silence around him.

Finally he heard the slight click of the gears as the clock prepared to strike the hour. A sudden drastic pallor spread across his face. He stood still and closed his eyes, like a man about to be taken ill. The first chime of two o'clock rang out in the silence. That sound pulled him out of his prostration; before the second chime had rung he'd seized a small silver bell that lay on the table and had shaken it violently, while speaking a single word: "Come!"

Anybody can have a small silver bell, anybody can shake it at exactly two o'clock in the morning while saying "Come!" But realistically nobody will have happen what happened next to Armand de Luizzi. The little bell he'd shaken so fiercely gave out only a weak sound and rang only once, a *ding* that vibrated sadly and without echo. When he called out "Come!" he put into it all the effort of a man who means to be heard across a vast distance; and yet his voice, projected forcefully from his chest, had nothing of the resolute, imperative tone he'd intended, and as it actually left his mouth it sounded like no more than a timid plea.

He himself was still registering surprise at that incongruous result when he noticed, in the chair he'd just left, a person who could be a man, because it had a man's self-assured manner, or who could be a woman, because it had a woman's face and graceful limbs, and who was certainly the Devil, because it hadn't walked in, it had simply appeared. It was wearing a dressing gown with plain sleeves that suggested nothing about the sex of the individual inside it.

In silence Luizzi studied that unusual person while it settled itself comfortably in the Voltaire-style armchair by the fire. The newcomer leaned back casually and reached toward the fire with the forefinger and thumb of one slender white hand. Those two digits stretched out like a pair of tongs and took hold of a coal. The Devil—for it was the Devil in person—used it to light a cigar he found on the table. No sooner had he taken a puff than he tossed away the cigar with disgust and said to Luizzi, "Don't you have any black market tobacco?"

The baron said nothing.

"In that case, have one of mine." From the pocket of his dressing gown the Devil drew a small cigarette case of exquisite taste. He pulled out two cigarettes, lit one with the coal he was still holding, and handed it to Luizzi. The baron refused it with a gesture, and in a quite natural tone the Devil said, "Ah, you're straitlaced, my friend—too bad!" Then he began to smoke, without spitting, leaning back and occasionally whistling a contradance tune, nodding his head slightly along with the beat in the most impudent way.

Luizzi still stood unmoving before this odd Devil. Finally he broke the silence: in the loud, staccato voice that typifies the modern dramatic style, he said, "Son of Hell, I summoned you…"

"First, my friend," interrupted the Devil, "I don't know why you're addressing me informally as *tu*; it's very bad manners. It's a habit people you call artistic have picked up among themselves—a false show of friendship that doesn't stop them from envying and hating and despising each other! It's a way of talking your novelists and playwrights use for the expression of passions pushed to their absolute extreme, but it's something well-bred people never do. Since you're neither a writer nor an actor, I'd be obliged to you if you'd address me the way you would a stranger, which will be much more appropriate. I'll also observe that in calling me the Son of Hell you're repeating a piece of foolishness that shows up in all known languages. I'm no more the Son of Hell than you're the Son of Your Bedroom just because you happen to be staying here."

"Still, you're the person I summoned," replied Luizzi with an affectation of great dramatic power.

The Devil gave him a dirty look and replied loftily, "You're a scoundrel. You think you're talking to your bellboy?"

"I'm talking to someone who's my slave!" cried Luizzi, touching the little bell in front of him.

"Just as you please, baron. But, my word, you're quite the young man of our time: ridiculous and boorish! Since you're so confident you can give me orders, you could afford to be polite; it wouldn't cost you much. Anyway, your manners are those of a jumped-up peasant—the kind who thinks sprawling in the back of his carriage makes him look like he's always had one. You're from an old family, you've got a reasonably distinguished name, you present a decent appearance, and you don't need this ridiculous posturing to make a good impression."

"The Devil, delivering a sermon! That's odd, and…"

"And you, don't try any politician's debating tricks. Don't put stupid words in my mouth just so you can triumphantly refute them. I don't make moralizing speeches; I leave that pastime to crooks and kept women. I hate phonies. If heaven had been gracious enough to grant me children, I'd rather have given them two vices than one affectation."

"You must have plenty to give away!"

"Many fewer than the most virtuous Parisian bourgeois. To take advantage of vices, you have to have none. To claim the Devil has vices would be like saying the doctor who lives off your ailments is sick, and the lawyer who gets fat off your lawsuits is litigious, and the judge appointed to punish crimes is a murderer."

The conversation between the supernatural personage and Luizzi had taken place without either of them moving. Up to now the baron had talked more to keep from looking dumbfounded than to say anything he meant. He'd gradually overcome the confusion and astonishment caused by his interlocutor's appearance and behavior, and he now resolved to broach another subject, one no doubt more important to him. He therefore took a second armchair, sat down on the other side of the fireplace, and examined the Devil more closely.

Now he could see better, and could admire the refined elegance of his guest's features and figure. Still, if this hadn't been the Devil, it wouldn't have been easy to decide whether this pale, beautiful face and this frail, restless body belonged to a young man of eighteen devoured by secret cravings or to a woman of thirty worn out by pleasure. As for the voice, it would've been too low to be a woman's—if we hadn't invented the contralto, that female baritone that promises more than it delivers. As for the look in the Devil's eye—the quality that betrays our own thoughts whenever it isn't being used to decipher the thoughts of others—that look gave away nothing. The Devil's eye didn't speak, it looked. Luizzi finished his inspection in silence; convinced he couldn't win a battle of wits with this inexplicable being, he picked up his little silver bell and rang it once more.

At that command—for such it was—the Devil got up and stood before Luizzi in the attitude of a servant awaiting his master's orders. That movement, though it lasted no more than a tenth of a second, had been accompanied by a total transformation in the Devil's appearance and dress. The fantastical being from earlier had vanished, and in his place the baron now saw a yokel in livery, with meaty hands in white cotton gloves, and a drunkard's face above a red waistcoat, and flat feet in big shoes, and no calves in his stockings.

"Here I am, Your Honor," said the newcomer.

"Who are you?" cried Luizzi, offended by the man's crude and insolent servility—the universal quality of the French domestic servant.

27

"I'm not the Devil's valet, I only do what I'm told, but I do what I'm told."

"And what are you doing here?"

"I'm waiting for Your Honor's orders."

"You don't know why I summoned you?"

"No, Your Honor."

"You're lying!"

"Yes, Your Honor."

"What's your name?"

"Whatever Your Honor wants."

"What were you christened?"

The Devil didn't move, but the whole castle, from the weathervane down to the wine cellar, began to laugh. Luizzi was afraid, and to hide it he became angry: it's a method as common as singing.

"Well, answer me: don't you have a name?"

"I've got as many as you please. I've served under all kinds of names. A gentleman who'd been exiled during the Revolution hired me in 1814 and called me Brutus to make fun of the Republic in my person. After that I worked for an academician who changed Pierre, the name I was using, to La Pierre, as being more literary. I was fired for falling asleep in the front hall while the gentleman was delivering a lecture in his parlor. The stockbroker who took me on next really wanted to call me Jules, because his wife's lover was named Jules, and the husband found it vastly entertaining to say in front of his wife, 'That animal Jules! That clumsy oaf Jules! That clown Jules!' and so on. I quit on my own initiative, I was so tired of being insulted by proxy. Then I worked for a chorus girl who was keeping a French peer…"

"You mean a French peer who was keeping a chorus girl?"

"I mean what I said. The story's not well known, but I'll tell it to you someday, if you ever want to publish a treatise on human morality."

"So you're already back to moralizing?"

"As a servant, I do as little as I can."

"So now you're my servant?"

"No choice. I tried coming to you in another role, and you treated me like a lackey. Since I couldn't force you to be polite, I resigned myself to being insulted, and so now I'm what I assume you want me to be. Does Your Honor have no orders for me?"

"Yes, in fact I do. But I also want to ask for your advice."

"If Your Honor will permit me to say so, asking your servant for advice is playing a scene out of a seventeenth-century comedy."

"Where'd you learn that?"

"From the serialized stories in the newspapers."

"So you read them? Well! What did you think?"

"Why do you expect me to think anything about people who don't think?"

Luizzi stopped again, realizing he wasn't getting any closer to his purpose with this new character than with the previous one. He picked up the bell; but before he rang it he said, "Even though you're the same person in a different form, I don't feel like discussing the subject we have to talk about while you're like that. Can you change?"

"I'm at Your Honor's orders."

"Can you go back to the way you were before?"

"On one condition: that you give me one of the coins in that purse."

On the table Luizzi saw a purse he hadn't noticed before. He opened it and drew out a coin. It was made of some priceless metal, and bore only this inscription: ONE MONTH OF THE LIFE OF BARON FRANÇOIS ARMAND DE LUIZZI. Instantly he understood the mystery of that kind of payment, and he dropped the coin back into the purse, which felt quite heavy—and that made him smile.

"That's too high a price for a mere whim."

"So you've become a miser?"

"How do you mean?"

"Just that you threw away lots of that money to get less than you're asking for now."

"I don't remember doing that."

"If I were allowed to reckon up your accounts, you'd see there isn't a single month of your life that you exchanged for something reasonable."

"Maybe so, but at least I lived."

"Depends what you mean by living."

"Does the word have more than one meaning?"

"Two very different ones. For lots of people, to live is to surrender your life to all the demands that surround you. Someone who lives like that is described as *good-natured* when he's young; when he grows up he's called *a fine fellow*; and when he's old he's known as an *excellent gentleman*. Those three names have one synonym in common: the word *sucker*."

"And you think I've lived my life as a sucker?"

"I think Your Honor agrees with me, since he only came to this castle to give up one way of living and assume the other."

"And can you define that other one for me?"

"Since that's the subject of the bargain we're going to make together..."

"Together? No!" interrupted Luizzi. "I don't want to bargain with you. I'd find it disgusting. Your appearance is absolutely repellent."

"But that's a condition in your favor: you won't give away too much to someone you don't like. A king who's negotiating with an ambassador he admires always makes some dangerous concession; a woman negotiating her seduction with a man who appeals to her always surrenders fifty percent of her usual terms; a father-in-law negotiating his daughter's marriage contract with a son-in-law he likes often gives the boy the right to ruin his wife. To avoid being cheated, you should only do business with unlikable people. Distaste will do the job of good sense."

"And it'll do me the job of getting rid of you," said the baron as he rang the little magic bell that forced the Devil to obey him.

Just the way the androgynous creature who'd shown up first had vanished, now the second manifestation—not the Devil himself but the version of the Devil who wore livery—also vanished, and in his place Luizzi now saw a fairly handsome young man. He was of that type of man for whom the term changes every quarter century, but which nowadays is known as a dandy. His white trousers stretched like a bowstring from his suspenders to his under-shoe straps. Resting his spurred and varnished boots on the fireplace surround, he leaned against the back of Luizzi's armchair. Perfectly gloved, the cuffs turned back on the sleeves of his tailcoat with glistening buttons, a monocle in his eye and a gold-headed walking stick in his hand, he looked exactly like some friend paying a visit to Baron Armand de Luizzi.

The illusion was so effective the baron stared at him like someone he knew. "Have you and I met somewhere?"

"I never go there!"

"Did I see you on horseback in the park?"

"I never ride!"

"Then were you in a carriage?"

"I never take one!"

"Ah, now I have it! I knew it—I played cards with you at Madame de…"

"I never gamble!"

"But you were waltzing with her."

"I never dance!"

"You weren't courting her?"

"I never go there, and I never pay court!"

Luizzi felt a strong desire to beat this gentleman with a riding crop to cure him of his insolence. But reason came to his rescue, and he began to understand that if he let himself be drawn into arguing with the Devil, given how many different forms that personage might assume, he'd never get to the point of the interview. So he resolved to be done with this version and with any others. As he rang the little bell again he cried, "Satan, hear me and obey!"

He'd barely finished speaking when the supernatural being he'd summoned appeared in all of his sinister splendor. It was indeed the fallen angel evoked in poetry: perfect beauty debased by pain, transformed by hatred, perverted by debauchery—and yet still retaining, when the face was at rest, some dormant trace of its celestial origins… But as soon as he spoke, the movement of his features conveyed an existence consumed by vile passions. Still, among all the repellent expressions passing across his face, the dominant look was one of deep disgust.

Rather than wait for the baron to ask him a question, he spoke first. "Here I am, to conclude the bargain I made with your family, by which I must give each Baron de Luizzi of Ronquerolles what he asks for. You know the terms of the bargain, I assume?"

"Yes. In exchange for that gift, each of us will be yours—unless he can prove he was happy for ten years of his life."

"And each of your ancestors," continued Satan, "asked me for what he thought happiness would be, so as to escape me at the hour of his death."

"And they were all wrong, weren't they?"

"All of them. They asked me for wealth, for glory, for knowledge, for power; and power, knowledge, glory, and wealth all made them miserable."

"So the bargain is entirely to your advantage, and I should refuse to make it?"

"If you can."

"Isn't there something I could ask for that would make me happy?"

"There is one thing."

"I know it's not up to you to tell me what it is; but can't you tell me if it's something I know of?"

"You know of it. It's been mixed up in everything that's happened in your life—sometimes within you, more often in other people—and I can assure you most people don't need my help to possess it."

"Is it some moral quality? Is it some material thing?"

"Now you're asking too much. Have you decided? Talk fast, I'm in a hurry to wrap this up."

"You weren't in such a hurry earlier."

"That's because earlier I was in one of the thousand disguises that hide me from myself and make the present bearable. When I imprison my being in the features of some human creature, however crooked or despicable, I find myself at the level of whatever century I'm in, and I'm not bothered by the miserable role I've sunk to. There's only one creature of your species who, having become ruler of the small kingdom of Sardinia, had the idiotic vanity still to style himself king of Cyprus and Jerusalem.[6] Vanity is satisfied with great words, but pride demands great things, and, as you know, that led to my fall—the hardest test my pride ever faced. After my struggle with God, after I'd led so many mighty souls, aroused such strong passions, unleashed such enormous catastrophes, I'm ashamed to be reduced to the shabby schemes and foolish affectations of this age; I conceal from myself what I was, so as to forget, as much as I can,

---

[6] The Italian kings of the House of Savoy, though reduced during the Napoleonic wars to ruling nothing but the island of Sardinia, still laid claim to long-meaningless Crusader-era titles to the kingdoms of Jerusalem and Cyprus. Soulié may have in mind Victor Emmanuel I (reigned 1802-21), or Charles Felix (reigned 1821-31), or Charles Albert (reigned 1831-49).

what I've become. The form you've now forced me to assume is therefore hateful and unbearable to me. So hurry up and tell me what you want."

"I still don't know, and I was counting on you to help me choose."

"I told you, that's not possible."

"But you can still do for me what you did for my ancestors: you can lay bare for me other men's passions, their hopes and joys and sorrows, the secrets of their existence, so that from that education I can find some light to guide me."

"I can do that—but you should know that your ancestors agreed to give themselves to me before I began my explanation. Look at the contract: I've left blank the name of the thing you're going to ask for. Sign it. Then, after you've heard me out, you yourself can write in what you want to be or what you want to have."

Luizzi signed the contract. "And now I'm listening. Speak."

"Not like this. The solemn formality this primitive form imposes on me would exhaust your frivolous attention span. Take my advice: go mingle in human life; I'm more present there than people think. I'll tell you about their lives."

"I'll be curious to hear it."

"Hang onto that feeling. Because from the moment you ask me to tell you someone's secret, you'll have to listen to the whole thing. Or you could refuse to listen to me, by giving me one of the coins from that purse."

"I accept, as long as there's no requirement that I stay in one place."

"Go wherever you want. No matter where you summon me, I'll be at the rendezvous. But remember, it's only here you can see me in my true form."

"Can I have the right to put down on paper everything you tell me?"

"You can do that."

"The right to reveal your secrets about the present age?"

"You'll reveal them."

"To publish them?"

"You'll publish them."

"To sign them with your name?"

"You'll sign them with my name."

"When do we start?"

"When you summon me with that little bell, anytime, anyplace, for any reason. Just remember: starting from today, you have only *ten years* to make your choice."

Three o'clock rang, and the Devil vanished. Luizzi found himself alone. The purse containing the days of his life lay on the table. He wanted to open it to count the coins, but he couldn't do it, and after carefully tucking the purse under his pillow he got into bed.

THREE NIGHTS

Chapter II: Three Visits

Luizzi left Ronquerolles the next day. Though he'd asked the Devil for a fairly generous period of time in which to find happiness, he behaved like a man who'd already made up his mind: he hurried back to Toulouse, meaning to go directly on from there to Paris.

Paris is the great illusion of those who think living means squeezing everything out of life. Paris is the Barrel of the Danaides,[7] into which you pour the illusions of youth, the plans of maturity, the regrets of white-haired old age; it absorbs everything and gives back nothing. You young people whom fate hasn't yet drawn into its all-consuming atmosphere: if your fine imaginations require days of calm and confidence, of romantic dreams lost in the heavens, if it feels sweet to you to devote your soul to someone you love, to follow her and cherish her—ah, don't come to Paris! The woman you follow will lead your soul into hell on earth, amid the insulting compliments of rivals who'll remain standing as they address the one you worship only on your knees—who'll cheerfully, lightly, carelessly proposition her and make her smile, while you tremble when you address her, if you dare speak to her at all. No, no, don't come to Paris if some harmonious strain of the eternal angelic chorus has echoed in your heart; don't cast into the common crowd the secret of that poignant delirium in which your soul weeps for all the joys it dreams of but that it knows exist nowhere but heaven: your only audience will be critics who'll bite your outstretched hands, and readers who'll sneer at your convictions because they don't understand them.

No—a thousand times no—don't come to Paris if you're driven by ambition for sanctified glory. No matter how strong you are, don't come to Paris: you'll lose more than your hopes, you'll lose your purity of mind. No doubt your mind dreamt only of the beautiful concerns of genius, the pure and holy song of good things, the sincere and solemn zeal for the truth—wrong, my young friends, wrong! When you've tried all that, when you've asked the public to pay attention to someone who speaks well and honorably, you'll find that public

---

[7] In Greek mythology, the Danaides (the daughters of Danaus) murdered their husbands on their wedding night, and were condemned to spend eternity trying to fill a barrel with water—impossible, since the barrel was perforated like a sieve.

hanging on the vulgar words of some petty scribbler, on the manic nonsense of some ink-spiller, on the frightening tales in some crime gossip sheet. You'll see the public—that old libertine—smile at the virginity of your muse and defile her with an indecent kiss before calling out to her, "All right, hussy, get out, or entertain me: I need astringents and burning Chinese remedies to wake my dormant senses. Have you got wild incest, monstrous adultery, horrifying criminal debauchery, or impossible desires to tell me about? If so, speak, and I'll listen to you for an hour—for as long as I can feel your acrid, venomous pen moving across my calloused and gangrenous feelings. If not, shut up, and go die in misery and obscurity!"

You hear, young friends? Misery and obscurity! Misery, that vice punished by contempt! Obscurity, that aptly named torture! Obscurity means exile from sunlight—when you're someone who needs the rays of the sun to keep your heart from freezing to death! Misery and obscurity—you don't want that! So then what'll you do, young friends? You'll take a pen and a sheet of paper, and at the top you'll write *The Devil's Memoirs*, and you'll say to your century, "Oh, you want to take pleasure in cruel things? So be it, my lord, here's a slice of your own story."

However, may God keep us from two things the world could forgive, but for which we couldn't forgive ourselves: God keep us from lies and immorality! What good are lies? Isn't real life more brazenly absurd and perverted than we could possibly make up? As for immorality, the great and the humble both enjoy it when they're safely alone: high-society women and shop girls swoon over an immoral book; one hides it in her boudoir, the other in her garret; and when their conscience is safely hidden away alongside the book, under a silk cushion or inside a straw mattress, they heap scorn and insults on anyone who brings up even the mildest sin in conversation.

All women behave toward an immoral book the way the countess in *Dangerous Liaisons* behaved toward Prévan: they surrender themselves utterly to him—then ring for a servant to throw him out like some insolent fellow who tried to molest them.[8] May God keep us, then, not from being guilty but from being gullible! To be gullible is the worst mistake in an age when success is the highest recommendation. What we're about to tell you, therefore, will be both true and moral; don't blame us if it isn't always flattering or honorable.

Meanwhile, in spite of Luizzi's plans, his slave's storytelling began sooner than he expected. Woe to anyone to whom hell has granted the power to tear away the veil of appearances from human actions! He who attempts that dangerous ordeal will know no rest. Twice cursed is he who gives in to that temptation even once! The cup in which he expected to quench his thirst leaves him still

---

[8] In Choderlos de Laclos's 1782 novel *Les Liaisons dangereuses*, Madame de Merteuil arranges an assignation with her would-be lover Prévan, but has her servants come in to break it up.

thirsty. In fact, the appetite that increases by being fed was wonderfully described by a drunkard to whom I jokingly offered a few more bottles of Bordeaux, and who replied innocently, "Sure—there's nothing like drinking to make you thirsty."

In any case, it wasn't some great desire that drove Luizzi to ask for the first mouthful of the corrosive poison the Devil would later pour out for him so generously. An escapade he hadn't in the least anticipated gave rise to the curiosity he'd thought he was safe from, and which then carried him so far.

Luizzi had a distinguished name and a great fortune. As a result, he was sought out by the most prominent families in Toulouse—a city well supplied with the upper aristocracy—and he was connected with several businessmen of good family. He was distantly related to the Marquis du Val. That name—so bourgeois when written without the *du*—belonged to the junior branch of an old noble family in that part of the country. Their original name had gradually fallen out of use, and each branch of the family had kept as its patronymic the modifier that at first had merely served to tell them apart from others with the same name. But when they had to show their distinguished ancestry they signed contracts with their almost forgotten real name, and people named H— du Val, H— du Mont, and H— du Bois[9] proved to be higher born, even with their shopkeepers' names, than the marquises and counts whose names referring to estates and manors gave them an air of quality.

Luizzi also had a business relationship with Dilois, a wool dealer. It was Dilois who usually bought the wool shorn from the splendid flocks of merinos raised on the Luizzi lands. Before handing over the management of his property to a steward, Luizzi wanted to meet in person the man who once a year would end up owing him a considerable sum; and the day he reached Toulouse he went to see him.

It was three o'clock when the baron made his way to the rue de la Pomme, where Dilois lived. After asking for directions to the wool dealer's house, he went through a carriage entrance into a square courtyard surrounded by a tall house. The ground floor contained storerooms at the back and on both sides, and offices on the side facing the street. Through the iron bars and the small panes of the tall windows you could make out the red labels and the glint of the copper corners of the account books. Above that ground floor on the courtyard side was an overhanging balcony, with a wooden balustrade supported on spiral posts and with doors opening onto it; the balcony was the only way to reach the rooms on the second floor of the house. The roof came down to that covered balcony and sheltered it.

When Luizzi entered the courtyard he saw a young woman on the balcony. Though it was cold, she wore only a silk dress; her black hair fell in curls around her face, and in her hand she held a book she was reading, while below her half

---

[9] H— of the valley, H— of the mountain, H— of the woods.

35

a dozen warehouse boys moved around bales of wool, urging each other on with the confused shouting that comprises half of all work in the south of France. It was a deafening din.

No one noticed the baron; the boys were caught up in their work, Madame Dilois—for it was she—had her eyes fixed on her book, and a young man with beautiful blond hair who was standing in the courtyard had his eyes fixed in turn on her. Luizzi waited at the entrance to the courtyard, observing the scene.

Madame Dilois raised her head, and the young man who was watching her so intently gave a peculiar cry: "Eeyaaow!"

All of the workers stopped. In the great silence that followed, the young woman's sweet, clear voice could be heard. "The bales of lanolin, numbered 107 and 108."

"In storeroom number one," came the young man's loud voice.

"This evening, to the laundry on the island," she added quietly.

"Bales 107 and 108 to the laundry on the island," cried the young man imperiously.

She went back to reading her book, the clerk kept his eyes fixed on her beautiful face, and, shouting once again to urge each other on, the workmen began carrying out their orders. A moment later Madame Dilois raised her eyes.

"Eeyaaow!" cried the clerk. Silence fell as if by magic.

The graceful young woman said calmly in her clear voice, "A hundred and fifty kilos, short staple wool, to pull from warehouse number seven and send to the spinning mill at La Roque."

The clerk repeated her order in his loud, commanding voice. Then he went to one of the barred windows and knocked on the glass with his finger. A small transom opened. Luizzi could see the pale blond head of someone young. In a quieter, more timid voice, the clerk repeated, "Invoice for La Roque for a hundred and fifty kilos."

"I heard—you shout loudly enough," replied the voice of a child.

The transom closed. Raising his eyes to Madame Dilois, Luizzi saw she was watching that window carefully, and that a slight sad smile, intended no doubt for the sweet face that had appeared at the window, still remained where it had formed on her lips.

At that moment Madame Dilois noticed Luizzi, as did the clerk. The latter took a step toward the stranger, but at the same time he glanced up at the mistress of the house, and at a sign from her he went back to his place beneath the balcony. Madame Dilois consulted her notebook again; then she closed it and put it into her apron pocket. Leaning on the balustrade, she gave an almost imperceptible sign with her head. The young man quickly climbed onto a few bales of merchandise so as to get close enough to Madame Dilois to hear her over the noise of the workmen. She spoke to him quietly. The clerk nodded, and was turning to go when Madame Dilois stopped him and added a few words while looking at Luizzi out of the corner of her eye. The clerk nodded silently again, and from the top of the pile of bales he cried, "Three hundred kilos, merino wool, Luizzi, to be hauled to Castres."

All of the workmen stopped. One of them, a hard-faced man, said brusquely, "You'll have to weigh it yourself, Monsieur Charles. I won't be responsible for it. The figures are never right with that Devil's wool—you ship a hundred kilos, and only ninety get there."

"It's easy to blame it on the Devil," replied the clerk. "You'll weigh the merchandise, and the figures will be right, you understand?"

"You weigh it, Charles," said Madame Dilois, who'd seen the workman straighten up with an insolent air while the clerk eyed him threateningly. The latter replied only with the silent nod that appeared to be his primary form of communication with her. Then, after Madame Dilois again drew his attention to Luizzi with a glance, the clerk jumped down to the ground in a single leap and approached the baron, asking him politely what he wanted.

"I'd like to speak to Monsieur Dilois," said Luizzi.

"He's away for the whole week, sir. But if it's about business, please go into the office and the cashier will help you."

"It is about business, in fact. But since the transaction I came to propose is a large one, I'd rather have dealt directly with him."

"In that case, there's Madame Dilois, and you can arrange it with her."

Since the clerk was pointing her out to Luizzi, Madame Dilois could tell they were talking about her, and she hurried down and graciously came to meet the baron.

"What is it you wish, sir?"

"Ma'am, I'd like to offer you an extension of a contract I already consider much to my advantage, since I'm able to make it with you."

Madame Dilois gave Luizzi a gracious look—though the clerk, having overheard, frowned at the compliment. Madame Dilois motioned for him to move away, and then replied in a friendly tone, "To whom do I have the honor of speaking?"

"I'm Baron de Luizzi, ma'am."

At that name she took a step back; Charles, the handsome young man, examined Luizzi with frightened, unhappy curiosity. But that lasted only a moment, and Madame Dilois pointed to the office door, saying, "Be so kind as to come in, sir. I'm at your orders."

Luizzi went inside, followed by Charles, who set a chair for him next to the enormous stove that heated the entire ground floor, and then sat at a desk where the day's correspondence awaited him. Looking around the interior of the house, Luizzi noticed, seated at a table, the lovely child who'd opened the transom; she was writing something with great care. She might've been nine or ten, and she looked so much like Madame Dilois there could be no doubt she was her daughter. In spite of her beauty, some kind of sadness and resignation made that young face look older. "Is Madame Dilois severe with her?" wondered Luizzi to himself. Yet the glance the mother had given the girl earlier had been loving.

The child lifted her eyes from her page only to ask an elderly clerk who was writing in another corner, "What price on the wool sent to La Roque?"

"Two francs, like always."

"That's all right," broke in Charles. "Give me the invoice and I'll enter the price myself."

If the Devil had been there, he would've explained to Luizzi the private meaning of that interruption. Luizzi attributed it to temper. This handsome Charles, so perfectly obedient to Madame Dilois's slightest gesture, was—Luizzi assumed—her lover, or at least in love with her. The arrival of an elegant baron must've alarmed him, and Luizzi thought the anger he read into the clerk's words was the result of fear inspired by his own presence here. But he was wrong. Charles was only thinking like a businessman when he interrupted the clerk: he saw no need to reveal the resale price of wool to a man who'd come to offer his own wool for sale. That was all Charles meant.

Madame Dilois soon joined them. Luizzi was able to study her more closely: she was a charming creature, and her surroundings only set off her rare perfections even more. She was tall, slender, delicate, with languid eyes hidden behind long brown lashes—a voluptuous veil that perhaps only intense anger could lift. She was happy to show off her slender feet and her white hands with their rosy nails. She looked so out of place among the rough features of her workmen and the counting-house faces of her clerks that Luizzi felt justified in thinking Madame Dilois was the beautiful daughter of some impoverished noble family, reduced to marrying a wealthy man beneath her. He therefore addressed her as an equal—which to the conceited baron seemed like the subtlest form of flattery.

Responding with no more than a smile to his polite commonplace remarks, Madame Dilois asked the baron to follow her. She opened a door with a key she drew from her apron pocket and led him into another room. Her looks and movements and languor were so romantic that the baron expected a scented blue boudoir enclosed in these dust-filled offices like an idea of love wrapped inside the sterile preoccupations of business. But the boudoir he imagined turned out to be just another office. The dim light in the room was produced by the curtain of dust built up on the glass, through which you could still see the heavy iron bars that protected the windows. A black desk, a steel safe with three locks, a Morocco leather desk chair, a file cabinet, a few chairs with straw seats—those were the furnishings of what he'd imagined would be such a suave and mysterious hideaway.

No doubt the look of the place ought to have shattered Luizzi's beautiful illusions. But, even without a temple, the goddess herself remained to keep the baron's faith alive. Madame Dilois, who'd settled herself gently in the desk chair, with her beautiful white hand resting on the scrawled pages of a loose-leaf notebook and her feet shyly placed against the cold damp brick hearth, looked to

Luizzi like an angel in exile, an exquisite flower among brambles. He felt for her something like what he'd once felt for a dewy white rose a cobbler had set on his windowsill between a pot of basil and a pot of ornamental grass. Luizzi bought the rose and put it in a porcelain vase on the sideboard in his parlor. The rose died, but it died with dignity. Luizzi acquired something of a reputation for chivalry.

The baron could hardly buy the drooping flower before him now; but perhaps he could pluck it. (I beg your pardon for both the thought and its expression: Luizzi had been born under the Empire.[10]) He therefore conceived the fantasy, or rather the desire, that he might be like a star in this woman's overcast sky and shine a bright light across the frigid shadows of her life. Luizzi was young and handsome, and his voice was filled with romance. He didn't have enough brains to miss having a heart, nor enough of a heart to miss having brains. He was one of those men who are successful with women: they're both passionate and cautious, they're both intimate and worldly, they make love without indiscretion. Luizzi had seen that kind of mediocrity succeed so many times, where more flattering or more devoted lovers failed, that he felt justified in considering himself an expert seducer. The self-conceit of men is usually just a reflected vice: they get it from the foolishness of women.

Luizzi therefore now allowed himself to stare so intently at the woman before him that she lowered her eyes in embarrassment and said softly, "Baron, I believe you came to propose a deal on some wool?"

"To you? No, ma'am. I came to see Monsieur Dilois. With him I would've tried to discuss prices and quantities, though I'm not experienced at that. But I'm afraid with you that kind of negotiation…"

"I have my husband's proxy," said Madame Dilois with a smile that finished Luizzi's sentence for him. "The deal would be good."

"For whom, ma'am?"

"Why, for both of us, I hope." She paused for a moment, then went on with a smile, "If you lack experience at business, I'm a… businessman you can trust, and I'll act with integrity."

"That would be difficult for you, ma'am, and I'm bound to lose something on the deal."

"Lose what?"

"I don't dare tell you if you can't guess."

"Oh, speak freely, sir: in this business we're used to unusual conditions."

"The condition I'm talking about, ma'am, is one you impose."

"I have yet to impose any."

---

[10] The First Empire, under Napoleon: officially 1809-1814, though Napoleon—and along with him the kind of social manners and style of gallantry Soulié is referring to—ruled France under various titles starting in 1799.

"Still, I've already accepted it, and that condition is to remember you, perhaps for too long, as the most enchanting woman I've ever met—a woman I'd like to leave with the same feeling about me that I have about her."

Madame Dilois blushed with coy modesty, and she answered playfully, "I have no proxy from my husband for that, sir, and I conduct no business on the side."

"If so, you must be acting out of either self-denial or generosity."

"I'm not merely a businessman you can trust," said Madame Dilois in a tone serious enough to cut the conversation short. She opened a file box, found a bundle of papers, untied it, and removed a document, which she handed to Luizzi in a manner that seemed to beg his pardon for the undue severity of her reaction. "This is the contract we made six years ago with your father. Unless you intend to raise the breed quality of your flocks, or else to lower it, I think the figures on this contract can and should be maintained. As you can see, it was signed by your father."

"Was it with you he negotiated?" asked Luizzi, still flirting. "Because if so, I wouldn't trust this."

"Don't worry, sir," she said, gently biting her lower lip and showing Luizzi the moist enamel of her dazzling teeth. "Don't worry—six years ago I wasn't married. I wasn't yet Madame Dilois."

Before she'd finished speaking the door opened and a child's voice said shyly, "Mother, Monsieur Lucas insists on seeing you."

It was the ten-year-old girl Luizzi had noticed earlier in the office. Her entrance now, just after Madame Dilois had said she wasn't married six years ago, was a revelation to him. Her addressing Madame Dilois as "mother"—perfectly natural if the child was Monsieur Dilois's daughter—prompted the baron to give the charming wool dealer a lively look. She was blushing and had lowered her eyes.

"Is this your daughter, ma'am?" he asked.

"I call her my daughter, sir," she replied simply. Then she went on, "Caroline, I'll come speak to Monsieur Lucas. Now leave us." Recovering her poise, she said to Luizzi, "Here's the contract, sir. Take your time looking it over. My husband will be back in a week, and he'll be honored to meet you."

"I'm leaving before then, but I'll have plenty of time to look over the contract. I'd sign it right now, if the extra time you're granting me didn't give me a reason to come back."

Madame Dilois had resumed all of her flirtatious boldness. "I'm always here."

"What time of day would be most convenient?"

"That's up to you."

With those words she gave the baron one of those bows women use to say unmistakably, "Do me the pleasure of going away."

Luizzi withdrew. Everyone in the outer office was at work. As she escorted him out, Madame Dilois held out her hand to a fat bumpkin who was standing by the stove and who said cheerfully, "Good morning, Madame Dilois."

"Good morning, Lucas," she replied with the same smile that had dazzled Luizzi—and that he saw on her lips when he turned to bow goodbye to her. He felt humiliated.

Leaving Monsieur Dilois's establishment, Luizzi went to the home of the Marquis du Val. Monsieur du Val was away from Toulouse. Luizzi asked for the marquise. The valet said he didn't know whether the marquise was receiving.

"Well, then go find out!" replied Luizzi in the tone that makes clear to a servant the speaker is accustomed to being obeyed. "Tell her Baron de Luizzi wishes to see her."

For a moment the valet just stood there in the anteroom, looking like he was trying to think of a way to get to the marquise. A woman went by; the valet ran to her and spoke quickly and quietly, as if he were delighted to pass on to someone else the errand he'd been given. The chambermaid gave Luizzi a deeply insolent look, examining him with a kind of dislike that suggested she knew his name and it brought back unpleasant memories. Then she answered sourly, "What did you say your name was?"

"My name isn't important, miss... I need to speak to the Marquise du Val, and I want to know if she's receiving."

"Well, baron, she isn't."

Luizzi found it so intolerable that his visit depended on the goodwill of a servant that he refused to withdraw. So he replied, "That's what I'll go find out for myself."

He walked straight toward the parlor, the door to which was open. The valet stood aside, but the chambermaid boldly blocked the way. "Sir, I told you, you can't see the marquise! It's astonishing that after I've told you..."

"Miss," replied Luizzi politely, "I beg you to be less impertinent and go announce me to your mistress."

"What's going on?" called a voice from a room beyond the parlor.

"Lucy," said the baron loudly, "at what time are you receiving?"

"Oh, it's you, Armand," replied the Marquise du Val in surprise. She came out to meet him, closing behind her the door to the room out of which she'd emerged.

Luizzi hurried to her and kissed her hands affectionately, and the two of them sat by the fire. Lucy gave the baron a look of delighted, protective surprise. The Marquise du Val was a woman of thirty, Luizzi was twenty-five, and that way of looking at him was allowable in a woman who'd seen him as a child of fourteen playing games, now become a handsome young man. Her examination took place in silence. Then, in a quick transformation, the marquise's expression changed to one of great sadness; a single tear appeared in her eye.

Luizzi mistook the reason for her sadness. "No doubt you're sorry, as I am, that the happiness of seeing each other again arises from such a sad occasion, and that the death of my father..."

"It's not that, Armand. I barely knew your father. And you yourself, having lived apart from him for ten years, the news of his death can't have made you feel the grief that's normal when you lose someone whose love you've been used to." He didn't answer, and after a moment of silence she went on, "No, it's not that. But you've come at a time that's... well, at a very odd time indeed." She smiled sadly, then continued, as if rousing herself to laughter, "The truth is, Armand, life is a very strange novel. Will you be in Toulouse for long?"

"A week."

"You're going back to Paris?"

"Yes."

"You'll find my husband there."

"What! He's only been a Deputy for a week, and he's already gone there? The session doesn't begin for a month. I thought you'd be traveling together."

"Oh, I'm staying here. I like Toulouse."

"You don't know Paris?"

"I know it enough not to want to go there."

"Why don't you like it?"

"Oh, it's my own fault. I'm no longer young enough to shine in the salons, and I'm not yet old enough for political scheming."

"You've got more beauty and more brains than you need to succeed everywhere."

The marquise shook her head slowly. "You don't really believe a word you're saying. I'm so old, my poor Armand—old in the heart above all."

Luizzi quietly moved closer to his cousin and lowered his voice. "Are you unhappy, Lucy?"

She shot a glance around the room and replied quickly and quietly, "Come back at eight and have dinner with me. We can talk." With a nod she asked him to leave. He took her hand, and she squeezed his in a tight grip. "Till this evening, till this evening," she repeated quietly. Then she hurried back to her room. The door didn't open right away: someone had certainly been listening and hadn't moved aside fast enough.

Now alone, Luizzi was so struck by that idea that he didn't get up to leave right away, and he soon heard the sound of a man's voice, speaking angrily. That disconcerted him, and he left preoccupied: a man hidden in a woman's room, and speaking in the tone of voice Luizzi had overheard—that man, if he was neither husband nor brother nor father, was a lover. A lover! The Marquise du Val! Luizzi couldn't believe it. He couldn't put those two ideas together in his head. He had so many memories that guarded poor Lucy against such a conjecture that instead he tried to figure out what kind of new unhappiness had befallen the young woman. For he'd known Lucy when she was unhappy: Lucy, a girl of nineteen, deeply in love, but able to resist it with all the strength of Christian virtue.

Luizzi found himself reviewing all of those memories as he made his way to the home of Monsieur Barnet, his lawyer, with whom he also wanted to meet. He soon got there, but it was a day for absent husbands: he was received by Madame Barnet, a skinny dried-up little woman with brown hair, dull blue eyes, and thin lips.

When the maidservant opened the bedroom door and announced a gentleman, Madame Barnet replied in a loud voice, "What gentleman?"

"I don't know his name."

"Send him in."

Luizzi went in, and Madame Barnet came to meet him with her left arm still inside a white cotton stocking she was mending. "What do you want?" she said, squinting—for she was very nearsighted; otherwise Luizzi's distinguished appearance would probably have made her soften the coarse tone she used.

"I'm Baron de Luizzi, ma'am, one of Monsieur Barnet's clients, and I would've been delighted to meet him."

"Baron de Luizzi!" cried Madame Barnet, pulling the sock with holes in it off her left arm and sticking the needle into her chest so fearlessly that Luizzi should've guessed the armor protecting her had to be at least a triple layer of muslin and a triple layer of cotton batting. "Have a seat! Not that chair, please, an armchair. What! Is there no armchair in my room? No armchair in a lady's room—that's so provincial, isn't it, baron? But we've got armchairs, I want you to know. Marianne! Marianne! Bring an armchair from the parlor. Take off the slipcover."

Luizzi tried to forestall all the fuss by explaining to Madame Barnet that even a straight chair was more than he needed, since he was leaving. But the lawyer's wife wasn't listening to his apologies: she was thrashing around, gathering the old underwear and filthy head scarves scattered around the room and throwing them behind the window curtains. Marianne soon appeared with an armchair of painted wood upholstered in elderly Utrecht velvet worn completely bald. She set it by the fireplace, which lacked only a fire, and Madame Barnet cried out again, "Marianne, a log for the fire!"

"My God, ma'am, you're going to too much trouble," said the girl. "I quit. I never thought much of Monsieur Barnet, and…"

"Monsieur Barnet would never forgive me for letting you quit, because I hope the baron will agree to have some dinner."

"I've already accepted another invitation, ma'am," said Luizzi, "but I'm very obliged to you. I'll come back to ask Monsieur Barnet for the information I'm hoping to get from him."

"Information, baron! No point waiting for my husband! Oh, I know Toulouse from top to bottom! My family has always been in the legal field"—Madame Barnet's father had been a bailiff—"and I know more than you'd think and certainly more than you'd want. Have a seat, baron. Whatever information you need, I'm ready to give it to you."

At first Luizzi didn't intend to take advantage of Madame Barnet's assiduous offer, but he sat down, hoping to be able to get away after some small talk. He was a little embarrassed about the kind of information he wanted, but his hostess didn't leave him time even to make a blunder. "Perhaps the baron would like to buy some property? If he wants to invest in a factory, my husband could check out the Jacques Brothers foundry. The owners lost thirty-one thousand francs in November and thirty-three thousand seven hundred and twenty-two in December. Three firms, two of them in Bayonne, with whom the Jacques Brothers do a huge business, went broke at the same time. They can't keep going past February, and since they're decent people, I'm sure if they got a cash offer they'd sell their foundry for a very good price—unless the younger Monsieur Jacques's wife wants to assume her husband's debts; she's got five excellent tenant farms she inherited from her mother—you know, old lady Manette, for whom Count de Fère lost everything?—it's property that didn't cost her much, nor her daughter either, but anyway she's got it. But Madame Jacques is just like her mother, she'd try to make an omelet with less than one egg, and she's certainly not going to risk taking out a mortgage of even a single sou on her property."

When Madame Barnet began talking, Luizzi hadn't bothered to listen; but now it occurred to him to question her seriously. It was when she shifted from Monsieur Jacques to his wife: he thought she might be able to tell him things he wouldn't have dared ask anyone directly—and he only had to start Madame Barnet down the path for her to tell him everything he wanted to know. So when she'd come to a stop he said, "I'm not looking to buy property, at least for the moment. But I have business dealings with several people in Toulouse, with Monsieur Dilois among others."

Madame Barnet made a face.

"Has Monsieur Dilois made any bad deals?" asked Luizzi.

"Well, baron, he made one bad deal, which is still in force."

"And that is?"

"He married his wife."

"Is she ruining him?"

"I'm not in Monsieur Dilois's office—I don't want to say anything bad about the business—the poor man knows no more about it than I do—his wife and his head clerk, Monsieur Charles, keep the books, and as long as the good man has enough to buy an espresso and play a round of dominos at Herbola's, he doesn't ask for more."

"But surely Madame Dilois understands the business?"

"She understands whatever she wants to, the sly thing. A hussy of a shop girl who had a child by everybody, and who snagged the biggest wool dealer in Toulouse! Oh, she could lead thirty men like her husband around by the nose."

44

"Including Monsieur Charles?"

"Monsieur Charles is another clever dog. I know him—he was an assistant here—he quit to go be a clerk at Dilois's. That was when we still saw those people socially—but I told my husband if he ever invited those bumpkins over again I'd slam the door in their faces. Oh, sir, till then Charles was a charming, considerate, dedicated, thoughtful young man!"

"But maybe he's still all those things—for Madame Dilois?"

"My God, baron, he can be whatever he wants to be for her—it's none of my business!"

"I think I caught sight of him: a very handsome fellow."

"Well, I mean, he was good-looking. But heartless, baron, heartless! And after all the good things we did for him…"

"I assume Monsieur Barnet liked him a lot?" asked Luizzi innocently.

Madame Barnet fell for it and said impetuously, "My husband? He couldn't stand him!"

The baron felt no need to point out to Madame Barnet the admission she'd just let slip, since he needed to question her further and didn't want to put her on her guard, so he affected a tone of indifference. "I'll profit from your good advice about Monsieur Dilois, with whom my business is nothing more than the sale of a little wool. But I have some capital to put out as loans, and I'd like to know the state of the assets of a certain very prominent man."

"For that, baron, there's nothing better than the land registry."

"No doubt, ma'am, but I can't go there myself: people know everything that goes on in Toulouse, and the Marquis du Val might resent me for it."

"The Marquis du Val wants to borrow money?" cried Madame Barnet, astonished. "Not possible! The Marquis du Val is a client of ours, and he's never mentioned it."

"Oh, you represent the Marquis du Val?"

"Him and lots of the best families in Toulouse—meaning no offense to yours, baron—and for a long time now. This firm has acted for the du Val family for more than fifty years, and Monsieur Barnet drew up the marriage contract for the current marquis. That event made such an impression on me I've never forgotten it—I can still picture Monsieur Barnet when he came back from the signing—as if he'd lost his mind."

"What happened?"

"Oh, baron, I can't tell you—a lawyer's confidentiality is sacred! If I know at all, it's because at that moment Monsieur Barnet was so upset that he spoke without knowing what he was saying."

"I'm very discreet, ma'am."

"The best way to keep quiet is to know nothing."

"You're right. I won't ask you anything… but I assume the marquise is happy?"

45

"God knows, baron, and God must know, because now he's everything to her."

"She's devout?"

"Fanatical—she lives for fasting and penitence. It seems to agree with her—so what can you say—we all make our own choices in life—but I fear her exertions will kill her."

Luizzi looked up at the clock set into the stomach of a wooden ape on the mantlepiece and saw it was almost eight. He rose; the little he'd heard about the Marquise du Val had stimulated his curiosity, and yet he didn't try to find out more. Seeing Lucy had awoken tender childhood memories in his heart, and—not being able to predict what Madame Barnet might say—he didn't want to hear her talk about Lucy anymore.

It's not always what's said about some people that wounds us, it's what kind of people are talking about them. There are names dear to our hearts that no one can utter to our satisfaction, names that voices we dislike injure merely by pronouncing them. Luizzi hadn't reached that point with Lucy; but even if she hadn't been related to him, or been his childhood friend, or been the dream of his youth, his pride as a gentleman would've taken offense no matter what judgment Madame Barnet rendered on the Marquise du Val. He bowed deeply to the lawyer's wife, and—full of reflections on the marquise's piety and what he thought he'd observed at her house—he made his way there.

Chapter III: The First Night: the Night in the Boudoir

Luizzi was still a good distance from the carriage entrance when he was approached by a woman who addressed him by name. By the light from a nearby shop he recognized her as the chambermaid who'd received him so impertinently at the marquise's house. Now she said quickly, "Go straight past the house and meet me at the far end of the street."

She kept on walking, and Luizzi, who'd paused for a moment, saw her turn onto a side street. He didn't know quite what to think of her instructions; but since following them wouldn't keep him from going back to the house later, he decided to comply. But as he passed the carriage entrance he glanced around inquiringly and saw a man nearby, wrapped in an overcoat, who appeared to be watching the house. Luizzi was tempted to walk right up to him and find out who he was. But that would've caused a scandal, which he had neither the legal right nor the personal right to do. Besides, he knew that in any quarrel between men in which a woman's name might be mentioned, it was always she who was the real victim, even if one of the rivals was killed.

He kept on walking, and at an intersection with a small side street some distance beyond the house the chambermaid met him and said, "Quick, follow me."

She walked so fast Luizzi had trouble keeping up with her. After taking several detours they reached a deserted alleyway flanked by garden walls. Still walking, the chambermaid said, "Don't stop, go straight inside."

And almost immediately she dashed through a partly open door, which she closed carefully once Luizzi had followed her in. No sooner were they in the garden than they heard rapid footsteps approaching from the far end of the alley. The chambermaid motioned to Luizzi to be silent, and they both stood still. Someone stopped by the little door, listened for a moment, then moved on. But no sooner had whoever was making all the noise gone a few steps than he returned.

With a gesture of impatience the chambermaid said in agitation, "I'm a fool! I forgot to bolt it!"

She rushed to the door and leaned her whole weight against it. She motioned to Luizzi to help her, and he obeyed automatically. He soon heard a key turning in the lock, and felt the impact of someone pushing on the door, which in yielding slightly made clear to whoever was outside that it wasn't being held shut by a rigid bolt, so that he pushed harder and called out, "Mariette! Mariette!"

But Mariette—since now we know the chambermaid's name—had taken advantage of that moment to correct her mistake, and had shot home the bolt.

Without waiting any further she took Luizzi by the hand and led him away, while the person outside turned his key in the lock over and over.

It was a large garden and a dark night. Luizzi followed his guide without thinking about what had just happened. He hadn't even had time to be surprised, because surprise requires some reflection. He didn't know where he was going, nor even to whose house he was going, when they reached the corner of a pavilion attached to the house by a long covered gallery. A small door opened. Luizzi climbed a carpeted spiral staircase. After a dozen steps he entered a small, dimly lit parlor, then another room with a hanging alabaster lamp, and a great fire burning in the fireplace; two places were set at a table, and powerful scents filled the small space.

"Stay here," said Mariette, and she left Luizzi alone.

Instinctively he looked around before it occurred to him to think about what was happening to him. The place in which he now found himself certainly offered plenty of surprises: it was a strange mix of the most sensuous and luxurious objects and the most fastidious furnishings of the religious life—images of saints and crucifixes appeared on silk draperies; softcover volumes of the latest novels and magnificently bound devotional books shared the shelves of a small bookcase; vases filled with wonderful flowers stood on a sideboard below a portrait of Saint Cecilia whose frame was crowned with a sprig of holy boxwood. A shallow alcove held a sofa filled with cushions, and behind it hung a large mirror framed by folds of blue watered silk; at the head of the sofa stood a Virgin of the Seven Sorrows, and at the foot was an ivory Christ on black velvet.

Luizzi looked around that boudoir or chapel in considerable confusion; and only then did he reflect on how he'd been brought here. The man who'd been watching the house, who'd come to the little garden door and who had the key to it, must surely be a lover. But didn't Luizzi himself look like one too? If anyone had seen him enter the Marquise du Val's house the way he had, wouldn't they have been justified in thinking he was the lucky man? And yet whoever thought that would've been deceived by appearances. Couldn't Luizzi also be deceived?

So he still hadn't decided what to think as he waited for Lucy to clear up the mystery, when the marquise herself rapidly entered the room. Her looks and her manner surprised him: this wasn't the sad, amiable woman he'd seen that morning. Her face wore was a bold, exalted expression he wouldn't have thought her capable of. Her eyes shone with an extraordinary light, and the smile on her slightly trembling lips looked bitter rather than happy.

"It's fine, it's perfectly fine," she said to Mariette, who'd come in with her, and who now threw her a questioning glance as she left. Lucy settled in an armchair by the hearth and stared into the fire without saying a word to Luizzi. He felt troubled and ill at ease. He could see there was something extraordinary in Lucy's face and manner—but he didn't know if he was supposed to have noticed. Still, as the marquise's absorption went on, he called to her several times by name.

"It's fine, it's perfectly fine," she replied without changing the direction of her fixed gaze. "Yes, yes, perfectly fine."

"Lucy, what's wrong? You're suffering, you're unhappy..."

"Me?" She lifted her head and made an effort to look calm. "Me, unhappy? Why, for God's sake? I'm rich, I'm young, I'm beautiful—am I not beautiful? You told me I was, Armand. What could a woman with all those advantages possible want?"

"Nothing, of course. And yet..."

"And yet!" repeated the marquise with nervous impatience. Clenching her fists fiercely, biting her lips, containing herself with difficulty, she went on, "Look, Armand, don't be like all the others, don't harass me with questions and remarks and complaints because I'm absorbed in thinking about something else. You know it doesn't take much to annoy a woman... But I invited you to dinner—let's eat."

They sat at the table, and she served him. She was obviously upset, and it made her clumsy. "There's champagne by you."

"Are you going to let me drink alone?"

She hesitated, then held out her glass for him to fill, and drained it at once. She let slip a look of distaste. Luizzi assumed she was making an effort to drive away the unwelcome thoughts that preoccupied her, but after a short sensible exchange about his travel plans she lapsed back into her heavy sadness.

Luizzi's interest and curiosity were aroused. He tried the same means she herself had used to drive away her unwelcome train of thought. "Will you have another glass with me?"

With tears in her eyes she said, "No, Armand, no. It hurts, it burns, it's killing me—yet as God is my witness I wish I could die!" She stood up and cried out, "Oh, to die, my God! To die quickly!"

She dropped onto the sofa in the shallow alcove and hid her face in her hands. Luizzi sat next to her and tried to question her, but she replied only with tears and sobs. He'd been a childhood friend of hers; he knelt gently before her and said, "Come on, Lucy, talk to me. If you're unhappy, confide in me. You know how much my heart belongs to you. Can someone who dared love you possibly forget you? Isn't he still your best friend?"

Her tears stopped suddenly. Looking at him, still on his knees before her, she replied, as if she were making an effort to flirt, "Seeing you like that, 'friend' isn't the description that comes to mind."

"Could I dare hope to fit another description?" he asked with a smile.

"Someone who's really in love can hope for anything," she replied rhapsodically.

"In that case I'd have more than enough reasons to hope," he said, spinning out those gallant clichés without attaching much meaning to them.

He was all the more surprised, therefore, when the marquise lifted her eyes to heaven and cried, "Oh, if only you were telling the truth!"

49

As we all know, it's dangerous to find yourself committed to a course from which you can't retreat without wounding someone who matters to you, and especially without the risk of looking ridiculous. So you push on, counting on luck—which got you unwittingly into that bind—to get you out again. And that's what Luizzi did. "Did you say 'if only it were true,' Lucy? Oh, loving you is a truth that everyone who knows you carries in his heart!"

The marquise rose, looked around quickly, and went on with the feverish agitation that she never shook off, "This is all nonsense! Let's go back to the table."

She sat back down and began to eat, like someone who's decided to do something distasteful because it fills the time. Unfortunately for her, what had just happened made Luizzi want very much to learn the secret of this soul in pain, and he resolved to satisfy his curiosity, or at the very least to try every possible means to do so.

"You're leaving soon, aren't you?" asked Lucy.

"In a week at the most."

"You're awfully eager to get back to Paris?"

"Ah, Lucy, that's where life is!"

"The life of happy people!"

"No, Lucy, Paris is where you have to go when you're sad. When there's a fire in your heart that you need to put out, a burning desire you have to extinguish, you have to go to Paris. That's where there's always something to engage the mind, and an enchanting feast for the eye and the ear. There, if you can't give yourself over entirely to happiness, you can distract your spirits with a thousand pleasures that are unknown here."

"You're right. It must be a great relief to hold back nothing of yourself. Were you in love in Paris, Armand?"

"Not the way I was in Toulouse."

Lucy smiled sadly and motioned to him to go on.

"Affairs in which anxiety is the perpetual torment and the only pleasure," he continued.

"Frightening husbands, right?"

"Not at all—but rivals on all sides. There are always ten men whom any slightly fashionable woman is forced to receive with the same expression and the same tone of voice. Among those ten men she hides a lover... or two... three... four..."

"Oh, you're slandering women!"

"No, Lucy, I'm not. And the truth is, when that happens, I haven't been able to hold it against them. Some of them are so unhappy!"

"You're right. Some women carry through life the secret of a suffering no man could imagine—but those aren't the ones who console themselves by taking lovers."

"Oh, no doubt you know more about it than I do," he said with a smile.

Those words shook the marquise, and all of her sad, preoccupied mood returned.

Luizzi was taken aback. Not knowing how to continue the conversation, he latched onto the first thing that occurred to him. "Are you ill? You're neither eating nor drinking."

"On the contrary," said Lucy, smiling again. To confirm what she said, she drank the glass of champagne he'd poured for her. Her eyes shone, and her voice shook. "Yes," she went on bitterly, "a lover keeps you busy and stirs up your life. But only if you love that lover."

"When you no longer love him, you dismiss him."

"A jealous tyrant who threatens you with dishonor at any moment, over anything! Who's suspicious of the least visitor, who even gets angry when you speak in a familiar way to a friend or a relative! A cowardly hypocrite, who turns an entire family against you to keep away the one he resents... Oh, it's an awful torture... My God! And yet a woman has to make it end somehow!..."

While she was speaking the marquise had gotten worked up. Luizzi, who'd remained calm, noticed her teeth were chattering as she spoke, and she was succumbing to a kind of fever. He was relentless; he casually refilled his glass and hers. She picked hers up, raised it to her lips, then set it down on the table in dread.

"You're a child, Lucy!" he said, leaning on the table and giving her a loving look. "A man like that, if one exists, is a wretch a woman should be able to silence instantly."

"How?"

"If he's a coward, there's no great credit to whoever steps up to defend the woman. If he's a brave man, all the better—to risk your life against him proves your devotion."

With a bitter smile she cried impulsively, "But if it's..." She stopped and clenched her teeth, as if to cut off the words before they left her mouth. She turned as red as if she were choking. She took a drink to recover.

Observing her growing agitation, Luizzi said, "Whoever he is, he can be silenced!"

She smiled again, with the same look of despair and disbelief.

"Yes, Lucy," he went on, "a man whose affection and loyalty have stood the test of time, a man you can trust absolutely, is someone in whom you can confide everything, and who would attempt anything for the woman who entrusted him with her happiness."

She laughed bitterly. "The test of time, you say? But I already told you, the very sight of that man would make him suspect." She hesitated, then, giving Luizzi a look as if she wanted to see to the bottom of his soul, she went on, "For a woman stuck in that position to get out of it, she'd have to find a heart that understood her right away, a generosity that didn't hold back."

"The moment you made clear you wanted it, I'd be on my knees before you."

"Nonsense! Men act only to get love in exchange for their devotion."

"Love that matches the love they feel," he said, drawing closer to her.

"And if the devotion has to be demonstrated on the spot, must the price for it also be paid on the spot?"

"Why wouldn't it be?" asked Luizzi, carried along by the oddness of the conversation and by the marquise's almost distracted manner. "Lucy, do you think there's no man capable of understanding a woman who gives herself to him, saying, 'I'm entrusting my happiness, my life, and my reputation to you—and so that you know without a doubt you're my only hope, take my happiness, my life, and my reputation! I put them at your mercy: you'll be their master!'"

"Oh, if only that were possible!" she cried.

"Lucy, it might be impossible for a thousand women, but for one as beautiful and as noble as you…"

Luizzi's voice was full of passion, and he'd drawn even closer to her. Lucy hid her head in her hands—but only for a moment, during which she pulled fiercely at the beautiful locks of her black hair—then she rose suddenly, and Luizzi followed her.

"My God!" she cried, "I'm going mad!"

"Lucy!"

"Mad! Mad!" she repeated. "Well then, so be it! I'll be completely mad!"

With a gesture that approached delirium, she seized the full glasses that stood on the table and drained them angrily. Then she turned to him, her eyes blurry, her gaze confused, and in a drunken madness of the senses and the mind she cried out, "Well then! Do you dare love me?"

During the whole scene the baron had allowed his mind to be affected by the strangeness of what he was seeing and hearing. Circumstances, occasions, surprises can induce a kind of drunkenness that makes your head spin and pulls you along and disorients you; and now he answered the marquise like a man who believes what he's saying: "To love you! To love you! That's angelic joy! That's happiness! That's life!"

"Yes! And you do love me, don't you?"

This time his only answer was to draw her into his arms. She didn't resist, and continually and as if madly she kept stammering, "You love me, don't you? You love me, don't you? You love me? You love me?" She repeated the word so many times it lost all meaning for her. She kept on murmuring it, right up till he'd overcome the instinctive resistance all women put up against a man's desires.

The delirium that had carried Lucy along, the drunkenness that had disoriented her reason, the madness that had driven her to commit a fault even love can't excuse, all of it—delirium, drunkenness, madness—was now quenched within her. The fever in her mind didn't extend to her body. Her mouth, which had shouted and laughed bitterly when she was angry, remained cold and silent in response to words of love. The woman who'd offered herself to Luizzi had been a lunatic or a libertine; the woman who gave herself was a statue or a victim.

There was some terrible secret there. Already he felt remorse and shame for his pleasure. The boudoir was silent. The marquise, sitting on the divan, now had the same rigid, quivering expression she wore when she first came in. With an anxious eye Luizzi followed all the tremors on her face. He wanted to speak to her, but she didn't hear him. He wanted to draw close to her, but she pushed him away with shocking strength. He wanted to take hold of her hands, but she stood up and tore herself away violently, crying, "Oh, it's disgusting!"

And then the storm in her heart and body, which had been threatening for so long, suddenly burst. She had a frightening fit of nerves. She uttered piercing cries, she spoke of a curse, of hell, of eternal damnation. Every time he tried to touch her she drew back as if from the horrible contact of a snake. He didn't know what to do.

Then the door to the boudoir opened, and Mariette came in, shrugging impatiently as she said, "I knew it!" She went to her mistress and undid her stays, speaking to her in a tone of authority that the marquise seemed to be used to obeying. The fit lasted a long time, and ended in a collapse Luizzi didn't dare interrupt.

"It's time for you to leave," said Mariette. "Come, I'll take advantage of this moment of calm to see you out."

Luizzi followed her. Mariette walked quickly, since she was in a hurry to get back to her mistress. He didn't feel like asking the chambermaid anything. He left after having spent five hours experiencing a series of astonishments that had drawn him into the unknown and beyond anything he would've thought possible. He crossed the garden, exited, and went back to his lodgings—so lost in thought that he didn't notice that, from the marquise's garden door to his own door, he was followed by a man wrapped in a long greatcoat.

The next day Luizzi paid a call on the Marquise du Val. He was told she wasn't receiving. He returned four times that same day and couldn't get in. The day after that he wrote to her, and got no reply. The third day he wrote again, and his letter was returned unopened. But he knew she wasn't ill: she'd been seen attending Mass every morning at the Saint Sernin Church, as was her habit. And every evening she'd gone to visit a pious old aunt of hers, who was going to leave her her fortune.

Luizzi couldn't get over his surprise. He had enough respect for decent behavior not to ask around about her, and especially not to talk about what had happened to him. And yet he didn't want to be treated like a sucker, and he resolved to see the marquise again, no matter what it took to achieve that.

Luck spared him the need to think of a way. He learned of a large soirée at a house to which his name would easily grant him access, and he found out the marquise had been invited and had promised to go. And yet, at the risk of being uncivil, he didn't ask for an invitation, and decided just to show up on the night of the soirée—fearing Lucy du Val would break her promise if she heard she'd meet him there.

Once he was sure of a way to have it out with her, he thought about business, and therefore about Madame Dilois. He studied the contract she'd offered him, and it looked acceptable. But he had some prejudice against her, since her flirtatious tone had aroused the pleasant fantasies that had later been shattered by Madame Barnet's revelations about her origins and her life. Those prejudices weakened his desire to sign a contract with Madame Dilois, so he visited several other dealers. The price they named for his wool was lower than what the Dilois firm offered. His financial interest overcame his prejudice, and he went back to the charming wool dealer.

Chapter IV: The Second Night: the Night in the Bedroom

He went there in the evening, when the warehouse and the offices were closed, so as to gain insight into Madame Dilois's life when she stopped being a businesswoman. He was admitted by a very polite servant girl, who, without announcing him, led him to the second floor and through a small room and, without warning, opened another door and let him enter the room, saying, "Here's a gentleman who wishes to speak to you."

Madame Dilois looked surprised and annoyed by the unexpected visit. She was seated by the fireplace, with the handsome clerk across from her. The modest but elegant clothes she'd worn in the morning had been replaced by a negligee notable only for its great cleanliness, which suggested she was willing to let Monsieur Charles see her no matter how she was dressed. The room was in a kind of bedtime disorder; the bed had been opened, and two pillows lay on the bolster.

The luxurious habits of high society can make you forget the visual appeal of dazzling white bed linens. You can barely see the snow-white refinement of the sheets amid the folds of silk on the bed and the gilt decor of a duchess's elegant bedroom; but in the modest bedroom of a middle-class provincial woman, amid walnut furniture blackened by age, under dark bed curtains, an alabaster white bed stands out like the figure of a virgin. The sight of anything unexpected or unusually graceful can prompt sudden bold desires in even the shyest and coldest man; and a man who, like Luizzi, had just come from an escapade in which a woman of high rank—for whom he had more respect than affection—had thrown herself into his arms, might well think he could get just as lucky with the little bourgeois woman he already considered a loose flirt. "By God! That's where I want to be, and this very night!"

That night, that very night, you hear? Some conquests are satisfying only for their speed. For a man like Baron de Luizzi to succeed with a woman like the wool dealer after a month or two of assiduous courting and lover's attentions would feel neither flattering nor stimulating. But to get his way in a matter of hours with a woman who, in Luizzi's mind, must be so accustomed to giving in that she had every resource for defending herself: that struck him as original, amusing, and desirable. Besides which, he had a rival to supplant—and, better than a husband, a lover: such luck! Persuading a woman to cheat on her husband was just conforming to the rules and expectations of marriage; but getting her to cheat on her lover, to betray a betrayal, to be unfaithful to an infidelity—that was much harder, a much more immoral act of love, and it made success worth attaining.

The long train of thought we've just laid out explained rather than drove Luizzi's decision. Seeing the handsome Charles with Madame Dilois, seeing the open bed, the baron was filled was an irresistible desire to take for himself the place he assumed was meant for Charles. He began by apologizing for the awkwardness of his timing. "Forgive me, ma'am!" he said, taking a seat between Charles and Madame Dilois. "Forgive me for showing up so late! People like me who do nothing—because I believe in fact we're good for nothing—start the day so late we sometimes get to the end of it without having had the time to take care of business. So please forgive me, ma'am, for coming to burden you with my business when yours is long since done."

"Unfortunately, sir," replied Madame Dilois with a little smile of annoyance, "we're never done with business here. When you came in I was already caught up in tomorrow's work: we were trying to locate a mistake in the accounts that has eluded us for a week."

Luizzi glanced at the handsome Charles, whose eyes were fixed on him. "That man is her lover," he thought. "Jealousy has already made him hate me instinctively." That idea served to spur on the plan he was already riding, making his desires gallop so fast that he vowed on his honor to get what he wanted. But it looked difficult, for the clerk showed no signs of being willing to withdraw, and—no matter how high an opinion you have of yourself or how low an opinion you have of a woman—it's difficult to seduce her, and difficult for her to let herself be seduced, while her lover is present.

And yet women have so many reasons for surrendering to a man that love can't be a factor in more than a quarter of their defeats, and Luizzi was too experienced not to know that. So, looking for a way to let Madame Dilois know he needed to speak to her in private, he took up what she'd said about never being done with business. "And here I am, with no right to bother you, coming to add to the persecution of business that follows you all the way into your bedroom. It's unforgivable, and I'll withdraw, if you'll just tell me what time you'd be free to meet with me."

"I don't want to give you the trouble of having to come by again. I know you said you won't be in Toulouse for long, and since you can't wait for my husband to get back…"

"Ah," he interrupted in the same tone as before, "I knew, because I was told, that in dealing with you, ma'am, I was dealing with the real head of the business…"

"Sir, I don't understand what you're…"

"The real head, meaning that the will, the authority, and the intelligence that have made this firm a success are yours."

"You're absolutely right," said Charles. "Madame Dilois understands this business better than the biggest dealer in Toulouse, and without her the Dilois firm wouldn't be what it is."

"That's exactly what Madame Barnet was telling me two days ago."

"Madame Barnet!" cried Charles and Madame Dilois together, and she added, "You know her?"

"Monsieur Barnet is my lawyer, and having gone there without being lucky enough to see him, I had an opportunity to meet Madame Barnet."

"Oh, that bitch!" said the clerk scornfully.

"You're not very appreciative, sir," responded the baron. "She spoke of you in the highest terms, she paid you such compliments…"

"Which are always well deserved," said Madame Dilois cuttingly.

"Maybe not from her," answered Luizzi with a smile and a look full of meaning.

Madame Dilois responded with a mocking smile, then added, "You must've talked with Madame Barnet for quite a while."

Charles wasn't following at all. He could tell from the looks on their faces only that there was some subtlety in what was being said, but that subtlety escaped him, and left him glum. Madame Dilois gave him a pitying, patronizing wink and said, "Charles, I believe you'd rather sleep than talk business. Why don't you go, and we'll talk about those accounts again tomorrow?"

"All right, ma'am," said Charles, rising obediently. Picking up his hat a little awkwardly, he gave a sad bow. "Goodnight, Madame Dilois! Goodnight, goodnight. And my regards to you, sir."

She rose to escort him out and give him some light. She wasn't gone long, but Luizzi could hear some words being exchanged in low voices. She came back, and he went on listening: he hadn't heard the street door close. Did Charles live in the house, or was he hiding? That wasn't an obstacle the baron should've had to worry about; he felt he'd been right in sizing up Madame Dilois as the kind of woman who takes care over the practical details of her affairs, who knows how to get rid of an unwanted man, how to lock and bolt a door—the kind of woman who brings all of her natural skill and foresight to the work of love.

And yet, when Madame Dilois had sat down again, Luizzi was quick to say, in a tone as full of meaning as possible, "Thank you for sending away that young man."

"You're quite right, because I think he'd have had trouble keeping up with me in the remaining negotiation over the contract."

She spoke in such a gently mocking tone, with such a gently veiled look, that Luizzi was almost confused. His theory about women was that they were always ready to surrender if you knew how to attack them; he had the lowest possible opinion of them when he talked *about* them—but he was often shy and almost always awkward when he spoke *to* them. In his mind he'd swept away the fine illusions of youth, but in his heart he remained emotional in the presence of a woman. He sensed that Madame Dilois's flirtatiousness was getting the upper hand of him, and he wanted to hide the fact so he could take advantage of it, so he replied, "It could be, ma'am, that the presence of that young man made me less agreeable on the terms of our contract."

"Why would that be, sir?"

"Oh," he said smoothly, "I'd have been less agreeable for lots of reasons, ma'am. The first is that maybe in front of him I wouldn't have dared say to you, 'Make whatever terms you want, I only want what you want.' I would've had to stay businesslike in front of him... And besides..."

"And besides?"

"Besides, when a man's presence irritates you, when the sight of him offends you, without your having the right to take offense, when you resent the gain he'll make from every loss on your part, it doesn't lead you to be very generous; and you have to be able to forget about that man so you can be comfortable with your own feelings."

She'd listened carefully; she must've followed his convoluted syntax, because she pretended not to understand. That's a commonplace tactic, but a surefire one, a tactic that works for men and for women, and which always leads the other person to say much more than they meant to. Madame Dilois therefore replied, "You're right, sir. Charles doesn't have a very friendly manner; that's why we haven't had him work directly with our clients. Still, he's an honest and capable young man."

"It wasn't in my capacity as a client that I took a dislike to Charles, ma'am."

Madame Dilois couldn't keep from laughing quietly. Turning to face Luizzi directly, she said, as if daring him to answer candidly, "Then in what capacity did you dislike him?"

"You can't guess?"

"As you can see, baron, I don't want to make guesses," she replied with a laugh so openly flirtatious it had to be either very bold or very innocent.

"Then you're forcing me to tell you everything."

"Is it so awful to hear?"

"It's difficult to explain."

"In that case, let's go back to that wool contract, because I have a very stubborn mind."

"As long as your heart doesn't have the same fault, that's all I ask."

"My heart, baron! The heart has nothing to do with this business."

"Yours, perhaps not. But as for mine..."

"Yours! Are you throwing it in as a bonus in the sale of your wool?" she replied, with the amorous look and tone of voice that in the south of France come naturally under any circumstances. But at the same time the way she'd said it was so innocently playful that he was both confused and aroused.

He had the presence of mind to hide his reaction and to answer in the same spirit, "No, ma'am, when I deliver it I expect to be paid for it."

"And what's the price?"

"The usual price." He allowed himself to take hold tenderly of her hands, and to throw a bold look at the open bed.

"And how long do you allow for payment?" she said, defending herself badly.

"I demand cash in hand."

"I'm all out, so I'll strike that item from the contract."

"But I'm keeping it in: it's all or nothing."

"You want the good merchandise to carry the bad?" she said with malicious glee.

"I'm not such a deal maker. I'll offer the good merchandise for free, on condition…"

"On condition that I buy the bad merchandise, and at a price…"

"Much higher than it's worth, I assume?" he replied gallantly.

"That's not what I was going to say. But the truth is, I can't accept. Enough nonsense, baron. I wanted to banter with you, but I got caught in the trap…"

"The most dangerous trap is your beauty."

"Quiet, we can be heard. If someone came in, what would it look like we were doing, so close to each other?"

"Talking about our contract."

"And in fact, here it is!"

"Sign it!"

"Is it up to a woman to go first?"

The baron took the quill pen and signed. Then, turning to Madame Dilois—who looked triumphant, and whose lowered eyes suggested she didn't dare see what she was about to allow—he took her hands and said, "And now I count on your probity."

Madame Dilois blushed deeply. In a voice full of flirtation she answered, "Here, baron." She offered him her tan and rosy cheek.

Luizzi was stunned, but he took the kiss she invited. "That's not all," he said gently.

"Really?" she said in the casual tone of someone who's just paid off a huge debt. "You also need…?"

"A little bit of happiness."

"Meaning?"

"When a husband's away…" he said, looking around the room as if to check.

"And when a chambermaid is awake?"

"You send her to bed."

"Without her having seen anyone leave?"

"You're right. But there are ways of getting back into a house you've left."

"You're awfully full of solutions."

"Are they impossible?"

"Of course not. There's a small door next to the main door."

"And it can be opened to let someone in?"

"Sure. But to come in you have to be outside. Let's start there."

"And we'll end…"

"Oh, baron!" she said, pretending to be deeply embarrassed.

"Yes, yes," he said triumphantly. "Throw me out fast."

Madame Dilois smiled and bit her lip. She opened the door and called. The maidservant appeared and lit the way out for Luizzi, who exchanged a private look with the pretty businesswoman. The entire last part of the conversation had taken place within bounds of humor and flirtation unthinkable for a Parisian. You had to be from the south of France, you had to be accustomed to the language and atmosphere steeped in romance that was normal for southern women, to know that what would be considered a compromising admission anywhere else might be nothing more than bantering there.

Luizzi, like any other man, must've thought Madame Dilois was one of those women, at once romantic and self-serving, who want a little amusing distraction from business—but who can only indulge it in their free moments, and who therefore have to move fast. That pleased him; and he was grateful to her for having put on the mask of playfulness rather than hypocrisy while she let herself be seduced. As he left he observed how beautiful and what a tease Madame Dilois was, and how white and charming the room looked. It was a sanctuary for pleasure, if not for love, and he was cheered by youthful thoughts, if not by romantic feelings.

When he reached the street he heard the big door being locked and padlocked behind him—and then his imagination, a little unsatisfied by his easy victory, began to wish it had been the husband doing the job of locking up. That would've made it truly entertaining, he thought to himself. But in fact it would be just as original if the lover had that chore. And that idea made him laugh out loud as he paced back and forth across the empty street with the long strides of a man who's pleased with himself.

A thin, delicate little mocking chuckle responded to his own as if it had been uttered into his ear. The baron turned and looked all around him and above him. All was silent. And yet that chuckle troubled him: it felt like so direct a response to his own that it must be significant—but where had it come from? He couldn't tell. He walked quickly to the small door, as if to say to the impertinent chuckle, "Here's my answer to your mockery!"

The door was closed—not surprisingly, since so little time had passed since he came out. But then the door remained closed, and a half hour passed, and he began to grow cold. Impatience and anger soon warmed him: had he been duped, or had some unexpected obstacle detained Madame Dilois? It took a long time for that second possibility to occur to him, because the idea was refuted by his natural male vanity, by his past success in love, by his recent escapade with the marquise, and especially by Madame Dilois's manner and by what he'd heard about her from Madame Barnet and by what he assumed about

Charles. It took him even longer to believe he'd been made fun of. But finally the cold in his fingertips got the better of his vanity: he'd been left standing at the door—and Monsieur Charles might even be hiding and laughing at him.

That awful thought tormented him, because now it was no longer a question of possessing the woman or not, but of having been tricked or not—of whether he was or was not ridiculous. Hamlet couldn't have been more troubled. And yet Luizzi still couldn't bring himself to believe he'd been played for a fool to quite that degree. A whole hour went by in that contest between his pride and the evidence. Self-esteem is an animal with more heads than the Lernaean Hydra,[11] and they grow back faster. Luizzi exhausted all other possibilities before he was convinced Madame Dilois had made fun of him.

And yet still another half hour passed, and by then he'd reached a conclusion that was proved by an unexpected event: the little door opened, and the baron ran to it and found himself face to face with handsome Charles, who was leaving. Both of them took a step back, and the look they exchanged in the night was angry enough for each to illuminate the other.

"It's awfully late for you to want to come in," said Charles.

"No later than for you to leave."

"Are you expected?"

"After you, apparently. But I swear, sir, you have nothing to worry about."

"Meaning?"

"That just once, maybe, I could've been allowed to go first."

"Do you dare imagine…"

"What I dare say, which is that the mistress of the house is the mistress of…"

"You won't say it, I swear!" cried Charles, seizing Luizzi by the arm.

The baron tore himself away with angry outrage. "Come now, sir! You must be out of your mind or rabid!"

The scorn with which the baron spoke infuriated Charles. He advanced on Luizzi. "Do you know who I am?"

"A peasant defending a…"

"Silence, sir!" cried Charles. "Do you know what you've just said will cost you?"

"Just as well as you know what a bale of wool costs."

"But I also know what a lead bullet costs, and I'll teach you."

"A duel! Oh, no, sir, no—being taken for a fool once was enough."

"Beware: I can force you to it."

"You can try."

"And sooner than you think… I'll come find you tomorrow morning."

"As you wish."

---

[11] In Greek mythology, the Lernaean Hydra was a giant nine-headed water serpent; two heads would sprout where one was cut off.

Charles walked quickly away. No sooner was he out of sight than the door opened partway and Madame Dilois said quietly in a shaking voice, "Come in, come in."

Luizzi felt a strong impulse to refuse.

"For God's sake, come in," she said.

Charles was already long gone. The baron went in. Madame Dilois took him by the hand; the poor woman was shaking. She led him to her room by a concealed staircase. The almost virginal serenity of that room had disappeared: the bedclothes were tangled, and only a night light was lit. By its trembling glow he could see she was even more undressed than when he'd left her: she wore nothing but a nightgown, and she'd come down in bare feet.

"Oh, sir!" she cried. "What did I do to you to make you want to destroy me?"

"Destroy you!" Luizzi chuckled. "I see no danger of that, and in any case it's not my fault." He was annoyed; he'd counted so much on a complete triumph that he considered himself utterly humiliated. Besides which, he was frozen and he felt ridiculous; he was pitiless.

"What!" she said. "All of that joking, everything we said, you took it seriously?"

"Seriously? I think any man in my place would've felt the same!"

"Any man! What do you take me for?"

"For a very pretty woman who loves to let herself be loved."

"You really thought I was waiting for you?"

"Yes, really, I thought you were waiting for me."

"What kind of opinion do you have of women?"

"My word, ma'am, a better opinion than they deserve—because I thought you were waiting for me alone."

"What! You think Charles…"

"Come, come, ma'am, enough joking, as you put it. To be tricked twice in one night is too much."

"Oh, don't talk that way, sir. And forgive me: I went too far in a foolish conversation, thinking you weren't taking it the least bit seriously." She stopped; then, shrugging with impatient sadness, she added, "Really, sir—a man I didn't know, whom I'd just met for the first time! And yet you thought… No, no, it's not possible…"

"It's so possible that I still think it."

"And maybe you'd speak of it, right? The way you threatened Charles you would?"

"Better stop that man from forcing me to speak; because I'll certainly not duel him without explaining the reason why to anyone who cares to listen."

"And if I have enough influence over him to stop him, what will you do?"

"Oh, ma'am, that's a different question. I apply discretion only to secrets, and I don't believe we have any between us yet."

"And there won't be any, I swear."

"As you please, ma'am. Let's each keep our freedom."

"But I'm married, sir!"

In his fury, he replied callously, "And you have children—among them a very pretty daughter!"

"Ah, now I understand you. Yes, you had enough contempt for me when you came here that you dared presume anything."

"It strikes me I didn't need that presumption, and you did everything necessary to inspire me with it."

"And that's what I don't understand. You come from a world, sir, where, as far as I can see, words are taken more literally than they are here."

"I come from a world, ma'am, where flirtation isn't a business tactic."

"Oh, sir, if that's how it is, here's your contract: you can tear it up." She held out the paper and turned away to hide her tears.

Unmoved, he replied, "In fact, ma'am, I'd rather sign it. And then I swear the most perfect silence…"

She gave him a look of horror.

"In that case," he said, "allow me to go."

She picked up a candle and lit it. The baron could see how pale and distraught the poor woman was. After putting on a shawl in silence, she motioned to him to follow her.

He was deeply stung by being so coldly and openly thrown out. "Think it over carefully."

"I've made up my mind."

"I can be vindictive."

"And I, baron, will be innocent."

"Then farewell, ma'am."

"Farewell, sir."

Without another word, she led him out, and he went back to his lodgings. He went to bed in great distress, worried above all about what he was going to do. Finally he fell asleep, and woke very late. As soon as he'd called for a servant he asked if anyone had come looking for him.

"No one."

"Ah," he thought, "Monsieur Charles changed his mind, or his pretty mistress changed it for him."

He got up and had breakfast, trying to think of a way to talk about what had happened to him. He didn't feel a moment's remorse for what he was about to do. Since men's indiscretion doesn't forgive women for the pleasure they give them, why would it forgive them for the pleasure they assume is being given to someone else? But giving away a secret isn't as easy as you'd think: you have to be prompted to do it, or else you're just a boor, an uncouth gossip. The baron still wasn't sure whom to tell, when the servant announced Monsieur Barnet.

"He's heavensent!" thought Luizzi, expecting him to be a worthy match for his wife.

Monsieur Barnet was a cheerful, affable fat man with a shrewd, witty manner. "You did me the honor of calling on me, baron, and my wife said you wanted information on the Marquis du Val's assets."

"True, true..." said Luizzi. "But what Madame Barnet told me was enough. And anyway my plans have changed, and now I'd like to know..."

"About the assets of the Dilois family? My wife told me everything. It's a fine, upstanding firm, baron, led by an honest, capable woman!"

"Hell! You're awfully quick to speak up for her."

"She's probity personified."

"I'm not disagreeing, but is she respectability personified?"

"I'd swear it on my head."

"All the better for your wife," laughed Luizzi. Then he collected himself and went on, "I'm sorry, I have less confidence than you do in the virtue of women. You only see them the day you sign the contract, and then it's all love and admiration and vows of fidelity. But later..."

"Do you have some reason to think Madame Dilois...?"

"I'll let you be the judge."

With that, Luizzi told Barnet the whole story, laughing and making himself look ridiculous to suggest he was doing it at his own expense—the villainous skill of the executioner smearing the victim's blood on his hands, as if he were the injured party! As we said, Luizzi recounted his entire escapade of that night.

"I would never have believed it," cried Barnet, "never, never! Really? Charles?"

"Yes, Charles, while I was playing sentry..."

"And then you went back in...?"

"Oh, for nothing, I promise you! It's already unpleasant enough to follow a husband—it's even less tempting to take the place just vacated by a lover!"

"A lover! Madame Dilois, with a lover!" repeated the lawyer, stunned.

Luizzi was delighted by what he'd just done. Tipping back in his chair, he added, "Oh my God, sir! In the three days I've been in Toulouse I've learned more than you could imagine about women who are above reproach!"

"Who'd have thought?" cried Barnet. "That little Charles! Oh my God! My God! Women!"

"I believe that one started out in a way that would make it easy to predict what she'd become."

"You're right. A good dog shows his breeding, and they say her mother... But that's a lawyer's secret, it's sacred!"

"Oh, yes, you must have some fairly odd lawyer's secrets, and especially one about the Marquise du Val?"

"Yes, yes, but I won't tell a soul. Poor woman! She's an example of someone who's faced life with virtue and courage!..."

Luizzi chuckled, but said nothing. He was too much an aristocrat at heart to toss the reputation of the Marquise du Val to a middle-class man like Barnet; if only the lawyer had been a minor viscount, the baron would soon have disabused him of his good opinion. Besides, he remembered he was going to see the marquise that evening; content with the first secret he'd given away, he merely advised Barnet to sell his wool to some other dealer in Toulouse. As for Barnet, he'd come to talk about the sale of a timber harvest, and he suggested the baron negotiate the deal with a certain Monsieur Buré.

"Is he married?" asked Luizzi in the smug tone that makes an insult of the most casual question.

"Yes, and to a wife I'd vouch for… But, my word, baron, I don't know what to think or say anymore about women… But she has reputation for spotless virtue."

"We'll see," said Luizzi, and he dismissed Barnet.

That evening the baron attended the soirée at which he knew he'd find the marquise. She turned so pale when she saw him that he pitied her. He approached her, and they withdrew into a corner of the room. She could barely answer him.

Luizzi thought they were being watched. "Do you refuse to hear what I have to say?"

"No, because I have a favor to ask you."'

"I won't be cruel."

"I know about your escapade with Sophie."

"Sophie who?"

"Madame Dilois."

"Madame Dilois!"

"Oh, I beg you, in heaven's name, don't tell anyone!"

"The fact is, I didn't come here to talk to you about Madame Dilois. Don't I have some right to be surprised at your refusing to see me after…?"

The marquise's pallor changed to a deep blush. "Armand, I'm going to die soon… I hope… Oh, yes, I hope!… And then you'll know everything."

He was moved by the intensity of her attachment to that awful hope.

"Never see me again!" Lucy went on.

"But…"

"I'm begging you on my knees. On my knees!"

The confusion he'd noticed before in her eyes was about to break out again. He replied, "All right, I promise."

"And promise me also," she went on more calmly, "never to speak of Madame Dilois."

Luizzi thought he could manage to stop spreading the story he'd told Monsieur Barnet, so he promised that as well. A moment later Lucy withdrew. All of the men present bowed deeply to her; the crowd around the door made way for her as if for a noble, saintly person for whom they couldn't do enough to demonstrate their great respect.

Luizzi remained there, lost in thought. A handful of young men nearby were talking and laughing a great deal. Just then the hostess of the soirée approached the baron and addressed him by name.

"Well, well!" said someone in the group near him. "Here's the hero of the Dilois escapade!"

It was clear to Luizzi that what he'd told Barnet was already the subject of every conversation, and—with a feeling new to him—he was sorry for what he'd done. Then, while pretending to be paying close attention to something else, he began to listen to what was being said.

"My word, he was a simpleton!" said one. "If it had been me, I wouldn't have left without showing the little woman you can't play tricks on a decent man like that."

"I guess that Charles is the lucky one: that little businesswoman is gorgeous!"

The conversation went on in that vein long enough for Luizzi to decide he'd blundered, and his recent remorse was absurd. A fairly natural train of thought carried him from his escapade with Madame Dilois to the one with Lucy du Val, and he told himself again that in the one case he'd been taken advantage of by a barefaced hypocrite, as he'd been in the other case by a shameless tease.

He'd reached that point in his reflections when the conversation turned to the marquise, and the chorus of admiration devoted to her changed Luizzi's mind yet again and filled him with unbearable anxiety. To make it stop he withdrew, with the idea of clearing up that first mystery thanks to his infernal confidant.

Luizzi expected to be alone, but a man was waiting for him at his house: the man Barnet had spoken of, Monsieur Buré, the wealthy owner of a foundry outside Toulouse. Monsieur Buré was an old man, but he gave an impression of solid, stable good health built on a busy, abstemious life. The business he discussed with Luizzi, and the way he presented it, gave the baron a high opinion of the man's abilities. He listened favorably to Monsieur Buré's proposal that he become a partner in some significant enterprise, and he agreed to visit the foundry with him.

In fact Luizzi wasn't sorry to be away for a few days, so he could collect his thoughts and escape for a moment from the whirlwind of mysteries that surrounded him. He was beginning to see, reluctantly, that what had happened must have some extraordinary cause. He'd never yet met such people nor had such escapades, and he wanted to give himself time to think.

When Monsieur Buré and Luizzi parted it was already late enough that the baron no longer had time for the explanation he wanted from his diabolical friend. Besides, he had to set out almost immediately. Two hours later he was rolling along in a post chaise, and by midday he'd reached Monsieur Buré's foundry. Without letting him rest for a moment, and after a hurried meal, Monsieur Buré led him on a tour of his establishment, and didn't take him back to his house till three, at lunchtime.

The whole family was assembled. Luizzi observed Madame Buré: she was a charming woman, gracious, cordial, filled with gentle serenity. Her parents and Monsieur Buré's parents were there, along with two girls of fifteen and sixteen who stood close to their mother—sweet flowers just starting to open shyly to a pure and saintly life, with no notion of evil; after all, in that family there was no one who could give it to them.

They were waiting for Madame Buré's brother. He'd been a captain under the Empire, and he still loathed everything connected with the Bourbon restoration.[12] Based just on that, a Baron de Luizzi was bound to displease him. And yet the captain greeted him with unguarded friendliness. Dinner was spent in casual conversation about business.

After lunch Monsieur Buré and his brother-in-law went back to work, and Luizzi was left alone with Madame Buré and the elderly people and the girls. They all busied themselves with small tasks or with serious reading. Luizzi, who'd picked up a newspaper, could see with what devotion, as a mother and a daughter, Madame Buré took care of all those around her. Her attentive consideration and protectiveness delighted him; as one easily led along by his impressions, he decided what he saw before him was the model of a perfectly happy life. Madame Buré above all struck him as the sweet, lovely personification of a woman whose heart was so rich in affection that it overflowed with love and spread it around her, like the great basin of one of those fountains in which the water rises constantly through hidden pipes and falls in a pure fresh cascade.

The scene made Luizzi joyful, and when evening came he withdrew with a happy heart. The day had been such a contrast with the days before it that he took pleasure in reviewing even its most trivial events. "What a woman that Madame Buré is!" he said to himself. "What exquisite beauty! What gracious simplicity! Certainly no one will ever try to upset such a calm soul, such a serene life; whereas Lucy du Val and Madame Dilois…"

As those names passed through his mind he remembered his intention of finding out the secret of their behavior. He vacillated for a long time, because some part of him warned him he would spoil the good feeling he'd been enjoying. But what should've restrained his curiosity instead made him determined to satisfy it: "Do I give the impression of being afraid of the Devil? And, being resolved to know human life in all of its darkest secrets, can I draw back from learning the probably very commonplace story of two fallen women?"

With that, he rose proudly and—after locking the door—rang the little magic bell. The Devil appeared before him. He was dressed like a dandy paying

---

[12] With the fall of Napoleon in 1814-15, the pre-Revolutionary Bourbon monarchy returned to power.

a call, the kind who smells good, who sees nothing except through a monocle, who talks with a yawn, like a carp nabbing a fly at the surface of the water. He looked bored, and as he eyed Luizzi through his monocle he gave a little chuckle the baron recognized immediately.

"Well!" said the Devil. "What do you want with me?"

"I want to know the Marquise du Val's story, and that of Madame Dilois."

"That'll take a while!"

"We've got time."

"And what do you expect to gain by it?"

"To know those women!"

"To know the secret of two women—that's all! You men are crazy. You think a whole life is contained in one escapade. Female virtue, baron, is a matter of circumstances. Chance can make it teeter and let it fall, without it being the woman's fault."

"It seems to me the marquise's behavior would give me reason to think..."

"She's a shameless libertine, right?"

"Well, yes. To give herself in less than an hour to a man..."

"Whom she's known for a long time and who once loved her. And what if she'd given herself to the first stranger who came along?"

"That's the act of a whore!"

"Not entirely."

"A madwoman!"

"Not at all. Listen carefully: I find you here, dazed by the virtuous air they breathe here. Well! I'd like to tell you a little story that'll show you your way of judging women is stupid, and so are your theories of human morality."

"Are you talking about Madame Buré?"

"Yes."

"Surely she's a virtuous woman!"

"You'll decide."

"Can she have committed some sin?"

"I don't know. But I believe Madame Dilois did by not giving in to you."

"In your interest, demon?"

"Not at all—in her own."

"I'd certainly like to know how."

"I'll tell you the story of Madame Buré."

"With reference to Madame Dilois?"

"That's my method. The best way to judge people is to see them in other people. If you want to go into politics, think about how you judge a king you've loved, and you'll be fair to one you've hated, and vice versa. If you get married, remember what you've assumed about your friends' wives, and you won't be surprised when yours cheats on you. If you keep a mistress, remember how many men have paid for her, and realize you're maintaining yours for others— certainly don't be fool enough to think you're an exception. Every man is born to lie to his father and to be cuckolded and to see himself cheated by his children. Those who escape that common destiny are rare enough that you don't know a single one."

"So Madame Buré has cheated on her husband?"

"What do you mean by cheat? She did him an enormous favor."

"By cuckolding him?"

"I bet in a while you'll agree with me."

"I doubt it."

"It's true that no one living could convince you of that. Madame Buré's escapade is a secret between her and the grave, and no one in the world could tell it to you, except for her and me. It's a little drama with two actors; because, in terms of people, I don't count in the cast list—though in fact I'm always a little involved in the resolution of that kind of play."

"Go ahead, I'm listening."

Chapter V: The Third Night: the Night in the Stagecoach

And the Devil began thus:

It was in 1819, in the courtyard of the stagecoach company in Toulouse: the fifteenth of February, at six in the evening. Night had fallen, and a crowd of travelers awaited the hour of departure. The driver appeared with his list and a lantern, and called for Madame Buré. At that name, a woman stepped forward and climbed quickly inside the stagecoach bound for Castres.

All was well. However, as she got in she allowed a tall, handsome young man who was behind her to see a leg of perfect elegance. Then she turned to take a parcel the driver was holding out to her, and showed the young man her plump rosy face, her teasing smile, and her admirably white teeth. That's when the mischief began.

In one movement the young man took off his hat, and took the cigar out of his mouth and threw it on the ground. With exquisite politeness he asked Madame Buré if she'd been given everything that belonged to her; on her answering in the affirmative he sat next to her and examined her by the light of the lantern, as if to make sure it was safe to attempt such a conquest.

It was in fact a completely dark night, and once they were on their way it would've been impossible for the handsome young man to assess his traveling companion. He was an artillery officer, and well trained in tactics, and he would probably not have taken a single step forward without an advance reconnaissance of the terrain against which he was directing his battery; even without that, the risk of committing himself with an old woman would no doubt have made him circumspect. But he'd seen enough of Madame Buré to know she was young, she was pretty, and she didn't seem unapproachable.

So as soon as the coach had left the suburbs and was rolling along the isolated road to Puylaurens, he began to move in on his neighbor. First, she wasn't sufficiently wrapped up, and he threw his fine new greatcoat on the floor to cover her feet. Then he began to question her, and didn't notice that in fact it was he who was answering Madame Buré's questions. They hadn't gone a league before he'd said his name was Ernest de Labitte, he was garrisoned in Toulouse, and he expected to leave that city soon and be transferred north. The business taking him to Castres wouldn't last more than an hour, and he'd go back to Toulouse by the return coach. Once all those circumstances had been stated, Madame Buré, who'd been fairly reserved at first, accepted the officer's attentions more casually than she had before, which is to say she was a little less on guard against them.

Cold weather is an excellent ally in that kind of affair: Ernest de Labitte took advantage of it fairly straightforwardly. "My God, ma'am, you must not be used to traveling alone; you couldn't have set off more recklessly! You have nothing to wrap around your neck. I have a few silk handkerchiefs my servant must've tucked into the storage pocket of the coach—allow me to offer you one."

"Really, sir, you couldn't be more gallant."

"You're mistaken, ma'am. I don't think much of the gallantry that puts a decent man at the service of any woman he meets."

"Your behavior toward me is proof to the contrary."

"It only proves that, when I meet a woman as perfectly gracious and charming as you are, I try to show her I understand the respect she deserves."

"Ah," laughed Madame Buré, "you may not be gallant, but at least you're a flatterer!"

"Me, a flatterer? You know that's not true, ma'am. Surely other men have told you how pretty you are, and they've told you often enough that you can't doubt it. I'm therefore no more a flatterer than I am gallant."

Madame Buré was a little embarrassed by the ease with which this stranger addressed bald compliments straight to her face, and she didn't answer.

Ernest waited a moment, then went on, "Have my words offended you, ma'am? Has my rough candor gone beyond the bounds of decency?"

"I can't say that, and yet I'd be grateful if you changed your tone."

"Ma'am, admiration for beauty is as involuntary as beauty itself, and when we get carried away by it..."

"You no longer know what you're saying, isn't that so, sir?"

"I beg your pardon—we know exactly what we're saying, and to prove it to you, I'll add that I'm beginning to suspect you're just as witty as you are pretty."

"Oh," replied Madame Buré sharply, "are you going to do me the honor of suspecting that?"

"Don't get angry, or I'll begin to think I was wrong."

"You'd admit at least that I'm nice enough to listen to you."

"I'd point out that you have no choice."

"You mean you don't know if I'm willing to listen?"

"I know you're willing to be here." He paused, then went on rhapsodically, "I know you're willing to be here, the way I know a fine day is willing to shine on my head, or a scented breeze to waft around me, or a fresh night to intoxicate me with its silence—the way I know anything unfamiliar is willing to show itself to me in a benevolent, heavenly light."

Up to that point the conversation had been tossed back and forth from one corner of the coach to the other in the bantering tone people use to be witty or at least try to be. But Ernest had delivered that last speech with such distinct feeling that it bothered Madame Buré. Unconsciously, Ernest had moved closer to her; but she didn't think it wise to let the scene shift to that terrain, and she wanted to return it to the ironic familiarity with which it had begun. Without moving out of her corner, and in the superficial tone she thought necessary to put an end to Ernest's flight of poetry, she replied, "I'm grateful to be admired the same way you admire the sun and the moon."

Her words had the desired effect. Ernest withdrew to his corner, and after a moment of silence during which he bit his lip, he said in a much less gracious tone, "Does tobacco smoke bother you, ma'am?"

The question was so absurd that Madame Buré turned to look at him, though in fact she couldn't see him. "I don't believe it's done to smoke in a public conveyance," she said coldly.

Ernest got what he deserved for his foolish question, and they fell silent. The exchange had begun in such a lively way that he was frustrated at seeing it end so abruptly. He looked for any possible way to renew the conversation, but found none. "I've been a fool," he said to himself. "I allowed myself to get carried away, talking to this woman with the feeling of happiness that meeting her inspired in me—because they don't come any prettier—but she answered me with a stupid joke, and now she's standing on her dignity. It's my fault, for turning poetic at the slightest excuse. If I'd gone on treating her chivalrously we'd be the best of friends. She's some little shopkeeper from Castres, who only takes such care of her appearance because it's good for business. I have to show her I'm not an idiot."

As soon as Ernest had come to that resolution he felt the time was right to carry it out. Sliding quietly across the seat cushion, he got close enough to Madame Buré to touch her knees.

She quickly withdrew. "Oh! Sir!"

So much was packed into those two words! How the sad, dignified tone in which they were spoken conveyed both her disapproval of Ernest and her unhappiness at being treated that way! And yet that simple remonstrance also showed that Madame Buré didn't think she needed any other defense against a man who seemed to be a gentleman.

Shamed and distressed, Ernest withdrew to his place in silence. He wanted to speak; and in spite of the darkness he gave Madame Buré a repentant look, as if she could see him. He could hear she was moving around slightly, but he didn't dare question her, and he felt too much in the wrong to dare apologize.

That was how they reached the first relay stop. All the travelers in the other compartments of the coach got out. Only Madame Buré stayed still; she seemed to be asleep, and Ernest didn't dare move. Suddenly the stagecoach driver poked his lantern through the door to get something out of one of the storage pockets, and Ernest finally saw what had made his neighbor move around earlier: she'd carefully pulled her feet out of the coat that was wrapped around them, and had pushed it toward him. The silk handkerchief he'd offered her and she'd put around her neck had been set down next to her.

Ernest was painfully taken aback. In the context of that one-hour liaison, it was like a breakup, like love tokens being returned. He almost cried out, but Madame Buré was asleep, and he didn't have the right to wake her to apologize. He sat still, watching her, till the stagecoach set off again. As soon as they were rolling he gently picked up his greatcoat and, fold by fold, set it back on her feet so carefully that she could easily pretend not to notice.

The moon was rising just then, and it cast a little light into the compartment. Ernest moved back as far as he could from Madame Buré. Then, seeing the silk handkerchief still lying on the seat, he tried to put it back around the sleeping woman's neck; but he couldn't manage it, and, fearing to wake her, he went back to his corner. As he was despairing for having forced this charming woman to suffer from the cold, he saw her hand feeling around on the seat. He gently set the handkerchief down; she found it, picked it up, and wrapped it around her neck without a word.

"Oh, ma'am!" cried Ernest with real feeling. "You're an angel!"

Making it clear she hadn't been asleep at all, and finishing wrapping the coat around her feet, Madame Buré replied in a charming tone of reproach, "Why would you treat a woman you don't know like an adventuress?"

He didn't answer. Too many unfamiliar feelings stirred him. He didn't say what he felt, because it would seem excessive and therefore offensive to her. It should be pointed out that, since they couldn't see each other's faces, they couldn't convey what they felt through their expressions, and they had to put everything into words.

Finally Ernest spoke, in a kind of cheerful anger. "You know, ma'am, a little while ago I was thinking I'd blundered; but I see I was just too abrupt. And now I don't dare tell you everything that's going through my mind, for fear of making you angry again."

"Is it that shocking?"

"Yes, it really is." He stopped, then suddenly went on, "The fact is, I think I'm in love with you."

Madame Buré burst out laughing.

Ernest responded with affectionate good humor, "Well, that's more like it! Make fun of me, show me I'm being ridiculous, that's more sensible. But, you know, back then, when I saw you'd pushed away my poor coat and my poor handkerchief!… It's foolish to have felt it, and foolish to tell you about it, but it hurt me—it sincerely hurt me, I swear. I was humiliated, but I was even more saddened." The emotion in his voice suggested he wanted to laugh but in fact hinted at genuine turmoil in his heart.

As for Madame Buré, she'd stopped laughing, and she replied gently, "You have a very young heart."

"And I thank you for making me aware of it. Would you like me to tell you what I was thinking an hour ago, and what I'm thinking now?"

"Well, I'm not sure…"

"You have too distinguished a mind and heart to take offense at what I'll tell you. Besides, I'll only put the blame on myself."

"All right! So, what were you thinking an hour ago?"

"I was thinking... You understand, I don't think so anymore... I was thinking you were a woman who has no one to answer to but herself for her behavior, one of those women who'll respond to chance... to a whim... to an opportunity... to a fleeting fancy... and who'll give..."

"That's enough of that," said Madame Buré in a tone that held as much sadness as disapproval. "And your good opinion of me placed me in that category of women?"

"Oh, don't believe that, ma'am. From the moment I saw you I was seduced. No matter what you call it, right away I wanted to leave you with a pleasant memory of the man you met by chance on the way to Castres. I'll even say that first feeling was almost unconnected to your beauty and your youth. If you'd been sixty I'd have surrounded you with care as if you were my mother. But as it happens, you were so pretty that I fought off that first impression: I brought you down from that improvised pedestal, and I hoped—so I could dare try to please you—you were less perfect than you seemed. I tried, but your charm overcame me in spite of myself; and if you're being fair you'll remember, just when you claimed I was comparing you to the sun and the moon, I'd been telling you from the bottom of my heart that your presence smiled on me like a fine day or a fine night. What can I say? I was speaking from the heart, and you answered me from your wit, and I was hurt. I was angry with myself for being taken in by your charm, and I've just punished you with the crudeness of my foolish heart. You see how frank I am! I've made you a very sincere confession, and that should be enough to show you I need your forgiveness."

Ernest fell silent, and Madame Buré didn't answer. She couldn't trust her own voice. To respond in a natural tone would've taken more skill than she had. And yet she couldn't remain silent, and to gain time to compose herself she gave him another opportunity to speak at length. "You've told me what you were thinking earlier, but you haven't said what you're thinking now."

"Oh, my thoughts now might be even more foolish and more blameworthy. But as I said, nothing I tell you should offend you. It's like confessing one of those momentary dreams you construct in your head, whose only excuse is that they evaporate in the morning. Mine will be over in a few hours."

"So let's hear that dream."

"All right. You should understand that when I realized I'd behaved so inappropriately toward you, I didn't give up all hope, or rather all desire."

"What! You still expect..."

"Let me explain how my mind and my heart work. To say I hoped isn't quite right; but to say I gave up desiring what was impossible isn't quite right either. And that impossible thing was that I wished some mad notion or some irresistible whim would make you give yourself to me. Maybe you don't understand me? And everything I felt was so crazy, I don't really know if I can articulate it. I said to myself, this woman next to me must love something, she has some passion or some specific taste. If she loved poetry, if she were one of those women who've given their hearts to literature for fear of losing them to love, if the magnificent, sacred language of poetry had occasionally soothed her sorrows or exalted her hopes, how sweet it would be to be able to tell her suddenly, 'My name is Byron or Lamartine,'[13] to discover my longtime intimate involvement in her thoughts, to inspire in her, for one forgotten hour, the idea of giving herself just for a moment to the man she dreamt of! If she were a musician, I said to myself, I'd want to be Rossini or Weber.[14] If she were a painter, what a pleasure it would be to be named Vernet or Girodet![15] Anyway, what can I say? I built up such extravagant fantasies between you and me so I could imagine that, if I'd been a great man, I wouldn't have met you only to leave you and say farewell the way I would to just anyone. You know, ma'am, I think I'm going mad—but I even thought if you were religious I'd have wanted to be an angel."

"Yes, you're right: you're quite mad, and all your dreams would've been useless. Because if you'd been Weber or Byron or anyone else, you wouldn't have found in me the passion or the taste to understand you. I'm just a poor, simple woman who decided long ago to be happy in my mediocrity. As you can see, all of your beautiful dreams are like all of your nasty suppositions: they refer to the wrong person."

"You're right, ma'am, and yet you're no ordinary woman. I don't know how exactly, but you have an aura about you, a charm that might be too delicate and subtle for the people around you but that smote me in the heart. People don't know you, and maybe you don't know yourself. Have you ever been in love?"

"Oh, no!" Madame Buré let slip that heartfelt answer suddenly, without thinking, and in such a tone of horror that it was obvious she'd always been afraid of her own heart and had kept it whole, being unable to give it to a legitimate lover and afraid to give it to an illegitimate one. Her words meant, "I've never loved—I've been careful not to—I would've loved too much."

That was how Ernest interpreted them. "Oh, so you've never been in love?" he cried. "All the better! You can love me."

---

[13] Lord Byron (1788-1824): a famous—and famously dashing—English Romantic poet. Alphonse de Lamartine (1790-1869): a French poet prominent in the 1820s, and later in life a statesman of the Second Republic.
[14] Gioachino Rossini (1792-1868): an Italian composer, mostly of opera. Carl Maria von Weber (1786-1826): a German composer and a pioneer of the Romantic style.
[15] There were several painters in the Vernet family, but Horace Vernet (1789-1863) best fits the pattern in this passage of artists both fairly young and prominent in the 1820s. Anne-Louis Girodet-Trioson (1767-1824): a French painter involved in the early Romantic movement.

"This is beyond madness."

"Oh, you'll love me, I'm telling you. I'm young, I'm rich, I'm free. My career is nothing but an occupation without a future—I can quit it as easily as I began it. All the energy I spent on tiresome training, and on pleasures even more tiresome than that training, all the hunger I have in my heart for a life of adventure, I'll devote all of it to looking for you, to pursuing you, to adoring you. Can't you see, ma'am, I'm going to trade my tedious life of maneuvers and mathematics and inspections and cafés for a wonderful novel about chivalry—the only novel about chivalry in this century?

"Inside this stagecoach compartment, you're the unknown lady of the manor some poor knight errant meets by chance in the forest, and to whom he devotes himself body and soul. In a few hours you'll escape from me, and I won't know where to find you. I'll let you flee, of course. Then I'll get my bearings, and I'll proceed, following your trail—not by the hoofprints of your mare along the road but by the perfume of refinement and happiness you'll have left behind you. I won't sound my hunting horn at the portcullis of every keep, but I'll knock at every parlor door; I won't look for you at some noble tourney, but I'll expect you at every fashionable soirée; I won't ask for your beautiful presence at the ogival window of some high tower, but there'll be a balcony laden with flowers, and a window with muslin curtains, behind which I'll see you someday after a long search; and then I'll still have to get to you. You have a father, a husband, a brother, who'll all protect you, and whom I'll have to get around and undermine and overcome. The portcullises, towers, and machicolations[16] separating me from my heroine will all fall before me, and I'll arrive at her feet and say, 'It is I, I love you, I love you madly, take my life and give me your hand to kiss.'"

"What a pile of nonsense! What gorgeous fantasies!"

"Oh, I'll act on that nonsense; I'll carry out those fantasies."

"Let's stop this. Can't you talk sense?"

"I may not talk sense, but I'm certainly speaking seriously."

"You expect to make me believe that?"

"Today? No. But soon, when I've found you again, when you see me again on your horizon, ceaselessly revolving around you like a planet enslaved by a beautiful star, then you'll realize I was telling the truth."

"But even I were foolish enough to believe you, sir, don't you see I might still consider your plans to be more than excessive?"

"Again, today you're right. But later, when you see I've carried them out, you'll admit to yourself I couldn't have acted otherwise and passion drove me to it."

---

[16] Machicolation: an open-bottomed overhanging portion in a castle wall, for dropping stones or boiling oil on attackers.

"The fact is, sir, now we're in a world completely unknown to me. Must it be that, because I had the bad luck to meet you, I'm condemned to have you persecute me? And speaking seriously, to follow your example: by what right—just to give your life some chivalric interest, to give your rich man's idleness the interest of a novel—by what right must I be disturbed in my life, my routines, my responsibilities? By what right must I have my reputation damaged? Because no one is going to believe that a man who's been given no encouragement is going to such trouble just to find a way to pass the time. So you can understand that, if I'm listening to you, it's because I feel like you're reading aloud from a novel that I'm hearing with my eyes closed."

"You think I'm going to leave it without an ending?"

"I'm counting on it."

"On my honor, ma'am, you're mistaken: there'll be one, sooner or later."

Madame Buré opened the window. "Stop! Stop!" she cried to the coachman.

"What are you doing, ma'am?"

"I want to leave this compartment, sir. I believe in the rear section of the coach there's room between a luggage handler and some lowlife woman. I'll be better off there than here."

"You can leave if you like. But my mind's made up, and I swear on my honor again, I'll find you sooner or later."

Madame Buré shut the window again. Affecting a casual manner that the sound of her voice belied, she said, "I'm really becoming as mad as you are. I believed you... I got alarmed... You frightened me... I forgot we were just joking... Well, sir, finish your fairy tale, it's very amusing."

"Oh, don't make fun of me, ma'am. I already love you enough to put up with your insults and your mockery. Can't you see you have only tonight not to believe me, and I have all of the future to make you admit my love?"

"Again, sir?"

"Always, ma'am, always, and wherever you meet me, it'll be the same feelings and the same words."

"Well then, sir," said Madame Buré gravely, "I want to talk to you seriously too... even though I'm ashamed to do so. Let's assume you're telling the truth, let's assume you love me—or rather you have enough time on your hands to do what you say you'll do—do you think I wouldn't know how to defend myself? I have a husband, sir, who's a man of honor. I have a brother who's a veteran of the Imperial army. It might be risky for you to force them to stand between us."

"Oh, ask for whatever support you want, ma'am, but don't set up obstacles that, given my age and who I am, can only give me more reason to persevere. To threaten a lover with a husband, or an officer of the Restoration with an officer of the Empire, is to summon combat and dueling. It would force me to do exactly what I've planned."

Ernest spoke those words with such truthful modesty that Madame Buré realized he wasn't boasting. She replied, "I wasn't threatening you, sir, and I didn't intend to. You've forced me to defend myself, and I'm doing what I can. I'm sure you're full of courage and honor and you're willing to risk your life over a word, but a love as frivolous as yours isn't worth it."

"It's certainly worth more than a word."

"You're clever, and you have an answer for everything. Well then, sir, I have a question for you. Will you swear to answer it sincerely?"

"I swear it on my honor."

"If I told you who I am, if I showed you that a young man's folly could compromise a respectable woman forever, that your invasion of our privacy would be a major event, that your pursuit of me would be a scandal, causing my ruin under the weight of slander and mockery, would you give up your plans?"

Ernest thought it over for a long time before replying, "No."

"No?"

"No, ma'am. When you leave this coach you take my life with you. I have a right to yours—that's the fatal law of love. You'll make me suffer, I'll make you suffer. We'll be united in misery. Misery is a bond as holy as happiness; I'll impose it on you."

Madame Buré was startled by the unshakeable resolve in Ernest's voice. When she thought about what she was hearing, it almost gave her vertigo. In a glance she foresaw the future of anxiety and suffering and madness this young man's folly was preparing for her. Having been reduced to genuine despair, she cried, "How can I escape from you, sir?"

The way she put the question was so real and so profound that Ernest was moved—but only for a moment. "The fact is," he said, "I can't explain the mad desire that filled my heart when I saw you. But that desire is so relentless, it's impossible for our meeting not to have been predestined. You must be mine…"

"Sir!…"

"Mine, because either I'll devote my life to having you, or you'll free yourself here and now from my eternal pursuit."

"I don't understand you."

"Listen, ma'am, listen. Of all the memories of childhood that offer us the sweet smiles and the comforting warmth of the past when our lives become solitary and cold; of all the happy children of our golden years who raise their blond heads next to our white hair and press their warm hands against our icy hearts; of all those memories, the most vivid and intoxicating are not those that, mingling joy and sorrow, span whole years but leave nothing but a word behind them. The most powerful memories are of those moments of astonishing happiness that burst into our lives like a bonfire, lighting it and heating it for a few hours, and which, when they go out, remain unburdened by all the trouble we went through to achieve them, unburdened by the despair of having lost them.

"Have you never, on some hot day or some still night, had the experience of hearing in the distance the mysterious music of hunting horns in the forest? That wild concert, whose performers remain unknown to you, those voices that last only a moment, haven't they triggered in you an ecstasy more profound than all the pleasure you've gotten from the most polished music you've heard in candlelit rooms or in a concert hall full of people? Have you never recalled them like some perfect happiness that remains between the mystery and you? Well, then! If that's ever happened to you, understand me now. I love you. I love you enough to pursue you relentlessly with my love. I love you enough to trade the long, stubborn passion that my heart is sworn to pursue... for an hour, a moment, a flash of happiness. Either you'll be the prize I'll pursue ceaselessly till I win it, or you'll be the lost treasure I'll have met by chance on a road I'll never travel again."

Ernest stopped. Madame Buré said nothing.

"You're silent! You're silent!..."

"Well, what do you want me to say, sir? I've let you talk—I've got nothing else to do. What you're saying, which at first I considered foolishness, has turned into a direct insult and a despicable threat."

"Oh, don't think..."

"What do you want me not to think? You happen upon a woman, and you indulge the fantasy of wanting that woman. And because she's not what you imagined, because you think you've figured out she has some self-respect to maintain, you threaten that self-respect by saying, 'Because you're a woman with a reputation to lose, give yourself to me like a woman who's lost her reputation!' It's vile and contemptible!"

Ernest now fell silent in turn. But a moment later he replied, "You're right, ma'am. You must think me very wicked. It'll take me long days of hardship, long years of perseverance, to win back from you the respect paid, even unwillingly, to any sincere passion. Well then, ma'am, so be it! Time is on my side. It'll justify me—it must justify me."

There was another silence, and it was Madame Buré who broke it. "You don't need justification," she said fairly coldly. "Promise me you'll give up your plans, and I'll forgive you. I can't hold a grudge against you—you don't even know me."

"But you know me, ma'am, and I've offended you deeply enough for the forgiveness you're offering me to be just a way of ridding yourself of a scoundrel..."

"Oh! What a word!"

"Could you consider me anything else after what I've said to you? And could I leave you with that opinion of me?"

"My opinion isn't as important as you imagine. Look, sir, you told me I was pretty and witty. Well then, I accept your compliments. For just a moment I pleased you enough to make you lose your mind, and I don't hold that against you. Go back to what you were at first—a polished, carefree man—and we'll part good friends, I swear."

"I believe you, but I don't accept the bargain."

"Why not?"

"Don't make me tell you. I might start insulting you again. But if—tomorrow, or in a few days, or sometime later—you find me following you everywhere you go, don't be surprised."

"What! You're not giving up, sir..."

"No, ma'am, no. But where do you live? What kind of men are there around you, that not one of them has ever made you understand the madness you're capable of inflicting on a man's head and heart? Maybe you think I'm just acting a role? Here, put your hand on my brow and on my heart: my head's burning up and my heart is pounding."

He'd seized Madame Buré's hand, and she could feel the spasmodic trembling that shook him. She tore her hand away and began to tremble as well—but with uncontrollable horror.

"Are you afraid?" he said. "Oh, be calm! I can keep my head from bursting, my heart from breaking, because I have hope. I'll see you again."

"But, sir!" cried Madame Buré in such a pleading voice that he could tell she believed he was sincere. "If I begged you not to try, if I asked you in the name of the very madness I've inspired in you?"

"It's love, ma'am!"

"All right, fine, then if I asked you in the name of that love, wouldn't you grant me that?"

"No, ma'am, no."

"But I've already told you, that would doom me, sir." She stopped, then went on in a halting, shaky voice, "Come, be generous... I believe you, you love me. Some inexplicable fate has filled you with this mad passion. But do I have to suffer from it too, or do I have to become as mad as you are to escape from it?"

"Oh, ma'am!" he cried, drawing closer to her.

"Come now, calm down, consider. What would you think tomorrow of a woman who could forget herself that far?"

"Tomorrow, ma'am, it'll be a dream that's over, if not forgotten. Tomorrow there'll be an impassable abyss between us."

"Madness! And what can guarantee that?"

"My word, which I give you, and my life, which you can dispose of if I break my word."

"Listen, Ernest! Everything I've just heard is so new and so strange that my head is spinning and I no longer know what I'm saying or doing. Oh, swear to me you'll never try to see me again! My tranquility, my life, my happiness depend on it. Swear it, Ernest!"

"Yes, I swear it: never, never..."

Ernest drew close to Madame Buré. She murmured softly, "Never, right? Never!"

"Never!" he said.

"Oh my God! My God! Have pity on me!"

"Unfortunately," said the Devil, "it wasn't God who was the third passenger in that stagecoach compartment, and I took no pity on the poor woman."

"And what did Ernest do when the stagecoach reached Castres?" asked Luizzi.

"He kept his word for an hour. He let Madame Buré go without following her, without inquiring about her."

"And later?…"

Later Ernest learned Madame Buré's husband was the owner of a foundry near Quillan, and the government had placed a large order with that foundry. He got the ministry to appoint him to inspect the fulfillment of that order. On his way there, he also heard that the family he was about to meet was large, and was known as a model of those patrician values that can still be found, far removed from high society, in a few obscure homes. He learned that Madame Buré's husband and brother were two of those strict Protestants of the south of France whose austere faith lives on in their honorable domestic life. He was even told of the strange misfortunes of that family, and of the disappearance of one of Monsieur Buré's sisters—a young woman who'd been seduced and abandoned, and who was so unhappy that no one blamed her, right up to the day when no one saw her again.

If Ernest had discovered that the woman he'd shocked with his wild threats was no better than an adventuress who'd compromised herself with him no more than she had with other men, he certainly wouldn't have applied to the government to be sent to her family's foundry. But she was a woman with everything to lose, and he felt he hadn't taught her to forget her duty permanently enough for his liking, and he didn't want to leave his victory incomplete. His arrogance as a seducer was reinforced by his vanity as a young officer. Her husband and her brother were daunting—but it would've been cowardly to give up his pursuit of the wife and sister of those two heroes: Ernest's honor and happiness were at stake. I can promise you he convinced himself of that. He considered himself enough in love to forgive himself for breaking his word, and he counted on Madame Buré to welcome with the same indulgence a love so true it was unfaithful to love.

Luckily for Madame Buré, word of Monsieur de Labitte's appointment reached the foundry before he did, so when he presented himself she was able to receive him with such well-acted composure and such polished ease that Ernest thought he'd have been wrong not to break his word. He was staying in Quillan, but Madame Buré invited him to dinner.

81

The young officer quicky found himself surrounded by that large and saint-ly family you met, into which he'd come to bring turmoil: elderly white-haired parents, serene and benevolent, with long honorable lives behind them; serious, confident men in their prime; guileless, reserved young ladies; shy, respectful children; and in the midst of them all, like the hub that connected all of those affections, Madame Buré, good and honorable, beautiful and calm. Though she didn't appear to be presenting that tableau of respectability as a lesson for Ern-est, he was touched even so, and the idea of leaving right away entered his heart. But his mind objected, and soon persuaded his heart the thought was nonsense. He even turned all that domestic saintliness to the advantage of a clandestine affair well hidden in the shadows of the prevailing purity: it just made the in-trigue even spicier.

That evening the men's business concerns and the young ladies' custom of retiring early left Ernest alone with Madame Buré. "Hortense," he said, "have I been forgiven?"

"Do you have to ask? But there are some precautions we have to take for my peace of mind. Tonight, wait at the far end of the little path that leads to the lodge in the corner of our grounds. I'll be there, and I'll open the door for you. Now go, and—with the pretext of showing you a shortcut—I'll point out the lodge and the path leading to it."

His happiness looked so easily within reach that Ernest was almost sorry he'd worked so hard only to find so little standing in his way. But he promised to be at the rendezvous. At midnight he knocked gently at the door to the lodge.

A window opened, and a woman asked, "Is that you, Ernest?"

"Yes, it's me!"

"You'll have to climb in through the window, because I couldn't find the key to the door."

The window was only five or six feet off the ground, and Ernest easily took hold of the sill. But just as he was about to apply his weight to his hands to climb in, he felt a circle of icy metal pressed against his forehead and heard these words: "You're despicable. You broke your word."

The pistol went off, and Ernest fell dead outside the lodge.

In that forested area, much frequented by poachers, nobody was surprised by a gunshot in the night. The watchmen at the foundry heard it, and one of them cried, "We might get some of that to eat tomorrow!"

"Some of what?" asked Monsieur Buré, who was making his last rounds.

"Oh, the hare or the boar one of our friends just shot in the forest."

"Be careful! You'll end up getting caught, and next time I won't pay the fine."

Monsieur Buré finished the inspection of his factory and went home, where he found his wife had gone to bed and was fast asleep—or pretending to be. The murderer was never found, and Madame Buré has watched her family flourish

82

without anything ever disturbing the saintly affection that binds sister to brother, wife to husband, mother to children.

The Devil stopped, and said to Luizzi, "So what do you think of her now?"

Luizzi was silent. After long reflection he replied, "That woman saved the peace and honor of her family."

"At the cost of adultery and murder! Is she a virtuous woman?"

"She's an unhappy woman."

"You think? Yet she seems so tranquil and so beautiful!"

"Can the lives of the Marquise du Val and Madame Dilois hold even more terrible secrets?"

"I'll tell you in a week."

The Devil vanished, and left Luizzi confounded by astonishment and lost in doubt.

Chapter VI: A Vision

When Luizzi left Toulouse he'd ordered that any letters that came for him in his absence be forwarded to him in the country. That way, he assumed, he'd stay informed of the results of his indiscretion, and he remained ready to return at a moment's notice, either to deny or to confirm what he'd said. That's how men are... at least that's how society has made them. If Madame Dilois had come to beg for his mercy, he'd have fought a duel to prove Madame Dilois was a virtuous woman; if Monsieur Charles had demanded that Baron de Luizzi retract his slanderous words, Baron de Luizzi would've fought a duel to prove Madame Dilois had a lover; and if you asked men of feeling what they thought about that, they'd say they'd do the same: they call that courage and dignity. If you looked closer you'd see it's only a trivial courage and a great stupidity. Anyway, after thinking it over at length, Luizzi concluded that what he'd said about Madame Dilois was one of those remarks without consequence that last only a moment and are soon lost in the thousand noises of a city as evil-tongued and troublemaking as Toulouse.

At the same time, Luizzi had been deeply affected by the story the Devil had told him. In possession for the first time of a secret thanks to which he could look at a woman and see her real self, so to speak, he decided to study Madame Buré. He tried to observe on her face any shadow of distracted or remorseful thoughts—one of those sudden reversions to the past in which, with your eye and heart fixed on some phantom, you remain trembling and immobile till some voice calling you, some hand touching you, alerts you that your preoccupied look has been noticed, and makes you smile to throw a veil across the remorse that stands before you like a specter, and makes you speak cheerfully to conceal it: graceful rosy winding sheets beneath which sleep a cadaver and a crime.

But Luizzi never saw anything like that in Madame Buré. The unchanging serenity of her expression wasn't disturbed even for a moment during the days he spent watching her. She was so consistently calm, good-natured, and friendly that at times he began to doubt the Devil's veracity. At other times Madame Buré's self-assurance offended him to the point that he was tempted to throw Monsieur de Labitte's name in her face. He could mention him as someone he'd known, speak of his sorrow over his unfortunate death, and date their acquaintance from a time that would make the guilty woman tremble.

He resisted the temptation. The motive that gave him the strength to do so, if he'd articulated what he believed it to be, would've been honorable. But the Devil wasn't inclined to preserve Luizzi's illusions about himself any more than about other people, and in shattering them he provided a hard lesson for the baron on the subject of what he called his honorable discretion. Here was how he learned that lesson:

When Luizzi had been there three or four days, he found the Buré family gathered at the usual hour, but with a look of displeasure on all of their faces. Luizzi was afraid he was the cause: some men are so pretentiously convinced of their influence that they attribute everything, even negative occurrences, to themselves. He assumed a family with a wife and two charming daughters might be alarmed by the presence of a handsome young man like him. The first words he heard relieved him of that flattering notion.

"I'm forced to leave you," Monsieur Buré told him. "I set off in an hour. I just got word of a bankruptcy that might cost me fifty thousand francs. My presence in Bayonne might save me a large part of that amount, so I have not a moment to lose."

Leaving Luizzi in one corner of the parlor, he resumed his conversation with his wife and his father. Suddenly Madame Buré's brother, Captain Félix, came in looking pale and distraught. "Is it true?" he cried. "Has that wretch Lannois suspended payment?"

"Yes, it's true," replied Madame Buré.

"At last!" said the captain with cruel joy. "I'm going to Bayonne, you understand? This is my business."

"It's mine more than anyone's," said Monsieur Buré.

"Yours?" cried the captain.

Monsieur Buré made a sign to him that an outsider was listening, and the two of them left the room. Madame Buré was shaking, the aged parents were upset, but the young ladies just looked astonished. No sooner were the two men gone than their raised voices could be heard outside. Madame Buré left the parlor, followed by the parents.

Luizzi remained alone with the Buré daughters. "This is a great misfortune," he said, "and I can appreciate your uncle's anger. It's awful for an honest man to find he's been cheated, and I share his outrage."

"For so little money!" said one of the girls.

"What are you saying, miss? Fifty thousand francs!"

"Oh, sir, our firm has suffered much greater losses without my ever having seen my father and my uncle in this state."

"Besides, my uncle should've seen it coming," said the other girl. "I've often heard him say Monsieur Lannois would end up making bad deals—and yet it was he who was always pushing my father to go into new ventures with him."

"Yes, it's surprising," said her sister.

And Luizzi repeated the word to himself: "It's surprising!"

The conversation ended there. When lunch was served they all sat down. The general calm had been restored. The meal was brief, because Monsieur Buré had to set off immediately. As he was leaving, he led Luizzi and Félix into a window embrasure and said to the baron, "Since I'm heading off to wind up some business my brother-in-law thought he was more involved in than I was, he'll stay here and wrap up the business I'd embarked on with you, baron."

The two men bowed to each other, but both were put off by having to do business together.

Though it was the middle of winter, after lunch Luizzi went out for a walk in the grounds. Soon he saw a servant walking by, leading a horse by its bridle. The man told him he was going to wait for his master at the door of a small lodge, from where a path across country shortened the distance from the foundry to Quillan. That description reminded Luizzi of the Devil's tale, and he deduced it was the same lodge outside which Monsieur de Labitte had been murdered. Though no trace of the crime would still survive, Luizzi wanted to see the spot where it had happened.

It's such a common curiosity that it needs no justification. Every year the royal castles are overrun by bourgeois who want to be shown where significant events of French history took place. Some people claim they can feel the importance of Napoleon's abdication when they see the shabby table on which it was signed; they're happy to see the frame that once held a picture that no longer exists; they can reconstruct the painting within that antiquated frame, imagining they understand it better that way.

Luizzi was like that, and when he reached the lodge he went out and crossed the road. Then, facing the building, he began to study the window where Madame Buré's escapade had ended in murder. He stepped back into the woods on that side of the road and leaned against a tree; from there he could philosophize in highflown phrases about the whole sad story. "So that's the spot," he said to himself, "where a woman coldly committed a crime that the boldest of men embarks on in fear! Her sense of honor and her pride in her reputation are that strong! Those prudent, circumspect motives, which wouldn't seem likely to stir a person to violence, can produce the same results as hatred, vengeance, and jealousy!"

Luizzi might've constructed an entire theory based on his insights, if he'd had time to extend his monologue; but he heard Monsieur Buré and the captain coming. When they reached the lodge door they dismissed the servant. Monsieur Buré took the horse's bridle, and he and his brother-in-law walked on slowly.

"So you swear!" said the captain. "No mercy! No pity!"

"You can count on my hatred for him."

"He has to die in the galleys!"[17]

"I've got enough to send him there."

"When Henriette reads about his conviction in the newspaper, maybe she'll finally start to believe us."

---

[17] In France, prisoners convicted of a variety of offenses were sentenced to serve their time rowing Navy galleys in the Mediterranean, and many were worked to death.

"I hope so," said Monsieur Buré, "because her suffering is appalling, and if she ever found out…"

Probably in response to a gesture from the captain, Monsieur Buré stopped short. Soon Luizzi lost sight of them, and could no longer hear even the horse's hooves on the road. He took advantage of that moment to go back into the grounds. Clearly beneath that occurrence and those plans lay some terrible hidden story. Those men with their patrician values, who were scheming at the downfall of a man whose only fault might've been to be unlucky; that woman of such apparent virtue, with two horrendous crimes on her conscience; the name Henriette mixed into the conversation—all of it made Luizzi badly want to know the intimate secrets of this family.

So instead of going back to the family parlor he took a long detour that would bring him to the house at a door by which he could reach his rooms without being seen. The path he followed took him to the far end of the grounds, and close to a lodge like the one he'd just left: it was where Captain Félix Ridaire lived. That lodge offered Luizzi fresh matter for thought: he'd noticed no one ever went to visit the captain, who always withdrew there quite early and had his supper brought to him. Luizzi had the odd notion that this lodge, the twin of the first one he'd seen, must contain some secret, which in the family history was itself a twin of the secret concerning Ernest de Labitte. That idea struck him so vividly that he approached the building and walked around it, listening as if some plaintive accusing voice would escape from it.

He heard nothing, and was going away disappointed—when he found himself face to face with Captain Félix. The captain let slip a muffled exclamation of surprise, and said fairly brusquely, "You here, baron?"

"Yes," Luizzi replied, disconcerted. "I didn't feel well, and I thought the fresh air would do me good."

"Fresh air is weak medicine," answered the captain, forcing himself to smile and talking a great deal to hide his discomfiture.

"For you, perhaps," said Luizzi. "For men used to spending all their time in the woods and fields, fresh air can't help, since it's your normal state, like good food for a rich man. But for city-dwellers like me, who spend our lives in carefully sealed-up rooms whose air we use up in a matter of minutes, to be in wide-open spaces where the body is immersed in air that's always fresh is like wholesome food for a starving man. Second only to freedom, fresh air is the greatest wish of the prisoner gasping in the noxious atmosphere of a cell. For someone from the cramped houses and narrow streets of our big cities to go strolling in the countryside is like a poor man invited by chance to share a rich man's table."

The captain had listened to him with an expression of dark mistrust, and the more he talked the more Luizzi could see the man was getting agitated. The baron's long, excessive hymn to walks and fresh air only deepened the already suspicious look on the captain's face, and he replied sourly, "No doubt. But the poor man invited by chance to the rich man's table rarely holds back from overdoing it. So beware, baron! The poor man risks indigestion, and rheumatism lurks in the fresh air. Time to leave the banquet table, I think: it's cold out."

"You're right. I feel the damp getting to me."

Without staying any longer, Luizzi went back to his rooms. Once he was alone he considered at length what he should do. The first time he'd consulted the Devil, the story he'd heard had quite entertained him, but it had disrupted his life. The delightful tranquility he'd found with this family had warmed his heart; but that sweet feeling had vanished, and unintentionally his visit to the foundry had turned into a kind of tacit obsessive inquisition. And yet the business deal he was being offered was profitable enough for him not to refuse it; all things considered, he felt he'd make the deal with greater confidence if he knew better who he was going into business with. After careful reflection, having attached that plausible motive to the curiosity consuming him, he rang the infernal bell. But the Devil didn't appear. He waited a few minutes and tried again.

The window opened immediately with a great clatter, and a hideous man appeared. He was dressed in rags—not the ordinary rags that are the mark of poverty, but the elegant rags that are always the livery of vice. Long greasy hair framed a pale face, whose red cheeks were inflamed by wine-soaked veins. The oily hair had left a shiny solid crust on the collar of a blue tailcoat with brass buttons. The man wore a hat whose gloss had been produced with a wet brush, which managed fairly well to conceal the lack of any felt nap, but which failed to hide the many cracks. A frayed collar of black velvet was attached to the coat in a way that suggested he wasn't wearing a shirt. His trousers, also black, were pulled so high on one hip and hung so low on the other it was obvious they were held up by only one suspender. The trouser stirrups did more to keep the down-at-heel shoes on his feet than to smooth out the creases in the fabric. Those trousers were spattered with dark stains, where he'd used ink in vain to blacken the white stitching, and the sewing needle had failed to tuck the basting under the hem. The man carried a stick with a massive knob on one end, whose weight was increased by the many little nails decorating it.

Luizzi stepped back at the sight, and the creature gave him a savage, despicable smile. "You're pushing it, Luizzi. I told you a week, and here you are, summoning me already. But you won't hear a thing about the marquise or the wool dealer till then."

"It's not about them I need to talk to you."

"Then about whom?"

"I have to know about Captain Félix and about this Lannois he's hounding so relentlessly."

"All right, tomorrow."

"No—now!"

"Baron, accept my secrets when I offer them to you. Don't make me tell you things that later you'll wish you didn't know. Not all secrets are as easy to carry around as Madame Buré's. You still have a conscience—be careful of what it'll make you do."

"A conscience can be silenced at will; Madame Buré is a great example of that."

"By the way, what do you think of her?"

"That it was fanatical concern for her reputation that drove her to murder."

"No, it was a low, shameful feeling."

"What feeling?"

"Fear."

"Fear! Fear! First you disillusioned me about her virtue, now you're disillusioning me about her crime. Will you never show me anything other than the ugly side of life?"

"I'll show you the truth as it is."

"So it was really fear that made her a murderer?"

"Yes, the same fear that kept you from saying a word in front of that woman, who can rely on the discretion of those who could compromise her; the same fear that made you retreat so fast from the captain, when he met you by his lodge."

"Mister Satan," replied Luizzi with scorn, "I'm no coward, and I've proved it!"

"You're a brave Frenchman, that's all. You're not afraid of a sword or a pistol in a duel, or a canon in battle, I know that. But beyond that, like so many men, you tremble at a thousand other dangers. You have the courage to face a quick death in the open; but the courage to face a slow death no one ever hears about, the courage to face everyday suffering, the courage to sleep in an open grave that might close on you before you wake—you don't have that kind of courage."

"So who can boast of that kind of courage?"

"People who might not have your kind."

"A fanatical priest?"

"Or a child in love: religion and love—the two great instinctive passions of humankind!"

"I'm not asking you for metaphysics, I'm asking you for a story."

"I'll tell you tomorrow."

"Right now: I want to hear it."

"I don't have time."

"I want to hear it," said Luizzi, and he picked up the little bell.

"All right, then," said the Devil. "Watch this if you dare."

At that moment the window, which had remained open, became a door into another room at the same level as Luizzi's. At first the baron could see nothing, because the room was lit only by a dim lamp. But gradually he began to make out objects, and soon he noticed a woman sitting in a large armchair with a child asleep on her lap. Luizzi had seen plenty of pale, sickly people whose looks inspire sadness and pity; he'd seen those who radiate the idea of imminent death and are just dragging around a rotting body; but never had he been faced with a sight like the one that confronted him now.

The woman before him was as white as one of those statues of wax that hasn't yet been painted in rosy shades to suggest life. Though the shape of her face suggested youth and innocence, that same dull, blank pallor was varied only by the blueish darkness around her eyes. The child in her lap, as pale as she was, sickly, thin, drooping, would've looked dead—if even death could look so inanimate—if it hadn't been for the slow, gentle movement of its breathing.

The young woman didn't move, and the child slept, so Luizzi was free to observe them. His eyes soon adapted to the low light in the room, and he saw it had thick carpeting on the floor, on the walls, and even on the ceiling. He could see no windows, no fireplace, no door—and yet the lamp flickered as if in a fairly strong air current. He realized the air entered through an opening installed at floor level and escaped by another opening installed in the ceiling. One corner of the room held a bed and a crib, and there was other furniture in good condition, suggesting care had been taken to make their stay here as comfortable as possible.

Luizzi was paying close attention, and in spite of the dim light he could make out the most minute details in the room, as if it was illuminated in some unusual way—as if his own eyes, when they turned toward some object, brought bright light to bear on it and make it stand out. It was some kind of superhuman vision, because he could even see through objects that stood between him and what he was looking at.

Astonished by what he was experiencing, he turned to ask the Devil to explain the unhappy scene, but the Devil had vanished. Annoyed at the disappearance of the creature who was his slave, Luizzi was about to seize the talisman that gave him command, when the young woman let out a long sigh and brought his attention back to that room. She'd risen and had laid the child in its crib. For a long time she listened to the terrible silence that formed an impenetrable rampart between her and the living world. Then she lifted a flap of the carpet and took out a book. She sat down at a table, on which she set the lamp, and opened the book. She rested her head painfully on her hand, bent over the pages, and read with great attention.

Thanks to the supernatural power of vision that allowed him to see even the smallest objects, Luizzi could read the title of the book—which surprised him more than anything else he'd witnessed so far. It was *Justine*, that filthy book by the Marquis de Sade, that debauched, disgusting anthology of every crime and depravity.[18] A painful thought occurred to Luizzi: might this young

---

[18] *Justine, ou Les Malheurs de la Vertu* ("Justine, or The Misfortunes of Virtue"), a 1791 novel by the Marquis de Sade, consists of a series of sexual "les-

woman be one of those people fatally destined for abomination and dysfunction? Had she been hidden away in this cell to lock up with her the savage lechery of her unbridled nature? Had she concealed this book from her jailers so she could feed her delirious imagination in secret—having already made her family fear she'd act out the repellent passions poured into that book by the mind of a man in whom blood and mud boiled like volcanic lava? Could such corruption be united with such youth?

In the grip of those thoughts, Luizzi watched the young woman; but he could see nothing in her pure features, heightened by the stillness of her hidden pain, to justify his assumptions. She went on attentively reading those obscene pages, and yet her whole being expressed such suffering that Luizzi couldn't blame her without also pitying her. "Poor thing!" he thought. "If she was born with that frantic lust, which medical science can explain but language can't describe, she's a victim of her family's insistence on their dignity and reputation. If, carried away by her amorous passions…"

Luizzi was free to follow his train of thought. But we who are writing this don't have that same freedom—or we lack the power needed. Language is such a feeble interpreter of our thoughts! It's so deficient in proper words for vulgar things that many of the passions that drive us, along with many of the occurrences that come at us from all sides, must be banished from our story. If the woman Luizzi was watching had been a daughter of Greece, a poet would've put the baron's thoughts into effortless lyrical verse. "It's the Venus of Pasiphaë," he would've said, "the Venus of Myrrha and of Phaedra,[19] it's the ardent courtesan Venus celebrated in the frenzied aphrodisiac rituals of Corinth and Paphos, it's the Venus of Aphaca[20] who has blown her burning breath into this girl's panting chest, it's Venus who has shot into her side the flaming poisoned arrow that irritates and pesters and distracts her and plunges her into mad love affairs—just as the horsefly on the nostril of a noble steed makes him uncontrollable, bad-tempered, enraged; and drives him, neighing wildly in pain, through forests and ravines and streams till he drops, wounded, dying, covered in blood and mire, still struggling, even as he dies, against the insect that bites him, stings him, and kills him."

---

sons": rapes, orgies, punishments, etc. An unexpurgated English translation wasn't published till 1953.

[19] Three figures of illicit lust in Greek mythology: Pasiphaë, queen of Crete, was the mother of the Minotaur, conceived from her adulterous and bestial union with the Cretan Bull. Myrrha, the mother of Adonis, was turned into a myrrh tree after having intercourse with her father. Phaedra, daughter of Minos and Pasiphaë, fell in love with her stepson Hippolytus; when he rejected her advances, she falsely accused him of trying to rape her, and he died cursed.

[20] The temple of Venus in the Greek town of Aphaca was notorious for the debauchery depicted (and perhaps performed) there.

But we, lacking native words for those thoughts, can only mistranslate those of Luizzi by borrowing words from a nation that had a poetic image for the most degraded things in life. All we can say is, he was observing the young woman with a mixture of pity and horror, when he noticed she was shedding a few meager tears, which hung from the rims of her exhausted eyes. Certainly what she was reading had nothing touching about it, and if Luizzi had been surprised by the book the poor thing was holding, he was made even more so by the effect it had on her. That prompted him to look more closely at the pages of that disgusting novel, and to his first astonishment was added an even greater one. He could see that below every printed line was a handwritten line, which stood out even more by being in red ink. Still full of his initial assumption, Luizzi wanted to know what kind of commentary an attractive young woman could've added to that foul work. Thanks to the powerful eyesight the Devil had given him, he could easily read the cramped, scrawled words, and the lines he read were:

This is my story. I'm writing it in this book, with my own blood, because I have neither paper nor ink. If I haven't crossed out, line by line, the text of the revolting book in which I'm writing—which a vile wretch put into my hands to destroy my soul after he'd destroyed my body—if I haven't crossed it out, it's only because my blood has become so scarce I have barely enough left to tell my tale of woe and ask for vengeance...

Those lines shook Luizzi to his core. Deep pity and bitter remorse stirred his very bowels. His earlier assumption now felt like one more torment added to the poor girl's incessant torment. Oh, what a horrifying torture it was to inflict on that soul, forced to pour out her innocent tears between those lines of filth, and to lift her prayer to God amid the blasphemous debauchery of those disgusting pages! Can you see her, forced to keep her eye on the words and letters that expressed her despair—lest she notice next to them some ugly, vile, depraved word! And her only reason for not crossing out the filth-stained account that ran alongside her own unhappy tale was that she didn't have enough blood left! O unfortunate, unfortunate creature!

So thought Luizzi, so he cried out, carried away by the strong emotion he felt. But his voice rang out only around him: the prisoner didn't react, and Luizzi remembered that what he was seeing was far away, and only a supernatural power had allowed him to witness it. But it was within human power to save the poor girl from that horrible prison, and to do so he had to know the causes of her misery. To know them, he had to read the manuscript that lay before his eyes. He resolved to do so, and this was what he read:

A MANUSCRIPT

Chapter VII: Maiden Love

I've already written out this account twice, and my torturer took them both away. I'm starting again, and may God give me the strength to finish!—because my mind and my soul are dying, just like my body. For a long time I reread what I wrote every day, so I wouldn't entirely forget the living world I once knew. And yet, in spite of that constant engagement with my memories, I feel them growing lost and confused. So I'm hurrying, so something of my soul remains in this world, so it can be known how much I loved, how much I suffered. Oh, yes, I loved and I suffered! In all of my forgotten past and in my present, those are the only two thoughts that still shine pure amid the chaos of pain in which my mind wanders: that I've loved so much and suffered so much! My God, my God! If the long torture I've been condemned to hasn't completely destroyed my reason and extinguished my memory—if it's true, as your holy words say, that much would be forgiven to one who's suffered much and one who's loved much—then have mercy on me, Lord, and let me die, die quickly! And let my child…

Would he kill my child if I died? Oh, yes, he'd kill her. So I'll live. Make me live, Lord, no matter what happens; because I sense that, even if I went mad, one thought would always prevail in me: that a mother must die to save her child. I'll write that in capital letters at the top of every page of this book, so my eyes always see it and can never forget it: *A MOTHER MUST DIE TO SAVE HER CHILD.*

And indeed those words were written on the page, and the poor woman turned to look sadly at the sickly creature sleeping in the crib. Then she held her head in her hands while Luizzi went on reading the manuscript, which he was able see through the pages he'd already read, just as if he were holding it in his hands and turning the pages at will.

Till I was ten I lived under the protection of my father and mother. At that point my brother married Hortense, who was barely fifteen. Hortense, who became my sister-in-law, was always good and kind to me. I don't think she betrayed me; I can't bring myself to believe she's one of my torturers. And yet she's afraid of her brother Félix, and she wouldn't have dared to defend me; she must be miserable! She loved me more than a sister—she called me her daughter. In fact my father and mother handed over their authority to Hortense, though we were all in the same house.

I can't think of anything significant that happened in the next six years. We were happy, and happiness leaves no trace. Happiness is like springtime: when it's over, there's nothing left to show how it was. The tree drops its leaves and remains bare; but when the storm and the lightning have lashed it, the scar is always there, even when spring returns.

I was happy in those days—yes, happy; and now I can remember how I was. I prayed faithfully to God; I played with my sister-in-law, who was such a young wife, and with my two nieces, who were such lovely children. It was like seeing my past and my future laugh and sing behind me and ahead of me: children as happy and loved as I'd been, a wife as happy and loved as I'd be someday! Oh, what a beautiful, beloved dream they made of my life! And how I welcomed it with a sweet smile! How I offered my heart to God when he came in the evening to speak quietly to me, in the long alley of sycamores where I went strolling alone as night was falling! I was sixteen, and my whole being breathed in life. Oh, how sweet and beautiful it is to go for a stroll in the evening, alone in the fresh air, with a ray of the setting sun, with birds singing quiet songs that drift away along with the dying day, and to sense an invisible being, a good being, walking alongside you, who says, "You're beautiful, you'll be happy, and you'll be in love, in love!"

To love, to love! What a joy it is in life to give your soul entirely to some noble heart, to revere him for his generosity, to cherish him for his goodness, to adore him for his saintliness! Because the one who loves you is a saint, he's the priest of your heart; the one who opened its tabernacle is a man set apart from other men, and God has touched him with his finger and crowned him with his glory. That's how I dreamt he'd be, and that's what I'd found him to be... Léon, Léon, do you still love me?... Lord, does he love me? They tried to make me doubt it; that's a great crime—their greatest crime!

So I was sixteen, and I was intoxicated with life. Yes, I was beautiful, yes, I had the strength and power of youth. Now that I'm dead, now that my withered limbs sag under their own weight, I can remember, like an inexpressible happiness, the unconscious happiness of feeling my whole being filled with life. How I breathed in the air! With every sigh of the evening breeze, I felt as if that air made me as drunk as the wine at the end of a banquet, I felt as if that air flooded my lungs with hopes and desires.

And then, when I'd stayed still for hours, absorbed in some secret, yearning thought, I began to run: I ran fast, and my hair flew in the wind, my feet were strong, I clapped my hands, I raised to the heavens a song as joyous as a skylark's, I listened to my heart beating and leaping, I watched myself becoming beautiful, I swore I'd be so good! I hoped, I hoped. I was too happy: it had to end.

One evening everything changed. That evening rises before me as if it were just yesterday. Nothing bad happened, but I felt fear in my heart, a fear I haven't fully understood and that's been cruelly suppressed in me. Ah, the vanity of reason misleads men, because God has no more left men defenseless against their enemies than he has the weakest and lowest animals. Some have instincts that tell them a plant is poisonous, others that a predator is nearby; the lamb turns away from a flower that freezes the blood, the dog shivers at the approach of a wild beast that smells its prey, and man too can sense intuitively when calamity prowls around him.

I had that intuition. Though I was innocent and good, I turned my head away from that man when he came in, I trembled when he said, "I'm Captain Félix, and I've just returned from the army." Oh, why didn't I obey my heart's instinct? Why didn't I nourish and strengthen the aversion I felt for him? Why, when he spoke to us of the great battles of the Empire and the misfortune of its fall,[21] of all those things that made me listen to him—why did I argue with my heart and say, "This man is brave, he's loyal to what he loved: that's honor, that's integrity, that's virtue!"

Why, when his harsh glance weighed on my brow like a beam of icy light, when his hard, cold expression made me hard and cold toward him, why did I tell myself it was childish to believe in those superficial appearances? And yet I'd been well warned, because from that moment, hope—the soul's life—came to me only veiled. No longer was happiness a nearby, accessible sanctuary; it had already become a distant land toward which I'd have to walk through canyons on rough trails. And one day, when my brother said to me with a smile that we should tighten the family bonds through my marriage to Hortense's brother, didn't I feel the shiver of death from my toes to the top of my head? And yet God was telling me, "There's the calamity!" But I didn't believe him.

I listened to all the foolish worldly arguments that depicted this man as virtuous, good, and honorable, and that made me ashamed of my dread, and blamed me for failing to recognize virtue, honor, and integrity. I was mad: they told me so, I constantly told myself so, and I had no answer for myself or for others except that this man had closed up my heart, had clipped the wings of my dreams, had smothered the deepest hopes of my life. How could I explain what I myself couldn't understand?

And can you not forgive me, Lord, for having allowed—in my self-doubt, amid the pressures that surrounded me—for having allowed that man to tell me he loved me, and to have answered that I would love him, and to have accepted, for some later time, the bond that would bring joy to my family? Oh, all that was fatal. Because inside I knew I'd never love him. And as for him, how could he love me? I couldn't explain it, and that's what doomed me. I said to myself, if the aversion I sense for him arose from all of our feelings being contrary, he

---

[21] The Napoleonic Empire, and its collapse at Waterloo.

wouldn't love me. Antipathy, which separates two hearts without giving reasons, would prevail over him the way it does over me.

But that's because I didn't know then that a man can love a woman the way the tiger loves its prey—to devour its life, to drink its tears, to hold it quivering in its bloody claws. He loves her, they say, since he'll commit a crime to have her. Ah, Lord, can that savage, corrupted love be love? Is love therefore something other than giving happiness?

So I'd promised to marry Félix, and our wedding had been set for the day I turned eighteen. Thanks to that promise, I'd bought myself two years of freedom. I'd recovered my serenity, but not my hopes. Oh, if only I'd carried out my sacrifice completely, if only I'd married Félix immediately! I wouldn't have fallen in love with Léon—or if I had loved him, I would've drawn back at the thought of betraying my husband. But they treated a child's promise as if it were a bond as solemn as a vow made before a priest. And yet, if I loved Léon, I'm not to blame, I didn't intend it, I'm innocent. I have to describe how it happened.

It was on one of those rainy days in the sad summer of 181*, on a Sunday. It was noon. I alone had dared to face the heat and damp of the day. I'd put on the wool cloak and straw hat belonging to one of our maids, and, in spite of the rain that kept falling, I'd been to see the wife of one of our workmen who was sick. I'd just turned off the main road to reach their house, which was a little ways off in the fields, when I heard someone calling to me, a man on horseback who, having seen me from a distance, had spurred his horse. The way he spoke to me made me realize my clothing had misled him about who I was, because from the far end of the path he began to call, "Hey, you! Girl! Girl!"

I turned, and he came closer.

"How can I help you?"

He looked at me with a slight smile, and in a tone both pleading and cheerful he said, "First of all, pretty girl, don't tell me, 'Keep going straight, just keep going straight.'"

"What do you mean?"

"I mean that for the four hours I've been riding this morning, I've asked my way thirty times, and not once have I failed to be told, 'Keep going straight, just keep going straight,' and I'll admit to you I'd just as soon go a different way."

"The fact is, sir, it all depends where you're trying to go."

"I'm going to Monsieur Buré's foundry."

I couldn't help laughing, and I answered, "Well, sir, I'm sorry to have to tell you, but you just keep going straight."

I don't know why having to tell that young man the way to our house, or why having to repeat the same directions that bothered him so much, had prompted me to speak to him in such a cheerful bantering tone; but he in turn replied with a kind of happy triumph, "You're sorry, pretty girl? Well, I'm delighted."

He hopped off his horse and came around to my side. I understood right away he was trying to pay me a compliment by saying he was delighted to walk with me. But I stopped him and said, still laughing, "I mean it's not straight ahead from here, it's straight ahead from there," and I pointed back to the road he'd just left.

The moment I said that, he blushed. He took off his hat and said with great feeling, "I thank you, mademoiselle."

Those words left me as dumbfounded as he was. I lowered my eyes from his gentle, anxious gaze, I mechanically gave him a polite curtsy, and I went on my way. Why had I shivered at the first sight of Captain Félix, about whom I'd heard so much good? Why had I smiled at my first encounter with that young man I didn't know? Why, as I walked away, did I listen so carefully for the sound of his horse returning to the road I'd directed him to? And when I reached a bend in my path, why did I turn to see if he'd gone on? Why was I happy to find him still standing where I'd left him, with his hat in his hand? He didn't move, but I sensed he was looking at me, and his eyes had never left me. He remained that way a long time; I could see him through the bushes that bordered the path I was on. Finally, after looking around, he gestured in a way I couldn't make out clearly, then got back on his horse and rode slowly away.

I'd begun the walk with a light heart and without thinking about anything besides the purpose of my visit; but I was deep in thought when I arrived at our workman's cottage, and it was only the sight of his wife Marianne's distress that reminded me I'd come to see a sick man.

"I was sure you'd come," she said. "I was watching for you from upstairs, and I recognized you when you left the main road, and when you stopped to talk to a man on horseback."

I felt myself blushing at those words, and I hastened to reply, "It was some stranger asking the way to the foundry."

"Then he must not have been in a hurry to get there, because he stood there like a signpost for fifteen minutes." That remark bothered me. She went on, "Anyway, he asked the right person, and he must've been surprised when you told him who you were!"

"Oh, Lord, I didn't mention it, and he took me for a peasant girl."

"Well! Won't he be embarrassed if he's still at the foundry when you get back!"

That made me realize I'd see him again, and I felt embarrassed too, as if he were present now. I was so disconcerted that Marianne noticed and said, "Did that gentleman say something to displease you?"

"Not at all."

"Then it's odd—you all troubled now, and him just standing there, as if nailed to the ground!"

Marianne was observing me as she spoke, and I thought I could see in her eyes that she didn't believe what I'd told her. I was offended, and I said ill-humoredly, "Here, this is what I brought for your husband."

"Thank you, thank you, you good young lady," she said with such sincere gratitude that it erased my resentment. Then she added, "I have a special favor to ask of you. Please get Monsieur Félix to promise not to give someone else the job of shop foreman; he threatened my husband he'd do that if he wasn't back at work in a week."

"My brother would never allow that."

"Oh, miss, ever since Monsieur Buré handed over the management of the workshops to Monsieur Félix, he doesn't want to get involved anymore."

"Well then, I'll speak to the captain about it."

"Yes, yes, speak to him," she said sadly. Prompted no doubt by cruel memories, she let herself say more than she probably meant to, adding, "Speak to him about my poor husband. A workman is already miserable enough under him, without him trying to take the bread from his mouth because he's unlucky enough to be ill. Monsieur Félix is not a good man... The firm has changed a lot since he arrived... If you only knew how he treated me when I went to ask him for an advance!"

She was in tears as she spoke, and I listened with fear in my heart.

"Woman! Woman!" murmured the workman from his bed.

Marianne understood better than I did what his interruption meant. "Oh, I beg your pardon! I beg your pardon!" she said to me. "I was forgetting that Monsieur Félix... he's certainly a fine man... a man who'll make you happy."

That last word startled me. With two years ahead of me, I'd forgotten I was to marry Félix. The reminder came so quickly after she'd guilelessly revealed the hardness of his heart that my blood froze. I turned pale, and felt so upset that I got up to leave.

Marianne hurried after me. "I've angered you. Oh, forgive me! You see, we're so poor! And I was afraid."

The wretched woman wept, and so did I. Now that I have the terrible leisure to examine everything that's happened in my life, I wouldn't know how to explain the despair that suddenly overwhelmed me. I burst out sobbing—I'd just read clearly in my heart that I'd never love Félix. Was it a forewarning that I'd love someone else? I don't know, but that moment revealed to me the misery of my whole life.

Marianne watched me without understanding my unhappiness. Often, when I was a child, I'd seen young ladies filled with sudden despair, and often I'd heard their elders—who'd forgotten their own hearts—say in a knowing tone, "It's just the vapors, she's suffering from being young, it'll pass with a little care." And they summoned a doctor. And at that moment when the heavens seemed to unveil my future before my very eyes, I myself responded to the horror that seized me just like those old people: I resisted my own despair, I fought

98

back my tears, I refused to credit my own soul as it rose in rebellion, and I replied, "I'm sick, I feel terribly ill!" As if it were more natural and more reasonable to suffer in the body than in the heart!

"Would you like me to walk you home?" asked Marianne.

"No, no!" I cried. "I'll go back alone." Alone! I needed to be alone. Before then, it was to walk more freely and more cheerfully in my happy dreams; now it was to cry. I headed sadly back along the path toward the house. When I reached the spot where the stranger had spoken to me, I stopped involuntarily. And yet I wasn't thinking about him. Do sympathetic emanations arise from our hearts and suffuse the air? Oh, poor child that I was! I stopped and looked sadly about me. That place on the path already held some memory I was searching for.

It was all momentary and elusive, it involved neither regret nor desire… but when I got back to the house my heart was aching and troubled, my despair had fled, and I no longer wanted to cry, but I would still have preferred to be alone.

Hortense found me in the parlor, and said, "Henriette, you need to dress. We have a guest for dinner."

"Who?" I asked, as if the news was a big surprise.

"A young man, Monsieur Lannois, sent here by his father for a few months to learn how to run a foundry."

"Oh! So he's going to be here for several months?"

"Probably… But why are you acting so surprised? Is this the first time it's happened? Go dress."

I was sixteen; all of my sad thoughts flew away, and I looked forward gaily to Monsieur Lannois's surprise. To make it complete, I wanted him to see at her most elegant the young lady he'd treated as a peasant girl. I chose my best dress, with the finest embroidery, and I got ready to appear before him in splendor, to heighten the contrast. I was filled with the happiness of childhood.

But my feelings as a young lady soon returned. Forgive me, reader. But alone as I am in the depths of my living tomb, I have the right to tell the secrets of a woman's heart. My mood changed suddenly. I drew back from the idea of joking with the stranger even in my thoughts, and I put away my dazzling dress and put on something modest, thinking I would look more beautiful to him if I were less decked out—beautiful the way a serious young lady should be, because I'd become serious.

When I went downstairs, they were all strolling in the garden. I recognized him talking with my brother. When he saw me his surprise was enormous. I was delighted. He was so taken aback that my brother noticed and said, "What's wrong?"

I'd come closer, with triumphant confidence. I can't express the innocent happiness I felt at finding him so shaken before me.

"My God!" Léon stammered. "Sir, I've already had the misfortune of meeting mademoiselle."

"What? The misfortune!" laughed my brother, and I couldn't help laughing as well.

Léon was utterly disconcerted. The more he lost his composure, the more I found mine. I was a playful child, and after experiencing unfamiliar emotions I laughed heartily—without understanding there was already some pride in my lightheartedness.

Léon was so upset he was actually sad. He too was so young! He was then eighteen. He was hurt by the mockery he faced, and didn't know how to respond.

"Come now," my brother said to him. "What exactly happened?"

I was so pleased with him in his shyness and embarrassment that I didn't want to help him. Finally, in a gentle, pleading voice, he murmured, "I met mademoiselle wrapped in a cloak, and I mistook her for a peasant girl, and I asked her for directions."

"Not too respectfully, I assume?" asked my brother.

"I don't think I was rude... but you know... you say things..."

"Yes," laughed my brother. "In this region we have a fairly crude way of speaking, and we're ready to call out, 'Hey, you! Girl!'"

"That's right, sir."

"Well then, apologize to the young lady, and I'm sure she'll forgive you."

My brother wandered off carelessly, and Monsieur Lannois and I were left face to face. Léon couldn't lift his eyes to meet mine. His embarrassment went too far, and began to affect me. Blushing, he pushed up the cuff of his sleeve, took a band made of hair off his wrist, and gave it to me. "Where you stopped," he said, "you dropped this bracelet, and I have to return it to you."

Though I attached no significance to the restitution, it came so late that I couldn't help asking, "When did I drop it?"

"When you brought your hand out of your cloak, I saw it fall."

"And you didn't say anything?"

"I was so disconcerted! Your hand—such a slender white hand—showed me I'd made a mistake... That's when I addressed you as mademoiselle... And then, after my rudeness, I didn't dare speak to you again. Anyway, by the time I picked up the bracelet you were far away."

"So if you hadn't met me again, you'd have kept it?"

Léon blushed like a guilty man, and the excuse he gave referred to something neither he nor I was thinking about. "This bracelet isn't so valuable that..."

"Maybe not to you, but it is to me!... I made it from my own hair as an ornament the day my sister got married, and I've never taken it off since."

Léon looked at the bracelet with a sadness I found delightful, and he replied feelingly, "I saw right away it was made from your hair, and that's why..."

"Well!" said my brother, coming back. "Have you made peace?"

"Absolutely," I answered confidently.

I was about to slip the band of hair back onto my arm. By one of those premonitions of the heart I can't explain even now, I looked up at Léon. His eyes were fixed on my hands and were carefully following the bracelet. His expression stopped me, and instead of putting the band on my arm I dropped it in my pocket. A sad smile crossed Léon's lips. I understood it was important to him that the bracelet he'd had around his wrist now go around mine, and he also guessed I didn't want to grant him that favor.

O sweet frail memories of the sacred love I devoted to him, come down into my tomb, as young and as tender as you were then! Come back, all of you, so that at the sight of your pale shadows my eyes can get relief from crying and from the icy view of this silent prison! Allow me to look sweetly back—I who have nothing to look forward to! Happy memories! Oh, how gently you soothed my heart when I understood you later, when I'd come to love him with all the power of my soul, and I realized all those fleeting feelings had been the first tremors of the passion that was about to overwhelm me!

Yes, the love that entered me and consumed me in the depths of my heart, the love that led me astray—it was that love whose beating wing stirred the warm wind I felt already then. Since Félix had arrived, I'd felt cold inside and out; and, like a child who's cold, I spread the folds of my dress to warm myself in that hot wind, and I breathed it in to bathe my heart in it. Yes, it was love that, without a word, was already pointing the way down the unknown path that has led me to my death! Alas! I followed that path without knowing what I was doing! Yet later I understood that if I'd wanted to I would've known what I was feeling—because you aren't transformed in a moment like that for no reason, without something more going on than a casual encounter with a stranger who'll soon leave.

My deep dread of Félix only made my heart ache during the day, and when I was alone; the slight palpitation I felt when I saw Léon kept me awake and restless all night. And yet it wasn't Léon I was thinking about, it wasn't his image I saw behind my closed eyes, it wasn't his voice that murmured in my ear: it was some formless unknown being who haunted me and spoke to me.

Only once in my life had I felt that kind of agitation: It was a day on which we were to go revisit the wonderful, marvelous Fairy Grotto in the mountains. We had to get up very early; I couldn't sleep, and all night long I dreamt of imaginary mountains and grottos—never of the real ones I was going to see. In the same way, it wasn't Léon who appeared before me, it was some emanation that came to me from him, the way the great boulders I imagined arose from the real fairy boulders. That premonition of love came to me like a friendly genie, like a heavenly wizard touching my soul with his magic wand, opening all the springs of love and making them flow. Then along came a thirsty traveler who held out his goblet, filled it with my heart's happy tears, and drank.

That's how it was for me the morning after that sweetly restless night. I got up before anyone else and opened my window—and the first person I saw was

Léon, standing there looking up at my room. If he still didn't realize I was going to love him someday, if, like the thirsty traveler, he didn't hold out his heart to fill it with the flood of emotion that flowed out of me, it was because he was so shy and good—because there was a moment, like a flash of lightning, when my joy must've burst out smiling all over my face. Then, just as quickly, all those scattered impressions in my dreams, all those vague, pale, ghostly shapes that had pursued me, suddenly grew clearer and gathered themselves together, with sharply drawn outlines, and I realized it was Léon who'd wandered through my night. Then I was afraid, and I drew back from the window, I stepped back quickly, and I sat down hard on the edge of my bed with my hand over my heart, which was pounding as if I'd run a long distance. Had I traveled so far, so fast, along the path of love?

Still, the activities of the day, the activities of the following days, soon calmed all that agitation, and I felt troubled no more. But my life had already become like a brook after a storm: the water was calm again, but it was no longer clear; my heart no longer shook, but it was unsettled. It takes long, peaceful days for the silt in a cloudy brook to settle back down to the bottom, so the water can become crystal clear once more. As for me, my troubled thoughts kept me from seeing down to the bottom of my heart, and I didn't have the tranquility needed to restore their innocent clarity.

For two weeks I saw Léon only at meals, and sometimes in the evening, when the family gathered. He was respectful and attentive to my aged parents, and cheerfully assiduous with Hortense, and so playful and indulgent with my little nieces that the two girls adored him. Only with me was he reserved and solemn; when I spoke to him he blushed; and though he was otherwise nimble and quick and capable, when I asked him to do something for me he always made me repeat myself and always did something awkward. I'd heard vaguely of the power of love to make the fiercest person gentle or the clumsiest person graceful; and I understood it was the same power that now robbed Léon of his gracefulness and made him ungentle.

I could tell that for him I was unlike other people. No, I didn't call that feeling by its true name, I didn't say to myself it was love—because he made me happy, and I'd been taught to fear love and think of it as an enemy. In loving Léon, and in feeling loved, I refused to look closely at what I felt. And when—in this solitude in which I've learned so much—I was able to read from books other than my own heart, I was always astonished that Juliet, the daughter of the Capulets, didn't say to the young man who enchanted her, the way Léon enchanted me, "Romeo, don't tell me you're a Montague, because then I'd have to hate you."

But a day came when I could no longer doubt Léon's love, when his feelings became completely clear to me: it was the day I realized he loathed Captain Félix. It had to do with the sick workman I'd gone to visit when I first met Léon. I'd gotten my brother to agree not to cross him off the list of workers, but the captain had refused to allow him to be paid for the days he'd missed. He said it would be a fatal example for all the idlers who'd find it convenient to earn their pay in bed. I hadn't thought about Marianne or her husband, Jean-Pierre, since that visit; already I had no attention to spare for others.

Here's what happened: It was dinnertime. The captain and Léon rarely met except at that time, because Léon generally left us in the evening to work. In a stern tone the captain asked Léon, "Did Jean-Pierre come to the foundry today?"

"Yes."

"Did he go to the office?"

"Yes."

"Did he get paid?"

"Yes."

"By whom?"

"By me."

"Out of what funds did you pay him, Monsieur Lannois?"

No doubt Léon—who I could see was boiling mad—knew the captain meant to object to the pittance the man had been paid; turning his back on Félix, he said disdainfully, "Out of my own, sir."

I believe the captain had been ready to lecture Léon about what he'd presumed to do; he was so taken aback at the answer that he turned pale. But, not knowing how to indulge his anger, in his powerlessness he added, "So it seems Jean-Pierre has done you some important service?"

The tone of those words irritated Léon enough to overcome his shyness. With a kind of triumphant exultation he answered, "Oh, indeed, sir, indeed! He's done me a great service."

"While he's been ill?"

"While he's been ill."

"And what would that be?"

Léon smiled, and his whole expression changed from anger to sweet, sad submission. He put his hand on his heart, and gave me a look that—for the very first time—spoke to me; and he answered, "Oh, that's my secret, sir."

"I assume it's also Jean-Pierre's," said the captain, "and I'd certainly like to know it."

"You're welcome to ask him."

"I don't need your permission."

"I don't doubt it, sir."

During that last exchange Félix had been studying me, because he'd noticed Léon's glance at me and the agitation it caused me. I'd understood that look; it meant, "It's when you went to visit Jean-Pierre that I saw you for the first time, and that's the service I rewarded him for."

Dinner passed in silence, because they'd all heard the conversation, and everyone was embarrassed. I alone pretended to be at ease. Just as I'd understood Léon's admission, I'd understood Félix's suspicions, and for the first time I felt a kind of glee at deceiving him.

Léon left, and we remained alone with my brother and his wife. Hortense complained quietly to her husband about Félix's harshness. "I don't dare speak to him. But you can try to make him see reason. That young man is good, and a hard worker, and Félix treats him badly."

I was so grateful to Hortense that my feelings must've been visible in my eyes. My brother, who was watching me, shook his head gently. "Yes, Félix treats him badly, and he doesn't like him. And because I don't want that young man to have any reason to complain about us, I'll find some excuse to send him back to his father."

"Oh!" I cried in sorrow and anger, "that would be too unfair!"

"It would be the most sensible thing," said my brother firmly, studying me carefully.

I lowered my eyes. He moved away—but not before he'd made a sign to Hortense, who was studying me as well. In guessing my secret, they let me know I had one. It was the first time the word "love" occurred to me as an explanation for my fondness for Léon.

If Hortense, my sister-in-law, had held out her hand to me at that moment and said, "Henriette, do you love him?" I'd have replied by throwing myself into her arms and dissolving in tears and vowing not to love him anymore—because in our family's estimation love was a crime. But Hortense—normally so good and so gentle to me—responded harshly and awkwardly; though she'd just criticized Félix, she now felt obliged to take his side, because she assumed he needed to be defended in my heart. With great authority she said, "Henriette, I was at fault in criticizing my brother's behavior. Don't commit a greater fault by condemning him thoughtlessly."

That reprimand wounded me. Taking advantage of the fact that I'd said nothing to motivate it—though of course deep in my heart I felt I deserved it—I replied bitterly, "I, condemn Captain Félix! I said nothing about him, I didn't even say his name."

The way I answered offended Hortense, and she said curtly, "You know very well what I mean, miss."

"What you mean?" I replied angrily, feeling it was unfair to attack me for something I hadn't done. "I really don't know what you mean. What do I have to do with the opinion you just expressed about your brother? Are you trying to make me believe I was the one who accused him of being harsh?"

"You didn't say it, but you were thinking it, when you exclaimed it would be unfair to send Monsieur Lannois back to his family."

"I was only repeating what you'd said."

"You're quibbling, Henriette. That's what people do when they're in the wrong."

"Wrong? Wrong in what way? Wrong about what?" I asked, feeling tears coming on.

My sister-in-law, who up to then had been looking at me sternly, came over to me; taking my hand, after a fairly long silence, during which she seemed to be searching my heart, she said, "Henriette, sister, beware of doing something reckless, and remember what you promised. Félix loves you."

I would've wanted to doubt my own heart, if I'd been forced to see into it clearly. Yes, I still think so, yes: perhaps without that warning I'd have let that unknown disturbance in my life settle down without learning what it was. But once it had been given a name, once it had been called "love," once it had been crowned with fire, once I knew what it was, I was curious to see it, to look at it, to measure it—if only to resist it. Before that moment, Léon had been present in my heart without filling it; with those words he became its only object.

I'd just been told I loved Léon: so was it true? Examining myself, I discovered surprising things. Léon's face, his clear, gentle eyes, his long, beautiful blond hair, his noble figure, his mellow, melodious voice, the graceful way he moved his head when he pretended to be angry with my nieces—all of that had been etched in me without my consciously observing it. I knew him better than I knew my father or my brother, better than all the people I'd been living with for years. I felt like I could've spoken with his voice, thought his thoughts, performed his gestures, so deeply had I been filled by—and in a sense been living off of—an existence that wasn't my own. I was appalled at finding myself so completely in the power of another. My pride was outraged at being at the mercy of a life to whom my own life perhaps meant nothing, and I was suddenly filled with the fear of not being loved.

Love! Ah, love is like all superior powers: everything serves its interests—neglect as much as resistance. I would've loved Léon if I hadn't been afraid to; I loved him because I was afraid to. My God! Could I not have loved him? Aren't there slopes so steep that you fall if you struggle to climb them, and you also fall if you don't make any effort to stop? I had that experience myself, because Léon's image haunted me; it sat so close to me at night, it stayed so near by day that I found it tiresome, almost pushy; it took hold of me and treated me like its mistress. I wanted to tear myself away from its influence; but everything that had sustained me till then—activity, prayer, work—all of it went missing, deserted me when I needed its support. It was like the sand at the edge of a pit, yielding as soon as you need traction. I felt like there was a fiery sun hovering over my life, reducing everything to dust, fertilizing only love. Alas! I'm explaining myself badly.

At the time I didn't see my own heart that way. But I took a solemn resolution: I didn't want Léon to suspect I was obsessed with thoughts of him, and for a whole month I made an effort to be disagreeable to him. It took all of my self-disgust to overcome my sympathy for his sadness. He was so miserable! But his misery showed me how much he loved me, so his misery pleased me, and I was secretly happy to see him suffer.

The only ordeal it was hard for me to bear—and may God forgive me the struggle, since I emerged victorious!—the only ordeal that weakened my resolve, was the captain's delight. I felt it was my right to make Félix miserable by my coldness, since I was suffering too. I didn't tell him so, but by tacit agreement with myself I understood I had the right to hurt the man from whom I was withholding so much consolation. But for Léon to have to endure the captain's triumphant looks and cold mockery—that's what upset me, that's what almost drove me a hundred times to say to Léon, "I'm lying when I avert my eyes from you, I'm lying when I avoid interacting with you, I'm lying when I speak to you without joy and listen without seeming to hear you!" Yes, I would've let him know, if I hadn't loved him so much that I was afraid once my heart was open my whole life would rush out to him. He loved me too, and I knew it.

That business with Jean-Pierre by itself had made it clear to me that no one else understood. Félix had questioned the poor man, and the poor man had told him he had no answer to his questions: not only had he rendered no service to Léon, but the first time he'd ever met him was when he gave him money. So Léon's explanation was considered to be some kind of childish stubbornness. Only I knew what service Jean-Pierre had done him: wasn't I on my way to visit the poor sick man when Léon met me?

But a day had to come that would bring an end to the hard duty of coldness I'd imposed on myself. No one was talking about sending Léon home anymore: he was so hardworking, so sweet, so obedient! The cloud of suspicion surrounding him and me had lifted; I'd even come to feel safer myself—when an unexpected event showed me I'd gained only an external respite.

Among the pleasures of my childhood, I'd retained that of caring for a small, distant corner of the garden with my own hands. Some storerooms had just been built nearby, and they wanted to put in a path so our merchandise could be moved there through the grounds. That path would rob me of my little flowerbed full of rosebushes I'd grown and that I loved. If my brother had just told me what was going to occur, perhaps I wouldn't have thought to object. But as it happened, I overheard Félix giving orders to the gardener to dig up all my flower bushes so the workmen could lay out the path the next day. I objected. At first he tried to joke with me, but I responded by complaining that he was tactlessly doing everything he could to hurt me. His true nature prevailed, and he answered me harshly, and I ran to my room to hide my tears. They left me alone there. I overheard a quiet conversation under my window that made me feel sorry for the speaker.

"It's a little girl's whim," said the captain. "I'd rather it be that than something else. There's no harm in letting her cry over her roses."

Hortense tried to persuade him to come up and comfort me. "She's attached to those pathetic flowers," she said.

"All right," replied Félix, "tomorrow or the next day I'll have them dug up carefully and transplanted wherever she wants. But for me to have to go beg her pardon for carrying out the business of the foundry? I'm not going to let her set that precedent."

At first his words and his tone didn't bother me. Yes, I was sorry for him, for making such clumsy efforts to win the heart he'd set his hopes on. But then unfortunately my brother showed up and said I should be touched by the captain's gallantry if he took the trouble to save my poor roses. To have to be grateful to Félix, to admit he could do something obliging for me, felt like a greater misery than any of the others. I don't know why, but it annoyed me, and I was consumed by a single idea—to go to my garden that night and destroy it, tear it up, so Félix couldn't save it for me: I would've hated my roses if he'd preserved them.

I was so angry that I realized you can kill your own happiness at a moment like that, to keep from owing it to someone's consideration that you find burdensome. So I waited, and when everyone was asleep I quietly left the house and slipped like a thief along the alleyways and flowerbeds. Filled with anger and sadness, I drew near the place where I was about to kill those fragile shrubs that had been the companions of my childhood. One thought above all was driving me: Félix had become the living embodiment of my unhappiness, and since he'd spoiled my beautiful dreams I liked to tell myself it was he who was destroying my lovely flowers. Needing to feel I was suffering by his hand, in my thoughts I cried out, "That man is the evil genius ruining everything I've loved!"

I was only a few yards from the flowerbeds I was heading toward, when I heard a slight noise. The fear of being caught in the act of what had at first felt like legitimate revenge—but that now suddenly looked like a ridiculous tantrum—made me hide. But since the noise continued I wanted to find out what was causing it. I tiptoed to my rose garden. Someone was working there: a man was bending down, digging the bushes out with care and laying them gently in a wheelbarrow, which he then pushed to another part of the grounds. I recognized him: it was Léon.

Oh, how can I explain what I felt? My heart was filled with heavenly joy—filled so full that it intoxicated me and overflowed. I had to lean against a tree, and I felt tears running down my cheeks. And my flowers, my beautiful flowers, how I loved them! How dear and precious they'd become! As soon as Léon was far enough away, I ran to the bushes that still remained, and looked at them all in turn. The idea of destroying them now appalled me; it would've felt like vile ingratitude.

I was alone, and night cloaked me in darkness. I took one rose, the finest, and I cut it. Right there, in a mad rapture of love, giving way to the passion I'd kept bottled up for so long, I showered kisses on the rose that had been saved. Then, hearing Léon coming back, I dropped it on the ground for him—as if he'd be bound to recognize it. I took another for myself, as if he'd given it to me. And then I fled, my head and my heart lost—as if that exchange of flowers, which I'd carried out by myself, had been the mutual confession of our love.

The next day I was radiant with happiness. Léon loved me, Léon had saved me from the need to thank Félix. I loved him for his love, and for my aversion to the other man. And yet I wasn't spiteful: if Félix had wanted to remain my friend, I would've appreciated him for what he was worth. But a cruel destiny always led him to do things that cost him a place in my heart and pushed me down a path I wouldn't have chosen.

That morning everyone knew what had happened, and they were talking about it before I came down. It was a Sunday, so everyone had gathered for lunch. I'd just kissed my family and returned Léon's greeting when Félix came in. He stopped at the door, eyeing me and Léon in the same glance. Then, trying to hide his anger under a tone of teasing good humor, he said, "I feel awful, Henriette! I'd prepared a fine spot on the grounds to transplant your rosebushes, but a quicker and more skillful hand beat me to it."

That look of Félix's, wrapping us both in the same accusation, suddenly gave me the idea to make myself the accomplice of the crime that had wounded him so much. "Really!" I said in pretended surprise. "Who could possibly have perpetrated such a misguided gallantry?"

"I don't know yet," said Félix with great irritation. "Otherwise I'd already have thanked him for his attention to you."

By the direction of his gaze, Félix had aimed that threat at Léon, who looked ready to explode.

I intervened. "So you really hold it against him?" I said with a laugh.

"Enough to teach him a lesson," replied Félix.

"The way captains teach lessons?" I asked, seeing the gathering anger on Léon's face. "Weapons in hand, I assume?"

"Why not?" asked Félix, still looking at Léon.

"Well then," said I, taking down a pair of swords that hung in the dining room, "I'm ready to be taught my lesson." I held one sword out to the captain, drew the other from its scabbard, and stood en garde.

"What?" cried Félix. "It was you?"

"It was I. I'm the guilty party. So, come on, captain, en garde!"

I advanced on him, sword held high. He retreated, reddening with anger. My family, who'd treated the whole thing as childish nonsense, began to laugh. My father and Hortense called out gaily, "Come on, Félix, defend yourself! Are you afraid of her?"

Only I could tell Félix was still angry, because only I understood I'd just made him look ridiculous in front of the man he wanted to destroy. Still, he recovered; and—not suspecting in the least I could be lying—he replied fairly wittily, "You're better at handling a sword than a spade, my dear Henriette: you did a rather peculiar job transplanting those rosebushes you love so much."

Léon was taken aback. Wanting him to be as happy as I was, I replied, "I like them the way they are."

"Well then," said my father, "after lunch Henriette will show us."

It was my turn to be disconcerted, because, though I'd seen Léon take the rosebushes away, I had no idea where he'd put them. "I'll be happy to," I answered boldly, counting on getting away before everyone else so I could find the spot.

During lunch I studied Léon's face. No doubt he didn't dare believe what my behavior should've made him suspect. Perhaps, if he'd looked radiant, I'd have been sorry to have given myself away to him so recklessly by accepting the devotion his kind actions implied. But he wavered so quickly between sweet joy and trembling doubt that I forgave him my recklessness. His shy hopes charmed me. The less bold he was toward me, the bolder I felt toward him.

Meanwhile everyone went on talking about my garden, and they asked me what spot I'd chosen to move it to.

"A lovely spot—you'll see."

"I had to follow the track left by the wheelbarrow to find it," said Félix.

I counted on that clue to help guide me there, but Félix added, "If the gardener had already finished raking the paths, as he has now, I believe I'd never have thought to look for a rose garden where you hid it."

The grounds were extensive enough I would've had trouble finding my new flowerbed. I began to tremble at my own lie.

"Well, where the devil did you hide it?" asked my father.

"I'll show you."

"Félix, tell me where," said my father.

"I won't commit another blunder by robbing Henriette of the surprise she's prepared for you."

Félix was unhappy, and he was getting back at me by refusing me the one favor he could've done me. As for Léon, he couldn't guess at my difficulty, because he couldn't understand how I knew my rosebushes had been moved.

Soon we all got up from the table, and Léon vanished. I was in a quandary about what to do. They were urging me on. I made my decision and asked them to follow me. My plan was to make my family wander all over the grounds, and when we happened upon my garden I'd pretend I'd chosen the most roundabout way to get there.

But my father was tired, and he took my arm. "Let's go," he said. "And don't make us run. These old legs aren't kidding anymore."

Just then, when my predicament was at its worst, the heavensent clairvoyance that inspires hearts came to my rescue. Lacking any word from the perpetrator, lacking any trace on the ground, I sought the fine, invisible thread that must've guided Léon. He had to have chosen my favorite spot on the property, an isolated, hidden place where I liked to sit alone on a wooden bench. I headed straight there, certain I was right. They all followed me. When I got there I found my rosebushes arranged around that bench, where so often I'd thought about happiness before I knew Félix and Léon. It gave me fresh joy: not because Léon had chosen it—I felt he could've chosen no other—but because I'd guessed it so exactly.

Alas! All those things, which may seem puerile to my readers, were the great events of my life. That was how I walked alone in my passion. Then came the day when we two walked together—because up to then I'd loved Léon, and Léon had loved me, but I think I wouldn't have dared say we loved each other. It was again because of that garden that our love joined together in one common thought. After the day I've spoken of, my rose bed had become the destination of our walks after lunch on Sundays. It had become such an exclusive property that, by unspoken agreement, no one dared pick a flower without my permission. That by itself made them precious: to get one was a favor. My father never failed to say, "Well, Henriette, do us the honors of your garden."

And I gave a rose to everyone present. Léon had come several times, and I gave him a flower along with the rest—but I gave it to him in front of everybody, and I understood that therefore I wasn't giving him anything. One day it happened that he joined us after I'd handed out the flowers. We were already leaving my garden. I wouldn't have dared to go back to pick a rose for Léon. I was leaving last, walking with my father, and Léon drew near to me.

"You came too late," said my father.

"So I get nothing?" asked Léon.

I didn't answer, but I dropped the rose I was holding. He picked it up and pressed it to his heart. I'd been waiting for a long time for a chance to reward him for his consideration; I can't express how delightfully he guessed my thoughts and carried them out before I had articulated them. I saw happiness in his eyes, and it made me happy.

After that, I never gave him roses, I just dropped mine. And then he had his own rosebush, from which I picked flowers only for him. To describe how we understood each other without speaking—to explain how, with some kind of shared intelligence, we conversed using words spoken by others, how a passing glance gave some casual word, spoken casually by someone else, a meaning that belonged only to the two of us—would be to try to write the story of our life, hour by hour, minute by minute. And yet it was all innocent: I'd have given any friend those ephemeral tokens he preserved so carefully, and not a word had yet been spoken to prove to Léon that I gave them to him in any other capacity.

But a day came when I received and gave a token that unbound, so to speak, the silence of our hearts. Forgive me for these details from the only days when I experienced life in all of its power, don't laugh at the fragile joys that are the only thing I have left to sustain me under the weight of the calamity that has struck me. It's only in those moments from the past that I can anesthetize my suffering with memories. And that memory was so sweet to me—not for the happiness it gave me, but for the happiness I was able to give. For I was right to believe that to love someone means to make him happy.

It was the day before my birthday. My father, my mother, my brothers, even my nieces were teasing me with warnings about the gifts they were giving me the next day. "You'll be surprised by what I'm giving you!" said one; "You'll see whether I know your tastes!" said another. All of them promised I'd be pleased. Only Léon said nothing; he didn't brag, he just looked at me. Oh, how awful it is no longer to see, no longer to love! Lord, when will you open or close my grave all the way?

Léon watched me. Lord, what attraction have you put into the eyes of the one we love? What heavenly light, what ethereal beam shines out of them, that it penetrates our hearts like a breath that grants life and perfumes it? Léon watched me, and I felt my heart melting with joy under his gaze. I was sure he'd thought of me. The next day, after everyone had gotten up and had brought me flowers or jewelry, I went out into the garden. Léon was there. I was determined to receive whatever his eyes had promised me. I went to him. He was trembling, he was about to speak—when Félix came up to me and gave me some beautiful jewelry. Léon withdrew, but my eyes called him back. I saw he was coming to some resolution, and I waited.

"I beg your pardon," he said. "I'd forgotten... This morning, while crossing the grounds, I found this handkerchief. It's embroidered with your initials, and I think it belongs to you. I've come to give it back to you."

At first I was hurt: he'd found one of my handkerchiefs and he wasn't keeping it! I took it back without looking at it, and I thanked him coldly. He went away embarrassed. Just then Hortense came up. Snatching the handkerchief from me, she said, "You sneaky thing! You finished your own fine handkerchief before me—you must've worked on it at night to get it done in time for your birthday. That's not fair! But it's so pretty! I wouldn't have thought it would turn out so well, you were so absent-minded while you worked on it!"

I didn't understand at first. But when I looked at the handkerchief I saw it was exactly like the one I'd been embroidering, which still wasn't finished. So that was Léon's gift: a gift I could keep without hiding it, a handkerchief that would belong to me more than my own—because only I would know where it came from. I accepted Hortense's explanation, and went immediately back to my room. I found the handkerchief that wasn't finished, and burned it over a candle. Why would I want to have anything of mine to compete with the one Léon had given me?

When I went down to lunch, Léon was withdrawn and sad. He looked at me. I was holding his handkerchief, and I dabbed my forehead with it. His whole face lit up with joy. I'd often heard it said you should dread the words of love. No—it's love's glances and sweet raptures you should fear. What could Léon have said to me that could match the joy I'd just given him? He'd come back into my heart, and I didn't speak, so that I might give nothing away.

Later we went for our walk. For the first time, Félix came along with us. I distributed my roses, and Léon got one of the last that remained on his bush. That day I handed it to him and said, "Thank you." He received it ecstatically.

Just then Félix came over. "And how about me?" he asked. "Do I get nothing?"

"Of course you do," I answered, and I turned to pick another rose.

"Do I get treated worse than Léon? Can I have one like his, one of those beautiful dewy roses over there?"

"There are so few left!"

"And you only notice that when it's my turn?"

I was so happy that I didn't want to jeopardize the feeling. I picked the finest rose and gave it to Félix, who thanked me. I wanted to give Léon a look so he could forgive me, but he tossed away the rose I'd given him, and stood there in despair. I understood his anger, because I'd just cheapened our secret. Félix was talking to me, but I barely answered. Someone called to him and he moved away. Abandoning all caution, I approached Léon. "You threw away your rose?"

"It wasn't mine anymore, it was everybody's."

"That's not a nice thing to say!"

"It wasn't a nice thing to do!"

"You, who are so good at returning something you didn't find, what would you say if I'd refused what didn't belong to me?"

"Oh, don't give it back to me," he said in alarm. He fell silent, then added quietly, while looking at me, "But allow me to regret not having kept something I really did find."

I followed his eyes: they were fixed on that bracelet of my hair he'd given back to me so shyly. Faster than thought, I took it off my arm and said, "Here."

He let out an exclamation. I fled immediately. I was afraid to see his happiness. Alas! They claim women are led astray by the suffering of those they love; that's not how it was for me. When I smiled at Léon, when I looked at him, when I spoke to him, it made him so giddy, so happy, I can't imagine how I could've shaken off the appeal of such powerful joy near me. Oh, I loved him! I loved him so he'd be happy. It was to make him happy that I did wrong. I go on suffering now because I believe in the happiness he'd feel if he saw me again, and that's also why I endure my suffering bravely.

The days that followed that one were truly the happiest of my life. I felt, in all of its intoxicating fullness, the happiness of loving and being loved. And yet I couldn't ignore the fact that an invincible barrier stood between Léon and me. I could see it, I could stare it in the face, but it didn't make me afraid. I had no way to change the destiny that awaited me, but I didn't try to find a way. I loved, I was loved! That feeling filled my heart. The intoxication was so complete that I no longer needed either memories or hopes—the present was my whole life. What I'd been, what I'd become, couldn't get my attention: I loved, I loved.

My God! My God! Now that reflection and solitude and despair have en-lightened me about what was being said around me, it seems to me the people who talked about love had never been in love—or else I was in love in a way no one else had ever been. My Léon was my soul, my mind, my life. I wasn't like people who make plans for the future so they can be happy together. That would've meant thinking beyond what I was experiencing, and I couldn't do it. I felt like my heart was floating in some state of serenity above all calculation and all foresight. My life, my thoughts, were barely strong enough to sustain me in that intoxication.

Oh, my Léon! I loved you—you can't believe how I loved you! For now, in giving you my life, in accepting the torture of death in which I live so as not to renounce your love, I don't love you as I did then. I think about my wasted life, about my ruined reputation; I know what I'm doing, I act by deliberate in-tention. Whereas then I had none: I loved, that was all—to love was duty, repu-tation, virtue... Poor Léon, how I loved you!

I couldn't say what happened between Léon and me for the month I was like that. Everything pleased me and intoxicated me. If he was near me I was happy; if he was far away I was happy: I dreaded neither his presence nor his absence. When he spoke to me his voice rang inside me and awakened an echo so strong that it kept humming continuously, and I went on listening to it when he'd stopped speaking. Did I share the life of others during that time? Was I of this world? Hadn't I been taken up into heaven, into some unknown atmos-phere? Wasn't it some dream where love alone stood watch, while caution and duty slept in my heart?

Yes, it was a dream, a delirium, a drunkenness without a name. Because when tragedy came and ripped me out of it, I couldn't have described a single event from those days so full of them; I felt only resentment—which had its own sorrowful joy. My heart had been torn from the heavenly embrace that had held it for so long. When I came back to ordinary life, I felt as if, had that state lasted any longer, my will would've melted gently like white wax over a low flame, and my soul would've evaporated like pure ether in the sun. That's how I should've died, Lord, not the way I'm dying now! I would've returned to you without having sinned, and you would've welcomed me, because you're the God of innocence. And yet I firmly hope you won't reject me, Lord! Because you're also the God of suffering.

I hesitate... I hesitate to begin the account that follows—for now all is fear, despair, and crime. Oh, Félix was exactly what I said he was: the tiger that loves its prey for the sake of devouring it, the tiger that crouches beneath bright cactus flowers, its striped coat blending in and getting lost in the bushy thickets, the tiger that bides its time in silence, then suddenly leaps on its prey, which sees it only at the moment of its death.

When winter came, I used to go out into the grounds and walk along a path that could be seen from the window by which Léon worked. I couldn't really see him, but I knew he saw me, and I brought him my presence. When the family gathered in the evening he found a thousand ways to tell me privately everything I'd done, my slightest gestures, how many times I'd passed by. We had our own agreed-upon signals for all that; those exchanges made us happy.

One morning Léon stopped me at a bend in a flowerbed. "Don't go any further," he said. "The captain has had my desk moved away from the window where it was. He suspects our love. I've seen him heading toward our path. I assume he means to spy on you. I slipped out to warn you."

As he spoke I saw Félix coming toward us. "Quick, get away!" I said to Léon.

"No, that would show him we have something to hide. Stay calm, and answer me when I speak to you."

The captain had seen us, but he didn't hurry his pace. That slowness frightened me, because it told me he was sure of what he suspected and of what he meant to do. From the far end of the long alley he'd come out on, all the way till he reached us, I thought I could feel his hard, cold eyes on my heart.

When he was only a few steps away from us, Léon said to me calmly, "I'll be sure to copy out that new score for you, miss."

"I'd be very grateful," I answered.

Félix stopped, and gave us a pitying, scornful smile. "Monsieur Léon," he said, "Would you come with me? I have a few orders to give you."

I suddenly wanted to find out what would be said, and I replied quickly, "I'll leave you together."

I feigned a quick withdrawal, as if I were running away. But, thanks to the thickness of a copse of yew trees, I was able to get close to the spot where Léon and Félix had stayed. The captain didn't speak immediately; no doubt he was giving me time to get far enough away. It was Léon who spoke first. His voice sounded strange to me: it wasn't the voice he used with me. In the same way that the voice I loved was sweet and submissive, the voice I heard now was proud and self-assured. "What orders has Captain Félix for me?"

"Just one, sir," Félix replied with surprising composure. "To be prepared to leave tomorrow."

"I didn't come to Monsieur Buré's foundry to get involved in outside business."

"And indeed, it's not on company business you'll be going, but your own. You've learned enough, Monsieur Lannois, and I think it's time to send you back to your father."

That news stunned me. I had to lean against the yews. I was close to fainting, when Léon's voice reassured me by frightening me. "You mean you're dismissing me?"

"I wouldn't have put it that way," said the captain quite calmly.

"Very well, sir," replied Léon in a slightly mocking tone. "It's not my place to make you even more discourteous than you are."

"Your insults are useless, little man," said Félix contemptuously.

"And your orders are equally useless, enormous captain," replied Léon with a snicker.

"And yet you'll have to obey them."

"When the one who's in charge here gives them to me."

"I'm the one in charge here!"

"Not yet, if you please, not yet! The master here is Monsieur Buré. I know you've been promised a partnership in the business when you receive Henriette's dowry. How convenient it is to make your fortune by marrying a rich girl! But the wedding hasn't happened yet. Till then you're an employee, captain, just like me. And if it pleases you to give orders, it doesn't please me to receive them."

I expected Félix to erupt in anger. I could tell by the sound of his voice that he'd resolved to control his temper. "All of your wishes will be honored, sir, and I'll ask Monsieur Buré to repeat what I've just told you."

"Meaning," cried Léon, outraged, "you're going to go denounce me!"

"Denounce you, Monsieur Léon! Why? I think you're an honest man, lacking neither diligence nor intelligence. But, what can I do, maybe it's just a whim, but I don't like your face: it gets on my nerves."

"Captain, do you realize I could take that as an insult?"

"And what would you do about it?"

"Ask you for satisfaction."

"I wouldn't be able to give it to you, my good sir. When your father sent you off into the care of upstanding businessmen, we received you in good health. We're returning you the same way, like the upstanding businessmen we are. Then, after your father has notified us that you reached home undamaged, if you wish to come wandering back this way, at that point I'll give you all the satisfaction you can ask for."

"I count on it," replied Léon with a scorn that pleased me even in the midst of my despair, because it must've humiliated Félix. "I count on it, my good sir, as you put it. But meanwhile I have to inform you, my good sir, that you're an imbecile."

All of the captain's self-control gave way at that insult. "Guttersnipe!"

"Well then, come along, captain, come along! I have swords at my place."

"No," said Félix, quickly recovering. "No, first we have to dismiss you." And, no doubt afraid he'd lose his temper again, he hurried away.

I wanted to go to Léon, but the strength that had sustained me suddenly fled, and I fainted. When I came to, I was in our parlor, with my whole family around me. They were all looking at me with stern suspicion. Only my brother looked at me with any kindness. I hadn't yet fully recovered my wits before my brother said, almost gently, "Henriette, are you guilty?"

Oh, woe, woe and curses on those who speak to innocent hearts in words that presume crime or vice! Those words, "Are you guilty?" must've meant something different to my family than they meant to me, because the answer I gave had a sense I didn't understand till later. Poor child in love, but who still loved like a child! I was thinking only of the one who was going to be dismissed, and I replied to that awful question—"Are you guilty?"—with the words, "Have mercy! Have mercy on Léon!"

"Wretch!" cried my father, rising.

"Oh, Henriette!" said Hortense to me quietly.

My father—whom my mother could barely hold back—was uttering muffled curses. I was stunned. I knew I'd done wrong, because I'd disobeyed my family's wishes; but I also knew I was innocent. Without understanding what the crimes of love are, I knew very well I hadn't forgotten all of my duty. So now I got up and replied firmly to my father, "You asked if I was guilty. Guilty of what crime? Guilty of loving Monsieur Lannois, it's true. Guilty of having said so to him, it's true. Guilty of admitting he loves me, it's true. If there are crimes besides those, I don't know what they are."

I left the parlor immediately, unhappy with all of them for having shown me nothing but harsh, accusing faces when the happiness of my life had just been shattered, despairing of the depths of agony I felt I was falling into, knowing in pain the love I'd known in joy: an immense love, a love that was the center of my life, and that would either kill me or drive me mad if it was snatched away from me!

Yet anger was mixed with my despair. I was angry that I'd heard not a single word of pity from all those happy people around me. I blamed them as much as they blamed me—and then something astonishing happened that intensified that feeling to the last degree of fury. I opened the door to my room, and found Félix at my open desk, rifling through the drawers, looking at my papers. I cried out in horror and contempt.

"What is it?" cried my brother, who'd followed me, along with Hortense.

"There's a lackey forcing the locks on the furniture!" I cried in my indignant rage.

"Henriette!" cried Félix. The fury of my insult didn't even give him enough time to blush at his own shameful behavior.

"Get out!" I said. "Get out of my room! I want you out of my room!"

My voice, my face, left my brother and his wife stock still in the doorway. Their blushes showed Félix they were ashamed of him for what he'd been doing. And anger must've given me a tone of command, because the captain left without a word, his face white, fury in his eyes. The look we two exchanged at that moment held our destiny: my eternal hatred and contempt for him, his eternal hatred and vengeance toward Léon and me.

No sooner had Félix left than I shut the door. And then I heard him saying to my brother, "I didn't find any proof."

Proof! Proof of what? Of my love? There was no need! I admitted it, I proclaimed it! So then, proof of my dishonor? Of my dishonor! Oh, you who are reading this wretched account, don't forget in what book it's written. Understand through what appalling calculation it was left—after many others—near me in my solitude. At first it was less horrible books. First a book called *Faublas*,[22] then others, many others—corrupters seated by my coffin to infect my soul, a few pages of which soiled my eyes before I understood what they were trying to do. Now I know what proofs Félix was looking for, now I know the meaning of that word "dishonor"! But then, God knows, the virginity of my thoughts was as pure as that of my body, and the love they tried to make me ashamed of was an angel from heaven whose white wings had never touched the ground.

And yet everything suggested my family's accusation wouldn't end where my transgression had ended. And in my anger at the harshness of all of them and the insulting impertinence of one of them, I tried to identify that transgression, and I was sorry I hadn't committed it. I envied my family, and Félix above all, the consolation they'd feel when they found out I was innocent: the chastity they didn't credit me with would bring them happiness!

That state of feverish fury was too intense, and it soon eased, and grief came to soothe me. I was losing Léon, losing him suddenly, without saying farewell, without making any avowals to him, without our telling each other, "Let's suffer and hope." It was awful! Sometimes I wanted to go downstairs to see my father, my brother, Hortense, to tell them I was innocent, to ask them not to let Léon leave, or to let me see him: I was as deranged from grief as I'd been from anger. At other times I wanted to go out and wander at random around the house, or around the grounds, to meet him or to see him from a distance. Of course I wouldn't have done it: I'd have stopped on the top step of the stairs, I'd have retreated—I feel it, I swear it. But at the moment that idea took hold of me, I tried to get out... and my door was locked! They'd locked it from the outside!

Oh, God forgive them for their crime! But they pushed me with all their might. What! For my innocent grief I'd found no consolation. For a grief that could lead to transgression, not a word of advice, not a word of appeal to my love for them, not a word begging me not to make them suffer, not even an order to respect their good name! Instead a lock! A lock—like for a hardened criminal! A prison, like for a convict! Oh yes, Lord, they deserved my crime, and from the depths of my punishment I still feel no repentance: they drove me to my fall!

Since I was imprisoned at my door, I opened my window. They hadn't yet imprisoned my eyes, and in spite of my family I saw Léon—but Léon leaving, Léon on horseback, going by on the path that passed in front of me. So: exile for

---

[22] *Les Amours du chevalier de Faublas* (1787-90) by Jean-Baptiste Louvet de Couvray, a popular trilogy of novels recounting the many tragicomic love affairs of Louvet's libertine hero.

him, prison for me—all of that in the space of an hour! Executioners don't move as fast as that.

I don't know which would've prevailed then, my despair or my outrage, but both would've led to the same result: I would've thrown myself out the window, if by a sign Léon hadn't told me, "Hope!" I hoped, and resolutely I watched him ride away, determined to resist all of them and to defend my happiness by all possible means.

No sooner had I lost sight of Léon in the distance than I heard the locks that held me prisoner turning. They were giving me back my freedom, because they thought it would now be protected by the absence of the one I loved. I rejected their freedom. Oh, my freedom would only have led me to futile hopes; I wouldn't have seen Léon again if they'd set me free to go after him. They didn't understand that, nor did they understand why I stubbornly refused to come downstairs. Though they were now sure of my innocence—because I learned later that Léon's dignified expostulations had enlightened them—though they were sure of my innocence, they didn't come back to me to apologize for their suspicions. They left me to rot under a vile accusation, because Félix said they shouldn't give in to a girl's mood, to a child's tantrum. So I was left to believe they still thought me guilty. Though they were reassured of my honor, they didn't bother to reassure me of their forgiveness. Perhaps I should've gone to ask for it. But to ask for forgiveness would justify Félix, and I couldn't do it. Oh, I've certainly experienced in all their power the two great passions in women's hearts: love and hatred. I loved Léon enough to die for him, and I would've died rather than give any joy to my torturer.

But soon it was time for lunch. They could've sent for me, but I was being punished. I was so young! They forgot I was in love, and love is the heart's supreme expression. I laughed at their punishment. So no one wanted to remember? And Hortense—who'd married my brother at sixteen—didn't want to recall that she'd been a wife and mother at the same age I was now, when she was letting me be treated like a temperamental child.

But eventually they sent someone, and a servant girl came to wait on me. I was about to dismiss her when she furtively slipped a piece of paper into my hand. A few words were written in pencil:

I'm leaving, but I'll come back tonight. I have to speak to you—we have to escape. At ten o'clock I'll be at the little door in the garden wall. Will you be there? I'm waiting for your answer.

It happened, oddly, that I'd never seen Léon's handwriting. The letter wasn't signed, but I didn't doubt for a moment it came from him, and at the bottom of the note I replied *Yes*, and gave it back to the servant.

I must confess, I took that action—which determined the course of my life—without thinking it over. The servant was standing there before me, Léon was waiting, and I needed to see him—not to receive his love at that moment, I swear, but to tell him what would become of me and ask him what he meant to do. It was like holding a conference about our future at a moment of crisis. Once the note was gone, I realized I'd just agreed to a rendezvous—and yet it wasn't what would be called a lovers' tryst. The day before, Léon could've begged on his knees for a meeting and I would've refused. But that day I would've asked him to come if he hadn't beaten me to it. Our calamity had already become a kind of protection.

Then I was shaken by another fear: maybe it was a trap laid by Félix! But to what purpose? To make me commit a sin? Well then, I'd resolved to do it, and—on my soul's salvation, which is the only hope I have left in my despair— the sin I was committing was just another act of disobedience, another rebellion against Félix, another way of trying to escape from him. Love played no part in it; and if I'd had to write down beforehand everything that needed to be said at that rendezvous, the words *I love you* would barely have made the list, which would've consisted of plans to get Léon's family to intervene, and to get mine to yield. Yes, I'll swear to it again, I had no thought of a guilty love affair, I was thinking about what my chances were of not dying, I had no idea I was risking even greater dangers.

In that way the time passed, and when night came I waited calmly for the moment I would escape from my room. But then, as I made my way down the stairs, which creaked under my footsteps, I began to shiver: vague images of some seduced girl fleeing her father's house passed before my eyes like ghosts. I'd seen a few paintings in which that was depicted, and now they rose up in the darkness—with me as the girl. If I'd been more experienced than I was, those somber warnings might perhaps have made me draw back, but I was handicapped by the innocence of my soul and the inexperience of my senses. What a pitiful child I was! My whole life had been lived in my heart, and I didn't understand that the heart can be put to shame.

I crossed the garden, I reached the door in the wall, I opened it: Léon was there. He came in, and took me by the hand. It was the first time he'd touched me. I was so agitated I didn't feel a thing.

"Come," he said. "Come inside this lodge. There we'll be safe from anyone seeing us. The captain might be walking around in the grounds. Come!"

I followed Léon, because I was afraid of Félix. We entered the lodge, in total darkness. Léon seated me on a sofa, and sat next to me. If I'd spoken first, what I would've said was, "And what'll become of us now?"

It was Léon who spoke. He must've forgotten our misfortunes, because he said, "Oh, Henriette, I've been dying for so long from the need to speak to you! For six months I've loved you, for six months your eyes have burned me and thrilled me, and not to have met even once, not to have told you how I was suffering—what a terrible calamity that's been!"

Those words, and the vehemence with which they were spoken, troubled and frightened me. I hadn't come to hear him say he loved me—I knew that perfectly well! I loved him so much! So on the first occasion in which he told me his thoughts freely, our hearts were in disagreement. Did he therefore love me less than I loved him, since he needed to say it to me? I didn't express those thoughts aloud.

"Léon, it's what happening to us now that's a calamity."

"No," he said, lowering his voice, "not if you love me the way I love you. I'm going away, I have no choice—but I'll be back soon. My father is enormously wealthy, his affection for me is boundless, I'll tell him everything, and he'll return with me to ask for your hand. They won't dare refuse it."

"Are you sure?"

"Yes, I'm sure I can get it... if I can be sure you'll save yourself for me."

"Léon," I said, taking his hand, "I swear to you that, even on pain of death, no one but you will be my husband."

He pressed my hands, and drawing me to him he said, "Ah! So you do love me, Henriette!... You love me... Will you be mine—do you swear it?"

I'd already told him so on my own. I thought that, given the way he was asking me again, I shouldn't answer. My heart sank—enough to hurt me—or filled enough to choke me. I felt my hands trembling in Léon's, I was shaking and gasping; and he, pulling me still closer to him, said, "You love me, don't you? You love me?"

An indescribable distress rose from my heart to my head. I felt I was losing my mind, that an attack of vertigo was going to make me fall. With difficulty I tore my voice from my chest to reply, "Leave me... Leave me." He didn't notice my terror, and took me in his arms. Uncomprehending, I pushed him away. "No! No!"

"You love me, and you'll be mine," he went on, "mine—my beloved Henriette! Mine later, and mine now. And can I believe in your love, can I believe you love me the way I love you, that your life is mine as mine is yours?"

"Yes. I swore it to you. I'll be yours, Léon. Isn't that enough?"

"Why are you pushing me away like this?" he said, using his strength to keep my hands trapped, and I felt his lips on mine.

Shaking, distraught, I stood up. "No! No! No!" I cried, rejecting my own distress more than his desire—because, I swear to God, I didn't know what he was asking for.

"Henriette! Henriette!"

"Ah!" I cried, putting into words an extraordinary feeling of horror. "Léon, Léon, you don't love me!" And I began to weep.

"What did you just say, Henriette?" he cried sadly, pulling me back to him. "That I don't love you! And yet for the sake of that love I've put up with six months of insolence from that man you're going to belong to! To keep from raising a barrier of blood between us, I haven't killed the man who dared to tell me you'd be his!"

"Never!"

"Never, you say? But he's staying, and I'm going, and your whole family will be around you, begging you, threatening you, telling you I don't love you, badmouthing me. And who knows whether, in some moment of doubt, of fear and weakness, you won't give in, you won't betray me?"

"Never, Léon!"

"Oh, you're so strong in resisting my love—you'll be too weak to resist their hatred."

"Léon, have mercy, have pity—I love you."

"Can't you feel your heart shunning me, your mind turning away from me, Henriette? Oh, don't you love me the way I love you?"

And I felt what he was describing. My heart was seething, I was shaking all over, my wits and my reason were going astray. I was in his arms, his breath burned my face, his lips found mine again, and even in the dark of night I closed my eyes. I let myself be pulled toward a crime I knew nothing of, but which I felt I shouldn't watch. I hadn't fainted, but in Léon's hands I was like an inert corpse. A painful annihilation of my body and my mind led me to surrender to him without a struggle; he could've killed me without it hurting me. I could feel nothing. In vain he embraced that soulless body, in vain he searched for my heartbeat, in vain he called for me to utter a word. I felt myself dying, that's all. I was guilty, dishonored, and debased—and still I didn't know why I was guilty, dishonored, and debased!

It was his cry of pleasure that roused me from my torpor. I wanted to push him away and curse him, but my words were smothered by his lips, and my tears were lost in his kisses. He'd taken me! I wept: I'd just had an illusion shattered, I'd just learned what it is that men call pleasure. Pleasure! Is it then the defilement of love? Poor fallen angel—I'd just plummeted from heaven. For I'd been an angel: If I'd been merely a woman, a woman like so many others, either I'd have resisted him, or I'd have taken pleasure too. But I was ignorant of men's love, and I succumbed.

Still, Léon's delirious joy calmed me, and I was letting my soul come down to him again, when—kneeling before me—he said, "Oh, thank you, light of my life! You're mine now, the way a child is its mother's. Now they'll grant me your hand or we'll die together. Henriette, Henriette, tell me you forgive me."

I thought I understood his euphoria: he'd finally been made sure I loved him. Oh, what a vile token of love a woman's honor is! I suppressed my remorse, because I didn't want to subtract anything from the joy I'd just given him.

It was only then he spoke of the future and his plans. I let him talk. All I needed to do was to trust myself to him—I'd lost the right to give him advice, to ask for any hope. I need take no further care for myself: he'd wanted my life, and I'd given it to him, and I felt now he alone was responsible for it. We parted then; he left, and I went back to my room. It was a night of tears, followed by a day of awful torture.

Can a more horrible punishment be conceived? The help that could've saved me came when I was already lost. Hortense, my father, my mother, alarmed by my stubbornly staying in my room, came to me the next morning and told me that Félix's jealousy had confused them, that they knew I was guilty of no more than falling in love, that they forgave me, that I was free to weep and suffer, and that they hoped the need to restore peace and happiness to the family would help me overcome a passion that was more imprudent than guilty.

So the next day—my God, the very next day!—my elderly father, my virtuous mother, my good sister-in-law, my fairminded brother, gathered around my bed, told me all of that with tears in their eyes and forgiveness in their voices... and I didn't cry out, "Fools! Torturers! It's too late, you let your child fall into the gutter, and now you come offer your hands to her! I don't need them anymore!"

I didn't tell them that. I only wept and writhed at their comforting words. They thought I was dying, and left me alone. Oh, at that moment, yes, if I'd known where to find Léon, I'd have escaped from our house, I'd have gone to him, and I'd have said, "You wanted me, so take me completely, give me a roof over my head, a family, bread, a name—because I'm ashamed of my family name, and of the roof and the bread I have now, because I'm stealing it shamelessly, none of it belongs to me anymore, I've renounced it."

My illness saved me from despair; fever took hold of me and held me for three straight weeks. When it left me, I had no strength for anything but cowardice, no courage for anything but deceit and trembling. I only became worthy of living again when an astonishing feeling—a feeling stronger, holier, harder to express than love—rekindled my heart: I was going to be a mother. I knew it before I felt it. Before the usual signs of pregnancy arrived to alert me to my condition, some intuition of my womb cried out to me that I no longer had the right to die.

And yet at first it was only a vague feeling of hope that came to me in my hours of solitude. I didn't know why I began to look at my sister-in-law's children with new curiosity. I remembered their faces and their cries when they were newborn. I took them lovingly on my lap and rocked them, while trying to recall their nanny's lullabies. Then one night, when I was on my knees in my room, praying to God with all the fervor of my despair, asking him to turn away from me the suffering I could foretell, promising him from my heart to redeem my sin by a life of penitence and virtue, I felt another life moving inside mine. O Lord, you who in your mercy have put so much love into the hearts of women, you put even more in their wombs! Wretched fallen girl that I was, I can't describe the cry of love with which I greeted the new being within me—who'd live to become the unanswerable witness to my crime; I can't describe the holy devotion I felt toward the being whose birth could only bring me either dishonor or death.

It was that devotion that drew me back to life, tearing me out of the awful despondency I'd let myself fall into. In the two months since Léon had left I'd had no news of him, and everyone avoided speaking to me about him, though I could guess from their whispering that my fate was a constant subject among some of my family. I was prepared for what was happening to me: I knew they'd hide all of Léon's efforts from me, right up till he triumphed over the obstacles that separated us. I was patient because I had faith in him. But when I was no longer alone, when I had to fear for two lives condemned to the same suffering, my anguish grew terrible, my worries robbed me of sleep, and I tried to break through the mystery that surrounded me.

A whole month passed that way—a month in which nothing suggested to me that my family's plans for me had changed. I remained in the midst of my family like a young girl saddened by a foolish crush, who out of pity has been allowed to indulge her sadness freely. They treated me with affection, they more than satisfied my wishes when by chance I said something that expressed a wish; but they didn't address my heart. Neither my mother nor my father nor Hortense ever came to me to hold out a hand and say that, to endure what I was suffering, I must have something in my heart besides a child's crush.

And then that situation, which I'd accepted because I wasn't conscious of it, became intolerable to me. What was Léon doing? Why had he not found a way to let me know what action he was taking? Why had I myself not let him know of my condition? All of that made me suffer from agitation, after it had made me suffer from despondency. The servant who'd given me Léon's note avoided me, out of fear of the consequences of communicating with me. I found out one day that a word of pity she'd let slip had almost cost her her job. "Poor miss!" she'd said, "she'll die in their hands without them noticing." And she was right when she said that: yes, I would've died if they'd just have let me die. But they wanted to kill me, and I defended myself. I resisted—I'm still resisting. How long will this last?

Meanwhile time was passing, and I heard nothing to let me know I hadn't been abandoned. Oh, what days and nights of torture, what sudden fears, what slow intense terrors! If some word spoken in passing referred by accident to my condition, I thought I'd faint. And when I was alone I imagined the moment when I'd have to tell the truth, or the moment the truth would be found out—and then in my insomniac nights I envisioned terrible scenes, with me on my knees, weeping and crying out amid my family's curses.

Strangely, Félix never appeared in those awful visions of delirium, neither in my waking nightmares nor in my dreams when I slept; but some unknown phantom hovered over my head with a hideous laugh. Did I understand in my heart that threats and curses weren't enough for him? Was my imagination simply unable to conjure up a torture worthy of that man's cruelty? I was already suffering so much that I thought I'd reached the last degree of my courage. I didn't yet know the soul's terrible ability to summon the strength to face every agony, so it can feel every cut before dying or passing out.

Soon I began to learn that terrible lesson. It came in the form of scorching wounds that consumed my heart, and icy embraces that froze it till it stopped beating in my chest. Today I'm not sure I'd want to leave this tomb if it meant undergoing those tortures again. The first, and the only one that contained hope, came to me at one of those hours when the soul is so low that even joy feels like torture—like those hours when sleep weighs on your eyelids with such an over-powering heaviness that you'd refuse to open them even to see your own child.

We were all in the parlor: a sad gathering, in which my bleak despair made the children's gaiety feel inappropriate. A servant opened the door with a kind of fear and said timidly, "A gentleman's carriage has stopped at the gate, and the gentleman is coming this way."

"Did he give his name?" asked my brother.

"Yes, sir."

"Well? What's his name?"

The servant hesitated. Then, with his eyes on me, he answered slowly, "His name is Monsieur Lannois."

"Léon!" I cried, leaping up.

"It's that gentleman's father," said the servant as he withdrew.

All eyes had turned to me when I cried out.

"Can't you see you're going mad?" asked my father with scornful anger. "Monsieur Lannois is announced, and—in front of a servant!—you scream 'Lé-on!' Go to your room. Withdraw. It's time we straightened out this business."

I could tell by my father's expression that he could barely contain his rage. I left, lowering my head and murmuring, "It's you—you're the one who can't see I'm going mad."

Then, no sooner was I out of the room, but I wanted to see Monsieur Lan-nois—Monsieur Lannois, Léon's father, sent here by Léon—my second father, my last hope. I wanted to see the man I pictured as a venerable, kindhearted el-der, an old man bringing benevolence and protection with him. I slipped into a small side room, and there, from behind a curtain, I saw Monsieur Lannois and heard the conversation.

Monsieur Lannois was still quite a young man: he was short and stout, with a ruddy cheerful face, a ludicrous pretentious demeanor, and a harsh common voice. It should come as no surprise that I noticed all of that so clearly in the first moment: each of the features I've described chilled my heart. If he'd been a man of austere and unsparing countenance, I would've trembled, I would've despaired—but not with the shameful despair that realizes in advance its request will be not so much dismissed as misunderstood. You can kneel in the presence of death, but in the presence of the bright face of cheerful folly you can only fall silent. Even if the severity of that judgment is held against me, I stand by what

I've written—because, it has to be said, that man was responsible for the worst of my suffering, and he robbed my misery of its dignity: he made me blush, not from shame but from disgust.

Yes, when I began writing this account I thought the picture of the tortures I've suffered would be the most cruel thing to draw—and now I see there are things I can't even make comprehensible. When I write about being locked up in this tomb and deprived of air and sleep, when I lay out the awful details of this captivity that's killing me, you'll pity me, you'll understand me. But can I make others understand the horrors of a brutality that withers and crushes a poor wretch's heart and life in its uncaring fingers? It doesn't matter. I'll try to explain, because all of my sufferings must be made known, and perhaps when they are, some woman's heart will understand me and weep for me and pray to heaven for the miseries I suffered in this world to be counted in my favor in the next.

The conversation between Monsieur Lannois and my family began with an exchange of compliments, followed by a discussion of business matters. Finally he sprawled in his chair and cried, "Hey, hold on! It strikes me there's someone missing!"

"Who?"

He chuckled. "By God, that beloved Henriette!"

"Monsieur…," said my father.

"Come on, old dad, don't get all puffed up with dignity. My boy Léon told me the whole story: he loves the little hussy, and she loves him back, which is believable enough, since I produced him and there aren't many like him around! So I'd advise you to take him: my wife is dead, so the mold that turned him out is broken!"

"Monsieur," repeated my father, shocked by his tone, "such a proposition, offered in such terms…"

"No, no! No terms!" said Monsieur Lannois triumphantly. "Cash down, always cash down. Fifty thousand écus to my boy Léon."

"We have other plans for Henriette," replied my father.

"That could be, but the two youngsters love each other, you understand? And in the old saying, the seed will sprout where it's planted, if you know what I mean."

Without a doubt, of all those listening to the man's strange words I was the most innocent, the least accustomed to the vulgarity of that kind of double-entendre, and yet I understood the vulgarity. Unable to listen any further, I fled into the garden. I wandered like a madwoman: I'd just been robbed of my last chance of rescue. I could see that my family must refuse an offer put that way—and given the dignified manners I was used to, I couldn't even resent them for refusing. My God, what would I have said if I hadn't sinned? Who knows whether that man might've made me turn away from the very happiness he was offering. Even now, as I write the vulgar words that were Léon's father's way of speaking, I feel myself blushing with shame.

But I have to describe what brought about this calamity, and how I could've been erased from the world without anyone knowing about it. I was in the garden, weeping, seized with the kind of vertigo that ends in suicide. Alas! If at that moment an abyss or a sea had opened before me, I would've thrown myself into it. But I was wandering through flowers, across a lawn, beating my breast, pressing my temples, weeping—when suddenly I noticed Monsieur Lannois leaving the house, looking angry and upset, and heading toward the gate where he'd left his carriage. No matter how crude and cruel his help was, it was my last chance of rescue. I hurried toward him, and, carried away by my distress, I called out, "What! Are you leaving, sir?"

I was so desperate, and my tone was so affecting, that Monsieur Lannois took a step back and considered me for a moment in surprise. Then he resumed the fatal manner that crushed all hope, like a machine whose uncaring cogs grind up either the steel that's tossed into it or the poor wretch who's caught in its inexorable teeth. "Am I leaving, by God? What do you expect me to do with a bunch of honey-mouthed boors? Protestants and Bonapartists, in a word!"

"Sir, sir!" I cried. "Have you forgotten I'll die if you leave?"

"You? And who might you be?"

"I'm Henriette, sir."

"Oh, right, Henriette, Léon's beloved, his sweetheart, his princess! Thanks, my dear! Go ask your puffed-up parents for a husband!"

Pushing me aside, he walked on. I stopped him. "But sir, sir!" I said, putting my hands together pleadingly. "Léon loves me, and I love Léon!"

"Well, if each of you saves that up, it'll make a nice nest egg for when you start out in life together."

Those words fell like blows against my heart; like the ruthless fist of a luggage porter beating a woman, each blow knocked me down, and after each blow I rose again bruised and cried out again. Finally I, a poor distraught dying girl, looked at that man one last time—that man who exuded life and health and good cheer—and I took hold of his clothes and, clutching onto him with all my strength, I said in a quiet, desperate voice, "But sir, I've sinned, I'm going to be a mother, and…"

And I dropped at his feet. The man looked at me while I panted, then turning away, he began to whistle and to sing softly, "I didn't know that, a-rat-a-tat-tat, I didn't know that."

I fell against the ground face first, and so choked was I with awful sobbing that I hoped to die.

Meanwhile I'd been spotted from the house. My brother, my father, and Félix all ran out to put an end to that scene, which they assumed must be degrading for them as well as for me. When they reached us, Monsieur Lannois was still singing.

As Félix was picking me up, Monsieur Lannois cried out with a triumphant cackle, "Gently, gently! Be careful with the child!"

"Meaning what, sir?" asked my brother.

"Meaning," replied Monsieur Lannois, repeating his own horrible play on words, "When two youngsters love each other, the seed will sprout where it's planted."

I fell to the ground again, and then looming over me I saw the terrifying face of the unknown phantom who'd haunted my dreams. It was Félix who was staring at me. A frightful spasm crossed his features. Then, straightening up, he looked Monsieur Lannois in the face and said, "You're a despicable slanderer! And you've just uttered a shameless lie!"

Monsieur Lannois trembled and turned pale. That brutal man was a coward. "Well, my word—she's the one who told me."

"Can't you see the poor thing is insane?" replied Félix.

"I didn't know," said Monsieur Lannois. "I'll tell my son—that'll cure him of his foolish crush. A madwoman! Good, good, that'll make him see reason."

I made an effort to get up and cry out, because Monsieur Lannois looked convinced of the truth of Félix's words, but no doubt my behavior only reinforced the idea... I crawled on my knees, and I was going to speak, when my strength failed me, and...

Chapter VIII: A Partial Conclusion

Luizzi was fully absorbed as he read that account; nothing so far had distracted him, neither Henriette's movements nor the cries of her child—a poor sickly creature, no doubt born in that awful prison. With his eyes locked on the words, he was following the narrative with all the eagerness of a cook or a noble lady devouring a novel by Paul de Kock,[23] when suddenly the unfortunate prisoner grabbed her manuscript and hid it quicky in the spot from which she'd taken it. A moment later Luizzi saw one of the panels of carpeting that covered the wall facing him move, and then Félix entered, carrying a basket.

The sight of the captain filled Luizzi with anger. He was about to call out, when he remembered by what kind of superhuman miracle he was witnessing a scene that was taking place far away, and he settled down to watch with the close attention of a man who doesn't want to miss a single thing.

The captain took dishes out of the basket and set them on the table—and Luizzi now understood why Félix never dined with his family, and why every evening food was taken to him in his lodge. The silence had continued for a while after he entered, but he had about him an air of triumph just waiting for an excuse to explode. "Well, Henriette!" he said finally. "Will the result be the same every day?"

"Every day, you say? Are there still days and nights, sir? For me there's only one eternal light and darkness, one calamity that knows neither yesterday nor tomorrow. I suffer, as I suffered, as I will suffer. I think what I thought, what I'll always think. In living life, the night that ends and the day that comes can prompt a change of heart. But I have neither day nor night, neither morning nor evening. In my life it's always the same time, always the same suffering, always the same thought."

"Henriette," continued Félix, standing before her as if to find some emotion on that pale face frozen in pain, "Henriette, it isn't day or night that could prompt some change in a resolve as adamant as yours. Six years have passed since the day when, taking advantage of your having fainted, our family hid the shame of your weakness from all eyes in this prison—from which a single word would free you, and that word you have yet to speak."

"And that word I will never speak," replied Henriette. "The only hope in my life was Léon's love; the only hope in my tomb is still his love."

"And yet he betrayed that love," said Félix. "He married another woman."

---

[23] Paul de Kock (1793-1871): a French novelist who, though popular and widely read in the 1820s and 30s, had a reputation as low-brow and in poor taste.

"No, Félix, you're lying. Léon could never give his heart to another as long as I'm alive."

"Have you forgotten you're dead to him and to the whole world?"

"Then Léon didn't betray me, and you alone have wronged both of us."

"Fine, I'll take responsibility for that, since it thwarts your hopes."

"In any case, as I've already said, sir, I don't believe you: Léon isn't married. The man who was capable of throwing me still living into this tomb, the man who's made himself guiltier than murderers and poisoners, the man who's destined by law to face the scaffold—that man won't have hesitated at a few written lies, a few forged letters, to add one more misery to my lot."

"There are some things that can't be faked, Henriette, like a judgment issued by a court. Soon I'll bring you the one that sentences Léon Lannois to hard labor, and then we'll see if you can keep up this love you think is so virtuous."

"If what you're telling me were true," cried Henriette, "I'd die in this tomb and with that love. And if by some chance I were taken out of here, if I found that Léon was unfaithful and dishonorable, I'd love him even beside his new wife, I'd love him even wearing the shameful chains of a prisoner."

"Henriette," replied Félix gravely, with a fierce look around the room, "don't you understand the time for patience is almost over, and your fate can't be put off?"

"The time for patience has lasted no longer than the time for suffering, and if it's my fate to die without seeing daylight again, bring it about right now! Because if you're tired of torturing me, I'm tired of suffering, and no doubt death is the only way to put an end to that suffering."

"Henriette, listen carefully! One last time, I'm offering you life. I misled you when I said you're assumed to be dead. Monsieur Lannois senior remembered and repeated what I said to him: you were thought to be insane, and we took advantage of that belief to spread the rumor that we made you leave France. You're believed to be locked up in an asylum in America or England, and while you might never return, you might also come back tomorrow. But obviously, Henriette, between you and me there stands a crime so great I must ensure your silence by bonds you won't dare break. You'll reappear in the world, but only as my wife, and only by leaving me this child as a hostage against your vengeance."

"You're right, Félix. A great crime does stand between us. But that crime will be even greater than you think. I want you to carry out that crime completely. The torture I suffer is the most horrible that can be imagined—but I swear to you I wouldn't shorten it by a day, not even by an hour. You'll have to kill me, Félix, you'll have to stand before men and God with my blood on your hands. Because I too have misled you: I no longer believe in Léon's love, and it's no longer for his sake I have the courage of my despair. The courage I have is for vengeance. Don't count on a moment of weakness. Oh, I've often dreamt of surrendering myself to you, of misleading you to the point of making you think I loved you, so as to buy an hour of freedom—an hour during which I'd go denounce you to the justice of man. I've recoiled, not at the crime itself, but from the fear of not being able to fool you sufficiently. I'd rather count on the justice of heaven—I'd rather make you a murderer."

Félix had listened to Henriette with the ruthless expression of someone choosing the right spot to strike his victim so exactly as to prevent any struggling or crying out. Then he turned away, and went to the door by which he'd entered. Closing it, as if to bury even deeper in silence the secret of that tomb, he returned and said quietly, "Henriette, my crime will be no greater, my remorse will be no worse, but my fear will be less constant. There's a man here, a man I've caught snooping around this lodge, who's probably surprised no one can get inside. That man has to be able to come in here tomorrow, so he doesn't begin to suspect something. He has to come in here before any cry for help betrays the fact that these walls enclose a living being. For that, Henriette, you have to be mine or you have to die."

"Die! Die!" cried Henriette.

"Don't forget, wretch, my crime is shared by your whole family: at first they were unwitting accomplices, but then they became accomplices under duress; at first they allowed me to hide you here for a few days, but then they let weeks, months, years go by. My past crime has therefore become theirs. The crime I might still commit will be theirs too. Don't forget, it's not just me you'd be sending to the scaffold, it's your father, your mother, your brother!"

"Well then, so be it!" cried Henriette. "Let those who began to kill me at your hands finish killing me at your hands! I have no pity for them, as I have no pity for you: I'll send my father, my mother, my brother to the scaffold if I can! Don't you understand, you just revived my crushed hopes! There's a man here, a man you suspect, a man who might be prowling around this lodge now, a man who might hear me! Oh, if it's God's will, may he come, and may my cries break through the walls of this prison!... Help! Help!"

Henriette began to cry out so piercingly that Luizzi, carried away by the awful scene, took a step forward as if to respond to her desperate appeal.

Félix, terrified, ran after Henriette, shouting, "Silence, wretch, silence!"

At that moment Henriette reached the door leading out of that terrible prison. With a quick and desperate movement she opened it and ran out, shouting even louder than before. In one unspeakable moment of anger and fear, Félix grabbed a knife he'd set on the table, and he'd almost caught up with Henriette on the first steps of a narrow spiraling staircase when Luizzi—forgetting the supernatural illusion that enabled him to witness that scene—hurled himself at Félix. "Stop, villain!" he cried. "Stop!"

Just as he believed he was about to seize the captain, Luizzi tripped and fell, with a sensation of violent movement. Sharp pains accompanied the intense dizziness that followed his fall. Gradually he came to, and opened his eyes. Everything had vanished. He lay on the ground beneath his window, out of which

130

he'd jumped, carried away by an uncontrollable emotion. He tried to get up and run to the lodge where that bloody tragedy was taking place, but he didn't have the strength, and he fell back to the ground in a faint.

Chapter IX: A New Bargain

When Luizzi regained consciousness he found himself in bed in his room at Monsieur Buré's house. There was a lit lamp next to him, and a servant was seated by his bed. It took the sick man a long time to gather his memories together precisely enough to understand his current position. His fall, and the cause of that fall, returned to him gradually—or rather came to him in the form of a terrible nightmare he'd had—and the reality of the experience still wasn't clear in his mind. When he sat up to look around he felt he lacked all strength. Slowly he discovered, from the bandages encircling his arms, that they'd let his blood; remembering confusedly the height of the window from which he'd fallen, he was surprised he hadn't been killed, and he was afraid he'd broken a limb. He felt himself, moved around, flexed his joints, and happily found he'd suffered no fractures.

After that attention to himself, he went back to thinking about the terrible scene he'd witnessed, and whose appalling end he'd tried to stop. Immobilized in bed by pain and weakness, he tried to think of something he could make use of, or someone he could ask for information and give instructions to if necessary. That was when he noticed the servant seated by the bed. The rascal was taking very casually the orders he'd no doubt been given, to keep an eye on the patient's slightest movement, because he was fully focused on the newspaper he was reading while he filed his nails, which were remarkably beautiful. With plenty of time to study him, Luizzi couldn't place him as any of the servants in Monsieur Buré's household. He found the knave's impertinent, uncaring manner supremely displeasing. Besides, sick people are like women: they detest anything being the center of attention other than themselves.

Luizzi's anger was about to boil over when the supposed valet, who was reading his newspaper with a lighthearted little smile on his lips and whistling gently, began to murmur, "Very funny! Very funny!"

"Apparently you're reading something entertaining?" asked Luizzi angrily.

The valet gave Luizzi a sidelong look and winked. "Decide for yourself, baron," he replied. "*Yesterday a duel took place between Monsieur Dilois, the wool dealer, and young Monsieur Charles, his clerk. The latter, hit in the chest by a bullet, succumbed this morning. The cause of the duel was a mystery, till word of Madame Dilois's sudden departure explained it to everyone.*"

"Oh my God!" cried Luizzi, sitting up. "Charles has been killed?"

The servant went on with his reading. "*It's alleged that certain comments made by the wife of one our wealthiest lawyers are not unconnected to Monsieur Dilois's discovery of the intimate relations between his wife and young Charles.*"

132

"What? They wrote that in the newspaper?" cried Luizzi in astonishment.

"Oh, that's not all. Listen: *10 p.m. We've just learned of perhaps an even more awful incident. The Marquise du Val has just put an end to her life by jumping out of the highest window in her house. An extraordinary circumstance of that suicide, which connects it in some inexplicable way to the Dilois matter, arises from a note found in the marquise's hand. Here are a few lines from that note: 'That A is despicable. He didn't keep his promise. He talked... He's doomed me... And you!... Poor Lucy, how I pity you!... (Signed) Sophie Dilois.' Everyone wants to know who the villain referred to as A might be... Is it the initial of his first name or his family name? Besides that, everyone is surprised at the familiar form of address[24] used between two women who weren't of the same social sphere and who wouldn't even have known each other as schoolgirls, since the marquise never left her mother (the former Madame de Crancé) till her wedding day, and on the other hand Madame Dilois was raised by the charity of an old woman who took her in as a small child.*"

Luizzi's astonishment and despair kept him from moving or speaking for several minutes. Madame Dilois, Lucy du Val, Henriette, Madame Buré—all those women, like white ghosts, hovered and circled around his bed. "I killed her, and I let her be murdered," he said to himself, as if some superhuman voice were whispering to him the words he kept repeating. He stared around him wildly, unable to act, with no one in the world to whom he could confide what he'd learned. In despair he looked toward heaven with his hands joined in prayer, and cried, "Oh my God! My God! What should I do?"

No sooner had he spoken those words than the valet beside him reached over and flicked him hard on the fingertips. "What's all this? You're going over to the enemy in the hour of danger? That's unworthy of a gentleman or a Frenchman!"

"Oh, it's you, Satan."

"It's me."

"Who summoned you, slave?"

"You, when you asked me for Madame Dilois's story and for the marquise's."

"You refused to tell me them."

"No, I just put it off a week. The week has passed."

"So I've been here in bed..."

"For forty-eight hours."

"And Henriette?"

"You'll hear the ending of that story later, master."

"Did Félix kill the poor thing?"

---

[24] In her note to Lucy du Val, Sophie Dilois uses the informal "*tu.*"

"If he did, he had good reason for her sake and for his. They're both freed from torture—she especially, since deep down she was getting tired of the part she was still acting out of arrogance."

"How can you say that? She loved that Léon with a love the world will never know."

"Oh no, master. She didn't love Léon anymore, and the truth is, it was never exactly Léon she loved."

"Satan, Satan, you debase everything!"

"No, I explain everything. Henriette didn't love Léon; she loved the feeling of being in love. The young man she met showed up just in time to open her heart and give her an object for her dreams. He happened to be there in front of her at the moment her soul wanted to fling itself at something that would catch it. But Léon was far beneath the passion he'd inspired; if he'd been aware of it, he wouldn't have understood it. Léon has forgotten Henriette; he thinks she's dead. Léon is married, Léon has children he calls Nini and Lolo, Léon's getting fat, Léon has a potbelly, Léon has two small glasses of brandy after dinner, Léon has just made a fortune by declaring bankruptcy. If Henriette had been free to give her life to Léon, she'd have been more miserable than in that tomb—because in that tomb all she saw die was her hope for the happiness she believed awaited her in heaven, and if she'd lived out in the world she'd have seen the death both of the religion in her heart and of her faith in love."

Satan spoke those last words with a kind of bitterness. Luizzi, observing him carefully, as if he could penetrate the demon's infernal secrets just by looking, said, "You consider losing one's faith and religion a misfortune?"

"It would've been a misfortune for Henriette, is all I meant to say. I scorn general theories that lay out universal principles that don't apply to everyone any more than the same clothes fit everyone. It's like if you tried to judge the Marquise du Val by comparing her to Madame Buré, just because both of them slept with a man they'd met only hours before."

"Oh! Is it true Lucy's dead, and that whole story in the paper?..."

"It's all true."

"And I killed her!"

"The gun was loaded, you just pulled the trigger."

"So she was much to be pitied?"

"Ah, yes, that one was much to be pitied! And you'll decide for yourself."

"Not tonight. Later."

"No, baron, you're going to hear it. I warned you: once you've asked to be told a secret, I said, you'll have to endure it to the end."

"I know that, but I can make an exception to the rule."

"By giving me a few of the coins in that purse."

"A month off my life?"

"Oh, no! I wouldn't spare you the account of the harm you've done for as little as that!"

"You can see I'm not strong enough to hear it."

"I'll give you the strength."

"I'll hide my head in my hands and plug my ears."

"My voice will pass through your hands."

"Satan, shut up, I beg you. I'm not refusing to listen to those sad stories—but later!"

"And why would I care to tell them to you when time will have hardened your heart and scabbed over your remorse? It's while your heart still aches and your wounds still bleed that you have to hear them. Am I your slave that I must obey you? Don't you know, wretch, that he who hires a killer has sold himself to him? You, who bought the Devil—you belong to me."

As Satan spoke, his figure half-hidden in the shadows of the room regained something of its infernal majesty, and he smiled—that beautiful frightening smile that makes God pity him, because it reminds him of the greatness of the beautiful beloved angel he was forced to punish, and who left an eternal wound in the divine heart: the impossibility of ever forgiving him.

Luizzi's feeble, pathetic character was unable to withstand that smile. It penetrated his heart like a saw-toothed screw that tears as it turns. "Mercy!" he cried. "Mercy! I'll listen to you whenever you like."

"All right. I'll decide when. And what will you give me?"

"A month of my life."

The Devil began to laugh. "Are you sure you've got a month left in your purse, that you can offer it so boldly?"

"My God, my God!" cried Luizzi, hunting under his pillow for the precious storehouse of his life. When he found it, it felt almost empty. "Am I so near death?"

"Our bargain doesn't include the future, so I have no answer for you. It only covers the past, and I'll tell you about the past." In a casual tone Satan began, "That Marquise du Val you killed..."

"Enough! Enough!" cried Luizzi in a dying voice. His head spun with terrible vertigo, fever hammered in his brain, pale emaciated ghosts crowded around him—he was losing his mind. Going mad frightened him even more than death, and he cried, "Here, take it, and leave me alone!"

The Devil seized the purse and opened it. Changing his mind, Luizzi reached out to take it back—but he remained glued to the spot. He watched the Devil's fingers slip into the purse and take out one of the coins. At that moment the baron's heart felt as cold as ice, all life ceased, and he felt nothing more.

The clock rang three.

PORTRAITS

Chapter X: Back to Life: the Stagecoach

The clock rang three. Luizzi felt someone tugging on his legs, and a man's rough voice called out, "Come on, let's go, all aboard!"

Luizzi woke and found himself in an unknown room, a shabby room. He jumped out of bed, and realized he felt full of energy and health. He noticed his purse and his little bell on a side table—but where was he? And why had he been awakened? He opened the window. In a large courtyard horses were being hitched to a stagecoach. It was a cold night. He remembered what had come before, and above all he remembered his bargain. He knew he was no longer at Monsieur Buré's house, and no longer in Toulouse. It was still winter—but was it the same winter? Hadn't many winters already passed?

He picked up the cheap candle he'd just been brought, and his first concern was to look at himself in the little mirror hanging from a nail over the small walnut chest of drawers in the room in which he found himself. He hadn't changed much, except now he had sideburns. "How much time did the Devil take from me?" he wondered.

"Come on, all aboard, all aboard!" cried the same voice that had awakened him.

A man came in. "What! Not dressed yet! And you were in such a hurry to go! You've only got five minutes left! Too bad for you if you're not ready!"

Luizzi dressed automatically, with the intuition that there was a lacuna in his life he couldn't account for, but that he had to keep from showing his surprise. A servant came to fetch his overnight bag, and the baron followed him, resolving to pay attention and to act according to circumstances. The night was very dark, and as he climbed into the stagecoach he could see only that there were three other passengers: two men and a woman, who was wrapped up in enough shawls, bonnets, and veils to smother her.

At the period we're speaking of, it was still the terrible custom to make overnight stops while traveling, and sleeping was like meals are today: you were barely in bed before it was time to go again. Nowadays the experienced stagecoach traveler doesn't much care about interruptions intended to spoil his dinner; he eats fast and stuffs dessert into his pocket. In those days the stagecoach traveler knew how to get up without waking up, and he took along—to finish later in the coach—the sleep he'd begun at the inn.

That was lucky for Luizzi, because it gave him leisure to reflect on his situation. How much time had gone by? How was it that he, a wealthy man accustomed to the good things in life, now found himself traveling by public stagecoach? Where was he coming from? Where was he going? All those questions crowded into his thoughts so quickly that he decided to have them settled by the only person with the power to do so. He pulled out his little bell and rang it, and right away the Devil showed up next to him, in the form of a traveling salesman he thought he'd seen riding up on the outside seat. Luizzi recognized him by the peculiar sparkle in his eyes as they shone in the dark.

"Is that you?" he asked. "How much time has gone by?"

"Six weeks. You can see I didn't cheat you. I behaved like a clever businessman: I was honest the first time, so I can rob you blind the second time. I'm warning you, so be on your guard."

"And what kind of life did I live for those six weeks?"

"Your normal life."

"What did I do?"

"It's not my job to tell you your own story."

"What! So I'll have no memory of that time?"

"You can find out about it from people other than me."

"So who am I supposed to ask?"

"That's not my problem."

"At least tell me where I am."

"You're in the royal mail coach."

"Bound where?"

"To Paris."

"Where are we now?"

"Three miles from Cahors."

"Why am I traveling by stagecoach?"

"That's part of your story. I'm not going to tell you anything about it."

"Come on—how am I supposed to live without knowing my own past?"

"You can make one up."

"A past?"

"Nothing could be easier. Most men furnish themselves with one: you know that better than anyone. You remember that frisky, dirty-minded little actress you were stupid enough to fall sentimentally in love with? You had a hundred chances to be one of her thousand lovers, and you let them all go by, because you loved her from your heart. Once you'd gotten over that stupid infatuation, you realized your friends all thought you'd slept with her—they couldn't imagine you'd been stupid enough not to go that far. You looked at yourself, and you saw you were ridiculous: you realized that woman had been alone with you three times, and you'd had her by right... if not in fact. So you let it be believed—and then you said, and now you're convinced—you slept with her. You count her among your conquests, don't you?"

Luizzi felt rather hurt by that little lesson—especially since there was no arguing with the Devil about feelings, into which his infernal eye saw so clearly. So he merely replied, "Wouldn't I have had her if I'd wanted to?"

"Do you always get the woman you love? It doesn't happen even once out of every ten affairs. Women always give in to men who love them so little they don't tremble in front of them. I can't think of even two women who took as their lover the man who loved them. And then they complain about being deceived! It's always their fault. Women's way of defending themselves, by bawling or by acting majestic, only works on those who believe them. A woman who dared to give herself, rather than letting herself be taken, would be the greatest woman ever created, and the most loved too... though that's a fairly fine distinction."

"Mister Satan," said Luizzi, who felt a newfound confidence, "among the reasons that forced the Almighty to hurl you down into hell, might your habit of spinning theories have been near the top of the list?"

"Just between us," said the Devil cheerfully, "there were no other reasons."

"Well, I feel like doing what he did."

"And for the same reason, I assume?"

"Yes, because of your endless chatter."

"No—because I don't tell you what you want to hear. If I told you about the last six weeks of your life, you'd be all ears."

"So you're really going to tell me nothing about that?"

"Have you so little imagination you can't make up a past? The humblest peasant is cleverer than you are. Riding in this coach is a certain Monsieur de Mérin, a man of good family who was caught cheating at cards at the royal court in Berlin, for which he got three years in state prison. There he met a one-time French spy, who'd been in India on behalf of Napoleon. Mérin learned all of his new friend's stories; he knows, down to the smallest detail, all about his going out to India and his stay there and his return. And now he's going to reappear in Parisian society as having just arrived from Calcutta. Right now he's contemplating a little book, two volumes in octavo, to be entitled *Recollections of India*. I'm willing to bet you whatever you want that fifteen years from now that man will become a member of the Academy of Sciences (Geography division) and will be decorated for his travels."

"I get it, but that man isn't going to be confronted at any moment by a traveler just returned from Calcutta who'll say he's lying—whereas anytime I might find myself face to face with someone who knows me!"

"That's what's going on right now."

"What do you mean?"

"The people traveling with you know your name, and that fat man next to you is even a friend of yours."

"And no doubt they're going to talk to me about what we did yesterday?"

"That's more or less the story of human life: talk a lot about the past so you can fill the emptiness and cover up the inanity, talk a lot about the future so you can imagine it'll be marvelous, and don't focus at all on the present. It's what you all do, it's what you call living. And the best proof I can give you is that you lived through six weeks of your normal life and you feel like you were dead that whole time, because you have no memory of what you did."

"But what do you expect me to say to people who talk to me about it?" asked Luizzi, now seriously alarmed.

"Really, you're pitiful!"

"Come on, be generous, and if I have to I'll give you a few more days of my life to find out the story of my past."

"What a fool!"

"Who are you referring to?"

"Me—for not reckoning the full extent of human stupidity, and for realizing only now, my poor boy, that if I'd wanted to I could've had your whole life for nothing!"

Luizzi was beginning to get annoyed. He said nothing for a while: silence is a wise counselor. "By God," he thought to himself, "if these people use the life I can't remember to embarrass me, can't I embarrass them in return by knowing their lives, which they imagine to be so well hidden? I'll treat them the way a brave man treats an attacker: instead of parrying his blows, just keep showing him the tip of your sword, ready to stab him if he lunges. I already know enough about Monsieur de Mérin for him to need my discretion. Let's find out about the others, and then we'll see."

Luizzi had said none of that aloud, and yet the Devil replied, "Not badly reasoned for a human and a baron! Who do you want me to begin with?"

"The fat man snoring next to me, who you said is a friend of mine."

Chapter XI: The Prankster; the Former Lawyer

And, propping his legs on the seat across from them, the Devil replied:

This one's named Ganguernet. He's the kind of man everyone's met once in his life: short, fat, bouncy, with his hair cut short and standing up, a low forehead, gray eyes, a broad nose, fat cheeks, his neck sunk into his shoulders, his shoulders into his stomach, his stomach into his legs—rolling and tumbling along, laughing and shouting—one of those men who grab hold of your head from behind and say, "Guess who!"; who pull away your chair just as you're about to sit down; who take away your handkerchief when you need to blow your nose; one of those men, in short, who, if you look annoyed at them, answer with amazing nerve, "It was just a joke!"

This Monsieur Ganguernet is from Pamiers, where he's always lived, up to now. He knows every trick of his prankster trade. He's very good at tying a piece of meat to the bell rope of a carriage entrance, so all the stray dogs in town come jump for the meat and wake up the servants ten times a night. He's an expert in the art of taking down shop signs and switching them with each other. Once he took down a barber's sign, cut it in half, and added the last part to a neighbor's sign to produce *Monsieur Roblot rents carriages and toupees in the Parisian style.* Another day, or rather another night, he tore down the sign painted on wood over a marionette maker's shop and hung it over a drugstore, and the next morning everyone in Pamiers could read *Monsieur F—, apothecary at the fairgrounds theater.*

Monsieur Ganguernet is just as entertaining in the country as in town. He knows exactly how to put hairbrush bristles in a friend's sheets, so after fifteen minutes in bed he's driven mad by the prickling. He's marvelous at poking a hole in a room partition and threading through it a piece of string he's carefully tied to your covers, so when he hears you're asleep he can tug gently till all the covers end up in a heap on the floor. You wake up numb with cold, because Ganguernet only plays that trick on cold damp nights. You pull your covers back up and wrap them around you carefully and go innocently back to sleep... and Ganguernet tugs on his string again, leaving you naked again, and frozen again; and when you give way to cursing all alone, he calls out through the hole, "It was just a joke!"

If Ganguernet meets a real fool, someone who's just asking to be tricked, while the man's asleep Ganguernet takes his pants and shirt and makes them smaller—doing all the sewing himself—then he wakes up the victim and tells him to get dressed so they can go hunting. The poor fellow tries to put on his pants and can't get into them. "Good God!" cries Ganguernet. "What's wrong with you? Did you swell up?"—"Who, me?"—"It's incredible!"—"You really think...?"—"Maybe I'm mistaken, but get dressed and we'll go outside, and everyone will agree with me. Oh, there's no doubt about it, you've swollen up! It's a sudden attack of dropsy!" And that'll keep going as long as Ganguernet hasn't delivered his famous line, "It was just a joke!"

Among his pranks is one I find revolting. He played it on a man whom people considered brave and who was terribly fearful. At night the man felt something cold and slimy down at the foot of his bed. He nudged it with his foot. It was something long and cylindrical. He put his hand on it: a coiled-up snake! He leapt out of bed, shouting with horror and disgust—and Ganguernet showed up, crying "It was just a joke!" The man had been frightened by an eel skin stuffed with wet bran. He was furious and wanted to thrash Ganguernet. Ganguernet poured an enormous pot of water over his head and ran away, laughing, "It was just a joke!" The owners of the house came running at all the noise, and calmed the victim down by explaining how Ganguernet was a delightful fellow, the stouthearted life of the party, and you couldn't do without him or you'd die of boredom, especially in the country.

Watch out for him, baron: he's one of those unbearable creatures who wander through other people's lives like a dog through a game of skittles, destroying with their paws every arrangement intended for your happiness or your sorrow. They're more unbearable and harder to get rid of than that dog, and they're on the lookout for all of your feelings and all the plans you've made, to upset them by a word or a prank. Those creatures are all the more to be feared because they expose you to the laughter of both your cruelest enemies and your dearest friends—which are equally enjoyable—and because almost always they make you an accomplice, through the pleasure you get from the pranks they play on others. As a result, when the prank is aimed at you, you're treated with exactly the same lack of pity you felt for others, and you're left all by yourself to look ridiculous for getting angry—if it's even possible to get angry.

Among men of that type there are a few whose vulgarity costs them their audience in the end; they tend to stick to a repertoire of well-known jokes. Poking your head through a piece of foot-tracing paper to ask the cobbler for the address of the finance minister or the archbishop; stretching a rope across a staircase to make people coming down "backslide"—that's the word for it; waking a lawyer in the middle of the night to send him urgently to draw up a deathbed will for a client of his who's perfectly healthy; and a thousand other practical jokes of the same kind... That's the bottom of the barrel for a prankster, as Ganguernet knows better than anyone. But he thought up a few tricks of his own, and they're the ones that gave him his stupendous reputation.

The only really witty prank he ever pulled happened at a country house where there were quite a lot of people. Among the ladies present, Ganguernet had his eye on a woman of about thirty, very preoccupied with Parisian fashions, who preferred the pale looks of some handsome young ninny to Ganguernet's beet-red face. Ganguernet gained nothing by making a fool of the fellow in the lady's presence: she took his awkwardness for poetical absentmindedness and his gullibility for admirable trust in others. One evening everyone retired after she'd stoutly stuck up for the pale young man—a defense Ganguernet tolerated with a patience that boded ill. Half an hour later the house rang with piercing cries of "Fire! Fire!" from the downstairs parlor. They all came running, men and women, half-dressed or half-undressed, as you prefer. They piled into the parlor, candlesticks in hand, and found Ganguernet sprawled in a chair. Making no answer to all their questions, he took the pale young man by the hand and led him to the pretty lady, to whom he said, "May I introduce to you the most poetical soul in all the company—in a cotton nightcap." Everyone burst out laughing, and the lady never forgave either Ganguernet or the cotton nightcap.

But most of Ganguernet's jokes weren't intended for revenge; his guiding principle was just to get a laugh. Before I come to the anecdote that'll show you the man in his true self, I want to tell you about a couple of his qualities he's proudest of. He was living in Pamiers, across from a venerable bourgeois couple who lived alone in a small house they owned. Those dignified persons were in the habit of having Sunday dinner and a round of piquet with a relative of theirs, who lived some distance away. They had a little rum punch, or a little fried millet dusted with brown sugar, and they washed it all down with Blanquette de Limoux sparkling wine, so that around eleven the couple went home singing and stumbling.

One fatal Sunday as they were staggering home they reached their next-door neighbor's house and went another ten paces, the distance between his front door and theirs. The husband felt in his pockets for his key and found it. He felt for the lock... no more lock. "Where's the lock?" he cried.

"You drank too much Blanquette, Monsieur Larquet!" said his wife. (His name was Larquet.) "You're looking for the lock, but we're still in front of the neighbor's wall."

"True!" said Monsieur Larquet. "Let's go a few steps further."

They walked on, but this time they went too far, because having first recognized the front door of the neighbor to their right, now they recognized the front door of the neighbor to their left. Their door stood between those two doors. They turned back, feeling their way along the wall, till they reached another door: that of their neighbor to the right. The two good people began to think they'd lost their minds, that they were completely drunk. They began their search again, and went from the right-hand neighbor to the left-hand neighbor: they could find those two doors—just not their own. Their door had vanished: who could've taken away their front door? They began to panic, wondering if they were going mad. Concerned about the ridicule they'd face as respectable bourgeois who couldn't find their own front door, they spent an hour feeling, examining, measuring... but there was no door, just an unfamiliar wall, an implacable wall, a hopeless wall. Finally they gave way completely to panic and began to shout and call for help.

It turned out their door had been meticulously bricked up and plastered over. When everyone asked who could've played such a trick on those worthy bourgeois, Ganguernet—standing at the upstairs window from which he and a few of his foolish friends had witnessed the devastation of Monsieur and Madame Larquet—shouted out to the crowd his inevitable catchphrase, "It was just a joke!"

"But it's going to make them fall ill!"

"Bah!" he said, and repeated, "It was just a joke!"

The local Crown magistrate was asked to dampen Ganguernet's appetite for jokes. It cost him a couple of days in prison, in spite of his skillful defense, which consisted entirely of saying over and over, "Your Honor, it was just a joke!"

Though he has his vanity, Ganguernet doesn't boast about all of his pranks; and there's one he's always denied—given that whoever did it is at risk of having his ears cut off if he's found out. That one was prompted by an insult to his personal dignity from a certain aristocratic salon—no less a salon than that of an elderly woman of great nobility, who received the highest society in town. Among other customs of her ancient lineage, she maintained (1) that of not letting lowborn men like Ganguernet into her circle, and (2) that of going about in a sedan chair with porters. She'd attended a ball thrown by the Deputy Commissioner; Ganguernet had been there too. She left around midnight, in pouring rain, riding in her sedan chair. As the chair was passing under one of those downspouts that empty the waters of the heavens onto the street in a long loud torrent, two or three whistle calls rang out in different directions, and four men appeared. The porters fled, leaving the sedan chair behind. Just when the noble lady thought she was about to be murdered, she felt a horrible cold wetness on her head instead. The roof of the sedan chair had vanished as if by magic, and the downspout was emptying a cascade of rain into the seating compartment— and she was unable to open the door. Struggling, she stood up on her seat, and there, like the Devil trapped in a pulpit, she began to call down divine wrath on the murderers who'd made her take such a cruel shower, and who responded to her curses only with humble bowing. The most outrageous part was that the lady was wearing powder, and the pranksters had umbrellas.

In Pamiers, surrounded by dead or brutish minds, for ten years Ganguernet has been considered the merriest, the friendliest, the funniest person in his circle. There are just a few who feel a kind of contempt for him, and a few more who are afraid of him. The rigid smile locked on his red lips is painful to look at; his implacable joviality in the face of all the vicissitudes of life must be disturbing, like the unchanging appearance of some hideous ghost; the disgusting phrase he throws out as a moral at the end of every prank—"It was just a joke!"—can sound as gloomy as the Trappist's greeting: "Brother, we must die!" He was bound to leave some disaster behind him in the course of his life; there was bound to be someone who died because Ganguernet felt like putting him through the fatal ringer of his amusement; the day was bound to come when his famous saying would be chiseled on someone's headstone: *It was just a joke!*

Three weeks ago, Monsieur Ernest de B— invited a few friends for a big hunting party. Ganguernet was included. As the guests arrived, Ernest was finishing a letter; he sealed it and set it on the mantelpiece. Curious, Ganguernet picked it up and read the address. "Well, well, you're writing to your sister-in-law?"

"Yes," said Ernest carelessly, "I'm letting her know we'll be at her place around seven this evening, asking for dinner. There are fifteen of us, I believe. We'd be at risk of dining poorly if she isn't warned well in advance."

Ernest rang for a servant and gave him the letter; no one noticed that Ganguernet disappeared along with the servant. They all set off. During the hunt, Ganguernet and one of the hunters went up one side of the valley, while their friends were beating the other side.

"We'll have a good laugh tonight," Ganguernet told his companion.

"Why's that?"

"Get this—I gave the servant a louis not to deliver the letter to that address."

"Did you take the letter?"

"No, by God! I told the servant it was a prank, and he should deliver the letter to the husband. He's presiding as magistrate at court right now. When he finds out there'll be fifteen hungry fellows at his house for dinner tonight, he'll be boiling mad. He's as miserly as Harpagon,[25] and the idea that we're going to pillage his wine cellar and his poultry yard will put him in such a foul mood, he's liable to sentence ten innocent men so he can get back to the country in time to stop the looting."

"That sounds like a pretty mean trick to me."

"Bah! It's just a joke! Anyway, the funniest part will be when we get there. The others will be dying of hunger and thirst, and they'll reach the house convinced they'll find an excellent meal there. But no! Absolutely nothing!"

"And you think that's all right with me, any more than it'll be for them?" replied the young man Ganguernet had chosen as his confidant. "Aren't you in fact the number one victim of your own joke?"

"No, no! I've got cold chicken and a bottle of Bordeaux here, and I'll split it with you."

"No, thanks! I'd rather go find Ernest and warn him."

"Oh my God!" cried Ganguernet. "I can't even share a joke with you!"

The young man went off to find his friends, to ask them where Ernest was. They told him he'd gone on in the direction of his sister-in-law's house. The

---

[25] Harpagon: the title character in Molière's play *L'Avare* ("The Miser," 1668).

young man headed that way, thinking to warn Madame de B— of Ganguernet's prank. At a bend in the path he saw Ernest going toward the house. He picked up his pace to catch him, and went fast enough to get there almost at the same time. But Ernest had already gone through the outside gate when the young hunter arrived. As he was about to follow, the gate slammed violently, followed almost immediately by a gunshot. Then a voice cried, "Well then, since I missed you, draw and defend yourself!"

The young man ran to a grating at eye level that opened onto the courtyard, and there he witnessed a dreadful sight: the husband, sword in hand, was attacking Ernest with desperate rage. "Oh, so you love her and she loves you!" he cried in a hoarse, furious voice. "Oh, so you love her and she loves you! Well, you first and then her!"

The letter delivered to the magistrate had revealed to him a secret that had remained hidden for more than four years; before imposing retribution for offenses against society he'd hurried home to avenge the injury against himself. In vain Ernest's friend outside the grating called out, appealing to them as brothers: with blind fury Monsieur de B— drove Ernest from one side of the courtyard to the other. Suddenly a window opened, and Madame de B— appeared, pale and disheveled.

"Léonie!" cried Ernest. "Go away!"

"No, she should stay," said the husband. "She's locked in—don't worry, she won't come separate us." And he threw himself once more on his brother with such violence that sparks leapt from their swords.

"I'm the one who should die!" cried Madame de B—. "Kill me! Kill me!"

The young man who was the unhappy witness to that terrible scene mingled his cries with those of Madame de B—. He called, he shook the grating, he was about to climb over the wall, when she—despairing, confused, mad, distraught—threw herself out the window and fell between her lover and her husband. The latter, whom fury had robbed of his wits, turned his sword against her. But Ernest parried the blow; and now, losing all fear on his side, he cried, "Oh, so you want to kill her? Well then, defend yourself!" And he in turn attacked his brother with unparalleled fury.

At that point no one could do anything to separate them: they were locked in the courtyard, and poor Madame de B— had broken her leg in her fall. It was an awful battle. Both brothers were already bleeding, and that seemed to do nothing but add to their fury.

Meanwhile the young hunter had reached the top of the wall, and he was about to jump down into the courtyard when he saw a few of his friends hurrying toward the house. Ganguernet was in the lead, and as he drew near he called out, "You've been screaming like a man being skinned alive—we've heard you for the last quarter league![26] What's going on?"

When he saw Ganguernet the young man ran to him, grabbed him by the throat, and pushed him furiously against the grating, crying, "Look! Just a joke, sir, just a joke!"

Monsieur de B——, who'd been run through by a sword thrust, lay motionless next to his wife.

"And how did that fatal encounter end?" asked Luizzi.

"Monsieur de B— died, Ernest fled forever, and Madame de B— took poison the day after that terrible duel."

As the Devil said those words, Ganguernet stirred and murmured, "It was just a joke!"

"This man's a despicable wretch!" said Luizzi. "How is it possible anyone still speaks to him?"

"Bah! Who knows about it?"

"At the very least the young hunter Ganguernet told about his prank."

"But," replied the Devil dryly, "what if that young hunter had done something just as horrible as Ganguernet? What if he'd ruined one woman and driven another to her death by a cowardly lie? And what if Ganguernet by chance finds himself able to add, to the initial letter used in a note written by a certain Madame Dilois, the rest of the letters that spell out the name of the cheerful slanderer responsible for those crimes? Then the young hunter will keep his mouth shut and will offer his friendship to that despicable wretch."

"What!" cried Luizzi. "That witness…"

"… Was you, baron. You, who've kept your mouth shut."

Luizzi forgot everything he'd just been told. Only one thing struck him, and he cried out happily, "You see? You're telling me about my own past life!"

"As long as it's connected to other people's, no problem."

"Ah!" said the baron, delighted—for he hoped to learn about himself by means of hearing about other people. "In that case, who's that skinny, anxious-looking man who keeps turning over and muttering, 'Yes, dear'?"

"That man's basically a cretin, and he has nothing to do with you."

"We'll see about that," said Luizzi, who didn't trust the Devil.

"As you wish, but it's your own fault if it ends badly for you."

"Don't worry, I won't throw myself out the stagecoach door the way I jumped out the window at the Buré foundry."

"Poor fool who thinks that, because he's prepared for one kind danger, there can't be other kinds that'll get him! You're like someone who, after hitting

---

[26] A quarter league is about a kilometer, though the metric term was not yet in common use at the time Soulié was writing.

his head while out walking, always walks looking up and thinks he's safe, and in his foolish confidence he falls into a hole he didn't see."

"Oh, well! I'll risk it."

"The first risk, baron, is to listen to me spinning theories."

"You can't skip it?"

"Come now, friend! Didn't you threaten to publish my memoirs? And do you really think the Devil is so principled a writer that he won't wallow like everybody else in general remarks and metaphysical pronouncements and moralizing digressions?"

"Go right ahead. It's a dark night, and I'm as wide awake as a man who's been asleep for six weeks. I'm listening."

And this is what the Devil told him:

It was back when the animals could talk, as La Fontaine put it; it was back in an even more extraordinary time—when young men with brains became lawyers. Those days are over. It was found that even moderate practice in the law led straight to obesity and moral laxity, and zealous application led to imbecility. Consequently men who wanted to be spared intellectual suicide fled that dangerous profession. The law has yet to be subjected to chemical analysis, so I can't say by what pernicious essence it achieves those unpleasant results, but the results are no less real. If you take the trouble to look around you, you'll see what I'm saying is no paradox.

The lawyer, once he's a lawyer, is a being apart. His studies are a soil in which he takes root and grows, like those animal-vegetable intermediates that natural science classifies arbitrarily among the lichens or the crustaceans. There's no profession that doesn't leave its practitioners some brain power to devote to the life of the mind: we've all known barristers,[27] doctors, bakers, and knife-grinders who have ideas about literary style and poetry; you can find moneylenders who love the arts, and there are even stockbrokers who understand painting and music and literature and can discuss them with insight. But I defy you to show me a fifty-year-old lawyer who has a single idea.

I don't mean to take on the subject of intimacy, but is there a class of men in the world more fertile than lawyers in producing cuckolds? It arises from subtle moral issues relating to the condition of women that I don't need to explain further to you. But it's easy to see that, in a profession that almost always leads to wealth, even for mediocrities, and that brings the practitioner into contact with people of every social class, it would be almost impossible for a wife not to find—either above or below her—a man who'll distract her from her boredom

---

[27] The Devil (or Soulié) makes a distinction between "barristers" who appear in court and "solicitors" who draw up contracts and wills—a distinction customary in France and Britain but not in the US, where the term "lawyer" covers both senses. The Devil's attack is aimed at solicitors.

with her husband. A man who's shut away in his office from eight in the morning till eight at night, and who leaves his wife without occupation and without money worries, is very likely to be cuckolded—because his wife is very likely to be idle and bored and to fall into wrongdoing. The wife of a stock market speculator, who gambles his entire fortune with every investment, can take some interest in that turbulent life; she can follow the success or failure of a deal on which her position and her circumstances depend. But a lawyer's wife! Money comes to her in her sleep, like it does to her husband, and she's got all the long days to chew her way through. When the chewing gets tiring, she finds someone to help her do it—it's perfectly natural!

"Mister Satan is delivering more than he promised," said Luizzi. "He warned me he'd be dull, but actually I find him stupefyingly tedious."

"That just shows it's impossible to improve humankind."

"How so?"

"Because people close their eyes the moment you try to show them why humanity is getting stupider."

"And what's the cretinism of a lawyer to me?"

"You'll see. Any man who's rich, or who's likely to inherit or get married, has to be interested in lawyers, those machines for making wills and contracts."

Luizzi deduced that the lawyer he was going to hear about would, like Ganguernet, be connected to his own life. He mustered his patience, and the Devil went on:

The moral atrophy of a lawyer needs time to reach its ultimate stage. So the head legal clerk is almost always a warm-blooded man, living in a world of fashionable women and card games and loud suppers. The lawyer in his thirties still cuts a certain worldly figure: he gambles for high stakes, he pays for a private loge at the theater, he holds dinners, he treats very young women to old-fashioned flirtatious remarks, he allows himself a few escapades with the least expensive of the pretty girls who are the subject of scandal for their wit or beauty. When he's past forty the lawyer falls back on whist, he dines alone, he's bored by the theater, he likes the countryside, for exercise he goes out on foot with an umbrella, he gives furniture to his doorman's daughter, he has his old hats reblocked, and he puts in for the Legion of Honor. At fifty cretinism sets in; at sixty it's absolute. The law is an unhealthy profession, for which I invite scientists to find a cure—something to add to the announcement of a prize for the discovery of a way to protect the health of tin-plate or gold-plate artisans.

Now, there was once in Toulouse a lawyer by the name of Monsieur Litois. He's not dead, but he is no more—meaning he no longer exists, though he's sixty-five and has an income of sixty thousand livres and has been practicing law for thirty years. Monsieur Litois is a human contract. If you invite him to dinner, he replies, "I've contracted another engagement." When he goes to Herbola's coffee shop to pick up a few delicacies, he says, "I wish to make acquisition of that partridge or that grouse; I'll take that boar's head with all of its dependencies; bring me that trout and all it comprises." He's so enamored of his profession that to become a lawyer, to be a lawyer, to have been a lawyer, has always seemed to him the pinnacle of human ambition, happiness, and reward.

So it won't surprise you to hear that Monsieur Litois practiced law for a very long time. But kidney problems—from too loyal an attachment to his Morocco leather armchair—told him it was time to stand up and walk around and leave the law. Twelve years ago he decided to sell his practice. He cast an eye on his head clerk, Monsieur Eugène Faynal, a bachelor of twenty-eight who was witty, charming, cheerful, and in love. Monsieur Litois knew all of his faults, but Eugène had no money, and that's why he chose him: to sell his practice to a wealthy man who'd pay him in shiny cash down would mean separating himself violently from his past life, casting into the arms of another man his beloved of thirty years, his ward, his ever-youthful, ever-faithful mistress. Monsieur Litois didn't have the courage.

He reasoned that a young man who owed him two hundred thousand francs would be much more at his mercy, and that he'd be able to slip furtively into the office a few more times to buzz from flower to flower again like a bee in the early morning, to peck at a sale contract like a songbird pecking at a piece of fruit, to brush a marriage contract with his quill pen like a butterfly brushing a rose, and to watch over his ward—that beloved priceless creature who, as Monsieur Litois put it, was becoming his daughter after having been his wife.

Eugène Faynal was delighted by Monsieur Litois's offer. The latter knew Eugène could pay off his debt by getting married; and, to keep the young man from worrying, he said he had a woman client in a small town near Toulouse whom he counted on providing to his successor, along with her dowry of three hundred thousand livres. It was such an opportunity to make his fortune that Eugène accepted sight unseen. In that first flight of enthusiasm, he even agreed to a few conditions whose consequences he didn't fully think through.

When Monsieur Litois made a deal, he liked to tie it up and leave no pending risks. Since Eugène might die before he married, his employer insured his life for two hundred thousand francs, so the law practice would be paid for even if Eugène died—leaving to the young man's heirs the burden of selling it again. Eugène was young and hot-headed, he enjoyed the world and all of its pleasures, and it was in part to satisfy his appetites that he so carelessly took a chance at making his fortune. Above all, however, he was an honest man, and his first priority was to pay his debt to Monsieur Litois. The latter had drawn up a payment schedule with the understanding that the young man had to build a reputation before he could be presented as a suitable match for such a fine dowry.

The first year, Eugène had to put up with no more than the nuisance of his former employer's visits. What was surprising was that Monsieur Litois—who in the past had done nothing without seeking the advice of his head clerk—now presumed to second-guess everything Eugène did as a lawyer. But those little annoyances didn't bother Eugène much, since he was rich and respected and happy.

Happy indeed! He was in love with a beautiful, amiable woman whose contract for the maintenance of separate property he'd handled. That woman had worldly sense, she'd been unhappy in her marriage, and she made good use of her characteristic pallor to leave an impression of deep sadness; she simpered languidly while growling her r's in the back of her throat; she dressed splendidly, and she adored Monsieur de Chateaubriand.[28] Professionally speaking, she was an ideal conquest for Eugène. He didn't mention it to anyone, but everybody knew about it. The word spread so far that her husband finally heard about it. He'd agreed to the separation of property with his wife; but since they hadn't separated their names, he didn't enjoy having his name bandied about in an unflattering way. He waited for an opportunity; and one day, when his wife and Eugène were leaving the theater together, the husband struck the lawyer in front of two hundred people. A rencounter was arranged for the next day.

At eight the next morning Eugène was at home with his witnesses, getting ready to go half a league out of town, when Monsieur Litois burst in, highly indignant. Before anyone had even understood who could be intruding like that without being announced, Monsieur Litois had leaped at Eugène's throat and grabbed him by the collar, crying, "You won't go! You won't go!"

"Sir!" said Eugène, breaking free. "What are you talking about?"

"I'm talking about keeping you a respectable man!"

"Sir! Meaning?"

"Meaning you're not going to fight a duel."

"I was insulted!"

"Could be."

"And I insulted my adversary."

"Could be."

"He's waiting for me, and I'm itching to meet him."

"Could be."

"And one of us will remain there."

"That cannot be."

"That's what we'll find out."

"No. You won't go!" cried the retired lawyer, standing furiously between Eugène and the door.

---

[28] François-René, Vicomte de Chateaubriand (1768-1848): a writer, politician, diplomat, and historian, preeminent in French letters and culture in the early nineteenth century. His royalist, Catholic, conservative, and yet proto-Romantic views allow him to serve here as a shorthand for good taste and a sign that the lady has safe, correct politics.

150

Eugène felt an urge to pick the old man up by the shoulders and toss him aside, but he restrained himself. "Come now, Monsieur Litois," he said, "be reasonable! Your concern for me is going too far: I'm not a dead man yet!"

"That's too bad!"

"What do you mean, too bad?"

"Yes, sir, too bad. Because if you were already dead you couldn't cheat me by going off to duel!"

"Sir!"

"Stop shouting, Eugène, and read this."

"What's that, my life insurance policy?"

"Read it, there, at the bottom of the page."

Eugène read: *The company will not be liable to pay the insured amount if the insured party dies outside European territory or if he is killed in a duel.*

"Or if he's killed in a duel! You see that, Eugène? Ergo, you will not fight a duel, unless you have two hundred thousand francs in good hard cash to pay me."

Flummoxed, humiliated, Eugène didn't know what to say. Turning to one of his witnesses, he said, "Please go beg my adversary to put it off till tomorrow."

"No more tomorrow than today!" interrupted Monsieur Litois. "I've alerted the police, and you'll be followed."

"Sir, you're dishonoring me!"

"You're trying to ruin me!"

"But sir, I wouldn't take your practice to the grave with me!"

"I no longer have a practice, I have a debtor for two hundred thousand francs! How do I know what's become of my practice in your hands? A lawyer who keeps a mistress in society, a lawyer who fights duels—who's ever seen such a thing? I wouldn't pay thirty thousand francs for your practice. But you owe me two hundred thousand for it, and your physical person is my guarantee. To risk your person is to dispose of what doesn't belong to you, it's a violation of fiduciary trust, it's committing a fraud, and I'll let these gentlemen be the judges of it."

"My word!" said one of the witnesses. "We'll come back when this argument's been settled."

Eugène couldn't get rid of Monsieur Litois. The hour for the rencounter had come and gone. In vain the young man had written to the husband to ask him for another rencounter: having learned what had kept Eugène away, his adversary refused, saying a man who misses that kind of appointment leaves it in doubt whether he'll miss a second one. Then, being a man of wit, and feeling sure he'd be better avenged using mockery than using a pistol, the husband spread the story of the lawyer trying to negotiate his freedom with his former employer. It was a highly comical scene, with the young man making one offer after another to the old man: "Ten thousand francs, and let me go!"... "No!"...

"Twenty thousand!"... "No!"... "Thirty thousand!"... "Thirty thousand times no! Two hundred thousand francs, or nothing."

The story made a lot of noise around Toulouse, and it didn't show Eugène to be a man of the world. Even his standing as a lawyer was noticeably damaged. A young man who didn't know how to fight either for himself or for the woman who loved him was a man without dignity. He lost clients, through their wives, either openly or in some veiled way. Monsieur Litois grew seriously alarmed at Eugène's loss of professional reputation, and did everything he could to stop it. But his first care was to make sure he got paid for his practice. He announced to his successor that the marriageable client he'd promised was arriving in two months.

Since his misadventure, since he could no longer show his face in the most select circles, Eugène had made a habit of socializing with a few of his humbler clients. On one of those visits he'd met a girl of extraordinary beauty and perfect modesty, with a gentle and yielding nature—an angel. In Eugène she saw only a gracious young man with elegant manners and polite wit and a good heart. She loved him, they loved each other, and Eugène—who in his transports of love forgot about his cruel debt—swore to marry her. She believed him, and then poor Sophie...

But that's another story, and it doesn't suit me to let you hear it yet. Coming back to Eugène Faynal... The day after that sacred promise, Eugène was invited to Monsieur Litois's for dinner. The poor fellow went there unsuspecting. No sooner had he arrived than his former employer led him mysteriously into his study and announced that he was about to meet his future bride.

Eugène turned pale. "I had no idea."

"What! You didn't know? I told you two months ago!"

"But..."

"What do you mean, but!... Have you forgotten your first payment of a hundred thousand francs is due, and if by a week from now your marriage contract hasn't been settled and payment made, I'm going to denounce you to the bar association?"

"Sir, that's inhumane!"

"What do you mean, inhumane? I'm handing you a wife who'll bring you a dowry of three hundred thousand francs!... You must be out of your mind!"

Eugène reflected that he might indeed be out of his mind, from a business point of view, and he let himself be led to the parlor. He entered, he looked, he saw—surprise!—a pretty, charming, gracious girl. In spite of being in love, he trembled with soft hope.

"Where's your aunt?" asked Monsieur Litois.

"Here I am!" answered a harsh voice out of a bony face.

"Mademoiselle Dambon, may I present our bridegroom."

Eugène bowed respectfully.

"Leave us, miss," said the old lawyer to the beautiful girl. "We have to talk business."

Eugène's eyes followed her amorously, and she laughed in his face. He turned his attention to the aunt.

"Come on, Eugène," said Monsieur Litois, "kiss the hand of your intended."

Ethically speaking, Eugène fell flat on his back, and if in fact his legs kept him vertical it was only out of habit, because he felt like he was at the epicenter of an earthquake. His aged prospective bride understood the effect she'd had on him, but she was pleased with him, and she assumed once he was hers she'd get what she wanted, willingly or not. She therefore gave Eugène time to recover, and soon she was talking with such animation and in such detail about her farms, her vineyards, her orchards that the young lawyer—already corrupted in spots by the practice of the law—began to find her less disfigured by rosacea, less bony, almost attractive.

Even so, the battle between his promise and his necessity was long fought. He was miserable enough to talk about it with a friend the day before the wedding. Plenty of lawyers have married ugly old maids for their dowries, but people know they've gone to a lot of trouble to do so, and they're considered clever. Eugène's marriage was considered an act of treachery. Plus which, ridicule had already cut into him once, and the wounds made by that dangerous weapon never heal; they only need to be brushed by another blow to become fatally infected.

The young lawyer and his old maid wife, as she was called, were a universal laughingstock. In fact Madame Eugène Faynal retained her old maid's primness, stiffness, and prudishness. To that misery Eugène added another, becoming father to twin boys; clearly women can make up for lost time. The twins were another cause for ridicule. The lady soon realized she was an object of curiosity who was invited to dinner just to hear her talk about her beloved twins. She accused her husband of being too weak to make people respect her. Eugène's life became an endless quarrel. His wife's bitterness broke out on her face as erysipelas, and she went from ugly to revolting. Within eighteen months of his marriage, Eugène's house had become a hell.

At that point, to escape, he spent all his time at his office, working. But by then it was too late—his clients had deserted his practice and taken their business elsewhere. He took a careful look at his accounts and saw that paying off the two hundred thousand francs plus interest had left only eighty thousand francs of the dowry; those eighty thousand francs had gone partly toward upkeep of their house, which the income from his law practice couldn't cover. He had to retrench significantly or renege on certain payments. Accepting neither the former humiliation nor the latter shame, Eugène decided to sell his practice. On the first of March, 1815, he was ready to sell for three hundred and fifty thousand francs; he delayed signing the contract for a week; a year later he sold the practice for fifty thousand francs.[29]

Monsieur Faynal now lives in Saint Gaudens, with a forty-eight-year-old wife, four children, and an income of twenty-two hundred livres. He's taken up the cultivation of roses. He wears calfskin shoes from Orléans, with cotton spats. He plays Boston whist for a penny a trick, and he plays the clarinet. Having once been a lawyer, he still has some spirit and a few ideas: he feels his misfortune and finds himself ridiculous. He's the one asleep across from you.

"And what's that man to me," said Luizzi, "that you've told me the troubles of his life at such length?"

"What!" cried the Devil. "You don't understand how a lawyer might be connected to your life?"

"If you're neither selling nor buying nor getting married—a double-edged contract in which you sell your name without buying happiness…"

"Bad! Very bad!"

"Excuse me?"

"Go on, I don't repeat myself."

"Well then, if you're not doing any of those things, you don't have much reason to get involved with a lawyer."

"Didn't you have a reason to get involved with Monsieur Barnet?"

"Of course, but Monsieur Barnet was my lawyer."

"But didn't you want to consult him because he was someone else's lawyer?"

"Well, yes, because he was the Marquis du Val's lawyer. What of it?"

"What of it? You poor boy, don't you understand? And you want to go live in Paris, where you have to guess at pretty much everything! Because that's a place where people say almost nothing about hidden motives, since they assume everyone understands them."

"You're too subtle for me, Satan."

"Well then, baron, it's almost guaranteed that in drawing up a marriage contract two lawyers will be involved: that of the groom's family and that of the bride's."

"Probably so."

"What was Monsieur Barnet?"

---

[29] Napoleon escaped from exile on Elba on March 1, 1815, and arrived in Paris on March 20 to reclaim his throne—which he lost again at Waterloo on June 18, ending the period known as the Hundred Days. The turmoil and instability of that time devastated the value of property, and of assets like a law practice. Soulié's readers in the 1830s would've understood just from his mention of the date that Eugène would never again see an offer as high as he'd received just before Napoleon's escape.

154

"The Marquis du Val's lawyer."

"And who was the lawyer who represented Mademoiselle Lucy de Crancé, who became the Marquise du Val?"

"The man asleep over there?"

"Very good! Very good!" replied the Devil in the nasal tone of an ignorant friar questioning a child on the eternal coexistence of God the Father and God the Son and satisfied with the answer he hears.

"And I assume he was present at the extraordinary meeting whose secret Barnet has kept so carefully?"

"Very good again!" replied the Devil in the same nasal tone.

"And you think he'll be willing to tell me about it?"

"You know I promised to tell you myself, but if he'll spare me the trouble he'll be doing me a favor, because I have other business here."

"On this stagecoach?"

"Yes."

"What in the world?"

"A trick in my own style."

"Such as what?"

"You'll see."

And with those words the Devil vanished. Thanks to the supernatural power of sight he was granted from time to time, Luizzi saw the Devil transform himself into a small fly—so small no one else could see it. It flitted around the compartment for a moment and then, still dancing, it stung the former lawyer on the nose. He instinctively clutched the knees of the woman next to him. The lady, who hadn't been stung by the Devil, struck Monsieur Eugène Faynal a humiliating blow across his fingers: there were three keys in her handbag. Faynal woke with a start, and Ganguernet leapt at his throat, shouting, "Your money or your life!"

"What's happening?" cried the terrified former lawyer.

"It was just a joke!" said Ganguernet.

And now that everyone was awake the conversation became general. But Luizzi, who was more interested just then in what was going to happen on the stagecoach than in getting to know his traveling companions, closed his eyes and pretended to be asleep—which didn't keep him from following the flight of the microscopic insect that was none other than the Devil. It left the inside compartment of the stagecoach and headed up to the outside seat.

Up there, next to Monsieur de Mérin, the India expert from the prisons of Berlin, sat a young man of no more than twenty. He was a handsome boy, but he had an air of inane ambition that Luizzi might not have noticed without the subtle power of perception the Devil had given him. That power enabled the baron to understand the young man's nature, but not to foresee where it might lead him. He could tell the boy had the gift of being extraordinarily impressionable, which constantly led him to dream of a life that was all the more fantastical for having been lived, so to speak, entirely in his imagination.

While still in secondary school, where he'd read Schiller's *The Robbers*,[30] the young man had fallen in love with the idea of long-faced wandering highwaymen. He pictured himself with a big mustache, wearing red pantaloons and yellow boots and black gloves, and armed with a saber and three pairs of pistols. His law studies, which he began a year later, taught him the folly of such vanities. French gendarmes seemed too numerous and French caves too few, and Fernand gave up the idea of being the hero of a German play.

Soon, as happened to lots of other young people, that repugnant novel *Faublas*[31] fell into his hands; and Fernand began to imagine a Marquise de B— in every box at the opera, and the young de Lignolle ladies in every smiling girl, and he thought he could invent riddles as well as the next man. A dancer cured him of that folly, and a doctor cured him of that dancer.

Another time, after he'd devoured *Werther*,[32] Fernand decided he ought to kill himself for love. Potier[33] put an end to that ambition when he came to Toulouse to perform. The chronicle of the wars of the French Revolution almost made Fernand enlist in peacetime, and if he could've crossed the Garonne River without getting seasick he would've become a sailor as great as Amerigo Vespucci or Captain Cook.

At the time Luizzi was observing the young man, Fernand had just been reading a history of the papacy, and delving into the secrets of the Vatican had enraptured him. That absolute authority, higher than that of kings, that direct power in God's name, the glittering pomp of Christian ritual, had dazed his susceptible imagination; whether he envied the debauchery of the Borgias or the refined artistic glories of the Medicis, whether he was carried away by the politics and philosophy of Clement XIV,[34] the fact was that the papacy had him by the throat. At the age of twenty, he thought to be pope was a greater destiny than to love and be loved. It was a kind of insanity.

In short, it was in that state of mind and heart that Fernand was traveling from Toulouse to Paris. Luizzi could see the Devil-fly circling the tip of the young man's nose as they reached a little village called Boismandé. Nothing

---

[30] *Die Räuber* (1781), Friedrich Schiller's first play, and a sensational success.

[31] *Les Amours du chevalier de Faublas* (1787-90) by Jean-Baptiste Louvet de Couvray—the same corrupting book Henriette Buré is given to read in her imprisonment in Chapter VII. The Marquise de B— and the de Lignolle ladies are romantic interests of Faublas's.

[32] *The Sorrows of Young Werther* (1774), a celebrated and deeply influential proto-Romantic novel by Johann Wolfgang von Goethe.

[33] Charles Potier (1806-70): a prominent actor and playwright.

[34] Clement XIV, pope from 1769 to 1774, was best known for refuting the medieval Blood Libel against the Jews, and for suppressing the Society of Jesus.

about it would draw it to a traveler's attention, except that the stagecoach stops there for lunch, and there are only two people in the world who really know the value of a meal they've anticipated: a man traveling by stagecoach, and a convalescent having his first porkchop. The great coach bearing the coat of arms of France therefore stopped at Boismandé, in front of the usual inn. It disgorged its many passengers, the men in scarves and silk caps, the women in crushed hats and greasy furs, both men and women wrapped up in shapeless greatcoats, threadbare pelisses, worn-out overcoats, etc.—all of them so encrusted with mud as to knock the brush out of even the nimblest hand. The only veiled woman didn't enter the inn, but pursued her journey.

Who isn't familiar with what it's like to make a stagecoach stop at an inn, and with everyone's first grotesque movements as they straighten themselves out? This man shakes his head and shoulders vigorously, rubs his hands, and coughs hard to escape for a moment from the sardine state he'd been in and return to the state of an ordinary human in full possession of all of his faculties. That man waves his leg around wildly to make his too-tight trouser cuff go back down over his boot after a neighbor's leg rubbing against it rolled it up as far as his knee. One woman, still looking fresh, uses her finger and her warm breath to smooth out the flattened pleats in her bonnet, which remains fairly elegant. Another woman plumps out her flattened russet quilted coat. After that short pause, everyone rushes into the enormous kitchen, where vast pots give off for all eternity the simmering sounds of a doubtful rabbit stew and a merciless fricassee; while turning on the spit over the fierce fire are a muddy duck from a nearby pond and a veal loin for those put off by the other choices.

When the men had slightly tidied up their faces and hands, thanks to the shiny copper sink in one corner of the kitchen, and the women had vanished for a moment and returned more comfortable and more cheerful, they all sat down at the long table that filled the great dining room; and that's when the meal—costing merely an écu a head—began. At first conversation centered on the excellence of the horses they'd had on the last stage, the skill of the postilion, the pleasantness of the driver, the comfort of the coach; then they discussed the towns they'd passed through, the region they were in now, the village they'd stopped at, the inn at which they were dining...

Luizzi listened with more than ordinary attention, because the conversation informed him about the beginning of his journey. But he never lost sight of the diabolical little insect obsessed with Fernand's nose. To be eighteen, to be a bachelor, and to have seen Toulouse and its city hall and Paris and all of its monuments is normally enough to make a man think he's earned the right to be contemptuous of everything; so Luizzi didn't really understand why the Devil took the trouble to leave Fernand's nose and go sting a short, rather impertinent young man who was on his way back to Paris to finish the law studies he'd begun in Toulouse. He didn't need that to make him say frankly that they were in a miserable inn in a miserable village in a miserable area.

Of course love of one's country, love of one's region, even love of one's domestic hearth, are noble sentiments. And yet they ill inspired pretty Jeannette—because if Jeannette hadn't sprung to the defense of her poor inn, what calamities her silence would've avoided! But the Devil had gotten involved, and God knows the Devil has always made use of good intentions to carry out bad deeds! The fly jumped from the student's nose to that of the young servant girl who'd been listening; and no sooner had the words "miserable inn" fallen from his lips than the girl, who was no more than sixteen, cried out, "Bah! Nobler lords than you, sir, have stayed here without speaking ill of it."

That drew the travelers' attention to the girl. She was tall, and the coarseness of her clothes couldn't hide the great beauty of her figure. Diminutive feet in clogs and delicate—though chapped—hands both suggested natural distinction and origins belied by her present status. Rest assured, anytime you meet among the common people one of those signs of a life not bound to hard labor, it's a girl forgetting her maiden self-control or her conjugal vows in favor of some handsome aristocrat that has produced the anomaly. No doubt manual labor and poverty quickly erode those noble features, the privilege of the idle rich, but at the age of sixteen they're still fresh and alive, and Jeannette was barely sixteen.

Did Fernand pay attention? Not at all. He was dreaming of the papacy, and nothing beneath that exalted sphere could reach him; a cardinal's purple would barely have made him look up. He'd therefore noticed nothing—not the remark, nor the reply it provoked, nor the delicate voice that had spoken, nor the mouth with its glistening white teeth, nor the long copper-blond hair, nor the big bluegray eyes whose vague expression suggested a heart easily carried away by chance circumstance.

One old man traveling alone looked at Jeannette with great care and asked her—in a polite voice rarely heard by inn servant girls—"Who were those distinguished travelers, miss?"

"Ha! By God," said Ganguernet, pausing his consumption of a chicken wing for the sake of the glory of France, "almost all the generals who fought in the Peninsular War!"

"They weren't the ones I was referring to," said Jeannette.

"Oh, I get it," went on Ganguernet. "You mean Pope Pius. Pius stayed here!"[35] And he began to laugh, with the big laugh he was famous for.

"Who?" cried Fernand. "What are you talking about?"

"Yes, sir," replied Jeannette in a respectful tone suitable for her next words. "Yes, our holy father the pope stayed at this inn."

---

[35] Either Pius VI, pope from 1775 to 1799, or Pius VII, pope from 1800 to 1823. Pius VII was imprisoned by Napoleon for five years, while Pius VI was not only imprisoned by Napoleon but died in captivity, which would make him the more likely of the two for Fernand to call a martyr.

"He did? He did? The pope?" cried Fernand, looking around wildly at the badly papered walls and the soot-blackened beams of the dining room. "Him! That great-hearted martyr!"

That shifted the group's attention from the servant girl to Fernand. As an untalkative and uncomplaining passenger on the outside of the stagecoach, seated between the driver and the "India hand," Fernand had remained till that moment almost a stranger to the small ambulatory world of which he was a part. But that exclamation, so odd coming from a young man of eighteen, made him stand out in the curious eyes of the whole company. Only now did they notice his great height, his austere features, and the high thoughtful forehead that almost always denotes either a tremendous capacity for great things or a mad obsession with trivial things.

"Yes, it's true!" said Jeannette, delighted to have found such an impassioned listener. "And that room has never been used by anyone else. We've changed nothing. We keep it carefully closed up, and we only go in respectfully and reverently."

At that moment the diabolical insect flew into Fernand's nose and seemed to want to get up into his brain. He cried, "Can it be visited? I have to see it!"

"I'll take you to it," said the girl. They left together.

Meanwhile Luizzi was trying to figure out what the Devil was up to with that servant girl and that young man. Their absence was beginning to draw comment, when they heard a loud noise in the kitchen next to the dining room. Jeannette's name, spoken angrily, reached the travelers' ears several times. Wanting to find out the cause of the uproar, they all went into the kitchen, just as Fernand returned to the dining room by another door.

A young man of about twenty-five, wearing a medal and dressed in hunting clothes, gripped Jeannette by the arm with indescribable violence. "Give me that key!" he cried. "Give it to me!"

The poor girl, pale and unmoving, looked back at him without answering, as if she were under a spell. Half a dozen gold coins that had fallen at her feet drew the greedy eyes of several peasants who were talking heatedly amongst themselves. The inn hostess, her face red and distraught, cried, "The key is in her apron pocket! Take it, Monsieur Henri, take it!"

Henri, at first so furious he was unable to think, finally understood what she was saying to him. After going brutally through poor Jeannette's apron pockets, he flung himself like a madman at the stairs leading to the second floor. The travelers were stepping forward to ask for an explanation for that violent scene, when Luizzi, from where he'd stayed by the door to the dining room, saw the young man with the medal leap down the stairs in a single bound. For a few seconds he looked around furiously.

One of the peasants approached him and asked, "Well?"

"It's true."

"In that room?"

"Yes, in that room."

"Sacrilege and abomination!"

"Is it possible!" said another peasant.

Just then, Luizzi thought he heard the mocking little chuckle he himself had been pursued by.

"What the hell's the matter?" asked Ganguernet.

"Up in that room," repeated the peasant, "in the room with the pope's bed!"

"All right!" cried Ganguernet, finally understanding. "Excellent! What an idea!"

But all of the peasants shouted him down with furious curses. They turned on Jeannette, who stared straight ahead, as if she'd lost her wits. Finally she cried out, "The pope's bed! I'm damned to hell!"

A voice only Luizzi could hear laughed at her words, and with a soft, plaintive sigh Jeannette collapsed, dropping as if every muscle in her body had failed. At the moment she'd spoken the words "I'm damned to hell!" she'd looked toward the door to the dining room, where the baron still stood. As it passed by him on its way to meet Fernand, her glance showed Luizzi it had something of the savage expression of Satan's own eye; and when the baron, looking at Fernand, saw in his fixed gaze a reflection of the sinister fire that seemed to have scorched him, he understood the Devil's menace.

But, carried away by pity, Luizzi slammed the door, leaving him alone with Fernand in the dining room. "Run!" he said.

"Yes," Fernand replied unemotionally.

"Run, or you're done for!"

"Me?" he said with a melancholy smile. "They can't do me any harm. I have my destiny. But I'll run for their sake."

"Then hide instead! Get up on the coach roof and hide under the tarpaulin!"

Fernand opened the window. He'd barely reached the top of the stagecoach when the dining room door opened and peasants armed with scythes, pickaxes, sticks, and flails burst in and rushed at Luizzi.

"It's not him! It's not him!" cried several voices, and they immediately demanded that he tell them where Fernand was. He hadn't even finished saying he'd seen him run away in the direction of the main road when they all hurried off uttering terrible threats and curses.

While the horses were being hitched, Luizzi told the driver where Fernand was hiding.

"That was a good idea," said the man, "because if he was on the road they'd soon catch up with him, and God knows what they'd do to him!"

"And what's happened to Jeannette?"

"At first they thought she was dead—that's why they didn't kill her. But Monsieur Henri had her carried into a room, where they cared for her."

"Who is this Monsieur Henri?"

"The postmaster's son," said the driver. "A soldier from before the Bourbon restoration. My former captain."

"Did he know Jeannette?"

"Him? Did he know Jeannette! Did he ever!"

The postilion cracked his whip.

"All aboard! All aboard!" cried the driver, and the passengers all came hurrying, sadly and silently. Luizzi got on last, and he noticed the driver give a start of surprise as the postilion got into the saddle. The postilion handed the driver a leather-bound box, and the driver muttered through his teeth, "Here's one of…"

The cracking of the whip drowned out the rest. At the speed they were going, they soon caught up to the peasants—who made the stagecoach stop, and demanded to climb onto it, since they thought Fernand was on the driver's seat. But the driver absolutely refused, and the postilion used his voice, his whip, and his spurs to lash the horses forward, and they soon left the angry mob behind. None of the passengers riding in the inside compartment had broken their silence till then. But when they felt sure they were perfectly safe from pursuit by those peasants, they began to ask each other what might've become of Fernand. Luizzi told them.

Just then, since they were in a fairly isolated spot, the stagecoach stopped abruptly. The postilion dismounted and called out, "Get down, wretch! Get down right now!"

Luizzi looked out the window, and beneath the postilion's smock he recognized the former captain.

Fernand got down and approached his adversary. "What do you want with me?"

"Your life! Your life!" cried Henri. "Right now, and right here!"

"I'll duel at the next relay stop."

"Oh, so you refuse—coward!"

As he spoke, Henri gestured threateningly, but Fernand was unmoved. Then, as quick as lightning, he grabbed the hand that had been about to strike him and dragged Henri toward the stagecoach. Placing his free arm under the rim of one of the wheels, he lifted the enormous vehicle more than an inch off the ground. He let go of Henri's hand and said with a smile, "As you can see, you'd soon be beaten at this game. I told you, I'm at your service at the next relay stop. Since I assume you're proposing a duel to the death, you'll allow me to make my dispositions before I undertake it."

Without listening to what his adversary answered, Fernand turned to Luizzi and said gently and politely, "Would you be so kind as to serve as my second? I'd like to speak to you for a moment; you'd oblige me by taking a seat next to me, up on the roof."

That arrangement being agreed to, and the driver having moved up onto the bench above the outside seat, Luizzi found himself sitting with Fernand and the

"India hand" from Berlin. Henri had gotten back in the postilion's saddle, and he was driving the horses on so furiously that the heavy stagecoach raced like the lightest calèche.

"Before I tell you the secret of what happened," said Fernand, "I'd like to ask you to do me a few small favors, and I hope you'll agree. I have to write several letters... would you deliver them in Paris?" Luizzi nodded, and Fernand went on, "You can have my luggage unloaded while I'm writing, and when we get to the relay stop, be so kind as to hire post horses for me. After the duel I'm going to change my route and leave the road to Paris—I won't go there."

The baron expressed some surprise at that decision, and especially at all of his calm thinking ahead.

"You're surprised I can speak so resolutely about a rencounter whose outcome seems doubtful to you?" asked Fernand. "Look at that man!" he added, pointing at Henri. "That man is as certainly dead as if he were already in the grave."

"Him?" cried Luizzi.

"Yes," said Fernand. "They say courage is the drunkenness of anger. I tell you, I'll kill that man! When I looked at him earlier, I saw death in his eyes. Look at how he's making the stagecoach fly: that man's in too big of a hurry to start fighting—he's afraid. But let's forget about it; he's the one who asked for it... Now," he went on almost mockingly, "I want to justify myself in your eyes for what I assume all of you consider my crime. The circumstances alone gave me the idea, and they alone gave what I did the taint of blasphemy. In truth, I consider myself less guilty for my half hour of fun than that man who wants my life, and who's spent the last six months persistently marching down the path toward seducing Jeannette.

"From the little interaction you've had with me, you must've gotten a sense of the obsessions that torment me, and you won't have been surprised at my crying out and at my ardent wish to see that unusual room. I'd barely entered it when, in some extraordinary moment of clarity, I—who've lived on little besides illusions—found myself suddenly brought back to reality. I looked at Jeannette, she considered me carefully, and as far as I could tell her soul was very far from the reverence called for in that holy place."

Luizzi listened to this man who was giving himself credit for his wicked act—whereas the baron himself knew he'd been nothing but the plaything of a demon's whim. The fly was laughing on the tip of Fernand's nose even as he melodramatically drew a hand across his brow. Speaking in a resonant voice, he went on, "Jeannette is no ordinary girl, so I can't tell which of my arguments her soul listened to. Even though they found the gold I gave her, I can't believe she just sold herself. There was a thought in her that answered mine."

The fly was still laughing.

"I'll find out!" said Fernand forcefully. "I'll see her again, because that girl is mine. I've already paid with the tranquility of my life, and I'll pay again with

162

the life of another man... Poor thing!" cried Fernand, chuckling tragically. "Do you know that what she said as she fainted was something I put into her mind? It was I who, in farewell, when even a tiger would've felt pity at her sobbing, called out as I left, 'You're damned to hell!'"

Luizzi started. He stared at Fernand as if to make sure the Devil himself hadn't disguised himself in his face and body. The fly laughed as it stung him fiercely. It seemed to Luizzi that Fernand was playacting, and turning a young man's crude desire into a romantic episode in some satanic poem. He wanted to make sure, so he replied feelingly, "Oh, that's terrible!"

"What can you do?" answered Fernand calmly. "The idea of battling the Lord, the surge of pride I felt in insulting his sanctuary and despoiling before his very face—and without his being able to protect her—his sweetest and most beautiful creation: that delirious thought scorched me like the fires of hell, and I dreamt that Milton's Satan might be no fiction."

Those words troubled Luizzi in spite of himself, and he turned to the "India hand," who calmly knocked the ash off his cigar and said, "The girl was pretty enough without the Devil getting involved."

The fly eyed Monsieur de Mérin sidelong, as if to make note of his disbelief.

"We're there!" cried Henri just then, and he tossed the reins to an ostler, called up to the driver, and retrieved his pistols.

How many of us have witnessed a duel? Who hasn't felt in his heart the anxiety of knowing for sure that a life is about to be extinguished? Luizzi barely knew Fernand, and yet he carried out all of his wishes as if they were those of his closest friend. Soon everything that belonged to Fernand had been handed over to the baron, and a post chaise was hitched up. Luizzi went to Henri, who sat on a rock with his head in his hands. Looking at the young man, Luizzi was afraid for him as he recalled Fernand's very different mood.

He called the driver over and, trying to reconcile the quarrel, he said, "Are we going to let these young men kill each other over an inn servant girl?"

"An inn servant girl!" replied the driver. "Of course that's her station in life, though you might say she was made to be served, not to serve others... But that's a whole other story."

"Tell me!" cried the baron. "Tell me!"

"It would take too long, and we're in a hurry. All I can say is, my captain has his own theory, and your young man will have earned it."

"Earned what?"

"The bullet that's going to smash his skull."

"Be careful!" said Luizzi. "If I'm concerned for anyone, it's not for Fernand."

"Him?" said the driver with a contemptuous smile. "A puppy who was never drafted, going up against an old dog, a member of the Imperial Guard, a veteran of Moscow and Waterloo! Because he was there, for all that he's only twenty-five! And skill! I'd hold a glass of champagne in my teeth for him at thirty paces, with those pistols." And he opened Henri's box.

"So they're very accurate?" asked Fernand coolly from right next to the other two. Taking the pistols in his hands, he tested the hammers, then gave them calmly back to the driver. "The excellence of those weapons grieves me, sir," he said to Luizzi. "It forces me to be merciless. I have no wish to throw my life away for that madman. Make things ready."

Seeing that Fernand had arrived, Henri made a silent gesture, and the witnesses followed him. Luizzi realized that between those two men no explanation was possible. Fernand handed him a few carefully folded letters, on which the handwriting was clear and firm. Then they all reached a small wood, in which stood a clearing suitable for a duel. The rules were that the adversaries would stand thirty paces apart, that at a signal they would each walk ten paces, and that they could fire at will while they walked. The pistols were loaded with care and concealed under a handkerchief. Luizzi handed them to the duelists, who then moved to their positions.

A hand clap was the signal. Fernand had no sooner taken a step than a pistol shot rang out. They watched as he staggered and stopped. "That man has skill, but lacks courage, otherwise he would've killed me," said Fernand, showing them the bullet hole through his right arm. And he moved his pistol to his left hand.

"Hurry up," cried Henri. "We'll start over again!"

"I don't think so," said Fernand quietly. And suddenly, without taking advantage of the ground he was allowed to gain, he fired, and Henri fell with a bullet through his heart, without a gasp or a shudder to show he'd ever been alive.

An hour later, Fernand was in his post chaise, and the Devil had resumed his seat next to the baron, who'd summoned him.

"Mister Satan, will you tell me why you breathed that foul desire into that young man's soul?"

"It's my secret. Besides, it's not a story I can tell you, since you saw all there is of it."

"True, but the characters in the story had antecedents I'd like to hear."

"Not in the least. An inn servant girl, young and an orphan, confused and ruined by unsavory books, that's all."

"But why choose them for that evil deed?"

"Because I needed two wonderfully attractive people, so they could become wonderfully wicked without anyone suspecting."

"You mean what they just did is only the beginning of a life of evil behavior?"

"Or of evil ideas, which subvert human morality and serve my diabolical interests much more effectively. I'd trade a whole century's crimes for one evil idea. So I've just condemned two people of strong, energetic character to a life apart, a life of exile from the world, a life at war with religion, marriage, and respect for social hierarchy. One of those two is a passionate, strong-willed, ambitious woman, in spite of her humble origins. She already regrets her ruined future more than her crime. Another week of good behavior for that soul full of lively, sudden impulses, and Captain Henri would've married her, and she might even have made Henri into a man of distinction and substance and prominence, so that alongside him she could be a distinguished, substantial, prominent woman. Now that's no longer possible, because Jeannette isn't one of those girls who believes in the power of repentance. Thrown into a state of ruin, she'll want to impose that state on the world."

"And for that reason she'll push Fernand to do wrong and even commit crimes?"

"Yes, in the light of your morality you'll have to call them crimes."

"Will you tell me about them?"

"You won't need me."

"How will I find out?"

"Someday you'll read Fernand's work, and you may even meet him again."

"How so?"

"I've destined him to be an author."

Chapter XII: The Start of an Explanation

The journey continued, and naturally the conversation revolved around what had just happened. They each used the opportunity to recount more or less extraordinary adventures they'd either witnessed or taken part in. It can easily be imagined that Ganguernet was a more fertile source than anyone else for that kind of tale. Among the stories with which he tired out his small audience, there was one Luizzi listened to with considerable interest and curiosity.

"It was a good prank, an excellent prank," said Ganguernet, "and I've never laughed so much in my life. You must've heard about it, Monsieur Faynal, maybe three or four years ago?"

"Hmm, hmm..." said the former lawyer. "Three or four years ago... Didn't something extraordinary happen in Pamiers?"

"Does anything extraordinary ever happen in Pamiers?" asked Ganguernet. "It was in Toulouse. It's the story about Father Sérac. Do you know Father Sérac?"

"You mean Monsieur de Sérac, Adrien Anatole Jules de Sérac, son of the Marquis Sébastien Louis de Sérac? Unless I'm mistaken I don't know of any other Sérac still living."

"Well, that's the very man. However it seems you know him as a man, and not as a priest, which is quite different."

"The last time I saw him," said the former lawyer, frowning and squinting as if to peer into the distance of his memories, "the last time I saw him, ten years ago, he was a fine young man of twenty-five, very much in love, and very little inclined to take holy orders. Ha! The truth is, I think I could specify the exact date," he added, pressing his index finger to his forehead. "By God, it was two days before the signing of the marriage contract between Mademoiselle Lucy de Crancé—whom I represented—and the Marquis du Val. And since you've made me think of it, I remember there was an extraordinary scene connected with that marriage."

"Wait your turn," cried Ganguernet. "If you tell your story, I'll keep mine to myself."

"As you wish," said Monsieur Faynal, settling back into his corner. "But try not to put me to sleep, because when I sleep I dream about my wife, and then there's no point in being away from her. Besides, I don't insist on telling you my story, because it takes me back to a miserable time—the time I spent as a lawyer—so miserable for me that I no more want to talk or hear about it than a galley slave wants to hear about hard labor."

"I beg your pardon, sir!" said Luizzi. "I think your story would be very interesting, and for my own part I'd be delighted to hear you tell it. That doesn't keep Monsieur Ganguernet from telling us his."

So Ganguernet began like this:

It was about three years ago. I happened to be in Toulouse for the Feast of Corpus Christi, and there was a big procession. To watch it go by, a few other pranksters and I had positioned ourselves in a house whose address I won't tell you—not its street, nor its number, nor its name—a house in a kind of gray zone, where lots of contraband was for sale, but which wasn't normally raided by Customs. On the ground floor, next to the alley, was a café. On the second floor was a shop selling suspenders and collars and neckties, run by two sisters in their early twenties. On the third floor was a shop selling collars and neckties and suspenders, run by three women, close friends in their late twenties, plus an old lady. On the fourth floor was a shop selling neckties and suspenders and collars, run by two working girls whose age and description I don't know—and if I did it'd be pointless to tell you, since they weren't involved in our prank. I just need you to understand that the house was fully occupied, and there was plenty of merchandise. But the higher you went in the house, the lower the quality of the merchandise... It's a play on words; get it?

Ganguernet was the only one who laughed. The woman in the corner gave him a look so sharp that it pierced through the thick veil that hid her face. Meanwhile the prankster went on:

Four or five of us fun-loving fellows had gathered, and we'd said to the third-floor shop, "You'll go down to the second floor," or to the second-floor shop, "You'll go up to the third floor, because on the second floor"—or the third floor, whichever it was—"there'll be a party, a feast, with ham and pâté and poultry and veal dumplings and plenty of Blanquette and Roussillon wine and rum punch—what you call a fine blowout!" Even though the second floor and the third floor were always quarreling, because they often stole customers from each other on the staircase, as soon as it was a question of eating they got along fine.

"I'm sorry if it offends the lady on behalf of her sex," added Ganguernet, bowing to the woman in the corner of the compartment, who still hadn't raised her veil. "I'm sorry if it offends the lady on behalf of her sex, but women are gluttons by nature. I don't know if duchesses and marchionesses love good food and brandy, but I've never seen anything as voracious as a working-class girl at a well-filled table: they suck down chicken wings like a stagecoach driver, and they drink their tot of liquor like an invalid. But that's not what this is about."

Let's just say that by nine o'clock in the morning the table was set and the wines were on ice, and my buddies and I had slipped up to the second floor by passing through the café, on the pretext of buying a cigar—because even when you're having fun you've got to keep up appearances. Now, the procession was going by. The young ladies were at their windows, flirting with the officers from the garrison, while we stood carefully at a side window, watching the good Lord go by through a curtain—when suddenly the sky turned black as ink, and in less than no time here came a downpour that soaked and scattered the procession. It came on so fast and the rain was falling so hard that everybody took shelter in whatever open doorway happened to be nearest. Several people, including a priest, came up the walkway of our house, and lots more followed them, so that the first comers were pushed all the way to the foot of the stairs.

Leaning over the banister, I could see the padre who'd come in when the first raindrops fell, and all of a sudden he gave me the idea for an excellent prank, and I said to myself, the priest has got to dine with us! I explained my plan to my companions of both sexes, and I was wildly applauded. I told them all to behave decently, and I put on an expression of solemn saintliness. I went down to the priest and said, "My God, sir, this is no place for you! If you'd like to come upstairs and wait for the storm to pass, my wife and I would be honored to be able to offer you shelter."

"I thank you for your kindness," says he, "but I'll be just fine waiting where I am."

I insisted, saying his refusal would wound us deeply, and the poor man finally followed me, just to make me happy. Ah, priest, what a fool you were! The moment he crossed the threshold and entered our young ladies' shop, I stretched out my hand over him and said to myself, "Priest, my friend, if you're not damned to hell by the time you leave here, I'll give up my own soul in exchange for yours!" Upon which I took my old lady by the hand and said to the priest, "May I have the honor of presenting my wife, Madame Gribou."

Gribou is a name I made up to spare my own name the annoyance of certain acquaintances, and which I use when I go out on bawdy adventures. As for Mariette, she was a wife of convenience—with whom I confess only the holy sacrament was missing to unite us by every possible bond. In those days she was a handsome girl with big black eyes shaped like almonds, lips as red and plump as cherries, splendid hair, and the figure of a queen in all her glory, and she had a loving, joyful, merrymaking spirit I can't even describe. I could never touch that woman's dark downy skin with the tip of my finger without being shocked as if by amorous electricity.

With her first look at the priest I saw she was entering completely into the plan of the trick I wanted to play on him. The priest was a good-looking fellow, as copper-colored as a mulatto, with a thick thatch of hair; and for a girl like Mariette it'd be well worth her while to teach him something besides the myster-

168

ies of the Eucharist. At first I was a little put out, and I'd just as soon it was one of the other girls who took charge of the lesson; but since it was my idea I couldn't ask one of the other gentlemen to make the sacrifice in my place. But I felt like Mariette had taken on the job a little too easily. Even so, the prank seemed too good to give up, and we lit a fire.

At first the priest was too hot, since he was wearing a chasuble that must've held twenty pounds of gold. We offered him something to cool him down, and under pretext of a glass of water and wine, I mixed him up a little drink made of Roussillon wine and Blanquette de Limoux and brandy. There was enough in it to make a mule drunk. The poor priest swallowed the whole thing without paying much attention, but a minute later I watched him go from pale to red, and his eyes seemed to be fluttering slightly. "Are you all right, Father?" I asked in a fake sweet voice.

"That wine made me feel ill."

"That's not surprising," I answered right away. "You probably haven't eaten anything, and wine always has that effect on an empty stomach. If you'll do me the honor of having something to eat, you'll see it'll soon pass."

He was stupid enough to believe me, and deigned to take a seat at our table; that was all I wanted. I placed him between Mariette and me. The table was narrow, so that while from his left I was pouring him some of that wine of my style, from his right Mariette was teasing him in her style. I can't describe—because there are some things you just have to see—the look on that poor man's face between my pre-mixed bottle and Mariette's eyes. The Devil falling into the baptismal font wouldn't have been more embarrassed.

I watched his head drooping little by little, and I realized things had reached a satisfactory point—and then I noticed he'd forgotten his hand in his neighbor's hand. Instead of staring at us in alarm, the way he'd been doing just a moment earlier, he was studying Mariette with an expression that would've made her turn even redder than she was, if that had been possible: because I believe that minx—with good intentions—had wound herself up, and besides the priest's good looks, which had attracted her right away, she'd also drunk a little of that apothecary's wine I'd mixed up so expertly.

Pretty confident my plan was working, I made a sign to the others, and they all got up, one to go look out the window, one to fetch another bottle, another some sugar, another who knows what—but one after another, casually, ending with me. On my way out I closed and locked the door, though clearly that precaution wasn't needed. The priest was in hands not likely to let him escape, and I knew Mariette too well to have any doubt he'd leave her shop as damned as a Jew…

"What!" cried Luizzi. "You used tricks like that to commit such a monstrous crime?"

"Come on!" said Ganguernet. "It was just a joke, my dear sir! You really believe in the virtue of all those rascal priests, who have nieces and grandnephews they make into choirboys and altar girls? That one might still have been young enough to believe in all that religious foolishness, but he wouldn't have for long, and if it hadn't been Mariette it would've been some pious churchy old maid who would've deflowered him less pleasantly. Anyway, I don't hide my opinions; I'm a liberal and I loathe Jesuits, and I'll never feel sorry for playing a good trick on those crooks who want to reimpose tithing and certificates of confession."[36]

"How did the story end?" asked Luizzi impatiently, because he felt he was in a worse position than anyone else to confront the man for his clumsy crudeness.

"Ah, that's the funny part of the whole thing!" replied Ganguernet. "Going on…"

After letting a couple of hours go by to give the wine and other vapors time to dissipate, I went down to the café. There, while I was sipping a little glass of brandy and playing dominoes, I began to describe, calmly and without emphasis, how as I was coming down from the third floor I thought I heard an unfamiliar voice in Mariette's apartment. "I'm not jealous," I added in a mortified tone, "but I looked through the keyhole, and I'd wager a hundred double pistoles in good Spanish gold against two six-liard coins I saw a priest's chasuble on a chair facing the door."

"Impossible! It's a joke! You're making it up! It's this! It's that!" they cried on all sides.

"I don't know," I said, "but I'll bet two bowls of rum punch there's something priestly up there."

"I'd be so happy to pay for them," said one, "I'd be willing to take the bet even if I were sure to lose!"

"Me too," I answered. "I'd happily pay for them to know Mariette hasn't done something like that."

"And I'd pay for ten bowls and give you a hundred francs to know she did! Oh, if I ever catch one of those padres who talked my aunt into leaving my inheritance to the hospital, I'll make the rascal sweat!…"

"All right," I said, "let's bet."

"It's a bet."

No sooner said than done. Meanwhile everyone in the café—there were at least thirty of them—had gathered around our table. The stakes had been set at ten bowls of rum punch for everybody.

---

[36] An obligatory document proving that its bearer had been to confession had been a controversial issue in France for over a century. The practice had originally been aimed at rooting out closet Jansenists.

"Well," I said, "if the whole company's in on the treat, the whole company should serve as witnesses to the thing."

That seemed fair to everyone, so off we went through the back room to the stairs, and climbed to the second floor on tiptoe. I'd taken a wise precaution: after locking the door I'd put the key under the doormat. When they step on it, I said myself, they'll notice it, they'll find it, and they'll use it. That was a stroke of luck, because in fact you couldn't see anything through the keyhole; and they were about to decide I'd been mistaken when the fellow who wanted to lose the bet as badly as I wanted to win it discovered the all-important key. He grabbed it and opened the door.

The first thing we saw was indeed the priest's square hat. We all rushed to Mariette's room; but they must've heard us, because the door was locked, and we were unable to catch the couple *in flagrante delicto*, as they say in the *ius romanum*.[37] The man who'd bet against me wanted to break down the door at all cost. Since I could see the business was well in hand without my needing to be mixed up in it any longer, I went back down to the café. Not everyone had gone upstairs with us; some of those who'd been in the café had stayed behind, talking, at the back door to the stairs. Gradually others had joined them—acquaintances, friends who were passing by—and it had grown to be quite a big group, all talking about what was going on upstairs. Since I don't like hanging around a quarrel if there's a chance it might come to blows, I went across the street to watch the outcome of my little prank. Up on the second floor they were shouting like madmen and hammering on Mariette's door, and the ones on the ground floor responded, shouting, "Throw the priest down to us!"…

"But that would've been murder, sir!" interrupted Luizzi.

"Oh, well," said Ganguernet, "it was just a joke. Anyway, it wasn't a long drop, and besides, priests are like cats, they always land on their feet—and that one proved it, because he didn't jump out the window overlooking the street, he jumped out the window overlooking the back yard. So after half an hour, when there were already more than four or five thousand people in the street, and the gendarmes had shown up and had broken down Mariette's door, they found the bird had flown. But he'd left his feathers in the cage, and if they weren't enough to identify the individual, they showed at least what species he was."

"So they didn't find Father Sérac?' asked Luizzi. "Then how did they know it was him?"

"By God!" replied Ganguernet. "They knew it because I recognized him two days later, at the Saint Sernin Church, where I found him off in a corner, praying and weeping like a madman. He recognized me too, because he stood up, and if we'd been in an isolated enough spot he might've tried to get revenge."

---

[37] Ancient Roman law, codifying the rights of Roman citizens.

"And maybe he'd have been justified," said Luizzi.

"Could be," said Ganguernet. "But I guarantee I'd have brought him back to his senses after making him lose them. After all, it didn't do him much harm: it didn't keep him from being named vicar general, because his family made the whole story go away, and even more because the Jesuits didn't want to give the liberals the satisfaction of seeing a priest punished. They didn't even send him away on retreat for a couple of months; that would've meant acknowledging the guilty party and singling him out for public mockery, which he certainly deserved."

"You think?" said Luizzi.

"Anyway," said Ganguernet, ignoring the interruption, "he was rewarded by learning something he might not have known, and by having the prettiest girl in Toulouse for his mistress."

"What!" said Luizzi. "Father Sérac saw that Mariette again?"

"To the point," said Ganguernet, "that one night I was forced to put him out the door by kicking him."

"To the point," remarked the veiled woman, "that one day when you wanted to see Mariette he threw you down the stairs."

Ganguernet and Luizzi started at that voice, which they both thought they recognized, and no doubt they were both about to question the veiled woman hiding in the corner—when the former lawyer, prompted by Ganguernet's story to tell his own, announced pedantically, "That's quite amusing. But what you obviously don't know is why Monsieur de Sérac became a priest."

"Do you know?" cried Luizzi, who thought he saw a way to clear up for himself the mystery surrounding poor Lucy's past.

"Hmm," said the lawyer. "It wouldn't be right to say I know it. But I think I can guess it, because here's what happened the very day Mademoiselle Lucy de Crancé got married to the Marquis du Val."

Chapter XIII: Così Fan Tutte[38]

"Let's hear it! Let's hear it!" said Luizzi.

And the former lawyer began like this:

As you know, the wedding took place during the Hundred Days. Monsieur de Crancé, Mademoiselle Lucy's father, had done what lots of other noblemen had done—I'm sorry to say it in front of the baron—he'd dedicated himself completely to the service of that bandit *Bu-o-na-par-té*. [We're writing the name that way to show how Monsieur Faynal pronounced it.] And when he came back from the army in 1814, after the fall of that bandit *Bu-o-na-par-té*, he discovered that his wife, whom he'd left in Toulouse to do the honors of the house while he went off to war for the usurper, was in the habit of receiving the Marquis du Val every day. General Crancé—for he'd risen to be a general in the service of that despicable *Bu-o-na-par-té*—asked his wife why the Marquis du Val came there to see her so often.

Madame de Crancé, a Creole who feared neither God nor the Devil when she'd set her mind on something, but who greatly feared her husband, Monsieur de Crancé—because he would've broken her arms and legs on the spot if he'd suspected even for a second what the Marquis du Val came there for—anyhow Madame de Crancé therefore replied that Monsieur du Val came to the house every day to court Mademoiselle Lucy.

"If he's come for that every day," replied the general, "he's come too often not to marry her."

At first that didn't bother Madame de Crancé much, because she thought with a little caressing and a little cajoling she could get her husband to change his mind. But the husband was as stubborn as a gray donkey and as mean as a red donkey. He'd said the Marquis du Val would marry his daughter, so he had to marry her.

Madame de Crancé only pretended to agree, because she was still very much in love with the marquis; but he agreed completely, because he was no longer in love with Madame de Crancé. Still he playacted well enough to make the mother believe he was only marrying the daughter to preserve her honor. As long as the mother believed that, she let matters proceed—and even helped them along, because she drove away Monsieur de Sérac, to whom she'd already promised her daughter's hand while the general was away. And, in spite of Mademoiselle Lucy's despair, she forced the poor girl to accept a marriage she loathed, while still not foreseeing how miserable it would make her.

---

[38] The title of a 1790 opera by Mozart and Da Ponte. The Italian expression means roughly "women are all like that."

Meanwhile things were moving along, and the day arrived for the signing of the marriage contract. Apparently on that day Madame de Crancé realized that what she'd thought was a sacrifice on the part of the Marquis du Val was in fact a genuine pleasure for him. Apparently she overheard him speaking to Lucy in a tone more loving than he'd ever used with her. Still, there was no way to break it off: the relatives and witnesses on both sides had been invited, the contract had been settled, and in the evening it was going to be read out in the presence of both families.

If I live to be a hundred I'll remember that day like it was yesterday. It was in the big parlor at Monsieur de Crancé's chateau. The whole family was gathered in a circle, with the general in the center, stretched out on a chaise longue; he'd had a severe attack of gout, and he needed all his courage to leave his bed and come witness the reading of the contract. My colleague Barnet did the reading, which was purely a formality, and as soon as he was done the couple signed, followed by the general and his wife and their relatives. The moment the general had put his signature to the contract, he excused himself on account of his health, and four servants carried him from the ground floor upstairs to the second floor, where his bedroom was. Right after that, the relatives withdrew, and we were left alone in the parlor: Madame de Crancé, her daughter, the marquis, my colleague Barnet, and me.

Madame de Crancé hadn't said a word all evening, but I'd noticed she looked as wild as a madwoman. When she signed she'd been so confused she couldn't find the place where she should sign, and her hand had dropped the pen twice before she could use it. Here's how we were arranged: I was seated at the table, where I was neatening up the documents; the marquis was with Lucy in a window alcove, and seemed to be apologizing for becoming her husband, while the poor girl couldn't stop crying; at the other end of the parlor, Barnet was explaining to Madame de Crancé the enormous advantages the contract gave her daughter—while she, instead of listening, had her burning eyes fixed on her daughter and her future son-in-law. As I watched the sinister expression on her face, I saw her suddenly leave Monsieur Barnet and hurl herself at the marquis. She tore his hand out of her daughter's, which he was holding, saying, "You lie, sir, you lie! You don't love this girl, you can't love her, or you're despicable!"

"I do love her!" said the marquis vehemently.

"Well then," replied Madame de Crancé, "if you love her, you won't marry her!"

"I swear to you I will marry her!"

"You won't marry her!" said Madame de Crancé, who'd reached a state of exasperation bordering on madness. Turning to the trembling Lucy, she cried, "Look carefully at this man! This man has been my lover—this man has been your mother's lover—do you want him for your husband?"

All of that had happened in a flash, and Barnet and I were looking at each other, horrified by what we'd just heard, when we saw poor Lucy fall at her mother's feet. "Mother, mother, don't say that!" she cried. "People besides me might hear you and believe you. Father might hear you."

"Well then, let him hear me!" said Madame de Crancé. "Let him come and kill me! If this man is despicable enough to marry you, and you, my daughter, are despicable enough to consent, well then, he at least won't allow this heinous incest!"

You'd have thought all of her Creole blood had risen to that woman's head. She seemed drunk with anger and jealousy. Turning to the marquis, she said in a voice full of fury, "You say you love her, you ungrateful wretch? You love her—but she doesn't love you! At least, she loves someone else, to whom she'll give herself, the way I gave myself to you. She loves another, who'll dishonor you, I hope, the way you made me dishonor my husband. She loves Monsieur de Sérac. Watch out—watch out for him!"

And she went on like that, heaping furious reproaches on the marquis, while he tried in vain to calm her, and her daughter, who'd fallen to the floor again, wept and moaned horribly. Barnet and I had withdrawn to the far end of the parlor, so as to witness as little as possible of that unfortunate scene. We'd even decided to try to escape, to avoid the danger of seeing such powerful people embarrassed before us, when Madame de Crancé—who I can testify had truly gone mad—grabbed the marquis by the arm and dragged him away violently, crying, "Come! Come! My husband must see us together! I must tell him the truth in your presence!"

At that very moment the parlor door opened, and the general appeared. I don't know if any of you knew him, but it was impossible not to lower your eyes before the cold, vacant look he gave you while speaking to you. Wrapped as he was in a long red dressing gown, with his long white hair and his long white mustache, he looked like some kind of apparition, like ghostly Death, who comes when you summon him with certain words. He stopped on the threshold and said in a low voice, whose tone I'll never forget, "What's going on here?" He asked that, but he had his unsheathed sword in his hand, forgetting that it showed he already knew.

His daughter ran to him, crying, "Mercy, father, mercy!"

The general turned to poor Lucy and replied—in a voice whose cruel, pleading tone nothing I can say could convey to you—"Mercy for you, isn't that right, Lucy? Mercy for you, isn't that right, daughter? Because in your heart you love someone else, and you're afraid it'll make your father angry? But I know that's an innocent love, and I forgive you for it. If it had been a guilty love, if that love had allowed the slightest suspicion to hang over the honor of a woman who bears my name, I would've killed that woman, I'd kill her even now."

As he spoke the general took several steps toward Madame de Crancé. Lucy threw herself in his way, crying, "Father, father! Mercy!"

And her father, taking her in his arms, replied in a soft but bleak voice, "Yes, my daughter, I would've killed you if you'd dishonored the Crancé name. And since I don't want that name dishonored…"

"I'll marry the Marquis du Val," said Lucy, falling to her knees before her father.

"Thank you, my daughter!" said the general, and he dropped his sword. Then, turning to us, he added calmly, "Till tomorrow, gentlemen. I invite you to the wedding ceremony."

When we were only a few steps away from the door out of the parlor, the general was attacked by such terrible pain in his chest that they had to hurry to help him lie down on mattresses, and they were unable to take him back up to his room…

"And the wedding took place the next day?" asked Luizzi.

"The wedding took place the next day," said the former lawyer. "Two days later, Monsieur de Crancé was dead, his widow had left Toulouse, and young Sérac had entered a seminary to become a priest."

Chapter XIV: Continuation

Luizzi had listened to that sad account with great interest. The stagecoach had just stopped at the foot of a long, steep ascent. All of the travelers had gotten out, and the baron was walking next to the former lawyer, lost in the somber train of thought the story had prompted in him, when Ganguernet—who wanted to hurry ahead to drink a couple of glasses of rum at a tavern they could see at the top of the climb—said as he overtook them, "It looks like you took the lawyer's tale to heart, baron!"

"Indeed," added Faynal, "you seem quite preoccupied by it."

"It's just that it began to unveil the secret of a misery and a turmoil I hadn't understood."

"And that I can explain completely," said the silent veiled woman who'd been on the stagecoach.

"You?"

"Yes. Do you recognize me, baron?" And she lifted her veil. Luizzi knew he'd seen her before, but he couldn't remember where or when, till she added quietly, "I'm the servant who let you in at night to see the Marquise du Val."

"Mariette!" cried Luizzi.

"Yes, Mariette. That's my name. It was my name when I was the marquise's servant, and it was my name when I helped Father Sérac escape from my room."

"What! That was you?" asked Luizzi, advancing from one surprise to another.

"Yes, that was me. I'd fallen madly in love with the priest, and I could think of no other way to tie him to me and to bring him back to me than to make him appalled at his own sin, and when I'd overcome his conscience, to make him gradually accustomed to debauchery... till the day came when, having become more debauched than I was, he forced me, by means of money and terrible threats, to assist him in his villainous schemes."

"Against whom?" asked Luizzi.

"Just listen!" said Mariette.

Seven years after Mademoiselle de Crancé was married, seven years after Father Sérac had become a priest, he still loved her, but he'd always loved her with a love made almost innocent by despair. When he'd become the lover of a whore—because I was more or less a whore—when he'd extinguished within him every higher feeling by continuing to immerse himself in orgies in which I no longer took part, Father Sérac still loved the Marquise du Val, but it was with a vile love, a love even dirtier than it was criminal.

Unfortunately, I hadn't foreseen how far that man's passionate spirit and stubborn nature would carry him, once he'd started down the wrong path. I was the first to suffer from the vice into which I'd pushed him: he mistreated me, he killed me every day with his wild flights of jealousy—even though he didn't love me. Six months after the adventure Ganguernet just told you about, Father Sérac was seized by the idea of becoming the Marquise du Val's lover. To manage that, he forced me to enter her household as a servant.

Since I'd been with him, he'd made me leave my neighborhood and had set me up in a little house on the other side of the river, where he came every night, sometimes disguised as a businessman, sometimes as an officer, never in the same clothes or uniform, so no one would suspect it was the same man coming to my house every night. He kept me completely hidden away, and he could've murdered me and no one would've asked him where I was. Anyway, I was afraid of him, and if he'd asked me to go commit some crime that would cost me my life, I'm not sure I would've dared say no. So I had to agree to what he demanded. I don't know how he managed it, what pious old women he got to recommend me, but as soon as I went to see the Marquise du Val I was hired. When I began working for her she was unhappy. She'd taken refuge in God; she spent all of her time in religious ritual, because the poor woman didn't even have the consolation and distraction of the sweetest and holiest occupation for women, that of raising her children.

Luizzi was listening to the young woman with interest and astonishment in equal parts. Observing that, she went on:

My words surprise you, sir, but in the three years I lived with the Marquise du Val I learned many things and experienced many feelings I'd never known before. As I said, she was unhappy. She was childless, because from the first day of her marriage she'd separated herself from her husband, and he'd never crossed the threshold of the room in which she slept—when she slept. Yes, baron, I learned many things, and the one that surprised me most was discovering how willpower and good manners can maintain elegance and grace when vice has turned body and soul gangrenous to the root.

I sometimes read the letters Father Sérac forced me to carry to the Marquise du Val, and I have to admit I've never seen such pure and respectful love expressed so sweetly and with such charm. I gave the marquise those letters in despair. After having refused for a long time to accept them, the poor woman had finally let me persuade her—I who lied to her because I was afraid, and who was sorry for my success at the very moment I'd just done all I could to succeed. Three months passed before the marquise was willing to read one of the priest's letters. After she agreed to read them, three more months passed before she allowed the priest to call at her house.

Against my will, I was pushing her toward a crime I dreaded much more out of my affection for her than out of the morality I'd grown up with: it didn't bother me that the marquise might take a lover; I didn't think it was sacrilegious for her to give herself to a priest; but I thought she was going to become the victim of a wretch who had every vice, and all the brutality of his vices. One hope still sustained me: I put my hope in the marquise herself. I thought the day that man began to speak to her in words she didn't want to hear, she'd know how to shut him up. And I knew the marquise so well, I couldn't imagine how that man could ambush the virtue of a woman both so pure and so strong. Unfortunately, baron, I forgot I myself had taught him a vile lesson…

"What!" cried Luizzi. "It was…?"

"Yes, baron," said Mariette. "It was by mixing noxious additives into the very little wine she drank, it was by making her drunk—that noble, saintly creature—it was by stupefying her, just as I'd stupefied Sérac and made him drunk, that he overcame her womanly virtue, just as I'd overcome his priestly virtue. He received her from her husband a virgin, just as I received him from his God a virgin. It's awful, isn't it, baron?"

She stopped, and Luizzi put a hand over his eyes, as if he'd been blinded by glare. Then he walked on silently beside Mariette, who still said nothing. It was a long silence, as if the baron needed all of that time to weigh the foulness of the act. Finally he said, "Oh yes, it's awful!"

"But," added Mariette, lowering her voice and coming closer to him, "one thing you couldn't imagine, if it weren't true and if I didn't swear to it on my life, is this…"

That noble, elegant young woman, surrounded by the most sparkling society, tried to forget the sin Father Sérac had made her commit by remembering the power that had delivered her to him. She made a vice out of what had been a misfortune. As soon as she was alone she obtained strong liquors, she stole them from her own servants in spite of me, and she abused them to the point of dropping to the floor, deprived of reason and strength; because for her, strength was the capacity to suffer, and reason was remorse and its heartbreak.

She lived that way for two years, under my protection; I hid her from the eyes of the world and those of her servants—and I would've tried to hide her from your eyes too, baron. One day, in one of those flights of folly her vice often inspired in her, she told me, "I'm going to get rid of this torturer who's killing me. Since I have neither a brother nor a husband who can tear me from his grip, I'll take another lover. Luizzi came to see me this morning—Luizzi, who seemed to be in love with me when he was still a boy, and who was also made unhappy by my misery when I got married. Luizzi came to see me. If he wants to love me, I'll love him. Am I not still beautiful enough for him to love? Oh, yes!" she went on, lifting her eyes to heaven and invoking God, so badly did her madness lead her astray at those awful times. "Yes, I'll love him, and you'll forgive me for that love, Lord, you'll have pity on that love. Because if he doesn't want to love me, I'll utterly defy your eternal damnation and kill myself."

"And it's because she would've done it, sir, that I waited for you at the gate of her house and led you to her, concealing you from discovery by Father Sérac, whom I'd seen waiting across from the door at which you were going to knock. It's because she would've killed herself that I let you into that chapel—which a priest had turned into a boudoir. And she'd calmed down when I left her. For a moment I hoped she'd dare to tell you everything, and you'd be generous enough to protect her without leading her into deeper sin. But she'd taken advantage of my absence to stiffen her resolve, as she put it, the poor thing! And when she entered the chapel where you were waiting for her, baron…"

Mariette stopped, as if unable to finish the sentence, and Luizzi slowly went on, "And when the poor thing gave herself to me, in the midst of sobbing and bursts of joy I didn't understand…"

"She was drunk, baron, she was drunk!"

Chapter XV

No sooner had Mariette said those words than a post chaise—going very fast and passing close by them, while the postilion cried, "Look out!"—forced them to step aside. Luizzi quickly glanced inside, and recognized Fernand and Jeannette sitting there. Fernand leaned out the window and, without stopping the horses, cried, "Don't forget my letter to Monsieur de Mareuilles! It's important! He's a very good friend of mine!"

It seemed to Luizzi that the fly that had stung Fernand was still with him, and that it had stirred and fluttered its wings when the young man had given him his instructions. Luizzi was so preoccupied by everything he'd just heard and seen—he would've paid dearly for a moment's quiet and solitude to be able to think at leisure—he didn't hear Mariette's cry of surprise when she spotted Jeannette in the post chaise.

Meanwhile as they were talking they'd reached the top of the hill, and they had to get back into the stagecoach. Luizzi was beginning to think the Devil was getting involved in his life in more ways than just by telling him stories; already he suspected that it was he—probably because he was tired of telling stories all the time—who'd put Luizzi in that stagecoach with Ganguernet and the lawyer Faynal and Mariette. And he was fully convinced of it when he saw Ganguernet running toward him, saying, "Wouldn't you know it! The main axle of the stagecoach just broke, and it'll probably be twelve hours before we can go on. We'll be stuck that whole time at this wretched inn, where there's nothing besides eggs to make an omelet, and plonk and potato liquor to wash it down."

"What?" cried Luizzi impatiently. "There's no way to fix the problem sooner?"

"Well, there is a way, if you've got money to spend and money to burn. Meaning, if you're willing to lose the cost of your seat in the stagecoach and take the berline post coach heading to Paris that's stopped to change horses up there."

"With pleasure. I'll take it on the spot, at no matter what price."

"I guess your pockets are full!" said Ganguernet, patting Luizzi on the stomach.

The baron was reminded that up to that point he'd given no thought to his present pecuniary status, and the remark prompted him to put his hand in his pocket: he drew out several handfuls of gold coins. He deduced that it wasn't for lack of funds, but due to circumstances still unknown, brought about by the Devil, that he'd been forced to take the stagecoach. He further assumed that this berline post coach happened to be here so conveniently for him only because the Devil had taken care to put it there. Firmly resolved to let himself by guided by the Devil, he had his belongings unloaded from the stagecoach—after first examining the driver's manifest to see what his luggage was, since he hadn't the slightest idea. Among his things was a large briefcase with a leather cover: something the baron didn't know he owned. He decided to put off examining the contents till he was alone in the berline; and he bid farewell to his traveling companions, after having given Mariette his address in Paris.

Once he was alone in his carriage he hastened to open the briefcase. Among the other contents he saw letters addressed to him, and he took care to learn his own address—though the seals had been broken, and it was clear either someone else or he himself had already read them.

The first letter was from the crown prosecutor in the arrondissement of —, and read as follows:

Dear baron,

The facts you've reported to us are of such gravity that I've had to refer them to the crown attorney general for Toulouse. That a woman could be locked up in prison for seven years without anyone having the slightest suspicion of it surpasses all belief. As soon as I've received a reply from the attorney general, to know how I should respond to the information you've given me, I'll forward his reply to you.

I have the honor to be, etc.

"Aha!" thought Luizzi. "It seems I denounced Captain Félix. Well, let's see how that business turned out."

He hunted through the briefcase, and opened another letter, which began:

Sir,

You're a villain...

"This must be from Captain Félix," thought Luizzi, "accusing me of not being willing to leave his crime unpunished."

... You've caused me to kill a young man and to dishonor a woman who bore my name. If you're not a coward you'll give me satisfaction for your shameful conduct.

—Dilois.

That second letter worried Luizzi a great deal more than the first one, and he wanted to know how he'd responded to that challenge. To find out, he looked through the briefcase for a letter telling him the outcome of the matter, but he found nothing but old exchanges about bills with his man of business and his accountant. When he examined them, it seemed to him he'd not at all neglected his business interests, and had in fact made sure of them to a degree that surprised him. Still hunting, still sorting his many documents, down in one corner of the briefcase he found a fragment of a letter whose edges were burned, as if it had been snatched from a fireplace just before it was completely consumed.

... Before she died, poor Lucy told me the secret of her birth. It was fated that it be you, Armand, who was the agent of my ruin and my dishonor! Heaven is just!

—Sophie Dilois.

Everything else Luizzi found by way of new information in his papers only further embroiled him in the inextricable maze of the events that entangled him. He still had the option of summoning Satan to demand an explanation of what he'd been reading; but, besides not being sure he'd get one, he wasn't in the mood to restart that life of constant turbulence in which he didn't have a moment to think. He put off till his arrival in Paris finding out what had come of his denunciation against the Buré family, how he'd responded to Monsieur Dilois's challenge, and why Madame Dilois called him Armand, as if he were her brother or her lover.

"My God," he said to himself, "it'd be a funny thing if, during that time I have no memory of, I'd been Madame Dilois's lover! I'm certainly capable of it. I probably tried to get her forgiveness for my stupid indiscretion, and got more than her forgiveness. That Madame Dilois is as pretty as an angel, and I must've been happy! How the devil did it come about? The fact is, I'm in an awful position! Not even to remember the pleasure—which must've been intensified by the great wrong I'd done her!"

Taken by that idea, he went on, "By God, I want to experience that pleasure someday. To win a woman whose vanity or love you've wounded, or whose reputation you've ruined—that must be an exquisite triumph. If ever I meet Madame Dilois again, I want to bring her back to me, I want... unless that's already happened."

Then he cried out impatiently, "Really, it's outrageous! And I'll let the Devil carry me off if ever I give him another day of my life, even if he tells me stories as frightening as those of Reverend Maturin or as boring as the venerable Monsieur de Bouilly's tales![39]

"I'll hold you to it," said a voice that seemed to come in by one window and go out by the other, and which frightened Luizzi so badly that for almost two hours he didn't dare move or speak or think.

Meanwhile his journey continued without incident, and on the twenty-fifth of February, 182*, he reached Paris, firmly resolved not to worry about what had happened in Toulouse, but to live his old life, and to leave it up to chance to reveal to him the mystery of all the events he'd witnessed since he first made Satan's acquaintance. Another resolution he thought he was making just as firm-

---

[39] Charles Maturin (1780-1824): an Irish Protestant clergyman and writer, best known for *Melmoth the Wanderer* (1820), a Gothic novel about a man who sells his soul to the Devil. Jean-Nicolas Bouilly (1763-1842): a French playwright and writer of children's stories, best known for the libretto for Beethoven's opera *Fidelio*.

ly was to summon the help of the Devil as little as possible, and especially not to make use—under any pretext, for any purpose—of information he might get from him. And to keep that resolution he pledged not to see any of the people who'd interacted with him during his recent journey.

Luizzi therefore thought he'd resume the life he'd had as a young man living in Paris, and reconnect with his old friends. So as not to fail in his earlier commitment, on the night he arrived he did no more than deliver to their addresses the various letters Fernand had given him—including the one addressed to Monsieur de Mareuilles, even though Fernand had brought it especially to his attention. That way, he expected to have put himself beyond the reach of any inquiries; but the morning after his arrival his valet announced Monsieur de Mareuilles.

Luizzi found him to be a handsome, well-dressed young man, nothing more. The baron just explained simply to him how he'd served as Fernand's second; but somewhere it had been decided Luizzi wouldn't rid himself as easily as he hoped of whatever was connected to the Devil, even by invisible threads. So this Monsieur de Mareuilles, a friend of that Fernand who'd fallen under the power of the Devil, took a real fancy to Luizzi, and—since the baron was the man of the world the least able to rid himself of a bore—he willingly let his new acquaintance tag along all day, to the Café de Paris, to the Théâtre des Italiens, to the Bois de Boulogne… everywhere men go whose society consists only of men.

But he also let Mareuilles take him to a house where the young man was received as a regular guest, and soon Luizzi began to think chance had served him well by connecting him to a nice boy who was rich, aristocratic, and stupid—but who could introduce him into social circles in which the baron was a complete stranger, and where regular attendance could only help give him a reputation as a man with a well-ordered life above reproach.

He didn't realize that in that world, as in any other, there'd be occasions when his curiosity was aroused, which would put him back in Satan's clutches; and that in his position he'd be better off living in the midst of naked vice than with vice that dresses up in hypocrisy and the false appearance of virtue. It should be said that Luizzi hadn't yet fathomed the real purpose of his contract with the Devil, and his exceptional destiny hadn't freed him from the ordinary fate of humankind, which is to endure life before assessing it, and to walk before having chosen a path. The adventure that would put Luizzi back in regular contact with his mentor wasn't long in coming.

THE THREE CHAIRS

Chapter XVI

Two days after his arrival, Luizzi became acquainted with a world that's not well known in Paris... that of capital in retirement. Let's be clear: we're not talking about the capital of the Bourbon Restoration, liberal capital whose wealth rivaled that of the great noble fortunes, papering in silk and gold the over-furnished apartments of stockbrokers when they hosted big receptions; liberal capital, who—aiming to establish a gallery of historic worth—had his portrait painted with a hunting scene, and included the faces of his coachman and his beater among those of his family; liberal capital, all of whose diamonds, awkwardly displayed on ostentatious wealthy women, could never match the seductiveness of a head simply held in an aristocratic manner, or a piece of ribbon amorously braided into the hair of a pretty girl from the Opéra.

The capital we're speaking of here predated the Restoration; it began with the Directoire,[40] and had been involved in that extraordinary looting of the national wealth and the pleasures of life. Indeed, when France reached the Directoire after surviving the Republic and the Reign of Terror it resembled an army that, having crossed a landscape riddled with chasms and enemies and cutthroats and ambushes in which it lost most of its vanguard, finally reaches a friendly town and finds a few hours of refreshment and safety. Then, by God, it's wonderful to meet again, to celebrate, to eat and drink, to embrace, to dance arm in arm, any old how, all together, without being too particular about cleanliness or dress or behavior, without worrying about funny looks or spiteful comments, because everybody's caught up in the same whirlwind.

People strolled, they ran, they stampeded toward the sound of orchestras, the sound of gold at the gaming tables, the sound of glasses clinking: a grand carnival, a splendid orgy, in which memories served as both excuse for and protection against memories! Because if one man said to another, "I saw you yesterday—you were tipsy!" the other could answer, "It's true, I remember—you were drunk!" And if one woman said to another, "You weren't wearing much at the Opéra last night!" the other could reply, "You were down to your blouse at Longchamp!" And if the first woman added, "So you've taken young Trénis as

---

[40] The Directoire refers to the era (1795-99) in which the revolutionary committee of that name ruled France, till it was overthrown by Napoleon.

185

your lover?" the other could say, "I've never stolen anything of yours!" and so on—and a thousand other things steeped in delirious drunkenness... which must've left quite a lot on the consciences of most of those women when they'd become old and ugly and prudish and devout. And this was how it all happened:

That delightful era, so revealing and so transparent, saw the return of lots of exiles. Many of them had been very young when they'd fled France, and most of them had spend the prime years from eighteen to twenty-five in poverty, in misery, and often in bad company. So now they threw themselves with amazing energy into that magical world that brought the distant nudity of the Opéra within arm's reach. The newcomers didn't have much money; their fortunes, shaken or toppled by confiscation, hadn't yet been restored or rebuilt. So they borrowed from husbands to give to wives, and mortgaged their future to gild the present.

Later, when the orgy was over, when the social classes had begun to separate again, when their fortunes were secure again, the nobility of the Faubourg Saint Germain couldn't completely break away from the capital to whom they still owed a great deal in principal and interest. Millions are quickly spent, but slow to repay. That liquidation lasted longer than the Empire. Already the capital of the Directoire had begun, little by little, to retire from business. It had skillfully handed over its affairs to intelligent clerks, who became the source of the capital of the Restoration, and who were mentioned above—but it had accepted neither their ill-bred world nor their shopkeeper's manners.

Accustomed to noble names and great political influence, the older capital couldn't reconcile itself now to receiving stock exchange and banking celebrities, after having mingled socially with men whose ancestors had made ancient French history and men who'd recently made modern French history. Later, after the Restoration, that regal capital turned completely inward. That way it kept its intimate connections with the Faubourg Saint Germain, and fairly capably mimicked its fine airs and pretensions and especially its attention to luxury and surface.

In truth, few women from the highest aristocracy could be found there; but the men were of the first rank. Many had maintained connections, whether of business or friendship, in that world of capital. There were pretty girls and handsome boys among them who had the faces and hands of an ancient noble lineage—though their father's title of count or baron dated only from the Empire—and the great lords who took an interest in them did so with a protective condescension so clearly understood that no one questioned the motive for their favor.

Now, of all the salons that seemed to him useful in establishing the wholesome reputation he needed, Luizzi most preferred that of Madame Marignon, or de Marignon, depending on whether the speaker did her the honor of visiting her or had the honor of being received there. At that time (182*), Madame de Marignon was a woman somewhere between fifty and sixty. She was tall, rather slender, and fairly bony. She had wonderfully preserved teeth, a face like parchment, fashionable bonnets, well cared-for gray hair, sparkling eyes, a thin nose, and thin lips. She was always tightly corseted, and she always wore quilted dressing gowns of the finest cloth, always cut in the same style. Since she'd embraced her role as an old woman so frankly, men found her perfectly ingratiating and women her own age cordially detested her. They claimed her shrugging off of all pretensions was insincere; they said it was a form of revenge, by means of which Madame Marignon (in that context the "de" was dropped), thanks to the inexorable aphorism about age, gave up conquests she was no longer allowed— but those conquests hadn't yet deserted her charms, which were better preserved than those of her rivals.

Madame de Marignon received lots of people, and at her house Luizzi made acquaintances of great value for gaining the right to bow to the finest male specimens in the best loges at the Opéra or the Théâtre des Italiens. Otherwise the rules of the house were quite strict. There were professional musicians; music performed by amateurs seemed too dangerous to Madame de Marignon, who had a daughter of ravishing beauty and exceptional musical ability. The paid singers entertained the guests, but it was forbidden for the guests to amuse themselves that way. They played whist for five hundred francs a card, but Madame de Marignon wouldn't have tolerated écarté for a hundred sous. They often ate dinner, they rarely danced, they never had a late-night supper. Everything seemed so correct, so well-ordered, so restrained in that house, that Luizzi hadn't yet been seized by any desire to know the deep secrets of that world—in which his name, his fortune, and his extravagance had made him perfectly welcome, though he was unknown there.

Here was the minor occurrence that gave him that desire and made him ring the infernal bell that put the Devil at his orders:

One evening, when there was a concert at Madame de Marignon's, in the middle of a piece sung by Madame D——, a woman of about thirty appeared at the parlor door, after having shushed the servants who wanted to announce her. The men crowding around the door stood aside, and she found herself standing at the entrance to a large circle. One seat remained unoccupied, by the piano. The woman, whom Luizzi didn't know, crossed the circle—making an apologetic gesture to Madame de Marignon, who greeted her without rising and with obvious ill humor—and took the empty chair. Her entrance made an impression, though the woman was pale and had a rather faded beauty. Luizzi noticed that, and also noticed she was dressed with perfect elegance.

But what struck him even more was that the two women siting on either side of the chair the newcomer had taken immediately rose and disappeared into the third parlor, where the card players had been relegated. The song was still going on, which made the insult even more blatant. The scandal it caused was enormous, but silent; only glances, questioning and responding, were exchanged; the singer finished the piece amid universal distraction. When the music was done, Madame de Marignon left to join the two women who'd insulted the newcomer so cruelly. As the lady of the house, she could've mended the damage by going to sit next to the victim and chatting with her for five minutes. But, though she looked put out by what had just happened, it seemed as if even in her own home she didn't dare take responsibility for that mending.

Luizzi knew the two women responsible for that scene, the way you know the people you meet in a salon. In the chair to the right had been Madame du Bergh, a woman of forty-five, renowned for her extreme piety and her connections with the most fashionable men of the cloth; she was known for her charitable works, her defense of religious schools, and her irreproachable conduct. The second woman, who'd been in the chair to the left, was Madame de Fantan. She was fifty, and so unexpectedly beautiful that she made a vanity of her age. Nothing was known about her, except that her first marriage had been unhappy, and she'd been separated from her children. It was also said that her marriage to Monsieur de Fantan hadn't made up for her earlier unhappiness, and people were surprised that such beauty could've survived so much grief. In any case people admired and respected both her and Madame du Bergh for their heroism in the face of their misfortunes, and for the first-class education they'd given their children; Madame de Fantan had a daughter, and Madame du Bergh had a son.

Luizzi didn't inquire further about those two, thinking he knew what there was to know. Instead he asked a neighbor as casually as possible who the woman was who'd been left so shamefully alone between two empty seats.

"By God!" the neighbor answered. "That's Madame de Farkley."

"I don't know her."

"The illegitimate daughter of the Marquis d'Andeli."

"Ah!" said Luizzi, in a tone that showed the name meant nothing to him.

"You know!" went on the other man impatiently. "Laura de Farkley, the one about whom the joke goes, *whoever wants her can have her*. You get it?"

"Yes, of course. But I'd like to know her story."

"Anyone can tell you that."

"You're quite right when you say anyone," interjected a gentleman who joined the conversation without disturbing the stranglehold of his starched white necktie; he was a dandy famous at that time for the line of his creases and the symmetry of his knots. "You're quite right to say anyone, because no one can know the whole story."

"There's Cosmo de Mareuilles," said the first man Luizzi had spoken to. "They say he was her lover, and he must have exact information to give Baron de Luizzi."

"Bah!" said the other man. "Cosmo's like the rest of us: he knows who was before him and who was after him."

"And who shared at the same time, perhaps."

"Probably so, but he's not the kind of man to keep a list. You have to be good at arithmetic to total sums above a certain magnitude, and that's not Cosmo's strong suit."

"I'd still like to know…" began Luizzi.

"My dear sir!" cried the second of the two dandies. "I'd just as soon recite you the *Thousand and One Nights*! Anyway, as I said earlier, no one besides Madame de Farkley herself can tell you the whole story—and even then, for it to be accurate, she'd have to publish a new edition every morning: updated, corrected, and above all expanded."

Luizzi wasn't present for that last charming piece of wit, because when he heard only Madame de Farkley could tell her story, he'd immediately remembered he could hear the whole thing from the source who'd already told him so many stories, and he promised himself he'd satisfy his curiosity. But to get more out of the experience than he had previously, he wanted to get to know Madame de Farkley in person first. He wanted to find out what kind of tale she'd tell about herself. He reasoned that he'd never have a better opportunity to assess vice at its highest state of development—whether this woman paraded her misconduct brazenly enough to defy all insults, or whether she tried to hide it under a hypocrisy that pretended not to see it.

As soon as he'd formed that plan, he made his way into the parlor that was now full of men. After greeting a few women he moved gradually closer to Madame de Farkley, and sat down next to her. She couldn't help glancing at the man who'd taken the empty chair. That quick, intense, fiery look filled Luizzi with a kind of dread. It seemed to him it wasn't the first time he'd been charmed by those eyes, and it struck him he'd known that wan, tired face in the prime of its youth and innocence. However, having searched his memory in vain for the source of that feeling, he decided to start a conversation. The performance they'd heard provided a natural subject, and he'd just opened with some harmless remark when Madame de Marignon suddenly reappeared in the parlor.

Seeing Luizzi sitting next to Madame de Farkley, the lady of the house gave him a look of sharp disapproval. However, she approached the two of them and said in a perfectly casual tone, "My dear Madame de Farkley, I've come to find you to ask for your advice about a cashmere shawl I want to give my niece. Not only do you have exquisite taste, but I know you're an authority on the question."

"I'm happy to help."

"I fear I'm taking advantage of your kindness."

"Not at all."

"By the way, how's the Marquis d'Andeli doing?"

"Thriving, like a man who's happy."

"He's not feeling his age?"

"On the contrary, he's expecting me tonight for the ball at the Opéra."

"That's what you call a good father!"

"Yes, indeed, he's wonderful…"

While that little exchange going on, Madame de Farkley gathered up from her chair her shawl, her fan, and her bouquet—all of the elegant accessories of a woman dressed for a ball. She left the parlor with Madame de Marignon. Immediately after that, Madame de Fantan and Madame du Bergh reappeared; and a moment later Madame de Marignon returned alone. A woman couldn't be thrown out of a parlor more blatantly than Madame de Farkley had just been.

Luizzi had remained where he was; he stood up when the two prudes came back in. But they thanked him so curtly for his politeness that he realized the great impropriety he'd just committed. Madame de Marignon expressed much more openly what the angry faces of the other two left him to guess at; as she passed by Luizzi she turned with a look of disdainful surprise and said, "What? You're still here? I thought you had a rendezvous at the Opéra ball!"

Those words produced in Luizzi the kind of strange bewilderment that can make a man the cruelest creature alive. His whole being rose up against the hateful accusation Madame de Marignon had just directed at Madame de Farkley. "What?" he said to himself. "She thinks that casual answer to a casual question was a signal thrown out by Madame de Farkley? Meaning she can be found tonight at the Opéra—it's a rendezvous! That's impossible. No woman is capable of such indecency. Madame de Marignon is blinded by a prejudice that makes her attach a dirty meaning to the most innocent words. Madame de Farkley may have behaved loosely, even improperly, but that's nowhere near throwing yourself at the first man who comes along. She's young enough and fashionable enough to be sure at least of being desired and pursued. That woman is being treated as lower than she deserves; she doesn't even know me—I'm nothing but an insignificant stranger to her..."

The flow of generous thoughts passing through Luizzi's mind came to a sudden stop as he noticed the whispering going on concerning him. In a sudden reversal he cried out—still to himself—"Am I just being a fool? Am I the only one who thinks that woman has self-restraint when in fact she doesn't? Am I—once again, like so many other times—going to throw away my chance for a few hours of pleasure, because of too high an opinion of others and too low an opinion of myself? I've been wrong too often about the false appearance of virtue to let myself be misled by scruples that arise from nowhere but within me. I want to find out for sure; let's go to the Opéra!"

How many betrayals, how many shameful deeds, how much bragging has that fear of looking foolish made men commit who would otherwise have remained reasonably honorable! As he left Madame de Marignon's salon, Luizzi committed one of those shameful deeds: he gave that woman's spiteful remark all the credit of a sure thing. Her remark had been overheard; Luizzi had been watched, and now was followed. One of the dandies who'd spoken so highly of Madame de Farkley pretended to be leaving at the same time; letting Luizzi go first, he overheard the footman call out to the coach driver, "To the Opéra!" He went straight back inside and told the story to half a dozen friends. They laughed loudly enough that everybody wanted to know the reason for their almost unseemly good cheer.

At first they replied, "It's nothing, a joke! That poor Luizzi—he looked so triumphant! A good fellow, really, but one who deserves no better."

"What's going on?" asked Madame de Marignon.

"It's not worth repeating."

"Were you talking about Baron de Luizzi?"

"About him, or about someone else."

"Did he leave?"

One gentleman nodded, with such a subtle smile that all the others burst out laughing.

"What's going on?" asked Madame de Marignon again.

"He went to the ball at the Opéra," said the same gentleman, articulating every syllable to give it emphasis.

"How dreadful!" cried Madame de Marignon disdainfully. "It's scandalous!"

"Even worse, it's in bad taste!" added Cosmo de Mareuilles.

"Yes," said Madame de Marignon. "I know you're hiding something."

"Oh, you wrong me!" said the dandy, prancing around.

"I'm wronging you? So you deny it?"

"No, no," said another man. "If you're wronging him, it's in accusing him of hiding something. He's never made a secret of anything."

"Ah, gentlemen, gentlemen!" replied Madame de Marignon in the tone—part outward indignation, part inward delight—that a prude uses for a perfectly expressed piece of malice. Then she went away and found her two friends. Between them, and a few people who came to join them, arose a conversation in which the cruel listeners feigned cries of astonishment while Madame de Marignon reported Madame de Farkley's reckless remark and Baron de Luizzi's departure. In referring to the poor woman who'd been thrown out, even the strictest among them eventually used words you rarely hear except on a street corner.

If Luizzi had been able to overhear that conversation, he would've learned a great secret about the prudishness of vocabulary in certain circles. A woman who'd refuse to listen to an even slightly lewd story veiled in respectable terms will permit—and if necessary even use—the most vulgar language if it allows her to insult another woman and condemn vice. In those circumstances, Madame de Fantan's virtue drove her to the limit in asserting that right.

"Yes, yes," she said to Madame de Marignon. "She came here to engage in the same trade some girls practice on the public thoroughfare."

"Oh, ma'am!" protested a man who was old enough to have known Madame de Fantan in her youth.

"Yes, sir," cried Madame de Fantan, annoyed by even a shadow of opposition to the justice of her judgments. "Yes, sir, Madame de Farkley came here to…"

"Oh, oh, oh! Don't say that!" interrupted the same man, his "oh, oh, oh!" drowning out the fatal word that, even if not heard, was certainly spoken.

The emotions stirred up in Madame de Marignon's salon by those events were such that for a long while all the skill of the singers who followed one another at the piano made no impression. Indeed, what music, no matter how excellent, can compete with a juicy piece of slander? But then something unusual happened. At the height of the whispering and the chatter, a man dressed in black—with a thin sharp-featured face, a high narrow forehead, deep-sunk eyes that sparkled with a savage glow under thick eyebrows, and a thin mocking mouth—sat down at the piano. As soon as his fingers touched the keys all eyes turned to him. It was as if the strings, instead of being struck by the instrument's leather-covered hammers, were being pinched by steel claws. The piano screeched and squealed under his frightening hands.

The man's appearance held the attention his musical prelude had summoned. Soon his sinister, mocking voice sent shivers all around the circle of his listeners, and he began the slander aria from *The Barber of Seville*.[41] The word "slander" rang out with such sarcasm that suddenly everyone fell silent. As the singer went on, his savage ringing voice and his biting intonation chilled the audience. The whole time he was singing he kept his eyes fixed on the principal trio, consisting of Mesdames du Bergh and de Fantan, who'd gone back to their seats, and Madame de Marignon, who'd taken Madame de Farkley's seat—as if to rehabilitate it for the injury it had suffered, the way a cross is erected at the spot where a murder took place.

The man's mocking stare, held so long it became insulting, seemed to frighten Madame de Marignon to the point that she clutched the arms of the chair in her tensed hands and pressed herself against the seat back. It was as if she were afraid the eyes fixed on her would project some scorching beam in her direction. Finally, when the singer reached the peroration of the aria, whose last words depict so vividly the slander victim's cry of pain and the slanderer's joy, the man gave his singing such an acerbic tone and his voice such echoing power that his listeners' hearts skipped a beat and all the crystal rang in unison.[42]

Everyone was filled with intense anxious anticipation. When the singer had finished, and an icy silence had lingered for a few seconds, he bowed and went away into the outer parlor. Immediately, as if the spell had broken, Madame de Marignon rose and, turning to the musician who was in charge of organizing her concerts, asked him who that man was. He didn't know, and had assumed he was an amateur performer from Madame de Marignon's social circle. She asked around to find out if he'd been brought here by someone who wanted to show-

---

[41] *The Barber of Seville* (1816), an opera by Gioachino Rossini based on a play by Pierre Beaumarchais, contains an aria, "La Calunnia," sung by the character Don Basilio: "Slander is a little breeze / a very nice little breeze / which subtly, imperceptibly / begins to murmur…"

[42] The last lines of the aria are, "And the poor slandered wretch, / vilified, trampled, / sunk beneath the public lash, / fortunately dies."

case a performer as yet unacknowledged; but no one knew him. Then she went to look for the man himself, but no one could find him; the servants said they'd seen no one leave for the past half hour. She grew worried and, while her guests talked in an uproar about that odd singer, she had her servants search her private apartment; they found nothing.

Madame de Marignon kept saying to everyone, "Who could that man be?"

"My word!" answered one of the dandies we've already met. "He must be a burglar!"

"Unless it was the Devil!" laughed the old man who'd tried to put a stop to Madame de Fantan's remarks.

That commonplace witticism, usually offered and accepted so casually in conversation, made Madame de Marignon turn pale; and she was upset enough to let slip, "The Devil! What a thought!…"

She withdrew almost immediately. A moment later it was announced that she was indisposed. The parlors emptied rapidly, and everyone went away with a bad feeling.

Meanwhile Luizzi had gone to the ball at the Opéra, that battlefield of beauty in the details. Indeed, that's where victory goes to slim lithe figures, small slender hands, fine arched feet. Lots of stories have been told about passions inspired by all of those secondary perfections, only to end at an ugly face and the shattering of a beautiful dream. But there's another experience that can only happen at the Opéra ball: the feeling a man has when, after turning away from a woman with a mediocre face, he discovers she has charms he hadn't noticed. As inferior as she is to other women in a salon, where a fresh glow and perfect features eclipse a muddy complexion and an ill-proportioned face, just as much is she their superior when she's at the Opéra ball, where observation, unable to see beneath her domino mask, finds attractions that are scorned elsewhere.

Luizzi experienced some of that. First he noticed a woman in a hooded domino cloak who stopped suddenly at the sight of him and studied him for a moment. It was only for a few seconds; the domino cloak resumed walking, and followed the ambling stream of people. Luizzi was at the entrance to the Opéra foyer, and that masked woman was walking along the corridor outside the second-floor loges. He followed her with his eyes, admiring first her graceful, flowing figure. The mask turned to look at him, and the slender, lithe figure twisted gently like a silk rope. Luizzi waited for the mask to pass by again to get a better look at her. He examined the woman's feet: they were narrow and slender, and so white that their brightness shone through the black silk stockings she was wearing. As she walked she set her feet down with elegant firmness. Those feet were at ease in satin shoes, and the ribbons that wound around her ankles merely showed off the tapered roundness of her calves.

The woman passed by several times for Luizzi's eager inspection. The gentle sway of her walk, the elegance of her figure, the refinement of all of it put together, struck him so forcefully that he took a step toward her to see her better. She noticed and, as if she feared being recognized, she raised her hand to press the fabric "beard" beneath the mask against her face. That hand was covered by a glove; but the glove, whose whiteness stood out against the black satin, revealed the most elegant, carefree, distinguished hand.

Luizzi cried out to himself, "Who can this beauty be?"

He stayed where he was while she passed and passed again. But already he'd begun to realize the absurdity of that pointless attention, and he was about go away in search of Madame de Farkley when the woman let go of her partner's arm and quickly approached Luizzi. She leaned close to his ear and said quietly, "You're Baron de Luizzi, aren't you?"

"Yes."

"At four, under the clock in the foyer, I have to speak to you."

Before Luizzi had time to reply she'd gone away, and Cosmo de Mareuilles was saying to him mockingly, "Well, well! And when is your happiness scheduled for?"

"What happiness?"

"Why, the happiness Madame de Farkley plans to give you."

"What! That was Madame de Farkley?"

"Herself."

"But, at Madame de Marignon's she seemed to be of a quite debatable beauty, whereas here..."

"Here she's ravishing, isn't she? She knows that perfectly well, which is why she makes her rendezvous for the Opéra ball, and she hooked you."

"Me?"

"Come on, don't act modest. It seems her advances were even a little over the top. Madame de Marignon is furious, but you're not at her salon anymore. I advise you to be punctual with Laura; she doesn't like being kept waiting. In any case, she's worth it, I swear!"

"You know that?"

"That's what people say."

Cosmo moved away, and Luizzi glanced around in search of Madame de Farkley. She was coming down one of the staircases leading to the ballroom, and the chandelier illuminated her in all her splendor. A few people spoke to her as she passed; when she turned to answer, all of her grace and style and elegance in motion were displayed in that moment.

Again Luizzi cried out to himself, "Isn't that woman splendid!"

He glanced at his watch: it was barely one-thirty; he still had two and a half hours to wait. He felt within him an impatience that surprised him. "Well!" he said to himself. "Am I going to get worked up about that woman? Could I possibly want her enough to trouble myself over her? Could I be in love with her? A woman everyone's had—a woman it's almost shameful to have had...

and not to have had! It's madness. And yet I've got too long a wait just to stand here like an idiot following her with my eyes. I need to find something to do."

Madame de Farkley passed again, and gave him a meaningful look. He found her wonderfully graceful, and his heart pounded. "All right," he said, "it's settled: I'm the favorite of the evening. Well, so be it. But I don't want to be more awkward than the rest—I even want to stand out in her memory. The men who came before me knew about most of her adventures; but there must be some secret stories only she knows, and those are the stories I want to reveal to her, after letting her believe she found a sucker in me."

He moved away from the crowd, pulled out his little bell, and rang it…

A gentleman dressed in black passed nearby. "Here I am," said Satan. "What do you want?"

"I want to know the history of that woman going by over there."

"The one who was thrown out of Madame de Marignon's so ignominiously?"

"Yes."

"And why do you want to know?"

"Because before I get to know her in person, I want to know her through you, to find out just how far a woman can push audacity in deceiving a man."

"You're right. Here you are in a completely new setting, in which you've barely set foot. It's good to recognize that, so you aren't at risk of frequent stumbles. But the picture wouldn't be complete if I didn't first tell you the history of the two women who got Madame de Farkley thrown out."

"Is there something to say against them?"

"In my capacity as the Devil, I can't judge whether the story does them credit or discredit. But you can't really understand Madame de Farkley, who's a woman dishonored in the eyes of the world, till you learn the worth of Mesdames de Fantan and du Bergh, who are women of honor in the eyes of the world."

"All right," said Luizzi.

Together they went into a loge. Cosmo de Mareuilles, who was passing by just then, turned to a young man who was with him and said, "Well! Madame de Marignon wanted to know who that peculiar singer at her salon was; Luizzi could tell her, since there they are together in the same loge."

"Presumably it was the baron who brought him there."

"He certainly could have—he cares so little about propriety!"

Chapter XVII: The First Chair

And the Devil began in this fashion: "Twenty-five years ago Madame du Bergh was named Mademoiselle Nathalie Firion. She was the daughter of Monsieur Firion, a purveyor: rich as royalty, fashionable, with a distinguished way of speaking, and who had in the highest degree the skill of making people accept his money. I've never seen a man buy more women while leaving them free to believe they hadn't sold themselves. Magistrates, army generals, government officials received millions from him they thought they'd earned legitimately; and in return they did him favors they considered freely given because the method of payment had been indirect. Don't imagine, my dear Luizzi, that corruption by means of money is an easy thing. You can buy a servant, a police informer, a kept woman, for an agreed-upon price, and it doesn't matter exactly how it's offered. But with a Member of Parliament, a writer, a woman in society, you need delicacy, tact, a light touch, and above all a strong will. If ever you enter the world of imperial princesses, I'll tell you the story of the crowned head who sold herself to a fashionable tailor. It's the best story I know of that kind."

"Another time," said Luizzi. "Right now I mostly want to hear the history of Madame du Bergh."

"So you can get to Madame de Farkley sooner? Fine."

As I was saying, Monsieur Firion knew better than anyone in France how to get his deals accepted; and of all the people who claim money can get you anything you want, he might've been the only one with the right to say it without boasting. As a result, he had a remarkable ability to promise and to deliver whatever was asked of him. No matter what his only child Nathalie asked for, she was never denied. To every request of hers, Firion replied, "I'll buy it for you," whether it was jewelry, a dress, a painting, a house, or even something belonging to a stranger.

People had often criticized Firion for his indulgence of her, without noticing it was a compulsion. The further he went in that kind of contest, the harder he found it to keep his promises, the more it interested him. As a result, this man, who'd almost never met an obstacle to getting what he wanted, had made a hobby of the challenges his daughter's whims created for him. He liked to talk about how he'd overcome them, to describe all of the skill, the cleverness, the trickery he'd had to use to get what she'd asked him for. His masterpiece, as he called it, was acquiring from an elderly German baroness the pug dog that was her pride and joy. A great prince, on learning of that negotiation, offered him the Saint Petersburg ambassadorship. Firion declined. "Tell His Highness," he replied, "I'm neither high-born enough, nor poor enough, nor stupid enough to make a good ambassador." Firion's political career went no further.

However, while he went to sleep at night delighted by his triumphs, Nathalie was growing sad and pensive. Instead of the bizarre wishes she'd constantly expressed as if to test her father's obedience, now she replied to him only with deep meaningless sighs: she was sixteen. Firion was both alarmed and delighted at the change—alarmed because his daughter was languishing; her eyes showed she'd been crying, her pallor was a sign of insomnia. For the first time there was sorrow in that heart, which up to now had been so innocently willful and despotic. Was it that she wanted to be married? Firion hoped so. He expected there to arise from that sorrow an extraordinary demand he'd be delighted to satisfy. If his daughter had been infatuated with a prince, he reasoned he had millions enough to give him. If she'd set her sights on a married man, he could arrange the divorce that would make the chosen one available.

As I said, Firion was in the grip of a compulsion, and he'd reached the point where he gave Nathalie what she wanted much more for his own satisfaction than for hers. So he waited and made ready in silence. He knew his daughter well enough to assume the barriers he'd have to overcome would only be those of social rank. Nathalie was tall, beautiful, refined; she was made to spark love and desire, but she wasn't made to feel it. A child's mind in an almost mature body gave her neither the burning desires that overcome reason and virtue, nor the attacks of feverish anxiety that produce the same result. Utter self-absorption protected her against those tender feelings that melt the hardest natures and bend the stiffest wills. Firion therefore believed he'd only have to satisfy her ambition and her vanity.

All of the doting father's expectations were undone by something he'd never even considered: the influence of the literature of his era.

"What do you mean?" asked Luizzi.

"You'll see!" said the Devil, smiling in delight—because he'd just spotted a pickpocket stealing a dandy's watch while the latter was ogling a masked woman outside the second-floor loges. He coughed, then went on:

One of humanity's greatest bits of nonsense is contained in the saying, "I want to be loved for myself!" If you ask the people who say it with such feeling what they mean by "myself," they end up, no matter how much you push them, at an astonishing series of absurdities. They say, "I don't want to be loved for my wealth—that's a mercenary love. I don't want to be loved for my looks—that's a superficial love. I don't want to be loved for my wit—that's a cerebral love. Oh!" they cry in their enthusiasm for pure love, "I want to be loved for myself! Yes, if I were ugly, stupid, and poor, I'd want to be loved; because the only true love is the one that speaks not to wealth or beauty or wit, but only to the heart."

Especially in those days, men had poisoned themselves with that fixation. But if a woman had decided to choose over one of those gentleman some peasant with all the qualities they aspired to, that wouldn't have kept them from utterly despising her. Besides leading to idiotic suggestions that salons be formed in keeping with the fashionable principle of being loved for oneself, that obsession had produced a flood of novels, tales, and comic operas with countless princes and princesses disguised as shepherds and shepherdesses. The consequent influence of the world on literature, and of literature on the world, had raised that fixation to a fervor, a delirium, a rage.

Meanwhile Nathalie grew sadder by the day, till Firion was alarmed enough to take it seriously. Though he'd made it his law to satisfy his daughter's slightest wishes, he'd taken care never to anticipate them. This time, however, he set aside his precautions. One evening, during a lavish party where Nathalie, sparkling with beauty and jewelry, was surrounded by submissive flattering praise, she gave way, burst into tears, and began to sob. Running into her father's arms, she cried, "Take me away! Let's get out of here! I'm suffocating, I'm dying!"

That scene frightened Firion; he worried that she'd succumbed to some passionate attachment, intensified by jealousy. He took his daughter away, lifting her half-fainted into his carriage. But no sooner was Nathalie alone with her father than she ripped the tiara of flowers from her head, pulled off her girlish jewelry, tore her dress of India muslin—a fabric hard to find in those days of the Continental blockade[43]—and trampled them all underfoot, crying, "Oh, I'm so miserable! I'm so miserable!"

"What's wrong? What do you want?" asked her father in alarm.

"I want what you can't give me."

"What could that be?"

"I want to be loved for myself!" cried Nathalie, giving her father a look of triumph.

That answer stunned Firion and undid all of his preparations. It's hard to buy a heart that loves unselfishly: you can't buy something that will cease to exist the moment it's paid for. Firion's business acumen was left helpless, and he fell into the shallowest commonplaces. "How can you imagine you're not loved for yourself? You're young and beautiful, you've got intelligence, you've got wealth…"

"And that's what makes me miserable! The Duke of —'s son pesters me with his attentions, but he only loves my money, with which he'll be able to polish his tarnished coat of arms. Colonel V— adores me, I think unselfishly, but he'd show off his wife just as arrogantly as he shows off his hussar's uni-

---

[43] Because of a trade embargo during the Napoleonic Wars, between 1806 and 1814 muslin from British India would've been impossible to buy legally in France, but some was smuggled in.

form: as long as she's prettier than General B——'s wife he'll be satisfied, because he hates General B——. A thousand other men court me assiduously, and it makes me blush for myself as well as for them, because not one of them feels true love, which speaks directly from one heart to another. If I were a poor girl, with no fortune, no doubt I'd meet a man who'd feel something simply for me. Oh, the poor are so happy! They can trust the affection they inspire."

Nathalie went on at length in that vein, and for the first time Firion, undone by his daughter's whim, couldn't answer, "I'll buy it for you." Still, he hoped the whim would pass, as had most of those he'd satisfied. But Nathalie had a newfound capacity for wanting the same thing for a long time; she clung stubbornly to her fixation, and soon she'd developed a profound revulsion for the world. Her health was affected, and for a moment her life was in danger. Firion, who'd placed all of his hopes and all of his expectations for his fortune in her, who'd dreamt fondly of making her into a great lady, dropped everything to save her; and to save her he gave in as far as possible to her fixation on being loved for herself.

So he took her secretly to the health spa town of B—— and settled in a modest house under the name of Bernard. They kept neither horses nor liveried servants. A single maidservant waited on both father and daughter. They went out on foot and dressed unassumingly, and if some Parisian dandy had passed them he'd have had trouble recognizing them. In fact, no one paid them any attention; and what Firion had thought would be just the thing to cure his daughter only worsened her condition.

"You see!" she said. "In plain sight you have proof of the falsity of all the men who were pursuing me with their compliments. I'm neither less pretty nor less good than I was in Paris, and yet no one here is courting me—because I'm no longer rich! Oh, what an awful misery it is to have a heart made for love and to find no one who can understand it!"

Firion didn't know what to say, because for once his daughter was cruelly right. Still, he watched for chances to show her off, and as soon as any man glanced at Nathalie her father felt so grateful he bowed and smiled and bothered the fellow. He played his part so clumsily that in the end people began to say the strangest things about him. It reached the point that people avoided them as if they were third-rate con artists. The father and daughter began to doubt themselves; Firion had lost his nerve, and Nathalie was growing awkward and ugly.

You have to understand, my dear Luizzi, success is like drunkenness; it truly multiplies the power of some wits and some good looks. There are men who know only how to win, and women who know only how to be happy; the slightest setback wipes out the former, and neglect makes the latter ugly. Those people are like racehorses: the moment they can't make the circuit of the Champs de Mars in less than three minutes, the best runners turn into old nags.

Meanwhile the season was almost over, and not one man had yet said a word to Nathalie, when Baron du Bergh showed up in B——. Baron du Bergh was a gentleman from Quercy, who came to the spa to use up what was left of his fine fortune and his fragile health. He was an orphan, who'd sacrificed a frail, delicate nature to the excitements of gambling and debauchery. Though he was still young, barely twenty-five, he'd reached the point where the contemplation of either cheating at cards or a woman produced no emotion; his heart beat neither from shame nor from love; he was vice perfected.

He was also a man of superior quality—at least enough that he took note of Nathalie as soon as he met her. The acquaintance wasn't hard to arrange: he introduced himself, and was made welcome. This girl, pretty though sickly and without a fortune, was the only conquest he could hope for in his condition as a ruined man. He therefore attached himself devotedly to her. He surrounded her with his attentions and his compliments, and soon Nathalie began to believe she'd found what she'd hoped for so long—she thought she was loved for herself, and once again she became beautiful and happy and sparkling, and her exhilaration even frightened her father.

Du Bergh took part in all of their walks, all of their pastimes, all of their conversations. Nathalie privately planned her marriage, and made it her joy, her glory, her triumph. Firion, who knew the moral, physical, and financial worth of du Bergh, turned a deaf ear. But since he wasn't aware of his daughter's emotional and physical coldness, he didn't understand where her exhilaration might lead her. In fact, he was wrong to be concerned.

To a nature like Nathalie's, to be loved for herself meant to be loved for nothing. Her wish was to inspire a pure, selfless passion; she barely allowed du Bergh to tell her she was pretty. Still, having no desire to disfigure herself to test the sincerity of his love, she acted as offended as possible, so as to impose on him the tyranny women claim the right to exercise to a greater or lesser degree. I need hardly tell you du Bergh didn't submit to that regime for long; he soon showed, by frequent absences, that he liked women for a reason. That neglect triggered a genuine relapse in Nathalie; she loved du Bergh out of vanity, and above all out of expediency.

"What?" asked Luizzi at the Devil's choice of words. "She loved him out of expediency?"

"Of course. Nathalie had gone down the wrong path, and—thanks to the stubbornness of petty minds—she'd stuck to it like a rebellious child. But she'd been delighted to find a man who'd help her escape from it. So she flew into an unspeakable fury when du Bergh seemed to be getting away from her. Her pride took a fall, and nothing is more dangerous for women; Nathalie fell seriously ill from it. Firion found a doctor…"

"For his daughter?" asked Luizzi with a yawn.

"No, for du Bergh."

"For du Bergh?"

"Yes."

He went to a sort of executioner, well known for the fatal care he gave his patients. Firion approached the doctor by telling him the simple truth about how he was worth millions and it was because of his daughter's whim that he was hiding the fact. Firion recovered all of his finesse in doing so, because it's difficult to use the truth to tell a lie. Then, without giving the doctor time to think, he told him his daughter had finally met the man she wanted, and that man was Baron du Bergh.

"Du Bergh?" said the doctor, stunned.

"Yes," said Firion, taking no notice, "and I'd pay a hundred thousand francs to the man who can cure him of his mortal illness."

"What? A mortal illness?" asked the doctor, whose ears and mind both pricked up at the mention of a hundred thousand francs. "It's a mild inflammation of the lungs, that's all. But if he'll follow my advice, in two months he'll be as healthy as you or me."

"Well then, see him and cure him, but keep it a secret. I'm putting all my trust in you."

"You won't be disappointed."

"I hope not." Firion had judged correctly: his trust in the doctor wasn't disappointed. No sooner had he left than the discreet doctor hurried to du Bergh and told him what he'd just learned from that so-called Monsieur Bernard.

At that point the Devil stopped. Studying Luizzi carefully, he seemed to abandon his story. Then he went on, "You're a reasonable man, my dear Luizzi, but like all reasonable men you can only allow something to be possible if it can be explained. The great secret of intuition is unknown to you. You dismiss as fairytale fantasies all of the wonderful discoveries made by a sense you don't have and that can only be called instinct. So you'll have trouble understanding the way du Bergh reacted to the news."

"It must at least have struck him as unlikely. A multimillionaire in hiding requires some explanation, and I assume du Bergh refused to believe it..."

"Not at all," interrupted the Devil.

"Then he must still have wondered why a man as rich and powerful as Firion would agree to give him his daughter."

"That's not a bad point. Then what?"

"Then he assumed paternal affection had blinded the father enough to make the sacrifice..."

"Wrong! Completely wrong!"

"Look," protested Luizzi, "I summoned you to tell me a story, not to pose riddles. What did du Bergh actually do?"

"He guessed immediately—I already told you he had a wonderfully developed instinct for vice—that Firion only wanted to have him treated by that particular doctor so as to be more sure to be rid of him."

"That's horrible!" cried Luizzi.

"Du Bergh thought it very clever, and he positioned his artillery accordingly."

He went back to Nathalie and—knowing now what part he was supposed to play—ended up persuading her as completely as possible that he loved her for herself. Nathalie, all the more delighted with her victory because for a moment she thought she'd lost him, wanted above all to reward a love so unselfish, so strong, so true. She announced to her father that Baron du Bergh was the only man she'd ever agree to marry.

Against all logic, Firion didn't refuse. He just put off the wedding for two months. He calculated that, thanks to the care of the doctor he'd chosen for him, du Bergh couldn't last longer than that. Indeed, du Bergh got paler and weaker by the day, and in spite of all his efforts he couldn't hide the true state of his health from Nathalie. The poor girl sincerely despaired. She blamed fate, she came up with a stream of ridiculous expressions cursing destiny, which seemed bent on persecuting her by robbing her of the only hope she had left in the world.

"By the way," said the Devil, taking a pinch of tobacco, "you humans have no end of astonishing words that are meaningless and that you use with impressive confidence. Like the word *destiny*, for example. Well! I say, if there exists in the whole universe someone who can explain to me what humans mean by destiny, I promise to be that man's servant, even if he's never had a servant or he's been a servant himself—two guaranteed ways of being treated like a slave."

The Devil grew pensive, and Luizzi—in whom the tale hadn't inspired much interest so far—said rather scornfully, "You're not in top form tonight, Mister Satan, and I don't know what I'm supposed to learn from the stupid story you're telling me."

The Devil eyed Luizzi with his cruellest look, and replied with a snicker, "Do you believe in Madame du Bergh's virtue?"

"You haven't told me anything yet to make me doubt it."

"Do you believe a woman who treated another woman so insolently this evening could be a poisoner and an adulteress?"

"Impossible!" cried Luizzi. "Madame du Bergh a poisoner and an adulteress!"

"Oh, it wasn't done in any ordinary way. It's a secret between her and me, and that's why I wanted to tell you about it."

"Is there nothing in this world that's genuine?"

"The truth is genuine."

"And, for God's sake, who knows the truth?"

"I do," cried the Devil, "and I'll tell it to you. Listen carefully, and don't miss a word of my story."

So du Bergh was dying, and Nathalie was in despair, and Firion was congratulating himself. But now a new whim of Nathalie's put the knife to her father's throat. Nathalie found a new sentiment ready-made in a sentence in a novel. Here's the passage from that novel:

Oh, if I can't be his, I want at least to bear his name! I'll never hear his name without it ringing like something sacred in my ears. Every time I hear someone call my name, I'll remember the love I lost and the happiness I looked forward to.

That was all Nathalie needed to construct a desire against which all of her father's objections could do nothing. "If he dies before I marry him, I'll kill myself over his grave... I want to bear his name... I want that... Let it be the pledge of a love that's worthy of me!" Nathalie had gotten herself so worked up by the idea that she'd acquired poison so she could carry it out.

Firion first thought it over, then consulted a doctor of some reputation and skill—not the one to whom he'd entrusted du Bergh. The second doctor, who'd found out from the local pharmacist what his colleague was prescribing, told Firion that without a doubt du Bergh was a dead man. Firion left with joy in his heart but tears in his eyes—a silly deceit he could've skipped—and he hurried away to tell Nathalie he agreed to everything. "By God!" he said to himself. "A woman widowed two days after her wedding, a virgin widow, that'll be extraordinary enough to give Nathalie the heightened attraction she lacks."

The wedding day was thus decided on, and du Bergh—who'd found out Firion's real name but still pretended to know nothing of his wealth—was carried to the chapel in a sedan chair. He got out dying, and was seated in the nuptial armchair to receive the priest's blessing at the very moment everyone thought he was about to expire. But he had strength enough to be carried to Firion's house and laid on the "hymenial couch"—the name in fashion at the time—which would no doubt be his deathbed.

To Nathalie the whole scene had a certain poetry to it, and she got caught up in it with enough enthusiasm that her father found it necessary to remove her from the room in which du Bergh was about to expire: he was worried about the effect of that death—no matter how inevitable and foreseen—on his daughter's mind. But as soon as Nathalie understood why she'd been forced to leave, she began to wail so loudly it seemed less risky to let her go back to her dying husband. Once she was free, she walked solemnly back toward the fatal room, announcing that she meant to keep a solitary vigil there.

Night had come. What a beautiful scene was about to be performed! Do you grasp it—this girl, in the presence of her first, sainted love, who was about to return to heaven? Can you see her, kneeling beside the dying man who adored her and who was using his final breath to say, "Nathalie, I love you!" Can you feel the heartrending beauty of the sight of that man in agony next to the pretty girl who'd just given herself to him, and who would sweeten the last moments of his life by telling him she was rich, and that if only he could've lived he'd have lived a life of luxury and pleasure? Is there anything more dramatic than raising joyful hopes around a dying man—ever greater hopes the more he loses the power to fulfill them?

By the hell of which I'm king, Nathalie certainly had a wonderful scene to look forward to! It would be enough to give a tremendous splash to her return to Paris... And that scene awaited her, behind the door separating her from du Bergh. That unquenchable thirst of the female heart, that thirst to extract from any situation all of its dreadful macabre emotions, drove Nathalie on; she opened the door and shut it behind her. Du Bergh...

"Du Bergh was dead!" cried Luizzi.
The Devil gave him a pitying look.

Du Bergh was sitting in a wing chair, holding a glass of Bordeaux, with a cigar in his mouth, humming the tune to "Boy Beloved by the Ladies"...[44]

"How imprudent!" cried Nathalie, looking at the wine.

"It's excellent, my dear," said du Bergh, rising and tossing his cigar out the window. "After you and his millions, it's the best thing your father has."

Seeing du Bergh full of energy and good health, Nathalie drew back. She stood there in a state of indescribable astonishment, while du Bergh, putting his arms boldly around her waist, went on, "It's a little surprise I've been preparing for you, my angel. Come now, don't be such a prude, my love! I didn't marry you to be treated worse than a lover, so don't act like a child."

"Ah," cried Nathalie. "My father has betrayed me!"

"My dear! Your father has betrayed you? What could you mean by that? Did you specifically ask him for a deceased husband? Were you in on the plot?"

"What plot?"

"Ah, here we go," said du Bergh, pouring himself another glass of wine. "I'll tell you everything, so we can be clear where all three of us stand relative to each other. First, your father, who's an eminent person, didn't agree to give his daughter to a man like me without a compelling reason. And what is a man like me? A libertine, a gambler, a forger."

"A forger!" cried Nathalie.

"A note for a trifling two thousand guineas. And his son-in-law's reputation is too important to your father for him not to hush up that business. We've

---

[44] *"Enfant chéri des dames"*: a popular song, possibly composed by François Devienne (1759-1803) for his 1792 opera *Les Visitandines* ("The Sisters of the Visitation"), or possibly a preexisting song merely used by Devienne.

got time; the bill of exchange won't come due at E—'s for a month. Daddy Firion will silence all complaints by paying it."

"A forger!" cried Nathalie, who had trouble keeping her thoughts straight under the shock of all the strange things she was hearing.

"I don't think your father was fully informed of the circumstances. But in any case he knew enough about me not to want to give you to me unless he hoped my death would soon rid him of his son-in-law."

"My father anticipated your death?" asked Nathalie, still without moving.

"The old fox did better than that! He helped it along."

"My father wanted to murder you?"

"No, no, I'm not saying that. He's too sophisticated for such villainy; but he found me a doctor who'd do the job for him. At my place I still have the whole pile of everything the rascal tried to make me take. I believe the pharmacist has sent me his bill; I hope Monsieur Firion is honorable enough to pay it."

"So... your illness, your weakness, your wasting away..."

"Nicely played, right, Nathalie?"

"And you knew who I was?"

"More or less, my angel."

"That I was rich?"

"Immensely rich, my darling."

"And you dared..."

"What's that, wife?" asked du Bergh.

Nathalie turned away and hid her face in her hands. Du Bergh forced them apart and looked at her. She was crying. "Are you crying because I'm resurrected? So would you have laughed if I'd died?"

Nathalie let out a muffled sob.

"Come now!" went on du Bergh roughly. "Let's explain ourselves a little. Is this what you mean by loving people for themselves? After making such a song and dance about that kind of love, do you only love me as a corpse? Thank heavens, I'm not a corpse, baroness. So cheer up: I still have enough strength to squander your father's entire fortune, if he'll give it to me. That worthy crook! Imagine the look on his face tomorrow morning, when—instead of finding me wheezing and ready to give up the ghost—he finds me lying amorously in his daughter's arms! I really want to give him that shock."

And du Bergh kissed Nathalie. He was half drunk, and she recoiled with loathing and disgust. He began closing the shutters and the curtains, muttering, "Oho, old Firion! Dear father-in-law, you wanted to kill me medico-legally! We'll see... We'll see..."

Nathalie tried to make a run for the door.

"Not a chance, my dove!" said du Bergh, stopping her.

"I'll call for help, sir."

"Why? So you can tell them you're sorry your beloved husband isn't dead?... My good father-in-law, your daughter's worthy of you!..."

Those words seemed to Nathalie to glow with some infernal light, but she shivered and turned her head away so as not to see it. "Sir," she said, "we must separate."

"Excuse me? Why's that?"

"Because we can't live together."

"I'm hoping for the contrary."

"Never."

"There are laws to secure husbands the possession of their wives."

"Well then, sir, let's go away, let's leave France..."

"My child," said du Bergh in an outrageously paternal tone, "your mind's been a little unsettled by everything that's happened. Tomorrow we'll leave for Paris. I'm a decent enough fellow at heart; and as long as your father guarantees us an income of two or three hundred thousand livres, a mansion in town, a chateau in the country, and so forth, I'll treat him with respect, and I won't even speak to him about what he was planning to do to me."

"So your mind's made up?"

"Completely. Remember, Nathalie, for the last two months I've thought about nothing else. Come along, child, it's getting late... My little Nathalie, do you love me?... Come..."

"In a minute," she replied, almost tenderly.

"What are you doing there?"

"Nothing... It's just a habit of mine... I'm putting my earrings away in this secretary."

"You've got a husband now, you don't have to be afraid of burglars anymore."

"Of course," said Nathalie, smiling and turning to face du Bergh, while her hand took a tiny vial out of the secretary.

"That's more like it!" said du Bergh. "Dear heart, let me show you how much I love you." And he laid his hand on her white head kerchief.

"Oh! Go see if there's someone at the door."

"Child!"

"Please!"

He went to the door, opened it a crack, then came back to Nathalie. She was standing by the table, pale and trembling.

"What's wrong?" he asked.

"I feel ill. I'd like a glass of water."

"Have that glass of Bordeaux, it'll do you good."

"Wine doesn't agree with me. But since there's only one glass, I'll throw out the wine and..."

"No need for that, my love. I'm thrifty where it concerns me—I only waste things when it's to my advantage." Du Bergh picked up the glass of wine and emptied it in one swallow. "And now?"

"Now I'm yours," said Nathalie.

"What!" cried Luizzi. "So then she gave herself to that man, and the young du Bergh who's alive now is the son?…"

"That young du Bergh," said the Devil, "is a whole different story. Because there were three drops of prussic acid in Nathalie's vial, and du Bergh hadn't even taken a step before he dropped dead."

"Dead!" echoed Luizzi. "And after that?…"

"My dear friend, it's three in the morning, and Madame de Farkley is waiting for you."

"Still, I want to know…"

"Don't you already know something that can guide you in your amorous adventure? I've told you a little about who the virtuous Madame du Bergh once was. Go find out who the depraved woman is who calls herself Laura de Farkley."

And the Devil vanished, leaving Luizzi alone in the loge…

Chapter XVIII: The Way Women Have Lovers

As Luizzi approached the clock where he was to meet Laura, he had to push his way through a fairly large group of fashionable young men crowded around two women who were making fun of them. One of the women turned to Luizzi: it was Madame de Farkley. She quickly took his arm and broke out of the circle surrounding her. The crowd made way for her with the mocking courtesy that shows respect for a woman because she's a woman, while at the same time making clear that the respect is addressed to the sex and not to the person.

They'd gone only a few steps away from the group when she asked him languidly, "You're Baron de Luizzi, aren't you?"

"Yes, ma'am."

"You're from Toulouse?"

"Yes, ma'am."

"Was it you I had the pleasure of meeting at Madame de Marignon's?"

"Yes, ma'am."

"Are you aware, sir, that your colossal reputation has preceded you here?"

"Me, ma'am? My God, reputation for what? I'm the least known man in France."

"The least known, because you're discreet, sir. But they say you've had adventures that would've made you the toast of the town, if they hadn't happened in Toulouse."

"The fact is, ma'am, I have no desire to dwell on the past when I'm with you."

"The fact is, sir, you're being ungrateful to the past; because I've been told it would be hard to find a woman more beautiful than that poor Marquise du Val, or a woman more charming than that little businesswoman, Madame... Madame... What was her name?"

"I swear those memories aren't exactly flattering, and even if I weren't with you I'd still want to forget them."

"That's very wrong, sir, and it shows men lack a sense of justice and generosity. I don't think a liaison has to be forever; or that a man drawn away by important considerations or great ambitions from a woman he has loved must remain unchangingly faithful to his lover. That's impossible. But if he's stopped loving her or has separated himself from her, then to disparage her or treat her as his enemy—that's what I think is despicable and contemptible."

"Those are crimes I'm not guilty of, and I protest that no one could have a greater respect than I do for the two women you mentioned."

"Oh, that's ridiculous in a different way," said Madame de Farkley, dropping gently back and then leaning even more gently on Luizzi's arm, to make

208

him aware of the lithe fragility of her body as it compressed and stretched with an inexpressible voluptuous carelessness at every step.

"What do you mean, ma'am? Ridiculous in a different way? Is it ridiculous to respect women who deserve respect?"

She turned toward him so that both of her arms were wrapped around one of his. Walking on like that, with her breast against his elbow, she said almost into his ear, "You're a child, baron."

The words were spoken in the tone of seductive superiority that, coming from a woman like Madame de Farkley, seems to say to a man like Luizzi, "You don't know what you're worth, and you're missing a thousand chances to succeed because you're too modest."

The baron assumed that was how he should take it; but he replied, "I understand why I'm a child no better than I understood why I was ridiculous."

"Neither ridiculous nor a child, if you like. I beg your pardon for saying so. You're not being sincere—or rather you're not acting natural."

"If there's one thing I definitely am, it's awkward, because I still don't understand."

"Well then!" replied Madame de Farkley, still keeping up the game of physical flirtation, so to speak, that consists of a way of holding the body, of a tone of voice, of an exquisite hand skillfully drawn from a glove to lift the veil of the mask and expose voluptuous lips playing over pristine teeth, of a thousand little tricks that slowly reveal a woman, one charm after another, to the eyes of the man who observes her... "Well then! I'll explain myself fully. You have an honest heart, baron, and personally I'd thank you for intending to behave well toward me—if you hadn't been as mistaken as everyone else about what happened this evening. That's why I can presume to give you—you who are still quite a young man—advice you'd do well to follow.

"You know neither how to admit nor how to deny a connection to a woman, and yet that's the whole key to the art of good manners here. Take you, for example: I just mentioned two women to you. Because I don't know the facts, I assume only one of them was your lover. And yet you responded with exactly the same empty, banal expression about both. If what you said has any meaning, if it's true, then you're insulting one of them by protecting with the same words both the one who surrendered to you and the one who didn't. But if what you said is empty and banal, as I suggested, again you're insulting the one who didn't give in by not defending her more than the one who did."

"But if neither one was my lover, ma'am, what could I have answered?"

"Oh, let's not change the question!" said Laura sharply. "I assume one of them gave in to you; in that case, do you think you gave me a good answer?"

"Yes, I do, ma'am, because at the very least discretion is a virtue in society."

"And that's the virtue by which almost all women are disgraced. Everything, every detail, gets found out in adventures like that, sir. But when you can't possibly be left in any doubt that an affair took place, and then you watch a man deny it, other women are grateful to him—and they're quite mistaken. If by chance the next day that man starts turning up regularly in their social life, it's quite likely people will take it for granted they're having an affair. And since those women didn't believe about another woman the virtuous denials you call discretion, neither will those discreet denials be believed about them."

"So by that reasoning, ma'am, the right answer to the first question would be to tell the truth?" Then, giving Madame de Farkley an impertinent look, Luizzi added, "There are some women for whom that theory would prove dangerous."

"Who knows, sir," she replied without apparent emotion, "which women would have reason to dread the exact truth? A lover, sir, is like the number one entered next to a woman's life. If after the lover some coxcomb comes along and boasts of getting what in fact he didn't get, society enters that zero next to the fatal one, and society reads ten—I repeat, ten. You can be sure, sir, that in a woman's life and in the rigorous arithmetic of gallantry, one lover and one coxcomb equals ten lovers."

It seemed to Luizzi that Madame de Farkley was pleading her own case fairly directly. Thinking that gave him permission to reply without much circumlocution, he said, "No doubt you can extend that numerical system to its logical conclusion; so, assuming a second coxcomb means another zero, the woman's reputation grows from ten to a hundred, then to a thousand lovers, and so on, depending on the number of coxcombs?"

"Exactly right, sir! I know women who wouldn't be able to devote more than a single day to each of the lovers attributed to them, if you made a complete list. But there are other women even more unfortunate than those I've already spoken of."

"It's hard to see how that could be possible."

"I mean to prove it to you. There are women who've been credited with all the lovers in the world, and who haven't had a single one."

"Not a single one!" he said, giving ironic emphasis to the words and eyeing her mockingly.

"Not a single one, baron! Not even you."

Embarrassed by that personal remark, Luizzi answered rather awkwardly, "I never presumed that, ma'am!"

"Then you were wrong not to, because you might be the only man for whom it would've been worth allowing slander to be nothing but the truth for once."

"And I assume I've clumsily made all that goodwill evaporate?"

"I can't answer that this evening, sir, because I see my father, and I have to go join him."

"Will I never find out?"

"Today's Saturday; Monday is the last ball at the Opéra. If you're willing to be here at the same time, perhaps I'll have something more to tell you—unless what I need to tell my father causes me to see you again before then."

Madame de Farkley moved away, leaving Luizzi quite embarrassed by what he'd just heard. Before he went home, he was the butt of jokes by all the dandies who knew him. Among others, Mareuilles said to him almost scornfully, "My dear Armand, it appears you have lots of time to kill?"

"How so, if you please?"

"Two masked balls to devote to Madame de Farkley, my good fellow—because we overheard your rendezvous for Monday. In truth, that's far too much, and you'll look like the biggest fool on earth if you don't call on her at noon tomorrow to beg her pardon for not being there now."

Luizzi considered for a moment. Then—wishing to escape from the perplexity into which his strange conversation with that woman had thrown him—he gave Mareuilles a serious look and said, "Monsieur de Mareuilles, are you sure you aren't playing the coxcomb on my behalf right now?"

Mareuilles was deeply upset by Luizzi's words, but the baron couldn't tell whether it was shame at being rightly accused of lying, or indignation at being wrongly accused, that made the dandy go pale. All of Mareuilles's friends seemed to think it was the latter, because they all burst out laughing. "Excellent! Excellent! Come on, Mareuilles, don't get angry! My word, Luizzi's splendid! He believes in our Laura's virtue. He might even become her third husband—because, as you must know, baron, she's already a widow twice over."

For a moment Mareuilles had seemed ready to answer Luizzi with a challenge; but now he suddenly put on an appearance of good cheer. Holding out his hand to the baron, he said, "See here, my dear Armand, let's not be childish! That woman has a fault even greater than having lots of lovers: she compromises them and exposes them in an undignified way. Her first husband was killed in a duel over her, the second likewise. And if it were up to her, lots of us would've cut each other's throats for the sake of her virtue if we hadn't had the sense to come to an explanation before we came to extreme measures. Anyway, Madame de Farkley gave you a rendezvous for the day after tomorrow; that's Shrove Monday. All right! If Tuesday morning you still feel like dueling over her, I'll be at your disposal that day—just that day, you understand? Because I like doing things at their appointed time, and I'm telling you, by Ash Wednesday I'll be done with Mardi Gras carnival foolishness."

"Good God!" said Luizzi—unhappy with himself, unhappy with everyone, truly not knowing what to think, and impatient with the never-ending perplexity in which he seemed to spend his life—"Good God, I'll give neither a yes nor a no; I'll see you Tuesday morning."

"Till Tuesday morning!" chuckled all the young fools. "We'll come ask you for breakfast, baron, and we hope Madame de Farkley will deign to do us the honors of her table."

Their great self-assurance left Luizzi baffled. He recoiled from the idea that society could speak so scornfully of a woman if she didn't deserve it. He went home firmly determined once more to depend only on himself for the opinion he should have about others, and he fell asleep full of that wise resolve.

But somewhere it was written that new events would force him to change his resolution in spite of himself. The next morning, as he was getting up, his valet brought him several letters. One of them was from Madame de Marignon, and both its tone and its subject astonished the baron. The letter read:

Sir,

When Monsieur de Mareuilles brought you into my house, he asked me for my permission. The name you bear and the respect that ought to follow from it were not, I have to tell you, sufficient authority for you to have felt entitled to bypass that formality. Certainly the performer you brought along without warning me is a man of great talent. But there are proprieties that take precedence over any merit, as there are proprieties that take precedence over any name; and though yours may be illustrious, baron, it isn't sufficiently so as to allow you to dispense with the proprieties society imposes on all those who wish to be respected in it. I'll explain no further. Please forgive a woman old enough to be your mother for offering you advice your youthfulness badly requires, and please believe in the sincerity of the regret I feel at no longer being able to count you among the persons who honor my salon with their presence.

When Luizzi had read that letter, which gave him his formal dismissal, he leapt out of bed, shouting wildly. "What! Have I gone mad or become stupid? What's all this about a singer I brought to Madame de Marignon's? How did I fail to observe the proprieties in such a way as to be thrown out—because I have been thrown out!—of her salon? Is it because I sat down next to Madame de Farkley? So that woman's a public whore, and I'm her customer? Is it compromising just to look at her, to talk to her? Oh, I want answers about all this!"

Having thought that far, he looked for a quill pen to write a reply to Madame de Marignon. But just as he was about to begin his letter, it occurred to him that the impertinence he'd just been subjected to deserved harsh punishment. "I've been shamed for having sat next to Madame de Farkley. She was thrown out, and I've been thrown out. Well then, by God! I'll teach Madame de Marignon that, if you choose as your close friends a Madame du Bergh and a Madame de Fantan, you should be less scrupulous about the people you receive!" Building on that idea, he added, "And who is Madame de Marignon herself, anyway? Where does she come from? What's her past? I have to find out right now—and it'll be her begging me out of pity to do her the honor of going back to her house!"

Upon which Luizzi rang his little bell, and the Devil immediately appeared.

"Mister Satan," said the baron, "no preamble, no philosophizing, no moral or immoral lectures: you're going to tell me—right now—the end of Madame du

Bergh's story, then Madame de Fantan's story, then Madame de Marignon's story."

"That's three stories to tell you—three stories about women! It'll take at least three weeks; you have to let me put it off a little."

"No! I want, I demand, that you start right now. And since the sound of this bell has the power to make you feel your eternal punishment even more cruelly, I'll make your torture so awful you'll obey instantly. Now start!"

"Starting right away is easy, it's finishing that's diabolically hard. I'm ready to begin, if you can tell me when you want me to be done. I asked you for three weeks."

"I won't even give you three days."

"I only need two. Today's Sunday, and it's noon. All right then, Tuesday at this same time, when you'll have learned from Madame de Farkley who she is, and when all of your friends show up here asking for an explanation, you'll be able to give them an answer, and you'll also be able to answer Madame de Marignon, because by then you'll know everything you want to know."

"Done! And since the telling's going to take so long, make sure you start right now."

"I'll especially make sure to abbreviate it. And there's an easy way you can help me, if you're willing."

"How's that?"

"By not interrupting me, and by letting me tell the story in my own way."

"Fine!"

Luizzi lay down, and the Devil sat in a vast armchair. He rang, and said to Luizzi's valet, "The baron is at home to no one, you understand? No one."

The servant withdrew. Having lit a cigar, the Devil turned to Luizzi and said:

Chapter XIX: The First Chair, Continued: One Kind of Affection

"Have you ever read Molière?"

"Satan, Satan! You're wearing out my patience! I asked you for the end of Madame du Bergh's adventures."

"I'm getting there, baron, I'm getting there."

"I'm sure, but by way of detours that are going to annoy me."

"And that you're making even longer."

Containing his impatience, Luizzi replied, "Go ahead and talk, tell it the way you want!"

"All right. Have you ever read Molière?"

"Yes, I've read him—read him and reread him."

"Well then, since you've read him, read him and reread him, did you ever notice that poetical jester was the deepest thinker of his era? Did you ever notice that writer, who always used the crudest possible language, had the most chaste mind of his time? Did you ever notice that mocking joker had the saddest heart of his century?"

"Yes, yes, yes, yes!" said Luizzi angrily, as if he'd understood even one of the questions the Devil had just asked him. "Yes, yes, I noticed all that. What about it?"

"Nothing at all. But I want to ask you again whether you noticed that in the work of that deep-thinking, chaste-minded, sad-hearted writer there's a line in the play called *The Hypochondriac*[45] that goes *Monsieur Purgon promised me to get my wife with child.*"

"Yes, I know the line, but I don't see…"

"You see nothing," interrupted the Devil. "But if you ever have these memoirs printed and published, as you intend to do, don't forget to use that line as the epigraph for the story I'm going to tell you."

"About Madame du Bergh?"

"About Madame du Bergh."

"Finally!" cried Luizzi.

"Here we go!" said Satan…

Now, when du Bergh was dead, Nathalie stood for a while looking down at the corpse, and the first thing she wondered was whether she should share the secret of her crime with her father. Nathalie was much too smart a girl to remain undecided for long: she knew her father's secret, and he didn't know hers, and she decided to keep quiet. That called for extraordinary courage: to spend the

---

[45] *Le Malade imaginaire* (1673), a comedy by Molière.

214

night with the corpse, to undress it, to put it in the bed, and to arrange things so that when people came into the room the next morning it would look like she'd slept next to it. From what I already told you last night, it won't seem remarkable that du Bergh's death didn't cause the least surprise, and he was buried quite legally, without anyone worrying about exactly how he'd died. Firion himself didn't have the least suspicion, and he believed completely in his daughter's despair. Still, he was curious about one question, which he very much wanted answered: whether du Bergh had died simply from his medical treatment or whether his wedding night—so imprudently undertaken by a dying man—had contributed to finishing him off. He soon got the clearest possible answer to his question.

The morning after du Bergh's death, Firion entered his daughter's room. She'd ordered the curtains closed, to shield her from the light that had become unbearable to her now that she'd lost the only man she could ever love. She greeted her father with that sentiment and others like it, and he listened with apparently sincere contrition, and even responded in the same vein—till in the midst of her sobbing she let drop a phrase that was certainly extraordinary coming from a young lady: "If only he'd left me some token of his love! If only, with him gone, I could love some being in this world who'd remind me of him!"

Wrapping the question he wanted to ask his daughter in every possible rhetorical protection, Firion said gently, "Poor child! Is there then no hope of that blessing coming to pass?"

Nathalie couldn't help looking her father straight in the eye and answering, in a voice unobstructed by tears or sobbing or lamentation, "No, father, no, I have no such hope. But I have another hope, which you'll understand better than anyone, because you know better than anyone what it is to love your child."

Firion was still wary, because he never knew where charming Nathalie's whims might lead. Her new manner frightened him, but he hid his feelings and replied in the most fatherly tone he could manage, "I'm happy to hear you still have some hope, and I'm sure this one's worthy of you, and it's reasonable, and it isn't built on sentimental utopias that would offer happiness if they existed, but that don't exist."

"You're right, father," said Nathalie, putting emotion back into her voice and her expression. "Oh, you're so right! I know now that love is an impossible dream. I know it's a cruel, egotistical passion, whose vile worldly calculations have robbed it of its divine essence. And I swear to you, father, I've shut my heart against that empty sentiment. No, I neither want to love nor hope to be loved... But there is a kind of affection—greater, holier, and more profound than romantic love—to which I want to dedicate my life. Father, father!" she added with tears, "your affection for me has shown me the strongest of all affections: father, I want to be a mother."

Those words made Firion jump out of his chair, more from the extravagant manner in which they were spoken than from the wish itself, and when he'd recovered from his shock he said, "Well, my child, when your period of mourning is over—or if you insist, after the ten months the law imposes on widows before allowing them to remarry—I'll provide you a new husband; and in the meantime I'll look for a suitable candidate."

That made Nathalie give her father a curious, thoughtful look. Like a client asking his lawyer to explain a legal clause he thinks he's found a way to get around, she asked, "Why is that delay imposed on women before they're allowed to remarry?"

Firion seemed a little embarrassed by the question. But he was one of those men who believe a woman can and should understand life and the obligations imposed by the letter of the law. Since his daughter had replied so straightforwardly to his question, he felt he could answer her own question just as straightforwardly: "During the ten months following a husband's death, a child might be born, since typically a woman's pregnancy doesn't last more than nine months. Since the child is the deceased husband's, the law in its foresight intends to prevent a woman from forming new ties before her position is absolutely clear, both toward the family she's leaving and toward the family she's going to enter."

Nathalie had turned pensive, while Firion went on casually, "But all of this is connected to the matter of assets and rights of inheritance—legal issues it would take far to long to explain."

"I believe you, father, I believe you. But what it means is, if I became a mother within the next ten months, my child would be Baron du Bergh's?"

"Certainly," said her father, growing embarrassed again.

"Legally speaking, I mean," added Nathalie.

Firion now felt he was failing to understand—or rather he began to be afraid to understand. Trying to change the subject, he said, "We're leaving tomorrow, and going back to Paris. There you'll find men worthy of you, and of your fortune, men who'll put you on such a pedestal that the joys of vanity will replace the joys of love you wish to renounce."

"Father, I'll bear no other name than that of the only man I've ever loved."

"But, Nathalie..." said Firion, driven back on his last defenses, "what are you trying to say?"

"Father!" replied the fascinating virgin widow as she fell weeping and sobbing at her father's feet. "Father, I told you: I want to be a mother!"

"Incest!" cried Luizzi.

"My dear fellow, you're an idiot!" said the Devil heatedly. "You don't have the least understanding of life's resources. You've absorbed the literature of our time without restraint, and right away you make some disgusting melodrama out of a story I think is very entertaining. There's not the least incest in the whole thing."

"Well! All right," said Luizzi impatiently, "tell me the rest of the conversation."

"The rest of the conversation," replied Satan, "lasted exactly the two minutes you've just wasted with your stupid interruption; and since you know the seconds are precious for us, I won't tell you the end of the conversation, I'll just tell you the result."

"I'm listening," said Luizzi, promising himself not to interrupt this time, no matter what absurdity the Devil felt like telling him.

And the Devil resumed:

The next day, father Firion went out into the countryside around B—, walking across the fields, stopping the peasants he met and chatting amiably with them. The first was an ugly man of forty-five, suffering from rickets; Firion moved on immediately. The second was short, fat, and hearty, but horribly poor and dirty. The third was an old man of sixty. Firion moved on quickly. He was about to head in a different direction, when he spotted a magnificent young man, about twenty-four or twenty-five, working with an energy denoting unusual strength, and singing; his voice suggested a deep chest.

After watching hm in silence, Firion, who'd just left his daughter, approached him and said...

"What!" cried Luizzi, choking on the outrageousness of the situation. "What! He said to him..."

"You're an idiot!" replied the Devil. "You're forgetting Firion was a clever man."

Firion said to the handsome lout, "Would you like to be a substitute, friend?"

"Whose substitute?" asked the young man.

"A substitute for one of my nephews, who's been drafted."

"No thanks! I'm exempt, as the only son of a widow, and I've got no desire to go do a job for someone else that I wouldn't have wanted to do for myself. Anyway, you'll find plenty of young men in the area willing to take you up on it."

"Damn! It's going to be difficult, because my nephew's a very good-looking fellow, and the government absolutely insists that it be given men equal in quality to the men it's letting go."

"Faith," said the lout, puffing himself up and putting one hand on his hip, "as you say, it'll be difficult, and I expect it'll cost you a bundle."

"Oh, money's no object. I'd gladly pay a fellow like you a thousand écus."

"I believe it!" said the peasant, picking up his spade and going back to work—an excellent way to listen without appearing to want to listen. "I believe it. There's an old widow around here who'd pay me more than that to marry her, if I wanted to replace the deceased."

"All right! I made a mistake. I didn't mean a thousand écus, I meant two thousand."

"Your nephew has a very kind uncle," said the peasant, stooping down to the ground and whistling a little tune that didn't seem to match the circumstances.

"Three thousand écus!"

"That might suit the big redhead across the road."

"Four thousand écus!"

The peasant leaned on his spade and said, in a voice he couldn't fully control, "What does four thousand écus equal?"

"It equals twelve thousand francs."

"Twelve thousand francs! That's a good chunk. What's the interest on twelve thousand francs?"

"Six hundred francs."

"Six hundred francs!" said the peasant, thinking it over and pretending to do the math. "Is that three francs and five sous of interest a day?"

"No. Three francs and five sous of interest a day would be about twelve hundred francs of interest a year," said Firion, who hadn't made his millions without a certain facility for arithmetic.

"All right," said the peasant, "three francs and five sous of interest a day, twelve hundred francs a year, how much money would you need for that?"

"Twenty-four thousand francs."

"If you've got twenty-four thousand francs, I'm your man."

"Deal?"

"Deal."

"Then follow me right now to the doctor."

"What's all this about a doctor?"

"Friend, I don't want to buy a pig in a poke. Since you're going to have to pass a medical inspection at the recruitment office, I don't want them to reject you for some physical disability I don't know about."

"Is that all? Come on now, I'm a healthy man, body and soul, you hear? And I've got nothing to hide, nothing at all."

"I'm delighted. Come on, let's go."

And without further discussion Firion took the peasant to the most respected doctor at the health spa.

At that point the Devil stopped and said to Luizzi, "You're not interrupting me anymore."

"Because I feel like I understand, and I don't need additional explanation."

"Well! What do you understand?"

"Mister Satan, there are things the Devil can say or think, but that a man of the world would be embarrassed to have to put into words. And everything you tell me is so peculiar!"

"Peculiar? In what way? The only peculiar thing is that it doesn't always happen like that: fathers don't take for their daughters' sake the same precautions the government takes for its armies. That reminds me of a play by the most truth-telling writer you've got, which was staged a few months ago.[46] He wanted to put a scene like that one on stage, but all the prudes in the cheap seats booed the scene for being immoral. I said all, because when it comes to prudishness women rank right behind men. Well! Of those three or four hundred imbeciles who were outraged that a father would want to know everything about his future son-in-law, there were surely a hundred and fifty who wouldn't have passed with such distinction the medical exam Firion's handsome peasant was forced to submit to."

"This is all very nice, but the final step seems difficult to carry off, especially with Mademoiselle Nathalie."

"It was especially with Mademoiselle Nathalie that the final step was the easiest thing in the world. There's nothing like being clear with yourself about what you want. I've already told you women are wrong not be more candid with men; they're also wrong not be more candid with themselves. They press their show of delicacy to the point of fooling themselves; and some of them, having carefully prepared for their own fall, manage to persuade themselves they were taken by surprise."

"I mostly agree with you, but I still don't understand how, in such circumstances, a girl like Nathalie could prepare for her fall."

"My dear friend," said the Devil scornfully, "you couldn't even write a comic opera. There are a thousand simple and a thousand ingenious ways to achieve a goal like that."

"Perhaps, but if the obstacles didn't come from the woman's prudishness, they might come from the peasant's reluctance. It seems to me you'd have to make the oaf understand he could please a woman whose father was paying him twenty-four thousand francs, and also console a widow who'd lost her husband the day before. You think that's easy?"

"Put in those terms, I admit it would be a difficult question to answer. Low-born men have both scorn and respect for well-born women, and both feelings are equally stupid. They're willing to believe well-born women have as lovers all the men in their social circle whom they receive, and as a result they have a bad opinion of them. But on the other hand they can't imagine those women's tastes could possibly reach as low as men like them, which means the

---

[46] *Le Faux Bonhomme* (1817) by Népomucène Lemercier. The play opened and closed the same night, after booing stopped the third act. (Soulié himself footnotes the title and author.)

women have to give themselves, or rather offer themselves, in the most explicit possible way before the men dare to imagine they want them. So from that point of view the thing would've been difficult to bring off. But, in a little isolated cottage where Firion took the peasant when they left the doctor, lived a pretty servant girl, who was lively and accommodating, and who welcomed the newcomer to her house and fairly skillfully let him see that her bedroom wasn't far from the one the substitute would be in."

"What!" cried Luizzi. "Nathalie put on an act like that! The woman degraded herself far enough to seduce a peasant with flirtatious advances?"

"My dear baron, you have a mania for stupid assumptions. I'm warning you, it's the height of idiocy to grab hold of a passing phrase or story and complete it in a way diametrically opposed to the truth. Lots of people in the world have that annoying habit. I don't know how other people react to it, but to me it's like those boors who put their hands in your plate and take a bite of your bread or your peach, and then take the piece they've bitten out of their mouths and say, 'Oh, that wasn't mine! Here, you can have it back. The rest of it's fine. You can finish it.' Avoid that habit—it can be fatal: there are men who'll never forgive you for having robbed them of a good punch line... In any case, if there was something shocking or unusual about Mademoiselle Firion's actions, it wasn't that she took a lover the day after her husband's death. The story of the widow of Ephesus is as old as the holy Bible,[47] and humankind has been made of the same flesh as long as it has existed. What does make Mademoiselle Firion's adventure quite exceptional is that she doesn't know and never saw the man who provided her with the strongest and most sacred of feelings, that of a mother for her child."

"What!"

"That's right, my friend. When the young servant girl had finally managed to make the peasant understand that handsome boys are made for pretty girls, Firion found a way, once night had fallen, to get him to go take a walk for an hour far away from the cottage. Meanwhile one carriage left and another came. When the peasant got back, Firion was sitting up alone, and the servant girl had gone home. Then Firion retired, inviting the boy to go to sleep. But the peasant didn't go to his own room, and he didn't mistake which door was his: he went to the pretty servant girl's door, and slipped into her room in total darkness."

"And Nathalie was there?" asked Luizzi in a proper tone of astonishment and indignation.

"Who can say whether it was Nathalie? The peasant certainly couldn't. He left the room before daybreak, and that morning Firion sent him twenty leagues away."

---

[47] In Petronius's *Satyricon* (late 1st century C.E.), the devoted widow of Ephesus, grieving at the tomb of her late husband, lets herself be seduced by a soldier right there on the grave.

"If the peasant didn't know, at least Firion did."

"He's no longer living."

"But Nathalie herself could say, couldn't she?"

"There's something else. Nine months and two days after the death of Baron du Bergh, an entry was made in the civil registry of the third arrondissement of the city of Paris, legally recognizing the birth of Edgard du Bergh, the charming young man said—by idiots who had the advantage of knowing the late Baron du Bergh—to bear a remarkable resemblance to his father."

"So that woman was…"

"That woman was what I said she was, a poisoner and an adulteress. For adultery consists above all in inserting an outsider's children into a living husband's family, but to me it seems even more creative to insert them into the family of a husband who's dead. That's posthumous adultery, something quite original."

"And there's no one in the world who can throw her crimes in her face and accuse her of them?"

"No one, unless it's you, and I'll let you decide whether you're up to it!"

"And… did she have any more whims after that?"

"Not a one."

"But… the whole story's impossible!"

"A frigid heart, a frigid mind, and a frigid body are enough to explain it. If Nathalie had been born in a different time, or if she'd been brought up more strictly, most likely she'd have become either one of those severe, dried-up abbesses who push to the point of tyranny the performance of a virtue that nature has made easy for them, or one of those virtuous old maids who are to other women what deaf-mutes are to the rest of humankind: they have no more conception of love than the deaf have of sound. But, like the deaf, they can see it exists; the communication love creates between two lovers looks to them just like communication by voice looks to the deaf—and since neither the one nor the other can understand the sense they're missing, they become envious of those who have it. As a result, old maids and deaf-mutes are almost always suspicious, slander-mongering, and pitiless. As long as you live, baron, beware of people with deficiencies: they're the only ones who are truly wicked."

Chapter XX: A Small Betrayal

Just as Luizzi was about to respond to that new theory of the Devil's, his valet entered and handed him a note, at the same time announcing Monsieur de Mareuilles. Before Luizzi could remind his servant of the order he'd given to admit no one, the dandy appeared at the bedroom door. Pointing with the tip of his cane to the note Luizzi hadn't yet opened, he said with a laugh, "I bet that's from Laura!"

"I don't think so," said Luizzi crossly, "because I believe I recognize this handwriting, and I've never received a letter from Madame de Farkley."

As his eyes moved from the door back to his own bed, Luizzi noticed that the armchair the Devil had been sitting in a moment before was empty. "Well! Where'd he go?" cried the baron in his startlement.

"Who?" asked Mareuilles.

"Um…" said Luizzi, who couldn't think fast enough of a name to substitute for the one he didn't dare speak, "um, the man who was here just now."

"You're losing your mind," said the dandy. "I didn't see anyone. Anyway, I'm sorry to disturb you so early, but yesterday, after you left the Opéra, I learned of Madame de Marignon's decision about you, and I've come to talk to you about it. I don't want to lecture you, because between a couple of young men there's no sense in that, but the fact is you compromised me in a pretty ungrateful way. You know on what footing I'm welcome at Madame de Marignon's; you know her daughter is a desirable match, which my family has long been thinking of for me; I'm as discreet as possible in my bachelor follies, so they won't harm my chances—so you have to admit it's unacceptable for me to be compromised for someone else's!"

"My word! Monsieur de Mareuilles, I'm glad to hear you're displeased—because the note I got from Madame de Marignon could only have been written by a woman without a husband or a son. If, in your position as future son-in-law, you're willing to take responsibility for her insolence, you'd be doing me a real favor."

"No problem, as long as it doesn't interfere with what we've already agreed on for Tuesday!"

"Quite right. And since I think it's just as foolish to duel over the respect owed to Madame de Marignon's world as over the faith I have in Madame de Farkley, it's a good thing tomorrow is a carnival day!"

"You're making jokes, baron!" said Mareuilles scornfully.

"And you're being conceited," retorted Luizzi.

"Not as much as you are," laughed Mareuilles. "You're conceited enough to think a woman who wrote to you the morning after meeting you for the first time couldn't have done the same for me, or for lots of others."

"But this note isn't from Madame de Farkley," said Luizzi, who felt more and more sure he recognized the handwriting.

"Well, if it isn't, I'll be proven wrong once for a change. But I'm so sure I'm right, I promise to apologize to her if I'm wrong. However, if it is from Madame de Farkley, I'll give you some friendly advice: don't make a big blood-and-thunder scandal out of all this; instead go to Madame de Marignon and tell her how sorry you are for what's happened; and don't make yourself a laughingstock over a woman who isn't worth it."

Without answering, Luizzi impatiently broke the seal and glanced at the signature: it was Madame de Farkley's. It's hard to express the pain and disappointment he felt on seeing it. If he'd better understood the emotions in a man's heart, he would've realized he wasn't indifferent to her, by his regret at seeing her justify the world's bad opinion of her.

He read the note, which ran like this:

Sir,

I fear I cannot keep the rendezvous I made with you for tomorrow at the Opéra ball. If you insist on an explanation of my parting words to you, I'm now able to give it to you. Expect me at your place this evening; I'll be there at ten.

Luizzi was baffled. Astonished at the woman's immodesty, he silently passed the note to Mareuilles, who immediately burst out laughing. "This beats all!" he cried. "Listen, if you take my advice you won't stay home tonight, and you'll go to Madame de Marignon's. I can hint gently at the sacrifice you're making for her sake; she'll be grateful to you, and all will be forgiven."

"You're right, though it'll rob me of my chance to show Madame de Farkley I'm not her dupe, and though I'll be sorry not to teach her the lesson she deserves."

"The best lesson, and the cruelest, is to tell her you'll be here for her, and then not to be here."

Luizzi thought he should follow half of that advice, while reserving the choice of whether or not to follow the other half, depending on how he felt in the evening. In other words, he began by replying that he would expect Madame de Farkley that evening.

When evening came, Luizzi had forgotten his dislike of her. He remembered the woman from the Opéra, so suave and so graceful. He blamed himself for sacrificing several hours of a pleasure he assumed would be quite memorable, for the sake of empty social respect. Luizzi was one of those creatures destined to a life filled with turmoil in the midst of the most mundane adventures. People like that turn the slightest decision into an internal battleground. It takes them as long to weigh crossing the street gutter as it took Caesar to weigh crossing the Rubicon;[48] and because they find their internal debate so fascinating, they think they've done something interesting. That was how Luizzi was able to spend two hours debating with himself the question of personal pleasure versus social respect.

As for Madame de Farkley's reputation, he didn't give it the slightest thought. To add one more scandalous adventure to all of her scandalous adventures didn't seem to him like a great crime. The only thing he regretted missing was the entertainment of witnessing her comeuppance. All of the struggles he faced that great day merely pitted egotism against vanity. Still, he overcame his regrets—but only because he imagined there was a much louder splash in not having had that woman than in having had her.

He left home at a quarter to ten, and, as ten was striking, Baron Luizzi was announced at Madame de Marignon's. It's impossible to depict the effect created by his entrance at that hour: all eyes turned to the clock, then greeted Luizzi with the most flattering congratulations. All of the women welcomed him with extraordinary charm and attention. Madame du Bergh's admiration for his heroism went so far that she introduced him to her son, Monsieur Edgard du Bergh. Madame de Marignon held out her hand to the baron, and almost begged his pardon for the letter she'd written to him. Mademoiselle de Marignon, who'd never yet said a word to Luizzi, consulted him in a delightfully intimate way about some new volumes of pictures she'd been given. As for Madame de Fantan, she made Luizzi promise to honor her with a visit.

That invitation soothed Mareuilles's bad temper a little; he'd been appalled by the success he'd pulled off for his friend Luizzi. Now he told him quietly, "Mademoiselle de Fantan is young and pretty, and she'll be rich. Remember that."

Luizzi's exultation was such that two hours went by without him feeling anything besides joy in his own success; never had he spoken so well or held his head so high. For those two hours he was truly the king of conversation at Madame de Marignon's: he had eloquence, wit, and inspiration. At midnight—superb, triumphant, filled with self-admiration—he left that salon, which the night before he'd gone away from almost furtively and guiltily. That was because the night before he'd tried to defy society over a woman society had cast out, whereas tonight he'd handed that woman over to society with yet another mark of shame. Perhaps that explains why man is a vicious animal, as Molière says.

The few minutes it took for Luizzi to get from Madame de Marignon's house to his own weren't enough to bring him down from his high, and never had he tossed aside his gloves and hat and coat with more poise and elegance

---

[48] By crossing the river Rubicon in 49 BCE, Caesar precipitated the civil war that ended in his overthrowing the Roman Republic and declaring himself dictator.

than that evening. He wasn't someone who showed off in the presence of servants, but just then he was so full of himself that he gave a particular flamboyant emphasis to his call, "Did anyone stop by tonight?"

"Yes, baron," replied his valet. "A lady."

"That's right," said Luizzi, feigning surprise. "I'd forgotten. I can't understand how I forgot. And what did she say?"

"She said she'd wait for monsieur to come home."

"Oh!" said Luizzi, his self-assured tone changing suddenly at the news. "And how long did she wait?"

"Well, baron, she's waited right up to now. She's in your room."

"In my room?" echoed Luizzi.

"Yes, baron. I'll go let her know you're back."

"No need," said Luizzi crossly. "Leave us, and don't come till I ring for you."

Then he entered his room.

Chapter XXI: The Second Chair: Whoever Wants Her Can Have Her

The dominant feeling in Luizzi's heart as he opened the door was a fairly incoherent mixture of anger, surprise, and disappointment. That woman had just spoiled the success he'd had at Madame de Marignon's, and her reason for staying was probably not the same one that brought her here. At the very least, he expected a scene; so he was surprised to find, rather than the irritated woman he assumed Madame de Farkley would be, a woman in tears. When he approached her she clasped her hands and said despairingly, "Sir! Oh, sir, you were fated to inflict the final blow against me!"

"Me, ma'am?" he replied casually. "I really don't know what you mean, nor what blow you're referring to."

She examined him in astonishment, then said more calmly, "Look at me carefully, sir. Do you recognize me?"

"I recognize you, ma'am, as the very attractive woman I saw last night at Madame de Marignon's, and whom I saw again at the Opéra, and whom I didn't expect to have the honor of seeing again at my house tonight."

"Well then, what made you sit next to me at Madame de Marignon's?"

Luizzi lowered his eyes modestly and, with the humble arrogance of a man who's reluctant to boast of a conquest, he replied, "But surely, ma'am, you can't find it surprising when... anyone at all... wants to know you."

At those words Madame de Farkley's expression grew troubled again, and she turned pale. In a different tone she replied, "I understand you, sir. I shouldn't be surprised when... anyone at all... expects to become my lover."

"Oh, ma'am!"

"That's what you meant, sir," she went on, barely holding back the tears in her eyes and the sobs in her voice. But suddenly, with an intense nervous effort, she seemed to master her emotions. She went on with painfully affected cheerfulness, "That's what you meant, sir, but I don't think you fully realized the boldness of your words. Don't you know it's dangerous to become the lover of a woman like me?"

"I'm just as brave as other men," said Luizzi, smiling arrogantly.

"You think? Well! I swear, sir, you'd have been afraid if I'd accepted your advances."

"Go ahead and test my courage, and you'll see what it's capable of."

"All right!" she said as she rose. "I'll be your mistress, sir. But first you need to know for sure what I assume you already suspect: I'm a fallen woman."

"Who says so?" he replied, trying to soothe her agitation.

"I do, sir, without overstating it; I, who for many years have suffered as the victim of slander; I, who for once would like to deserve the insults; I, who chose you for that purpose; I, who am yours… if you dare take me."

That abrupt, explicit avowal found the baron unprepared, and for a few seconds he was nonplused.

Madame de Farkley sat back down and said with a sad smile, "Like I said, sir, you'd be afraid."

"That's not the right word," said Luizzi, trying to recover. "But I admit that so great and sudden a reward confused me, it was so unexpected…"

"You're lying, sir. You just thought it wouldn't be as easy as that, and you were counting on me defending my honor—a defense you can now see I've freed myself from."

Luizzi felt unmoored. He'd never conceived of such brazenness; nor conceived that, if Madame de Farkley just wanted to toy with him, she'd have done it in his house and at such an hour. He was silent for a moment, then finally said, "The truth is, ma'am, I don't understand you…"

"In that case there's nothing left for me to do but withdraw. However," she added as she reached for her gloves, "I assume you're honorable enough to declare, in a way people will believe, that the woman who came to you at ten at night, and who left you at one in the morning, didn't yield to you, the way they say she's yielded to so many others."

She rose as if to leave, and at that moment Luizzi saw the enormous ridicule he was about to be covered in, relating to this woman. He also predicted the arrogance that had brought him success at Madame de Marignon's would just look silly to his friends. Besides, what passed for tasteful arrogance at ten in the evening became gross vulgarity at midnight. You can decline a rendezvous with a beautiful woman—but you can't throw her out if she shows up. So he took Madame de Farkley's hands and, forcing to her sit back down just as she was about to leave, he said, with more politeness than he'd shown so far, "What nonsense we've both been speaking! You have the right to be angry at my rudeness for not being here, but is there any fault that can't be remedied? Can't an hour or two of bad behavior—or rather of actual madness—be forgiven in exchange for the devotion or the love you know so well how to inspire?"

Madame de Farkley settled in her seat again, and replied with great seriousness, "I'd be curious to hear, sir, how you account for that bad behavior or that madness, as you choose to call it."

Just then a strange idea occurred to Luizzi—the same idea he'd promised himself to put into action if ever he found Madame Dilois again: To have had Madame de Farkley at ten o'clock, when he'd found her here, to have had her like so many other men to whom she'd yielded or to whom she'd given herself, didn't have much appeal. But to have this woman after showing her he didn't want her, to get her to believe seriously in a sincere and almost mad passion after having insulted her with utter contempt—that struck Luizzi as something fresh, original, and worth the trouble of attempting, especially with a woman as clever as Madame de Farkley. From that moment on, he desired her as if he were in love with her.

Those thoughts passed like a flash through his mind; leaning gently toward her, he said, "No, ma'am, no, it's not difficult to account for that bad behavior and that madness. You've been open enough with me for me to be able to give you that explanation. But if you hadn't been so completely candid, I admit it would've been impossible for me to explain myself."

"I'd be delighted if for once in my life my candor was good for something. It will have done some good, sir, if thanks to that you find a way to prove your absence wasn't an affront, and everything you've said since you got back wasn't another insult."

"I wouldn't respond to your candor by a lack of candor on my part. Yes, ma'am, my absence was an affront and my words were an insult."

"And you claim you can excuse them?" asked Madame de Farkley bitterly.

"I don't know if I'll succeed, but in any case I'll tell you the truth, and you can be the judge."

"I'm listening."

"You used a very serious word, ma'am, and I beg your pardon from the bottom of my heart for repeating it... You said, 'I'm a fallen woman'..."

Hearing that word, which she'd spoken in the bitterness of her anger, now coming out of Luizzi's mouth, made Madame de Farkley turn pale. He noticed, and was moved. He drew closer to her, but she stopped him with a slight movement of her hand, and said in a choked voice, "It's nothing, go on."

"Well, ma'am," he went on, like a man who has to force himself to speak, "that word explains my behavior."

"Yes," she said sadly, "I understand your contempt. And yet it's rare for a man to slap a woman so cruelly with it, no matter who she is, especially when that woman has done him no harm."

"Oh, it's not that, ma'am," he replied. Captivated by the idea that was guiding his actions, to the point of speaking very emotionally, he went on, "It's not that, ma'am, that made me insult you. What made me so offensive, so disgraceful, so cruel, was that I felt I was about to fall in love with you."

"You!" cried Laura. "You, who couldn't suppress an anxiety full of hope—you, in love with me!"

"Yes, ma'am," said Luizzi, delighted with his own performance. "Yes. And you have to understand that at the moment I felt that love kindling within me, I was afraid, just as you said. Because, as you also said, you're a fallen woman! And yet you're beautiful, ma'am, with the kind of powerful beauty that distracts the mind. You have an inexplicable attraction that makes men fall at your feet as your slaves. You're one of those women for whom we feel ready to give up our lives, or more than that, our honor, our reputation. That's how you

228

penetrated both my heart and my mind: as a fallen woman and as a woman I could adore at the sacrifice of everything else.

"Well, ma'am, at the moment when I still felt able to do so, I drew back from that love; it terrified me. The slight touch of it I'd felt had given me a foretaste of the suffering I'd have to endure if I gave it my whole life to extinguish. A love like that, ma'am, must be hideously jealous; because I think I've already been jealous—not jealous over the future or the present, but jealous over the past, jealous over what no power on earth, not even that of God, can keep from having happened. You can kill the lover of a woman who's cheating on you, you can kill a former lover whose memory is hateful to you, but what you can't kill, ma'am, is a lost reputation, a life I won't call guilty but gone astray. Can you see the horror of an absolute love, given unconditionally, confronted with a love the past pulls away from you in shreds, and that this man, that man, ten, twenty, thirty lovers can each claim a part of? That would be the tortures of hell, ma'am, and rather than face that torture I preferred to face your hatred."

As she listened to Luizzi, Madame de Farkley was pale and trembling. He noticed, and went on more gently, "I seem awfully brutal, don't I? And certainly I'd have been less brutal if I'd had as little respect for you as so many others do, if I'd seen you as a woman good for no more than an affair a few days long, if I hadn't been overwhelmed by the extraordinary allure that envelops you and that at this very moment distracts me to the point of making me say things you shouldn't hear."

While Luizzi spoke like that, Madame de Farkley watched him with an anxious joy, an ecstasy she couldn't shake off. Finally she made a violent effort, and replied, "Armand, are you deceiving me? Armand, consider that you hold in your hands the last hope of a life that's been nothing but misery. Armand, consider that to deceive me is to murder me. Armand, answer me the way you'd answer God: do you love me as you say you do?"

The baron, who'd just played his part with some conviction, wasn't sorry to find out exactly how she'd play hers. He answered with sublime exhilaration, "Yes, Laura, yes! That's how I love you—it's a mad passion! A passion from hell!"

"No!" she cried. "It's heaven that inspired you, Armand. This love is an atonement. This love will be a blessing, because you won't have to blush for it."

At those words Luizzi could barely contain a grimace. He sat back in his chair, waiting for some fantastical story from which Madame de Farkley would emerge as white as a dove.

But instead of going on, she suddenly stopped. "Not tonight, Armand, not tonight!" she said in a soft, sad, happy voice. "Tomorrow I'll tell you the story of my life. A single word would explain everything, but I don't yet have the right to speak that word. Till tomorrow!"

Luizzi didn't detain her. He was content to answer urgently, "Till tomorrow! Where?"

"Not here. But I'll send you word—because now I can only enter this house again as the Baroness de Luizzi."

At those words he was polite enough not to burst out laughing, and he contained himself till he'd seen her out. But when he got back to his room he couldn't help saying to himself out loud, "This has gone too far, and my stratagem worked too well. Madame de Farkley, Baroness de Luizzi! Either I'm a great actor, or that woman takes me for a great fool!"

Luizzi had reached that point in his soliloquy when he noticed the Devil sitting in the same chair from which he'd vanished that morning, and calmly finishing the cigar he'd begun then.

"Ah, there you are!" laughed the baron. "Why'd you take off this morning as if you yourself were at your heels?"

"You think I'm not bored enough having to waste my time with you, so I'd agree to play third fiddle in a conversation with the likes of Monsieur de Mareuilles?"

"You're right. I'd forgotten he was the one who drove you away. And what are you doing here now?"

"I've come to tell you the story of Madame de Fantan, which you asked for."

"Oh, my word. I don't want to hear it. More scandalous adventures, I assume? I can see women's lives consist of nothing but, and I'll admit I'm beginning to get tired of them."

"Baron, you made a big mistake by forcing me to talk when I didn't want to; don't make an even bigger mistake by refusing to hear me when I feel like confiding in you! Look, it's one o'clock. You still have an hour to listen to me, and an hour to…"

"Mister Satan," interrupted Luizzi, "I'd like to sleep. In any case, I don't need to offend Madame de Marignon anymore. I really don't care about Madame de Fantan's past. So, please, leave me in peace."

Satan obeyed, and Luizzi went to bed with a satisfied heart, like a merchant who's paid off his debts, or a regimental chaplain who's just given first communion to a dozen old soldiers.

Chapter XXII: The Second Chair, Continued: A Correspondence

Monday morning, when Luizzi awoke, he received the following letter:

Armand,

I'm happy, with a happiness you can't imagine, happy to have found a man to whom I can tell everything and who'll understand everything about my life. I'm carried away by that happiness, because I'd sworn not to reveal this secret till the one who's as concerned in it as I am gives me permission. But when I left you my heart was so full of sweet hope that I couldn't wait. I'm writing to you, and sharing a strange kind of secret with you, because I won't use the names of the people involved. But your heart, your memory, your regrets—I won't say your remorse—will guess the names. So listen to me, Armand, listen to me, you who've told me you love me.

You remember that almost mad conversation we had last night at the Opéra ball, in which I told you how a woman who's forgotten her principles once can pass for having forgotten them a thousand times? Well, today I'll show you how a woman who's never done wrong can be condemned by an extraordinary combination of circumstances.

"Hmm, hmm!" said Luizzi at those words. "Here's some fancy rhetoric! I just want the story I'm going to read not to be the fiftieth printing of *The Works of Madame de Farkley*, and for her to have taken the trouble of composing a new unpublished version for me!"

With that observation Luizzi settled himself comfortably in his armchair, like a subscriber to a circulating library who's just received the latest fashionable short story or tale or novel. That short story or tale or novel began like this:

You know I'm the illegitimate daughter of the Marquis d'Andeli. I myself didn't know it till after misfortune had already ruined me. You don't know who my mother was, and I myself know only her name. My mother came from a great Languedoc family. She was married very young to a man who had to go to the wars, and who left her to herself. She had a daughter; but the child's love wasn't enough for that passionate heart. She met the Marquis d'Andeli. The Marquis d'Andeli fell in love with her. She fell in love with the Marquis d'Andeli. At that time he held a very important administrative position in the city where my mother lived. He lost that position and was forced to leave her six months before I was born.

My mother gave birth in a peasant's hut, where she'd gone to hide. Her maidservant took me away and gave me into the care of another old woman, who raised me till I was fifteen. People said she'd found me on her doorstep and had taken me in out of charity. I believed it, and I didn't notice anything that would've made me suspect it wasn't true. So I was already fifteen when my mother's first daughter got married. There's no need for me to tell you how she learned of my existence; but one day one of the wealthiest and most beautiful women in town came to our miserable hut. In an interview in which unfortunately I learned only part of the truth, she told me I was the daughter of someone of very high rank, who was related to her, and whose mistakes she deplored without being able to condemn them.

I didn't know then what a mother is, and the respect that word commands; I thought only the arrogance of her high status kept that woman from telling me my mother's name. So you can imagine my astonishment when she added, "Your mother's lapses haven't ended. When she was widowed, she dishonored her widowhood just as she had her marriage. She has abandoned another child; another child who will live in misery; another child who will face misfortune, perhaps without finding pity like the pity that protected you. You must take charge of that child. She's your sister. Be the mother she lacks. I'll give you both the wealth you don't have."

I accepted, Armand. The first good deed I was in a position to do in my life brought me my first misfortune. I was fifteen, and pretty. No one imagined that at fifteen I could be motivated by the charity a woman of sixty had shown for me; and because no one was willing to acknowledge a little virtue in me, I was accused of a sin. I'd said I'd be a mother to that child, and they made me its mother in fact.

Luckily a decent man, who lived in the same house as me, knew better than anyone that the life I'd led made that sin impossible. He defied all of the tales told about me, and honored me with his name. My father, who'd finally learned of my existence, reimbursed him for that service—to the extent a service like that can be reimbursed—by promising me a considerable dowry. I lived like that for a while, happy and almost respected, or rather forgotten by slander.

Another extraordinary event brought on or rather set up my ruin. My little sister's father, whose name I didn't know, the father of the child I loved like my own daughter in spite of all the sorrow she'd brought me, had once sown trouble in another family besides my mother's. The noble stranger who'd already entrusted one orphan to me told me a young man, abandoned as I'd been abandoned, as my sister had been, was languishing in poverty. Knowing as I did the awfulness of a solitary life, without affectionate support, I wanted to rescue him too. I opened my husband's house to him, I gave him a place of honor there, I gave him a family.

That second good deed was the cause of my second misfortune. A man who should've thanked me for what I'd done—a man who should've said, "Thank you for my sake for what you did for this poor wretch!"—that man thoughtlessly added cruel remarks to the local gossip, which already faulted me for my new protégé. He made some terrible joke, and the orphan I'd saved was taken for my lover. My husband heard of it; his honor was insulted, and in his anger he asked for no explanations. He goaded the young man into dueling, and killed him. He few days later he learned the truth, and he demanded satisfaction from the slanderer for his wife's lost reputation and the blood he's shed.

At that point in Madame de Farkley's letter, Luizzi was left confounded. It seemed so strangely like what had happened in Toulouse that he felt a sudden terror taking hold of him. But comparing the dates, and remembering it was only two months since he'd so recklessly risked Madame Dilois's reputation, he was reassured. Then—since bad behavior is infinitely skillful at finding excuses for itself, and infinitely skillful at condemning bad behavior in others—he said to himself, "Madame de Farkley must've heard what happened to me in Toulouse, and now she's attributing it to herself and embedding it in her own past life so I'll be more likely to believe it. But it's too obvious a trick, and I won't fall for it."

Having freed himself of that slight pang of anxiety, he picked up the letter again and read what followed:

Meanwhile, before that fatal duel, in my initial horror, I'd gone to find the woman who'd first told me of my birth and of my father's identity. My first despairing impulse was to reproach her for having brought me the child that had led to all my troubles. But I could respond with nothing but tears when she said, "That child is your sister! That child is... our sister!"

"Our sister!"

"Yes. All three of us are children of a guilty mother."

Noble, sainted martyr—wretched sister who is no more—can I complain of what I've suffered, I in whom you confided the secret of your life? But I knew nothing of that then, and I cried out, "And what's become her, who delivered us all into misery?"

"She's left France. I didn't want to find out what she's become. I don't know under what name she disguised herself, and God protect us from ever learning it! But what you don't know, what's even more horrible, is that the man who wants to ruin you is the brother of the orphan you rescued."

I went home—only to find out my young protégé had died. Imprudently, I wrote my sister the fatal letter that was made public. I fled from my husband's house, and I learned he'd been killed in his second duel, and that he died knowing I was innocent.

Now you understand me, Armand; you understand the letter I wrote you and that you must not have received, since you never answered it... For now this story is no longer mysterious to you, is it? You can guess it all. I won't remind you of what my poor sister confided—alas, she admitted everything, the unfortunate girl! I'll say no more. Memories that are too painful would be elicited by my story, and at this point, Armand, I don't want to give way to useless recrimination...

Luizzi rubbed his eyes. He wasn't sure he was awake. He felt as if some kind of madness had taken hold of him. He was like a man who's dreaming, and who chases shadows that always elude him. He got up and paced around his room, hunting for an explanation for what he'd just read, and forced to believe either in his own madness or in the madness of the woman who'd written to him. Finally, to tear himself out of that horrible state in which he was losing his mind, he went on reading the letter. It ran like this:

I'll move on to another period in my life. When he learned of all my misfortunes, my father summoned me to him; he took me to Italy, and married me to Monsieur de Farkley. He made me change even my given name, so there'd be nothing to remind the world of what I'd been and what slander I'd been subject to. But in Milan a man from our part of the country, who was named Ganguernet, recognized me. Two days later everybody knew—not the true story of my life, but the story as appearances had rendered it. I was insulted, and driven out of society. My husband tried to defend me, and he too died in doing so.

Can you understand now how a woman, of whom it can be said that a lover and two husbands have died in duels over her misbehavior, can be taken for a fallen woman and be treated as one? I'll stop here. Tonight—tonight—you'll come see me, won't you? My father will be here. I'll see that he forgives you, and perhaps he'll agree to tell you what became of my mother. He told me she's alive, and that he'd find a way from now on to make her protect the daughter she ruined.

Love me, Armand, love me. We've shared many a tear; and, in spite of my father's promises, you're still my only hope.

—Laura

Luizzi's head was spinning more and more. He felt as if his thoughts were blundering around his mind like a crowd stricken with vertigo; he could neither calm them nor gather them together. With a gesture of despair he cried, "Oh, I can't wait that long! It'll drive me mad!"

With an angry spasm he instantly rang the infernal little bell. The Devil didn't appear, but the doorbell of Luizzi's apartment seemed to reply with a sinister echo. The sound iced his veins, and he hadn't moved... when Madame de Farkley entered his room.

"Laura! Laura!" he cried. "In heaven's name, explain this letter! I think I'm losing my mind!... Laura, Laura, who are you? What was your name before?"

"You're asking me?" replied Madame de Farkley with graceful mockery. "Ah, that's pushing too far the forgetting of your own wrongdoing!"

234

"Laura, I beg you! Who are you? What was your name when that child was given to you?"

"I was named Sophie. The children of adultery don't have a last name."

"But when you got married?"

"My name was Sophie Dilois."

"You!" he cried. "But it's barely two months since…" Then he started over. "Oh, it's impossible… It's…"

The door to Luizzi's bedroom opened, and his servant handed him a letter. He couldn't stop himself from opening it, and this was what he read:

You are requested to attend the funeral procession, the memorial service, and the interment of Madame de Farkley, which will take place Monday morning the — of February 182*…

Luizzi dropped the letter, and—frozen, devastated—turned to the woman who stood next to him. She seemed to dissolve in the air like a thin mist, and he found himself looking at the Devil, whose face wore the fiery smile that had already done him so much harm. In his fury Luizzi wanted to hurl himself at him, but a supernatural force kept him nailed to the spot.

"Will you explain this awful mystery, Satan?" he cried, choking with rage and despair.

"It's easy to explain. It's just a matter of dates and numbers," cackled the Devil. "In 1795, at the age of sixteen, Madame de Crancé bore an illegitimate daughter named Lucy. In 1800 she bore a daughter out of adultery named Sophie. In 1815, having become a widow, she had an illegitimate daughter, the one you saw at Sophie's house, to whom you yourself can give a name, because she's the child of your father, the noble Baron Hughes de Luizzi…"

"That child was my sister?"

"And Charles was your brother, another child of adultery abandoned by your father, the virtuous Baron de Luizzi."[49]

"But I met all those people alive, barely two months ago. I saw Sophie two months ago, and now I find her remarried and unrecognizable. Oh, it's impossible, I tell you! You're tricking me."

"I'm not tricking you today, master, but I did trick you."

"You did?"

"You remember the first time we met, when you claimed to be so careful about the spending of your own life? Poor fool, for once handing it over to me!"

"You told me you took six weeks."

"I took seven years."

---

[49] All of the complex relationships described here are diagramed in the Appendix at the end of Volume Two. However, that family tree necessarily also contains information about other character identities and connections that will not be revealed till much later in the novel. To avoid spoilers, therefore, the first-time reader is advised not to consult the Appendix before finishing the book.

"Seven years!"

"It's been seven years since Lucy died, seven years since Dilois died, seven years since Charles, your brother, died. It's been seven years since you killed all three of them with a joke."

"And Laura? Laura?" cried Luizzi, whose head could barely contain all these horrible events, coming one after another.

"Laura… She died only twelve hours ago, such a martyr in this life that God himself couldn't pursue her beyond the grave. The affront you gave her yesterday was the last blow against her exhausted courage. She came here to tell you the story of her life, which you'd misunderstood. She knew why you weren't home, and to whose salon you'd gone to sacrifice her. You killed her twelve hours ago."

"But last night, the woman I saw here…"

"That was me," laughed the Devil. "I felt a kind of pity for that woman, and I came to play the scene that would've taken place if she'd waited for you. I pulled it off pretty well, don't you think?"

"And this letter?"

"I wrote it myself. You can include a copy of it in those memoirs."

"Wretch! Wretch that I am!" cried Luizzi. "Such crimes! Such crimes, and I can't make up for them!"

"Yes, you can," said the Devil, caressing Luizzi with the fire from his eyes, like a flirt trying to seduce a simpleton. "You can, because as an honorable man you still have two duties to carry out: The first is to care for your father's child, whom poor Sophie put in a convent; imagine the suffering the world has in store for her, based on what her two sisters suffered! The second is to avenge Sophie for the injury done to her by Madame de Marignon's friends, the injury responsible for everything that happened. But will you dare, master?"

"Oh, give me the power to do it!" cried Luizzi amid sobs and cries of rage. "And I'll repay evil with evil—because now I finally see I'm forbidden to do good. Tell me who the women are who so cruelly insulted the poor woman I killed!"

"I told you story of one of them."

"But what about the other one?"

"The other?" said the Devil, prancing around. "The one whose story I wanted to tell you at one o'clock in the morning, when Laura was still alive, and I thought I'd gotten you interested in her fate?"

"Yes, that one!" cried Luizzi.

"That one, whose story would've made you run to Laura to beg her pardon, to vow to defend her, and perhaps to save her from despair—if only you'd been willing to listen to me?"

"Yes! Yes!" cried the baron wildly. "Speak! Speak!…"

Chapter XXIII: The Third Chair

The Devil settled himself, as if he were about to begin a long story, then replied carelessly, "In 1815 Madame de Fantan was named Madame de Crancé."

"Her mother! Her own mother! Horrors!" cried Luizzi, trembling convulsively at the thought of so much perversity.

The Devil began to laugh, and the baron, crushed and devastated, felt his head spinning and his heart failing, and he fell in a faint.

Chapter XXIV: The Devoted Servants

Luizzi remained unconscious for thirty-six days. That was a long time to go without eating. So the first sensation he felt when he came to was fierce hunger. He wanted to ring, but he couldn't move his arms or legs. "Well!" he said to himself. "I've had another fall. Yet it seems to me I didn't jump out a window like last time; this is just an overall numbness." He tried once again to move, and discovered he'd been solidly tied to his bed. He called out feebly, but no one came. But a woman who was sitting by his bed, dunking a fine chunk of bread into a big glass of sugared wine, got up slowly, looked at him, swallowed a bite of bread and a mouthful of wine, and calmly sat down again. She set her glass down next to her, picked up a novel, and began to read, muttering each sentence aloud.

Luizzi would've rubbed his eyes to make sure he was awake, but—as the woman with the bread and the wine put it—he was "hermetically" bound.

"Pierre! Louis!" he cried. "Louis! Pierre!"

A few bursts of laughter, accompanied by the clinking of glasses, were the only response.

"Louis! Pierre!... You rascals! Hey, anybody!" Luizzi called out much louder.

"My God, he's annoying!" murmured the woman. Without getting up, she took an enormous sponge that sat soaking in a bucket of ice water, and applied it vigorously to his face.

The remedy worked: it made the baron think. "All right," he said to himself. "I've been ill. I assume I've had a brain fever. Still, I must be completely cured, because all I feel is a certain weariness in my body; I have no difficulty thinking. I can remember exactly what happened to me—I could describe it from beginning to end." Enumerating his recollections to himself, like a beggar tallying his fortune on his fingers, he began to speak out loud. "I remember everything: Madame de Fantan is Madame de Crancé. Laura de Farkley is Sophie Dilois; she's dead, poor thing—I killed her!... Ah, Satan! Satan!"

"Well!" mumbled his nurse. "There he goes again. He's so tedious!" Now in turn she called out, "Monsieur Pierre! Monsieur Pierre!"

Pierre appeared, wrapped up in his master's dressing gown and dunking a Reims cookie in a glass of champagne. "What's up, Madame Humbert?" he said, swaying and stuttering.

"What's up is, we'll have to send for the leeches again. Doctor Crostencoupe told me very clearly, if the delirium starts again, apply seventy leeches to his stomach and refresh the mustard plaster on the insides of his thighs and the soles of his feet."

"That doctor sure goes through a lot of leeches and mustard powder!" said the valet. "The baron may be rich, but Doctor Crostencoupe could easily eat up his entire fortune in apothecary prescriptions!"

"Good health is worth every penny, Monsieur Pierre. It's the greatest blessing on earth," said Madame Humbert.

"Maybe so, but I'd rather be sick my whole life than pay thirty sous for each nasty leech."

"You can tell it's Doctor Crostencoupe writing the prescriptions. The last time I tended a sick man with no family, they only cost thirteen sous apiece. It's true, the deceased was just a fraudulent insurance broker who'd only declared bankruptcy three times."

"I hear you were able to skim off a little extra income?"

"Not much, Monsieur Pierre! Not enough to make you lick your lips like that."

"The baron seems to have calmed down. Couldn't you skip the leeches?"

"What! I told you, he was delirious. He began talking about those ladies again, you know. Anyway, what's bought is paid for. I don't want to deprive the apothecary of his sale."

"It's not the baron's purse I'm telling you to go easy on, it's his skin. His chest and his stomach are as pockmarked as a slotted spoon. It's like he caught smallpox from the leeches. Put them on the tab, but don't put them on his stomach."

"We'll carry out your prescription right away, Monsieur Pierre. As long as Doctor Crostencoupe doesn't notice tomorrow! He'll look for the holes; that man insists on the right number of holes. Speaking of which, get a hundred leeches instead of seventy, because there are always some that don't bite…"

"And which you'll take home to resell to the trade, Madame Humbert?"

"So? You want me to leave them here, strolling around, walking stick in hand?"

"Hey, Madame Humbert, I've got an idea!"

"What now?"

"With all of your experience tending sick people, have you ever seen leeches having sex?"

"Shut up, you big animal!" said Madame Humbert, making herself sound prudish. "Go get me what I asked for, and while you're at it send me in a little glass of wine and a cookie. I feel hungry all the way down to my feet."

"You want champagne?"

"No thanks, I hate the bubbles, they give me acid. Just another of the same."

"Bordeaux?"

"Yes, Bordeaux."

"You've got strange tastes! A heavy wine like that'll put you to sleep."

"By the way, don't forget my coffee. I feel so drowsy."

"All right, all right, I'll get you what you want. Louis will go to the apothecary."

"The coachman? He hasn't sobered up all morning."

"That's when he's at his best. He never drives as well as when he's dead drunk, so he'll be all right when he's only had a little."

"Wine doesn't do you any harm either; you're friendly enough."

"You think I'm drunk?"

"Not at all. Your eyes are shining like coach lanterns."

"The better to see you with, Madame Humbert," said the valet, drawing closer to the nurse, who—contrary to custom—was neither so old nor so ugly, but thirty and curvaceous, better than Monsieur Pierre deserved.

"Well, well, Monsieur Pierre! Your wine's a little too sweet!"

"Oh, if only you'd be sweet!"

"And what would Monsieur Humbert say?"

"Oh, there's a Monsieur Humbert?"

"I beg your pardon! Is there one? How do you think I got the name Madame Humbert? Out of the almanac, maybe, or a rag-picker's sack?"

"Don't get angry, there are lots of madames without a monsieur!"

"Could be, but I'm not that type, you understand, Monsieur Pierre?"

"Does that stop anything, Madame Humbert?" cried Pierre.

"Go get me my leeches, you nasty red-faced man! And if you start this again, I'll sock you in the nose!"

"It would do me good, and you too."

"Don't talk nonsense."

"I'd rather talk nonsense."

"Hey, rascal!" cried Luizzi in annoyance.

That put a sudden stop to the valet's amorous advances. He stood still, then began to laugh. "What a fool I am! I forgot he's crazy."

"He's got more sense than you do. Listen, it's ringing midnight. The apothecary's going to close and I won't get my leeches."

"I'm going, and I'll be right back," said Pierre. As he left he blew Madame Humbert a tender kiss.

"Hmm. You big lug," murmured the nurse. "If I wanted a lover, he'd have a little more initiative than you do."

That observation didn't keep her from clearing off the table next to the baron's bed and pulling up two good armchairs—an unequivocal sign that she hoped to spend a little more time with the gallant valet.

The reader might perhaps be surprised at Luizzi's silence during that long conversation; but the reader shouldn't forget this wasn't the first time Luizzi had found himself in this position, following a lacuna in his life devoid of memories. The ice-cold sponge applied to his face, and the immediate threat of seventy leeches, were enough to warn him that if he made a fuss he'd be treated like a madman. He also understood that, in his ignorance of what had happened to him since his last conversation with the Devil, he might say things that would truly make him appear to have lost his mind. So he chose to keep silent, and—partly thinking, partly listening to what was being said—he looked for a way to get out of the awkward position he'd been put in.

He thought he saw an opportunity when he was alone again with the nurse, and to prove he was in his right mind he began to speak in a feeble voice. "Madame Humbert, I'm thirsty."

"My God, what a sponge of a man! I gave you a drink no more than five minutes ago."

"Excuse me, Madame Humbert," he replied gently. "It's been more than five minutes, because you were talking to Pierre for half an hour."

"Well!" said Madame Humbert, picking up a candle to see him better. "Well! You'd almost say he's in his right mind when he talks like that!"

"I'm completely sane, Madame Humbert. To prove it, I'd like you to untie one of my arms so I can take a drink by myself."

"Oh yes! Just like the other day. So you can throw the herbal tea in my face, and tear a bonnet off my head that cost me sixteen francs, new, just last year? Here, drink this and be quiet."

"I swear, Madame Humbert, I won't do you any harm, and I'm completely sane."

"All right, all right. Drink this first, then go to sleep."

"What's up?" asked Pierre, returning with a bottle under each arm, a salad bowl full of sugar in one hand, and a plate of cookies in the other.

"What's up?" asked Madame Humbert, turning just as she was holding a cup of herbal tea out for the sick man. "What's up is, he's having one of his lucid moments, and he's asking me to untie him."

"Don't do that," said Pierre. "Remember last time? He gave us enough trouble getting him back into bed: it cost me a good dozen kicks."

"And you'll get the same again when I'm up!" cried Luizzi angrily.

The valet stood at the foot of his master's bed, still holding the bottles of wine under his arms and the salad bowl and the plate in his hands. He gave the baron a rather drunken grimace and said politely, "I'd like a better tip than that, thanks!"

"Wretch!" cried the baron, making a violent effort to rise. In doing so he bumped the teacup Madame Humbert was holding out to him, and tipped it over.

The nurse cried angrily, "You must be crazy to tease a madman like that! That was the last cup of herbal tea, and I was rationing it to make it last all night. Now I'll have to make another one, or he'll have to go without."

"Well, hell, he can go without," said Pierre.

"Easy for you to say! He's going to howl all night that he's thirsty, and I won't be able to sleep a wink. Anyway, it won't take long. There's a kettle on the fire, and I'll put some hemlock in it."

"Jut a second," said Pierre. "First we need your hot water to melt this chunk of sugar."

"What for?" asked Madame Humbert.

"Well, besides the bottle of Bordeaux, I brought this excellent cognac, and we'll make a little salad bowl of caramelized sugar in flaming cognac that we can eat without a fork."

"You and your flaming cognac!" said Madame Humbert. "It's the same thing every night with you! You'll singe yourself body and soul till one day you catch on fire like an old bundle of rags."

"The fire's already lit," said the valet, giving her an annoying smirk.

"Are you going to start your nonsense again?"

"I'm talking about the fire in the punch," said Pierre, feeling clever. "Look at the pretty blue flame it makes!"

"It's true. It makes you look all green, like a corpse."

Suddenly she gave a cry, and said with genuine fear, "My God, Pierre, you're an idiot! Don't put out the light like that! It terrifies me!"

For a harmless little joke the valet had blown out the candles and was standing behind the flaming punch bowl. Lit by that sinister glow, his face had taken on a greenish tinge, and the horrible grimace he was pulling to make his joke funnier gave him a frightful look. From his chest came a long, hoarse sound.

Terrified, Madame Humbert said, "Come on, Pierre, that's enough. Light the candles."

"Ho, ho, ho!" cried Pierre in a sepulchral voice.

"That's horrible!" she cried. "How stupid can you get!"

"Ho, ho, ho!" he cried in an even more impressive voice.

"Look, if you don't stop I'm going to call for help," she said, truly shaking as she went toward the door.

"You will not leave this place," he went on in a cavernous voice. "I've come from hell to take you away, you and your patient."

"Will you shut up?" she cried. "Pierre, Pierre, please stop it!"

"I am not Pierre, I am the Devil!"

"Satan, is that you?" cried Luizzi, whose imagination, unsettled by his long illness, easily lent itself to a scene that, to him, had nothing supernatural about it.

At the baron's exclamation, the valet and the nurse screamed and threw themselves into each other's arms, while in his delirium Luizzi went on calling, "Satan, come to me! Satan, I summon you!"

"Nicely done," said Madame Humbert, still trembling all over. "Now you've sent him into a relapse, worse than he was a week ago. He's summoning the Devil again like a maniac."

"Wouldn't it be funny," said Pierre, trying to sound relaxed, "wouldn't it be funny if the Devil had appeared?"

"Come on, that's enough," she said impatiently, "or I'll call for help."

She relit the candles while Pierre poured the flaming cognac into their glasses.

"Here you go," he said. "Drink that. It'll make you feel better—because you sure were scared."

"Don't act so cocky," she replied. "You're as white as a sheet… Give me another glass. It gave me such a turn when he began calling for the Devil, my legs are still trembling."

As she spoke she sat down at the table. Pierre sat next to her, and while he poured her another glass of punch he said, "Still, this isn't the first time you've heard the baron summoning the Devil."

"Certainly not!" she said, sipping her drink. "At the beginning of his illness he did nothing but!"

The hallucination of sorts that had seized the baron had now been dissipated by the nurse's and the valet's terror. Realizing there was no use speaking to them reasonably, he resigned himself to keeping silent; he decided to listen quietly to their conversation, no matter what they talked about.

"Still, it's a strange kind of madness," said Pierre, "imagining you can order the Devil around."

"There are stranger kinds of madness than that. I myself have seen some much more amazing. I spent a whole year taking care of a young lady from Gascony who thought she'd had a child and she'd been locked up in a cellar for seven years."

In spite of his resolution to keep quiet, Luizzi was so surprised by those words that he cried out, "Wasn't that Henriette Buré?"

The nurse jumped, and Pierre said, "What's wrong?"

"That was her name," she said. "How could your master know that?"

"Oh, he's from Gascony too. He must've known her back home. Let him jabber away by himself, and tell me about it."

"I don't know anything more, except she was brought here by a man in her family. Anyway, she wasn't at all dangerous, and she did nothing but write out her story from morning to night."

What Luizzi had just heard filled him with horror. He understood how, using a diagnosis of insanity, the revelation of certain crimes could be suppressed for life. He reflected that he himself was considered mad, and perhaps there were people around him whose interest it served to support that idea. He'd just learned he'd emerged from a long illness in which he'd been in the grip of delirium. During that time he might've told the story of Madame du Bergh and of Madame de Fantan, and if word of it had reached those two women, there was no doubt they had more reason than anyone to claim he was mad. He reflected further that it wasn't only for a few days they needed that diagnosis, and he had to assume they'd use any means possible to make a man disappear from the world who'd shown he knew their sordid secrets.

The silence following Madame Humbert's remark had given Luizzi time for that train of thought. The two servants had spent the same silence eating a few cookies lightly sprinkled with punch. Now Pierre went on, "Still, it's peculiar for someone to lose his mind like that, all of a sudden and with no warning."

"Your master never gave any sign of madness before these past six weeks?"

"None. But I'd only been in service with him for a couple of weeks, and he was more or less like everybody else, except for talking to himself when he was alone in his room with the door closed."

"And that didn't tip you off?"

"Oh, no, because I'd just left the service of a politician who spent all day declaiming speeches in front of a mirror facing a podium he'd had built in his parlor so he could practice his eloquence."

"He must've looked like a complete idiot!"

"On the contrary, he's a well-respected lawyer, who's considered even smarter than he is fat."

"Even so, you'd have to be a pretty stupid man to stand in front of a mirror and make speeches to yourself."

Luizzi could tell the conversation was wandering away from what interested him, and to bring it back around to himself he asked to have a drink again.

"Is he ever thirsty tonight!" said Madame Humbert irritably.

"Well, the herbal tea you gave him must really have satisfied him, since it all spilled on the sheets."

"Say, that's true, and I forgot to make him another. And now there's no water in the kettle and I'll have to relight the fire."

"Don't bother, Madame Humbert, I'll take care of it. Where's the little packet I'm supposed to put in it?"

"On the left, there, on the mantelpiece, next to that oddly shaped little bell."

At that word, Luizzi lifted his head and saw his talisman. His first reaction was a feeling of satisfaction; but little by little, as he considered the situation the Devil's confidential stories had put him in, he promised himself firmly never again to have recourse to him.

While Pierre made the tea and Madame Humbert went on drinking her flaming cognac, the coachman, Louis, entered, carrying a fish bowl full of leeches in one hand and an enormous package of mustard-seed flour in the other. The sight of them did more than any of his reflections to convince Luizzi to keep quiet. He trembled at the thought of having those topical remedies applied to him, and to keep his excellent servants from wanting to help him out in his illness, he pretended to be asleep. To make it even more convincing, he even tried out a gentle snore.

"Hey!" said Pierre, turning around. "I'll be damned! I think he's giving his last gasp!"

"No question," said the coachman, going toward the bed.

"Not possible!" said Madame Humbert, barely stirring in her chair.

"I'm not surprised," went on Pierre, coming over to examine the patient himself. "He's been lingering like this for more than a week. Check his pulse."

Madame Humbert got up, but the flaming cognac had affected her more than she knew, and she stumbled, and instead of taking the sick man's wrist, where the pulse was still vigorous, she pressed her finger to the back of his hand. Feeling no pulsations in the vein, she announced pompously, "My word, I believe it's over."

"*Requiescat in pace*," said Pierre, pulling the sheet up over Luizzi's face. "I'm going to make a tidy pile out of this."

"*De profundis*," replied Louis through his nose. "The horses have eaten up all the hay and all the oats."

"Hold on," said Madame Humbert. "I'm responsible here. Don't touch his things, it'll be noticed. I'm not talking about his cash."

"There is no cash," said Pierre.

"How do you know?" asked Louis. "Did you check the chest of drawers and the secretary?"

"I'm telling you, I know there's nothing."

"All right, all right," said Louis. "But you can bet on it, the gendarmes aren't just good for catching dogs. You give me my share right now, or I'm going to the magistrate and telling."

"You try it, and I'll have them ask you how the horses ate six hundred bales of hale and twenty sacks of oats in the last six weeks."

"Pierre's right," said Madame Humbert. "He keeps his nose out of the stable, you keep your nose out of the bedroom."

"How much is he passing on to you to take his side?"

"Nothing at all, you hear? I'm an honest woman, and I've never taken anything besides what my patients give me, and Monsieur Pierre is my witness that a little while ago the deceased offered me a half dozen silver table settings to repay me for the good care I always took of him."

"Did he put it in writing?" asked Louis.

"No, since he's been hermetically tied to his bed."

"Well," said the coachman, "if you plan to eat off that silver service, you're likely to have your soup with your fingers."

"He's right," said Pierre. "It's a nuisance we never gave him the idea of writing a will. I bet he would've given us all enough to live off of."

"Maybe so," said Louis. "He was a little stupid. But what's done is done, so forget about it. Let's just make sure to come to an understanding, like the honest people we are."

"Fine," said Pierre. "Let's have a seat and keep our voices down: we don't want the porter to hear us."

"Oh, I left him snoring on the sofa in the parlor. If he wakes up, it won't be to come bother us, but to go get in bed."

"Still, close the double doors," replied the valet, "and let's talk it over together."

Luizzi could tell, by the sound of chairs being moved, that the three worthy speakers had gathered around the table, and the clink of glasses told him the flaming cognac was being put to work again.

"All right," said Louis. "Be honest, Pierre: what did you find in the secretary?"

"Ten thousand five hundred francs," said the valet, "and not a sou more."

"Word of honor?"

"Word of honor! And you, what did you make out of the oats and hay?"

"Eleven hundred and twenty-two francs."

"That isn't much," said Madame Humbert.

"Damn!" said the coachman. "We all contribute what we can."

"My word," went on Madame Humbert, "considering the man had millions, that's not much of an inheritance."

"The fact is," said Louis, "a proper will would've done us more good. Is there no way to get one?"

"I'm not handy at writing," said Pierre. "Besides, monsieur had terrible handwriting, like chicken scratches."

"You have a sample?" asked Madame Humbert.

"I don't know," said Pierre. "The only time I ever saw monsieur's handwriting was when he gave me little notes to deliver."

"Son of a bitch!" said Louis, striking the table. "Educated people are so lucky! To think, my beggarly parents didn't even teach me to read, and I might miss out on a fortune because of that!"

In spite of the horror the conversation inspired in Luizzi, the idea of a will gave him some hope. Just as the coachman struck the table violently, the baron let out a long sigh. The three frightened servants listened carefully.

"Louis!... Pierre!..." murmured Luizzi softly.

"He isn't dead!" they all muttered to themselves. Pierre, the steadiest of the three on his feet, got up and pulled the sheet off his master's face.

"Ah! Is that you, Pierre?" asked Luizzi, as if he were just coming to. "Where am I? What's happened?"

"Say!" said Madame Humbert. "It sounds like he's recovered his wits."

"Who's that woman?" Luizzi asked Pierre.

"I'm your sick-nurse," she replied with a bow.

"Have I been in danger for a long time?"

The servants exchanged a glance, not yet quite sure the master had fully recovered his senses. Then Louis answered, "You've been in bed for six weeks, baron."

"And you good people have been watching over me every night that whole time?"

"It's true," said Pierre. "We've hardly slept since you fell ill."

"You'll be well rewarded for your zealous care," said Luizzi, "whether I get well or whether I succumb... because I still feel very weak."

"I went to get the leeches. Would monsieur like some? It might help him feel better."

"I don't think that'll be necessary," said Luizzi. "The first thing I want to do is write a note to my lawyer."

The servants looked at each other.

"I'm not afraid of dying," he went on. "But you never know what might happen, and I need to put some order in my affairs. I won't forget you, good people, I won't forget you."

Crude as it was, Luizzi's trick worked perfectly. That's because it was targeted directly at greed; and we have to acknowledge that, if that passion is among the most ingenious at finding ways to succeed when it acts on its own, it's also the most prone to taking the least disguised bait; that's true of all the greedy instincts, whether physical or moral.

The wish the baron had just expressed was quickly carried out. But he noticed that, while Louis was getting him the necessary paper and ink, Pierre and Madame Humbert were conferring in lowered voices. A new fear seized the baron: if he summoned a lawyer and drew up a will, shouldn't he be afraid that, once they knew it contained clauses in their favor, the wretches surrounding him would try to hasten the moment when they could profit by it? He paused to think of a way to stave off this new danger.

"Monsieur isn't writing?" asked Louis, observing him.

"Hey! How's he supposed to write with his hands tied?" asked Pierre. He approached, pulled off the covers, and undid the ropes that bound the baron's arms.

Luizzi lifted his hands off the bed with childish glee—but his joy was quickly dampened by the sight of his terribly thin arms. A patient whose face gets thinner day by day, and who follows the ravages of his illness in a mirror, has trouble keeping track of the gradual change in his features; but a patient who sees himself suddenly after a long period of time, and discovers all at once what his illness has done to him, often suffers a fright more fatal than the disease itself. That's how it was for Luizzi. No sooner had he seen his arms than he cried out in terror, "A mirror! Bring me a mirror!"

The obsequious servility that had replaced the earlier despicable indifference in the servants' hearts responded promptly to the baron's request. Madame Humbert gave Luizzi a mirror and helped him sit up. When he saw his pale face, his long beard, his tangled hair, his hollow eyes bright with fever, his pinched nose, his white lips, he froze for a moment at the sight. The supposed courage

247

our hero thought he had in plenty suddenly fled, and in tears he cried out, "Oh, my God! My God! My God!"

Then, letting the mirror drop, he fell back on his bed, utterly crushed and despairing. He let the tears roll down his cheeks without hiding them from the avid curiosity of his servants; because at that moment his cowardice had trumped his vanity, which is most men's courage.

Luizzi's faithful servants must've been genuinely alarmed by that spasm of weakness, because Madame Humbert said to him as gently as possible, "Doesn't monsieur want to write to his lawyer?"

"Am I that ill?" he asked, looking anxiously up at her.

"No, no, baron. But it's good to take precautions, and it's always better to die after putting yourself in order with men and with God."

"With God!" he cried, bursting into tears. "With God! Me, reconciled with God! Never, never! Hell has me in its clutches, and…"

"And there he goes again!" said Pierre. "It was a false recovery. Come on, we'll have to tie him up again."

"Oh, I beg you!" cried Luizzi, near tears again. "Don't tie me up! I won't say anything, I'll keep quiet, but don't tie me up. I'll write—I'll write to my lawyer."

That new promise worked, and Luizzi took the pen they handed him. But he couldn't see the paper and his hand no longer knew how to guide the pen; and he could barely write a few words before he fell back on his bed, exhausted by the effort.

"Hurry up, Louis," said Pierre in a low voice. "There's no time to lose."

The coachman rushed out and slammed the door behind him.

"Don't leave me alone!" said Luizzi, trembling. "Don't leave me alone!"

Pierre and Madame Humbert sat down by the bed in silence, watching the sick man's slightest movements and taking care to arrange his pillow and to make him as comfortable as possible. The mess in the room had disappeared, taken away by Pierre while Luizzi was writing; so when he looked around again no trace remained of the nocturnal festivities he'd witnessed. With his mind weakened by illness, and by the vivid shock produced by the embarrassing scene that had just taken place, he had trouble keeping all of his recollections straight, and soon he began to question whether it hadn't all been one of his delirious dreams. Reassured by that uncertainty, he let himself drop into a feverish slumber, in which sometimes he saw his apartment ransacked, sometimes he saw countless leeches pursuing him on all sides.

Finally exhaustion won out; he slept deeply and didn't wake till dawn the next morning. What yanked him from sleep was the sound of his doorbell being rung violently. Then he saw Pierre come in and say quietly to Madame Humbert, in a significant tone, "The lawyer's here."

A moment later Louis came in, and Madame Humbert said quietly to both of them, "He's asleep."

The baron decided to take advantage of his servants' mistake to learn the truth about what had happened during the night, so he listened to what they were saying to each other.

"You took your time," said Pierre to Louis.

"The lawyer wasn't at home. They told me he'd gone to a concert in the Faubourg Saint Germain, and then I had to run from the boulevard to the rue Babylone. When I got there I asked for him, but a footman told me he hadn't seen him in any of the rooms, and I was going to come back here, when a coachman who's a friend of mine told me he'd just seen the lawyer's carriage leave, and heard him give the order to take him to the Place Royale, where one of his clients was giving a big ball. I ran all the way there, and had no trouble asking for him, since there were really just four or five of them sitting playing écarté. But I had to wait another hour and half, because the game had heated up. Finally I caught him on his way out, and I've brought him here in his silk stockings and top hat."

"All right," said Pierre. "As long as the baron hasn't had a relapse, we're set."

"Has he noticed anything?" asked Louis.

"Nothing," said the valet. "He thought we were watching over him."

At that moment voices could be heard in the parlor, and Doctor Crostencoupe entered, followed by the lawyer, Monsieur Bachelin.

"I'm telling you, it's impossible," the doctor was saying peremptorily. "These idiots must've mistaken a moment of calm in the madness for a recovery of sanity. He has acute persistent encephalitis, and we're far from a cure."

"Damn!" said the lawyer. "So there was no point disturbing me and making me get up so early! When you've been up half the night on business, it's no fun getting up again at the crack of dawn."

"You're quite right," replied the doctor. "I think your presence here is quite unnecessary."

"I'm sorry to hear it," said the lawyer. "But let's have a look at the baron and check on his status."

They both approached, and Luizzi opened his eyes to take a look at the doctor in whose care he'd been placed. He was a tall man, bald in front though he didn't seem especially old, dressed with considerable elegance, and holding his head in a very theatrical way. He stopped at the foot of the baron's bed. Staring at him with a slight frown, he pointed at him and announced pompously, "Look! The cheekbones are prominent, the face is purple and puffy, the eyes are red and restless, the eyeball rolls, the respiration is irregular and hesitant, the skin is damp with sweat: the intensity of the disease has not diminished."

"I think you're mistaken, doctor," said Luizzi quietly.

"You see?" went on Doctor Crostencoupe with a smile. "He's still delirious: he says I'm mistaken."

249

"I swear to you, doctor," said Luizzi, "I'm fully in my right mind, and the best proof I can offer you is to tell you why I summoned my lawyer."

Then the baron described to the doctor the way his servants had cared for him, and their intentions when he died.

"God almighty!" cried Madame Humbert. "What nonsense! I spent the whole night quietly by myself next to him, and I had to go wake Louis, who was sleeping in the outer room."

"To prove that," added Pierre angrily, "all you have to do is look in the secretary and in the closets and see if there's anything missing!"

"All right, all right," said Doctor Crostencoupe. "You don't have to defend yourselves. Obviously the madness is still going on."

"You're the one who's mad!" cried Luizzi furiously as he sat up in bed.

"What! You untied him?" cried the doctor.

"Hell! We had to so he could write to the lawyer," said Madame Humbert.

"Well, tie him back up again!" said the doctor.

"Don't you dare, you rascals!" cried Luizzi with growing anger.

"Hurry, hurry," went on the doctor. "Pay no attention to what he's shouting."

"What's going on? What's going on?" asked the lawyer, waking up with a start. Tired out by his long night spent on what he called business, he'd sat down in an armchair and let himself fall asleep during Luizzi's account.

"My God!" said the doctor. "The delirium is coming on stronger than ever!"

"Monsieur Bachelin!" cried Luizzi. "Help me! This is premeditated murder!"

"You hear him?" said the doctor. "The insanity is total."

"Send me another doctor!" said Luizzi. "I don't know this one. He's a schemer, a villain. I'm in the clutches of people who are banking on my death!"

"Tie him up tighter than ever," said the doctor, while the baron defended himself as well as he could. Finally, exhausted, choking with fury, he collapsed panting on his bed.

"Poor man!" said the lawyer. "He was so strong, so full of life when I knew him before! It'll be quite a fine inheritance for the Crancé family."

"Never!" said Luizzi. "My fortune will never go to a family that includes the despicable Madame de Fantan."

"All right, now he's completely lost it," said the doctor. "Step away, Monsieur Bachelin. The idea of making a will can only aggravate his condition."

As he left, the lawyer glanced pityingly at Luizzi, then took away his last hope. As soon as he was gone, the doctor turned to Madame Humbert. "So, what was the effect of the leeches and the mustard plaster you applied last night?"

"I didn't apply them, since it was such calm night."

"That seems unlikely—his pulse has never raced like this. You'll apply them immediately. You can apply a hundred."

"Very good," said Madame Humbert.

"I'll come back tonight," said the doctor, "and see where we are." Then he left.

As soon as he was gone, the three servants looked at each other questioningly. But, at a sign from Pierre, they too went out, leaving Luizzi by himself. The poor baron therefore lay there alone with his thoughts. He was in the hands of an ignorant butcher whose treatment was bound to kill him, and at the mercy of servants whose criminal plots he'd unmasked without convincing anyone, and who had a clear interest in keeping him from recovering, so as to escape the punishment he'd be able to inflict on them.

He felt lost. He had no way to alert his friends—and anyway what could he have told his friends if he'd had any? Without a doubt, he was done for. His servants were holding a conference in the outer room to carry out a crime that had become unavoidable. What to do, where to turn? To the Devil? Luizzi still shrank from the thought of reopening relations with that infernal figure: wasn't it he who'd put the baron in the awful position he was in now? What if Satan rescued him from this predicament, only to throw him into something even worse?

Still, it was his only chance; and in his despair of finding any human help, he summoned Satan. But Satan didn't appear, and Luizzi realized even that last hope had been taken from him. It was true, the mighty little bell was out of reach, and he had no more power to make himself obeyed by his infernal slave than by his human servants. As a result, the hope Luizzi had invested in Satan, despairing of any other, now seemed to be denied to him as well—and he wanted it all the more since he couldn't have it. He bitterly regretted not having taken advantage of the times when his servants were obeying him, and asking them to give him his talisman, and now in his rage his cried out, "Oh, I'd give ten years of my life to have that bell!"

"Really?" asked the Devil, appearing suddenly at the foot of his bed.

"Oh, Satan, it's you! Help me, save me!"

"And you'll give me ten years of your life?"

"Haven't you already taken enough years from me?"

"Not enough, since you did so much harm."

"It was you who drove me to it, villain!"

"By obeying you."

"By hiding the truth from me."

"By telling you the truth. But you should know one thing, baron. He who made this world is a skillful worker. When he put eyelids on men's eyes, it was to keep them from being blinded by the brilliant light of the sun. When he gave them ignorance, error, gullibility, it was to keep them from being reduced to idiocy and insanity by the lethal light of the truth."

"If that's how it is, I guess I have nothing more to ask you."

"That's up to you."

"Can I get out of the fix I'm in?"

"If you can."

"All right, then just give me that bell!"

"No, damn it! I came here on my own time; I'm free."

"Then why did you come?"

"Because you were offering me an attractive deal."

"I don't want to go through with it."

"It's up to you."

"Ten years of my life!" said Luizzi sadly. "Never!"

"What good has it done you, that you're so attached to it?"

"It's exactly because it's done me no good that I want to be careful in spending what's left of it!"

"Well then, in return for that bit of wisdom, I'll give you some advice. You've just put into words the greatest of truths: man only clings to life because he spends it so badly, so wastefully. He never stops believing tomorrow will give him what he let slip away yesterday, and he's always running after something he's always left behind him."

"You haven't changed, Mister Satan: you're forever moralizing. What's the advice you want to give me?"

"Get married."

"Me?" cried Luizzi.

"Look, master, if you weren't single right now, none of this would've happened to you."

"This is a trap you're setting for me."

"It's a deal I'm offering you. Take a wife, and I'll get you out of that bed without asking for anything in exchange."

"A wife you give me would be a shabby present."

"You can choose; I won't interfere in the least."

"You know I'll choose badly."

"On Satan's honor, I haven't looked into it, but the odds are on my side. You're vain, weak, rich—you'll fall for some gold digger."

"And how much time are you giving me?"

"Six months."

"And if after six months I haven't chosen?"

"I'll take ten years of your life."

"But if I get married, how does that benefit you?"

"I'm buying my freedom," laughed Satan. "Your wife'll keep you busy enough you won't think about me anymore. You're vain, so you'll pick a pretty one, which means you'll be jealous—a huge waste of time. You're weak, so you'll be a slave to all of her whims. You're rich, so she'll have the right to ask for enough that you won't have time to waste with me."

"You're taking advantage of the situation, Satan: you wouldn't dare talk to me like that if I had my bell."

"You can see I'm not such a devil as they say, since I'm behaving like a man."

"I'm quite sure your advice is some kind of treachery."

"Saint Paul said, '*Melius est enim nubere, quam uri*': better to marry than to burn.[50]

"But am I going to die here?"

"Who knows?"

"You're trying to be awfully clever, Satan," laughed Luizzi, "but I've caught you in your own trap: you asked for ten years of my life, which means I've got at least another ten years to live."

"Sure, but what kind of life? You're in the hands of a doctor who thinks you're mad."

"He'll have to be persuaded I'm not."

"Do you think Henriette Buré is mad?"

"Excuse me?" cried Luizzi. "So you think I might end my days in an insane asylum?"

"People who were saner than you have died there."

"You're slandering civilization, Satan."

"I'll let you be the judge of that someday."

"When?"

"Maybe tomorrow, maybe in ten years, depending on what you decide to do."

"But can you just tell me one thing? Was that shameful scene I witnessed last night real, or the effect of delirium?"

"You saw right, you heard right."

"That lifts my spirits!"

"That's because you're ill, baron, and you have perverted tastes."

"You advocate of vice, would you dare defend it even in that sleazy form?"

"Fine. I'll leave that to the best circles."

"The best circles?"

"The best and the most straitlaced, my friend," replied the Devil, pursing his lips as if he'd just caught a whiff of an unpleasant smell. "You've just had a living preview of the literature that'll be in fashion in a few years."

"In France? Among the wittiest and most elegant people in the world?"

"Yes, master, among the wittiest and most elegant people. There'll soon come a literature devoted to stories set in dressing rooms, in garrets, in night-clubs. The heroes will be doormen, rag pickers, used clothes dealers. The dialogue will be in shameful slang, the morals will be the vices of bottom-dwellers, the descriptions will be caricatures…"

"And you think anyone's going to read books like that?"

---

[50] From 1 Corinthians 7:9.

"They'll devour them: great ladies and shop girls, magistrates and stock exchange clerks."

"And those books will be admired?"

"I'm not making this up. That literature will be like a notorious woman: both scorned and sought after."

"Those are quite different things."

"They're absolutely the same thing, baron. That's the privilege of easy pleasures. To find pleasure in a refined woman's love, you need a certain loftiness of feeling and thought; you have to know how to find satisfaction in a word, a glance, a gesture, in something veiled and delicate, pious and solemn. With a prostitute, on the other hand, pleasure comes running—candid, open, messy; you don't need to chase it, it throws itself around your neck, it arouses you, it leads you on, it turns your head. The next morning you blush over it; the next night you start in again. It's the same with literature: you don't go around telling people you've been with a bad book, but you go there anyway."

"And it might even include scenes like what I witnessed?"

"Aren't you going to write my memoirs?"

"And you want me to include scenes like that?"

"Why not? You think, at the distance I stand from humanity, I see much difference between the vices of a great lord and those of a peasant? You think, for someone who sees Man naked, it matters what clothes cover his deformities? You've seen greed in its lowest-class form; you want to see it in what's called society?"

"What do you mean by society?"

"Oh, there are lots of levels, but I've never seen much difference except in dress and concealment."

"Meaning there's more hypocrisy above than below; that's just one extra vice."

"My dear friend, hypocrisy, properly understood, is humanity's great social bond."

"Excuse me?"

"Listen, baron! In a city struck by the plague, if the local government is foolish enough to let the streets fill up with the dead and dying, if they let the air get polluted and people's imaginations run wild, there's no doubt pretty soon the plague will carry off three quarters of the population. But, on the other hand, if they make all traces of the disease disappear, if the sick are hidden in hospitals and the dead are quickly taken away, the epidemic will be restricted to its natural limits. Vice is just like the plague. It has its miasmas that corrupt the moral air: that's what you call setting a bad example. So don't blame hypocrisy for covering up humanity's wounds—that assures the moral health of society."

"So then what's virtue?"

"Virtue, master, is health."

"Where is it?"

"Look for it."

"And how can I find it after what you've just told me? Who'll guarantee me that hypocrisy, that deceitful clothing, isn't covering up vile diseases?"

"Look beneath the clothes."

"Meaning I have to listen to the stories you tell me? I've heard about nothing but crimes so far."

"I'm not the one who chose the subjects."

"But if by chance I meet a pure soul, won't you stain it with your stories?"

"I don't lie and I don't slander; those are the weapons of the weak and the cowardly."

"Since that's the way it is, Mister Satan, since I'm sure to hear the truth about every woman I meet, I accept the deal you're offering—but on one condition: that I'll have two years to choose."

"Two years, agreed."

"It's a deal?"

"Deal."

"All right, make me healthy."

"I can't. I don't interfere with the material things of this world, you know that."

"So you've tricked me?"

"You're always the same: untrusting, because you're untrustworthy! Look, in three weeks you'll be as well as you can be."

"How?" asked Luizzi.

The Devil was gone.

Chapter XXV: An Excellent Cure

Luizzi was disappointed by Satan's sudden disappearance; but, reassured by his promises, he considered his predicament more calmly, and finally realized it wasn't as desperate as he'd thought. Fear had turned the obstacles confronting him into monsters.

The next moment Madame Humbert returned. But instead of the enormous bowl of leeches or the bag of mustard flour he expected to see in her hands, she was carrying a little tray holding a cup of broth and a glass of excellent wine. We've said Luizzi had awoken with a fierce appetite, and hunger gave him the idea of secretly seducing Madame Humbert and removing her from his servants' plot: how true it is that in most men the stomach is the seat of invention!

He called to her. "Are you bringing that excellent meal for me?"

"For you, sir! Oh, no, you're much too ill to have anything."

"Are you going to start treating me like I'm crazy again?"

"Lord God above! I know perfectly well monsieur is in his right mind, but even so I can't give him anything to eat. My duty is to carry out the doctor's orders."

"Of course. But it's not in your interest."

"Interest isn't what governs me, baron."

"That's too bad! Because if you'd been willing to give me that broth, I'd have paid you for it as if it were liquid gold."

"And if Doctor Crostencoupe found out?"

"If he got angry I'd throw him out."

"And then he'd throw me out, and he'd replace me with some mean old sick-nurse who'd do everything he said."

"You're right, Madame Humbert. I won't say a thing to him. Let's see that broth."

She stirred the cup. "You'll also have to tell him you took all your medicine."

"I'll tell him, Madame Humbert. Give me the broth."

She brought the cup toward his bed. "There's also Pierre and Louis who could tell him you're not following his orders," she added, looking troubled; and she put the cup back on the tray.

"I'll forgive Pierre and Louis, if they agree to keep my secret. But give me that broth."

"At least drink it slowly."

"Fine, fine."

"Wait till I undo the ropes tying you down."

"Thank you, Madame Humbert, you're an excellent woman."

Luizzi drank his broth, and was so restored that hope rekindled in his heart while the heat reached his stomach.

Toward evening Doctor Crostencoupe arrived, and asked if his instructions had been carried out exactly.

"Ah, doctor!" said Luizzi. "A strange thing happened to me today! It was as if a haze fell over my eyes. My chest felt like it was being stung repeatedly, and my thighs were burning."

"All right," said the doctor with a frown, "the leeches and the mustard plaster. What else?"

"What else, doctor? As the pain increased, I felt my head clearing, and soon it was as if I was emerging from a dark night."

"Finally!" cried Doctor Crostencoupe. "You're saved, baron! We just need to persevere with the same treatment: another two hundred leeches and fifteen mustard plaster applications, and you'll be fit to go riding."

"I hope so, doctor."

"But what I recommend above all is strict fasting."

"What, doctor, no food at all?"

"Not even a glass of sugar water. The least nourishment would mean death."

"Death?" cried Luizzi in alarm.

"Instant, annihilating death."

"Bah!" said Luizzi mockingly.

"A new brain congestion, delirium, frenzy, softening of the cerebellum, coma, and death."

"O Moliere!" thought Luizzi.

"You hear me, Madame Humbert?" asked Doctor Crostencoupe.

"Absolutely, doctor, absolutely."

"Till tomorrow." And he left.

He returned the next day, carrying a large container of pills and a sealed bottle, which he set down on the sick man's bed. "Here, this should complete the cure. You'll take one of these pills every hour, and in between, without fail, you'll take a teaspoonful of this syrup."

"I'll do it, doctor, don't worry."

Doctor Crostencoupe left again, and Madame Humbert immediately brought Luizzi some broth, which he drank with a child's glee. A week passed that way, during which the doctor never failed to stop by every morning and every evening, and ordered the exact administration of his pills and his syrup— which exactly every hour on the hour they tossed out the window. The baron assured the doctor the regimen was doing him so much good he wouldn't miss a dose. Still, at the end of a week he took a risk and asked the doctor's permission to have a little broth.

"Broth!" cried Doctor Crostencoupe. "Broth! So you want to undo the results of all my care! Broth! Take arsenic, it'll act faster!"

"The thing is, doctor," said Luizzi with a smile, "I've been having broth for a week already."

"Bah!" said the doctor without much surprise. He considered, then went on, "I see: the pills and the syrup have counteracted the effect of that noxious beverage. I'm delighted to hear it—it proves they're even more effective than I thought."

"So I can continue having broth?"

"Yes, but diluted with water, and doubling the dose of the pills and the syrup."

"I'll remember."

No sooner had the doctor left than Luizzi called out triumphantly, "Madame Humbert, make me a porkchop, and every hour on the hour toss two pills and two spoonfuls of syrup out the window! The count has to come out right for the doctor."

Doctor Crostencoupe came back the next morning, and, on being assured that the patient had swallowed a double ration of pills and syrup, he marveled at how much he'd improved just to the naked eye.

A week later Luizzi played the same scene again. "Doctor, I wonder if maybe it's time to let me have a porkchop or a chicken wing?"

"Oh, oh, this time no, baron. To submit the stomach to indigestion, to bring disorder to the nervous papillae of the stomach, which connect directly to the brain, would be to bring on all the violence of the illness once again."

"You think?"

"I'm sure of it. You see, that would be understood by even the lowest practitioner; why, it's the bridge of asses of medicine."[51]

"Well then! I have to tell you, doctor, I've been eating a porkchop every morning for a week!"

"Astonishing!" cried Doctor Crostencoupe, drawing back. "And you've felt nothing?"

"Nothing except perfect well-being."

"Admirable! No mental problems?"

"None."

"No ringing in your ears?"

"No."

"No vertigo?"

"No, nothing, absolutely nothing."

"I wouldn't have believed it."

"Believed what?"

---

[51] The bridge of asses (*pons asinorum*) is the traditional name for the isosceles triangle theorem in Euclid's *Elements*, because the proof separates those who can understand it from the "asses" who can't.

"The invincible power of my syrup and my pills. Look, baron! In spite of your reckless behavior, here you are, almost cured! Double the dose again: four pills an hour, and two large soup spoons of syrup!"

"And I can go on having my porkchop?"

"Hmm... I'm not sure about that."

"But those pills are so powerful!"

"Half a porkchop."

"That syrup is sovereign!"

"Fine! The porkchop is all right." Then the doctor called out, "Listen, Madame Humbert, I'm holding you responsible for the baron's life. I've allowed him a porkchop, by which I mean a lean porkchop, well done. Make sure he doesn't exceed my instructions by so much as a mouthful of bread. And no raw foods—above all, no raw foods!"

"Of course, doctor."

Doctor Crostencoupe left, and Luizzi threw off his covers and got up, crying, "Madame Humbert, I want a three-course dinner, and especially a salad, and artichokes in pepper sauce."

"Oh, baron, be careful!" said the sick-nurse, dropping her eyes and blushing.

"Well! Is it the casualness of my dress that shocks you? I'd have thought that was nothing new to you."

"Nothing new, baron," she said with an unexpected smile, a nod, and a look of satisfaction.

The baron kissed Madame Humbert—and Pierre came in. It occurred to Luizzi that in the high spirits of his returning health he was making himself a rival of his valet. Ashamed of himself, he resumed his tone of command.

"It appears monsieur is completely cured!" said Pierre.

They brought him his dinner, and he ate very well. Another week passed in that way.

One morning the doctor found him up, and said with a smile, "He, he, baron, I assume you see the benefits of my caution in forbidding you to eat anything besides a small porkchop?"

"Come now, doctor! For a week already I've been gorging myself on excellent stews and all kinds of raw foods."

"Incredible! Incredible! Incredible!" cried the doctor, pacing around the room with great strides. "This is the perfect case outcome to add to my memoirs. Yes," he went on, pulling a manuscript from his pocket, "this memoir will bring me fame and fortune: it's the case study of your illness and your cure. I'm submitting it to the Academy of Sciences tomorrow; I have no doubt they'll be struck by the astonishing results of my treatment, considering the risks the patient himself voluntarily introduced. To have cured you if you'd followed my orders exactly would've been simple; but to have cured you in spite of your constant noncompliance with the prescribed regime—that's the clearest proof of the supreme effect of my pills and my syrup! They will pass down to posterity, baron! Crostencoupe's pills! Crostencoupe's syrup! Tomorrow I'll announce them in all the newspapers. Allow me to make use of your name, baron, that's the only fee I ask."

"Go right ahead, doctor," laughed Luizzi. "I'd be delighted to hear the thoughts of the Academy of Sciences on these medicines."

"Then I'll just put the finishing touches on this account, baron. I'll be honored to read it to you. I'm sure to find you at home, since you're not yet fit to go out."

"What! Not go out? But what if I took eight pills?"

"You can take eight, but I still forbid you to go out."

As soon as the doctor was gone, the baron opened his window and threw out the whole container of pills and all the bottles of syrup. In a stentorian voice he cried "Louis, harness the horses!"

In his glee he grabbed his bell to summon the valet. The Devil appeared.

"Who rang for you?" asked Luizzi.

"You did."

"Indeed, you're right. In my haste I used the wrong bell."

"Well! What do you think of your doctor?"

"I wouldn't have believed medicine was so idiotic."

"Your valet's right, you're completely cured. You've become self-righteous again."

"How so?"

"I asked what you thought of your doctor, not of medicine. In any case, human folly is the same everywhere. It always blames things for individual people's mistakes, religion for priests' failings, the law for magistrates' errors, science for the ignorance of its practitioners."

"Could be," said Luizzi impatiently, "but I have no wish to hear a sermon."

"Would you rather hear a story?"

"Even less—for the moment, that is. Because you remember what you promised me: if by chance I meet a pure and honorable woman, you know you have to tell me the truth about her."

"I will."

"Are you sure you can do it?"

"You child!" said the Devil with melancholy, jealous rage. ""You think I don't recognize the angels? Have you forgotten I lived in heaven?"

"So, according to you, a pure and honorable woman is from heaven? So where am I supposed to find her?"

"Start looking," chuckled the Devil. "Start looking, master, and don't forget you have only two years."

"And don't you forget I've got my talisman back."

"I have a better memory than you do, because I kept my word and gave you back your health."

"You? Didn't you refuse to interfere in my recovery?"

"Materially speaking, yes, but mentally…"

"How so?"

"With wicked thoughts. I gave Madame Humbert the idea of making you delirious again by letting you eat, and I gave you the idea of disobeying your doctor."

"You put everything in the worst possible light. I'd forgotten my servants' treachery."

"You think they're any worse than you are, for plotting to kill you for their benefit?—you who for a moment's amusement are going to let a quack make use of your name to sell poison to the public?"

"I'll fire all of them."

"Quite right, baron. You wept in front of them, you conspired with them to play schoolboy's tricks on your doctor, you tried to outsmart them, and they have contempt for you."

"Contempt, from my servants!" cried Luizzi furiously.

"Baron," laughed the Devil, "that's the first contempt you earn, just before society's contempt."

"You mean?…"

With a mocking look at the baron, the Devil left. A few minutes later, Luizzi showed up on the Champs Elysées in a splendid carriage. It was a warm, languid spring day. He ran into all of his friends, some in carriages, others on horseback; but not one of them acknowledged him. Among them was Madame de Marignon, who passed by in an open caleche with Mareuilles, and who clearly turned her head away. The baron went home furious, bent on revenge. Then it occurred to him for the first time to ask for the list of people who'd come to call on him while he was sick. There were only two names: Ganguernet and Madame de Marignon.

PLATONIC LOVE

Chapter XXVI: *A Marquis*

When Luizzi saw those two names he was stunned, both that they were on the list and that so many others weren't. The absence of Monsieur de Mareuilles's name left the baron in no doubt that he shared in Madame de Marignon's insult in cutting him dead, and he looked for a way to punish them. Left to his own devices, a man has no shortage of wicked thoughts; so a man in league with the Devil must be crammed with them. Mareuilles was supposed to marry Mademoiselle de Marignon; was there a way to steal his bride from him? Luizzi thought it over at length, but he couldn't see any way to pull it off except to marry her himself; and in spite of his need to find a wife within two years, he wasn't at all tempted to search for one in a social world about which he already knew so much that was criminal.

Imagination wasn't the baron's strong suit, and he probably would've stalled at that point in his plot without finding a way to carry it out—when a visitor was announced: Monsieur Ganguernet.

"Hey, morning, baron!" said the prankster from the far end of the parlor. "What did I hear? You've been sick? And here you are as fresh and rosy as an apple!"

"Yes, I'm fully recovered."

"Well! What do you think of Paris? What a city! What a crowd in the streets! What a commotion! It's the land of the gods."

"And goddesses too, right, Monsieur Ganguernet?"

"Oh, baron, the women are hellish frigid. They don't have the dark eyes, the come-hither movement of our shop girls in Toulouse!"

"And what did you come to the capital for?"

"What! I never told you? I'm here for a wedding!"

"You too?" asked Luizzi incautiously.

"Well! So you're getting married! To whom?"

"To the perfect woman. And you?"

"I didn't say I was getting married. I'm here for a wedding, but it's my son's."

"You have a son? I never heard any mention of a Madame Ganguernet!"

The prankster smiled. "I couldn't legally marry the woman."

"Really!" cried the baron, disgusted. "So your son bears a name that doesn't belong to him?"

"I beg your pardon, it does belong to him—he bought it."

"What? He bought a name?"

"It wasn't expensive. He's a clever rascal, I promise you. You know the play by Monsieur Picard called *The Foundling*?"[52]

"Yes, I believe I saw it performed not long ago."

"Well, my son put the plot into action. He's a good-looking fellow, and he'd been playing Elléviou's roles in provincial theater for quite a while.[53] He was a huge hit with the ladies. When he was between jobs he came to Paris by way of Toulouse, and we painted the town red together. No sooner was he gone than I got a letter from a prankster friend of mine, an old veteran from the days of the Empire, who was in Toulouse with Field Marshal Soult.[54] He invited me to come have fun at his estate in Taillis, near Caen, and he told me he had a niece and a grand-niece to marry off, with a dowry of two million francs."

"A dowry of two million francs!"

"It's a funny story, actually," laughed Ganguernet.

"I believe you, but let's not lose the thread of the first story."

"Here it is. On the spot I wrote to my son, inviting him to join me in the adventure. 'If we play our cards right,' I said, 'you'll have one of the chicks. It'll be an excellent joke to play on my friend Rigot.' There was only one problem: my son was named Gustave, period; and Rigot is too much of an old scalawag, and from a working-class family, not to want a respectable man with a distinguished name for his niece or his grand-niece."

"You surprise me!"

"Bah! Everybody's trying to get out of the gutter by his own means or by means of his family. That's how it is with courtesans: they almost always raise their daughters very correctly."

"You think?" laughed Luizzi.

Ganguernet puffed out his cheeks and went on melodramatically, "Since they know the reefs, they can keep others from running aground on them."

"Could be. But how'd your son get his name?"

"Like this. When he got my letter, he was in the middle of a run with the Opéra Comique. That theater has an extraordinary fellow, the leader of their claque."

---

[52] *L'Enfant trouvé* (1825), a comedy by Louis Benoît Picard and Edouard Joseph Ennemond Mazères.

[53] Pierre Elléviou (1769-1842) had a short but brilliant career in Parisian theater as a singer, actor, and librettist.

[54] Jean-de-Dieu Soult (1769-1851) rose to the rank of general during the Napoleonic Wars, and in the 1830s and 40s served as prime minister of France under Louis Philippe.

"Every theater has one."

"But this one's different, because he happens to be the Marquis de Bridely."

"The Marquis de Bridely, from Toulouse?"

"The youngest of the four sons of the Marquis de Bridely you're thinking of. At the time of the Revolution he was at seminary. He threw his cassock into the bushes; and while his father and his three brothers joined the Army of Condé,[55] he bravely enlisted in the army of the Republic. His father and his three brothers were killed, and he became the Marquis de Bridely, but that's all: he remained an ordinary soldier, to the extent he could. He was as brave as a lion, and was decorated at Austerlitz, but he was never promoted to corporal, because he got drunk fourteen times a week, except during battles. He was discharged from the army in 1815, and began working as a veteran."

"What does that mean?"

"You don't know?" said Ganguernet, putting on an act like a veteran of the Old Guard, with military posture and a deep voice. "'An old soldier of the Empire, who's seen all the capitals of Europe, damn it! Long live Napoleon! A brave Frenchman, loyal unto death! Decorated on the battlefield, twenty wounds! Long live the Emperor!' With that, and a pretty good service record, for two or three years he picked up hundred-sou coins with the Emperor's effigy on them from all the Bonapartists and officers and generals and so on to whom he introduced himself."

"That's a hell of a living!"

"It's very widely known. But all the competition wrecked it, and he had to find something else. So he started working the opposite side: the ruined noble family racket."

"And what's that?"

Ganguernet put on a long disdainful face and a posture both pliable and arrogant, and began talking through his nose and his pursed lips. "'The Marquis de Bridely! Absolute devotion, which they think has been sufficiently repaid with a meaningless decoration'—in this case the red ribbon of the Legion of Honor repurposed as the red ribbon of Saint Louis![56] 'Unshakable loyalty to the Bourbons, in spite of their ingratitude!' And that's how you trick royalists into giving you napoleons with the effigy of Louis XVIII."

"And that career failed, like the other one, because of the competition?"

"No, by getting used up. The marquis was moving fast: he exhausted Paris in three or four years. He could've kept going in the provinces, but he needed to

---

[55] The counterrevolutionary Army of Condé was led by exiled aristocrats and nobles, and was financed by England and other powers hostile to revolutionary France.

[56] In other words, a Napoleonic honor masquerading as a Bourbon honor.

be in Paris. So, after a spell as a ticket scalper, he became the head of the claque at the theater where my son wanted to be hired."

"Finally we get to the point! And what did your son do?"

"When he got my letter, he went to the marquis and offered him a thousand écus if he'd marry his doorkeeper, adopt him, and legitimize him. The marquis agreed, and the son of Monsieur Aimé Zéphirin Ganguernet and Marianne Gargablou, maiden name Libert, is now Count de Bridely, if you please."

"Is your son good-looking?"

"He's the spitting image of Elléviou."

"Does he have good manners?"

"Elléviou to a tee."

"This calls for thought, Monsieur Ganguernet."

"What does?"

"Oh, nothing, nothing! And when are you off to visit your friend, Monsieur…"

"Rigot? In a week or so—enough time to have clothes made for his father the marquis. We're taking him along: he'll drink with Rigot and charm him. The mother's allegedly ill… I expect it'll be a good prank!"

"Very funny indeed," said Luizzi thoughtfully. Then, seeing Ganguernet get up, he said, "What! You're leaving already?"

"It's getting late, and I have to meet Gustave at a restaurant before we go see *The Two Convicts* at the Porte Saint Martin.[57] The marquis got us tickets."

"If I weren't ill, I might join you there. I've heard a lot about it."

"They say it's very good. It's about a convict who, knowing the secret of one of his prison mates, forces him…"

"To give him his daughter's hand in marriage," said Luizzi quickly.

"No, since it's his wedding day. It's not like you couldn't write a play based on what you've just told me."

"Perhaps something better than a play," replied Luizzi, still thinking about his idea for revenge.

"That's true: when you've got hold of somebody's secret, there are lots of ways of making use of it."

"You're right," cried Luizzi. "Come back and see me tomorrow morning."

"Till tomorrow, then."

"Please accept my apologies for not calling on you; I still have to be careful when I go out."

Ganguernet withdrew. No sooner was Luizzi alone than he rang the little bell and the Devil appeared. He was dressed in a black suit and carried an enormous briefcase under one arm.

"Where've you just come from?" asked Luizzi.

---

[57] *Les Deux Forçats* (1822), a musical melodrama by Boirie, Carmouche, and Poujol.

"I've been drawing up a marriage contract, whose terms you might find out someday."

"Is it mine?"

"I told you, I'm not getting involved in this business, except to tell you what you ask for."

"I assume you know why I've summoned you?"

"I know, and I approve. You finally understand the world, and you're re-paying evil with evil."

"No more sermons! I'm doing what I want."

The Devil smiled scornfully.

"Slave!" cried the baron.

The Devil burst out laughing. Luizzi rang the bell. The Devil fell silent.

"I want to hear Madame de Marignon's story."

"Right now?"

"Right now, and skip the commentary."

"Are you sure you won't be doing the commentary? The world's awfully small if you look down at it from high enough up, master, and you can't predict what you're going to learn."

"More horrors, I assume?"

"Maybe."

"Crimes?"

"You take me for a writer of melodramas?"

"Aren't you their muse?"

"I'm the Prince of Evil, baron; I leave mere wickedness to human minds."

"But you'd make a perfect man of letters, since you've got the most important of their gifts—vanity."

"The only gift I have is for doing evil. Let them have it, and they'll justify it as well as I do."

"You're always such a wit, Mister Satan!"

"You can see, I'm no scribbler of melodramas."

"No more, please," said Luizzi. "Let's get started."

"Here it is," said the Devil. And he began like this:

Chapter XXVII: *Madame de Marignon*

She's the daughter of a certain Madame Béru. To understand the daughter, you have to know the mother. Madame Béru was the wife of Monsieur Béru. To understand the wife, you have to know the husband. Monsieur Béru played the violin at the Opéra; he was an immensely talented man, but he was no artist—artists didn't yet exist in those days. When a musician went without dinner in 1772, it was because he didn't have the money. Sometimes he laughed off his poverty, sometimes it made him angry. But he never wrapped himself in it to pose as a high and mighty victim. Art—that veiled god whom all of your great men mold in their own image—didn't yet have a cult and martyrs.

Béru was a great violinist, and he'd spent many years wading through the muck in pursuit of a fee, without imagining he was a genius with wings of fire whose thoughts rose beyond the mud of the gutter he paddled in with his shoes full of holes. He wore a threadbare suit, not glorious rags. His violin was his violin and his breadwinner, not the divine voice by means of which he bared his soul to the multitude, nor the immortal manna nourishing him with a ray of harmony stolen from the angelic choir. If Béru's wig was disheveled, it wasn't because artistic delirium had tangled it, it was because the neighborhood wigmaker had refused to tidy it up decently.

Béru said openly, "I'm the greatest violinist of my time," but he would've considered an idiot anyone who told him, "You're one of those passionate beings to whom God has confided a word of the great mystery! And when that harmonious word sings and weeps on your submissive obedient strings, men listen with astonishment and women dream in their hearts, because then you awake one of those eternal echoes that murmur within us every time genius—that voice from heaven exiled on earth—speaks to us in a language that thrills us without our comprehending it."

If you'd said that to Béru, he wouldn't have understood a thing. Still—though he hadn't made his talent into the metaphysical, imaginary Pylades of some living, angry Orestes, the way our young artists do nowadays[58]—even so, Béru was well aware of his own worth. As soon as the conversation turned to music, he became impassioned, eloquent, angry, cutting, pitiless. Béru was a fol-

---

[58] In Greek mythology, Pylades was the cousin and possible the lover of Orestes. Pylades encouraged Orestes to murder his mother Clytemnestra to avenge her murder of his father Agamemnon. Pylades therefore represents—in general and in the Devil's comparison here—a spirit of resolve and commitment to some terrible and fateful action.

lower of Gluck, and called Piccinni a clown, a fraud, a rascal, a thief.[59] Béru had all the intemperance of a musical passion. He was a great and genuine musician, and the surest proof I can offer is that his talent was as impervious to success as it had been to poverty.

Around 1770 Béru got married. He married Mademoiselle Finon, who kept a house where the young noblemen of the court were in the habit of going to eat and gamble. In those days Finon was a woman of thirty, for whom having a lot of company, a liberal table, and sumptuous clothing was life at its best. At first she'd made use of her own beauty to procure all those good things. Later, as an intelligent woman who could accept reality, she'd counted on the beauty of others to keep up the kind of establishment her own beauty couldn't sustain anymore. But, to keep her house from drawing too much attention from the police, she thought it prudent to find herself a husband who'd give her legal standing. It was a difficult choice. She needed a man who not only accepted the awkward status of the house, but who wouldn't get upset at the proprietor's own dalliances—because if Finon was no longer the goddess of the old businessmen and the young aristocrats, she still knew how to take care, here and there, of a few wealthy tenant farmers who were treating their suppliers, or a few Knights of Saint Louis, as noble as they were threadbare, who took her out to the play and went for walks arm in arm with her.

She heard about Béru, a violinist with an income of twelve hundred francs, whom all the noblemen had known forever because he sometimes played in their little house orchestras. Finon thought he wouldn't impose on her life a presence that had to be acknowledged or that might be displeasing; and if he had a decent personality she could get along with him. She sent Béru word to come see her. At their very first meeting she decided he suited her needs in every respect. He was sublimely indifferent to all the jokes people made about his personality and his looks. He ate and drank with an energy nothing could discourage, and at the end of dinner he was drunk enough to have to be carried to bed.

The next day Monsieur Béru was married. That great event affected him only superficially. His wife provided him with a tailor and a wigmaker, and left him his income of twelve hundred francs to do as he pleased with. Once the wedding was over, life went on as before: the house continued to be a meeting place for fashionable women and the richest and highest-born men, and Béru went on playing the violin at the Opéra on Opéra nights, and spent his evenings at the Café Procope when he had the night off. He never reacted to any of the jokes his friends made about his wife, and he never gave those who envied him the satisfaction of seeing that he understood what they meant, and with sublime

[59] Christoph Willibald Gluck (1714-87) was a German composer who radically reformed early Classical opera, with lasting influence on later Classical practice. Niccolò Piccinni (1728-1800)—not to be confused with the much later Giacomo Puccini—was a popular but conventional Italian opera composer.

composure he went on getting drunk and playing the violin. By the end of a few months his inertia had worn down even the worst mockers, and they could barely summon a few quips when, a year after he was married, he was declared the legal father of a newborn girl.

A satirical piece on the occasion was posted on the stovepipe at the Café Procope, and it ran like this:

Yesterday Madame Béru
Said to her husband triumphantly,
"You have a child!"... "A child—me?"
Replied the good fellow,
"And may I hear what her name might be?"
"Béru, sir, just like you. That's the law."
"Will she be noble or bourgeois?"
"Bourgeois, sir—isn't that what you are?"
"Bourgeois will do, ma'am, but can I inquire,
Whose is this beautiful child?"—"She's mine, sir!"

When Béru entered the café he did what everybody else did and went straight to the stove. He read the poem from beginning to end, while he rubbed his hands on the hot stovepipe to which the sheet of paper was glued. Nothing on his face betrayed the slightest emotion. He picked up his hat, which he'd set down on the marble stove top, and his cane, which he'd propped against a chair, and he was humming as he went over to his usual table.

One of the regulars, outraged by his cynical indifference, called out, "Hey, Monsieur Béru, did you read anything on the stove that interested you?"

"I don't know how to read, sir," replied Béru with admirable calm.

"Well, you know how to listen, anyway," said the regular. "So I'll tell you what it says there."

Béru leaned on his elbows as if to listen better; and, as portentously as possible, the regular declaimed the ten wicked lines I've already quoted.

"Oh, is that on the stovepipe?" asked Béru, leveling an almost threatening look at the regular.

"Yes, sir," replied the regular, squaring off like a man getting ready for a fight.

"Well then," said Béru, finishing his glass of liqueur. "If that's where it is, let it stay there."

"Are there really husbands like that?" asked Luizzi, interrupting the Devil.

"There are, master, and some with even longer horns, believe me. If I were in Parliament, the first thing I'd do would be to add something to the laws governing the promotion of civil servants: *One third of the positions will be award-*

269

ed by seniority (meaning by incapacity), one third by favor (meaning by corruption), and the last third to women (meaning to cuckolds)."[60]

"What a charming government you'd produce!"

"The one you've got is just like it, baron. Things run so smoothly because what isn't written in the law is maintained by custom."

"All right, all right, let's get back to Béru."

The Devil continued:

Nothing could be done against such courage, and after Béru had passed that formal test all the jokes and all the satires came to an end. Life went on much the same, except there was a child in the house. The child had been named Olivia. She grew up without anyone paying her any attention, ignored equally in the kitchen and in the parlor, listening both to theories of servants' crookedness expounded in below-stairs slang and to theories of amorous corruption expressed in the language of libertine foppery upstairs. When Olivia was ten she didn't know how to read and write; but, to make up for that, she was constantly being fussed over by gentlemen with the finest manners, and she played in a parlor where the most distinguished representatives of fashionable vice gathered, and as a result she could babble charmingly on any subject with perfect elegance. And then suddenly she could come out with the most unexpected remarks, born of the servants' quarters, which were wildly successful as humor in the salon.

Around that time, two important events took place in Madame Béru's household: her husband died of apoplexy brought on by indigestion, and she came down with smallpox. When she rose from her sickbed she left behind her the remains of a beauty that had preoccupied all of Paris—or rather that had been preoccupied with all of Paris. That's when Madame Béru noticed her daughter, and realized she'd be a dazzling beauty. Finally she thought about the girl's education. Olivia was taught only two subjects: writing and music. Music to make it possible for people to hear the most beautiful voice in the world, and writing to make it possible for her to put down on paper the meticulously crafted phrases she learned from conversation in her mother's salon.

My opinion is, Olivia knew everything a woman should know, because to the two talents I've already mentioned she added those of dressing to perfection and of walking like a goddess. One of the great faults of fashionable women of your time is not knowing how to walk; most of them drag themselves along feebly, imagining it's a sign of idleness—and therefore of wealth—to find it painful to set your feet on the bare ground when they're accustomed to the carpets in parlors and carriages. Women are mistaken: one of their liveliest attractions can

---

[60] The Devil isn't proposing that women would actually hold the positions, but that they would effectively do so through their submissive (cuckolded) husbands.

only be seen in a firm, straight, quick walk. Only a walk like that can show off a sudden decisive reaction to an unexpected encounter, or the slight bow which the speed of the walk keeps from being deeper, and therefore more awkward and formal. A walk like that makes it possible, without it seeming brazen, to toss out one of those clear, well-articulated glances that spark and flare like lightning, and like lightning last only a moment—those glances right in your eye that stun you and make you turn around as if someone had bumped into your heart. Women nowadays don't know any of that. What's in fashion is limp head movements, weary posture, and a hazy look that barely meets your eye. As a result, you have yellowed, leafless, tired affairs, and almost none of the fresh green romantic adventures that take place in just twenty-four hours, like a classical comedy. Is the way women walk a cause or an effect of your literature? I can't say, but it has to be admitted there's a remarkable connection between them.

Now Olivia—intelligent, a fine musician, a splendid dresser, with an exquisite walk—was a perfect woman. The only thing nature had denied her was the kind of original wit needed to make her fortune; and luckily for her, her bad education had supplied that. I mean that Olivia—who was lively, good-hearted, witty, with no vices except a weak will—would've lacked that spicy, unexpected attraction that provokes passion and drives it to delirium, without her sudden shifts in tone from the most refined expression to the most ridiculous. That had given her a particular style all her own, which to a careful eye explains—much better than her perfect looks or her genuine talents—the phenomenal success she achieved.

On the first of March, 1785, Olivia turned fifteen. She was taller than average, and perhaps a little thin. Her bust was ample but indistinct, still that of a child. Her arms were thin, her hands small and slender. Her feet were narrow, her ankles bony, her face long and almost colorless. Everybody could see she was one of those women destined to great beauty, but whose full splendor is slow to develop, because nature, just like man, takes its time to create something perfect.

That day Madame Béru threw a big dinner; she'd gone to extraordinary expense to celebrate her daughter's birthday. The dozen gentleman guests were the elite of the regulars at her house. A fine dinner, worthy libertines. They told stories, true or false, about the most distinguished women at court or in the financial world; at the feet of a girl of fifteen, who was destined to be a courtesan, they immolated the highest reputations and the most honored names; they taught her how to cheat on a husband, and—much more entertaining—how to keep two lovers. In short, they taught her such contempt for what are called decent people that it was almost better morally not to be considered one.

When in their drunkenness they'd emptied both the bottles and their hearts to the bottom, the Marquis de Billanville, counselor to the king, who'd served with distinction in a number of embassies, motioned to Madame Béru to make her daughter leave. Madame Béru took Olivia away, in spite of the pleas and protests of the other guests, and a moment later she returned alone.

Then the marquis stood up, posed like an orator about to harangue the company, and delivered the following speech: "Gentlemen, I'd like to propose a deal to you. If you're sensible, you'll accept."

"Of course, of course!" they all replied.

"You've all admired Madame Béru's daughter—the excellent Madame Béru, whom I'll ask to listen to me carefully, because it's especially to her maternal affection I want to address myself now, to help me make you understand my proposal. Olivia is fifteen: a fine age, gentlemen, the age at which women owe the debt of love! And yet, if you'll consent, we won't make her pay what she owes yet; we'll give her another year…"

"What's that supposed to mean?" they all cried.

"It means, the more the flower has opened, the better it'll be to pick."

"That's awful!" said Luizzi. "That's vice undisguised!"

"And that's the only thing wrong with it," replied the Devil. "Like I said, hypocrisy is the great social bond."

"Fine," shrugged Luizzi. "You're like a very full goatskin. If you open it just a bit, the water gushes out uncontrollably. You're so full of pedantry, the slightest interruption sets you off. You're why La Fontaine wrote the fable about the pedant and the schoolboy."[61]

Luizzi stopped, but the Devil didn't go on with his story.

"Well?" asked Luizzi. "What are you doing?"

"I'm listening to you putting that fable into practice."

Luizzi bit his lip and replied angrily, "Go on."

"So," continued Satan:

The marquis added, "It means, gentlemen, that till a year has passed none of us will try to have Olivia. Meantime, each of us can try to please her, but go no further. Let's swear on our honor to show her respect for a year. At the end of that time the gates will open, and happy will be the man who bears away the prize! He'll win the most perfect and most fully developed beauty."

"But, marquis," cried Viscount d'Assimbret, "who knows where I'll be in a year? That's a secret known to God alone. So for my part I don't agree with you. Besides, while we're doing no more than promenading in front of Olivia, someone who's not in this company might steal her from us! I'm taking the field tomorrow."

---

[61] In La Fontaine's poem *L'Écolier, le Pédant, et le Maître d'un jardin* ("The Schoolboy, the Pedant, and the Owner of the Garden," 1679), the pedantic schoolmaster cites all of the ancient Latin authors on the evils of theft… while the schoolboys plunder the orchard.

"Gentlemen, gentlemen!" said Madame Béru with all the dignity of an ugly woman. "You forget in whose presence you're speaking."

"On the contrary!" cried the Marquis de Billanville. "It's because I know you're a sensible person that I think you'll agree with me."

"Not so!" cried the viscount. "My good Béru doesn't want to wait, she won't wait: she needs the money. I know the state of her bank account, and I'm offering a hundred thousand livres in cash."

"Oh ho ho!" cried a fat man who hadn't spoken yet. "A hundred thousand livres, that's quite a sum! I'll offer five hundred thousand."

"In cash?" asked Madame Béru, carried away by the offer.

The fat man, a financier who held the contract to collect the salt tax, paused. "I can pay it in a year," he went on, "because I agree with the marquis: we should wait."

"You, Libert? You fat sack of money, you want to wait?" said the viscount.

"Libert!" cried Luizzi. "I know that name, don't I?"

But the Devil paid no attention to the baron's interruption—or rather he didn't choose to hear it—and he went on with the viscount's remarks to the financier.

"Shut up, Libert!" said the viscount. "You're just waiting for your wife to die—the wife who'd tear your eyes out if she knew you had a mistress who was even slightly in society. You must've found her a good doctor if you're sure you'll be free in a year!"

"Two of us want to wait a year," said the king's counselor. "Are you with us, father? You can't have Olivia till you're sure of your bishop's miter."

"That's true," said the priest. "I'm for the year's delay."

"All right, then," said the viscount. "I accept, but on one condition. Listen, fat Libert here is going to steal Olivia from us, that's for sure. Isn't that true, Béru? Because he bought you for six times what you're worth. No rank, no name, no advantage, no brains can compete with that moneybags's gold. So I propose that each of us deposit a hundred thousand livres with a lawyer. That'll make twelve hundred thousand livres, since there are a dozen of us. So, as long as Olivia chooses one of us, she'll get the twelve hundred thousand livres. That way in a sense we all have twelve hundred thousand livres to offer her. Do you agree?"

"Yes! Yes!" they all cried.

"Yes, yes," said the financier proudly.

"Very well, mister moneybags," said the viscount. "But we're all on our honor not to offer a single écu more than that figure, and a penalty for you of a hundred strokes of the cane if you offer a red cent more."

"In that case I withdraw," said Libert.

"No, no," said the king's counselor. "That would raise the stakes without increasing our chances! Because whether he's in or not doesn't change anything."

"Except for the money, right?" said the financier angrily. "Well, I'm in, and I swear I won't do anything beyond what you do, and I'll have the girl."

"And I'll be delighted to let you have her, if I don't," said the viscount, "because she'll make you a cuckold the next day."

"We'll see about that," said the financier.

"I'm sure we will," said the viscount, "and a toast to Olivia! And so you don't suffer for it, Madame Béru, the sixty thousand livres of interest on the twelve hundred thousand will be paid out to you monthly."

Madame Béru, delighted with the deal, nodded her agreement.

"But what if one of us dies?" asked the financier.

"You're a numbers man: that'll just improve the chances for the survivors."

"So it's a kind of tontine?"

"You said it. Béru, bring Olivia back in."

As Madame Béru rose, Olivia entered and said sullenly, "You're treating me like a little girl, mother. I'm fifteen, and I don't see why I can't stay to the end of dinner!"

"I beg your pardon, miss," said the marquis solemnly."We had important business to discuss, and you'd have been bored, since you're so intelligent!"

"Bravo!" said the viscount. "The war has begun. Olivia, my girl, if you ever take a lover, beware of king's counselors!"

"And don't trust the military nobility," said the marquis.

"Why not?" asked Olivia.

"Because if a pretty girl wanted to have two lovers," laughed the financier, "military nobles run their swords through their rivals, and king's counselors have them locked up in the Châtelet dungeon!"

"Whereas tax contractors are willing to share, right?" said the marquis.

"I'd rather have fifty percent of a good deal than nothing."

"That must be why you've never had more than one percent of your wife!" cried the viscount.

"It's true," said Libert. "As much as possible, I try to reduce my stake in bad investments."

"My God!" cried the viscount. "You remind me of poor Béru, except he had some brains."

While dinner went on in that fashion, Olivia studied the guests with an interest that must surely have had some hidden motive, so alert and attentive was she. In fact, she'd overheard her mother's friends' conversation. She was much more mature than they knew: she was already a grown woman, and the best proof I can give you is that she immediately began thinking about how to deceive her suitors. Surrounded as she was by the twelve men's jealous concern, it would've been difficult if she'd tried to have a man from their world; but, while they were all watching each other, Olivia looked beyond their circle and found her opportunity in the form of her harpsichord tutor.

He was a well-built bachelor of about thirty, with a shapely leg and good teeth, and he'd do just fine for a lover. Olivia resolved to love him. But deep down the man had so coarse a nature, and he felt so much like a peasant in fancy dress, that Olivia would never have succeeded without her mother's help. Indeed, Madame Béru had noticed the care with which Olivia dressed whenever her tutor was coming, and right away she began to keep watch over her daughter. Monsieur Bricoin felt the attraction of forbidden fruit. The blood of Eve, my first mistress, ran in Olivia's veins.

"What! Eve?..." cried Luizzi.

"... Cuckolded her husband, just like all the rest. Cain was mine!" replied the Devil. Then he continued:

Till that point Olivia had been struggling not to find Bricoin unbearable; now suddenly she saw him in the most seductive light. Bricoin wouldn't have to have been very conceited to notice the girl's attentions; he sensed that she admired him, and in spite of Olivia's beauty the rascal brazenly tried to make himself desirable, because she desired him. Her head had been turned, and soon she was genuinely besotted with her harpsichord tutor. They exchanged confessions of love, and eluded Madame Béru's supervision.

A week later, Olivia had no more illusions. Presiding every evening at the center of a circle of men who dressed their vices in elegant forms, and whose bantering wit always caressed her with the flattering devotion granted to beauty by debauchery, she made unfavorable comparisons between the men she'd meant to deceive and the man for whom she'd deceived them.

Bricoin was a true fallen woman's lover: tyrannical, brutal, insulting, always threatening to give away Olivia's secret if she didn't obey his every whim. He soon turned her life into a never-ending torture; and the poor girl, with an innocent heart and a depraved mind, kept saying to herself, "Of course I'll have lovers, but I'll never love again."

The fatal year passed like that. At a dinner like the one we've already seen, when it came time for Olivia to choose among the twelve suitors, the pretty girl rose and said firmly, "I choose the tax contractor."

"In two days," cried the financier, "in two days, my queen, you'll be installed in the finest mansion in Paris!"

The rest of them were stunned. Only the viscount said nothing, and later that evening he approached Olivia. "I don't get it. You chose that gold-painted ball. It's not greed, not at your age. There's something else going on. If you need an imbecile as your official lover, it must be to hide another lover."

275

Under pressure by the viscount, Olivia confessed everything to him. A week later, when Bricoin arrived at the new mansion in the morning to give Olivia her lesson, instead of finding the tax contractor with her, he found the viscount. Bricoin tried to make a scene, and threatened to tell the financier everything. The viscount took his walking stick and broke it all the way up to the handle over the rascal's back. Then he said to him, "That's to warn you never to come back here again. As for the tale you're threatening to tell, if you say a word, I'll carefully cut off both your ears."

Some time later, meeting the financier, the viscount said, "Well, the golden calf! Are you happy with little Olivia?"

"Hmm, hmm! I'm afraid Béru played a trick on us."

"And I," said the viscount, spinning around and thrusting his sword between the financier's legs, "I swear Olivia is cheating on you."

Chapter XXVIII: An Elléviou

Satan had reached that point his story when Luizzi heard a knock at his door. "Who's there?" he cried impatiently.

"Sir," said Pierre, "it's Monsieur Ganguernet and Count de Bridely."

Luizzi paused uncertainly for a while, than called through the door, "Ask them to wait a moment. I'll see them."

"Weren't you in a big hurry to hear Madame de Marignon's story?" asked Satan.

"The thing is, I feel like I'll understand it better after I've spoken a little with Ganguernet. There was a certain interruption you didn't respond to, which that man might be able to explain to me. Meanwhile, don't go away."

As he spoke, Luizzi looked at the Devil. His black suit and his briefcase had vanished. He was dressed in a long silk gown and slippers; a single lock of hair hung from the crown of his scalp, and he was cleaning his teeth with his pinkie fingernail.

"Are you going to a costume ball?" asked the baron.

"No, I'm going to China. I'll be back in a moment."

"China!" cried Luizzi, stunned. "What for?"

"To arrange another marriage. Isn't today Friday?"

"The bad-luck day."

"Meaning the day of Venus."

"And what kind of marriage are you going to arrange?"

"I'm going to persuade a mandarin official to marry his mortal enemy's daughter, so as to end a family feud."

"How admirable of you! But will you succeed?"

"I certainly hope so! It should have splendid results."

"To set aside hatred is almost a virtue; and you think you can do it?"

"That's to say, I expect to bring it to a boil. The marriage will produce ten children; five will take their father's side, and five their mother's. From that will come quarrels, discord, fratricide."

"That's villainous!"

"A moment ago you thought I was so good!"

"I hope you won't succeed."

"We'll see. The groom has already sent the bride the usual gifts."

"Excuse me? It seems to me I read in a book by one of our most eminent scholars of geography that in China it's the bride's family that send gifts to the groom."

"Well, for a scholar he's not far wrong. There were at least some gifts involved, that's the main thing. So many of your academics put cities where there are swamps, and deserts where there are cities; so the one you mention certainly deserves the high reputation he enjoys."

"Don't forget, I'm going to summon you back."

"I told you, I'm running to Peking and I'll be back in a moment."

The Devil vanished, and Luizzi asked for Monsieur Ganguernet and Count de Bridely to be brought in. The latter was actually quite a handsome young man, with his fingers hooked into the armholes of his waistcoat; he would've looked fairly distinguished if not for his enormous crown of curly hair, the diamond studs and gold chains that covered his shirt, and the rings on his fat fingers.

After the usual greetings, the baron was somewhat at a loss how to broach the subject about which he was seeing Ganguernet, because he wasn't sure whether Gustave knew he was in on the secret. However, since he couldn't retreat he advanced boldly, saying to Gustave, "So you've decided to leave the theater, sir?"

"Oh, baron," said Gustave, thrusting his pomade-coated hands into the thickets of his corkscrew hair, "what do you expect a man with any talent to do in the theater anymore?"

"But I had the impression there was room for everybody there!"

"True enough," said the Elléviou imitator, prancing around, "because everybody's quit! But mediocrities are in fashion now, and I'm not enough of a schemer to drive them out."

"Again," said Luizzi, "I had the impression the public was better than scheming at sorting out who the real talents are."

"For that to be true, baron, the public would have to be able to recognize real talent."

"Directors want to hire them."

"Do they know what they're doing? The only talent they recognize is for flattery. Anyway, you can't overcome the jealousy of certain people in important positions. For example, a week ago, before I'd found my father—you know I had the joy of being reunited with my father, the Marquis de Bridely?"

"Yes, yes," said Luizzi, glancing at Ganguernet, who began laughing with his big laugh.

"Well, as I was saying, sir, two weeks ago I went to see the director of the Opéra Comique. He was in a spot, because his lead tenor refused to perform that evening, a Sunday: that meant four thousand francs of ticket sales lost. While we were discussing the terms of my contract, he sent a doctor to the tenor's dressing room to check on the state of his health... I won't say of his voice—that's been ruined for a long time. We were about to sign my contract when the stage manager came in to say the lead tenor had agreed to perform a little one-act piece. 'Aha!' I cried, 'he knows I'm here!' 'He might've seen you come in, sir,' said the stage manager. 'Well then,' I went on, 'would you like me to make him perform?' 'Hell, you'd be doing me a big favor,' said the director. 'Then ask him to come down,' I said. So the tenor came down in a huff. I stayed in a corner. 'I can't perform,' he cried when he came in. 'I'm tired and sick.' I didn't say a thing, but I began to sing a scale rising from low C to high C—do re mi fa sol la ti do re mi fa sol la ti do, do, do—with considerable flair. The tenor looked at me, then said to the director, 'Tomorrow I'll appear in two full-length plays.'"

"That's amazing, sir," said Luizzi.

"Well, baron, would you believe that a moment later—after I'd just saved him four thousand francs in ticket sales by singing one scale—that rascal of a director refused to give me a job for a thousand écus?"

"I understand it very well," said the baron, whose ears were still raw from the Elléviou's two-octave scale.

"It's quite simple," said Count de Bridely with a bow. "He's the slave of that wretched tenor."

"Probably so," said Luizzi. "But I forgot to ask Monsieur Ganguernet to what I owe a second visit at this time of night."

"First of all," replied Ganguernet, "I wanted to present Count de Bridely. As I was passing I saw light in your windows, so I figured you weren't asleep yet. And then I wanted to ask you to keep your lips sealed about the story you heard this morning; I know you're fond of scandal."

"Me? I swear I'll never breathe a word to anyone, not even to Count de Bridely."

"What's this all about?" asked the count.

"I don't think it would interest you, sir," replied Luizzi loftily. Then, turning to Ganguernet, he said, "For me to keep your secret, you'll have to answer one question. Have you ever heard of a certain Monsieur Libert, a financier?"

"What?" cried Ganguernet. "Do I know my own brother-in-law?"

"I had a feeling," said Luizzi. "So he was the brother of that Madame…"

"Marianne Gargablou, maiden name Libert. Antoine Libert, an important man in Tarascon, a Provençal grafted onto a Norman—greed and ostentation grafted onto crookedness and rapacity."

"A real Turcaret, am I right?"[62]

"A perfect Turcaret, because he dumped his wife so he could maintain mistresses, and he let his sister die of hunger."

"Well," said Luizzi, "I expect I can give you news of him."

"He's dead."

"I hope at least I can give you news of his wealth, and it's not impossible that it'll revert to Monsieur Libert's legitimate heirs."

"To me!" cried Gustave, carried away by the memory of his uncle's many millions.

"What's this got to do with you, count?" asked Luizzi scornfully.

---

[62] In *Turcaret* (1709), a satirical play by Alain-René Lesage, the title character is a ruthless, dishonest, and dissolute financier.

"You know very well what, baron," said Ganguernet. "It's all right," he went on, addressing Count de Bridely, "no need to make signals at me. Baron de Luizzi knows the whole story."

"And I'm part of the plot."

"Anyway," said Ganguernet, "this business with old Rigot is very risky: he has two million francs to give as a dowry, but to whom?"

"To his niece, didn't you say?"

"Oh, no! Rigot's too much of an eccentric! He's giving a dowry of two million francs, without anyone knowing whether it's going to the mother or the daughter. He's decided they'll be married the same day. But it's only on leaving the church that the lawyer will open the tightly sealed dowry contract Rigot gave him."

"Hell!" said Luizzi. "That's peculiar!"

"Certainly, but that's not the issue. How will we recover Uncle Libert's millions?"

"I'll tell you tomorrow. Go see *The Two Convicts* and study it carefully, along with *The Foundling*."

"I get it! There's some secret we can use to force the holder to pay up."

"Something like that. Goodnight! I'm expecting the person who'll bring me the latest news."

"Well then, goodnight, and see you tomorrow!" said the two Ganguernets, one of whom was a count; and they left.

Luizzi rang for the Devil.

"Well, well, my friend," said Satan as he appeared, "you seem to have become more than a little insolent."

"Me?" said Luizzi, surprised by the accusation.

"Yes, you. You've been keeping me waiting for twenty minutes!"

"You're quick," said Luizzi scornfully. "You must've have finished with your mandarin official?"

"Like you with the Ganguernets."

"You've sown evil to harvest crime."

"That's good coming from a simpleton like you! I've sown good to make crimes grow; I've preached reconciliation to foment hatred."

"That sounds like a masterpiece whose glory I don't envy."

"You're working hard enough on your own of the same kind to have nothing to envy me for."

"Are you talking about my plan to get Mademoiselle de Marignon married to Monsieur Gustave Ganguernet?"

"That strikes me as a fairly nice piece of villainy."

"Come on. That's revenge, or more like a hoax."

"I know you humans have pompous and resounding names, as well as pleasing and inconsequential names, for your crimes. You're already quite good at it. A little more and you'll be like Ganguernet and call it a good joke."

"Are you trying to talk me out of my plan?"

"Neither to talk you out of it nor to help you with it."

"But that's exactly what you're going to do by telling me the end of Madame de Marignon's story."

"Poor woman!" said the Devil, in such a pitying tone it made Luizzi laugh.

"She's certainly worthy of your sympathy!"

"Poor woman! Poor woman!" replied the Devil, shaking his head.

"You're becoming ridiculous, Satan: you're getting soft."

"You're right. I'm getting soft, and you're acting wicked: we're both breaking character."

"So get back in yours, and especially get back to your story."

"Here it is."

Chapter XXIX: The Story Continued

Before I show you Olivia in society, I have to go into some detail about her state of mind. She began her career as a woman of fashion with a particular error in her heart. She thought she'd known love: the childish whim that had thrown her at Bricoin had brought with it worries, hopes, violent scenes, a few moments of pleasure that are easy to mistake for happiness when you don't know the difference, followed by remorse, tears, fear... in short, the affair had brought with it all of the paraphernalia of true love. Olivia, who was inexperienced, was fooled, and she formed a very negative idea of that passion. So, being a wise, intelligent girl, she vowed, as I already told you, never to fall for it again.

You might rightly be surprised that the heart of a sixteen-year-old hadn't preserved enough fresh illusions, vague desires, and languishing thoughts to find, for a moment now and then, the true feeling of love; but that's how it was. In other circumstances, and especially in another era, Olivia would no doubt have seen her error. But what idea of love could Madame Béru's daughter have? What could the word "lover" mean to her? From Madame Béru's point of view, love was a transaction whose mastery required beauty. From the point of view of the world around her, love was nothing but an exchange of pleasures, in which it was understood that wealth and flattery would substitute for passion in the man, and faithfulness in bed would substitute for true affection in the mistress. Don't forget also, the corrupt society Olivia lived in was the most naive expression of the mores that were the norm at the end of the eighteenth century. Sensuality and the denial of all rules and all moral standards reigned supreme over that decrepit society; and even if Olivia had stepped outside the special sphere of corruption that enclosed her, it still would've been difficult for her to find any shelter against the erosion of morals that, at such a young age, tore away from her the soul's flower, her belief in love!

Still, she found some compensation for the loss of all the amorous emotions that make youth a time of suffering almost as long as it lasts, and which is always missed when it's over. Her compensations were that she became accustomed to a glittering world and she acquired a taste for exquisite things, a quick and decisive judgment of men and events, a kind of passion for the great concerns of humankind—a passion based on the philosophy forever dominated by the teachings of the *Encyclopédie*—and, in the midst of the dissolute gallantry in which women choose a new lover like a new dress, an unusual preference for the life of the mind, the pleasures of conversation, the triumph of witty expression, and a reputation as a superior woman.

Not that Olivia, having reached the full flowering of her beauty, wasn't also the slave of her ardent and imperious nature; but it must be said she never made the same man the choice of her mind and the choice of her eyes. She almost always had both a lover she wanted for his name, his reputation, his success, and of whom she was proud… and a lover from whom she required none of those things, and whom she kept carefully hidden. She gave herself to both of them, but the difference was that she made the former pursue her for a long time, and she surrendered easily to the latter. And another difference between the two men was that she belonged to the first and the second belonged to her.

Olivia spent her youth in that double debauchery. The financier had multiplied the fortune he'd won from the association of the dozen; and princes, ambassadors, businessmen rapidly took their turns in Olivia's favor, and soon she'd made the kind of fortune that's the disgrace of the society in which it's possible to earn it. When the Revolution came, she was in England with a Member of the House of Lords, who was spending beyond the income of an immense fortune on her. She was ready to return to France to save her property from confiscation, when the wave of exile sent all of her Paris friends to London. In those circumstances Olivia proved herself to be generous and honorable and clear-thinking. She reduced her household expenses to make it easier to welcome all those ruined lords without them facing accusations of latching onto the bandwagon of a nobleman's mistress. And she used her savings secretly to help the poorest exiles. She was tactful enough in her generosity to require the recipients to sign IOUs, and—while knowing she was giving them money—she was careful to make sure they thought she was just extending loans.

Meanwhile she went through lovers just like before, the more so since Olivia, always picky in her choice of her public lovers, had long since gone downhill in her choice of her hidden lovers. And perhaps she'd have ended by getting completely trapped in her shameful habits—if a lethargic illness, brought on by the London climate, hadn't put her life in danger. All medical care having proved useless to defeat the melancholia that had almost extinguished her physical strength and was already beginning to cloud the powers of her mind, it was decided that Olivia must leave England or die there. All of her exiled friends advised her to go to Italy; the suggestion was made with a certain envy—forced to abandon their fortunes, their rank, and their country to the upstart peasants who'd driven them from France, they felt a kind of bitterness at the thought that those bloodthirsty men, as they called them, could also rob them of their pleasures.

And they were certainly right to fear that, because Olivia's virtue was even more fragile than the fallen monarchy. Olivia didn't listen to them; she wanted to see Paris again, a different Paris from the one she'd known, ruled by different men, driven by different ideas, hurrying to different celebrations—because at the time I'm speaking of, the Directoire was already in power at the Luxembourg.[63] Olivia had no trouble getting her name removed from the list of exiles, and the scraps of the fortune she brought back from England provided her with a comfortable living, leaving her free to do as she pleased with herself and negotiate her own terms.

Thought she was already past thirty, Olivia was such a pure, sublime beauty that she was soon surrounded by the attentions of the men most celebrated in Paris for their magnificence. As a woman of luxury and pleasure, she was noticed at the gauzy festivities at Longchamp and at the mysterious balls at the Opéra and at Frascati's.[64] She didn't, however, recover either her health or her carefree lightness of spirit. Her attacks of melancholy and despair grew more frequent by the day, and it was with the greatest difficulty that she was persuaded to attend a small party one evening in the winter of 1798, given by one of the richest purveyors to the army. Olivia didn't fit in: of all the women present, only she lacked wit, flirtation, or fun. Of all the men, only one also remained cold, indifferent, and seemingly weary of the gaiety that surrounded him.

That man, who might've been thirty-five, was named Monsieur de Mère. He was said to have been driven by his passions. When he was still very young he'd left his family and abandoned all the advantages of a great fortune to a younger brother, to follow a woman he loved to Holland. He loved her enough to respect her chastity for three years—after which she casually gave herself to another man. That first disappointment drove him into shameful debauchery; though of superior name, rank, character, and intelligence, he plunged into every kind of excess.

He returned to France and to better company, where he fell in love again, with a woman to whom he swore to devote his life. That second affair was more violent and less respectful than the first, but again he was betrayed. Monsieur de Mère was twenty-seven when that happened. Just like the first time, he was filled with such despair that he sought revenge—but this time he didn't choose himself as the victim. He wanted to make all women pay for the misdeeds of two of them, so he dedicated his life to the peculiar task of seducing those women who were said to be the most virtuous, and abandoning them the morning after they'd given themselves to him.

That miserable campaign of vengeance soon exhausted the man who'd dedicated all of his happiness to it, and after two years of that life he confronted himself: still young, but withered by the contempt he'd shown toward all wom-

---

[63] The Directoire was a five-member committee that ruled the French Republic from the dissolving of the National Convention in 1795 to Napoleon's coup in 1799. The Revolutionary legislature met in the Palais du Luxembourg.

[64] The Hippodrome de Longchamp was a fashionable horse-racing track. The Maison Frascati was a popular First Empire café and pastry shop, with gardens and ballrooms and gambling tables.

en. The Revolution pulled him out of that profound self-disgust and turned his mind toward public interests. In 1792 he joined the volunteers from his province, happy to feel his heart beating in time with the drum, and to be stirred by any emotion at all. In those days destiny greedily took hold of so many men on whom it could lavish its favors that Monsieur de Mère couldn't help being blessed. By 1798 he was already a brigadier general; and he hadn't reached an even higher rank only because a serious wound had required him to stay in Paris.

Just as Olivia was the least young of the women who'd been invited to that party, Monsieur de Mère was the oldest of the men present. They'd been seated far apart, because Olivia was the object of desire of the youngest and most ardent men, and Monsieur de Mère the victim of the silliest and most annoying flirts. Neither the former nor the latter had the least success. Olivia and the general observed with pity the feverish gaiety, the amorous delirium they'd both drunk to the last dregs. Olivia was too beautiful to accept the love of a young man whose passion would've placed her among the women of a certain age who educate young men, and Monsieur de Mère no longer cared enough for pleasure to risk disillusion again.

When evening came, chance—or rather the solitude they both sought in a side parlor—brought them together. Monsieur de Mère knew who Olivia was, but she didn't know about him. He opened a conversation with her, not with the respect due to an unsullied reputation, but with the restraint a refined man shows to any woman who moves in fashionable society. At first they exchanged a few words about how little they were enjoying the pleasures of the party, and both blamed the poor state of their health—because both of them assumed they were too much the exception in that world to speak of the poor state of their souls. Being not much interested in each other or in themselves, they gave up that conversation in favor of topics of general currency. The wars of the French Republic and the triumphs of Napoleon were then at their height, and Monsieur de Mère spoke of them with a warmth and enthusiasm that showed he still had more fire and youth in him than he imagined. In another direction, literature, theater, art, and music were all beginning to revive, and Olivia spoke about them with a tact, an insight, and an interest that also showed her heart was more susceptible to the tender emotions than she believed. In that way they spent the long hours of that evening, each listening to the other with pleasure but without judgment; then, aware from the silence that the party had ended, both realized they'd long overstayed the time by which, with their settled habits, they would normally have been home. They had to part.

Monsieur de Mère, who still had a few weeks to kill in Paris, didn't want to let slip away a chance to lessen the boredom of his stay in the company of a woman he'd found intelligent and likable, so he asked Olivia for the favor of receiving him at her house. He put it in the most flattering terms, and without expressing surprise or rebuffing him she replied, "I don't need to know your name, sir, to be delighted to receive a man as distinguished as you; but I do need to know it so as not to be surprised by your call—if by chance you don't forget you've asked to call on me!"

"Well, ma'am, if tomorrow evening Monsieur de Mère is announced, will you receive him?"

"Monsieur de Mère!" echoed Olivia. "There's a name that would've made its bearer welcome even without this evening to recommend it."

Clearly, both of them were unembarrassed to express the pleasure they'd felt at their meeting. And both believed themselves so safe from flirtation or seduction that they heard each other's declarations equally without embarrassment. Neither of them left that party infatuated. Olivia went through the next day without remembering that Monsieur de Mère was to call that evening; and he thought of his upcoming visit to her as no more than a better use of his time than a performance at the Opéra or an evening of cards at some politician's salon.

At nine in the evening Olivia was at home with Libert, the fat financier she'd chosen long ago at sixteen, and whom she'd retaken as her official lover because he was the most slavishly devoted of all those who'd held that title. His great fortune, made off the profligacy of the monarchy, had grown off the profligacy of the Republic; and Olivia used it to satisfy her whims—which were perhaps more exacting and more demanding than the whims provoked by vanity and the love of pleasure, because they were prompted by boredom.

Just then the financier, now a purveyor, was telling her about the odds of some upcoming deal; and Olivia, with nothing better to do, was having fun showing him how stupid his entire business was—though at heart she knew Libert's greedy instincts were impervious to any argument she could offer. They were on the verge of a quarrel when Monsieur de Mère was announced. Olivia was made very unhappy; though all Paris knew she was Libert's mistress, she was remarkably upset at being found with him by a man like Monsieur de Mère. Still, she received him with a poise due more to habit than to good feeling. The subject of conversation was the party at which they'd met. Olivia's tone was mocking and awkward; the general was scornful about the other guests the previous evening. The financier's presence made both of them self-conscious and embarrassed, because it expressed too clearly what Olivia was.

Libert left the room before Monsieur de Mère. As soon as he was gone Olivia said, "You made a mistake, general. No doubt you thought you'd be coming to a salon where you'd find a lot of people and witty conversation; and instead you've stumbled on one poor woman all by herself, who spends most of her evenings like this."

"I only came here to find you, ma'am."

"And it wasn't just me you found: is that what you're trying to say?"

"No, really. But I have to admit I didn't expect to interrupt such a private get-together."

"I'm not sure how to take that."

"As an expression of my astonishment at finding the beautiful Olivia alone."

"Alone!"

"Yes, truly. I'd thought I'd detected in her a superior mind that wouldn't be satisfied with interaction on a certain coarse level."

Olivia gave the general a look in which sadness and mockery were mixed. "If I were the bold flirt you think me, I might reply that I was alone only because I was waiting for you. But in fact that would be a lie, and it's been a long time since I've taken that kind of trouble."

"So you weren't expecting me, ma'am?"

"I swear, sir, I'd forgotten all about you."

"Thank you for your candor, though it's not especially complimentary."

"It might be more complimentary than you imagine, because I devote a lot of thought to avoiding people who are nuisances."

"Well!" said the general more cheerfully than he'd felt in a long while. "You're bantering with me! You're not acting natural, the way you were yesterday, and that makes me cross."

"Maybe I'm cross too."

"About what?"

"About your coming here."

"Really? And can you tell me why?"

"If I tell you, you won't be too conceited?"

"My God! For me as well, it's been a long time since I've taken that kind of trouble."

"In that case, I'll tell why I'm cross. I met you yesterday in unbearable company, as bored as I was among people who were having fun. You made the evening sweet and pleasant for me. I lost track of the time, which is unusual for me; you didn't seem to think you were wasting yours, which I assume is also unusual for you. I would've remembered that evening later, and you would too. No doubt it pales next to other evenings in your life, and it would've been unmemorable for me, if I'd had to retrieve it from among the boisterous times of my youth; but in the empty life I lead now, as do you, it would've stood out happily."

"And why should it lose that distinction?" interrupted the general.

"Oh, don't pass off tired old gallantries on me. I'm worth more—or less—than that. The memory lost its distinction because you came here, because you met Monsieur Libert, because I sensed you were judging me for my position, and because in fact you did judge me, as I say."

While Olivia was speaking, the general observed her; he noticed her sublime beauty, more affecting because she was made languid by physical pain and by sadness. After a moment of silence he replied, "In everything you've just said, the only part I don't understand is the empty life you speak of."

"And that baffles me. It's not that I couldn't have a glittering circle of admirers around me; the success some women have makes me think I couldn't fail if I cared to summon them. But, tell me, what interest would I have in that? That of being maintained pleasantly? I have to admit, I've been spoiled in that respect. Maybe the need for amorous flattery? I'll admit again, since men in the social world open to me have lost the attraction that a great name and fine manners used to give them, I'm not especially tempted to welcome them and start a new apprenticeship in love."

"Love! But that's the thing you haven't mentioned, and that strangely I don't find here."

"What!" she said in surprise. "I think I just explained to you that I've given it up."

"I beg your pardon," he said with a gentle smile. "For my part I think you've talked about everything except love."

"About what, then?"

"I hardly know how to put it."

"Oh, be honest," she replied with energy. "Say it; I can listen to anything— I'm a good little woman. Or if it would put you more at ease: speak, speak, I'm an old woman."

Monsieur de Mère shook his head, and, still smiling, he went on, "I'll speak because you want me to, that's all. It seems to me it's not love you've given up, according to what you yourself say, but what we common soldiers call amorous adventures."

"Ah, I understand," laughed Olivia. "But I have to tell you I'm even more careful to repel what you'd probably call love than to give up what you call amorous adventures."

"Has love made you suffer so much?"

"Yes," she said, with a look of shame and almost disgust. "It hurt me. It did me terrible, vile, shameful harm. I was only in love once, and I'd like to forget it."

"Well, me too! I've suffered terribly from love. My purest feelings were deceived, my total devotion was betrayed, my trust in and worship of the one I loved were mocked; and yet I wouldn't give up the memory of those long-ago torments for anything."

"Really?" asked Olivia, leaning on the arms of her chair and looking at the general in uncommon surprise.

"Don't you understand it as I do?" he went on, growing animated. "Don't you understand that when the heart is weary and impoverished, it's happy to remember the time when it was rich and overflowing with sweet ambition and honorable hopes? To love! To love, knowing that beside you there's a soul that sees and rejoices in everything good and beautiful you do, a fragile being that has faith in you, that entrusts its happiness to you to protect, that sleeps and wakes peacefully in the shelter of your protection; one that, if it finds itself constrained by more urgent duties, still thinks of you regretfully while it waits, that lives in you as you live in it, that understands you at a glance if you're silent, that knows what you're thinking better than you do, whose happiness is more precious to you than your own life, in short that keeps your heart in a constant state of joy and desire, magnifying existence and giving it an immense capacity for either happiness or suffering! Oh, you're deceiving me, ma'am: either you don't reject memories like that, or you've never loved!"

At those words, Olivia pressed her hand to her heart; something painful and unfamiliar seemed to have resonated there. She looked at Monsieur de Mère in silent contemplation, as if her eyes had been dazzled by a new day, in which she couldn't yet see clearly. Finally she said to him slowly in a low voice, "And you've loved like that!"

"And you must've been loved like that too, or at least you've felt for someone else an emotion like the one I've just described to you!"

Olivia lowered her eyes and blushed. She felt ashamed of herself, and regret for a life given over to pleasure. To escape from her thoughts she picked up the conversation that had been broken off by her silence, and said, "And you, at such a young age, you're left with your memories! And you think that passion you know so well will never overpower you again!"

"I hope not," said the general with a smile, "and yet I wouldn't count on it. It would have to be a woman like you, taking the trouble to make me fall in love with her."

"Oh!" she cried with true childish joy, "how I wish you were in love with me!"

"Would that amuse you so much?"

"Oh, don't say that," she pleaded. "I swear, I'd be very clumsy if I tried to toy with feelings like that. I've been silly and giddy; but I've never aimed to hurt a passion as sincere as that."

"So you must often have acted out of pity, if you never made unhappy those in whom you inspired that passion."

"If I did inspire it, I never realized it."

"Meaning you never shared it?"

"Never!"

The artless way that was said by that woman of thirty-two in turn astonished Monsieur de Mère. He examined her to see if she were playing a part; but there was so much sincerity in Olivia's manner and her surprise that he couldn't doubt the truth of what she was saying. For a long time he sat silent before her, admiring in that beautiful face—which seemed to have been tested by passion—the innocent surprise of a girl who's just discovered her heart and who's astonished by the new emotions she feels.

Still Olivia said nothing, and still Monsieur de Mère watched her. Finally she lifted her eyes to him and cried sorrowfully, "Truly, you've just done me harm!"

"How so?"

"I can't really say. But this life I lead, which I already found unbearable, will now become impossible. And that man's presence, which was unpleasant, will now fill me with shame. And all the pleasures I thought merely frivolous will now seem odious. What I thought was repletion was only an emptiness in my heart."

"Have you given up on filling it?"

"At my age," she said with a smile, "to fall in love, to love like a child, would be foolish. Worse than that, it would be ridiculous."

"You can never be ridiculous, ma'am, when you're as beautiful as you are and you have a genuine emotion in your heart."

"If someone told you to expose yourself to the turbulent emotions you were speaking of earlier, certainly you wouldn't consent."

"I'd bless the hour, ma'am, in which I could feel again what I once felt. I should tell you the whole truth: I feel as if my heart has been mute for so long that while it rested it recovered all of its youth, its strength, its impulsiveness."

As he spoke, the general looked at Olivia in a way meant to make her believe she was the one to whom his hopes for that passion were addressed.

She was disconcerted, and said to him with a laugh, "Come now, no childishness! You forget that in terms of love we're elderly, and the young fools we were with last night were more in control of themselves than we are. Here, let's talk about you and your hopes—hopes for glory, I hear."

"Why start with me?"

"Oh, because there's nothing more to say about me, because I've thrown a veil over my past and I don't want to look into the future. A life of boredom, robbed of all interest, that's what I have ahead of me. I'm resigned to it—or I'll resign myself to it. But you: you have a splendid career. You've already made great strides, and there are greater still to come. It's so wonderful to realize it's possible to make your name resound across France, the world, posterity! And you men have all that. When the passions of love have died, you still have ambition; you're very lucky!"

"But, believe me, ambition would be even more powerful for knowing another heart was interested in its success."

"Come, come!" she said with a smile. "You've become quite a young man again. You've taken on the mad ardor of your youth, you're sustaining your beautiful illusions."

"Why not do the same on your side?"

"The thing is, you can go on doing it at your age, but you can't start at mine."

She was clearly upset and unhappy as she spoke those last words. Before the general had time to reply she rang firmly, then said to him. "I'm dismissing you. To be clear, I'm dismissing you for this evening. I'm not telling you to come back, but I'm always at home. I need to be alone; I'm not well. That party last night wore me out. Goodnight, and see you soon."

She was lying; it wasn't the party the night before that had tired her, or rather disturbed her so deeply. Since she was lying, what was she feeling? The general withdrew, after kissing her hand—which she impulsively tried to pull away. Olivia remained alone with her new thoughts...

Luizzi had been listening to that account with great attention, and he noticed the interest with which the Devil was telling Olivia's story. "I understand why you want to depict that woman as less odious than she is in fact," said the baron. "But try as you will, you'll never make me see in her story anything but a lot of debauchery ending in some ridiculous passion on the part of a used-up woman."

"You wicked fool!" cried Satan so loudly it made Luizzi jump. "Will you never judge things by anything deeper than the stupid appearance your ideas give them? Can't you see that woman had come to the most terrible of misfortunes?"

"Excuse me?"

"Yes! The supreme misfortune of having no more illusions about the past, the awful misfortune of knowing, as much as the human heart can know it, that every mistake is irreparable. What's more, for her that terrible knowledge remained uncertain, whereas I know it in all of its stunning clarity. Don't you understand, you poor cold dried-up wretch, what it's like to have been able to inhabit the heavens, and to find yourself condemned to the mire of hell? And, speaking only of Olivia, do you understand the despair that gripped her when she discovered she could've loved and been loved—which is your heaven—and that she'd never been anything but the merchandise of lust—which is your lowest degradation?"

"I understand a little your predilection for that woman," said Luizzi scornfully. "She's a distant echo of the regrets that eat away at you."

"With this difference: I made my destiny, and hers was made for her."

"And I assume that's what Olivia was thinking about?"

"And maybe someday it'll be what you're thinking about."

"Tell me your protégée's thoughts; it might spare me having the same regrets."

"Then listen, and try to understand if you can..."

So Olivia had remained alone, surprised at feeling upset in a way she'd never experienced, with her hand over her heart as it pounded violently in her chest, feeling at the same time somehow happy and anxious, both afraid of her own emotions and abandoning herself to them willingly, finally engaged in the instinctive battle of a heart in the grip of first love, which defends itself with dread, understanding that it will become the slave of a passion stronger than its willpower.

That turmoil, which lasts so long in the heart of a girl, soon gave way to other emotions in a woman like Olivia. A virgin, in whom love kindles the first desire whose fire brings her whole being to a boil, couldn't be more astonished than Olivia was; but the former's unawareness of where that great passion will lead makes her less suspicious. For a girl, falling in love is an intoxication she can't imagine waking from; for Olivia, on the contrary, that intoxication seemed like it must end, like all the rest, in disgust. Unhappy is the man whose lips touch the cup knowing that once the wine is drunk there'll be nothing left in his mouth but a fetid, nauseating aftertaste! Unhappy is the woman whose lips can't receive a kiss without being sure it'll revolt her before it's over!

That's the position Olivia was in. For her, falling in love could no longer mean hoping for happiness; to crown that love by becoming Monsieur de Mère's mistress merely meant to her probably giving and definitely receiving disillusionment. She spent that whole night sometimes full of dread, sometimes full of the extraordinary delight of the sweet feeling in her heart at the memory of her conversation with Monsieur de Mère—like a traveler wracked by anxiety and fever who comes upon a clean white scented bed, where for the first time in a long time he can find relief from his perpetual weariness.

However, worldly thoughts soon began to mingle with those feelings in Olivia's heart, and they dictated a solution that seemed reasonable to her. What she feared above all was ridicule. To avoid it, she wanted to flee from a passion that would make her ridiculous in the eyes of everyone who knew her. But she didn't want to flee that passion like a woman who's afraid of it; and, wanting neither to avoid Monsieur de Mère nor to suffer any further the distress he'd caused her, she decided to resume for a while a life so filled with pleasure it would leave no room for obsessive thoughts about him.

So when he returned the next day, instead of finding Olivia alone, as he'd probably hoped, he entered a parlor where he found gathered the few men then remaining in Paris who were good company, along with the few splendidly flirtatious women who were the subject of every piece of gossip. One of the latter in particular had been a former object of the general's attentions. Seduced in a matter of days and abandoned in a matter of hours, she still carried a vivid grudge against him. With any man other than the general, she might've attempted the most refined vengeance women can inflict in those circumstances: that of inspiring love in the man who humiliated her, so as to humiliate him in turn with the most insulting rebuff. But that woman thought she knew the general too well to hope a trick like could work on him; and as his open enemy she aimed to get her revenge by a frontal attack.

It's always easy to bring the conversation in a salon around to the inexhaustible subject of love. Madame de Cauny, for that was her name, led the way; and after a few general observations she began a bitter diatribe against men in whom debauchery has used up every noble quality, all respect, all pity, and to whom it has given the worst of vices, cowardice. The general, who'd listened fairly scornfully to Madame de Cauny's rant, couldn't keep from starting at that last word. She noticed, and turning directly to him she went on in a tone full of sarcasm, "Yes, general, it's the lowest cowardice that attacks a woman, and I don't mean to say the vilest attack is to damage her reputation by words. For if the woman is pure, the testimony of her honor defends her, and there are still people in this world decent enough to listen and to understand. But if the woman deserves no respect, then the damage done to her isn't much, and she has a chance to find a new lover, not necessarily with a pure heart, but at least with enough courage to punish the villain who insulted her."

In short, the general found himself under such fierce and unexpected attack that he was unable to hide his discomfiture. As he listened to Madame de Cauny his brow grew pale and he clenched his teeth nearly to breaking point, because Olivia too was listening to her while watching the general. Madame de Cauny came to a stop, choking with rage. You shouldn't assume, however, that by "rage" I mean her accusations had been addressed to the general in the panting, shrieking manner of a woman who's carried away and whose eyes are starting out of their sockets. Everything had been said in an elegant, mocking tone, with eyes half veiled beneath long lashes. Only the slight trembling of her lips and an almost imperceptible change in her voice gave away the fact that the anger escaping from that tightly controlled opening would've exploded in fury if she hadn't been held back by the powerful brake known as the world's respect.

That's the way I think most of your modern novelists are wrong in how they depict emotions. In whatever social circle and whatever period they place their characters, they always push them to the most animated expression of their thoughts; they make the volcano erupt over anything and everything—forgetting that, under the pressure of your civilized manners, it burns deep down and rumbles more often than it throws out fire and lava.

Olivia was too much a woman of the world not to have sensed, under Madame de Cauny's nonchalant mockery, the fury raging within her; but, not caring to moderate it, and wanting instead to learn the full extent of that fury, she asked, "Then what cowardly attack is it that's even lower than those you've already described?"

"It's this," replied Madame de Cauny, sitting forward with her elbows on the arms of her chair so as to look Monsieur de Mère up and down where he stood leaning against the mantelpiece. "That cowardice is to take advantage of your good name, of a few personal qualities, and of a mind that has the gift of speaking the language of the heart, to approach a woman—a woman you don't know, you understand, a woman you've never met, and who therefore has never injured your interests or your vanity or your affections, a woman who's a bystander you could pass without even looking at, but at whom you point while saying to yourself, 'I'm going to hurt that woman'…

"As I was saying, you approach that woman. At first you flatter her by making her proud of the attentions of a distinguished man. You take her unawares and preoccupy her with a love affair she wasn't looking for. You wrench her out of her peaceful life and give her the anxieties of a passion she'd resolved to avoid. You offer her boundless devotion, and persuade her of the sincerity of that devotion. You give her the joy of being loved, and you ask her to surrender herself to the joy of loving. You stir her up, you intoxicate her, you confuse her, you take everything from that woman...

"And the next day you stop seeing her—without a pretext, without a quarrel, without an accusation, without reason, without necessity. At first you leave her with the love she has; then with the shame that follows, with the awful waiting and the bewilderment that nothing can clear up, because she doesn't know what she's done wrong; and finally with the certainty of humiliating rejection that you don't even take the trouble to make into a clean break. And then you pursue another woman to do the same cowardly thing again. That's what I call cowardice, base vile cowardice, general, and I'm sure you agree with me."

It was perhaps the first time the consequences of a romantic adventure had been described in such a serious way in that social world. In any other circumstances, jeers and jokes would've served to reply to Madame de Cauny's tragic grievance. Olivia might've led the way; the general might've found some excuse against that terrible accusation. But Madame de Cauny's tone squelched all of the mockery habitual in that salon. Olivia had gone on listening, her eyes fixed on Monsieur de Mère; and though she hadn't said a word, he'd understood she was horrified by the vision of a similar fate for herself.

But the general couldn't stand there without trying to make some answer, no matter how futile, so he replied, "What can you do, ma'am? The heart's easy to fool: you think you're in love, and you find out you're not; the desire kindled by any beautiful, intelligent woman can go too far and look like true love; and then when the desire's quenched you realize nothing else remains."

"Not even an honorable man remains?" asked Madame de Cauny. "Not even a man who, though deprived of his illusions, spares the woman the pain he's going to cause her? You say nothing remains, general—not even a man of good breeding who can wrap the lowest, most shameful insult in polite words? Ah, you're right, nothing remains, absolutely nothing, except a villain who strikes the weak and a boor who offends against all decency."

"To know men like that so well, ma'am," cried the general, carried away by his anger, "you must've met some. Do you dare name them?"

"Perhaps that would be a service to other women," said Madame de Cauny, glancing at Olivia. "But I can't push courtesy so far."

The conversation ended there, because Madame de Cauny stood up and withdrew. No sooner was she gone than frivolity regained its sway over the company, and a few people even began to mock her for her anger. Only Olivia—Olivia who just the night before would've been the most eager to make fun of such despair—remained serious, and more than serious, sad. While congratulating herself for the decision she'd made, she was appalled at the danger to which she might've been exposed, and she was sorry to see so completely robbed of enchantment the man she wanted to keep from persuading her, but whose words had so deeply moved her.

On his side, Monsieur de Mère could see he'd been significantly lowered in Olivia's opinion, and he felt a kind of aching impatience he didn't want to admit to himself. But it was strong enough that he thought he ought to try to justify himself with one of those crafty maneuvers that had once been his pride; while the company was breaking up into small groups and Olivia was alone, he approached her and said, "Madame de Cauny's tirade must've given you a pretty low opinion of me."

"No," she replied candidly. "It wasn't what she said. Lots of frivolous behavior could account for such cruel treatment. But what astonished me was your reply."

"What about it?"

"That you can be mistaken about what you call love. That desire can prompt all of the same emotions, all the distress, all the intoxication… and that once the desire is quenched nothing else remains. Is that true?"

He thought for a long time, then replied, "No, it's not true. It can't be true, though I feel like I've experienced that. It must be that the person is dishonest with himself, that he fails to examine his own feelings, or rather that he's careless in doing it."

At that word she looked at him in great surprise, and echoed, "Careless?"

"Yes, I don't know how else to put it. You don't pay attention to your feelings in spite of the intensity of your emotions, because they lack an intimate sense that belongs only to love, a sense that speaks up when it's truly love you feel, a sense that warns you and says, 'Look out!' No, Olivia, no, when you're in love or you're truly in danger of falling in love, there's no mistaking it."

"Are you sure about that?"

"Listen, and don't make fun of me. Earlier you saw my embarrassment, my anger—let's go further and say my humiliation. A few days ago, honestly, what happened to me tonight would've delighted me. I'd have been proud—I who've suffered so much—to have paid back to someone a fraction of the hurt that was inflicted on me. I might've recovered enough of the sarcastic wit I used to have to turn Madame de Cauny's abuse to my advantage and reflect the humiliation and ridicule of her attack back at her. Well! Tonight I was ashamed, defenseless, wounded, miserable."

"And what do you conclude from that?" asked Olivia, searching in Monsieur de Mère's words for an explanation of what she felt, because in any other circumstances she herself wouldn't have been saddened and wounded by what had just happened.

"This: it's because I needed the esteem of someone before whom I was being cut down, I needed that person's trust in my sincerity. It's because in my heart I feel despair at having lost her trust. It's because I just found out I love her—because if I didn't love her none of that would've happened."

"How strange!" she murmured, very moved.

"That's one of the symptoms you can't mistake, one of the unquestionable warnings that tells you, 'You're no longer in command of your heart—it no longer belongs to you—it belongs to you so little that if it frightens the one to whom you want to offer it, you'll be left in shame and despair.'"

"Is that how..." she said with an effort, but without being able to express either in her voice or in her glance the mockery she meant her words to carry. "Is that how you played the scene with Madame de Cauny?"

The general bit his lip. Then, rising and bowing, he replied, "Perhaps."

He left the salon. Olivia retired so she could be alone. As she entered her room she felt weak and terrified. She leaned against a dresser and pressed to her heart a fist clenched in anger. And, as if to shake off the weight that suffocated her chest, she cried out in a loud voice, "My God! My God! I think I'm in love with that man!"

"Olivia, in love!" snickered Luizzi, interrupting the Devil. "What kind of love?"

"The youngest, holiest, purest love," said Satan. "Because that immodest woman had forgotten that beneath her shame lay her heart's virginity, a virginity you can't give up without joy, without suffering. And she found it again at that moment, and it happened that the courtesan fell in love—not like someone falling in love for the tenth time, but like a girl at the dawning of her heart, like Henriette Buré: as happy as she was, as filled with dreams and deep contemplation as she was. And yet that love was even more pure in the fallen woman than it was in the confused girl."

"I find that strange."

"Listen," replied the Devil, whose voice had almost descended to a human emotion, "listen!"

Indeed Olivia loved that man, and Monsieur de Mère likewise loved that woman. But each of them, confused and surprised by that passion, carefully avoided the other. Monsieur de Mère returned to the army, and they went almost six months without seeing each other. It was at the Opéra that they met again. They recognized each other at a glance from opposite ends of the hall. The general, trusting in his long absence, went to present himself in Olivia's loge; he assumed he'd find her just as she'd been when he knew her before. Indeed, she was beautiful in all the perfection of her beauty, dressed as elegantly as her exquisite taste could make her; she was smiling, almost cheerful; and when the general entered her loge she held out her hand and pressed both of his with charming warmth—with irresistible grace, which coquetry can never imitate!

"Hello!" she said with a fine sweet smile. "I'm so happy to see you! I have so much to tell you! What wonderful things you did in Bonaparte's immortal campaigns! I told you, you have a great, distinguished career ahead of you! I'm so pleased I predicted you'd follow it to glory!" As she spoke to the general so joyfully, Olivia almost had tears in her voice.

Very moved, very surprised, he replied, "Thank you! You've just given me a greater reward than I got on the battlefield. Your approval is more than approval, it's the fulfillment of a hope I carried away from Paris with me, the hope that you wouldn't forget me."

"Forget you? You've been brought much too clearly and too vividly to the attention of those who know you."

"There are so many others who accomplished more than I did!"

"Oh, but we don't think about them."

The orchestra began, and the general had to leave. "When do you receive?" he asked.

"Always. I'm always alone."

"And always bored?"

"Less bored," she replied softly, "but perhaps sadder. Come, and we'll talk about all that."

The next day Monsieur de Mère found Olivia completely alone, but already both of them had their defenses up against the unexpected emotions of the previous night. At first the conversation was tranquil. She asked about the general; it pleased her to have him tell her all about his daily routine, the dangers he'd faced, the great battles he'd taken part in.

Finally he said, "Tell me about yourself. What have you been doing? What's become of you?"

"It's silly to question me, a poor woman, given how happy you are! What's become of me? On the outside I've remained what I was: avoiding society or only seeking it out where there are enough people not to be tiresome; weary of being excluded and pushed to the fringes of a social world I now feel scorn for and yet that I don't have the right to scorn; thinking a great deal about you—you who did me so much harm—and finding only in that some consolation for the harm you did me."

"Olivia, is that true?"

"Yes, it's true. I love you. Oh, I can say that without danger. But where will it lead me? To become your wife? I know that's impossible: please believe me, I have no such ambition. To become your mistress? Never, Victor, never!"

"You know my first name!" he said in surprise.

"Yes, I asked Madame de Cauny."

"You love me!" he went on. "You love me! And you believe I don't deserve you—though nothing matters to me anymore but what you think. You understood me yesterday, when I thanked you. You understood me just now, when I explained how hard I was working to give you by public reputation the little bit of glory I didn't dare dedicate to you. And you still think I wouldn't want all of your love?"

"No," she said, turning away her head. "No, because you've got all that's good and pure in that love. Don't ask anything of the woman herself, you understand? Don't make me blush; it wouldn't be modesty on my part, it would be shame. Let's stay as we are. Don't take away the happiness you've given me."

"Folly!" he said with a smile. "Aren't you more beautiful than any other woman in the world?"

"You think I'm beautiful?" she replied, smiling and caressing him with her eyes. "Good!" she laughed. "Because I too find you handsome, in truth very handsome! That fine brow tanned by the Italian sun, that scar that crowns it so nobly... Yes... Yes, I find you handsome, and I love you."

The general took her hands and moved closer.

Olivia asked, "Will you be in Paris long?"

"Two months."

"Two months! That's a lot, for someone who has such great things to do elsewhere."

"Won't you help me make the time pass quickly?"

"Not often. I'm not as free as I used to be. I have a lot of people around me now. I found some of my father's relatives, living in misery. There were two girls, and I've taken them in. I've taking charge of them and I'm raising them." Then with a sigh and a tear she added, "I'll make honest women of them. So, you understand—I'll see you occasionally, not often, and we'll talk the way we have today."

Olivia had left her hands in his, and as she spoke she squeezed his hands. The general, who'd been watching and listening eagerly, drew her gently into his arms. But she disengaged herself firmly and said, "No, no, Victor! What difference does one more woman make? Don't risk my affection against a moment of triumph. I could hate you, Victor. I could even do more, I could stop loving you..." And then, gazing at him lovingly, she leaned quickly closer and kissed his brow, saying with delightful joy, "And I do love you!"

Then she opened the door of her room and fled toward her young piano students. "Goodbye," she said to him. "It's time for our lesson. There's no one here but the mother of a family, who receives her old friends in the family circle."

Monsieur de Mère left. The best way for me to explain his feelings is to quote the letter he wrote when he got home:

Olivia,

I thank you for loving me, and I thank you for my loving you. You don't know how grateful I am to you. You've given me back my life, my soul, my future. I'm proud, I have hope in everything, trust in everything. I've become young again; I've become jealous again. Yes, jealous. Because as I was leaving you I saw, stopping at your door, the carriage of one of those dashing young men who were with you in your loge at the Opéra, which I entered as a stranger. Olivia, I beg you on bended knee, don't deceive me. I knew it was possible to start one's life and fortune and glory over again. I didn't know it was possible to restart one's heart, and you taught me that. My heart beats, my head burns, I laugh and I cry. I'm in love, I'm in love. Oh, don't deceive me, Olivia. Don't make one last mockery of this one last happiness. I thank you, I thank you on my knees. Love me! Love me!... I love you so much I'm afraid of you.

His letter received no answer. A few days later, he went in search of Olivia. She wasn't alone; one of the preeminent dandies of the day was with her. The general suffered all the impatience, all the perturbation of a jealous lover—and Olivia felt all the submission of true love. She sent away the dandy; she sent him away rather clumsily, clumsily enough that by the next day all Paris had heard that Monsieur de Mère was her official lover. He heard the rumor, and in anger and sorrow he went straight to Olivia.

She'd heard it too, and she responded to his anger with a smile. "I'm glad you're upset with me. You've just done me more good than I've ever felt in my life. But I have to admit, the slander didn't offend me. I have the right to call it slander, not blaming the world but blaming myself; I didn't want to be yours, and I'll never be yours."

And that word "never" was true. It must seem all the more surprising to you, since Olivia had to resist not only the inclination of her own heart, but also the attraction of that passionate man, whose voice rang and whose eyes shone with love, and whom she could neither listen to nor look at without getting as excited as a child and shaking with desire. The struggle wasn't over in a day; it was a long, painful struggle, from which twenty times she emerged triumphant, a struggle against all the fevers of passion; because Monsieur de Mère sought her out everywhere, all the time.

Forced to return to the army, he took advantage of two weeks of leave, a short rest period, to travel two hundred leagues back to Paris. He arrived suddenly at her house, while she was daydreaming about him, thinking he was far away, and as he came in he said, "I've come from Rome to spend an hour with you."

Olivia opened her arms and pressed him to her heart, which leapt with ineffable happiness. Then she gazed at him a long time without looking away, a gaze that devoured him, that sent out her soul to him and drank in his own... and that was all. If he tried to break the firm resolution she'd taken, she fled—because Olivia liked the new love she felt, she like the proud, commanding, exclusive feeling that filled her and inspired her, and she didn't want to risk losing it by a surrender she knew better than anyone would lead to so much disappointment. That lasted two whole years.

"Two years!" cried Luizzi. "Two years! But I assume at the end of that time..."

"At the end of that time," replied the Devil, "Monsieur de Mère was killed. Olivia mourned him chastely, as she'd loved him chastely. She preserved every little keepsake of his she could find. Then, after a year, having created out of love the need for a more respectably established life, she married the only man so ruled by her as to commit the greatest of follies: she married the financier Libert, who bought the Marignon estate and became Monsieur de Marignon."

"Ha!" cried Luizzi. "My instinct about vengeance didn't lead me wrong! Olivia, the courtesan, the prostitute, had to be that insulting Madame de Marignon who threw poor Laura out of her salon! And she ended up marrying that wretch Libert, an upstart sated with gold and robbery! What a worthy conjunction of libertinism and rapine, which together probably gave birth to insolent vanity and a hunger to be noticed. Ah, Madame de Marignon, you deserve a son-in-law like Count de Bridely, and you'll have him, I promise!... Well, Satan, you have nothing to say?"

"I'm waiting, so I can finish Madame de Marignon's story."

"It isn't finished?"

"Not yet. After her marriage, she took advantage of her husband's fortune and his old connections to create for herself the social world you saw. It cost her dearly; she became the slave of its slightest demands. Since she was vulnerable on so many sides, she had to accept the cruelest humiliations with servility. But she suffered them patiently, because she was a mother; she had a daughter, and, needing not to blush before her, she had to accept the veil of prudery she was forced to throw over her past."

"So it was in honor of her past that she threw out Madame de Farkley?"

"Yes, master. And what's most admirable about the whole thing is that vice and crime, pushed to their most shameful depravity, have taken weakness and unhappiness by the throat and forced them to serve their villainous purposes; I mean that Madame de Fantan and Madame du Bergh have forced Madame de Marignon to exclude Laura de Farkley from her salon. But if you'd seen, if you'd known how to look, you'd have realized that she softened the insult as much as she could; you'd have seen that only she, out of all that world, asked after the health of the poor man lying sick in bed."

"Ah!" said Luizzi, pacing energetically around his room. "You've made up my mind. I was afraid a firm character would present a fatal obstacle to my plan. But Olivia is exactly the woman I need: trembling at the fear of scandal, weak at the fear of memories."

"The woman who's like that, however, isn't the wickedest of those who've injured you. What about Madame du Bergh and Madame de Fantan?"

"Oh, enough, Mister Satan. You won't change my mind. I know you. By turning my anger against those two other women, you want to make me think your predilection for Madame de Marignon is disinterested. I'm not going to fall into that trap; and I swear, if I only strike against the least guilty of them, it's because I have no way to get at the others."

"Well then, would you like me to name the guiltiest of all the characters in this story, the one whose memory you can debase without remorse? He's the one who led Olivia by the hand to her first debauch."

"Who's that?"

"Don't you remember the cheerful Marquis de Billanville who thought up the shameful arrangement that would hand Olivia over to one of the dozen?"

"Sure. And?"

"When you learn his real name, you'll know the truth about the whole story, and you'll know whom to hold up to the contempt of all. And you know that man. His name was the Baron de Luizzi."

"My father!"

"Your father."

"Always! Always!" cried Luizzi furiously.

The Devil was no longer there.

As our readers will have noticed, Luizzi was already no longer the self-assured, trusting young man who'd set off gaily into the world, not examining it too closely, indulging every passing emotion, ready to do good and to believe in it, having the faults of his rank without its vices, a little smug, a little mocking, as forgetful of yesterday's favors as of yesterday's hatred, assuming everyone was in the right station in life and envying no one's.

But the Devil had come—the Devil who'd blown away appearances and torn off masks; and then Luizzi had been revolted by what he thought was the true condition of the world. Anger had given him bad counsel, and he'd listened. Having, like most men, done evil without thinking about it—innocent evil, so to speak—now he dreamt of calculated evil, evil long premeditated, guilty evil. That's because Luizzi, it has to be said again, was like almost all men who out of vanity are ruled by false notions, who do bad they think is justified or even good. Luizzi was a commonplace man, and he took the commonplace path because he had neither virtue nor reason strong enough to hold him back or enlighten him. He didn't understand how a strong man could choose good because he knows good leads to good, because he knows society accepts vice and crime, but doesn't welcome them the way humankind accepts flaws, and doesn't willingly open its doors to them. He was far beneath those men to whom Providence has given the unfailing guide known as faith, and who, seeing a lighthouse on the horizon, stride toward it without worrying about or even looking at the rabble that goes astray. He wasn't one of those fortunate souls who advance, and advance unceasingly, and who, if they're not alone in attaining virtue, are almost always alone when they attain happiness.

Here's where Luizzi stood a few days after that conversation with Satan: firmly committed to carrying out his plot against Madame de Marignon, and believing himself to be very much in the know because he'd listened to the Devil describe some wicked behavior. Then, because he was engaged in vengeance, he tried to think of a way to have revenge on Monsieur Ganguernet: he liked the idea of punishing him in his own style, by playing a prank on him. The plan grew rapidly in his mind, and soon—shaping it at will the way a writer composes a play—he found all the conditions needed for it to succeed. He decided to let Ganguernet and his son the count go after Madame de Marignon while he himself would go visit Monsieur Rigot, the man who had a niece and a grandniece to marry off. Luizzi had found that out by chance, and he welcomed the knowledge all the more because it had come to him by chance.

"I looked for an honest and virtuous world in fashionable society," he said to himself, "and I was mistaken. To look for a pure and honorable woman in that world would probably be another mistake. Let's follow the road that's open before us. The Isles of the Blessed[65] were discovered by people who didn't know where they were going. Here's what I've decided: I'll try for a marriage at Monsieur Rigot's. I think I'm aristocratic enough to marry a nobody, and rich enough not to have to worry about choosing the wrong woman. And if I end up addressing my suit to the one who doesn't get a dowry, I'll have even more right to demand her respect for the name I'm giving her, and her gratitude for my wealth after her poverty." That was Luizzi's train of thought as he set off in search of an honest woman, while relying only on egotistical calculation and the attractions of rank to find her, and already trusting neither the restraint of morality nor the holy love of the good that is a quality of certain souls.

Though he was leery of Satan, he still kept him as a last resort to defend himself from being duped. Having lost half of his good intentions, Luizzi's position relative to the Devil was like that of a gambler at the roulette table who's already left the larger and more liquid part of his fortune in the devouring hands of the casino. He picks up the crumbs of his capital and decides to try a risky business speculation that he already foresees will lead to failure and ruin. So he keeps one last hope alongside that bad risk: he reserves a small sum with which he'll return to the tables and perhaps repair both the losses he's already suffered and those he anticipates. Luizzi was that gambler; or rather, in his own mind, he was the navigator who embarks in a stout ship to go in search of new lands, who loads it with plenty of supplies and cautiously fortifies his vessel against every possible danger—and who, in spite of all that, takes along a rowboat and a dinghy to save him when the ship goes down, expecting those fragile craft to preserve him when his powerful ship has failed to do so.

Once he'd made up his mind, Luizzi put his plans into action with the speed of a man for whom money provides all resources, eases all transactions,

---

[65] In Greek mythology, the Isles of the Blessed were a terrestrial paradise inhabited by the heroes of myth. They were thought to lie somewhere in the Western Ocean, on the edge of the world.

and especially removes all hesitation. Two days after the Devil's revelations about Olivia de Marignon, the baron was riding in a post chaise on the high road to Caen. Before he left he'd told Ganguernet and his son the count everything he knew about her, and had given the son a letter of introduction to her. It showed a certain skill, and Madame de Marignon would definitely fall for it. It ran like this:

Ma'am,

Your name is the only one I found in my visiting book throughout my long illness. If I don't come to thank you in person, it's because I fear it would be un-grateful of me to reveal such uncommon goodness and charity to the world. However, since I don't know how to put in writing all the gratitude I feel, I've given the task of coming to you to express it to one of my friends. That friend is Count de Bridely. He bears one of the finest names in France. If you'll permit him to join your circle, he'll learn how to carry that name. The need for fresh air forces me to leave Paris, and I go regretting not being able to express to you myself the feelings, the respect, and the gratitude you've inspired in me.

—Armand de Luizzi

A DOWRY OF TWO MILLION FRANCS

Chapter XXX: The Last Relay Stop

It was seven in the evening when Luizzi reached Mourt, a small village a few leagues outside Caen and the last relay stop for the post coach from Paris to the capital of Lower Normandy. No sooner had he reached the door of the post inn than he called for one of the postilions and asked him if there was still time before nightfall for him to be taken to Taillis, Monsieur de Rigot's estate.

The man he asked was already old and thin, having left in the saddle everything nature had given him in the way of flesh on his thighs and calves—but he hadn't left at the bottom of his jug of cider what his Norman nature had given him in the way of cunning and guile. Instead of answering Luizzi directly, he called a stable boy and said, "Do you know how far it is from here to Taillis?"

"My word, no!" replied the boy, exchanging a slight smile with the postilion on his way back into the inn.

"What!" cried Luizzi. "You local people don't know how far it is from your village to a neighboring estate?"

"True enough! Nope, I don't know," said the postilion. "We Normans are decent people who stick to our own ways, and my way is the high road. As for what's going on to my right and my left, I give it no more thought than I do to a glass of cider."

"Maybe you'd give a little more thought to a hundred-sou coin, and it would help you recover your memory!"

The postilion eyed the coin with a leer. "Ha, ha! You could give me ten times as much, and I still couldn't tell you what I don't know!"

"In that case, have horses provided for me. I imagine the postilion whose job it is to escort me will know the way better than you do."

"You're out of luck. Right now there are no postilions here other than me, and no horses other than mine, and we just got back from Caen five minutes ago."

"Well then, get me those horses, and ask the way."

"So you think I'm going to kill my animals," said the Norman as he walked away, "for a lousy thirty-sou ride and fifteen sous for the guide? You'll have to wait like everybody else."

"Are there any other travelers like me, who aren't going on?" asked the baron.

"Why, sure. There are three or four waiting in the big parlor who are as much in a hurry as you are, and who are yakking away with each other."

"In that case have my carriage put away. I'll spend the night here at the inn, and I'll leave in the morning. It's already late, and I don't feel like floundering around on a lot of side roads and getting to the house of a man I don't know in the middle of the night."

At those words the postilion stopped. Then, still with an ambiguous smile and the Norman eye that sees all the better for not seeming to see, he said, "You don't know Monsieur Rigot?"

"Not from Adam. Do you know him, my good man?"

"Course I know him! I'm the one he always chooses to take him places."

"Damn! And yet you don't know where his estate is?"

The Norman's cunning manner gave way instantly to a look of total stupidity, and he replied, "It's simple. Monsieur Rigot comes here with his horses, and I take him to Caen or Estrées, but I've never been to his place."

"And yet, to know him as well as you do, you must've seen him somewhere besides on the high road, because it's not when you're on your horse and he's in his carriage that you could've gotten to know him!"

"And what about at the bar? Monsieur Rigot's a good man, who takes pity on people and animals. He never sees a tavern on the road without calling out from inside his carriage, 'Hey, Little Pierre! Let your horses catch their breath a while, my boy!' Then he gets out, and he never has a glass of brandy or a jug of cider without generously splitting it with me. He's a true Norman, with his heart in his hand. And while we're toasting we talk."

"And what do you talk about?" asked Luizzi, delighted to be gathering some information on Monsieur Rigot.

"Oh, my word, we talk about this and that, anything and everything. Then I get back on my horse and go straight on my way—because, you see, I don't stick my nose in these people's or those people's business."

"So you don't know Monsieur Rigot's nieces?"

"Why, sure I know them, the mother and the daughter and the grandmother too."

"And... are they pretty?" asked Luizzi, eyeing the postilion.

"Oh, the grandmother was a fine-looking woman in her day."

"But the daughter and the granddaughter?"

"As for that, it depends on your taste. But the grandmother, see, she was, if I can put it this way, the perfection of beauty."

"So you knew her when she was young?"

"Damn! They're from here. I grew up with old Rigot and his sister. That was forty-five years ago, when she was a lower servant in this inn, and he was a postilion like me. They left the area and settled in Paris, where the little Rigot girl got married. As for her brother, he enlisted in the cavalry, where, knowing horses, he rose quickly to the rank of farrier. Anyway, good people, decent people, real Normans, hearts in their hands like me, keeping to their own ways, like I've done all my life! That's the worst I can say about them."

Just then a servant girl approached Luizzi, who'd stayed in the courtyard with the postilion, to tell him they were about to serve supper to the travelers who were waiting for the horses to be hitched up, and to ask whether he'd like to join them or would rather be served separately. Luizzi, who had nothing better to do and no reason to do it alone, said he'd have supper with the other travelers. He was about to follow the servant girl when the postilion made him a little private sign.

"Though you were the last to get here," said the Norman, "you can be the first to leave if you like. In the middle of supper I'll pass through the dining room, you'll say you're going to bed, you'll find your carriage hitched, back there behind the big barn, and we'll take off quickly without anyone suspecting."

"But if you don't know the way..." said Luizzi.

"I just found out by asking around," replied the imperturbable postilion, who hadn't been out of Luizzi's sight for a moment.

"Good God, no," said the baron. "I'm not in such a hurry to get there."

"Well!" said the postilion, truly stunned. "You're not going there to get married?"

Luizzi fell silent for a moment, so surprised in turn was he by what he'd just heard. On the off chance, he replied, "No, no, I'm here on other business."

"Good for you!" said the postilion, stepping back to examine him and looking not at all convinced.

He went into the barn, and Luizzi could hear the sound of horses and of voices murmuring. He moved closer to the door to test a suspicion that had just occurred to him, and he overheard the postilion say quietly, "Another one going to Taillis, but he's not the smartest of the bunch."

The bell announcing that supper was ready kept Luizzi from hearing any more; but the little we've just reported had been enough to inform him that the travelers with whom he was about to eat probably had the same goal he did. As a result, he entered the dining room prepared to observe his companions and to fend off their curiosity.

At the beginning of every play there's a page unfamiliar to the novelist, and which would be very helpful if he made use of it in his own work. That page is the *Dramatis Personae*. I intend to seize hold of that speedy and rational way of putting my actors on stage—without asking for a patent for my invention, as I would if I'd discovered Lion Pomade or Arabian racahout.[66] On the contrary, I

---

[66] Lion Pomade: a patented nineteenth-century hairstyling product. Arabian racahout: a patented porridge mixture, made of acorn flour and potato flour, among many other ingredients with supposed nutritional benefits, and alleged to be based on an Arab dish.

offer my invention freely to whoever wants it—for fear that playwrights, whose entire living consists in stealing novelists' ideas, should file suit against me for lowering the value of their literary property.

Dramatis Personae

Monsieur Rigot, a wealthy landowner from the outskirts of Caen: aged fifty-five, blue suit, shiny buttons, light gray stovepipe trousers, satin waistcoat embroidered in gold, brush-cut gray hair, hands black with dirt and no gloves, nails untrimmed.

Madame Turniquel, his sister: aged sixty-five, fat, short, hoarse voice, hands on her hips.

Monsieur Bador, an attorney: aged thirty-six, dressed all in black from head to foot, notable for the shine on his boots and on his hair.

Monsieur Furnichon, a stockbroker's clerk: aged twenty-seven, a handsome fellow, chinstrap beard, hat by Bandoni, jacket by Chevreuil, trousers by Renard, waistcoat by Blanc, shirt by Lami-Housset, boots by Guerrier, gloves by Boivin, cravat by Pouillet, never takes off his hat.

Monsieur Marcoine, a lawyer's head clerk: nice feet, nice hands, nice face, nice figure, nice clothes, nice voice, nice handwriting, nice hair, nice, nice, nice.

Countess Lémée, the widow of a peer of France, and a neighbor of Monsieur Rigot, whose property adjoins hers: aged forty-five, thin, tall, plain, with grand airs and big teeth, an aquiline nose, has her dresses sent from Paris and her hats made in Caen, knit gloves, eyes a little rheumy, rosacea on the lower half of her face, foams a little at the corners of her mouth when she speaks.

Count Lémée, her son: aged twenty-two, less well dressed than the stockbroker's clerk and much more elegant, less handsome than the lawyer's clerk and much more pleasing, smokes Havana cigars, wears a big mustache and long spurs, eats with his gloves on.

Madame Eugénie Peyrol, Monsieur Rigot's niece: aged thirty-two, tall and blonde, white muslin dress, peacock-green shoes, solid lisle stockings, hair in a headband, unusually slender hands and feet, large languid slightly uncertain eyes, nearsighted.

Ernestine, her daughter: aged fifteen and a half, tall and already fully developed.

Akabila, a Malayan king: tattooed face, shaved head, boots with upturned toes, leather trousers, jockey's waistcoat.

The first scene takes place in the dining room of the inn at Mourt. Present at the start of the scene are the attorney, the lawyer's clerk, and the stockbroker's clerk.

When Luizzi entered the room in which they were sitting, they were all busy reading papers, which they immediately put away in their briefcases. All three gave Luizzi a look of surprise and displeasure, then looked at each other, as if to see whether anyone knew the newcomer.

"Gentlemen," said Luizzi with a bow, "I'm ashamed to be depriving you of part of what's yours, because I fear the supper that was planned for one seemed to the innkeeper to be sufficient for two, then for three, then for four."

"Whoever you are," replied the attorney, bowing graciously, "welcome! If I allow myself to receive you as if I were the master of the house," he went on, glancing alternately at his two companions, "it's because I have certain incontestable rights..." Monsieur Bador paused in his artful speech to see what effect it had produced; and after a moment's silence he went on, "My claims, however, amount to two: one, to have reached this inn first, the other, to be, so to speak, from the area."

"You live in Mourt, sir?" asked Luizzi.

"I have a few clients here. I'm from Caen, my whole family is from Caen, I have some influence there; my practice, while not the leading practice in town, isn't the worst."

"You're a lawyer, sir?" asked Monsieur Marcoine.

"An attorney," replied Monsieur Bador, "and formerly a barrister, when we attorneys were allowed to argue cases in court. Unlike my colleagues, I happily welcomed the decree forbidding us to speak. I don't much like speaking, I'm not talkative, it tires out my lungs. And in spite of my clients' chagrin and their pleas, I didn't sign the petition all of my colleagues drew up against the king's decree. I've added a few young barristers to my practice, and I'm giving them the opportunity to launch their fortunes, their speeches, and their reputations. Thanks to me, the Caen bar offers great expectations; those fine young men take advantage of it, I use good judgment, and all's going well."

"In that case," said Monsieur Marcoine, "your clerks must be very happy, sir. They must find the work handed to them on a plate—not like in Paris, where our employers let us do all the work while they reap all the benefits."

"Ah! You're in the clericature, sir?" asked Monsieur Bador, turning to look at the young man.

"And in the law," Monsieur Marcoine replied, giving Monsieur Bador a scornful look.

"Well, gentlemen," said the baron, "since each of you is willing to say what you do, I feel I ought to be equally forthcoming. My name is Armand de Luizzi, and I do nothing."

"There's an excellent profession!" said Monsieur Furnichon, rising to his full impressive height and turning to look at himself in a small mirror. "But we can only hope we'll get there, since I've had enough of the stock exchange and the three percents."

"Say!" said Monsieur Marcoine, the little lawyer's clerk, "in fact, I feel like I've met you in Paris."

"Ha, ha! I recognize you too," replied Monsieur Furnichon, his loud voice issuing from his thick pink lips. "We played écarté together at the Suckling Calf, at the wedding of one of my buddies, who married the daughter of a former shoemaker."

"The one who brought him a dowry of four hundred thousand francs," added Monsieur Marcoine, "with which he bought Monsieur P—'s practice six months later: a nice haul for him."

"There are better hauls out there," said Monsieur Furnichon, stroking his cravat.

"Not around here," said Monsieur Bador, the attorney.

"Who said anything about around here?" replied Monsieur Marcoine.

"Yes," said Monsieur Furnichon, "who said anything about around here?"

"They say, however, there are some big fortunes in Calvados," said Luizzi, as they all sat down to the supper that had just been served.

"Yes, yes," said Monsieur Bador, taking a bite of his stew so carelessly that he burned his mouth badly. "A few fortunes in real estate, money invested at two and a half percent; but besides that, no liquid capital, no dowries in cash—just income from property mortgages, that's all you'll find around here."

"Might there be some exceptions?" asked Monsieur Furnichon with labored slyness.

"Do you know of any?" asked Monsieur Marcoine casually, serving himself a cream puff with the tips of his fingers.

"Perhaps," replied Monsieur Furnichon grandly, taking hold of an enormous veal cutlet in parchment paper.

"And you've come to pay them a visit, sir?" asked Monsieur Bador, watching his face closely.

"No, I'm here to do some hunting in the area."

"In May?" asked Luizzi.

"No doubt, sir," said Monsieur Bador, eyeing Monsieur Furnichon, "every season is open season for the game you're after?"

"Indeed," added Monsieur Marcoine, with a wink at his companions, "you must be fond of big game, sir."

But Monsieur Furnichon didn't get it, and he went on, "And how about you, Monsieur Marcoine? What the devil are you doing here?"

"I'm not as lucky as you: I'm not here for pleasure. I came to see a property for one of our clients."

"If you tell me what it's called, I can give you all the information you want," said the attorney. "I know all the substantial estates in the area."

"Sure!" said Monsieur Marcoine. "So you can outbid us?"

"You must think I'm from Paris," replied Monsieur Bador mockingly.

"No," said Monsieur Marcoine, "but I don't think you're from this village."

That accusation of bad faith passed quite casually in the conversation; and the Norman attorney, believing he knew what had brought the two Parisian clerks to Mourt, turned his attention to Luizzi, who struck him as more dangerous than the others. Indeed, one of the clerks had come on the stagecoach and the other on the mail coach, getting out at the last relay stop, whereas the newcomer had arrived in a magnificent berline pulled by four horses.

"And you, sir," said the attorney, "would it be indiscreet to ask what brings you to our area?"

"Me?" said Luizzi. "I came for more or less the same reasons as the rest of you: to hunt on the same grounds as this gentleman, and to visit the same property as that gentleman."

The lawyer's clerk and the stockbroker's clerk exchanged a look, and the attorney seemed quite surprised by the answer.

"Bah!" said Monsieur Furnichon. "You've come to hunt on the grounds of...?"

"Bah!" said Monsieur Marcoine at the same time. "You've come to see the estate of...?"

"Yes," replied Luizzi, seeming to choose his words carefully, "I've come to hunt on the grounds of... and to see the estate of... That's funny! I'm just like you, I forgot their names. Help me remember them."

"Well! You're going hunting on the grounds of... of... of... Monsieur Rupin," said Monsieur Furnichon out of the side of his mouth.

"Well! You're going to see the estate of... of... Valainville," said Monsieur Marcoine.

Both spoke at random, so as not to seem taken at a disadvantage.

"I don't know a Monsieur Rupin, nor any estate called Valainville in this area," said the attorney.

"It's a name something like that," said the two clerks together.

"Yes," said Luizzi, still pretending to search his memory, "Rupin, Ripon, Ripeau, Rigot—that's it, that must be it." The others all looked at him as he went on, "And that Valainville estate must be something like Valainvilli, Vailli, Taillis—that's it, Taillis!"

"Ah!" said the attorney, while the two clerks sat stunned at Luizzi's joke. "You're going to Taillis, to see Monsieur Rigot?"

"That's right, sir," replied the baron, "and if these gentlemen don't have a way to get there, I can offer them seats in my carriage. We leave first thing tomorrow morning."

"Oh, you're going in the morning?" said the attorney. "Around ten, right? You don't want to get to Taillis too early: they aren't early risers at the chateau."

"We'll go whenever these gentlemen wish," said Luizzi. "We've had a fine supper, and we'll add a few bottles of champagne if we can, and we'll pass the time cheerfully till we go."

"Please yourselves, gentlemen," said Monsieur Bador. "That's a Parisian schedule you must be used to, but it doesn't suit our provincial habits. I'll therefore beg your permission to go to bed, and wish you a good night."

Upon which the attorney rose and withdrew.

"Well, gentlemen, it's up to us!" said the baron, uncorking a bottle of wine and pouring for both the stockbroker's clerk, who resolutely held out his glass, and the lawyer's clerk, who seemed to be listening to what was going on in the courtyard.

A moment later, indeed, they heard the sound of a cabriolet leaving the inn. Monsieur Marcoine got up from the table, opened the window facing the high road, and watched the carriage rolling off into the distance.

"What's wrong?" asked Monsieur Furnichon. "What's come over you?"

"Oh, it's nothing," said Monsieur Marcoine. "I'm just a little lightheaded… The journey made the blood ring in my ears."

"That's funny," said Monsieur Furnichon. "Me too: my legs are swollen."

"I really don't feel well," said Monsieur Marcoine, pulling out his watch and thinking to himself, it's only ten. "I'll have to ask your permission to withdraw, like Monsieur Bador."

"Please, as you wish, just like Monsieur Bador," said Luizzi. "I hope this other gentleman won't abandon me the same way."

Monsieur Marcoine withdrew, and Monsieur Furnichon, now left alone with Luizzi, went on, "What a funny notion they both had to go to bed! I'd rather pass the night drinking than stretched out on a bad inn-room bed between clammy sheets."

"And I say I don't believe it's the clamminess of the sheets that's going to give those gentlemen head colds."

"Why's that?"

"You'll see in a moment."

Indeed, just then they saw Monsieur Marcoine going by, led by a postilion and perched on a tall horse, whose saddle he was holding onto with both hands.

"Hey there, jokester!" called out Monsieur Furnichon. "Where are you off to like that?"

But Monsieur Marcoine made no reply. Monsieur Furnichon turned to Luizzi and repeated the question. "Where's that jokester headed?"

"Probably to have a look at the grounds you came to hunt on."

The clerk cursed viciously and went on, "Where'd he find a horse?"

"I expect if you asked for it in the most peremptory way, they'd find you one."

Now in turn Monsieur Furnichon left the dining room, and Luizzi could hear him raging and shouting in the courtyard. A moment later an old rattletrap pulled by two nags left the inn, carrying the stockbroker's clerk and his great quantity of luggage.

Luizzi was on the verge of laughing aloud, when he was interrupted by someone tapping him gently on the shoulder. Turning, he recognized the old postilion.

"Well!" said the man in a confidential way. "All three of them are gone: the attorney in his cabriolet, the little lawyer in the saddle, and the big ladies' man in a cart. Aren't you going to hit the road too?"

"Are your horses rested?"

"They just need to be hitched up. I gave them a triple ration of oats."

"In Normandy a triple ration is good for making beasts and men go."

"In Normandy, like everywhere else."

"Yes, but even so we shouldn't start too late."

"All right. I know a way that'll cut the distance in half. You'll get there before they do, on my word of honor."

Luizzi thought it over for a while, not at all eager to take part in that race for a dowry. But the idea of witnessing his competitors' successive arrivals won him over, and he replied, "Listen: two louis for you if I get to Taillis first; fifteen sous as your guide fee if I'm only second."

"In that case, nothing doing. That attorney's a clever one, and he took the shortcut; he'll be at the manor before we are."

"Three louis if we're first."

"There's no way," said the postilion, shaking his head. "It's too late, as you yourself said before. And I'm losing your three-louis tip on account of the miserly six-livre coin that miserly attorney gave me earlier! He owes me!"

"What!" cried Luizzi. "Was that the six-livre coin he paid you to keep me from going?"

"And you're stupid too! Why don't you say something?" The postilion turned to leave.

"One moment, rascal. Don't forget, I want to be at Taillis tomorrow morning before anyone's up."

"All right. I'll be ready."

Indeed, day hadn't yet begun to dawn when the baron, who'd flung himself onto his bed fully dressed, heard the horses being hitched to his carriage. He got up, paid his bill, and set off immediately.

His introduction to the three men who'd dined with him reminded Luizzi of something the Devil had said: "You've seen greed in its vulgar form; do you want to see it in society?" He reflected that the coincidence that had brought him face to face with those three wife-chasers might only be the working out of one of Satan's schemes, and he resolved to take advantage of the lesson without having to call on the Devil's secrets.

As he was forming those fine plans he reached the gate of the Taillis estate, which was closed; behind the wall, for quite a long time already, he'd been hearing the formidable growling of two or three dogs. He thought it was his arrival that had aroused the beasts' attention, till he noticed, along the outside of the perimeter wall, two shadows coming and going on either side of the gate. Luizzi wasn't easily frightened, but the presence of two men at the gate when it was barely daylight, and especially the fury of the dogs, made him begin to worry he was up against people of some malevolence.

He quickly rang at the gate. The bell had barely sounded when he saw the two shadows come running. Luizzi had just enough time to set his back against the grille and draw the little dagger sheathed in his walking stick before he found himself face to face with Monsieur Furnichon and Monsieur Marcoine. They were both frozen, numb, shivering; their faces were purple, and their hair hung lank with the damp. Luizzi looked from one of them to the other in astonishment.

"Ring!" cried Monsieur Marcoine. "Ring all you want! Hell if anyone comes!"

"A thousand damned devils! We've been here eight hours!" said Monsieur Furnichon, in such a state of rage it ought to have heated him a little. "We've been ringing like a carillon from hell, and if it weren't for those damned dogs I swear I'd have climbed over the wall."

"So the gate was closed when you got here, gentlemen?" asked Luizzi, feeling more and more like laughing. "Why didn't you go back to the inn?"

"How?" asked Monsieur Marcoine. "I got here, the postilion took down my two trunks and said, 'Just ring loudly and they'll come open up.' With that I paid him, but as I was trying to count out his money—which took a while since my fingertips were numb—this gentleman showed up in his cart. He'd been cleverer than me: he'd paid in advance. As soon as he saw me he jumped out and cried, 'Unload my luggage! Ha, ha, Monsieur Marcoine, I've been as sly as you have! You won't be the first to see Monsieur Rigot!' etcetera, and a lot of other nonsense."

"I beg your pardon?" said Monsieur Furnichon.

"Well, yes, nonsense, sir. You think I'm here to… But let's drop it. Anyway, sir, while we were arguing, the cart turned around and left this gentleman, like me, standing at the gate. I began ringing… once… twice… nothing. I rang again… we rang again… nothing. Finally after an hour we realized we'd been tricked: we'd been taken to an uninhabited estate."

"Or inhabited only by dogs," laughed Luizzi.

"So the two of us were forced to stay here, forced to stand guard over our bags, unable to take them away."

"Bloody hell!" cried Monsieur Furnichon. "I'll be hanged if I don't break my walking stick over the back of the rascal who drove me out here."

"Oh, there's no doubt," said Monsieur Marcoine, the lawyer's clerk, "I'm going to file suit against whoever played that trick on me."

"Why's that?" asked Little Pierre, Luizzi's postilion, drawing closer. "You asked them to take you to Taillis, Monsieur Rigot's estate. Here you are."

"Impossible! They would've let us in. We rang the bell till it almost broke."

"Which one?" asked the postilion.

"Well, damn, that one!" said Monsieur Furnichon, yanking angrily on the chain and making the bell peal out loudly, while the dogs howled louder still.

"The thing is," said the postilion, "that's not the one. You can't hear it from the chateau, which is more than a quarter of a league away across the grounds. Here's a different one, which would've done the job." He pulled a little knob hidden high up in a recess of the wall.

"My God, you're useless!" cried Monsieur Furnichon, addressing Monsieur Marcoine. "You spent an hour searching for another bell!"

"How could I have found it? I can't reach that high!" said the little man angrily. "You're even more useless: you're as tall as Goliath and you stood there cursing like a porter instead of helping me look! You'd have found it just by stretching out your arm."

"Well, why'd you have to be as short as you are?" replied Monsieur Furnichon furiously.

"Well, why'd you have to be as dumb as you are?" replied Monsieur Marcoine even more furiously.

"Gentlemen, gentlemen!" said Luizzi, laughing heartily as he tried to calm them.

"You go take a walk," said Monsieur Furnichon, "you and all your laughing, with your 'I have a berline'! Here's my suit ruined, my hat lost, my boots impossible to save!" He got carried away, slamming his fist into his hat and crying, "And you stupid little lawyer's clerk!"

"I think you're hilarious," said Monsieur Marcoine. "I'm frozen to the bone—I might even catch a pulmonary congestion because of you."

"Because of me?" asked Monsieur Furnichon.

"Leave me alone," replied Monsieur Marcoine, beside himself. "Worry about your hat."

"Hop in, baron," called the postilion. "Here they are now to open the gate."

"Gentlemen," said Luizzi, laughing as he climbed back into his berline, "I'll send someone out for you, and I'll tell them to light a fire for you."

As soon as Luizzi was aboard, the postilion rode triumphantly into the grounds, passing right by the stockbroker's clerk and the lawyer's clerk, who remained at the gate with their trunks and their bags. A half hour later, from the window of the room to which he'd been led by an old servant woman, Luizzi watched as the two suitors arrived, encumbered with luggage, dragging their belongings after them as best they could, helped clumsily by some kind of jockey wearing odd clothes, half red, half blue, who strongly provoked Luizzi's curiosity.

Chapter XXI: The Four Suitors

Luizzi had already been at Taillis for two hours without any word coming that he was to be presented to the master of the house, for whom Ganguernet had given him a letter of introduction. Then he heard a soft knock at his door, almost immediately followed by the entrance of a fat woman of at least sixty, as wrinkled as the surface of a pond full of paddling ducks, wearing a silk dress of a dreadful flame red, and topped by a bonnet bristling with yellow satin knots. She made Luizzi a deep curtsey, into which she put a lot of effort, while a graceful smile raised the corners of her toothless mouth. The baron bowed in return.

"Sir," said that worthy person, "I've come to see if you need anything. My brother is Monsieur Rigot; I'm Mademoiselle Rigot, married name Turniquel. I had the misfortune to lose my husband in 1808, of a burst blood vessel he got in a fall he took from the fifth floor, off scaffolding up which he was carrying mortar."

"Ah! Your husband was a…"

"An architect, sir. But he was setting an example for his workmen, because he was an architect for the government, and the Emperor liked for his leaders always to be the first on the job. A fine man, sir! My daughter, who was his, is as like him as two peas in a pod; she also has all of my looks. You'll see her, sir. Ah, if she hadn't had such misfortunes… Anyway, it's neither her fault nor mine, since I raised her like a duchess, always swaddled in cotton wool. I came to see if you needed anything, because my brother is an excellent man, but he doesn't understand the considerations due to a visitor like yourself."

"I've been made perfectly welcome, ma'am. I lack for nothing."

"The thing with servants is," went on Madame Turniquel, pulling out a rag and dusting the furniture, "they're lazy. As long as they can eat and drink and sleep, they don't care at all whether the work gets *done*. For example, here's a room: it's only been swept in the middle—the sides can just come closer if they want some. It's no surprise: when you're raised up among savages like my brother, you can't have any concept of proper society, like someone who's always lived in it."

"I can imagine," said Luizzi, opening the window to escape from the clouds of dust Madame Turniquel's attentions were raising all around him.

"Look out!" cried the worthy woman. "Don't open the window. It's not healthy in the cool weather this time of year. I can tell you that, because I've got a background, having studied medicine to be a midwife."

"I have an excellent way of counteracting its noxious influence: I'm in the habit of smoking a cigar every morning."

"And you're quite right, sir. It's excellent for the stomach. I learned that when I was at sea, where I smoked a great deal because of the scurvy that had stricken the entire crew."

"Ah! Have you traveled a great deal, ma'am?"

"I've been to England twice to visit Genie and bring her her child. Genie's my daughter, sir... Say, there she is, going by in the yard, down there!"

Just then, indeed, Luizzi saw a tall, good-looking woman pass quickly beneath his windows.

At the top of her lungs Madame Turniquel called out, "Morning, Genie, morning!"

The person being addressed lifted her head, and seemed quite surprised to find Luizzi's face next to her mother's. She waved in some confusion, then made a sign to the sort of jockey Luizzi had already noticed earlier. Acting timid and submissive, the creature approached, listened with great attention to what his mistress told him, then immediately dashed off into the chateau.

Luizzi had barely lost sight of him before he heard his door open and saw the jockey coming over to Madame Turniquel at the window, crying, "Ha, ha! Mama she below, ha, ha!"

"What does this tapestry figure want with me?" asked Madame Turniquel, turning around.

"Ha, ha!" cried the jockey. "Ha, ha! Mama she below... Genie, Genie!"

"Oh! My daughter wants me, is that right?"

The jockey nodded, then pointed to the door.

"All right, all right. Good news, sir: we'll breakfast in half an hour. You'll hear the bell."

"I thank you for your kind visit."

Luizzi showed the worthy woman out, while she tripped over herself in magnificent curtseys. No sooner had he closed the door than he gave way to laughter—and then he heard a harsh little laugh echoing his own. Turning, he saw the jockey, who began to mimic Madame Turniquel's heavy, awkward movements while laughing loudly. The jockey was quite a singular being: a face covered in tattoos, smooth black hair, sparkling mischievous eyes, long, sharp, shiny teeth. He seemed to be about twenty-five. His appearance cut short Luizzi's laughter, and the baron began to study him with a certain curiosity. As soon as the jockey realized he was being watched, he fell silent, lowered his head, and stood against the wall, glancing suspiciously in the baron's direction. As Luizzi went on observing him with the same care, the jockey began to look around more and more anxiously. Then, noticing a pair of boots in a corner of the room, he seized them with a cry of joy and quickly carried them off before Luizzi had had time to ask this odd creature a single question.

When he was gone, the baron began to wonder whether he was in a lunatic asylum, and he was thinking over the two peculiar visits he'd just had, when he heard a carriage stopping in the courtyard of the chateau. He went to the window to find out what new comical figure had just arrived to join those he'd already seen. But it was Luizzi's destiny almost always to be mistaken. A woman dressed with a certain elegance and a handsome young man got out of the carriage.

No sooner had the newcomers set foot in the courtyard than Madame Turniquel ran out to meet them, crying, "How you doing, countess?"

"Fairly badly," said the elegant lady as she embraced the old woman. "This west wind has given me a terrible attack of nerves."

"Oh, don't I know!" replied Madame Turniquel. "It always hits me at this season; it gives me awful leg cramps." Then, turning to the young man, she said, "And you, the son, how's it going this morning?"

"Very well, very well," replied the young man, shaking Monsieur Rigot's sister by the hand. "Except the roads getting here are so bad I'm quite broken."

"Oh, I know all about that," said the old woman. "When I used to take the animals out to the fields, there were potholes you could sink into up to your knee."

"Oh, Madame Turniquel," said the dandy, "you must've made a charming shepherdess. You were Estelle, and there must've been more than one Némorin."[67]

The elegant lady motioned to the young man with displeasure, while Madame Turniquel was saying, "Who are Estelle and Némorin?"

"Oh, God," said the lady. "It's a novel by Monsieur de Florian."

"Monsieur de Florian!" said Madame Turniquel. "I knew him well. He had great respect and esteem for me, and he used to read me all of his books."

No doubt the conversation would've gone on like that for a long time, if Madame Peyrol hadn't come out again to interrupt her mother's stories. They all went into the house, and a moment later Luizzi heard the bell announcing breakfast. He went downstairs, and—thanks to the sound of Madame Turniquel's voice—found his way to a fairly handsome parlor, where a dozen people were already gathered. Luizzi recognized the attorney, the lawyer's clerk, and the stockbroker's clerk; he also saw the lady and the young man who'd gotten out of the carriage, as well as a girl of uncommon beauty, whose resemblance to Madame Peyrol led him to conclude she must be Monsieur Rigot's grandniece. Monsieur Rigot himself was in a corner of the room, talking to the attorney and glancing questioningly at all the guests present.

When the baron was announced, Monsieur Rigot turned around and came to meet him. "A thousand pardons," he said straightforwardly. "I'm an ill-bred old soldier. Those of us born in the gutter, as they say, don't know good manners. I realize that as master of the house I should've paid you a visit, but we

---

[67] *Estelle et Némorin* (1788): a novel by Jean-Pierre de Florian, described as a "pastoral melodrama."

317

common people don't know etiquette. Isn't that right, Countess Lémée?" he said, turning to the lady who'd arrived by carriage.

Turning back to Luizzi, he went on, "I got my friend Ganguernet's letter telling me you were coming—that's to say I had it read to me, because we peasants are ignorant, you know, we don't know anything. But I declare I'm delighted to welcome Baron Armand de Luizzi—a man with two hundred thousand livres in income, according to Monsieur Ganguernet. It's my honor to greet you."

Monsieur Rigot moved away—leaving Luizzi with all eyes studying him curiously, especially the eyes of young Count Lémée—and approached the two Parisian clerks who'd had supper with the baron. "Which of you gentlemen is the lawyer?"

"That's me," said Monsieur Marcoine pleasantly, pulling papers from his pocket. "The purchase of your mansion in the Faubourg Saint Germain is completed, and here's the contract. This business was especially entrusted to me, and I think it was done with some skill. I got the mansion for a hundred thousand francs below the estimate."

"I thank you," said Monsieur Rigot, "because, you know, we humble people are easy to dupe."

"I wanted to bring you the contract myself," went on Monsieur Marcoine in an affected tone, "so as to make you better appreciate its advantages."

"You're very kind," said Monsieur Rigot. "Because, you know, we simple Normans don't understand anything about business." Then, turning to the stockbroker's clerk, he said, "And you, sir? To what do I owe the honor of your visit?"

"Sir," replied Monsieur Furnichon, "I came about the matter of investing the funds you left with your banker."

"Didn't I tell your boss to put it in the three percents?"

"That seemed to him a very disadvantageous investment."

"I want the three percents," said Monsieur Rigot. "I want the nobles and exiles fund. I already have a marquis's estate, I have a duke's mansion, and I want the exiles' indemnity fund."[68]

"But we have something better than that to offer you."

"I want what I want," said Monsieur Rigot angrily. "Maybe we little people are idiots, but that's how it is."

---

[68] After the Bourbon Restoration, compensation for the property losses of the nobles who'd fled the Revolution into exile became a politically fraught issue. In the end they got an annual payment worth three percent of the assets they'd lost, for thirty-three years. Monsieur Rigot—though neither a noble nor an exile—wants his own wealth invested in that fund, which was government-backed and therefore risk-free.

Just then a servant came to announce breakfast was served. Monsieur Marcoine, passing close to the baron, said slyly, "I don't think Monsieur Furnichon has much chance of success."

Madame Peyrol and her daughter Ernestine did the honors at breakfast with a grace and an elegance that contrasted sharply with Monsieur Rigot's and his sister's manners. Luizzi and Count Lémée sat on either side of Madame Peyrol, and the two Parisian clerks on either side of Ernestine. The attorney sat at one end the table, between Monsieur Rigot and Countess Lémée, and Madame Turniquel sat at the other end, between two people we haven't mentioned yet, one of whom was the parish priest and the other the local tax agent. Since the former was celibate, and the latter already married, they were to play mute roles in this scene, given how little stake they had in its results.

When they were seated, Madame Turniquel, having counted, declared, "We're exactly twelve! That's lucky! If we'd been thirteen, I wouldn't have eaten."

"How can a woman as distinguished as you have such superstitions?" asked the attorney.

"What are you calling superstitions?" asked Count Lémée. "I agree completely with Madame Turniquel. I've seen cases of terrible misfortune that came about because people defied that popular belief."

"Come on!" said Monsieur Furnichon. "Notions like that are good enough for the Ignorantines!"[69]

"Don't be so scornful," said Countess Lémée. "People of the highest rank have shared those beliefs you call superstitions, and Queen Marie Antoinette, whom it was my honor to serve before the Revolution, was terrified of the number thirteen."

"I know it well," said Madame Turniquel. "The queen told me so herself one day, on the occasion of the birth of the Duchess of Angoulême, when I went to see her as part of a deputation of market women."

"Mother," said Madame Peyrol quickly to drown out the last part of her mother's words, "would you like a little of this chicken?"

"Thanks, I'm finishing my smoked herring, then I'll have a little cream, and that'll be all."

"As for myself," said Monsieur Rigot, "I'm a fatalist. The great Napoleon was a fatalist. All great men are fatalists."

"Don't I know it," said Madame Turniquel. "I who's speaking to you right now, I heard the Emperor say so a hundred times."

"Oh?" said Luizzi. "You knew the Emperor, ma'am?"

---

[69] The Ignorantine Brothers: the Brethren of the Christian Schools, a religious fraternity dedicated to the free education of the children of the poor. Their rules forbade the admission of any priest with a theological education—hence their nickname.

"Like I know you…"

While Ernestine interrupted her grandmother to offer her the cream, Madame Peyrol said quietly to Luizzi, in a pleading tone full of charm and dignity, "Spare my mother, sir, I beg you."

Then to change the subject Madame Peyrol addressed young Monsieur Marcoine, who'd prudently kept silent. "Well, sir, what interesting news do you bring from Paris?"

"I'm not well informed, ma'am," he replied modestly. "I'm very taken up right now with the business of the firm, and I'm training the assistant clerk who'll replace me."

"Oh," said Monsieur Rigot, "are you leaving the law, young man?"

"No, sir, no," said Monsieur Marcoine with a casual air. "I'm buying a practice—the best practice in Paris, without a doubt."

"Then you must be getting married!" said Monsieur Furnichon.

"Of course," said Monsieur Marcoine. "I have some excellent offers. The law, you see, is a profession that appeals to parents. It's a safe and respectable investment, a secure and honorable position in the world, with connections to the best of everything in the capital, and after a certain time it means a considerable fortune, and a reputable name that opens the door to every ambition, if you have any."

"Less so than the profession of stockbroker," said Monsieur Furnichon. "In terms of fortunes, if you need one, that's the place to look. In terms of society, the world of banking is a little more elegant than the law, and as for ambition, I think you get there quicker through the stock exchange than through a law practice."

"In Paris, three lawyers are Parliamentary Deputies, and four are arrondissement mayors or members of the departmental council," replied Monsieur Marcoine with some emphasis.

"Maybe so," replied Monsieur Furnichon, "but two stockbrokers are colonels in the national guard. Count P—, who was a banker, and who's now a peer of France, began as a stockbroker. A career in the stock exchange can't really be compared to the law."

"And I assume you mean to stick to it to the end?" asked Monsieur Rigot.

"And to get a start in it, you also need to buy a position?" asked Luizzi.

"That's right, sir," replied Monsieur Furnichon.

"And to buy that position," went on Monsieur Rigot, "I assume you'd marry a woman whose dowry…"

"Oh, no!" said Monsieur Furnichon in a sentimental tone, with a look of enthusiasm divided equally between Madame Peyrol and Ernestine. "Oh, I would never marry anyone except the woman I love. I'm no fortune hunter. I ask only for a heart that loves me."

"My word," said Count Lémée smugly. "I agree completely, sir, and I have to admit sometimes I regret the brilliant rank luck has given me. I'm twenty-two, my father's death made me a peer of France, I have a name with a certain prominence..."

"Are you sorry you have all those advantages?" asked Luizzi.

"Yes, indeed, sir," said Count Lémée. "I have reason to fear that, if ever I marry, what you call my advantages might be the only thing that interests the woman I propose to. There are so many who are looking more for high worldly status than for sincere affection and a man of feeling; and perhaps, if I weren't who I am, I might find them choosing over me an ugly, stupid, selfish little monster to whom luck had given all the assets I possess."

"What, son?" asked Countess Lémée sententiously. "How can you speak so ill of a rank that must be the ambition of every well-born woman?"

"Oh, you're right about that," said Madame Turniquel. "If I ever got remarried, I'd be happy to be the wife of a peer of France."

"Not mine, though, Madame Turniquel, isn't that right?" said Count Lémée with a gracious smile. "Because I'm poor."

"Son!" said Countess Lémée.

"Why hide something everybody knows?" replied the count. "That's my consolation: if ever I meet a woman who's able to understand me, I can be sure it'll be neither my name nor my rank that's won her—if she dares to share my poverty."

The meaning of that speech was addressed so directly to Madame Peyrol that Luizzi concluded Count Lémée, as a neighbor and a regular guest at the Taillis estate, must have fairly exact information about which of the two potential brides the dowry of two million francs had been settled on. To confirm the truth of that, Luizzi turned to Monsieur Bador, who he assumed was also in Monsieur Rigot's intimate confidence. "You must have a low opinion of both the law and the stock exchange as professions, and I assume you'd advise a woman not to choose between them."

That question—so bluntly direct that everyone was embarrassed—made Madame Peyrol look at the baron with astonishment, as if she hadn't expected something like that from him.

The attorney alone was unruffled, and he replied with scornful indifference, "For my part, sir, I think a man's profession is unimportant. But it seems to me his position must be secure, settled, steady, and not dependent on expectations that are almost always illusory. In short, I think a man must've proved himself before he can think of marrying."

"Well reasoned," said the baron, "and spoken like a man who's firmly established."

"Yes, sir," replied the attorney, "like a man who knows the world and has lived; like a man who knows happiness doesn't come from the extravagance of parties and balls at which the wife of a stockbroker or a lawyer spends her life; like a man who knows happiness for a woman doesn't come from what you call high rank, where the fortune she brought to her marriage is often paid back in insolence. In short, I speak as a man who thinks happiness is to be found in a quiet, decent, retired life, in the midst of a respectable family, with a husband whose first thought is to anticipate his wife's least desires, and to carry them out, and to have no thought but for her."

The attorney delivered that little speech with great affectation, keeping his eyes fixed on Ernestine, who seemed to be listening with real interest. While Luizzi observed that new maneuver—no longer sure which of the two, the mother or the daughter, was destined to have the dowry—Monsieur Marcoine didn't want to leave the attorney's touching theory unanswered. "You're talking about provincial happiness; and in any case, do you think you can't find men just as assiduous about anticipating and fulfilling their wives' needs in Paris as well?"

"Of course," said Monsieur Furnichon, who thought he should side temporarily with the lawyer's clerk to defend the Parisian happiness so sharply attacked by the attorney's speech. "Of course there are husbands who make their wives happy in Paris."

"But that happiness," went on Monsieur Marcoine, "is a little more elegant. Instead of the coarse pleasures of the provinces, it's more refined pleasures; instead of your sad, cold gatherings, it's sparkling balls."

"With Collinet and Dufresne," added Monsieur Furnichon.[70]

"Instead of your dull evenings spent doing needlework, it's the Théâtre des Italiens and the Opéra," added Monsieur Marcoine.

"With Monsieur Tulou and Rossini," added Monsieur Furnichon.[71]

"Instead of your bucolic pleasures," added Monsieur Marcoine, "it's…"

Monsieur Furnichon interrupted, "It's races at the Champs de Mars, with splendid horses and women in magnificent clothes."

"And still that's feeble enough!" said Count Lémée. "Let's talk about a man who can introduce his wife to all the salons, not just of France but of Europe, who can give her access to the courts of all the great nations, who can make her sought after and admired everywhere he presents her—and who can present her everywhere."

The attorney, the lawyer's clerk, and the stockbroker's clerk, seeing themselves under attack as commoners, felt obliged to answer Count Lémée, and they'd all begun talking at once, when Monsieur Rigot spoke up, and immediately silence fell. "How about you, baron?" he said to Luizzi. "What do you think about all that?"

He was about to answer, and everyone leaned forward to listen, because by his silence he'd acquired the authority of a man who has yet to speak, who's as-

---

[70] Jean-Louis-François Collinet (dates unknown, but active in the 1830s): a celebrated Parisian chef and the creator of Béarnaise sauce. Louis Dufresne (1752-1832): a renowned naturalist and explorer.

[71] Jean-Louis Tulou (1786-1865): a French composer.

sumed to have ideas in reserve, and whose words are expected to put an end to all discussion. Luizzi began, "I think…"

He got no further, because he was interrupted by a pair of wonderfully polished boots, which the jockey we've mentioned earlier set down on his plate with a little satisfied laugh. That made Monsieur Rigot burst out laughing, and everyone in turn followed suit, even Madame Peyrol, who couldn't keep from giving in to the epic laughter of the whole table. Meanwhile Akabila leapt around the dining room like a wildcat, and they all rose from the table without learning Luizzi's opinion on the important question they'd been debating.

Chapter XXXII: A Fair Deal

A few hours had gone by since that memorable meal, so strangely inter-rupted by the plateful of boots Akabila had served to Luizzi. The baron tried to ask Monsieur Rigot for an explanation, but his answer was to laugh like a mad-man. Madame Turniquel said only, "That wild beast always behaves like that, but he's a fixation with Rigot; it amuses him, so you just have to let it go."

As for Ernestine, she wasn't a girl you could ask about anything that didn't concern her directly. She was preoccupied with her looks, her face, and her clothes; and she seemed to have the greatest disdain for Luizzi's casual, unpre-tentious ways. She barely deigned to listen to the few words he occasionally ad-dressed to her.

He'd had to resort to Madame Peyrol, who'd explained away the jockey's mad behavior fairly plausibly. "My uncle brought that Malay back from Borneo, and he wanted to make him useful. He tried to make him a page, a coachman, a valet, who knows what. But having failed at all that, he gave him as his only job that of shining boots. The fact is, my uncle treats him a little like a monkey, and when Akabila has done his work well he gives him a glass of rum, which the little wretch is very fond of. Today they must've forgotten to give him his ration, so to get it he grabbed the first boots he could find and polished them and brought them in triumph to get his reward."

Luizzi was satisfied with that explanation, though the Malay's presence in the household astonished him in spite of himself, and though the incident with the boots disturbed him without his knowing why. Still, he went back to observ-ing what was going on around him, and he enjoyed the spectacle of the torments endured by the lawyer's clerk and the stockbroker's clerk as they paraded their homages to the mother's daughter and the daughter's mother, while Count Lémée held his own with Madame Peyrol and the attorney did the same with Ernestine.

The minimal attention Ernestine paid to what Luizzi said to her prompted him to direct his efforts toward Eugénie Peyrol, and he saw in her an upright, serious, superior character, with great intelligence in her dutiful behavior toward her mother and her daughter and a dignified resignation to the ridiculous role her uncle had imposed on her. Still, Luizzi had more or less made up his mind that even if he'd found an angel here, it was next to impossible for someone as young, handsome, fashionable, and rich as he was to become connected to such a family, and he'd decided to leave that house the next day.

He was a little embarrassed about how to explain that to Monsieur Rigot, but that very evening the latter gave him an opportunity. After dinner the master of the house asked the gentlemen to keep him company and empty a few bottles together. When the ladies had withdrawn and they were alone, Monsieur Rigot said, "Gentlemen, I know why you've all come here. There's two million francs to win, and you all want it."

They all protested, except Luizzi, who, having come to his decision, reserved the right to reply haughtily to that insolent suggestion.

"I say there's two million francs to win, and you all want it. So don't act so prim, and listen to me."

"You're always such a joker, my dear Rigot," said the attorney, pouring him a drink.

"And we understand joking," said the others, clinking glasses with the former farrier.

"Well then, gentlemen, I have to tell you something. I'm getting tired of all the visits by suitors who, even if they don't snag the dowry, snag a lot of dinners. So I have to warn you, I've told my nieces to make up their minds within twenty-four hours. Here you are, five handsome young men of all ages and all professions. I've received excellent word about you, and you all suit me fine. So work it out among you to make up your minds and choose. Make sure to guess right—because I'm telling you now, the dowry of two million francs has been settled, and the one who doesn't get it won't get a penny."

The young count and the attorney exchanged a knowing glance, and the two clerks looked very disappointed.

Monsieur Rigot went on, "The choice will be made tomorrow evening, the banns will be published the day after tomorrow, and we'll hold the wedding in a week, unless these gentlemen from Paris need more time to send for their family documents."

The two clerks looked at each other with even more embarrassment. But then that good-looking Monsieur Furnichon, drawing boldness from his foolishness, dared to reply, "My word, it won't be me who'll keep you waiting. I have all my papers in my pocket."

Monsieur Rigot began to laugh. Turning to Monsieur Marcoine, he said, "And you, young man?"

"I'm no dumber than Monsieur Furnichon," he replied shamelessly.

"As for those gentlemen," said Monsieur Rigot, "they've been ready for a long time, so it only remains to hear the baron's intentions."

Luizzi had just received one of those rare lessons few men are granted: he'd just seen to what point greed driven to desperation can endure humiliation. He was revolted by so much abjection, and in the cause of human dignity he replied, "I'll never make a shameful bargain of the most sacred bond, the most solemn commitment; and these gentlemen can take their chances at the two million francs without any competition from me."

That answer made Monsieur Rigot turn red with anger. But he immediately calmed down, and gave Luizzi a look of such malevolence it would've alarmed the baron if he'd thought this man could do anything to him. Meanwhile the four suitors all cried out that the baron had insulted them and they all demanded satisfaction.

"Silence!" shouted Monsieur Rigot. "If anyone's been insulted, it's me. If I feel like getting revenge, that's my business. Say no more, baron. The field is clear for the rest of you gentlemen. Let's go rejoin the ladies."

He rose immediately and headed to the parlor. The attorney and Count Lémée followed him, but as they went out the door Monsieur Bador pulled his handkerchief from his pocket and let fall a piece of paper, which Luizzi picked up. He was about to call to the attorney to give it back to him, when he saw Monsieur Marcoine make a sign to Monsieur Furnichon, who came back to him. Luizzi paused to listen to them.

"All right, look," said Monsieur Marcoine. "Let's get straight to the point. We're being played for fools here. Haven't you noticed the attorney and the count have an understanding?"

"I don't see what they could have an understanding about," said Monsieur Furnichon. "Either Madame or Mademoiselle Peyrol will have the dowry, and good for whoever chooses right!"

"And too bad for whoever chooses wrong, eh?"

"It's that simple."

"You're the one who's simple, my friend," laughed Monsieur Marcoine.

"Excuse me?" said Monsieur Furnichon.

"That's right, and we'd be a pair of idiots if we didn't understand business a little better. Let's join forces, and we'll get the two million francs."

"How?"

"Listen carefully. This is how to go about it. Let's imagine the daughter chooses me, and she gets the two million francs, so you're stuck with the mother and nothing."

"True enough, and I admit that frightens me."

"And me too. But there's a way to prevent that calamity, or at least to soften it."

"What way?"

"Now let's imagine one of the two brides gets a dowry of one and a half million francs, and the other one gets half a million. Wouldn't that encourage you?"

"It sure would!"

"So now you understand?"

"Not at all."

"My God, for a man on the stock exchange you're pretty feeble at money matters!"

"Explain yourself more clearly."

"You really need every i dotted, don't you? So, let's agree that whoever gets the wife with two million francs will give five hundred thousand to the one who gets the wife and nothing."

At first Furnichon was too stunned to answer. Finally he said, "Letting go of five hundred thousand francs like that—that's expensive!"

"But if you're the one with nothing…"

"That's possible, yes."

"Well then, do you agree?"

"It's a deal."

"Have a seat here. I'll draw up a little contract in pencil. We'll agree to it, then I'll run up to my room and copy it out. I'll come back, we'll sign it, done."

"Hurry up—the others are gaining ground in the meantime."

"Do you have a blank piece of paper?"

"Certainly not."

At that moment Luizzi came back in and said, "What are you two looking for?"

"Oh, nothing, a piece of paper."

"Here's one," said Luizzi carelessly. "But one side is written on."

"That's all right," said Monsieur Marcoine, "I'll write on the back."

While he was scribbling away, the attorney returned, followed by Count Lémée. Monsieur Bador seemed to be looking for something. He turned over everything in the dining room, then turned it over again. Then, noticing Luizzi sitting in a corner, pretending to read a newspaper, he asked him, "Did you happen to spot a little scrap of paper lying around here?"

"I believe those gentlemen have it."

"What!" cried the attorney, addressing Monsieur Marcoine. "You found that paper, sir, and you were indiscreet enough to…"

"Not at all," said Monsieur Marcoine casually. "It's this gentleman who gave it to us, and I assure you I haven't read a word of it."

"In that case I'll ask you to give it back to me," said the attorney. He turned and whispered into Count Lémée's ear, "It's our statement of agreement."

"How careless!" said the count.

"Well?" said the attorney to the clerk. "Are you done?"

"Jut a moment," said Monsieur Marcoine. "I didn't know this paper was yours, and I wrote some things on it in pencil that I'll ask you to give me time to erase."

As he was about to start erasing, Luizzi approached the four men, motioning to them to draw closer, and said to the lawyer's clerk, "Why erase it, Monsieur Marcoine? It's very likely that what's written on the front in ink is the same thing that's written on the back in pencil."

"Excuse me?" said all four suitors.

"Come on now!" went on Luizzi. "A contract drawn up by an attorney and reviewed by a lawyer—what could be more soundly worded? Read it, read it. I'm sure each of you will be delighted with the other's craft."

Monsieur Marcoine, who was holding the paper, turned it over with irresistible curiosity. He read aloud the first words the attorney had written: "*The undersigned, Count Lémée and Monsieur Bador, etc., etc., agree that if either of them marries Madame or Mademoiselle Peyrol, etc. etc...*"

"Go on," said Luizzi.

Monsieur Marcoine turned the paper over and read, "*The undersigned, Monsieur Marcoine and Monsieur Furnichon, etc., etc., agree that if either of them marries, etc. etc...*"

"How about that!" said Luizzi.

Monsieur Marcoine went on mumbling a few more sentences, sometimes from one side, sometimes from the other. Then, when he reached a certain point on the side written in ink, he cried out as he read, "*Whichever party earns the dowry specified above agrees to give five hundred thousand francs to...*" He flipped over the paper to the side written in pencil and read, "*... agrees to give five hundred thousand francs to...*"

"What!" cried Monsieur Furnichon, still stunned.

"My word!" said Monsieur Marcoine. "You won't find a better-written contract in Paris."

"But it seems they do it just as well there as in the country," said the attorney, taking the paper. Then, having read it, he cried, "It's the same, word for word!"

"In fact," said the count, "it's as if it was copied."

"Or traced," said Monsieur Furnichon.

"As the proverb puts it," said Luizzi, "great minds think alike."

"Well then, so be it," said the attorney. "One pact against another, two against two."

"But why war instead of alliance?" said Monsieur Marcoine quickly. "Why not make one pact with four parties? Because in the end neither of you might be chosen, and the same with us, and then you'd have nothing. They might choose the attorney and me, or the count and me, or the stockbroker's clerk and the count, or the stockbroker's clerk and the attorney: that's four combinations that would leave us all with nothing."

"He's right," said the attorney. "This is very smart. Let's make a four-way pact: whoever gets the wife and the dowry will pay five hundred thousand francs to whoever gets only the wife, no matter who it is."

"And the two who get nothing?" asked Monsieur Furnichon.

"Well," said Monsieur Marcoine, "they get nothing."

"Yes, they do! Yes, they do!" said Monsieur Furnichon. "We have to cover our expenses at least. I suggest ten thousand francs in compensation to the two rejects."

"Agreed as stated," said the attorney. "Let's hurry. Since someone might come interrupt us, let's each make our own copy, so it'll go faster. Here's some stamped legal paper, pens, and ink." He drew the supplies from his briefcase.

They all sat at the table and began to write as the attorney dictated: "The undersigned gentlemen…" And each of them in turn, as the attorney looked at him, dictated his full name and titles.

The count went first. "Alfred Henri, Count Lémée, peer of France."

"Louis Jérôme Marcoine, lawyer's head clerk."

"Désiré Anténor Furnichon, stockbroker's clerk."

"… and François Paulin Bador, attorney in Caen, agree that, etc., etc., etc.,…"

For ten minutes the attorney dictated, each of them repeating the end of the sentence aloud to show he'd finished. It was a shameful spectacle, and Luizzi was standing there watching, unsure whether to laugh or protest, when he felt a light tap at his elbow. It was old Monsieur Rigot, who asked, "What are they up to in there?"

Luizzi didn't want to tell the truth, either because he had no reason to denounce those four dowry sharks, or because he wanted to draw the pleasure of that little comedy out to the end, and he replied, "I believe they're each writing a love note to one of the ladies."

"Excellent, excellent! I just have a little secret to share with those gentlemen."

"But it would be a real pity to interrupt them. Romantic inspiration is so quick to dissipate!"

"Still, I can't leave them in ignorance of this circumstance."

"What could be so important?"

"It doesn't concern you, since you're not one of the contestants. Though I didn't say anything about your withdrawal, think it over: I'm giving you twenty-four hours to think it over."

"My mind's made up."

"Well! We'll see about that," said the old man, nodding his head. "Meanwhile I'll give them the news."

"Go ahead. I'll leave the room."

"You can stay. It might amuse you."

As he spoke, Monsieur Rigot moved from the door, where he'd been standing with Luizzi, all the way into the dining room. The four lovers had just signed and exchanged their contracts, and when they heard the voice of the master of the house they turned around guiltily.

"I beg your pardon, gentlemen!" said Monsieur Rigot. "I didn't share all of my plans with you, because I didn't think it concerned you. But my sister has just made me see that she shouldn't be treated any worse than her daughter and her granddaughter, and I've come to tell you what I intend to do for her."

"What!" cried the four horrified partners. "Is she in on the two million francs?"

"No, no, gentlemen," replied Monsieur Rigot. "I'll keep my word. The two million francs will go either to Madame Peyrol or to her daughter; but I've decided there'll be another million for Madame Turniquel. And that million won't be a gamble: I'll certainly give it to my charming sister. As a result, whichever of you manages to please her can be sure of his reward. You'll just have to decide whether you're tempted; you've got till tomorrow evening."

Monsieur Rigot left the dining room without saying another word about his new plan, leaving the rivals in considerable perplexity.

"Damn!" said the attorney. "That complicates things oddly."

"Would you have the courage to take on the grandmother?" asked Count Lémée.

"I think that's beyond human strength," said Monsieur Marcoine.

"Bah!" said Monsieur Furnichon. "Stranger things have been known, and speaking for myself, if I were sure to succeed…"

"Yes, but I can promise you, you won't succeed," said Monsieur Bador. "There exists in the world a certain Little Pierre, a postilion in Mourt, who was in favor with Mademoiselle Rigot before she became Madame Turniquel, and I believe that fellow will have first refusal."

"Are you sure about that?" asked Monsieur Furnichon.

Luizzi felt a happy anticipation; but, Monsieur Bador having declared the old woman unassailable, they all outdid each other in protesting against the idea of sacrificing themselves to a woman like Madame Turniquel—and no one louder than Monsieur Furnichon.

"Well, well," said the baron to himself. "Greed hasn't yet gone as far as I thought."

They'd reached that point when Monsieur Marcoine asked, "But why do you think this changes matters, Monsieur Bador?"

"Because the fortune that used to be only two million francs is now three, since someone's going to acquire that million, and that's guaranteed, whereas at the rate old Rigot is going he'll be ruined in a year."

"It's true," said Monsieur Furnichon. "The man will end up living off of us."

"That's another expense we'll have to keep in mind," said Monsieur Marcoine.

"But where the devil did Monsieur Rigot get all his millions?" asked Monsieur Furnichon.

"Oh, as for that, God knows!" said the attorney. "All I can tell you is, it's invested in good property, with clear title, and in funds deposited in the Bank of France."

"My word," said Monsieur Furnichon. "That's his business, and it doesn't concern us!"

Upon which they all moved to the parlor, where they found the ladies gathered. Ernestine was radiant, and old mother Turniquel had put on another bonnet, even denser with pink and blue knots than the one she'd worn in the morning. Just then Countess Lémée was complimenting her on her good taste in dress—the noble lady humiliating herself before the old woman's unshakable silliness. As for Madame Peyrol, she sat in a corner by herself. She'd obviously been crying, and it was only with an effort she managed to overcome her sorrow and respond to the gentlemen's assiduous compliments.

Luizzi found the scene so comic that he wanted to add to it: he went to sit by Madame Turniquel, and began to sing the praises of her beauty and her jewelry, to which the old woman responded with a multitude of toothless smiles and with a gracefulness elephantine enough to make a calvary regiment bolt.

The joke went so far it made Madame Peyrol blush. Going to Monsieur Rigot, she said, "Uncle, I beg you, put an end to this cruel embarrassment, if not for my sake—though it pains me to see my mother so ridiculous—then for the sake of my daughter, who's already too tempted to show disrespect to her grandmother. It's wretched and mean, coming from a man like Baron de Luizzi!"

"Bah! Bah!" said old Rigot. "Who knows? More unlikely things than that have happened!"

Madame Peyrol shrugged and turned to the baron, who just then was saying to Madame Turniquel, "Yes, ma'am, happy is the man who, having recovered from the foolish illusions of youth, has learned to appreciate a mature heart and a spirit that's impervious to the vain seductions of a tenderer age!"

"Excuse me?" said Madame Turniquel haughtily. "What are you calling illusions? I'm not so decrepit, I'll have you know. I've got a superb body, and a leg…"

She was about to show off her leg when Madame Peyrol interrupted her, glaring at Luizzi to put him to shame and saying to him quietly, "This is barbaric, sir!"

Luizzi was embarrassed at what he'd done, and he went after Madame Peyrol to apologize. He managed it successfully, by admitting honestly that he'd meant to teach a lesson to those four bloodhounds who were after the two million francs and were pursuing both her and her daughter.

Madame Peyrol listened to him carefully. Then, with a violent effort, she replied, "Well, sir, I'd like to speak with you for a moment."

"I'm at your command, ma'am."

But for Madame Peyrol and Luizzi to have that interview, the league of suitors would've had to be kept from panicking at the little private aside that had just taken place. In spite of Luizzi's announcement that he was withdrawing from the contest, they all approached Madame Peyrol en masse and forced the baron to retreat. Soon the time came for everyone to retire; and as Eugénie Peyrol left the parlor she gave Luizzi a long look that communicated some kind of rendezvous.

Chapter XXXIII: A Very Busy Night

When Luizzi got back to his room he was surprised to find Akabila there, holding the famous boots he'd served him at breakfast. After the explanation the baron had heard from Madame Peyrol, he assumed the jockey had come for the glass of rum that was the usual price for his labors. Curious to study that extraordinary creature more closely, Luizzi nodded to suggest he would satisfy his desires; but, having no rum in his room, he was going to ring for a servant to bring some. Just as he was about to take hold of the rope, the Malay reached out to stop him, shaking his head vigorously and saying in a guttural tone, "No! No! No!"

"What!" said the baron, accompanying his next words with pantomime to make himself better understood. "You don't want a drink of rum, which you like so much?"

The Malay again replied no. Then, going to the door, he listened to make sure there was no one on the other side before coming back to Luizzi. Now began a pantomime scene it would be difficult for us to describe exactly. He mimicked to marvelous perfection the attorney's arrival in his cabriolet, then that of the two clerks dragging their luggage behind them; and after each of those caricatures he shook his head scornfully. Then he came to Luizzi, and depicted him comfortably seated in his berline, with his four horses, entering the courtyard of the Taillis chateau at a gallop. He went on puffing himself up and making himself large, till Luizzi understood he took him for a great lord. Pointing to the baron, Akabila said with a grand air, "King! King!"

Luizzi, who wanted to see this performance to its end, nodded to the Malay to say he wasn't mistaken. The jockey immediately dropped to the baron's feet as if to beg for his protection. Then, rising once more and puffing himself up again, he stood beside Luizzi as if to suggest he was his equal. Pointing at something that seemed to be far away, he repeated, "King! King!"

Luizzi was following this pantomime show with great interest, and he motioned for the Malay to continue. Now, as the creature ran around the room, pointing to the gilt candlesticks, and the buttons on Luizzi's shirt, and the cut-glass stopper of a carafe, whose facets resembled a diamond, he communicated—for his gestures were so expressive, words would've added nothing—that he'd possessed a vast quantity of objects like those.

Up to that point Luizzi had perfectly understood everything the Malay tried to tell him. Akabila kept going. Using his voice and gestures to imitate howling wind and rolling thunder, he depicted a storm, then a ship drifting at sea, and the gust of wind that threw it onto a reef, and a man swimming desperately amid furious waves, reaching shore, and collapsing from exhaustion. Luizzi couldn't tell who exactly Akabila was trying to depict; but then the Malay pantomimed the poor castaway struggling to rise with such a perfect imitation of the rich old man's gestures and demeanor that it was clear he meant Monsieur Rigot. He went on to show him drained by fatigue, dragging himself desperately up the beach, meeting natives who wanted to massacre him, and finally being saved by an old man who came to his rescue and took him into his hut. At that point Akabila's pantomime grew less clear; Luizzi deduced that it concerned a murdered man and a stolen treasure, but the specifics of that strange tale were lost in the Malay's contortions and tears. The baron was trying to get him to explain more clearly, when suddenly Monsieur Rigot's loud voice rang out in the corridor, calling for Akabila at the top of his lungs. The Malay began to tremble, and he was going to hide behind a curtain—but Monsieur Rigot threw open the door and spotted him.

"What are you doing in here?" he said angrily.

The jockey put on his most charming smile. Pointing to the boots he'd set down on a chair, he said sweetly, "Rum, rum!"

Monsieur Rigot kicked him hard in the usual place to kick someone, and said, "You animal, do people put on boots to go to bed?"

The Malay didn't make the least complaint, but he threw Luizzi a glance to suggest he was counting on him. A moment later Monsieur Rigot left the baron's room, after first apologizing for the little scene that had just taken place. "We peasants are a little too quick with our fists and our feet. But with a brute like him there's no better way to make yourself understood."

When he was alone, Luizzi thought over the strange secret he'd just learned, and asked himself whether duty required him to inform the magistrates of what he suspected. Still, he was reluctant to get involved in another ill-considered legal action, as he had over Henriette Buré—an action whose consequences were more or less unknown to him, except that the unfortunate victim had wound up in a madhouse. The baron therefore wanted to learn the whole truth about this adventure, whose general outline he believed he'd deduced; and he was about to summon the Devil when he heard a soft knock at his door.

Madame Peyrol came in immediately and stood there a moment in confusion, as if appalled at what she'd just done. But Luizzi stepped forward and motioned her to a chair. "May I learn, ma'am, to what I owe the honor of this visit?"

The poor woman's embarrassment and distress were indescribable. Stammering, she tried to apologize; then, pressed by Luizzi's questions, she finally seemed to gather her courage, and with her eyes lowered she replied, "You know my situation, sir. I'm penniless. Monsieur Peyrol's death left me destitute, because since he died childless his family claimed and took back all of his property."

"What!" said Luizzi in surprise. "Mademoiselle Ernestine…"

"Is not Monsieur Peyrol's daughter," she replied, lifting her head. "It's a sad story, sir..."

"Which it might be too painful for you to tell," he said a little coldly. "I don't mean to impose that burden on you, but I'm ready to hear your reason for coming to my room tonight."

"No!" she said sadly, hurt by his tone. "No, it's impossible! Forgive my reckless gesture, sir, and forget it."

"As you wish, ma'am," he said, ready to see her out.

But just as Madame Peyrol was about to open the door, she stopped and turned quickly toward Luizzi. "Still," she cried decisively, "your presence in this house gives me permission to speak to you. My daughter has made her choice. In addressing himself to her, Monsieur Bador has shown he knows her well, and knows me too. He knows if my uncle's fortune falls to me, my daughter will be as rich as I am; he knows if my uncle chooses Ernestine, she won't pass along any of her fortune to her mother."

"What! Ma'am, you think..."

"I'm sure of it, sir. That calamity might befall me, but it might also happen that I gain the fortune; in which case, I'm telling you, I'd be even more appalled at sharing it with one of those men you've met in this house than I'd be at remaining in poverty. Only you, sir, have demonstrated neither greed nor base eagerness. I've had only a day to judge you, and I have only an hour to tell you who I am; but since you came to this chateau for the same reason as all the other men I've seen, I can speak frankly and tell you I've chosen you. I tell you that, sir, because I have to ask for your word of honor that you will allow me to give away half of that dowry, if my uncle has decided to give it to me."

Luizzi was quite embarrassed by that strange declaration; but he resolved to cut short her new proposition, and he replied, "If your uncle had been more open with you, ma'am, he would've spared you a solicitation that was no doubt painful to you, and that was useless: I've told Monsieur Rigot I withdraw from the competition for a favor I don't think I deserve."

At those words Madame Peyrol turned pale, and making a deep bow to the baron she withdrew without another word.

No sooner was Luizzi alone than he locked his door to prevent any more visits; and, more determined than ever to consult the Devil on the secrets of that house, he pulled out his little bell and rang it energetically. As usual, the Devil appeared immediately; but, contrary to his normal practice, he had neither the mocking air nor the look of cruel malice he seemed to assume at will. His expression had regained all of its sinister splendor, his smile all of its bitter pride, and he greeted Luizzi with obvious impatience, his voice harsh and serious.

"You seem awfully anxious, Mister Satan!" said Luizzi.

"What do you want from me?"

"Don't you know?"

"More or less. But speak: what do you want?"

"You're quite laconic for someone who's usually so talkative!"

"That's because it's no longer one man's interests that concern me, but those of a whole people."

"One you're going to push toward rebellion and sedition?" The Devil was silent, and Luizzi went on, "All right, since you're in such a hurry, tell me: what's that Malay's story?"

"He told you."

"You mean I think I deduced it!"

"You showed some intelligence for once in your life—that's a lot."

"Your impertinence is turning into insolence."

"I rise to the occasion. Farewell!!"

"Just a second! That's not all. I understood Akabila's story up to the point where Rigot was rescued by an old man. Then what?"

"That old man was Akabila's father. He had an immense treasure, accumulated by his family for a century. I assume you know the island of Borneo is rich in diamonds and gemstones. The civilized European came to that Malay race whom you detest because they show no pity in massacring the men who come to seize their land; civilization added its crimes to the crimes of barbarism. Rigot, at first Akabila's slave and then his friend and confidant, persuaded him to murder his father and seize his immense treasure. He promised to take him to a country where he'd find pleasures unknown at home. But once they set foot on the noble soil of civilization, the roles were reversed: Akabila became the servant of his former slave, and you've seen how much good his parricide did him!"

"But why would Rigot keep around him an eyewitness to his own crime?"

"Ah, that's beyond your intelligence, master. To understand Rigot's actions, you'd have to be his age, of his background, and to have been a slave."

"What do you mean?"

"You'd have to have been a peasant on the estates of the gentlefolk who ruined Rigot's family over a little poaching; you'd have to have suffered the bastinado for not having filled your master's pipe fast enough."

"So it's revenge?"

"And pleasure. You can't imagine the delight he gets from kicking a king's son in the seat of his pants. You can't conceive his joy in seeing all the groveling greedy wretches who fill up his house."

"They certainly are despicable."

"What right do you have to judge them so severely?"

"It seems to me they could hardly be more shameful."

"There are men even more shameful than that."

"What men could go further than they have in abandoning all dignity?"

"You, perhaps."

"Me!" cried Luizzi.

"You, master, if ever poverty struck you, if ever you were cut off from those pleasures you think you scorn, only because you have them in abundance; you, who believe you're free of ambition because nothing stands in the way of your desires; you, who might be the most transparent of those dowry chasers if you were intoxicated by the luxury next to you that you couldn't touch by other means; you, who have such utter contempt for those whose only fault is to be poor."

"You're mistaken, Satan," said Luizzi disdainfully. "I may love wealth, I may be ambitious, but I'd never stoop to marry a woman under the conditions imposed by the wretch who's master of this house. Never would I give my name to a woman who no doubt started out in life by giving herself to whatever peasant was Mademoiselle Ernestine's father."

"You're awfully severe, master. You forget Henriette Buré committed the same error."

"Oh, that's completely different! That was a well-brought-up girl with a respectable education, whose honorable feelings were taken by surprise by an influence to which her family's strictness drove her."

"That makes her error even less forgivable, because Henriette should've been protected by the example of good morals and the guidance of a decent education. But a poor girl from the lower classes who falls isn't surrounded by the thousand defenses guarding a well-born girl."

"So now you're going to plead the cause of vice again."

"Or maybe that of hardship."

"In that case, become a novelist and stop bothering me."

"So you're resolved not to marry Madame Peyrol?"

"Quite resolved."

"God help you!"

The clatter of a messenger riding noisily into the courtyard interrupted their conversation, and the Devil said immediately, "You're the one he's looking for, baron. I'll leave you to your concerns."

336

Chapter XXXIV: Ruin

No sooner had the Devil vanished than Luizzi's manservant Pierre, whom he'd left behind in Paris, came in.

"What momentous news is there, for you to have ridden here like mad?" asked Luizzi.

"Urgent letters from Toulouse, from Paris, from everywhere, and bailiffs who showed up at your apartment for a repossession."

"My apartment?"

"Your apartment, baron."

At those words Luizzi turned pale and cold. The idea of ruin didn't seem possible to him, but the Devil's menacing insolence, and the mocking farewell he'd given him as he vanished, terrified him. He motioned to Pierre to withdraw, and opened the letters he'd just received.

The first announced that his banker had absconded. It was a terrible blow, but Luizzi still had landed property amounting to a considerable fortune. He opened his letters from Toulouse, from which he learned that everything he thought was his didn't belong to him: a man had shown up armed with legitimate documents proving that all of the property belonging to the late Baron de Luizzi, Armand's father, had been sold to him by private contract, on condition that the purchaser allow the baron its enjoyment during his lifetime. If that man hadn't come forward when the will was read, it was because he'd been in Portugal, from which he'd communicated his rights to a certain Monsieur Rigot, who was carrying out the expropriation.

It would be pointless to try to depict Luizzi's rage and terror as he read those fatal letters. For a moment he thought he was dreaming, and he shook himself as if to shake off the awful nightmare pursuing him. He opened his window, as if fresh air would drive away the delirium filling his head. Then he thought for a moment Satan was giving him this scare to punish him for having judged others; and in a violent rage he rang his infernal bell once again. The Devil appeared, still sad, still calm, still serious.

"Is it true?" cried Luizzi.

"It's true," replied the Devil.

"Ruined?"

"Ruined."

"This is your doing, Satan! This is your doing!" cried the baron. And in a moment of inexpressible distress he threw himself at the Devil. But his hands were unable to take hold of the powerful figure before him, which slipped through his fingers like a snake. Driven to the brink of madness by his impotence, Luizzi redoubled his pursuit of that elusive being, till, exhausted by fury and fatigue, he fell to the floor shouting, weeping, and sobbing with rage. His misery collapsed rather than easing; he hadn't yet collected his thoughts when he found Satan standing before him, watching him with his sad, cruel smile. Then Luizzi, comforted by his tears, held his head in his hands and cried, "What can I do? What can I do?"

"Get married."

When the baron had completely recovered from his furious despair, he found himself alone, and he noticed the house was plunged in the deepest silence. Then he began to think over his position, and gradually he began to talk to himself in the following shameful monologue: "Get married, Satan said. But to whom? To one of the two women I rejected? Become part of this family, the baseness of whose morals is matched only by the baseness of its manners? And who knows whether, in choosing one of those two women, I might end up with the very one who'll be poor? Because I was foolish enough not to join in the contract those men drew up together. Oh, if I still could! Only crooks are happy."

At that moment something like a flash of lightning passed before Luizzi's eyes, showing him the notions to which he'd sunk, the way a flash of lightning on a stormy night shows a man the muddy abyss he's fallen into. Luizzi was disgusted with himself, and for a moment he returned to healthier, more reasonable thinking. "No," he said to himself, "I won't commit that infamy. Besides, what good would it do me? Ernestine's choice is made; her mother told me so. As for her, I've rejected her... But there might still be time."

He paused on that thought; already it seemed less awful. But he sought distraction from his misery in his misery itself, so he reread the letters he'd trampled underfoot in his transports of rage. They only confirmed his ruin, and soon a total collapse followed the turbulence of his first reactions. He considered the life that lay ahead of him, a life of poverty and privation, and above all a life as the butt of mockery and scorn from everyone he'd ever known. Vanity—after poverty, the worst of counselors—vanity made itself heard; and Luizzi, pursuing wrong the way a madman pursues death, without looking where he's going, decided to try to make his fortune by marrying.

Without giving himself time to reflect, once again he summoned Satan, who appeared looking just as sad and just as calm.

"Slave," said Luizzi, finding the courage to do wrong that he'd never found to do right, "for once in my life can you tell me something true that's useful to me?"

"I've told you twenty truths you didn't want to believe."

"Well then! Tell me which of those two women will get the dowry their uncle means to give one of them."

"So you've decided to do the thing you found so shameful?"

"Enough with your moralizing, Satan!" said Luizzi angrily. "I don't claim to be better than other men, because I'm beginning to think that's a fool's job."

"You've never been worth more than anyone else. You've been—even at this very moment you are—lower and more despicable than anyone you blamed so cruelly; because they had many long years, one step at a time, to reach the point of forgetting all generosity and all good feeling; they had humiliation imposed on them by people richer than they were; they knew poverty, misery, scorn. While you, who've suffered nothing of all that, you've lost all generosity and all magnanimity, just like them—but at the mere threat of the suffering they've experienced."

"But then what is this life I have?" cried Luizzi, in whom shreds of honor and pride still stirred.

"It's human life; the life other people spend ten or fifteen years going through, but that for you has taken only a quarter of an hour. I stole seven years of your life, but you've made up for lost time; you've got nothing to complain about."

"You cold, pitiless mocker! Finish your appalling task, tear away the last of my illusions, tell me the woman I'm going to marry is a fallen woman, tell me all of her abominations, don't hide a single one, so I can drink to the dregs the bitter cup of my own vileness."

"So you're absolutely resolved to marry that woman? Wouldn't you rather give me ten years of your life?"

"So I can wake up not only poor but old? No. No—no matter what that woman is, I'll marry her."

"You still have two years to make your fortune by honorable means."

"No," said Luizzi with a kind of irrational stubbornness. "What would I do? What do I know how to do? Would I go ask for a lowly job from all the men I've crushed with my wealth? Do I have to beg for work I wouldn't know how to do, and demonstrate a uselessness that would double my shame and my despair? No, I want to marry that woman, and I will marry her."

"You're quite sure?"

"Yes," said the baron, motioning for Satan to take a seat.

"Well then, listen to what she is."

EUGÉNIE

Chapter XXXV: Poor Child

Eugénie was born on the seventeenth of February, 1797—or rather: on the twentieth of February, 1797, a child was brought to the town hall of the second arrondissement of Paris and registered under the name Eugénie Turniquel, daughter of Jeanne Rigot, married name Turniquel, and Jérôme Turniquel, her husband, the said girl having been born on the seventeenth of that month.

"Why that qualification?" asked Luizzi, interrupting the Devil. "Was the declaration false?"

"I didn't say that."

"Was that child not the one referred to under those names?"

"I didn't say that either. I just reported a fact. And I can assure you the woman you know, Madame Peyrol, whose story I'm going to tell you, is the one who was registered at the town hall of the second arrondissement on the twentieth of February, 1797."

"Go on then. Because, considering where you're starting your story, I'm a little afraid it'll take till tomorrow night."

"So stop interrupting me," said the Devil, and he resumed:

You have no concept of the life of the common people, master, and few people have any concept of the life of the common people of Paris at that time. Nowadays it's rare, even among the poor, to live a long time in the same house. People change addresses as easily as they change their clothes; and just as provincialism has been destroyed in France, so neighborliness has disappeared in Paris. At the time I'm speaking of, on the contrary, every neighborhood had a sense of community that allowed its residents to say, "I'm attached to my neighborhood, I was born here, I'm known here, I'll die here."

That sense of community, which tied the residents of a street to one another, bound the tenants of a single building together even more closely. The building Eugénie's parents lived in was on the rue Saint Honoré, at the place where since then a street has been cut through leading to the Marché des Jacobins. It was an immense building, the second floor of which was occupied by the Marquis de La Chesnaie, his wife, his daughter, and his son. All of the upper floors were divided into small apartments, of which Jérôme Turniquel had the smallest.

What you know of Madame Turniquel won't give you any sense of what her husband was like.

Jérôme was a bricklayer. He was twenty, while Jeanne Rigot was thirty. In the poverty into which Jérôme was born, he'd begun life working; he was an orphan, and by the time he was barely eight he was working for the bricklayers to earn his bread. A certain sense of integrity—which must've been innate, since he'd received no education at all—had always kept him from following bad examples. So by the age of twenty Jérôme had already risen above the rank of laborer; his bosses entrusted the management of important jobs to him, and held him up as an example to all their workers. The firm hand Jérôme took with himself he rarely imposed on others, unless it was a matter of carrying out his duty rigorously.

Jérôme had one of those good, simple, open natures that injure themselves when they ought to be striking others. And maybe, mixed with his goodness, Jérôme had a certain... I wouldn't call it disdain for his profession, which he carried out with enthusiasm, but a kind of distaste at finding himself constantly in contact with brutal, coarse, insolent men who could only be driven by brutality and insolence. All of Jérôme's hopes were therefore focused on quickly making his fortune, or at least reaching affluence, so that contact would no longer be so direct. It wasn't arrogance, it was sensitivity; he didn't have contempt for his fellow workers—his fellow workers injured him. It was like a fine white hand forced to shake a harsh, calloused hand whose grip was painful to it.

In fact the women in the rue Saint Honoré neighborhood always called him "good-looking Jérôme." Indeed, Jérôme was very handsome, and his reserved, solemn, melancholy character gave his looks a distinction whose influence the people of his class refused to acknowledge, out of jealousy, but which was perfectly summed up in a single word by the children of the neighborhood: they called Jérôme "Monsieur Jérôme." He was twenty; and with his brow always bent toward the furrow of work he was plowing before him, he'd never yet lifted his head to look at the fine expectations he was building for the future: he was afraid of finding it was too far away from him, and of losing courage. He'd never yet loved, or dreamt. He was a child-man, with the character of a man and the heart of a child.

He was suddenly yanked out of his absorption in his work by a letter from the mayor of the arrondissement, notifying him that he would soon be drafted. Jérôme was devastated. He—who'd progressed step by step toward a lessening of his poverty—knew better than anyone you can't make a fortune overnight. He had no illusions about his military career, because he could neither read nor write. And the place he'd started from was far behind him: a long road he'd traveled for a dozen years, the whole distance separating an assistant from a foreman, and now suddenly he'd have to give it up and start all over again. All of his courage and perseverance left him in the same place as the good-for-nothings who'd spent their lives in cabarets and idleness: he had to be a soldier like them, and Jérôme thought that was unfair. And—just as there are bold, adventurous souls who know how to leave one career and start another, who bravely and quickly rebuild a new fortune on the ruins of the old—so there are others, powerful only in their patience, who lack the ability to recover what a disaster has taken away. Jérôme was like that, and the obligation to turn soldier filled him with genuine despair.

In keeping with his character, that despair was profound and silent; he didn't burst out in curses like lesser men. Nor did he calm down in a few days, worn out by the violence of his own emotions. None of his friends guessed it, because he confided in no one. He knew all too well they wouldn't understand him. Only one woman noticed that Jérôme's usual melancholy had turned to despair. That woman was Jeanne Rigot, a local vendor on the rue Saint Honoré, who lived in the same building as Jérôme. Her door was across from his, and in the evenings, when he came home from work, he sometimes chatted with her, and she told him what she'd earned that day. He'd often lent her small sums to help her through the day's business; and she'd often made him a little soup when his fragile health suffered from his perseverance in his rough work. I should tell you right now, the old woman you've met here was once a very pretty girl.

"I know," said Luizzi. "Little Pierre the postilion, who must've known her then, told me something about it."

"Little Pierre the postilion lied! Conceit, master, is not the exclusive privilege of great lords, though of all their vices it was the last to be adopted by the common people."

Jeanne was a pretty girl, and a well-behaved one, though she was interested in Jérôme. Besides, trust me, as large a part as low morals play in a life of idleness, they have correspondingly little room to make their way into a life of hard work. Jérôme and Jeanne got up at four in the morning, stayed out all day, and came home in the evening only to sleep. Desire is worn out by bodily fatigue, and between hardworking Jérôme and energetic Jeanne there'd never occurred the disturbance of the senses that leads so many people astray.

I'm not talking about romantic dreams. Jérôme could at least have dreamt, but if he had it wouldn't have been about a big, cheerful, lively girl who was eager to please. And yet the two of them liked each other; they had a bond in common, and that bond was incorruptible integrity. Jeanne was the most honest woman Jérôme had ever known; Jérôme the most disciplined, upright, punctual worker Jeanne had ever met, the most worthy of making his fortune. If Jérôme's sadness had only been expressed in his words, Jeanne might not have noticed it; but for several days—instead of pausing for a moment at her place, instead of wishing a friendly goodnight to all the neighbors whose doors, always open down the long corridor, made each person's life visible and gave them all a view of each other's lives—instead of that, Jérôme went back to his room without saying a word and without responding to the "Welcome home!" that greeted him on all sides.

One evening, when he seemed even sadder than usual, Jeanne made an important decision: she waited till everyone was asleep, then knocked on Jérôme's door. He opened it, surprised anyone would call on him so late, and still more surprised when he saw Jeanne, who he assumed had long since gone to bed. The poor girl didn't take long to explain her reason for coming over: she told Jérôme she suspected he'd lost the little money he had, and she offered him her own pitiful savings to help him out of his difficulties. That was Jérôme's first experience of a gesture of selfless interest in him—because his bosses' favor to him had always been motivated by his superiority to his fellow workers.

The poor boy was moved to tears. But he corrected Jeanne's misconception; confiding in her in a way quite new to him, he told her the real reason for his unhappiness. That left the poor girl discouraged and saddened too: the misfortune that had struck Jérôme was far beyond her power to mend, and the two of them parted without any hope of fending off such a terrible blow.

The next day the whole corridor, the whole building, the whole neighborhood knew the reason for Jérôme's unhappiness. Some mocked the overgrown boy afraid to be a soldier, others were sorry for the good workman forced to lose his job. Jeanne, who paid attention to everything people were saying, found little comfort in it—till a suggestion by one of her neighbors led her to think more seriously than she'd done yet. "Hell," the neighbor had said, "there are only two ways Jérôme could get out of being a soldier. One's to be married, and he isn't; the other's for a girl to declare he got her pregnant and demand that her seducer marry her."

Those words had no sooner been spoken than Jeanne had resolved what to do. She decided to go before the magistrate and declare she was pregnant by Jérôme. To say Jeanne understood the full extent of her devotion, or had weighed the sacrifice she was making of her own honor and good reputation, would be to credit her with feelings she didn't have. For Jeanne, doing what she intended to do meant lying to the government, and to common people the government is a natural enemy that always reserves the right to tell lies itself; and then it meant telling the neighbors the trick she'd played on the municipality, without imagining for a moment that even one person would be skeptical when she said her pregnancy was a fiction.

So one morning she set off early and went to the town hall; and there, before the whole municipal council, she made that declaration without shame or embarrassment, and went home very happy with what she'd done. She planned to make a surprise of it to Jérôme, like good news. A few days later he got a letter from town hall, and as always he had a neighbor read it to him. Both of them were astonished to find the mayor was asking Jérôme whether he acknowledged the truth of Jeanne Rigot's declaration, and, if so, inviting him to get ready to marry his victim.

Jérôme swore to God it was all false, and within ten minutes the whole corridor had heard the big news. There was talk of throwing Jeanne and Jérôme out of the building, and of going en masse to the landlord to ask him to evict those two misbehaving hypocrites. All those workmen had young daughters for whom Jeanne's indiscretion could be a fatal model. That day all the doors stayed shut; the corridor was in mourning. Jeanne came home in the evening, still happy, humming a popular song in her loud voice; then she cried out in surprise at all the closed doors on a workday, as if it were a holiday. She was already calling out to one neighbor and another, when Jérôme opened his door a crack and motioned to her to come in. Several eyes glued to peepholes noticed that visit, and it only added to the general indignation. People opened their doors quietly and exchanged a few furtive words in the corner; they decided the petition to the landlord should be presented immediately. An old shoemaker and a stocking weaver took off their aprons, rinsed their hands in water, and went downstairs in the name of the whole community.

Meanwhile Jérôme was asking Jeanne what had led her to do what she'd done, and Jeanne was explaining naively how she'd wanted to save him from the draft while putting one over on the mayor. Then Jérôme told her the awful consequences of her recklessness. It wasn't despair or grief that filled the big girl's heart, it was anger and outrage. She was already talking about silencing malicious tongues by tearing people's eyes out, when they began to hear a great muttering in the corridor. The shoemaker's voice stood out as he cried, "Yes, sir! They're shut up in there together!"

Right away there was a knock at Jérôme's door. Fearing Jeanne's frenzy even more than his neighbors' anger, Jérôme stood in the doorway to keep her from getting out and them from getting in. A thousand accusations flew, and everyone—men, women, children—cried out to the landlord, "Jeanne's in his room! Jeanne's in his room!"

"Yes, she is," said Jérôme.

"In that case," replied the landlord, "you'll understand I can no longer let you stay here. I can't allow such a scandal in my building."

"She's his mistress! She's a slut! He's a good-for-nothing! He made a baby with her!" came the cries on all sides. "Evict them, if he won't marry her!"

"Well then," said Jérôme, "I'll marry her. And anyone who dares insult her now had better watch out!" Then, turning to Jeanne, he said, "Come, Jeanne. Don't worry about anyone making the least little remark to you now, because now you're my wife."

That was how Jérôme, the good-looking young man with the gentle, melancholy soul, married the big, cheerful, coarse girl whose residue you see now. Eight months after they were married, Eugénie, as I already told you, was taken to the town hall and entered in the civil register as the daughter of Monsieur and Madame Turniquel. For a long time Eugénie was a weak, sickly creature: pale, listless, unhealthy. She was as playful as a butterfly; whenever she could she es-

344

caped from her mother's supervision, and her mother punished her severely for the slightest childish faults.

The fact is, she stood up to her punishment with a stubbornness that only annoyed that blunt, brutal woman, whose coarse nature couldn't understand such courage in such a frail body. But when evening came and Jérôme returned from work, if he saw his daughter doing penance in a corner, and if he said to her gently, looking at her with his beautiful, sweet, sad eyes, "Eugénie, you didn't behave," then the child dissolved in tears and humbly begged her father's forgiveness, not for having done wrong but for having caused him sorrow.

Jeanne observed with hatred the child's submission to Jérôme and defiance of her; it was by beating her cruelly that she got revenge for the child's preference for her father. He often had to intervene to save the child from her bad treatment. To give Jeanne fewer opportunities to be angry with her daughter, he sent the girl to school, where she made such rapid progress that her father was delighted. But Madame Turniquel had no appreciation for an education she lacked, and for which she'd never felt a need. To her, a pale, sickly, feeble, wild child was nothing but an intolerable burden; when any of the wealthy tenants in the building, meeting her by chance on the stairs, asked Jeanne about her daughter Eugénie—that elegant, charming child—she replied bluntly, "I don't know how I ever gave birth to that puny, ugly thing."

Jérôme, on the other hand, adored his daughter; and, as small as she was, Eugénie became a comfort to him. Both of them—without the father daring to tell the child—suffered in silence under the brutal tyranny that walked alongside them, its words in the flat of its hand and its fist raised. Eugénie was a peculiar child, who made the building ring with her shouting and laughter while her father was away, fleeing from her mother and being chased by her from floor to floor.

She often found refuge with the Marquis de La Chesnaie, who was amused by her babbling. That was one of the most significant circumstances in her life; because when the servant girls in the apartment found Eugénie in the entry hall, hiding behind a butler while her mother stormed up and down the staircase, they seized her and entertained themselves by dressing her up in a thousand different ways, all of which suited her wonderfully, there being so much uncommon grace in that young body and that sweet, naive face. Eugénie enjoyed that pastime; she especially liked to hear, not that she was pretty, but that she looked like a well-born young lady. That bantering fed in her some innate need for elegance.

But as soon as her father showed up she dropped everything for him. She went back up to her miserable garret, and in vain the little girls her age passed her door calling, "Eugénie! We're going out to play in the garden!" She'd stay by her father's side, reading to him from a serious book, a chapter about Roman history she didn't understand, but happy because she could see he was satisfied. Then, taking his child onto his lap and gently squeezing her delicate little feet and her little hands, he'd say to her quietly, "Oh, you'll never be a laborer's wife, some brute's wife. It would kill you, poor little thing." In fact it was killing him—that unhappy young man, that poetic, illiterate soul who didn't know how to express his sorrow and sometimes even blamed himself for it.

Other days he'd go away with his child, taking her into the country, carrying her in his arms to beautiful places he loved, so he could show her nature. Inspired by holiness, he'd say to her, "Look how beautiful it is! How good it feels to breathe here and sleep here!" And he rocked her on his lap, and the child, who soon fell asleep, sometimes woke to the sound of Jérôme's muffled sobbing, and she threw her arms around his neck, saying, "Poor father! Poor father!" And he replied, "Poor child! Poor child!" Then they went home together slowly, as slowly as they could, and Jérôme said to Eugénie, "You won't tell your mother we've been crying."

Still, Jérôme had to give way to his wife's clearly stated will, and let the useless child's small strength be directed to some purpose. Jeanne thought her clever enough, but unproductive. They apprenticed her to a seamstress. There again she showed uncommon skill and lively intelligence. But there again, as she grew accustomed to seeing all the superb fabrics and the fashionable dresses, she found more and more hateful the heavy clothes her mother forced her to wear. Her natural discontent with her miserable life showed itself in the only way it could: in an excessive care for her appearance, in a desire for material finery—during the time before she could become conscious of the finery of the soul.

But don't assume, baron, that this child, so badly treated by her mother, had been taught to rebel against her. When she was no more than a small child, her natural antipathy instinctively resisted the coarseness of her mother's authority. But as soon as her young mind could understand the idea of duty, Jérôme taught her the sacredness of motherhood, and everything that title required in the way of submission and obedience; and Eugénie, trusting her father's words, accepted that obedience and submission without complaint.

When she was eleven, nothing about her yet hinted at the lovely, statuesque woman you've met. Her apprenticeship was nearing its end, and she loved that work, in which she could always touch silk, muslin, batiste—materials as soft and delicate and elegant as she was herself. One day another child from her building, named Thérèse, came to find Eugénie, weeping and calling out that her father had been brought home hurt. She ran straight home from the shop. When she entered the room where they lived she saw Jérôme lying on the bed, passed out and covered in blood. Jeanne was weeping and shouting, and the neighbors were crowding around, but no one was helping the poor injured man in any practical way.

Eugénie, who cried so easily, didn't cry. She asked, "Who sent for the doctor?"

"We couldn't find one nearby," someone said.

"I'll go get one," she replied firmly.

And she ran out immediately and went from door to door asking for a doctor, and when she found one she climbed the stairs and rang the bell and asked for the doctor, and told him briefly and urgently, "Go right now to number —, rue Saint Honoré: my father's dying."

She went to three or four doctors in the same way, and didn't go home till she was sure they'd come. That action was the first manifestation of the firm, decisive, quick-thinking character that has formed that woman's entire destiny, and that you yourself witnessed tonight when she came to tell you to your face what she hoped for and what she thought of you.

Eugénie returned to her father's bedside only in time to hear the doctors say he was doomed. Still, they attempted to bleed him. The child held the bowl into which her father's blood fell. That operation succeeded only in restoring Jérôme's consciousness temporarily. His eyes sought his daughter, and when he saw her by his bed he held out his hand and murmured softly, "Poor child!" Then, in the grip of the delirium of his final agony, he died, stammering even with his final sigh, "Poor child! Poor child!"

Jeanne had loved her husband after her own fashion, without ever understanding he wasn't the happiest of men. She was at least as worthy as the wives of the other workmen who were happy. So she felt a mighty despair at those fateful words, "He's dead!" and her despair was such that the neighbors had to take her away and keep her with them. They forgot Eugénie, who hadn't cried out, and who'd stayed, kneeling at the foot of the deathbed. When night came the child watched over her father's corpse without anyone thinking of her.

You've never seen anyone die, baron; you've never spent the twelve hours of a long night by a deathbed. You don't know what it's like to contemplate by wavering lamplight a face that only a few hours earlier smiled lovingly at you; to look at cold, still lips that said to you, "I love you, my child"; to hold in your hot hand an icy hand that only a few hours earlier rested on your head and held you in its protection. You don't know the vast education you acquire in those few hours, the reflection and maturity of thought they bring, the resignation they give the soul.

Oh, if I—Satan—were allowed the wish to make men good and holy, I'd often send them to look at the dying, and I'd often send them to spend time with the dead. You can't understand life at eleven, but you can understand your own suffering at any age, and Eugénie was suffering. Those words, "Poor child!" that her father had spoken in all of his pain, and that he'd left her as a final farewell, rang unceasingly in her ears. As small as she was, she stood on tiptoe to look into her father's sweet, calm face, hoping those sad words she used to summon with a smile, "Poor child!" would come once more to give her hope; but nothing spoke. Oh, what a terrible despair it was for her—the stillness of death, that you strike against in vain without disturbing, the stillness of death that says without a voice, "Nothing, nothing, nothing ever again!"

Then, across the small distance separating her from the room where Jeanne had been taken, she could hear her mother's moans and the assiduous words of consolation poured out to her; and seeing herself abandoned like that, Eugénie felt that life, like death, was telling her, "Nothing, nothing, nothing ever again!" Then she veiled her father's face, and knelt and prayed to God.

Luizzi had listened to the Devil in rare mute astonishment since the start of his tale, but he couldn't keep from protesting at the sad, solemn tone in which the fallen archangel had spoken those last words.

Satan turned his savage burning eyes on Luizzi and went on, "She prayed to God, master, she prayed to God and regained hope. Because God, you see, holds hope in his hands and showers it on those who pray to him. The child prayed to God, and he sent her a drop of that celestial dew I've been denied from eternity to eternity—because I don't pray to God. No, no, master; I'm too proud. I don't pray to him: he'd forgive me!"

If the example of human motivation could make it possible to understand what Satan seemed to feel, you might've said he scorned blasphemy against the Eternal when he spoke of the support God gave such a small, weak creature; you might've said he sought to magnify himself by proclaiming that the stubbornness of his rebellion was not a necessity imposed by God but the result of the implacable will of the Lord of Evil; you might've said, finally, he only praised the Eternal's inexhaustible goodness so highly, the better to boast of his own inexhaustible defiance to it. Then he went on:

As lightly and carelessly as the child had entered that death chamber, so serious and wise did she leave it. In any case, she'd missed no lesson of the great education we call death. Having seen life leave that body, she saw the body leave that room; and having stayed alone with a corpse, she stayed alone with nothing. The neighbors wouldn't let Jeanne go back to her room for several days, and Jeanne didn't ask for her daughter. When Eugénie was alone, completely alone, she was frightened, she wept, and she left. What welcome did she receive? Stares that followed her with more curiosity than sympathy; whispering as she passed, without anyone addressing her; and then children, more cruel or more pitying than their parents, who asked her, "Is it true, poor Eugénie, you're going to be sent to the foundling home?"

Those words terrified Eugénie, and reminded her of something she'd paid little attention to before then. Her father had a box, whose key he kept, and he'd often said to his daughter, "You see this box? There's a secret inside it that concerns you, and that I'll tell you someday." In a spasm of fear she wanted to take possession of that box, as if anything belonging to her father would protect her. She returned to the room she'd just left. Her mother had come back, and in her hands she held the box, which she'd opened, and whose contents, a bundle of papers, she'd thrown into the fire. By a kind of astonishing intuition, Eugénie understood something was being taken from her, some last hope was being taken from her, and she ran to her mother, crying, "That box is mine, what's inside is mine!"

"There's nothing here of yours," said her mother, pushing her away brutally. "There's nothing here of yours, not even the bread you eat, because you don't earn it."

"I've eaten nothing since my father died," replied the child bravely, "and I wouldn't eat your bread, mother!"

That's how the mother and the daughter met again after the death of the husband of one and the father of the other. A moment later Jeanne left, for the needs of that day and the next had to be thought of. The poor have the misfortune of not even having time to recover from their misfortune. Jeanne left to her daughter the task of restoring the room in which her father had died.

"If ever Eugénie is yours," said the Devil, breaking off, "and you see a little bag hanging around her neck by a silk cord, don't tear it off like some offensive souvenir of a first lover; it holds a small scrap of cloth on which there's a drop of Jérôme's blood. It's the only remnant of that honorable life, the only object to which she can address her adoration for her father. It's her private religion—the holiest to her after the one I've renounced."

Meanwhile the child's proud reply to her mother hadn't been empty talk. Eugénie left the room in turn, and went to the seamstress for whom she worked, and asked to be paid a salary for whatever she could do outside the hours she owed her for her apprenticeship. The child, whose days were committed, sold her nights, and when she went home she could say to her mother, "I earn my bread!"

But soon it wasn't just her own bread the child had to earn, it was her mother's: Jérôme had made Jeanne give up her trade as a street vendor, and when she wanted to start again she found her old place taken and people's buying habits changed. Don't assume Eugénie spent the money she made: she gave it to her mother, and every morning her mother cut her a slice of bread, gave her one sou, and told her, "Go work!"

Don't laugh, master! Don't laugh, arrogant millionaire who's about to be poor! You'll soon learn the value of a sou. One sou to spend on pleasure is nothing; one sou for necessities is a treasure. When evening came, the poor child, who was almost always home first, set the table and made the frugal supper; and after eating, more work—nights spent by the light of a feeble candle! The first nights were cruel, believe me: she had to make mourning clothes for her mother and herself.

And yet that was an important experience for her, and here's why: For the first time she had at her own disposal the fabric that would clothe her, and for the first time her instinctive hatred for clumsy tailoring had free rein; she gave her simple dress the latest, most fashionable style. Don't assume she did it unthinkingly, out of some imprudent vanity. She knew very well it would nettle Jeanne's rustic fashion sense. She expected to be beaten, and she was beaten; but she was also beautiful. People said she didn't seem made to be a laborer. Her new clothes marked a new turn in her development, and she was pleased.

"Ah, I understand why you like that woman," said Luizzi. "She represents the lowest rung on the ladder of pride."

"Pride is never low, master. It's only vanity, no matter how superior it is, that always grovels in the mud."

Luizzi received the Devil's insult without comment, and motioned for him to go on. The Devil continued:

Chapter XXXVI: Poor Girl

I told you, baron: the child was finished, and the girl had begun. Now let me tell you what life is like for that kind of girl. Of course it's work, but it's also freedom. Jeanne and Eugénie left the house at six in the morning: the mother to rebuild, as much as she could, the business she used to have—a woman of the common people, always harsh and coarse, but always honest and hardworking—the daughter to go to her workshop, drawing on that pride you criticize to carry out her duty. Do you understand now that in that self-reliant life it takes a kind of virtue to resist all the seductions that surround it, with no lack of opportunities to give in? Because, apart from her own good sense, a girl like that has no protection around her, the way your young ladies do: the ever-present vigilance of a mother and the material obstacles of your world, which don't leave what you call a young miss a single hour to get through a conversation that no one listens to or watches over.

Do you understand that her virtue must be very great to resist not only that freedom but the vast power seduction has to spread itself before her? Because with your women, baron, when you seduce them—or rather when they let themselves be seduced—you don't have to show them the infernal paradise of wealth and luxury: they already live there, just like you. When they stray, their only excuse is a thirst for love. But the unhappy girls at the door of the beautiful garden with golden fruit, which they can see but not taste, those girls face temptations much greater to resist. Your women fall in palaces and woods where they flaunt their idleness; poor girls also fall sometimes, but it's because the road they're on hurts their feet and the burden of their poverty crushes them. You people stuffed with gold think you're rich in youth and expectations, but you're actually poor in the only true human wealth—because your dreams can reach no further than a step ahead of you, while the dreams of those who have nothing can fill vast spaces.

The loveliest tales that entertain the young about the future aren't told in fine salons; it's not the girl in the silk dress who's at the mercy of every desire; it's the girl in the burlap dress who dreams of every experience. The greatest and most delightful hopes, the handsomest lovers, the finest dresses, the most glittering pleasures, the most unexpected conquests are born in a workshop full of girls who are pretty but poor; that's where almost all hope, the joy of youth, can be found.

Do you understand, in short, that in this situation familiar to all the daughters of the common people, when there's a girl to whom nature has given not a desire for a life of refinement, but a need for it—do you understand that when such a girl adds to those commonplace dreams the dream of elevated conversation and superior occupations and the refined pleasures of wit and the flourishing of talent, she needs great virtue not to buy herself all that by one mistake that she's told is her only route to happiness? And I'm not talking about love, master, because you use that as an excuse for your women, who otherwise would have none.

Eugénie was the girl I'm referring to. She was already seventeen when the event I'm going to tell you about turned her spirit's passive, resigned suffering into active misery. She'd become beautiful. Her fragile, sickly body had suddenly blossomed: she'd quickly grown taller; she was as lithe and slender as a young tree planted in the shade, which hurries to reach the sun. Still, the dazzling pallor of her face showed that the vital energies of that fine body hadn't developed as quickly as her height; and Eugénie, once a sickly little child, was now a tall but fragile girl.

At the time I'm speaking of, she was working for Madame Gilet, one of the best-known dressmakers in Paris, who was also located on the rue Saint Honoré. Her workshops occupied one side of a courtyard, on the other side of which lived Monsieur de Souvray, a bishop without a diocese who, having stagnated for years in England, had returned to France to live on the pension Napoleon had granted to unemployed priests. Eugénie had found one friend in Madame Gilet's workshops: the same Thérèse who'd been her childhood friend in happier times, and who pleased her with an air of refinement and an elegance of dress that disguised how poor she was. As I say, that's the way she pleased Eugénie, who more than ever was driven by an innate need for refinement; and their friendship was based on nothing more than the superficial bond of being the prettiest and best-dressed girls in the shop.

Being his neighbors had allowed the two girls to meet Monsieur de Souvray. The introduction between a man like the former bishop and two girls who were so distant from him socially had been brought about by means of a certain Madame Bodin, who was the old bishop's housekeeper. Madame Bodin was a woman of about thirty, whose beauty had given rise to suspicions that I can tell by your smile you share. And yet it wasn't like that at all, and if Monsieur de Souvray was attached to her it was because she served him zealously and devotedly; and if he enjoyed making the two girls talk, it was because old men take enormous pleasure in letting the rosy words of youth brush their faded cheeks. Monsieur de Souvray's social circle consisted of a few elderly gentlemen, and Eugénie had never seen a young man there besides Monsieur de Mednitz, a naval lieutenant who was the bishop's nephew and who'd lived at his house for a few months in early 1813.

One day, the thirtieth of March, 1814—a terrible day for the whole nation and an even more terrible day for Eugénie—the rumble of canon could be heard all around Paris.[72] The breathless city was terrified at the thought of seeing the enemy host, who'd gathered against France for so many years from all corners of Europe, finally burst into the streets of Paris. The city was especially afraid of the barbarian Cossack horde, which they knew had crisscrossed the Champagne region with such ferocity. Everyone was quaking—and yet in the middle of Paris the young workers at Madame Gilet's had gathered as usual to make elegant muslin canezou jackets and light gauze shawls, simultaneously terrified and laughing while the Empire collapsed around them.

At ten o'clock Madame Bodin suddenly entered the workshop and asked Eugénie to come talk to her. The girl followed her out, and Madame Bodin, pale and with clenched teeth, barely suppressing terrible suffering, said to her, "Eugénie, take me to your place right now. Your mother's out, isn't she?"

"Yes. Why?"

"I'll tell you, but come, come quick."

The poor astonished girl led Madame Bodin there, but the woman could barely drag herself along. No sooner had they reached Eugénie's room than Madame Bodin fell into a chair, crying, "Help me! Help me! I'm having a baby!"

"Here?" cried Eugénie, backing up.

"Yes, here or in the street, because Monsieur de Souvray fired me this morning when I told him I was pregnant."

"Pregnant?" echoed Eugénie.

"Yes, it's his nephew who jilted me—his nephew, who was supposed to come back to Paris and who's abandoned me."

Before Eugénie had time to reply, the agonies of childbirth became so sharp and so awful that Madame Bodin began using her teeth to tear the sheets of the bed she lying on. Eugénie ran around the room, crying, "What should I do? My God, what should I do?"

"Oh, shut up! Don't let me die. I'll be strong enough not to shout, though I'm suffering the agonies of hell. Go get my doctor, he's been warned. Go!"

Eugénie now saw only a woman who was about to die, and she ran and brought back the obstetrician…

"Ah, master," said the Devil, breaking off and giving Luizzi a sad mocking look, "your sisters and your daughters don't witness anything so horrible, they're not privy to such secrets. In their lives there's a veil that doesn't rise, or at least shouldn't rise, till their wedding day. That's not how it is with the poor. They have countless opportunities to learn everything; and the moment Eugénie left behind her maiden ignorance was the moment she helped with a delivery, to

---

[72] Russian, Austrian, and Prussian armies surrounded Paris on March 30, 1814. After a day of fighting in the suburbs, the French surrendered on March 31, and Napoleon abdicated the Imperial throne and went into exile.

receive into the world an illegitimate child and hide the shame of a woman she barely knew."

Madame Bodin's delivery was easy and fast. While the doctor was finishing taking care of her, Eugénie went to see Monsieur de Souvray and told the old man what she'd been forced to do. He listened without understanding, or without wishing to understand, the child's heroic dedication, and he replied coldly, "That's all I wanted. That childbirth couldn't happen here—it would've compromised me too much. You must see that, Eugénie, especially at a moment when the return of the Bourbons gives me hope of recovering the position that was taken from me. All it would've taken to doom me is the wicked rumors this could've given rise to."

Baron, don't you admire the coolness of the man, who was building his expectations on the fall of an empire, and was afraid of a little spiteful neighborhood gossip? And that at the age of seventy, when he was already too weak to put on his miter and carry the pastoral crozier! Then, having exposed the utter egotism of his own self-interest—forgetting that what could cost him at most the remnants of an old man's ambitions could rob a young life of its entire future—he promised to take every precaution to hide the child.

As soon as it was dark enough to leave Eugénie's building without being seen, the innocent girl and the doctor set off together. Under her shawl she was carrying the newborn, whose cries she stifled. Meeting her mother on the dark stairs, she said to explain her going out, "Madame Bodin was here, and she burst a blood vessel and had to be bled. I'm off to let Monsieur de Souvray know, and to find a hackney cab to take the lady home."

The bishop was waiting for Eugénie and the doctor at his door, and the three of them went to the Saint Roch Church to present that child of sin to God, and to ask him for mercy and hope for the baby. They'd have done better to ask it for themselves, especially Eugénie—Eugénie, who didn't know she'd just stained her life with another woman's sin.

Over the next few days Eugénie noticed the neighbors giving her strange looks, and examining her demeanor, her walk, her face. But she was so lively, and sang so happily while she did her housework, that their suspicions dissipated—or at least were no longer visible. Suspicion, master, is like a body you throw into a lake. Rarely does the water throw it back out again; sometimes it sinks to the bottom and is hidden in the mud, but it's still there under the water. If a strong wind agitates the lake, the body comes back to the surface, covered in slime and mud. Eugénie didn't know that; and, because the neighbors went back to their usual behavior with her, she assumed they'd accepted the explanation she'd given for all the noise they'd heard from her room. Only Thérèse understood, and guessed the truth. But in vain she urged Eugénie to give her permission to make fun of Madame Bodin, whose pretensions to being an upright woman annoyed her. Eugénie had sworn silence, and she had integrity, even about giving her oath.

A few days after the events I've just described, during the fine midday hours late April sometimes grants the earth, Eugénie, Thérèse, and another girl had gone for a walk in the Tuileries Garden when Mass was over. After one turn around the garden they noticed they were being followed by two Englishmen; the invasion had brought many to France at that time. That should be enough to tell you how hateful they were to those daughters of the common people, who'd always loved the Empire, out of that instinctive attraction the masses have for great size, since the masses themselves are great in size. The two men seemed to them not only odious but ridiculous.

You men, and especially you Frenchmen, excel in the worst aptitude I know of: that of getting excited about what's fashionable, of being infatuated by whatever trivial thing some pushy fellow offers for your admiration because it's new or made to look new. Second to that wretched quality, you have the most shameful trait of all for humankind: that of contempt, the most profound contempt, for whatever you've loved, and loved to excess—and that within a few years, a few months, a few weeks! To those two qualities, however, you add another tendency that seems irreconcilable with them: obliviousness to anything that didn't originate with you, and haughty disdain that leads you to ignorant mockery of whatever you don't know about. It's as if your minds have two great flaws: it's as if they're simultaneously too narrow to hold two different attractions side by side, and too obtuse to get quickly to the essence of things. And yet you have a reputation as the wittiest of people, and it's accurate. Explain that if you can; maybe someday I'll tell you the secret.

Anyway, at the time I'm speaking of, nothing could be more ridiculous in your eyes than an Englishman, simply because he wasn't shaved like you or dressed like you or shod like you. I could understand it from, say, Oriental people, in whom the magnificence of their own clothing makes it natural for them to scorn European dress, with its affectation of poverty. But for you, who'd just been through the square-cut coats of the Incroyables and the fishtail cutaway coats of the Muscadins and the skinny muslin cravats of the Merveilleux,[73] it took all the insane vanity in your power to mock the Englishmen's tight tailcoats and sober clothes.

However, our three young ladies, noticing they were being followed, let the Englishmen tag along behind them, instead of making clear by their stern reaction how unwelcome the pursuit was, as they would've done with Frenchmen. That gave the girls the opportunity, during the whole of a long walk, to

---

[73] The Incroyables and the Merveilleux were fashionable aristocratic subcultures, with outrageous clothing styles, in Paris during the Directoire (1995-99). Both grew out the Muscadins, an earlier dandyish subculture among street gangs during the Revolution and Thermidor period (1789-93).

make fun of them, to examine them, and to laugh together endlessly at those odious islanders who were so ugly and so ridiculous and who had the vulgar, stupid vanity to imagine they had only to show up to inspire love at first sight in Frenchwomen.

What I'm describing to you has no doubt happened to countless other women, but for them the encounter and the joke has no consequences. It took a peculiar set of circumstances for that encounter to have such serious results for one of those three girls! Listen, and be aware that I, the Devil, am allowed to tell you something implausible, because I'm telling you the truth. Besides the circumstances I'll tell you about, you need to know that one of the men they were making fun of was the kind of person who devotes serious attention, even zeal, to everything he desires; he was vain, egotistical, and corrupt; he was one of those idle people who learn from a wicked book what kind of life to live, and who pursue that life with all their might.

At the age of twenty Arthur Ludney had taken Lovelace as his model.[74] But not the Lovelace who, in passing from the original to the translation and from the translation to the imitations, has become merely a good-looking bonehead who makes women fall in love with him just by parading his conceitedness before them. Arthur Ludney had gone back to the source: the true English Lovelace, with all of his ardent, corrupt, stubborn desire, followed by his utterly dry, cold, implacable scorn when that desire has been satisfied; all that, not frivolously, with the gracious light touch of a butterfly, like your ordinary seducers, but with calm, serious perseverance and a mind bent on its goal of seduction, the way it might be toward ambition or fortune.

You know that handsome D—, from the British embassy, who approaches a diplomat and a tailor with the same seriousness of mind, who discusses the buttons on a waistcoat with the same care as the terms of a treaty, and who, trusting no one but himself for whatever is difficult, draws up the most important diplomatic dispatches with his own hand and cuts the cloth for his own trousers? Since you've seen how far a man with honorable intent can take a love of dandyism, you should have no trouble seeing how far an even more persistent man can go in emulation of Lovelace. In any case, a Lovelace is an English type you don't have: he's too despotic for you, and above all too patient and too wicked.

So that's who one of the men was who was pursuing the three girls; and, annoyed—as a Lovelace, as an Englishman, as a great lord—that those children, those French girls, those working-class girls, weren't struck by his beauty, he vowed to punish them; not just one of them but all three. It seemed, however, that Eugénie would be saved from that man's pursuit and vengeance: when they

---

[74] Robert Lovelace, a libertine, a seducer, and eventually a rapist, is the villain of the novel *Clarissa, or the History of a Young Lady* (1748), by Samuel Richardson.

left the Tuileries, she parted ways with Thérèse and Désirée and went home, and after a moment's hesitation the two Englishmen followed her two friends.

The next day at Madame Gilet's workshop everyone laughed over their adventure and over Thérèse's comical telling of it, as she mimicked the stiff, awkward, starchy Englishmen muttering behind them, "Hoo hoo! The pretty mademoiselles! Hoo hoo! What chiarming bustlesses! Hoo hoo! Verry chiarming!"

They all congratulated Eugénie for having been neglected by those wicked Englishmen, but Thérèse protested, "Oh, I wouldn't call them wicked. One of the two is as beautiful as a dream: a small young man who can't be more than twenty, with big black eyes and long black hair and teeth like pearls."

"So he's not English," they all said. "Englishmen are all red-faced."

"He's English, he told me so."

"What!" they cried. "So you talked to him?"

"Yes," said Thérèse, "when Eugénie left us. Because she's such a prude, you know: when a man looks at her, it's like he's stolen something from her. We talked to them for the fun of it. I remember one of them is named Back, like the rue du Bac; he's the ugly one, the redhead. The other one's name is Arthur... Arthur, then an English last name, I don't know what. He's the son of a wealthy lord."

"And what did they say to you?"

"Bah!" said Thérèse, standing in front of the flounces of a dress she was finishing to see if they hung well. "Bah! Englishmen's nonsense! That they'd give us cashmeres and carriages if we loved them. That is, it was the ugly one who said that. The other one's much more romantic, and he kept saying, 'Hoo hoo! I'll verry much lerve yew, verry much, if yew'll lerve a little bit me.'"

"And they kept on following you?" asked Eugénie.

"Yes, all the way to Désirée's door."

"And then when you went home alone?..."

Thérèse blushed deeply, and as she was taking away the dress she replied, "They weren't there anymore."

That encounter had made no impression on Eugénie's mind, and by the next Sunday she'd forgotten it. She went to Mass as usual, and she was about to leave the church when she noticed the handsome Englishman, who seemed to have been watching her for a while from behind a pillar. The man's bold stare would've offended her anywhere; in church it struck her as an insolent sacrilege, and she moved away quickly. As she was going down the steps of Saint Roch she noticed she was being followed; prompted by an initial impulse of fear, she ran home. But when she reached her building it occurred to her she'd be revealing to that stranger where she lived, so she doubled back quickly and went into a perfume shop.

Listen carefully to all these childish circumstances, master; they'll help you understand what I'm going to tell you. The perfumer, seeing Eugénie come in so alarmed—Eugénie, whom he'd known as a child in the neighborhood—

asked her what was wrong. She told him and his wife about the Englishman who was following her, and the perfumer got angry, and blustered, "All right! All right! I'll go send him away. Point him out to me."

"That's him," said Eugénie, "looking in the shop window."

The perfumer opened the door, and the Englishman gave him a look so filled with menace and scorn that it stopped the man short; instead of advancing on Arthur, he began humming carelessly on his doorstep, and after a moment he went back inside.

"Well!" said his wife. "Is that all you found to say to that playboy of an English?"

"Hell!" said the husband. "I can't just go tell the man to walk on. He's looking at the window display; that's his right; the street belongs to everybody."

"Come on, you old coward!" said his wife. "He scared you. This is our place, and I won't hear it said that rascals can come insult us on our street and at our door! I'm going to go send him packing the way he deserves."

"Never mind, never mind," said Eugénie. "I'll wait till he's gone."

"Oh, sure! He'll just stand there like a sentry. Don't worry, my girl, this won't take long."

The wife went out, and the Englishman immediately approached her. Before she could open her mouth he bowed and, pointing to a small vial in the window, he asked, "How much is that?"

It was an item worth one écu. But the woman replied angrily, "Forty francs, sir!"[75]

"I'll take it," said the Englishman, going into the shop and pulling out his purse.

The perfumer's wife, stunned, opened the display, removed the vial, and handed it to Arthur, who paid for it without taking his eyes off Eugénie, who'd retreated to the back of the shop. "Very good, very good," said the Englishman loudly. "I'll come back and buy a lot more."

He left, and, by the perfumers' lack of enthusiasm in continuing to offer her the protection that had been so helpful to her, Eugénie understood they didn't want to risk losing such an excellent customer for her sake. One thought was uppermost in her mind: the man's stare, which had frightened her, had also frightened a man—the perfumer—and that made her afraid of meeting him. The stranger became a terrifying being to her.

She also though about the solitude in which she lived, with no father, no brother, no relatives to care about her. It was during that period she saw her uncle Rigot again; not wishing to remain in France after the fall of his Emperor,

---

[75] Since one écu was five francs, she's charging him eight times what the item is worth.

he'd begun talking about going abroad to seek his fortune. But it was only after the events of 1815[76] that he carried out his plan.

Meanwhile Eugénie had left the perfume shop, determined to elude the Englishman's pursuit if she saw him again. To do that, instead of going back to her mother's, she went to Madame Gilet's. Arthur was still following her, and he didn't leave Madame Gilet's street till he'd waited two or three hours. Then Eugénie went home.

I haven't mentioned Madame Turniquel for quite a while, and you might be assuming that, moved by Eugénie's courage, the woman at least left her in peace after her stressful day. Here's what really happened. No sooner had Eugénie reached the corridor on which they lived than her mother came running, shouting, "Where've you been, you little tart, you floozie?" etcetera, etcetera. I'm not even using her real words, baron; because if, as you've threatened to do, you ever publish these memoirs, the words would be useless to you, since you wouldn't dare have them printed. Eugénie tried to speak up to defend herself, but as soon as she opened her mouth she got slapped. I'm speaking plainly. It wasn't the first time it had happened, and it wasn't the only abuse the poor girl had to endure. To prove it, I have to tell you about a wretched detail of that wretched life.

Eugénie gave her mother the entire fruit of her labor every day. Her mother knew what she earned, so there was no way for her to keep anything back. Once she was home she worked again till bedtime. Jeanne had calculated how much more that would bring her, and she'd said, "Since you make another ten sous every evening, you have to give them to me." But Eugénie couldn't help loving her clothes; and when her mother was asleep in her rough way, she got up again and went on working, and she slowly accumulated the wages of her work by night, after having given Jeanne everything she made by day—and all that for a caprice, to have a silk spencer jacket.

After a great many nights, she was able to buy the material and make the jacket. And one day she carried it into her mother's room to be punished for what she'd done. The mother and the daughter were engaged in a struggle you can't really understand, because it was manifested in details too mundane for what you know of life. It was the struggle between the jealous hatred of the common people for anything that seems to show contempt for its coarse habits, and the insurmountable disgust a refined nature feels for those same coarse habits. The fury Jeanne felt was all the more intense because it was her own daughter who continually insulted her by her seeming scorn for the life into which she'd been born.

And I have to say, both of them went at it with notable stubbornness. So, when Eugénie came in carrying her spencer and admitted to her mother that it

---

[76] Meaning Napoleon's 1815 escape from his exile in Elba and return to power for the "Hundred Days" ending with his final defeat at Waterloo.

belonged to her, Jeanne was stunned by so much audacity. She wanted to tear the jacket out of Eugénie's hands; but when her daughter tossed the spencer back into her room, Jeanne struck her, and Eugénie let herself be struck, because she'd calculated the jacket would cost her thirty nights of work and her mother's violence. But when Jeanne spoke of tearing up the spencer, Eugénie protected it; she stood in the doorway, saying her mother would have to kill her to take it from her.

Violence like that was an everyday matter, baron, and right up to the incident I'm describing it had resulted in nothing more than tears, which youth soon wipes away. But the day Eugénie was frightened by the English stranger's pursuit, she went home full of generous, dutiful thoughts: she was coming to her mother to confide her fears to her, and to ask her to walk her to work and back for a few days; she was coming with the conviction that her mother wouldn't begrudge her that precaution—and instead right away she was greeted with insults and blows.

She was so outraged that she pushed her mother away and cried, "Look out, mother, look out! You'll drive me to do something bad."

"The wretch is threatening me! She's threatening me!" Provoked by a defiance she'd never experienced, she threw herself on Eugénie, and the neighbors had to wrest the girl from her hands, while Jeanne made the corridor echo with shameful insults against her daughter.

"She made Jérôme die of sorrow, and she'll kill his child!" someone murmured in Eugénie's ear. And for the first time the girl wondered whether, on top of all of her life's work, she'd have to sacrifice her life itself to the woman who called herself her mother.

"That woman was a monster!" cried Luizzi.

"No, master, no. If Jeanne had had a daughter like herself, she wouldn't have beaten her so often, because the girl would've had a nature she was accustomed to. But your world has been so thoroughly reformed that what's a virtue on high is a vice below; and the care you insist on for your children, the common people begrudge to their own; and while in your world it's a disgrace for a woman to neglect her appearance, in that world it's a disgrace for a woman to dress up. If Jeanne had beaten a daughter who resembled her, the girl would've suffered less: only her body would've ached. That's how Jeanne had been brought up: it had made her a respectable woman—because she was a respectable woman—and it had broken neither her arms nor her legs. So she considered it right to treat her daughter the way she'd been treated."

That day, after they'd lectured her sternly, she swore to her neighbors she'd do nothing to Eugénie when the girl came back to their apartment. But when she came back, her mother greeted her with fresh insults. When she'd gotten that out of her system, Jeanne said, "Apologize to me!"

"For what? For your having beaten me?"

"Apologize!"

"For the fact that I won't be able to go to work for a week?"

"Apologize!"

"For not wanting to be a wicked daughter?"

"Apologize! Apologize!" cried Jeanne, driven to furious rage by her own powerlessness to overcome the passive courage that lay on the floor and said, "Beat me, kill me—I'll never give in!"

Jeanne had promised not to beat her daughter, and she didn't touch her. But she said to her menacingly, "You'll pay for what you just did to me!"

Such was Eugénie's life! A few days passed without further trouble at home. But outside Madame Gilet's workshop Eugénie found the man who'd been responsible for her recent suffering. She stepped back in horror, and when he began to come toward her she fled, terrified, crying out, "Leave me alone! Leave me alone!"

In telling you all this, baron, there's something I want to make you understand above all: Arthur didn't leave Eugénie indifferent, as he might've left any other girl. He inspired fear and even aversion in her, maybe, but he filled her thoughts, he made his way into her life and settled in. Not a day went by without the memory of that man coming back to trouble her.

The next Sunday, Thérèse wanted to take Eugénie to the Tuileries with her. But that was where she'd run into that Englishman, and she refused to go. Still, she wept at being forced to give up a fine Sunday out, the only day on which she could fill her lungs and straighten up her frail body, which all week long was bent over her work, and she wept bitterly. As for Arthur, oh, he was a man just like all of you are, you impertinent little great lords: in his vanity as a dandy, as the son of a lord, as a rich Englishman, he was astonished that a chit of a girl, to whom he'd deigned to suggest he found her pretty, wasn't instantly thrilled and grateful.

"You're always exaggerating," said Luizzi, interrupting the Devil. "And since you seem to be aiming your remarks at me, let me tell you that, aside from a few fatuous idiots, in my circles I've never met a man like you're describing, and I've certainly never met one so young."

"That's where you're wrong, baron. There's no greater egotism, no greater conceit, than in the very young. At twenty you've lost innocence of heart and you've not yet gained experience of life, so you lack restraint and you lack pity, because you know neither the punishment for bad behavior nor the regret it can lead to. So Arthur pursued Eugénie without thinking about, or really without even understanding, the harm he was doing her. And if he'd known, he might've snickered scornfully at the pain she felt. After all, it's such a little thing for a man whose idleness is a burden to him to rob a poor girl of the one day of leisure her mother allows her! Besides, wasn't he there to compensate her for her loss? And didn't the delight of knowing she'd pleased him make up for all of the pathetic joys she was giving up?"

Anyway, Eugénie didn't want to go to the Tuileries that day; but, urged by Thérèse, she agreed to go the painting exhibition. It was Sunday, a day for the working class, and there was no risk of meeting the handsome Englishman. And yet they ran into him, either because he was favored by what you call luck, or because he was led there by the sovereign hand that had chosen him to be an instrument of evil.

Eugénie's pride rebelled against the man's presence and the horror he inspired in her. She was ashamed of seeming to run away again, and she wanted to show him that, as small as she was, her scorn for him was big enough to be bigger than he was. She dared look him in the face to demonstrate her contempt for him clearly; but once more she lowered her eyes before the young man's implacable, despotic expression. Still, she managed to disappear into the crowd and get home without being followed. Only there did she think she was safe.

Then, alone at home, looking around despairingly at the wretched room he'd made into her prison, and that held for her only one important memory, that of her father's death, and so many awful memories of her mother's mistreatment of her, she began to weep and weep and weep from the misery that has no name if you don't insult it by calling it envy, the misery that always looks above itself and doesn't stop even when it lowers its eyes and is called resignation; she began to weep from the misery people of her class wouldn't have understood, because they were beneath the feelings she had in her heart; from the misery people in high society wouldn't have understood either, because they wouldn't have wanted to admit she had feelings as refined as theirs. Exiled from the world below her by her nature, exiled from the world above her by her poverty, she wept all alone.

Still, she wanted to be able to hope the Englishman would tire of his pursuit in the face of her untiring resistance; and for a few days she thought she'd proved to the stranger his attempts were useless... But one evening, just as she was leaving Madame Gilet's, the neighbor, Madame Bodin, stopped her on the stairs and said, "Come in for a moment and see Monsieur de Souvray. It's been more than three weeks since you paid him a visit."

Eugénie saw it as a reason to stay past the normal hour she left work, and thereby to elude Arthur's watch for her, and she entered the old bishop's apartment.

"Go on, girl, go on," said Madame Bodin. "His Grace is in the parlor."

Night was beginning to fall, and when she entered Monsieur de Souvray's parlor Eugénie could only tell he wasn't alone, without being able to recognize the person with him, who'd just risen to leave. Just then the old bishop was saying to him, "Yes, Monsieur de Ludney, I'm delighted your father remembered the fine welcome he gave me long ago in England, and that he counted on me enough to be sure I'd repay that welcome to his son in France. Please come see me often. You won't find only old men here, whose company wouldn't suit you; you'll also find a few young men your age whom I'd like you to meet. They're the sons of old friends of mine from the country, whom I was responsible for introducing at court, brave and faithful royalists who all know how much the Bourbon cause owes to the support of England. You can rest assured they'll be happy to offer their friendship to the heir to one of the finest names in that generous nation."

The bishop, who felt sure of regaining his crozier and miter, had delivered that speech with a little sermonizing air, like a man who wants to get back in the habit of facile, unctuous oratory. Eugénie had noticed it, and a silent smile lit up the normal melancholy of her features, till she heard the brief reply: "Your Grace, it'll be my honor to call on you often, and I hope to find in those visits more pleasure than you can know."

That voice and those words extinguished Eugénie's smile and struck fear in her heart: it was Arthur's voice, which she knew very well, though she'd heard him speak no more than the rapid words he murmured to her as he pursued her. The emotion she felt was so intense that, out of an impulse of fear and doubt she cried, "Who's there?"

"The one who loves you and will have you," replied Arthur in a low voice as he passed her quickly on his way out.

"Well, my child!" said the bishop, who'd remained on his chaise longue. "What's this I hear from Madame Bodin? You've become sad and melancholic and you cry all the time? Is your mother still mistreating you?"

"I'm used to it."

"So it's something else? Is Madame Gilet displeased with you? Does she want to fire you?"

"No," said Eugénie sadly, "she gave me a raise a week ago."

"Well then! Can what I've heard be true? Are you an ambitious little striver who's satisfied with nothing and who's aimed her expectations higher than she should?"

"No, my God, no! I ask nothing more than to be left in peace right where I am."

"Come, come!" said the bishop, motioning for Eugénie to draw closer. "Might there be love in the air? Beware, Eugénie, beware! It ends badly! Remember Madame Bodin!"

"But I don't love him!" said Eugénie, bursting into tears.

"Aha!" said the old bishop. "So there is someone!"

"Yes," said Eugénie resolutely, "and it's the young man who just left, who's been following me everywhere, who's been annoying me, and who I'm sure only came to visit you, Your Grace, to see me and speak to me."

"My word!" said the bishop haughtily. "Your vanity certainly puts me in my place, miss! Please resist the silly conceit that's made you think a man of rank and fortune like Sir Arthur has any interest in an insignificant girl like you. That's my advice to you, though I know you've got grand pretensions and you think you're a splendid young lady because you dress fashionably like women in high society."

The child of the common people had come to the priest of the religion established to liberate the people, the girl who'd been neglected had confided her fears to the powerful old man, and that's how she'd been received, that's how she was thrown back on her inexperience and her neglect! I won't say it was done out of wickedness or corruption—because I can see again by your smile, master, that you assume I, Satan, take pleasure in badmouthing a useless old priest. No, it wasn't wickedness or corruption in that old man, it was the vast contemptuous indifference of the great for the small, it was the enormous self-esteem of the great lord and the gentleman, who can't admit that a gentleman and a great lord could possibly be at fault toward those miserable creatures out of which society has made its bedding, so that arrogance and lechery can keep their feet warm.

After that scene Eugénie went home and resolved not to go out again for a long time. She sent word to her employer begging her to have her work brought to her room, and she locked herself in, hoping she'd finally found sanctuary, a place her persecutor would never dare enter.

A week passed that way. When Sunday came around again, Thérèse went to see Eugénie and offered to take her away, far away, out to the country. "Your mother won't be home today," she said, "because you know Madame Bodin found her a good job."

"Yes," replied Eugénie, "for two days now she's been looking after an old Englishwoman, so for two days I've been alone here."

If Madame Bodin had found Jeanne an old Englishwoman to look after, you must suspect, baron, who'd introduced the old Englishwoman to Madame Bodin.

"But aren't you bored out of your mind, girl?" went on Thérèse.

"It's true, I'm not having much fun," said Eugénie, who was beginning to miss her simple carefree life back when the horror of encountering Arthur had eased a little a week after she'd first met him.

"Well, come on then!"

Eugénie hesitated for a moment, then replied, "No, definitely not. Next Sunday, or in two weeks, I'll go out, but not today."

"Well, I don't want to leave you alone. I'll spend the afternoon with you. I'll go home and tell them I'm here."

Thérèse left, and soon returned. They sat together at a small table, and Eugénie's sorrow naturally became the subject of conversation. But she'd already had her trust too badly received, by a man who should've understood it, to give it to a girl she knew was flighty, shallow, and thoughtless, and who'd sometimes given her advice that appalled her. It wasn't that Thérèse was so skilled in the ways of corruption; it wasn't that she boasted with great artfulness of everything a pretty girl can gain by her downfall; it was that Thérèse had powerful allies in Eugénie's unhappiness and the disgust she felt for the wretched, shameful life that had been imposed on her. In vain Thérèse pressed her friend with the most direct questions; she could get nothing out of her.

Then there was a soft knock at the door of her room, and almost immediately a man entered. It was Arthur. Eugénie screamed, and Thérèse said casually, "Well yes, it's him."

"You know him? You dared let him come here?"

"Come on!" said Thérèse. "Don't be a bad friend. I can't see him at home because my parents say no. You're lucky: you're free, your mother won't be back, all the neighbors are out for a walk—you can certainly let us talk together for a bit."

A strange sensation went through Eugénie's heart at that moment, and it took all of her confusion, prompted by her reaction to the discovery of an understanding between Thérèse and Arthur, to keep her from throwing both Arthur and Thérèse out together.

Based on what she'd just heard, Arthur was pursuing Thérèse; it was Thérèse he'd come here to see. Then what did she, Eugénie, have to fear? Had she been dreaming? Had her pride led her so far astray as to believe she'd inspired a love that hadn't even occurred to him? Had a man like Arthur rated all the beauty and elegance she thought she possessed lower than Thérèse's beauty and good cheer? Eugénie felt humiliated in her own eyes. Remembering the old bishop's words, she wondered whether in fact she'd been madly presumptuous, misled by her own vanity. She didn't realize that, if that had been the case, the question would never have occurred to her: at no time, no matter how great the disappointment, does vanity ever doubt itself.

"You certainly do loathe vanity, Satan!" said Luizzi.

"Because in your foolishness you humans sometimes set it next to pride—and pride belongs only to me. You understand, master?"

"To you, and to Eugénie."

To her as well, that poor child who wanted to punish herself just for having hoped to be insulted; and who, in her shame at the position the discovery left her in, allowed that man to talk of love to Thérèse right next to her, while reinforcing in her heart the conviction that she was neither desirable nor beautiful nor sought after, and that Arthur had played on her fears for nothing: because Thérèse had said to her, "Now that you know everything, you can stop being stupidly afraid about nothing. And you, Monsieur Arthur, stop tormenting her for fun. She's such a child you'll make her lose her mind."

You can't imagine how crushed Eugénie was. One hope had kept the young woman alive—that someday what was superior and distinguished about her would be noticed. Arthur's pursuit had wounded her because it was insulting, and she wanted both love and respect. The conviction that she'd been tricked shattered her hope and her self-confidence, and she sat there, unmoving and silent, oblivious to what was going on next to her, fixated on a single thought: that she was nothing, absolutely nothing, less than Thérèse.

Thérèse, it should be said, was a true commonplace daughter of the people. She liked fun, pleasure, laughter, silly excitement. At a word from Arthur she jumped up, crying, "Oh, we're going to have a great evening! We'll have supper for three, it'll be fun!"

And she went out to get what they needed. Had the man planned that scene? Or did he have the destiny for evil that shows up exactly when there's a breach in a soul by which he can get in? That's his secret—or mine. But only one circumstance could make Eugénie listen to him, and he possessed that circumstance: there sat the poor girl, in despair, her pride bowed low till it lay flat on the floor, doubting herself like a man of genius who sees mediocrity favored over him, and in his despair wonders if he isn't beneath mediocrity.

That was the moment he dared tell her the truth. "I've deceived Thérèse!" he cried. "You're the one I love, you're the one I wanted to see. In my anger at all your rejections, I wrote to London for letters of introduction that would get me in to see that old man you visited sometimes."

Eugénie listened, her pride listened, rising a little at the idea that she hadn't been a vain fool, like so many girls she scorned.

Arthur went on, "You fled from me once more. But I swore I'd see you again, and I persuaded that girl I loved her so I could come tell you I love you."

Oh, how Eugénie's pride listened, and how it rose, watching the girl who a moment earlier she'd thought was above her now sink far beneath her!

"Yes," continued Arthur, "I deceived her, I sacrificed her to my need to see you for a moment, a minute, to tell you I'll stop at nothing to get to you."

So she wasn't mistaken! She was loved, madly, to excess, by a man people assumed was too far above her to have noticed her; she was loved by a man whom the girl she'd just thought herself beneath loved to the point of forgetting her duty—and whom Eugénie herself didn't love! Yes, baron, yes, Eugénie listened with delight to that declaration of love, and before Arthur was finished the poor girl's pride had risen till she was almost ready to thank the man who'd made her doubt herself, but who'd so suddenly restored her confidence, a confidence now greater than ever.

Thérèse returned just when Eugénie must've realized Arthur's presence in her room was a sin she'd allowed herself to commit. But she felt a need to see how, between the two girls, this man would keep up the act he'd put on. Though still very young, he was skillful at—or rather he had the diabolical gift of—speaking the artful language of love. And while he charmed Thérèse with his fatuous declarations, he fed Eugénie's pride by respectful attentions the vain Thérèse took for indifference; and in her pride Eugénie happily noticed the distinction someone was making, for the very first time, between herself and the girl who was considered to be her friend.

That was enough for Arthur; he knew at certain times on certain days he could enter this room with impunity, and though Eugénie had ordered him never to come back, he did come back. He returned once, ten times. After having found a way to get into Monsieur de Souvray's, after having forced Madame Bodin to bring Eugénie there, after having seduced Thérèse so as to enter the home of the girl he was pursuing, he found a better way: he got his mother to introduce him to Madame Gilet as her dressmaker, then he got Madame Gilet to introduce him to Eugénie as her best worker, then he got his mother, Lady Ludney, to climb the stairs to the sixth floor with him to offer Eugénie work she couldn't refuse, because he made the offer in front of Jeanne, and the price they settled on was so high that the greed of that woman of the people would've repaid a refusal on Eugénie's part with the most shameful abuse.

There comes an hour, master, an hour that belongs to me, an hour in which virtue wearies of the struggle against bad luck, against neglect, against all temptation. That hour began for Eugénie when she told her mother Arthur's secret, and she replied, "My God! He's not going to eat you! You just have to defend yourself—it's not that hard. You think no one's ever going to try anything with you? One time Little Pierre tried to start something with me, and I gave him such a welcome his face bled for a month!"

That was what Jeanne meant by defending herself! Her daughter, blushing with new modesty, tried in vain to make her understand there were dangers in Arthur's visits besides the risk of assault. Perhaps Eugénie wouldn't have known how to explain, how to tell her that a man with so despotic, so persistent a nature can't enter a girl's life with such authority and menace without consequences. Indeed, the horror Eugénie felt in Arthur's presence couldn't stop her from listening to the young man, who came every day on his mother's behalf, and talked endlessly of love, making her young head spin with all the thoughts of greatness and superiority she'd dreamt of; because he'd made himself her slave to the point that he—a great lord with white hands—had wormed his way into the material concerns of that humble household.

He didn't do it with the good humor of a Frenchman, to whom everything's a game and who reconciles himself to things so cheerfully as to make them trivial; it obviously pained him to do what he was doing: it was steel that bent. Finally that man, at whose feet Thérèse was groveling because she could tell he was getting away from her, groveled in turn before Eugénie's every arrogant whim. "Do you want me to drop Thérèse?" he asked her. "To dismiss her?"

"What do I care?"

So when Thérèse came to Eugénie's that evening, sure she'd find the man who'd pursued her so hard and whom she was now pursuing in turn, Arthur mistreated her—because she couldn't even arouse her rival's jealousy.

But time was passing, and Arthur was making no progress into Eugénie's heart, because while he flattered her pride with his servility, he wounded her by offering her a love that spoke of nothing but love. In a heart as hardened and despotic as Arthur's, that state of things couldn't endure long; sensing his inability to conquer this girl by seduction, he tried threats.

One Sunday—take note of the day, it plays a role in almost all the sins of the Catholic peoples—Arthur came in the evening. As usual, everyone was out, and he'd given Thérèse a rendezvous so far away she wouldn't be able to get back in time to surprise him. He entered Eugénie's room, and there he tried to seize by violence the triumph that had eluded his wicked seduction. She got away from him again, but only after the kind of long, painful, awful struggle that may not cost a girl her honor, but costs her her purity, in which she sees sacred veils torn away, in which she wrests away from some villain's arms the bruised white virgin body whose beauty was known to her eyes alone.

So when Arthur tired of his villainous assault and stood still, panting and furious, before her, Eugénie was standing on her shabby chair—still chaste, but weeping for the flower of her purity, the soft down that envelops the ripe fruit and that a coarse hand can tear off, but without the fruit dropping or being picked. And as she wept, with heavy sobs and copious tears, Thérèse returned: Thérèse, who was jealous, and who'd guessed Arthur had promised too definitely to meet her for him to have kept his word. And now Thérèse, seeing both of them disheveled, had the nerve to blame Eugénie; she accused her of conspiring with Arthur and deceiving her with him. It was too much for the poor girl; she rose and threw them both out, and that night she wrote to Lady Ludney to say she could no longer do work for her.

There's something you don't know, master, and that's how low love can stoop once it has broken the bounds of honor; I'll enlighten you. Thérèse—who was jealous of Eugénie, who knew she'd been dropped because of her, who hated her—Thérèse came back the next day to beg forgiveness for herself and for Arthur. Arthur had asked her to do it, and she'd obeyed. That was the price, he promised her, for him to love her again; and she'd believed him, and had gone to her rival to abase herself and obtain forgiveness for her lover.

Ah, master, you men are cruel tyrants when you hold in your hands a poor girl whose heart or whose head you've driven mad; when, after ruining her in her own mind, you can ruin her before her family and see them throw her out and expose her to contempt. Arthur knew he had that power over Thérèse, and he made use of it. Such profound humiliation filled Eugénie with pity; she herself would've suffered so terribly at sinking so low, that she didn't want to add more to a suffering that seemed so awful to her. She forgave Thérèse for having suspected her, and let her back into her apartment.

Arthur had the effrontery to return in broad daylight, while Jeanne was there; he came on behalf of his mother, who was surprised that the poverty-stricken girl who'd promised to do a job for generous pay now refused to keep her word. Eugénie tried to justify herself, but on hearing of her daughter's decision Jeanne turned white with anger and merely replied, "Never mind, sir, never mind, I'll see to it she finishes the job."

Arthur withdrew, either because he didn't know by what means Jeanne planned to overcome her daughter's resistance, or because the ferocity of his desire didn't balk at the idea of handing her over to her mother's abuse, so that the girl would be delivered to him broken in spirit and in body. But Eugénie had the courage to tell her mother everything, and Jeanne had to agree that her daughter had defended her honor resolutely.

Still, though forced to concede that point, she blamed Eugénie for the insult she'd suffered. "If you didn't put on airs like a great lady," she said, "if you didn't make everybody look at you by dressing as if you were made of money, no one would chase after you. But that's the end of that. I'm going to throw all those muslin dresses and embroidered shawls into the fire, and when people see you're nothing but a poor, honest working girl, they'll treat you with respect. People only look down on those who act like they despise their own condition; and if that young man hadn't looked down on you he wouldn't have treated you that way."

You think there are many hearts strong enough to withstand that kind of interpretation of their misfortunes? You think there aren't times when you'd rather have committed all the sins you're accused of, than be reduced to cursing your own innocence or your virtue—the lowest form of despair? That time was coming for Eugénie. She'd had enough of those crude insults, enough of that abuse, enough of her misunderstood resistance, enough of her hidden tears and her daily torture. She felt she'd reached the point of fulfilling the warning she'd given her mother: "Look out! You'll drive me to do something bad."

In her dread of the despair that might lead her to commit a sin, she preferred committing a crime. That's what I call pride, master! Rather than surrendering feebly to her misfortunes, she preferred ending them along with herself. Maddened, distraught, Eugénie ran to the window and threw herself out... Her mother grabbed her by her long hair, which had come loose in the desperate agitation leading up to that decision; she held onto her and with all her strength she dragged her back into the middle of the room, where Eugénie lay on the tile floor as if dead, with one shoulder dislocated and her head bleeding.

"You see, master: those little shop girls you speak of with such scorn are happy to have your love, and the honor you do them gives them enough joy to last their whole lives!"

"Enough sermons!" said Luizzi. "You're preaching to a man who at least doesn't have anything that bad to blame himself for."

"I'm preaching," replied Satan, "to a man who not too long ago said to me pompously from the height of his rank as a baron, 'Tell me every vile thing about that woman.' Oh, you want to hear vileness? I'll tell you about it."

A few days later, when Jeanne had been forced to leave her sick daughter to go back to work, Arthur returned. It was evening. He was very dressed up, and hatless. He came in quickly. When she saw him Eugénie cried out, and shrank down in her bed as much as she could with her arm in a sling.

"Eugénie!" cried Arthur. "I only heard you were ill an hour ago, and here I am. My mother found out why I brought her here, and she's forbidden me to go out. She ordered the servants to watch me, and threatened to send me back to England if I saw you again. But tonight there's a ball at her house, and I got away. I came without my hat; I came, running the whole way, to beg your forgiveness."

The man who spoke those words was only twenty. You think, at seventeen, you ought to mistrust a boy of twenty who's panting as he speaks, with his voice halting and with tears in his eyes? Eugénie, that poor girl who was all alone, sick in bed, took pity on the suffering of this man who'd left a ball to come see her. She believed in the madness of his love, though she didn't share it, and she replied gently, "All right, I forgive you. But leave me and never come back. You'd kill me."

He promised never to come back, and he came back every evening, during a brief interval when he knew he could elude his mother's surveillance, which to tell the truth was fairly nonchalant, lulled to sleep by his appearance of submitting completely to her will. Meanwhile a doctor—whom luck seemed to have sent Jeanne's way, and who claimed he'd learned of Eugénie's illness from a neighbor, but who had in fact been sent by Arthur—was now treating her. Every night Arthur himself secretly brought the medicines the doctor prescribed. His devotion, his repentance, and his respect touched Eugénie. After a few days she no longer told him never to come back; and after a few more days, when she was beginning to regain hope in life and faith in the sincerity of his affection… that relentless skirt-chaser, who'd promised himself, "She'll be mine," began once again—with a girl who was lying in bed, deprived of her clothes, weak from her injuries—the terrible struggle he'd lost the first time.

I won't describe for you the victim's horror and desperation, nor the attacker's savagery and determination; but when she fell out of bed onto the tile floor, Eugénie, shattered by pain and despair, lost all strength of body and spirit. And it was there on the floor that she closed her eyes and said to herself, "There is no God!" She was mine.

"She was yours?" cried Luizzi. "She was yours because she'd lost her strength, poor girl, because she was the victim of a monster whose fury you'd instilled! Oh, no, Satan, no, she wasn't yours."

"Poor fool," replied the Devil, "you think I'm almost as wicked and stupid as men are! She wasn't mine because some wretch had raped her, but because her pride had to hide a blemish, because she'd fallen so far as to doubt God. Listen carefully, and don't ask me to prove what I'm about to tell you. What I'm about to tell you is the truth; explain it if you can, if your mind can grasp the inflexibility of a nature steeped in pride. Eugénie had fallen as a virgin; she got up as a guilty woman. She didn't love that man, she hated him, and when he said he'd come back she told him, 'Come back, come back, and I'll be your slave, and I'll be yours till you're tired of me. But you won't say you ruined me. To keep your crime a secret, I'll take the blame for it, if you'll spare me the shame.' Ha, ha!" laughed Satan. "As you can see, she was mine."

"Did she escape from you later?"

"You'll see. But what you can see already, master, is that all vices lead to the same end."

Thérèse's weakness and her confused thirst for love had made her Arthur's slave; and Eugénie's pride, and the thirst for distinction that had been her life-long dream, reduced her instantly to the level of the rival she'd scorned. When Arthur threatened to divulge her shame, Eugénie deceived her mother to receive him; when he threatened to say she was his mistress, she went to him in secret, disguised as a man. Thérèse could've done no more. And yet, of all the knowing looks Eugénie dreaded, Thérèse's look would've humiliated her more than any other, and she made Arthur swear he'd given up Thérèse completely and forever.

I have to tell you also that, as strong as he was, Arthur hadn't come out of his struggle with Eugénie unscathed. Though he'd won, the battle had left him with serious wounds. The triple bronze shell of his vanity, his egotism, and his libertinism had been shattered against that heart of steel, and wide cracks had been left open for fear and for love. Arthur was afraid of Eugénie; and the wretch was afraid of her because he hadn't been able to look down on her. He was all the more tyrannical because he felt she was superior to him. He knew he'd only had her body, and he wanted her soul. That's why he was deceiving her. Here's how:

Thérèse had come back to Eugénie's, quieter now and no longer talking about Arthur. Listen carefully, master. I'm about to describe a sordid scene, but it determined the course of Eugénie's life, so you need to hear it in every detail to understand her. One day Thérèse asked her friend to lend her a few clothes, which she needed for the next day. She said she was going to meet a great lady who wanted to help set her up in business, and she needed to look decent. Eugénie gave her the finest things he had.

Don't forget, I'm telling you the story of a working girl; by explaining the refined feelings she had, I might perhaps have made you lose sight of the external realities of this story, since you're not used to understanding a superior spirit if it isn't dressed in a distinguished name and doesn't frequent the highest circles. So I'm coming back to the material poverty of that very poetic life.

As I said, Eugénie lent Thérèse the most beautiful clothes she had. She didn't do it out of indifference or fear; it was out of pity for the poor girl from whom she'd taken, without meaning to, the lover she adored, without even the excuse that she loved that lover. She wanted to help her, as much as she could, to find compensation elsewhere for her despair, and she offered to dress her herself, to make the best impression on the people she was going to meet. But Thérèse refused, and soon after that she left Eugénie, promising to let her know the next day how her visit had gone.

Arthur was supposed to come that next evening; but for quite a while his visits had been noticed, and Jeanne, alerted by the neighbors' gossip, told her daughter that if she ever believed what she'd been told she'd throw her out of the house. If Jeanne had made that threat two weeks earlier, Eugénie would've defied her, and might've forestalled the threat by leaving her mother's house. Then it would've been just another calamity, and an undeserved calamity; but now it would amount to public degradation and righteous punishment, at least in strangers' eyes. She therefore bowed her head without replying, and without her mother taking her obedience as an admission of her guilt.

But the next day, instead of going straight to Madame Gilet's shop, where she'd begun to work again, she wanted to go warn Arthur not to come to her building, where she knew she'd be spied on. She hurried to his house, and got past the concierge by tossing out Lady Ludney's name; but instead of stopping on the second floor she went up to the small suite Arthur occupied on the third floor. His apartment consisted of a small anteroom, a parlor, and a bedroom, one room leading into the next. Oddly, Eugénie found the door onto the stair landing open; she quickly crossed the anteroom and the parlor and came to the door to Arthur's bedroom, which she found locked and bolted.

Hearing the attempt to open it, Arthur called, "Who's there?"

"It's me, Eugénie," she replied, trembling all over, and almost immediately she thought she heard another voice besides Arthur's.

It was seven in the morning, and Eugénie wasn't surprised when Arthur answered through the door, "Give me a minute. I'm getting up, and I'll be right there."

She sat in a corner of the parlor, listening for a repetition of the murmuring she thought she'd heard. She was about to go closer to the door, when she noticed a bit of pink ribbon sticking out from under the folds of a closed curtain. As if the sight had struck her a sudden terrible blow, she rose and walked, pale and trembling, toward that ribbon. She hesitated a moment before touching it, as if she were about to put her hand on a hot iron. Finally she moved the curtain aside, and recognized the bonnet she'd lent Thérèse the day before. She looked around with unspeakable horror and indignation, and under a sofa cushion she found the beautiful shawl she'd lent Thérèse the day before. She kept on looking, and thrown into a corner she found the pretty stockings she'd lent Thérèse the day before. All of the clothes were soiled, all of them had been tossed shamefully across the room, all of them attested to the pandemonium of the moment that girl had stripped off the clothes Eugénie maintained so carefully and chastely.

That shabby detail loomed large for the poor girl; it gave her an eloquent vision of what Thérèse had become—she who'd been such an attractive, elegant, tidy working girl! Horrified, she wondered whether she herself, being in the hands of the same seducer, wouldn't reach the point of tossing aside all sense of restraint, the way those clothes had been thrown. And since a disgust for vice was so strong in Eugénie's nature, that emotion prevailed over the anger and indignation any other woman would've felt in her position.

Arthur entered the parlor while Eugénie still held the bonnet, the stockings, and the shawl in her hands. He noticed and came closer, not sure whether he should head off a violent, shocking scene by threats or by tears. Eugénie didn't give him time to make the wrong choice; she looked at him with cold disdain, and said with the utmost contempt, "Milord, when you're the son of a peer of England, and you have a poor mistress, you don't make her go around begging for clothes so she doesn't have to come to her lover's mansion wearing rags. Tell your mistress, milord, that out of charity I'm giving her what she borrowed from me."

She threw everything she was holding at Arthur, and turned to leave. Meaning to stop her by force, he moved quickly to block the door. But she didn't fight; she just gave him the same contemptuous look once again, and sat down in an armchair.

"Eugénie," he said, drawing closer, "Eugénie, listen to me, and forgive me."

The poor girl looked him straight in the face, and for the first time Arthur's savage, burning eyes dropped before a woman's cold, determined expression.

"Eugénie," he said again, falling to his knees, "won't you listen to me? You're the only one I love, the only one I want to love." As he spoke he took her hands, and tried to take her in his arms.

"Be careful!" she said. "You'll hurt your child."

"Good God!" he cried. "Are you going to be a mother? Oh, Eugénie, if that's true, you can count on me. I'll take the child, I'll raise it, I'll give it my name!"

"That would only be fair, milord; since you know it's yours."

She got up and left. Only then did her tears burst forth, and her weeping broke the dam built by the pride of a humiliated girl, and for a moment she was seized by the self-disgust that leads straight to suicide. But that despair lasted only a moment, because what made her weak also made her strong, and she saw that her death would be too great a victory for the villain who would thus have triumphed over her all the way to the grave. She resolved to live, but she didn't want to live surrounded by all those who could guess at her misfortune and humiliate her for it. Before she'd reached home her decision was made; before she'd seen her mother again, she'd sold her life to be able to leave France.

Chapter XXXVII: Poor Girl Again

In those days, when French fashions were in such high demand, wealthy entrepreneurs looked everywhere for intelligent working girls they could bring to England. When possible they chose young, pretty workers, who could show off by their personal attractions the new clothes the businessmen wanted English-women to adopt. At Madame Gilet's they'd often talked about the wonderful rewards being offered to girls who agreed to go abroad. But the idea of living in a foreign land frightened Parisian families, for whom a journey within France was already extraordinarily bold, and the entrepreneurs had trouble finding workers suitable for their needs.

So when Eugénie came forward she was welcomed eagerly. Her skill was known, and if she didn't secure an arrangement even better than the one she was offered, it was because to her it didn't matter whether her salary was higher or lower, but only that she leave France immediately. She stipulated that the salary she'd been granted be paid directly to her mother, keeping for herself only enough to live on, and reserving the right to return to France if she didn't like England.

Human nature has limited strength, and no matter how hard you try, it eventually tires and gives up. Anyone other than Eugénie would've used theirs up in shouting and weeping and despair; she used hers to carry out her sudden resolve. When she got home she collapsed, exhausted; and it was because of that exhaustion she allowed Arthur's pleas to reach her. He'd written to her. By strange coincidence his letter advised her to do exactly what she'd done.

Leave Paris, he wrote. *Thérèse overheard the terrible confession you made to me, and she's threatening to reveal your condition. Leave for England. I'll supply you with the means. In a few weeks I'll come join you. Don't forget, you told me the child you're carrying in your womb is mine. You owe me that child; you're no longer mistress of your own life: it belongs to me till I possess the treasure that's mine. Between now and when it's born, I hope to obtain a forgiveness I now feel I can't live without. If Arthur who loves you has lost the right to beg you to live, the father of your child almost has the right to demand it.*

That letter, of which I'm quoting you only a part, was given to Eugénie by the friend of Arthur's who'd been with him the day she first saw him at the Tuileries. Eugénie read it from start to finish without saying a word. When Back asked her what answer he should take to Arthur, she thought for a moment, then said calmly and with resignation, "Tell him, sir, that I'll be in England in two weeks, and that if I see him again there, I'll listen—but not to his excuses, for a father needs none toward a mother to convince her of the interest he takes in his child. But tell him also that it's only there, and only in that regard, that I'll ever see him again."

For Eugénie to keep the resolution she'd made not to see Arthur again, he would've had to agree to stop pursuing her. But she was forced to go out every day to make preparations for her departure, and he dogged her footsteps. He made her listen over and over to his promises of repentance. It was no longer the violent young man who spoke, it was the father who understands the full extent of his responsibilities, the decent man who, having strayed for a moment, is determined to atone for his crime.

Eugénie wanted to believe him. She wasn't in love with him, but she'd been his, and he was the father of her child, and she welcomed joyfully the hope that in that capacity at least he deserved her respect. Finally he went far enough in his promises that she felt justified in believing there might come a day when she'd no longer have to blush; and for the first time in her life she allowed herself to say to that man, "No, Arthur, I won't hate you if you're willing to be honorable and good."

Eugénie didn't know where in London she'd live. When she left Paris, the company that had hired her was still negotiating to rent several apartments, among which they had yet to decide; so she had to arrange with Arthur that she'd write to him from London to tell him her address, and to do that he gave her his address. He had clever little ways of making her believe in his devotion. He pretended to be afraid Eugénie would lose that precious address, and—unable to retain words in a foreign language—she wouldn't remember it. So he wrote his address in her passport, and in the bottom of her trunk, and on a handkerchief, and inside a hatbox—on everything Eugénie was taking with her. He had it engraved on a ring, which he forced her to accept.

Eugénie was grateful for such small attentions. The poor girl who was escaping her country without escaping her misfortunes, the child who was leaving her mother with her brow marked by a shame she'd never admitted to, the unfortunate creature who was going among strangers whose manners and language she didn't know, in the company of other strangers from her own country whose character she didn't know, didn't dare reject the hope of finding someone where she was going whom someday she'd have the right to ask for help and support. And that day would surely come: its date was certain.

"I've reported that last sorrow of Eugénie's, and her decision and her hopes and her departure, awfully quickly, master. My account was short, like the time necessary for all those events. But the tale would've lasted too long for the hours you can grant me if I'd tried to describe all the despair that passed through her soul in that short interval. It'd give you vertigo; it'd be like making you stand on the edge of a river in flood and listing everything that was rushing by—trees, rocks, houses, coffins, cradles—all bumping into the banks and tearing them away, and to go on talking about them when they were long downstream and had been replaced by other things. Eugénie's old troubles and her new troubles were as different from each other as the miner's pickaxe, which takes long hours to dig a hole in rock, is from the gunpowder charge he tamps into that hole, and which shatters the rock in an instant."

"Yes," said Luizzi, "I understand the poor girl's misfortunes."

"Poor girl! All right," replied Satan, "keep calling her that, because your language doesn't have a different word to describe her till the time comes when, having called her poor child and poor girl, I'll call her poor woman and poor mother. So listen."

Eugénie had reached England. Just as there are miseries so quick you can't glimpse them in every detail, there are others so deep you can't measure the small sorrows that move at their bottom. So I don't know how to make you understand that, in Eugénie's sad situation, a thousand cruel circumstances still wounded her. I'm not one of those who think the benefit of a great misfortune is not to feel the small irritations. Napoleon on his rock at Saint Helena still suffered from the insolence of an English sergeant who wouldn't salute him, or from some lapse in service at table. That's because all those little events are louder or softer echoes that bounce back your cry of despair and make it ring constantly in your ears.

So Eugénie's journey all alone in a public stagecoach, the coarseness of the English customs inspectors, people's rough curiosity about a traveling Frenchwoman, all of it constantly reminded her, "You've fled France, you've fled your mother, you've fled the life of your childhood, all because on your path you found a villain who pushed you violently onto another path."

Some lives are fatally doomed to crime, others to sorrow. You blame God, without noticing that the whole secret of what you call outrageous unfairness is written on a single page of the holy books you've never understood. The entire human race has misunderstood the Lord's plan in the first man's sin, and the entire human race has been condemned to expiate that original sin; but God didn't choose the victims, God isn't unjust, God only said to all of humanity, "You'll suffer and you'll hope."

But just as there's enough room in your social world for all men, and there's enough work for all men, and enough harvest for all men, and yet there are men who do all the resting and take all the harvest and leave all the work to others; in the same way there's enough sorrow for all and enough joy for all, and here too the rich take all the joy and leave all the sorrow to the poor. The blame for that faulty social division belongs to the political laws you've made; the blame for that faulty human division belongs to the moral laws you've made. God had nothing to do with it, and still Christ's mission had no other goal than to teach you that God would take into account the sorrows of those who'd paid more in suffering than they owed in the great expiation; that's why believers are so strong.

But in the time of sorrow she'd now reached, Eugénie was no longer a believer; or rather she doubted. She stood on the lip of the abyss where I reign, and it would take no more than a nudge to make her fall in. That nudge came. Before I tell you about that great work of evil, I need to describe for you the people among whom Eugénie now found herself.

The wealthy businessman who was trying to establish a firm in London dedicated to French fashion—meaning the trade in everything needed to dress women—was named Legalet. He had a prosperous business in Paris, whose management he'd entrusted to his wife and to his daughter Sylvie; and he was building up the business in London, which was managed by his sister, Madame Bénard. Now that I've stated their names I'll go on with my story, because the hours are passing, master, and the night's going by, and the position you're in is too serious for you not to know everything.

This Madame Bénard was the widow of the orchestra conductor at one of your biggest theaters, and before her marriage she'd had the opportunity to know a great many actors and actresses. No sooner had she reached London than she reconnected with a few of her old acquaintances, and to her house came an odd mix of French merchants established in London and French actresses who happened to find themselves there. Among the latter was one already old in debauchery, next to whom Madame Béru selling her daughter to the association of the dozen was a model of virtue of the highest order. Even her own friends had nicknamed Madame Firet "vice on two legs." She secured her introduction to Madame Bénard by arranging to supply her with the most fashionable actresses in London; she was soon like one of the family.

Just then, meaning early in 1815, a French hat, a French dress, a French shawl, fetched outrageous prices: they represented women's luxury to the highest possible degree. Men looked for their fashions in the same direction, and a French mistress was the peak of fashion for a dandy—racehorses and bellboys were reduced to second place. The girls who got there first had all been snapped up for insane prices, and the fad was such that the rates rose every day. Madame Firet knew all that, and when she heard Madame Bénard had arrived with a party of beautiful girls, she realized it was an opportunity to earn a commission. Madame Bénard hadn't been in London for a month before the most extravagant libertines were quarreling over who'd get the pretty French girls. The betting had begun, and offers came in from all sides. Wanting to protect the most susceptible girls from temptation, and to protect from insult those who'd justifiably have been offended, Madame Bénard, whether from virtue or from the calculation of a good businesswoman, blocked all attempts to enter the parlor in which she kept her seamstresses; only ladies were allowed in. But with the ladies came

Madame Firet, and Madame Firet had sworn to deliver Eugénie to Lord Stive, who'd spotted the pretty French girl one day at the Argyll Rooms.[77]

Don't assume it was the need for entertainment or the love of pleasure that led Eugénie to that theater, which at the time featured French actors under the patronage of the most eminent people in London, and which was open by invitation only. But the craze for French fashions was so strong that a duchess who wouldn't have allowed in a gentleman of doubtful rank used all her credit to extend an invitation to the theater to that businesswoman Madame Bénard, in exchange for a promise to let her have the latest Paris styles forty-eight hours before anyone else. Madame Bénard usually chose to bring along the most elegant of the girls from her shop, and she dressed them with a care that you could say showed off the quality of her own taste. Eugénie, who was young and charming, and whose beauty embellished anything she wore, was always a favorite; and in spite of her resistance Madame Bénard had finally made her come along. That was how Lord Stive had seen Eugénie.

Meanwhile the poor girl had been in London almost two months, and she'd sent to Lord Ludney's several times to find out if his son had arrived, but the answer she always received was that he was still in France. The foolish hope the poor thing clung to therefore faded day by day, and her normal sadness was turning into bleak despondency, when one evening Madame Firet approached her and asked her if she'd ever noticed a second-rate dancer who sometimes came to buy things in the shop. Eugénie said she remembered her. So then Madame Firet told her—with astonishment, because of the dancer's mediocre looks and figure—about the extraordinary good luck that had just befallen the girl. Several great lords, all of them millionaires, had quarreled over her, and in the end she belonged to a lord who gave her horses and servants and a house.

Eugénie, who hadn't paid much attention to the story, replied nonchalantly, "She's very lucky."

The old scoundrel took that casual remark as an expression of envious desire. "Well, you pretty little thing, all that's nothing compared to what I know a certain lord wants to do for a girl he's in love with. First, he's offering her an annuity of thirty thousand pounds all her own and which he can never take back from her; then, for the whole time she stays with him in England, a mansion in London, a villa in the country, two four-horse carriages, diamonds, the retinue of a princess, and in short a fortune beyond anyone's wildest imaginings."

"And who's the lucky girl who's inspired such a grand passion?" asked Eugénie, who was bent over her work, making the pleats of a lamé dress.

"The lucky girl is you, and the man is Lord Stive."

---

[77] The Argyll Rooms were a popular London venue for concerts and other entertainments. They hosted concerts by serious musicians, including Liszt and Mendelssohn, but also comic operettas, vaudeville, and dances put on by a fashionable association called the Pic-Nics.

Before Eugénie had a chance to spurn that vile proposition, the old woman moved away, probably repeating to herself the saying she always used when speaking of her infamous profession: "I've thrown the yeast into the dough; now we've got to give it time to rise." The skillful old corrupter knew you can't accept an offer like that on the spot, and an initial refusal blurted out in a moment of indignation sometimes leads to a later willingness, but one that can no longer be expressed. In a nature like Eugénie's, propositions of that kind don't torment a girl by seduction but torture her with doubts: they make her see where vice comes from and where virtue leads.

In spite of Eugénie's indignation, that thought made its way into her mind; and soon, as the days passed slowly without Arthur returning, a doubt about what was right took hold of her to the point of making her think she was capable of giving way to sin. But for that temptation to take effect, she would need to have no accomplice. Though she might perhaps, in the distress of her wounded pride, have gone to offer herself to a man, Eugénie recoiled at the idea that a woman like Madame Firet could play a part in the wrong she'd be willing to do. So when the old woman returned, Eugénie demanded that she speak no more about it, with a contempt Madame Firet accepted, though she didn't consider it insurmountable.

Meanwhile at Madame Bénard's they noticed Eugénie's sadness: nights spent in tears had hollowed out that beautiful face and spoiled that youthful health. She'd been told they wouldn't object to her returning to France, in spite of how the business would suffer, because all the fine ladies of London had grown fond of the pretty girl who seemed to be neglecting her looks. Eugénie always replied that her problem was only a lassitude brought on by the climate, and she'd soon get over it.

Still, a day came when, unable any longer to stand the doubt that ate at her, she decided to go check on Arthur's absence in person. Giving as her excuse a need to go for a walk for her health, she took along as her guide and interpreter a young Englishwoman who spoke French, and had her lead her to Lord Ludney's. But when the young Englishwoman reached the door of the mansion she refused to go in, and Eugénie entered the house alone. After a fairly long wait she was ushered into a parlor, where she saw a severe-looking old man, next to whom sat a man of about forty who ogled her with more astonishment than impertinence.

She addressed herself to Lord Ludney, who replied in English, "I don't understand French."

"His lordship says he doesn't speak French," said the stranger right away. "I'll translate your question." Turning to Lord Ludney, he repeated Eugénie's question, asking whether Arthur was in England.

The old man spun around and cried in English, "Who is she?"

"He wants to know who you are, miss," said the dandy in a tone that softened the old lord's question.

"I'm French, sir, and my name is Eugénie."

No doubt the old man recognized that name, because he stood up and shouted threats at the poor girl. Though she couldn't tell by his gestures what insults he was offering her, in her fear she retreated toward the stranger, who was trying to calm the old man, and who at least could understand what Eugénie said. She practically threw herself into his arms as she cried, "Oh, I'm innocent, sir, I'm innocent!"

Lord Ludney's fury was rising by the moment.

"Be calm," the stranger told Eugénie. "He thinks you're the one who's kept his son from coming home for three months."

"But I've been here in London for three months."

The stranger translated that for the old lord; and while he was speaking Eugénie thought she heard him mention a name she knew: Thérèse. Lord Ludney gradually calmed down. He looked at her less angrily, and after saying a few words he withdrew from the parlor.

"Lord Ludney has asked me to apologize on his behalf, miss," said the stranger. "Since you're French, he took you for a woman who's kept Arthur in Paris longer than he was permitted to stay. But I disabused him, because I know that woman's name isn't the name you gave."

"Isn't her name Thérèse?" cried Eugénie forcefully.

"Yes, Thérèse. At least that's the name Arthur told me."

"So he's in London?"

"Yes, as of a week ago."

"Where does he live?"

"At number — in Covent Garden."

"Oh, I'm going there," she said desperately. "I'm going there!"

"Would you allow me to escort you there?"

In her mental turmoil Eugénie accepted, without paying attention to the implications of the gesture. Perhaps if outside she'd found the young English-woman who'd accompanied her there, she'd have remembered she had a more suitable guide than a man she didn't know; but that girl, tired of waiting, had left, and Eugénie got into the carriage that was standing there for the great lord. For the whole ride the poor girl, choked by sobs and tears, failed to notice the lecherous pleasure and the anxious curiosity with which her companion watched her.

Finally they reached Arthur's house. The door opened immediately at the rapid knocking that announced an important visitor. The stranger entered, leading Eugénie by the hand. He brushed past the servants, went up to the second floor, and threw open the door of a parlor. Arthur was stretched out on a sofa with his back to the door, reading a newspaper.

"Arthur," said the stranger, "I've brought you someone I met at your father's who was asking for you."

The young man got up without turning around and replied nonchalantly, "It's one of my creditors whom you've taken under your protection, isn't it, milord? You're certainly capable of playing a trick like that on me."

"Arthur, it's me," said Eugénie, stepping forward.

At her voice Arthur turned around. He looked at her carelessly, and smoothed down his hair in a mirror as he replied, "In that case the encounter isn't quite so unpleasant. Well, Miss Eugénie, what do you want from me?"

The poor girl stared at Arthur in such astonishment that it was clear she wasn't completely sure of what she was seeing and hearing.

"Be so good as to hurry up," said Arthur. "I'm expected for lunch somewhere. Come now, what do you want from me, miss?"

"What I want, Arthur, what I want... but... have you forgotten who I am? The child I'm carrying..."

"And who'll probably look like his brother," said Arthur, cleaning his teeth.

"His brother, you said, milord?"

"Yes, a delightful child."

"Ah! Either you're mad or I'm mad. Who are you talking about, what child?..."

"Why, the one who was born on the thirtieth of March, 1814, in the same room where six months later I was base enough to make an attempt on your virtue."

That accusation struck Eugénie a terrible blow, but it gave her back her strength. It seemed to reawaken her reason, which she was about to lose. She understood there'd been slander and a mistake, whereas such awful cruelty would've driven her mad if unmotivated. Enlightened by that very slander, she cried, "Ah, I see where the blame lies. It's Thérèse, Thérèse, who told you..."

"Thérèse, and even better than Thérèse, an eyewitness... Madame Bodin."

Crushed by so much wickedness, Eugénie gave a muffled cry and hid her face in her hands. That gesture of despair could just as well have been prompted by her shame at seeing all her sins exposed, as by her justified horror.

Arthur read it as the reaction of audacity when it sees its mask stripped away. With insulting condescension he went on, "Still, I forgive you, miss. I know that's just how French shop girls have fun, by making those naive Englishmen pay for the peccadilloes of their youth. So you're no more guilty than any other girl, and I want to show I can be generous. If your situation is desperate, I'll help you; my creditors haven't completely ruined me yet."

"Enough, milord. Stop talking... I'm leaving.... Stop talking... I'm going... Stop talking..." Eugénie tried to rise from the chair into which she'd dropped, but no sooner was she on her feet than her strength deserted her and she leaned against the wall to keep from falling onto the carpet.

"Oh," said Arthur, "I know you're a good actress."

Hearing that gave Eugénie back enough strength to get out of the room without collapsing, but she'd barely reached the top of the stairs before it deserted her again, and she fell onto the first step in a faint.

"You're overdoing it, Satan," said Luizzi. "No man is as barbaric as that."

"Have you forgotten he was practically a child, barely twenty-one?"

"And that's why so much cruelty surprises me."

"You're surprised at everything, you people who don't know how to see into the essence of things. You pick up some general ideas that you adopt without examining them carefully, then you walk around with them as if you had truth by your side. Of all those ideas, the most true might be that great generosity is the property of youth. But that idea has its opposite, which is that the most pitiless cruelty also belongs to the young. Stop on a Paris street someday, baron, and read the posted judgments from your courts of assize from beginning to end; you'll see nine tenths of the crimes committed in your society are the work of the very young. That's the inevitable result of all their desires and their strength. Depending which path they take, they can achieve either great deeds or great crimes. Caution restrains middle age, and impotence stops the old. That's what you need to know now, for the rest of this story not to prompt more of the naive surprise you've already displayed."

Then the Devil went on:

When Eugénie awoke from her faint she was in a magnificent apartment she didn't recognize. The stranger who'd taken her to see Arthur had followed her out to catch up with her, had found her collapsed on the stairs, had put her into his carriage, and had brought her to his house. As she regained consciousness Eugénie saw she was being tended by an old woman who gave her smelling salts, and who withdrew immediately at a sign from the stranger.

"Where am I?" asked Eugénie.

"At my house," said the stranger. "With one who won't abandon you like that scoundrel Arthur; with one who believes in your innocence, because he knows what the rival who slandered you is capable of; with one who offers you shelter."

"And—my God!—who arc you?" asked Eugénie, her heart melting at hearing such unaccustomed words.

"I'm Lord Stive, miss," he replied, studying her face carefully to see her reaction.

"Lord Stive!" she cried, sitting up and looking around in terror. "Lord Stive!" she repeated, drawing back.

"Don't be afraid, miss. I can tell by your concern you've been misinformed about who I am, and misinformed about my hopes. I love you, miss—but not the way Arthur did, before abandoning you to your poverty and your misery. I love you, but I want to give you the rank and the eminence you deserve, to rescue you from a life that's unworthy of you, to set you far above the wretched women who slandered you. Because I believe in your innocence, and I can forgive the sin that delivered you into Arthur's hands. I can forget that sin; it's forgotten... my love doesn't want to know about it. What I've learned will change nothing about what my heart has resolved; and if you're willing to listen to me, in a few days—tomorrow—from the heights of your fortune you'll be able to scorn and defy all those who've meant you ill, even that insolent Arthur."

"The temptation was nicely constructed, I think," said Satan, interrupting his story. "The timing couldn't have been improved, and the wording of it couldn't have been better suited to the ears that received it."

"Yes," said Luizzi, "but to me all these encounters seem implausible at the very least."

"That's because the truth is almost always beyond the reach of your intelligence. That's why your men of genius invented plausibility; it's a little cowardice on their part, a little pandering to the common stupidity. Besides, what would be the point in being the Devil if I didn't arrange the events in my narratives a little better than your novelists?"

"So you made use of every trick in your power to get one poor girl to surrender?"

"Yes. And I was beaten."

"Beaten?"

"Yes."

After what Eugénie had just heard, she replied, "Milord, in telling me you believe I'm innocent, you've made it clear what I have to do. I want to believe in the respect you've shown for me—though the proposition you've just made to me proves your respect isn't serious. Still, I want to make you believe in it too, by proving I deserve it."

"Miss," said Lord Stive, "think—don't refuse a man who can consider himself one of the most powerful in England..."

"No, milord, no," Eugénie went on, her voice cold but broken by the heaviness of her heart. "I can't accept... I don't want to accept... I forgive you... I don't hold it against you... I only ask that you allow me to withdraw."

"Not like this, miss, not like this. Such calmness after such violent despair makes me fear it'll lead to something terrible."

"No, milord, no. I'm not going to die. I'm going to be a mother; I'll live."

"That's when she got away from me," cried Satan. "Three time I held out suicide before that woman, and three times she escaped it. But I still had the horror of poverty. I tried that."

Lord Stive, who wanted to understand Eugénie's soul to its very depths, the better to be able to possess it, immediately replied, "Throw yourself on our English law: go before a magistrate and name the father of your child, and he'll be forced to acknowledge it and support both the child and you."

"Oh, milord," said Eugénie, turning away, "we French girls don't know how to display our shame like a legal right. I'd far rather die."

"Still, believe me, Miss Eugénie, don't reject that last resort, don't resign yourself to poverty, because it too leads to death. And if going to a magistrate is so repugnant to you, believe me, it'll be enough to threaten Arthur with it to make him atone for his villainy. Believe me, if I speak to him…"

"If you ever speak to him about me," interrupted Eugénie as she rose, "tell him, milord, the victim will live to bring her torturer's child into the world, the poor woman will work to feed the rich man's child. Tell him there's a name that will never again come out of the mouth he sullied, and the daughter of the people has pronounced before you for the last time the name of the noble Sir Arthur Ludney. Farewell, milord, farewell. We now have nothing more to say to each other."

"She left that house, and got away from me again."

"Ah!" said Luizzi with uncommon delight.

"Yes," went on Satan in a sinister tone, "yes, she got away from me. But I promised myself I'd hand the victim over to the Lord her master so tortured and so wounded it would be hard for him—all-powerful as he is—to heal such injuries. Keep listening, and don't be afraid."

She left that house, and at her first step I grabbed her. I don't disdain small evils; I invented the art of scratching large cuts to make them hurt more. She left that house, but she didn't know where she was going. For a long time she wandered, her body lost on the route she kept asking about and kept being shown, because two steps after being shown the way her head and her memory got lost in the maze of her sorrows. If you really want to understand what she was like then, picture her coming, going, coming back, looking at the houses, stopping passersby, getting no answer but curses, and continuing on her way again, coming, going, and coming back again to the same spot. Now picture that inside she was just the way she was outside, that her thoughts came and went among the sorrows of her life, wandering, stumbling, falling, without quite going mad, and with neither God nor me taking pity on her.

An old man found her in that terrible state and took her home to where she lived, almost dead of sorrow and fatigue. That night a burning fever took hold of her, and it wasn't till a week later she was able to be back among her companions.

That week had been used productively. Lord Stive hadn't given up on making the girl his, and he tried to use despair to get what he couldn't get using corruption. He told Madame Firet Eugénie's secret, and suggested what it would take to make her surrender. I like Madame Firet: she's an intelligent, capable woman. She understood evil instinctively, and she didn't need a long explanation. Once the channel was open the water flowed by itself. Contrary to Lord Stive's rather mundane wish, the old woman wasn't going to tempt Eugénie again by making her ashamed of her condition and showing her how lucky she was to have found such a powerful protector after so shameful a fall; she was cleverer than that. She went to Madame Bénard and told her, with indignation in her eyes and sorrow in her voice, that she, the worthy Madame Bénard, had been shamefully deceived by Eugénie's hypocrisy, and that she'd found out the wretch had only left France to hide a pregnancy.

If Madame Bénard had been the only one to hear the story, the plan might not have worked; but Madame Firet spoke in the kind of voice that pretends to whisper and that penetrates a thin dividing wall. Two minutes later the entire shop knew Eugénie's condition; and for the next several days when she came downstairs she was greeted only with mocking smiles and scornful laughter and jokes whose meaning she trembled to understand—till the moment came when, unable to endure the continual insults any longer, she cried out in a fit of rage as a girl was walking disdainfully away from her, "What is it with all of you? It's like you're afraid to touch me!"

"I'm afraid I'll hurt your baby,"replied the other girl.

That's how what she'd said to Arthur in a moment of despair came back at her. And I should tell you everything, baron, so you can learn about the human soul, which you want to understand. The girl who'd insulted her so cruelly had given birth six months earlier, and had killed the baby, and now she walked away with her head held high, confident that no one knew about her crime.

"You're telling me about monsters!" cried Luizzi.

"No, only about the inevitable result of your society's morals. Since you're without pity for a sin that's exposed, people commit crimes to conceal the sins they don't want to blush at, that's all. If you had justice as precise in your morals as you sometimes have in your laws, if you evaluated sin the way you evaluate crime, if you bothered to consider that there may be extenuation for some moral lapses as there is for some killings, if the human tribunal sometimes absolved those who've sinned the way your courts of assize sometimes absolve those who've killed, perhaps there'd be fewer of those fallen women who are the worst enemies of women who are merely unfortunate, and perhaps there'd be fewer crooks to disgrace an honest debtor and drive him into bankruptcy. People don't become malicious because they feel like it, master; everything in this world has a cause. But you're all too lazy or too stupid to find the root of all your vices and cut it out with a firm hand."

"You might be right. But really, how could Eugénie endure so much sorrow without it killing her?"

"Because the soul is built like the body, and one might die after falling a couple of feet while another can sometimes survive having all of its limbs broken and its flesh torn apart."

In fact, one woman did take pity on Eugénie—or maybe she just wanted to restore peace to her house. Madame Bénard offered to send her back to France; and, so the torment of her lapse wouldn't follow her there, she also offered to give her a recommendation to her brother for a job in Paris, which would provide her with a change of setting in that enormous city, where, as in the smallest village, everything can be hidden and everything is known.

Eugénie had come to England by herself with little hope; she returned to France by herself with no hope at all. She hadn't confessed her pregnancy to her mother before she left, and she couldn't confess it in writing to a woman who wouldn't be able to read the news without broadcasting it everywhere.

"This is a terrible story you're telling me," said Luizzi. "I shudder to think what you're going to say about the welcome Jeanne gave her daughter."

"Well, master," replied Satan, "you're wrong again."

Neither Eugénie's sorrows as a child, nor her sorrows as a delicate girl, nor her unhappiness as a misfit, had managed to pierce the tough bark enclosing Jeanne's heart. But utter misery that was real and intelligible to her moved her to the depths of her bowels. She didn't curse her daughter, she didn't insult her, she pitied her. She helped her hide her pregnancy and hide her labor; because amid all the other miseries I've told you about, I didn't describe the miseries of the perpetual need to hide a condition that grew more visible every day. Eugénie was staking her life on the outcome, and she lost only her health; that woman experienced every possible suffering.

So as to make it completely clear to you, master, what it means to suffer, so as not to leave you thinking you're the most miserable of beings if you have to face misery, I want to paint you a picture that actually won't be the saddest of all those I've painted for you. Eugénie's mother, supported by the money her daughter sent her, had left her old apartment and gone to live in a room whose windows looked out on a small square courtyard. Eugénie shared the only bed in that room with her mother.

She'd arranged to go to a midwife's house for the delivery, but, since it cost six francs a day to stay at that woman's wretched house, she had to put it off till the last minute so her stay there wouldn't be too long and too expensive. They'd already spent a lot of money on baby clothes, and what was left had been budgeted, almost down to the last sou, for the period she'd have to be away from home. To exceed that span of time would be to risk being unable to pay in cash,

387

and to risk having the midwife come to their house loudly demanding her fee for services rendered for the girl's childbirth.

Eugénie kept waiting for the fatal moment. One night at two in the morning she felt the first labor pangs. She had to get up and think about going; she had to dress haphazardly in the dark, because a light in their room at that hour would've revealed, through the windows bare of curtains, the mother and daughter getting ready to go out in the middle of the night. She had to go downstairs quietly, on tiptoe, though her legs almost refused to support her body. She had to hurry past the porter's lodge, though she barely had the strength to walk. She still had far to go, a distance that could've been covered in twenty minutes but that took them four hours, the mother dragging her daughter along and pulling her up from every curbstone she sat down on, unable to go any further.

Finally Eugénie got there, and dropped onto a bed and into the hands of an ignorant woman who let her suffer more pain than even God in his anger promised for woman's childbirth. It was only the next night that she gave birth to Ernestine, whom you know. Five days later she was back home, and two weeks after that she began working at Monsieur Legalet's prosperous shop at the top of the rue Saint Denis.

The Devil stopped, and Luizzi inhaled deeply, like a man who reaches a summit after a hard climb and sits down to catch his breath.

"Onward, master, onward!" cried the Devil. "The hours are passing, it's almost dawn, and we have no time to lose. Onward, if you want to be well informed at the moment when you have to make your life choice!"

"Go ahead."

"The poor girl…"

"Again?"

"Still a poor girl, master. The poor wife and the poor mother are yet to come. Listen and you'll see."

Chapter XXXVIII: Poor Girl Still

Eugénie had gotten away from me, as I said. But though she'd withstood a quick tug, I didn't lose hope of seeing her give in. I had too much experience not to know that someone who holds out against a violent shock can sometimes fall at the gentlest touch. The art lies in choosing the right occasion: sometimes when you've shaken the body hard and it's staggering, other times when you give it a sudden unexpected shove. Eugénie had been so constantly miserable that she was always on her guard; and since she was strong she'd always stayed upright. So I wanted to give her security, and for the first year of her time at Monsieur Legalet's she lived as happily as possible: she rested after her sorrows. She was well paid for a girl her age and with her job, and she made it possible for her mother to live in a small village outside Paris, where she'd placed her baby with a wet nurse. Every two weeks she went to spend her Sunday off with her mother and her child.

The only torment she had to endure came again from Arthur; he ran into her one day and followed her. But the time had passed for pleading or threatening. He tried to stop her, and she said loudly enough for passersby to notice, "What do you want with me, sir? I don't know you."

"I want my child, my son!" said Arthur, pale with rage and humiliation.

"What's the child's name?"

"Be careful, Eugénie!"

"Be careful yourself!" she replied scornfully. "There are gendarmes around to arrest drunks who insult women."

Arthur—that merciless villain Arthur—was beaten; the insult was a slap he could do nothing about; and before he'd recovered from his mute fury Eugénie had vanished into the crowd. That encounter took place soon after she'd returned to France, and—thanks to me—no other disturbed the peace in which she slumbered.

At the end of that year a young man named Alfred Peyrol arrived in Paris from the provinces. He'd come to finish his business training at a Paris banking house, and his father had given him an introduction to Monsieur Legalet. He was welcomed at the merchant's house as the son of an old friend. He pleased Madame Legalet, and he pleased her daughter Sylvie even more. He was young, cheerful, passionate, and a witty storyteller, with the touch of originality that comes from the informality of provincial manners. He was extremely funny when he described how Paris astonished him. He was so sincere about what he admired, and he admired such odd things, that he provoked laughter, but not ridicule—because rarely has a person been more gifted at detecting ridicule in others and more anxious to avoid being the butt of it. Apart from that, he was bold, resolute, capable, and patient, and he could've gone far if he hadn't had such a puerile fear of what people thought; there was a constant war between his nature and his education.

Eugénie hadn't noticed the attention he paid her, but she was made aware of it in an unusual way. Mademoiselle Sylvie had fallen for the handsome young provincial who spent almost every evening in the workroom where a dozen girls were gathered. Though he was already twenty-four, he was much younger at heart and in mind; and the retired life he'd grown up in with his family had sent him out into the world with a character well formed for business but a mind quite ignorant of the most mundane things. All that made him a likable young man.

One evening Sylvie, who'd stayed alone with Eugénie to finish an urgent job, approached her and said quietly, though everyone else had gone to bed, "Have you noticed Monsieur Alfred is courting me?"

"No, I really haven't," said Eugénie, who'd glanced at Alfred no more than once or twice since he'd started coming to Madame Legalet's.

"You really think he doesn't fancy me?" asked Sylvie in alarm.

"I'm not saying that, just that I haven't noticed anything. It's my own fault: I'm so absent-minded!"

"Well then, Eugénie, pay attention, please."

"Why?"

"Because… because I'd like to know… whether I'm mistaken."

"Why does it matter to you?"

"Because I'm in love with him," said Sylvia, lowering her eyes.

Eugénie looked at her. For her, love was a word she'd often heard spoken, but which had a terrible meaning. It evoked on the one hand all of her own suffering, and on the other the turmoil of Thérèse's life. But as she observed Sylvie's open, charming face, she thought she saw another kind of love, one she didn't know and that felt sweet to the heart. She replied slowly, "Ah! You love him?"

"Yes, I love him. When I see him come in, I have what I've been waiting for all day. When he speaks to me, I don't hear his voice the way I do anyone else's, I feel like it touches me as if he were touching me with his hand. I hear him everywhere. When he compliments me, oh, I'm so happy! So happy I could cry! When he laughs at me, I'm so sad, sad enough to cry as well."

"Oh, he must love you for loving him like that!"

"But he doesn't know. We don't say those things to each other."

"And he's never said anything to you?"

"Would he dare? Louis, who married my sister, was in love with her for two years without saying anything to her, till my father was forced to tell my sister himself."

What a different life that was from the one Eugénie had known! What a different kind of love from the one she'd heard about! What fresh, entirely new shade for a heart that had crossed such terrible chasms, and that no longer ran into a thousand sharp obstacles only because it was walking through a desert! Tears came to Eugénie's eyes, but she held them back, because she couldn't have explained her secret to the girl who had so innocently shared her own.

Curious to see someone going down the beautiful path she herself could no longer take, Eugénie promised Sylvie to find out whether Alfred loved her. The next day she paid attention to the young man. She noticed he acted toward Sylvie the same way he did toward all the other girls, and that if he singled out anyone for particular attention it was Eugénie herself. But she didn't linger on that observation, which wasn't even a thought.

That night Sylvie came to Eugénie. "Well then!" she said. "He loves me, doesn't he? He thought my hat was ravishing."

"Yes, of course," said Eugénie, who was worried the naive girl would commit herself recklessly. "Yes, he said that. But he said it to me too."

"He had to, so it wouldn't be too noticeable. And then, the way he picked up my embroidery when I dropped it! The way he admired it! The way he held it in his hands a long time, to touch what I'd touched! And the way he looked at me when he gave it back! Why, the embroidery almost burned me when I took it!"

"It's true... it's true," said Eugénie, bowing her head and looking away sadly.

"What are you thinking about?"

"Nothing, nothing." Then Eugénie went on, "But I don't want to mislead you and let you love him if he's not going to love you, because it must be awful to be rejected."

"What is it?"

"Didn't you notice when one of the girls dropped her handkerchief and he picked that up too, and held onto it for a long time?"

"Yes, yes, but it was yours. And he crumpled it while tying and retying it, and turned it into a veil that he put over his face. But then he was just playing, he was laughing and funny; that's different."

The day before, Eugénie had learned what love could be like in the heart of a child. Now she discovered the naive blindness that always accompanies that passion. Afraid of wounding that delicate soul by ripping away its delusion, she waited, not daring to tell her the truth. Besides, might not she herself be wrong? Wasn't it possible she no longer had the capacity to understand innocent things?

The days passed in that fashion; and Eugénie, constantly studying Alfred's smallest actions, was almost forced to acknowledge that it was toward her he directed the attentions, the words with a double meaning, the moments of joy, the flashes of sadness, by which love expresses itself when it can't yet be spoken aloud. Sylvie still saw nothing, or rather she saw only what flattered her own hopes; and in confiding to Eugénie every night the faint signs she read as hints of Alfred's love, she taught her rival that the much clearer signs she alone saw were those of genuine love. Eugénie pitied the child, and blamed herself for being loved, as if she'd betrayed her.

Still bruised by the brutal attacks she'd recently escaped, Eugénie wanted to avoid anything that might bring turmoil back into her life. She tried to put obstacles between herself and Alfred that would be hard for him to overcome. Using the excuse that her seat at work was too far away from the lamp that burned by Madame Legalet, she moved into that corner, behind a long row of her young companions. But all that did was give Alfred a chance to show her he'd seek her out everywhere and find a way to approach her everywhere. He stole one girl's work from her, he had another girl called away, he bothered another girl; and gradually chair by chair he got next to Madame Legalet and Eugénie—to whom he could say nothing and dared say nothing, but whose air he breathed.

Madame Legalet laughed a lot over the young man's silliness, and she jokingly called him the tyrant of the workshop. The next day Sylvie wanted to sit in that corner with her mother; and since Alfred sat there again she imagined he'd come there for her—because she'd followed him. Another evening, when Eugénie had put a black ribbon around her neck, he declared black ribbons were a delightful accessory; and afterwards Sylvie said to Eugénie, "You see, he wants me to wear a black ribbon, because he thinks a black ribbon would look good on me too." The next evening she put on a black ribbon, and Eugénie took hers off, and Alfred said unhappily to Sylvie—quietly, but so Eugénie could still hear— and while looking reproachfully at Eugénie, "You're nice and friendly. You're not afraid of wearing something that pleases me." Later, in private, Sylvie said to Eugénie, "You saw how he thanked me for wearing a black ribbon! Oh, he certainly loves me."

Eugénie's heart echoed the words, "He loves me." What a strange spectacle it was: the naive and ignorant girl drawing her rival's attention to all the compliments being paid to her, and thereby alerting her to the love she was being shown—without which she might not have understood it. Eugénie's displeasure at being forced to be Sylvie's confidante, and the cold manner in which she received her secrets, did nothing to silence a girl so much in love. No matter what she tried, Eugénie had to listen to her endless chatter. One day she told Sylvie her mother might hold it against Eugénie if she found out the girl had been encouraging an attachment she disapproved of, and Sylvie replied right away, "Oh, my mother knows, and she doesn't mind. Alfred is such a decent young man, so respectful, so well brought up! My mother told me that herself, and he'll certainly be accepted the day he asks to marry me."

The child's words were a blow to Eugénie; the word "marriage" was painful to her. Could she, a poor fallen woman, ever get married? And, assuming Alfred's love was as sincere as she thought, based on what she'd been told about true love, shouldn't she renounce it? You see how ingenious passion is at finding its way into the heart! As soon as Eugénie imagined that someone found her worthy of loving, she suffered at the idea that she wasn't worthy; and having been afraid to let Alfred's love for her grow, now she was afraid of losing it.

So now she began to doubt herself, and she wanted to know whether she too, like Sylvie, was caught up in some mad blindness; and now she avoided Alfred, no longer to escape him but to test him. He pursued her with the same skill and the same perseverance. He managed to get close to her by means I can't even describe. Eugénie anxiously observed all of his little maneuvers, and when he'd succeeded, and she could no longer doubt he was happy to be near her, she was happy to be near him. She was grateful to him for loving her in spite of her past—as if he'd known it—and sometimes she fell asleep dreaming of happiness, because she too was in love.

But she wasn't aware of that, till one day, when she returned from seeing her daughter in the country, she learned that Madame Legalet had hired a new worker. The next day, when she saw the new girl, she was terrified: it was Thérèse. She greeted Eugénie brazenly as a friend. But Eugénie couldn't suppress her indignation; after replying coldly to all of Thérèse's advances, she moved far away from her and avoided speaking to her.

Life moves fast in certain circumstances: Eugénie spent the whole day consumed by the fear that Thérèse would give away her secret. But that fear hadn't affected her as much as you might think. The serenity of her nature gave her strength, the testimony of her conscience supported her, and she told herself that as a desperate last resort she could quit that job and find another refuge. But when evening came and Alfred showed up, the fear Thérèse inspired in Eugénie, and that she'd thought she was strong enough to conquer, completely overwhelmed her. Her first impulse in that fear was to conceal Alfred's love for her and to increase her precautions against him. Clearly she enjoyed his love for her, since she was trying to protect it from exposure.

But before the evening was over she knew Thérèse had guessed it; and she felt she wouldn't have the strength to withstand Alfred's contempt the way she withstood other people's contempt; and for a moment proud Eugénie thought of begging Thérèse for pity—Thérèse, who'd caused her fall! She spent the whole evening with her eyes on her work, and filled with tears, and when she got up to go home Thérèse approached her and said, with the base sarcasm of vice, "Your new lover's sweet. But he seems a little naive. He's a good sucker to catch."

Eugénie was too disgusted by the vileness of her words to have the strength to reply, and she turned away in revulsion. Thérèse got revenge for the contempt she deserved by turning it back on the one who didn't deserve it. In a few days that worldly-wise girl knew about Eugénie's love, and also about Sylvie's. So she approached Sylvie and invited the same confidences Eugénie had been fending off for so long. Once she was sure of Sylvie's misconception, she tore it away, pitilessly breaking the girl's young heart, so that in her despair Sylvie would break Eugénie's heart just as pitilessly.

"Oh, that's impossible!" said Sylvie when Thérèse told her Eugénie was in love with Alfred. "I told her everything, I confided everything in my heart to her, and she was deceiving me! She was laughing at me—I'm sure of it! There's never been such cruelty and such treachery! I'll tell my mother everything."

"And that's the right thing to do," said Thérèse, skillfully managing the tools of her revenge.

Sylvie ran to tell her mother about her great betrayal. Madame Legalet was even more indignant than her daughter, because she felt she had a right to blame Eugénie even more than Sylvie did. The next day she summoned Eugénie, and before entering into explanations with her she handed her a letter: the letter in which Madame Bénard had recommended Eugénie to her sister-in-law. That letter revealed all of the poor girl's secrets. Eugénie hung her head as she read it, then handed it back to her employer.

"As you can see, miss," said Madame Legalet, "I knew everything, and yet I never said a word, I never said anything that would've humiliated you in front of the other girls, I even spared you the pain of making you blush before me. And you've repaid me by using your flirtatious charms to entice a young man I intend for my daughter, a young man she loves, the poor child, with an innocent love, whereas yours is base vile calculation."

So, having slandered Eugénie's life, now she slandered her love. Eugénie felt tears coming, but she composed herself and replied, "No, ma'am, no: I did nothing to attract Monsieur Alfred, and I'm not in love with him."

"Well then, miss, since he's the only one who needs to be cured, I'll tell him who you are and what you are."

"Oh, ma'am!" cried Eugénie, falling to her knees. "I'll leave your shop, I'll go away. But don't tell him anything, don't shame me in his eyes. Why would you need to do me harm if I'm no longer here?"

Madame Legalet thought for a moment, then replied, "Yes, I know you've been more victim than sinner. But don't become one now by stealing the love of a decent man. Stay away from him, make it clear to him he has no hope. A girl can always find a way when she wants to, and you'll find one if you want to. On that condition, I won't fire you. On that condition, I'll promise to keep your secret."

"Finally," said Luizzi, "a good woman."

"Bah!" said the Devil. "If you were willing to examine her leniency carefully, you might find it involved a little vile calculation."

"Again?" cried the baron.

"Yes. Madame Legalet might've realized that if Eugénie left her shop, Alfred might well not come back, and then farewell to all of her pretty plans to set her daughter up with a young man with an income of a good twelve thousand livres of his own and whose father was rich!"

"You're a cruel commentator, Satan."

"No, but I'm the spirit of contradiction in devilish form, and I almost always find what you scorn as stupid as what you admire."

"Time's passing, and…"

The Devil resumed:

Eugénie accepted Madame Legalet's deal, and even more: she accepted the long evenings spent in Alfred's company while a watchful eye observed her, and she had to rebuff sharply the advances everyone could now see. She was teased when she'd managed to make Alfred angry enough to go address to another girl the words that led Eugénie to think the love that had made her so happy wasn't strong enough to withstand the slightest check. She was insulted when she hadn't exhausted his pursuit, because then she was told she hadn't tried hard enough. She was always threatened with having her secret revealed. And she endured all that because she was in love: and love conquers even the strongest nature, love forces even the most refined nature to drink the bitterest repugnance down to the dregs. It's like with hunger and thirst, master: when a man is in the grip of those two needs, whether he's lived on black bread or on fine fare, he'll drink and eat greedily what would've turned his stomach before.

Alfred's presence and the sound of his voice were the food Eugénie lived on, and she didn't have the strength to do without that nourishment, no matter what vile filth was stirred into it. I should also tell you, so you can understand the full extent of her love, that Eugénie's secret, as a flail with which to thrash her, hadn't remained in Madame Legalet's hands alone: Thérèse, impudent Thérèse, had let it slip among all the girls in the shop, and the insults and torments Eugénie had known in London began again—but more pointed, more intense, because now they were aimed at a heart in which they wounded both pride and love.

Alfred, meanwhile, had understood that such a sudden change in Eugénie's behavior and in the attitude of her fellow workers must have some cause. He reasoned correctly that they'd discovered his love, and he could deduce what Madame Legalet's plans were. One evening, determined to let no one have false hopes, and to give strength to the girl who was presumably being tormented because of him, he announced, seemingly to no one in particular, that he expected to get married, because a week earlier he'd turned twenty-five. He announced also that he didn't care about marrying a fortune, because if he didn't find one ready-made he was capable of building one on his own. He added that no intrigues would keep him from marrying the wife he chose and loved, whether she was of the lowest class, or poor, or a servant.

Madame Legalet understood at whom a speech like that was directed, and she was all ready to tell Alfred not to set foot in her shop again; but she wanted revenge for the shattering of her hopes. No sooner had he finished speaking than she replied, "Noble sentiments, sir! But I assume that in addition to the other qualities you're looking for in a wife, you'd also want her to be a respectable girl."

At those words Alfred stood up, and so did Eugénie. Alfred looked at her and Eugénie looked at him. The expression on her face made him turn pale: there was an eternal farewell in her eyes. She put her work down on the table and left—so as not to collapse, broken by despair and shame, before the man she loved. She ran from the shop, which was on the ground floor, all the way up to the sixth floor of the building. I had a great opportunity, master; the window was tall and open, and Eugénie was racing—panting, furious, out of her mind— toward her suicide: a few more steps and she was mine. Alfred had followed her. Forgetting all the proprieties, breaking the constraints—so weak, but so strong for him—that you call respectability, he'd chased after Eugénie, and he caught up with her just as she was about to cross the threshold of her apartment. He stopped her.

"You understood me," he said. "I love you. I know you're poor, I know you live by the work of your hands, but I love you still more for that. Don't be afraid of anyone; I'll give you my name, I'll make you rich, and then I swear no one'll dare insult you or slander you."

Eugénie looked at the honorable young man who knelt before her and pressed her hands lovingly between his. "Do you love me?" she asked. "Well, I love you too, and I'll prove it by showing you I don't want to deceive you."

She opened a drawer, took out a letter, and handed it to him. The letter consisted of only two lines:

Miss, be sure to come Sunday. Your daughter is a little sick, and your mother accuses me of not taking good care of your child.

When Alfred had read the letter, he remained unmoving before Eugénie. She watched him, because her life or her death depended on what came out of Monsieur Peyrol's mouth. She could see his face was troubled, his hands shook, his wandering eyes avoided her. Finally, feeling that he was losing his mind amid the clash of such disparate ideas, Alfred replied, "Tomorrow— tomorrow—I'll give you an answer."

With those words he fled, not waiting to hear anything, and Eugénie was left alone.

"Listen, master, I want to make you feel what a day of waiting like that is like, what that uncertainty feels like. Here's what I want to tell you: you might not be as ruined as you think…"

"Good God!" cried Luizzi.

"Or maybe you're more ruined than you think. Anyway, you'll know by tomorrow night."

"Is that true?" cried Luizzi; and immediately, instead of listening to the Devil, he began to pace around the room, uttering the wildest and most desperate exclamations. "Oh, if only that were possible! But no, you're tricking me,

396

you're teasing me, you're giving me hope so you can make my destitution even more awful. I'd accepted the burden of misery, and you must've thought I was showing too much courage, and you want to double the burden by causing a relapse... Still, you wanted to tell me... And why wait till tomorrow?... Satan, speak to me, don't leave me in uncertainty more awful than my ruin!"

The Devil looked at him scornfully. "Eugénie was more dignified and stronger than you. She didn't cry out convulsively, she didn't pace about like a madwoman, knocking over the furniture and shouting loudly enough to wake the whole house; and yet what she stood to lose was more than a fortune, it was her heart's last and greatest hope."

"And she won it, since she became Madame Peyrol!"

"Yes. The next day Alfred wrote to her, in just these words: *Will you be my wife?*"

"So then she was happy?" asked Luizzi, no longer listening. "She was rich, she was loved, she had a family and friends, and that sad story ended happily. She didn't need as much pity as I thought."

"Then began the next chapter of her story: *Poor Wife!*"

Chapter XXXIX: Poor Wife

"I assume," said Luizzi, "this'll be a chapter that's so commonplace: a husband who's in love for a few months, then abandons his wife, then resents her for everything he did for her and exposes her to scorn and loneliness..."

"No, master," said the Devil, "that isn't it. This chapter, if you could listen to it, would take a lot longer than all those that came before it. But in fact you're unable to listen to me anymore. Now that you have some hope personally, egotism has entered your heart along with it. You're like the world into which Eugénie was thrown: you're afraid thinking about her is a waste of your time, because she's no longer the last chance of rescue you have left."

"You're wrong, Satan. I'll listen to you, but dawn is coming, so hurry up."

"Fine. I'll tell it to suit the way you're listening: without lingering over details, without demanding a level of attention you're no longer capable of. Now, here's why Eugénie was a poor wife..."

It was because she entered society with a living testimony to her fall; because she had a husband who loved her enough to believe she was innocent, but who wasn't strong enough to make her accepted as innocent; because, for her, ordinary actions lost their everyday meaning when those actions had no personal meaning.

At first Monsieur Peyrol took his wife to his home in the country; but he'd married her against his family's wishes, though with his father's consent. His father received his daughter-in-law, and defended her almost as much as her husband did; but some things can't be defended against, like the icy reception she got from her sisters-in-law and brothers-in-law, like the insolence of some kinds of politeness and some kinds of oversights, like the cold formal "ma'am" always used in addressing Eugénie by people who only used first names with each other, like the malicious skill that—though unable to drive her out of a parlor—found ways to exclude her from the family, like the thousand little things that hurt her without her being able to complain about them. It was, when she went out walking, a bow that wasn't returned—something Eugénie couldn't dismiss as an inadvertent lapse, the way any other woman could. It was a visit declined, its refusal made even more glaring by the perpetrator passing under Madame Peyrol's windows a dozen times before coming in to visit someone else in her new family.

It was especially that child, to whom Monsieur Peyrol had been unable to give his name, and about whom people were always asking for an explanation, though they knew perfectly well who she was and what she was. If Eugénie happened to bring her into a salon or along on a walk, people immediately fastened on the child to say, "Oh, what a pretty little girl! Who's your mommy?"

"Madame Peyrol."

"And your daddy?"

"I don't know him."

"Poor little thing! She's so pretty! It's too bad she doesn't have a daddy!"

They said that to Eugénie's face; so she sent Ernestine out with a maid—and they said it even more cruelly behind Eugénie's back, and the child came home and innocently repeated everything to her mother, who then kept her from going out at all. That provided a new cause for tears, because the little girl, who could see other children playing, asked in tears—which provoked her mother's tears—why she couldn't play with children her own age. To compensate her for what she couldn't have, her every whim was indulged, and as a result Ernestine soon became the most willful, tyrannical, difficult child.

Monsieur Peyrol was completely devoted to Eugénie, and persisted in the struggle against his family—persisted to the point of falling out with his brothers and sisters. He saw his father only in secret and when he knew he was alone. In fact his father's courage had finally yielded: threatened with either the loss of all of his other children, who'd done nothing wrong, or the loss of Alfred, he'd taken sides against the one son whom in his heart he valued the most. For he was a worthy old man! But to reach that point there'd been a thousand awful little scenes: at table, where everyone got served except Eugénie; at cards, where no one would be her partner; at a ball, where no one asked her to dance—if she'd been invited to come, which wasn't always; it was the same, everywhere and always, till they just left her alone in her room. Alfred followed his wife into the isolation imposed on her, and Eugénie knew one final sorrow: that of seeing she'd cost the happiness of the man who'd devoted himself to her own happiness.

What I'm telling you here in a few words lasted for years; it lasted till the moment Alfred grew tired of fighting against all the petty provincial hatreds that couldn't be appeased either by Eugénie's exemplary conduct or by the respect in which her husband held her. To tell the truth, it wasn't a matter of terrible calamities; it was the torture for which you've found such a good image—death by a thousand cuts. So Alfred decided to go back to Paris. For a short while he was able to lose himself in that immense city, by concealing who Ernestine was and calling her his daughter. Thanks to that lie he got a few days of respite. He was beginning to regain hope, when he was killed, eighteen months ago, coming home from Le Havre, in a steam engine boiler explosion.

So the miseries of their false position were followed by the miseries of ruin. You know about them, and they almost drove you mad, though you're a man, and you have no one to support but yourself; whereas Eugénie was left with a child accustomed to luxury, a child who blamed her for her poverty, who…

"This is the beginning of the chapter called *Poor Mother*, isn't it?" said Luizzi. "Hurry up, I'm listening."

"No, it's morning, and you'll see for yourself."

Chapter XL: Poor Mother, etc.

The Devil had vanished, and when Luizzi opened the shutters and the windows he saw the day wasn't as far advanced as he'd thought. The first thing he noticed was the correspondence that had brought him the news of his ruin; he reread it. The hope the Devil had given him, and that had disoriented him for a moment, was erased by that second reading. He knew too well the Devil had only offered him a way out to lure him into some trap. Besides, hadn't the Devil said, "You might not be ruined, or you might be even more ruined than you think"? He therefore resolved to act as if his ruin were certain. Anyway, he hadn't listened to the Devil's story in vain: Eugénie seemed like the wife he'd dreamt of. All the unpleasantness arising from her situation would no longer threaten her, once Ernestine was married and bore a name behind which no one would go looking for the name they must assume she'd had.

Luizzi headed downstairs to the parlor, determined to accept Madame Peyrol's offer and to add his name as the fifth man on the suitors' contract. But he was surprised to find that the feeling of good cheer, instead of growing and rising to a splendid climax, had dropped noticeably. He was filled with an odd fear: had the story, which he'd thought had lasted only part of the night, been stretched out by the Devil to the end of the decisive day? He was sure of it when he passed through the dining room, where the table was only half cleared, as if after dinner. Caught off guard by this new trick of the Devil's, Luizzi ran toward the parlor and burst like a madman into a large circle of people silently arranged around a long table. His entrance and the astonishment on his face gave them a start; they all looked at him pityingly.

Monsieur Rigot came to him and said, loudly enough for everyone to hear, "Ah, baron, here you are! I've heard the bad news you received, and I forbade anyone to disturb you in your room. Damn! When you're ruined in one stroke, from top to bottom, it's got to affect you, especially you great lords, who aren't accustomed to poverty like we peasants are. But I thank you for having pulled yourself together enough to join our family gathering."

Luizzi, partly recovered from his shock, stammered a few words and glanced at Eugénie, who was sitting humbly in a corner. He could see she'd been crying all day. She returned his look, and he bowed to her with a respect he hadn't shown her when she came to his room, but which he now tried to make clear as he went toward her. Among the persons present was one Luizzi hadn't seen before: Rigot's own lawyer, who was considering him with a very particular look through his glasses. It seemed to Luizzi that he knew that man: the look on his face, more than his features, had already made an impression on him, and he was about to search his memory for where and when he'd met him, when the clock rang seven.

"The time has come!" cried Rigot. "The proceedings are about to begin. First, let's put the names of the three ladies into a hat; we'll draw them out one at a time to determine who'll choose first. The baron can render us that service, since he isn't one of the contestants."

"I didn't say that," mumbled Luizzi, driven by his fear of the poverty that awaited him, and yet held back by some residue of integrity.

"Ha, ha!" laughed Monsieur Rigot. "I see the night has brought good counsel, baron. I'm delighted."

Luizzi bowed his head at that insult, submitting in a way he'd found cowardly when the insult was aimed at others. Then he heard Rigot's lawyer give a dry, harsh little laugh; and it seemed to him he'd already heard that malicious cackle, but he couldn't recall the circumstances. The harsh little laugh rose over the discontented murmur that broke out among the rivals and finally burst into rude remarks.

"Ha, ha!" laughed the attorney, Monsieur Bador. "The night brought good counsel, and bankruptcy too!"

"Yes," said the Paris lawyer's clerk, Monsieur Marcoine. "I'm sure, if he had time, it wouldn't just be a marriage contract the gentleman would like to sign."

"The baron's decision," added the peer of France, Count Lémée, "does him the more honor the later it comes: it's only in the face of danger that great courage shows itself."

"I wish it took any courage to tell you you're a smug popinjay," replied Luizzi, "so you'd be convinced of that courage."

"I'll seek that proof whenever you please."

"Right now, sir."

And they were about to step outside when Monsieur Rigot cried, "Anyone who leaves this room to go fight a duel will be banned from the contest!"

It must be said, for the baron's honor, that it was Count Lémée who sat down first.

Monsieur Rigot went on, "And the first one who makes any threats will also be banned."

"I didn't say a word," said Monsieur Furnichon, the handsome stockbroker's clerk.

Absolute silence followed that little incident, and Monsieur Rigot continued, "Sister, niece, grandniece, here are five handsome fellows, all of them suitable, and of all ages. Take care to make your choice on that basis: compatibility of age is the foundation of happiness. Let's review: Count Lémée is twenty-five..."

"You mean thirty," said the little man, with a glance at Madame Peyrol.

"Fine," said Monsieur Rigot. "Monsieur Bador is a little older, isn't he?"

"Twenty-nine!" said the attorney, drawing himself up before Ernestine.

"Monsieur Marcoine is…"

"I don't know how old I am," said the lawyer's clerk.

"And Monsieur Furnichon?"

"I'm whatever age you like."

"As for the baron, he's thirty-two, that I know. So we can get started. But since the baron is now one of the contestants, he can no longer help us by drawing the names. It'll be that clown Akabila who serves as lottery boy. Come on, move it, rascal, or I'll make the skin off your backside into bedroom slippers!"

And before poor Akabila had understood what was wanted of him, he was reprimanded by Monsieur Rigot's foot, as if it were seeking information on its future slipper. When the king's son understood, he put his hand into the hat and drew out a name. It was Ernestine's. Monsieur Bador, who was near her, let out a sigh that was echoed in unison by Monsieur Marcoine and Monsieur Furnichon. Akabila put his hand into the hat again, and this time Rigot's lawyer read out Eugénie's name. Now it was Count Lémée's turn to sigh deeply, echoed once again by the two clerks.

Only Madame Turniquel's name remained; she made an ugly face and said, "After the others, if there are any left! What a treat!"

"There'll be some left, you can be sure of that," said Monsieur Bador with a satisfied air.

"Some good-looking ones!" said Monsieur Furnichon.

"And some good ones!" said Monsieur Marcoine.

"And some noble ones!" said Count Lémée.

Luizzi said nothing.

"And some who're in love!" cried a voice from the parlor door. It was Little Pierre, who came in with his boots still on, saying, "I'm looking for you, baron. I've come on behalf of a gentleman from Paris, who told me you should go see him right away or he'd come here."

"Just a moment," said Rigot's lawyer. "We can't proceed like this. If this gentleman leaves, I insist he be excluded."

Luizzi paused, torn between the hope the Devil had given him and the threat he'd made. He asked Little Pierre, "Who was the man?"

"A tall, thin, dark type, with a briefcase under his arm and two couriers following him. He looked to me like a legal man."

"A bailiff?" cried Luizzi.

"Could be," replied Little Pierre, "because he asked for the address of the justice of the peace, and I left him scribbling on stamped papers."

"It seems the baron has some letters of credit to discharge?" asked Rigot's lawyer.

"If I have any, I'll pay them," said Luizzi disdainfully.

"With what?" asked the peer of France.

That made Luizzi turn pale. Rigot's lawyer, after laughing again with his little cackle, went on, "Are we finishing this or not?"

"Quite right," said Monsieur Rigot. "Those who aren't interested should leave."

Luizzi was ready to go. He felt clearly that he was shaming himself in the eyes of the woman who'd spoken to him so contemptuously about the men who were chasing after her for a chance at a dowry. But at the same time he remembered he'd accepted letters of credit adding up to a considerable total, in a reckoning with his banker, and that he'd endorsed them. To the fear of poverty was now added the fear of prison; and—since nature hadn't allotted the baron a sufficient dose of determination and good sense to guide him through difficult moments—he stayed.

Little Pierre settled into a corner, and Mademoiselle Ernestine was called upon to announce the choice she'd made. We won't attempt to depict the faces of those assembled, because situations like the one we're describing occur so rarely in human life; but if you can imagine a gathering of heirs on the day the will is read, who act indifferent while biting their lips to keep them from trembling, whose mouths gape and whose eyes bulge with a searching look, whose feet shuffle and whose hands, fingers, and noses twitch, whose legs wobble, whose whole demeanor expresses failure, then you'll have some idea of the behavior of that company.

Ernestine stood up and lowered her eyes graciously; and—while Monsieur Bador sighed heavily enough to make his heart burst inside him—she said modestly, "I choose Count Lémée."

The count, who'd been eyeing Madame Peyrol amorously, lifted his head, uttered a cry of joy, ran to Ernestine, and kissed her hands. "You understood my heart! Oh, you sensed that I loved you and you alone!"

Madame Peyrol couldn't suppress a smile of contempt; while Monsieur Bador, maneuvering skillfully closer to her, affected an air of delight and cried out, "It's straightforward: youth with youth—a judicious choice. You need to be about the same age to be happy together."

"So how old are you?" asked Monsieur Rigot. "You told us you were twenty-eight."

"By God, I'm easily thirty-five," said the attorney, looking at Madame Peyrol.

"Who isn't thirty-five?" said Monsieur Furnichon angrily. "As if that's a virtue!"

"And anyone who isn't thirty-five," said Monsieur Marcoine, "will be someday."

"Silence, silence!" cried Monsieur Rigot. "It's Eugénie's turn."

She stayed seated, and looked all around her. Then, as if the words were tearing her chest, she said, "I choose Baron de Luizzi."

"Me!" cried the baron. Then he remembered he'd asked Satan for the secret of the dowry recipient, and the Devil hadn't answered.

"Do you accept?" asked Monsieur Rigot.

"He, he, he, he!" cackled his lawyer.

At that moment Luizzi recognized the Devil's laugh, and stopped abruptly.

"Do you accept?" repeated Monsieur Rigot.

"Just a moment," said his lawyer. "The baron wasn't present when the contracts were read, and perhaps he'd like to make himself acquainted with them before deciding. He should know that in the event of the wife's decease the contract gives the surviving husband a child's portion. Come look it over, baron, come look."

Luizzi approached Rigot's lawyer with his heart sinking—because if he accepted Madame Peyrol's offer he might be condemning himself to poverty even greater than he feared, if she got no part of the dowry; and perhaps that was the news the Devil had threatened him with. He reached the table and leaned on it to keep from falling, and next to the contracts he saw a thick sealed envelope that contained the act awarding the dowry of two million francs.

"There it is," said Rigot's lawyer, setting his sharp-pointed fingers on the contract. "Read that!"

Luizzi couldn't do it: his vision was blurry, and he was seized by a kind of vertigo.

"Use my glasses, baron," said the lawyer. "You'll see better."

And without further ado he set his glasses on Luizzi's nose, while still pointing to the place he should read. No sooner had Luizzi glanced at the document than he realized Satan's glasses had given him that power of vision thanks to which he'd been able to read Henriette Buré's manuscript through walls and dark of night. So, while everyone watched him anxiously, he leaned over the table and looked at the dowry, and through the envelope he read that Monsieur Rigot gave the sum of two million francs to Ernestine Turniquel, natural daughter of Eugénie Turniquel, married name Peyrol.

"Well, then! Do you accept?" asked Monsieur Rigot for the third time.

Luizzi sank into the lawyer's chair and replied, "No."

All of the rival suitors cried out in joy, and Eugénie cried out in shame and despair. As for Monsieur Rigot, he repeated furiously, "No? Oh, you're saying no... No!... We'll see about that... Come along, Eugénie, choose another husband. I guarantee those other gentlemen will accept."

"Now it's my turn to say no," replied Eugénie. "Give your fortune to my daughter, uncle, and let me go live in some humble village."

"Well then, no again!" cried Monsieur Rigot in a fit of rage. "You'll each have a husband, or you'll have nothing!"

"I prefer poverty," said Eugénie.

"And I'll keep my millions!"

"Keep them, uncle. I haven't forgotten that work supported me; I know how to work."

"Good," said Madame Turniquel. "And I'll help you."

"Oh!" cried Ernestine. "It's disgraceful!"

"Ernestine!" said Eugénie.

"Yes, ma'am, yes, it's disgraceful! It's bad enough to have given me a wretched life and no name, to have made me spend my childhood in shame and exile everywhere, to have refused to tell me who my father was, who I know was a man with a distinguished name. By your refusal now, you're robbing me of my only chance to have a name and a fortune. Yes, it's disgraceful!"

"Oh!" cried Eugénie, hiding her face in her hands. "Ernestine, my child!"

"And you're letting a hussy like that talk to you in that insolent way?" said Madame Turniquel. "I'd know how to make her sing a different song!"

"Ma'am," said Ernestine, "I don't know what you want with me. I don't know you."

"Oh, you don't know me, you little wretch!" cried old Jeanne. "And when your mother worked to feed you, instead of giving you up to the foundling home like so many others, who was it who rocked you and took care of you at the wet nurse's, you wicked bastard child?"

"If I am," cried Ernestine, "it's not my fault, it's my mother's."

"Oh, you wretch! You wretch!" cried Eugénie, racked with despair and choked by tears. "You wretch!"

"Is there no decent man here to whom to give this decent woman?" cried Monsieur Rigot, beside himself.

The baron felt a sudden desire to run to Eugénie. He rose halfway out of his seat, but the Devil pointed to the dowry and said, "Read it, read it."

Luizzi fell back into his chair.

Monsieur Bador, understanding Monsieur Rigot's anger and catching the ball on the rebound, cried out, "Sir, whether Madame Peyrol is rich or poor, there are decent men here who are ready to offer her their hand."

"Yes, yes," cried the two clerks together, "yes, we're here."

"Me too," said Little Pierre.

"Eugénie, listen," said old Rigot. "Pick a husband. These fellows aren't as bad as I thought. Here I am, reconciling myself to these gentlemen."

"No, uncle, no, I can't do it. It's too vile."

"Beg your mother's pardon," said Count Lémée quietly to Ernestine, "or we're sunk."

For a moment Ernestine remained undecided.

Luizzi, observing the scene and recognizing Satan's hand everywhere, said to him quietly, "You were right: poor mother!"

"Wait, wait," replied the Devil.

Then Ernestine approached Eugénie and got on her knees, and said in a touching voice, though her eyes were quite dry, "Forgive me, mother, it was a momentary madness and confusion... I got carried away by my love, which is perhaps too intense. Alas, you yourself know into what mistakes that can lead one."

"Be quiet, be quiet, you wretch!" said her mother. "Don't insult me with your excuses the way you did with your anger. Be quiet. Since God has destined my existence to be the lifeblood for others, I'll give it to the end. Since you can only be rich and happy through the ultimate sacrifice I can make, I'll make it."

She paused and, turning to Monsieur Bador, the attorney, she was about to speak; but her strength failed her, and she looked once more at Luizzi, with a glance in which she offered herself again to him—believing him to have some honor in his soul because he'd refused her. But the Devil cackled his harsh little laugh, and Luizzi lowered his eyes.

"Sir," said Eugénie to the attorney, "do you want me?"

"Yes, ma'am," said Monsieur Bador, "and God is my witness that I'll always honor and respect you."

"All right! That was well said!" cried Monsieur Rigot. "And now, Niquet, unseal the dowry. I'll stand by it, whether you marry or whether you don't marry. Those who aren't happy can just leave. Read it, Niquet, read it..."

Rigot's lawyer slowly picked up the envelope and broke the five seals one after another. He seemed to be toying with the suitors' patience. The two clerks, with nothing at stake, snickered at the dumbfounded faces of the two betrothed men, while Luizzi sadly watched poor Eugénie, who hid her face in her hands. The lawyer solemnly unfolded the document and picked up his glasses, which he spent several minutes wiping.

"All right, all right," said Monsieur Rigot. "Don't hurry, all in good time."

Finally Rigot's lawyer put on his glasses and, after all the usual coughing, read the dowry act without skipping a syllable of its barbaric terms, till he reached the famous clause by which Monsieur Rigot declared he was giving the sum of two million francs, currently deposited at the Bank of France, to his grandniece Ernestine Turniquel, natural daughter of Eugénie Turniquel. Ernestine gave a cry of joy and Count Lémée fell at her feet, while Countess Lémée enfolded them both in her long and inordinately maternal arms.

Eugénie dried her tears and said to Monsieur Bador, "Oh, forgive me, sir!"

"Don't worry, don't worry," said the attorney. "I have in my pocket a rigorously drawn up agreement, and as of this instant Count Lémée owes you five hundred thousand francs."

"What!" cried Ernestine to her intended. "You presumed to dispose of my dowry?"

"And what if you hadn't gotten it?" asked the attorney.

"We'll contest the wording of that agreement," replied Count Lémée.

"It's perfectly correct," said the attorney.

"We'll see."

"Well, well," said Monsieur Rigot. "You know you're free not to get married, because what's done is done, and the dowry will be given as it says."

"Will Count Lémée recognize the validity of the agreement?" asked the attorney.

"I forbid it!" cried Ernestine to her intended.

"It's an immoral agreement," said Count Lémée, "which was extracted from me by deceit."

"How about that!" said Monsieur Furnichon, the stockbroker's clerk. "And my ten thousand francs?"

"Now him!" cried Ernestine.

"And mine?" added Monsieur Marcoine, the lawyer's clerk.

"And the baron's too, I assume?" asked Monsieur Rigot.

"I'm not involved in this despicable transaction, sir," said Luizzi.

"He, he, he, he," cackled Rigot's lawyer, so quickly and so piercingly that everyone stopped to listen. "It's just that the act of dowry isn't over, gentlemen. Listen." And he went on, "The aforementioned sum will be invested in government funds at five percent interest."

"Good," said the stockbroker's clerk. "The interest will be a hundred and ten, which comes to ninety thousand nine hundred and nine francs and nine centimes."

"I'd have done better than that with a mortgage," said the lawyer's clerk.

"Just listen," said Count Lémée.

"And that aforementioned interest," went on Rigot's lawyer, "considered as the usufruct of the sum of two million francs, shall be paid to Madame Eugénie Turniquel, married name Peyrol, who will enjoy it to the day of her decease, her daughter having only the naked possession of the property."

"Now that's admirable!" cried the attorney.

"Now that's stupid!" cried Count Lémée. "And what are we supposed to live on in the meantime?"

"You've got the agreement that guarantees you five hundred thousand francs," said the lawyer's clerk. "Monsieur Bador was so much in favor of it a little while ago."

"True," said Count Lémée. "And that agreement…"

"Is null and void," interrupted the attorney. "I can't touch the money, so I can't pay out."

"You're a crook," said the count.

"And you're a scoundrel."

"Come now," cried Monsieur Rigot in his stentorian voice. "Do you accept, count, yes or no?"

"My word!" said the count, pacing about with long strides. "Two million francs, that must be waited for, who knows how long… No doubt it's a fine future, but it's an awfully distant future…"

"Ah, so that's your love, sir!" said Ernestine.

"Well, miss," he replied, "your mother's still young!"

"Monstrous!" cried Eugénie.

"Don't get upset like that," said the attorney. "You'll make yourself ill."

Eugénie turned away, and met Luizzi's eye once more; he looked like a man suffering from vertigo.

Just then Monsieur Rigot cried again, "Well, count, do you accept?"

The count hesitated, and Rigot's lawyer said to him quietly, "Madame Peyrol is young, but the grandmother's old, and by buttering her up a little, in less than two years you'll get the million francs that are going to her."

"That's true," said Ernestine.

"Well? Well?" asked Monsieur Rigot.

"I accept," said the count.

"Will the gentlemen from Paris be needing post horses?" asked Little Pierre.

"The devil take you!" cried Monsieur Marcoine.

"That's guaranteed," observed Rigot's lawyer.

"The devil take you all, and me too!" added Monsieur Furnichon angrily.

"That's his duty," said Rigot's lawyer again, "and he'll carry it out." Then he went on, "We're not done here; we still need to hear Madame Turniquel's choice."

"That's right," said Little Pierre, stepping forward gallantly.

"I'm not involved," cried Monsieur Furnichon.

"Me neither," added Monsieur Marcoine.

"In that case," said Rigot's lawyer, "that leaves only Little Pierre and Baron de Luizzi."

"Me?" cried Luizzi.

"It's worth pointing out," said the lawyer in a voice so piercing it could be heard over everyone's murmuring, "Madame Turniquel's marriage contract is entirely to the advantage of her fiancé; because instead of putting a million francs in the form of a dowry, it acknowledges that the fiancé brings a million francs to the marriage—meaning that the fiancé is the true possessor of the fortune and can dispose of it at will."

"That's different!" cried Monsieur Furnichon.

"That changes everything!" added Monsieur Marcoine.

"Not so fast," said the old woman. "You've made a show of your disgust, gentlemen—thank you very much, you coxcombs!"

"That's right," said Little Pierre. "Paris dandies aren't your type, pretty Jeanne."

"Maybe they are," said Madame Turniquel. "And since my granddaughter is so proud to be a countess, I wouldn't say no to being a baroness."

"Oh, that's how it is?" said Little Pierre. "So long, Jeanne. You're scorning your old friends, and you'll be sorry."

He made as if to leave, then suddenly came back. "By the way," he added, "baron with four horses, I was about to leave without passing on a letter the tall thin man in black gave me and that I'd forgotten in my pocket."

Little Pierre tossed the letter on the table, and Luizzi picked it up to read it, while everyone else was pacing around the parlor, the attorney calming Eugénie, and the count quarreling with Ernestine because her grandmother's inheritance was getting away from them.

The letter ran like this:

Sir,

A warrant for your arrest, enforceable immediately, has been issued against you for a debt of one hundred thousand francs. All necessary measures have been taken to carry out your arrest, and the authorities have been notified. Therefore either surrender the balance of your debt to me, or surrender yourself at Mourt, where I await you, if you wish to avoid the unpleasantness and scandal of a public arrest.

—Signed, Laloguet, High Bailiff

"A million francs!" cried Rigot's lawyer, as if to restore order and calm to the gathering. "A million, did you hear me? A million francs, of which the future husband will have full possession and free disposition!"

"Are you withdrawing completely, Little Pierre?" asked Monsieur Rigot.

"She doesn't want me, that ingrate!" said the postilion in a tearful voice.

"Don't leave, Little Pierre. Because if I'm not a baroness I want to be a peasant—one or the other, all the way."

"Well said," observed Rigot's lawyer. "One or the other, all the way. That's lots of people's destiny: rich or poor, living the good life or rotting away in Sainte Pélagie."[78]

"Come now!" said Monsieur Rigot. "Are you asleep, baron? Will you be my brother-in-law or my prisoner? Because I should warn you, I'm the bearer of your letter of credit, and I swear you'll serve your five-year sentence. Will you do it?... Going once..."

The baron dug his nails into his chest.

"Going twice..."

The baron tore at his skin in fury.

"Going three times... This is your last chance: will you do it?"

"Yes!" cried the baron, rising and looking about him with such a menacing glare that no one dared laugh or say a word.

"That was hard," said Monsieur Rigot.

"Not as hard as I thought it would be," said his lawyer.

---

[78] The Maison de Sainte-Pélagie was a prominent prison, in use from the 1790s to the 1890s.

Chapter XLI: Vertigo

"Since that's settled," said Monsieur Rigot, "come to the table, gentlemen, come to the table! Supper awaits us, a supper to which I've invited all the rich landowners in the area. Come to the table, and let each man take his bride by the hand: we're going to do a proper introduction."

Count Lémée took Ernestine's hand, Monsieur Bador offered his arm to Eugénie, and Luizzi fell into step beside Madame Turniquel. The baron was moving like a drunkard, knowing neither what he was doing nor what he was saying. They seated him at the table between his intended and a man of about thirty, named Monsieur de Carin.

As supper began, Luizzi overheard his neighbor quietly asking Count Lémée, "So, old friend, did you do well?"

"Not too well: two million francs, after the mother's death."

"That's the opposite of my position: you're waiting for a fortune, I'm waiting for a peerage."

"Indeed," said Count Lémée.

Luizzi was listening, searching everywhere for infamous behavior that would justify his own, when Rigot's lawyer cried, "Come, let's drink! Who'll give me something to drink to?"

"I will, by God!" said Monsieur de Carin. "There's nothing better than drinking when you've just done something foolish."

And the two of them clinked their glasses. When the lawyer drank, white smoke wafted out of his mouth, as if the wine had been poured into a red-hot cylinder and evaporated into smoke.

"Drink up, baron," said Monsieur de Carin. "It helps make old women, fathers-in-law, and mothers-in-law more bearable."

"Yes," replied Luizzi furiously, "let's drink. I need to keep from thinking."

He drank. He drank glass after glass in such a rage that soon he saw the room and the guests dancing all around him. And he wasn't the only one: Rigot's lawyer asked everyone for something to toast to, and unleashed on the whole company a kind of drunken madness, whose influence spread even to the most reserved of those present.

"Bravo!" cried Monsieur Rigot. "Now things are picking up! Let's get the party started properly—the big glasses!"

The servants brought immense glasses, each of which could hold almost an entire bottle of champagne, and filled them up.

"To the lovely young Ernestine, future bride of Count Lémée!"

"To the beautiful Ernestine!" they all cried.

"Kiss your bride, count!" cried Monsieur Rigot, half drunk.

And Count Lémée kissed his bride.

"Keep the toasts going, and double the portions—the other glasses!"

The servants brought even bigger glasses.

"To my niece Eugénie!" stammered old Rigot.

"To the beautiful Eugénie!" they all cried.

"Monsieur Bador, kiss your bride!"

And the attorney, who'd taken part in the festivities, kissed Eugénie, who drew back in shame from the whole debauch.

"That's right! Keep the toasts going!" went on Monsieur Rigot. "The really big glasses!"

The servants brought colossal glasses, and when they were filled Monsieur Rigot cried, "To the magnificent Jeanne Rigot, widow Turniquel, future Baroness de Luizzi!"

"To the magnificent Jeanne!" they all repeated.

"Kiss your bride!" cried Monsieur Rigot.

And Luizzi kissed her.

A harsh, piercing laugh rang out over all the shouting of the party, and it seemed to Luizzi that everything he looked at took on an extraordinary appearance: it was a gathering of bizarre, monstrous horned devils with napkins tied around their necks, drinking from glasses that never emptied. And it seemed to him that Rigot's lawyer—or rather Satan—had climbed onto the table and sat down on the point of a knife and was laughing his huge devilish laugh.

Then he heard him shouting, "Ha, ha, ha, master! You've now sunk lower than all those you despise! You could've married the only angel, the only woman on earth I couldn't conquer, and you spurned her because you thought she was poor. Ha, ha, ha, master! Greed blinded you enough to keep you from reading to the end of the document that would've enlightened you and that I'd put into your hands. And you, Baron de Luizzi, of a lineage ennobled since the year 908, worth millions, thirty-two years old, accepted as your wife a laborer's daughter, the widow Turniquel, aged sixty-four! Ha, ha, ha, master! There's something truly great and noble about you!... Come, to your health and to your honor! Now drink with me, master, drink with me!"

His looks, his words, drove Luizzi into a kind of frenzy. Seizing a knife, he threw himself on the satanic wraith and plunged it into his chest. A horrible cry rang out, and in an instant the spell was broken, and he heard twenty voices all around him murmuring, "He killed the lawyer. He killed the lawyer."

"No!" cried Luizzi. "I killed the Devil! The Devil is dead!"

Then he collapsed under the weight of the horror that oppressed him.

When he came to, he found himself lying on a bed in a room whose barred windows made clear to him he was in prison. Satan stood before him.

"Not yet," said the Devil. "I'm not dead yet, master."

"Where am I?"

"In prison."

"Why?"

"For murdering the lawyer Niquet."

"Me?"

"Yes, you. In a moment of drunkenness, it's true. That's probably what'll give you a chance to end your days in the galleys."

"Me, in the galleys?"

"Would you rather be guillotined?"

"This is just another dream I had, Satan."

"Could be."

"Ah! Will you never give me a straight answer?"

"I don't have time today."

"And when will I see you again?"

"In the next world, I imagine."

"Have I lost my little bell?"

"It was confiscated by the warden."

"Then I'm doomed!"

"That's a charming word out of a melodrama."

"Leave me, Satan. I've lost my talisman, but I've gotten more out of your lessons than you think. I haven't forgotten Eugénie's story, and how she got away from you."

"My word! You remind me of her."

"What's become of her?"

"Every day the attorney prays to God for his wife's safety, and every day her daughter prays to me for her mother's death."

"Poor mother!"

"He, he, he!" cackled the Devil. "You see I keep my promises."

"Except with me."

"Didn't I get you out of bed? Didn't I make you free and healthy and hearty?"

"Yes, only to throw me into an even more terrible mess."

"From which I can still rescue you."

"How?"

"That's my concern."

"I mean, at what price?"

"This: I made a bargain with you to get you out of bed, on condition that you get married within two years or give me ten years of your life. I'm going to offer you another bargain."

"Which is? It seems to me you can't do better than the position you've already put me in. I'm a condemned man, I can't get married, so you'll have those ten years of my life."

"Who knows, master? I might have need of you in two years."

"And what's the new bargain you're offering me?"

413

"It's now two months since we made the old bargain, so you still have twenty-two months to find a wife. Give up twenty months to me, and I'll forgive you the rest of the terms, even the marriage."

"That means you know I won't be sentenced, Satan."

"It's possible. Do you want to risk it? Farewell."

"Just a moment."

"Hurry up, master. Today is the twenty-sixth of July, 1830. On the twenty-sixth of February, 1832, I'll rescue you and give you back your freedom, your fortune, and your good reputation, all of which you've lost."

"You're tricking me again."

"Look!"

As the Devil spoke that word, the door of the cell opened, and a judge came in, followed by a clerk of the court. Behind them came a doctor—and Luizzi recognized the dreaded Doctor Crostencoupe, whose scholarly paper on Luizzi's cure had earned him a position as head prison doctor.

The judge said to the doctor, "See if the accused is able to undergo questioning, sir."

"Have you heard any news of the victim?"

"The injuries are severe and seem likely to prove fatal, so the accused will probably be found guilty of murder. People around here adored Niquet. He was a leading voice in liberal ideas. The jury is made up of liberals, who'll be all the more harsh because the accused is a man with a distinguished name and a title, a man descended from the ancient nobility. It's a bad business. Niquet's next of kin have filed a civil case, at Bador's instigation, and he'll move heaven and earth to have the accused condemned. He's taken over the case. Besides, the murderer's background isn't the kind likely to earn him any favor with the judges: when he was arrested for the killing he was about to be arrested for debt, and after that for a swindle he had a hand in."

"So he has a criminal record?"

"Not yet."

"And what was that swindle?"

"In Paris he introduced into Madame de Marignon's salon a certain Count de Bridely, though he knew the man had assumed a false name by a false act of legitimation. And since that Count de Bridely stole a fairly substantial sum of money from the lady and has since vanished, it's assumed that Baron de Luizzi was his accomplice."

"Baron de Luizzi!" cried Doctor Crostencoupe, who'd been chatting in that fashion with the judge while the turnkey prepared everything necessary for taking notes. "Baron de Luizzi! I know him!"

"Well, here he is."

"He's a madman—a raving madman. I'm the one who cured him the first time, but he escaped, and the madness must've returned immediately, since he left without even paying me."

"In that case, you think it's pointless to question him?"

"Utterly pointless."

"Good enough. We'll file a certification of madness."

Luizzi was about to cry out, but the Devil motioned to him, and they were left alone.

"You see your only chance of being saved, baron. A proper certificate of madness will protect you from the risk of a trial and a sentence."

"You're deceiving me again, Satan."

"When have I ever deceived you, master? Was it when you asked me to tell you Madame de Marignon's life story, which you took advantage of to attempt the wicked scheme for which you're now in trouble? Did I deceive you when you asked for Eugénie's life story, though it almost allowed you to escape from me and find what would've freed you from servitude to me, namely happiness? Didn't I even point straight to what should've made you decide to marry that woman? Is it my fault you didn't read all the way to the end, if like all men you trusted to the surface appearance of things, and if you remain what you are and what all men are—selfish, greedy, and arrogant? No, master, it's not my fault. And no, I never deceived you."

"But what about my fortune?" cried Luizzi.

"Give me the twenty months I'm asking for, and I'll get you out of here a rich, innocent, and what's more a well-regarded man."

"How will you do it?"

"I'll tell you then."

"It's twenty months of sleep."

"That's all it is."

"Then take them."

The Devil touched Luizzi with the tip of his finger, and he fell asleep.

The next day, when he awoke, he found himself in the same cell. Nothing had changed—but he noticed his little bell next to him. He summoned Satan and said, "I've had a wonderful sleep, though somewhat short. But knowing that to-night I'll fall asleep for twenty months, the main thing worrying me is how I'm going to spend the day. The idea of twenty months of sleep is enough to drive a man mad."

"Read to pass the time," suggested the Devil.

"Can you have them bring me books?"

"I can do better: I can provide them myself. I can even supply you with unpublished manuscripts. Follow me."

The Devil led the way, and Luizzi followed him. They soon came to a fairly nicely furnished room. Luizzi put on the famous glasses the Devil had already lent him before, which could make him see perfectly on the darkest of nights. Then he saw a woman of uncommon beauty, fast asleep.

"Who's this woman?" he asked.

"Madame de Carin, the wife of the charming fellow with whom you spent that delightful evening."

"That terrible evening!"

"Perhaps for you."

"But not for you, Satan."

"Oh, I had a good laugh. You were all such vile scoundrels."

He laughed again with the lawyer's little cackle, which filled Luizzi's heart with remorse and struck his ear like a falsehood. The baron shook his head vehemently and replied, "You're the one who's vile, you who are determined to show me the world in the ugliest light. But never mind that; tell me why this Madame de Carin is in this prison; has she committed some crime?"

"You'll find out," answered the Devil. He opened Madame de Carin's writing desk, took out a manuscript, and handed it to Luizzi. "Since you're afraid of my stories, since you think the way I present the world to you is a vile parody, judge for yourself. I'll do no more than put the articles of evidence before your eyes. This one here is the first and the most important."

Luizzi opened the manuscript and read carefully. It began like this:

Édouard,

You—whose care for me has helped me bear my sufferings and the horror of my situation—have asked me for an account of the misfortunes that brought me to this point. Here it is, and forgive me for the minute detail in which it's told; for I must persuade you even more of my sanity than of my misfortune.

"What's the meaning of this?" asked Luizzi.

"Read it," replied the Devil. "When you read a modern novel, do you stop at every sentence you don't understand?"

"No, I'd never get to the end. But I assume this isn't a novel, and therefore it's different from them."

"And the result will be different too, because you'll understand it."

"Is it going to be more calamities?"

"Maybe."

"Crimes?"

"Maybe."

"Where'd this woman come from?"

"From one of the noblest families in France."

"And she's suffered misfortunes?"

"Perhaps even more than Eugénie."

"But I'm sure she wasn't the object of a shameful auction, the way that poor woman was. Her high birth would've have protected her from that."

"Read it. You'll find out whether the daughter of the noble family and the daughter of the common people have any reason to envy each other."

Luizzi, who knew the Devil's wiles, and knew he couldn't be made to say what he wanted to conceal, decided to take the manuscript away with him. Worn out from having walked only a few steps, he threw himself onto his bed and began to read.

TO BE CONTINUED IN
"THE DEVIL'S MEMOIRS"
(VOLUME 2)

.